NOBEL PRIZE WINNER

PATRICK WHITE

HIS TOWERING NOVEL OF STRUGGLE, PASSION, AND TRIUMPH

The Tree of Man

"Mr. White's technique is closer to poetic drama than to that of conventional fiction . . . He expresses 'the great simplicities of life in simple, luminous words for people to see.' He conveys a sense of the flow of time as it shapes and dissolves in the human consciousness."

San Francisco Chronicle

". . . The novel has unforgettable scenes, marvelous characters, wide range of mood, strikingly fresh imagery—all those ingredients which make a novel outlive its season and become a permanent part of our memory."

Washington Post

"THE TREE OF MAN becomes a grander and more meaningful book with each re-reading . . . A Lawrence-like vitality runs through the book . . . His focus on a man and wife, their children and their children's children, is a means of showing Australia in action and, more deeply, of showing the world in operation, given meaning by the presence of man."

New York Post

Avon Books by
Patrick White

THE EYE OF THE STORM   21527 $1.95
THE TREE OF MAN   22665 $1.95

PATRICK WHITE

The Tree of Man

 AVON
PUBLISHERS OF BARD, CAMELOT, DISCUS, EQUINOX AND FLARE BOOKS

To

Manoly

The lines of poetry on pages 397-98 are from
A. E. Houseman's A SHROPSHIRE LAD, XXXI.

AVON BOOKS
A division of
The Hearst Corporation
959 Eighth Avenue
New York, New York 10019

ISBN: 0-380-00282-5

First Avon Printing, March, 1975.

AVON TRADEMARK REG. U.S. PAT. OFF. AND
FOREIGN COUNTRIES, REGISTERED TRADEMARK—
MARCA REGISTRADA, HECHO EN CHICAGO, U.S.A.

Printed in Canada

PART I

Chapter 1

A CART drove between the two big stringybarks and stopped. These were the dominant trees in that part of the bush, rising above the involved scrub with the simplicity of true grandeur. So the cart stopped, grazing the hairy side of a tree, and the horse, shaggy and stolid as the tree, sighed and took root.

The man who sat in the cart got down. He rubbed his hands together, because already it was cold, a curdle of cold cloud in a pale sky, and copper in the west. On the air you could smell the frost. As the man rubbed his hands, the friction of cold skin intensified the coldness of the air and the solitude of that place. Birds looked from twigs, and the eyes of animals were drawn to what was happening. The man lifting a bundle from a cart. A dog lifting his leg on an anthill. The lip drooping on the sweaty horse.

Then the man took an axe and struck at the side of a hairy tree, more to hear the sound than for any other reason. And the sound was cold and loud. The man struck at the tree, and struck, till several white chips had fallen. He looked at the scar in the side of the tree. The silence was immense. It was the first time anything like this had happened in that part of the bush.

More quickly then, as if deliberately breaking with a dream, he took the harness from the horse, leaving a black pattern of sweat. He hobbled the strong fetlocks of the cobby little horse and stuck the nosebag on his bald face. The man made a lean-to with bags and a few saplings. He built a fire. He sighed at last, because the lighting of his small fire had kindled in him the first warmth of content. Of being somewhere. That particular part of the bush had been made his by the entwining fire. It licked at and swallowed the loneliness.

7

By this time also the red dog had come and sat at the fire, near, though not beside the man, who was not intimate with his animals. He did not touch or address them. It was enough for them to be there, at a decent distance. So the dog sat. His face had grown sharp with attention, and with a longing for food, for the tucker box that had not yet been lifted from the cart. So the sharp dog looked. Hunger had caused him to place his paws delicately. His yellow eyes consumed the man in the interval before meat.

The man was a young man. Life had not yet operated on his face. He was good to look at; also, it would seem, good. Because he had nothing to hide, he did perhaps appear to have forfeited a little of his strength. But that is the irony of honesty.

All around, the bush was disappearing. In that light of late evening, under the white sky, the black limbs of trees, the black and brooding scrub, were being folded into one. Only the fire held out. And inside the circle of its light the man's face was unconcerned as he rubbed tobacco in the palms of his hard hands, a square of tinkling paper stuck to his lower lip.

The dog whistled through his pointed nose. In the light of the fire the bristles of his muzzle glistened. As he watched for an end to this interminable act.

Till there it was, with the smoke coming out.

The man got up. He dusted his hands. He began to take down the tucker box.

How the dog trembled then.

There was the sound of tin plate, tea on tin, the dead thump of flour. Somewhere water ran. Birds babbled, settling themselves on a roost. The young horse, bright amongst his forelock, and the young and hungry dog were there, watching the young man. There was a unity of eyes and firelight.

The gilded man was cutting from a lump of meat. It made the dog cavort like a mad, reddish horse. The man was throwing to the dog, while pretending, according to his nature, not to do so. The dog gulped at the chunks of fatty meat, the collar working forward on his neck, the eyes popping in his head. The man ate, swallowing with some ugliness, swallowing to get it down, he was alone, and afterwards swilling the hot, metallic tea, almost to get it finished with. But warmth came. Now he felt good. He smelled the long, slow scent of chaff slavered in the nosebag by the munching horse. He smelled the smell of green wood burning. He propped his head against the damp collar discarded by the horse. And the cavern of fire was enormous, labyrinthine, that received the man. He branched and flamed, glowed and increased, and was suddenly extinguished in the little puffs of smoke and tired thoughts.

The name of this man was Stan Parker.

While he was still unborn his mother had thought she would like to call him Ebenezer, but he was spared this because his father, an obscene man, with hair on his stomach, had laughed. So the mother thought no more about it. She was a humourless and rather frightened woman. When the time came she called her boy Stanley, which was, after all, a respectable sort of a name. She remembered also the explorer, of whom she had read.

The boy's mother had read a lot, through frail gold-rimmed spectacles, which did not so much frame her watery blue eyes as give them an unprotected look. She had begun to read in the beginning as a protection from the frightening and unpleasant things. She continued because, apart from the story, literature brought with it a kind of gentility for which she craved. Then she became a teacher. All this before she married. The woman's name was Noakes. And she remembered hearing her own mother, talking of things that had happened at Home, tell of a Noakes who had married the chaplain to a lord.

The woman herself did no such thing. By some mistake or fascination, she had married Ned Parker, the blacksmith at Willow Creek, who got drunk regular, and once had answered a question in a sermon, and who could twist a piece of iron into a true lover's knot. This was not genteel, but at least she was protected by a presence of brawn. So Miss Noakes had become Mrs. Parker, became also, in a way, more frightened than before.

"Stan," said his mother once, "you must promise to love God, and never to touch a drop."

"Yes," said the boy, for he had had experience of neither, and the sun was in his eyes.

In the drowsy bosom of the fire that he had made the young man remembered his parents and his mother's God, who was a pale-blue gentleness. He had tried to see her God, in actual feature, but he had not. Now, Lord, he had said, lying with his eyes open in the dark. Sometimes he would hear his father, swearing and belching, the other side of the door.

9

His father did not deny God. On the contrary. He was the blacksmith, and had looked into the fire. He smote the anvil, and the sparks flew. All fiery in his own strength, deaf with the music of metal, and superior to the stench of burned hoof, there was no question. Once, from the bottom of a ditch, on his way home, after rum, he had even spoken to God, and caught at the wing of a protesting angel, before passing out.

The God of Parker the father, the boy saw, was essentially a fiery God, a gusty God, who appeared between belches, accusing with a horny finger. He was a God of the Prophets. And, if anything, this was the God that the boy himself suspected and feared rather than his mother's gentleness. Anyway, in the beginning. At Willow Creek, God bent the trees till they streamed in the wind like beards, He rained upon the tin roofs till even elders grew thoughtful, and smaller, and yellower, by the light of smoking lamps, and He cut the throat of old Joe Skinner, who was nothing to deserve it, not that anyone knew of, he was a decent old cuss, who liked to feed birds with crusts of bread.

This was one of the things, the young man remembered, his mother had not attempted to explain. "It is one of those things that happen," she said.

So the mother looked upset and turned away. There were many things to which she did not have the answers. For this reason she did not go much with the other women, who knew, most of them, most things, and if they didn't, it wasn't worth knowing. So the mother of Stan Parker was alone. She continued to read, the Tennyson with brass hasps and the violets pressed inside, the spotted Shakespeare that had been in a flood, and the collection of catalogues, annuals, recipe books, and a cyclopædia and gazetteer that composed her distinguished and protective reading. She read, and she practiced neatness, as if she might tidy things up that way; only time and moth destroyed her efforts, and the souls of human beings, which will burst out of any box they are put inside.

There was the young man her son, for instance, who now lay with his head on a horse's collar, beside his bit of a fire, the son had thrown off the lid. He had sprung out, without unpleasantness, he was what you would call a good lad, good to his mother and all that, but somehow a separate being. Ah, she had said, he will be a teacher, or a preacher, he will teach the words of the poets and God. With her respect for these, she suspected, in all twilight and good faith, that they

10

might be interpreted. But to the son, who had read the play of *Hamlet* in his mother's Shakespeare, and of the Old Testament those passages in which men emerged from words, reading by day to the buzz of fly or at night while puddle cracked, there seemed no question of interpretation. Anyway, not yet.

He was no interpreter. He shifted beside his fire at the suggestion that he might have been. He was nothing much. He was a man. So far he had succeeded in filling his belly. So far, mystery was not his personal concern, doubts were still faint echoes. Certainly he had seen the sea, and the hurly-burly of it did hollow out of him a cave of wonderment and discontent. So also the words of songs floating in the dust and pepper trees of a country town at dusk do become personal. And once some woman, some whore, neither young nor pretty, had pressed her face against a windowpane and stared out, and Stan Parker had remembered her face because he shared the distance from which her eyes had looked.

But the fire was dying, he saw, with such cold thoughts. He shivered, and leaned forward, and raked at the fragments of red fire, so that they shot up into the night on a fresh lease. His place in the present was warm enough. On the fringe of firelight stood the young horse, his knees bent, trailing from his head the nosebag, now empty and forgotten. The red dog, who had been lying with his nose on his paws, crawled forward on his belly and nuzzled and licked at the wrist of the man, who pushed him away on principle. The dog sighed at the touch. And the man too was reassured of his own presence.

Night had settled on the small cocoon of light, threatening to crush it. The cold air flowing sluiced the branches of trees, surged through the standing trunks, and lay coldly mounting in the gully. Rocks groaned with cold. In the saucers that pocked the face of stone, water tightened and cracked.

A frosty, bloody hole, complained the man, from out of the half-sleep in which he had become involved, and twitched the bags tighter round his body.

But he knew also there was nothing to be done. He knew that where his cart had stopped, he would stop. There was nothing to be done. He would make the best of this cell in which he had been locked. How much of will, how much of fate, entered into this it was difficult to say. Or perhaps fate is will. Anyway, Stan Parker was pretty stubborn.

He was neither a preacher nor a teacher, as his mother had

11

hoped he might still become, almost up to the moment when they put her under the yellow grass at the bend in Willow Creek. He had tried his hand at this and that. He had driven a mob of skeleton sheep, and a mob of chafing, satin cattle; he had sunk a well in solid rock, and built a house, and killed a pig; he had weighed out the sugar in a country store, and cobbled shoes, and ground knives. But he had not continued to do any of these things for long, because he knew that it was not intended.

"There goes young Stan," people said, pulling down their mouths and blowing the air through their noses, because, they felt, here was somebody assailable.

Because they had looked through the doorway and seen him, as a little boy, blowing the bellows for his father, there, they felt, he shall stay put.

To stay put was, in fact, just what the young man Stanley Parker himself desired; but where, and how? In the streets of towns the open windows, on the dusty roads the rooted trees, filled him with the melancholy longing for permanence. But not yet. It was a struggle between two desires. As the little boy, holding the musical horseshoes for his father, blowing the bellows, or scraping up the grey parings of hoof and the shapely yellow mounds of manure, he had already experienced the unhappiness of these desires. Ah, here, the sun said, and the persistent flies, is the peace of permanence; all these shapes are known, act opens out of act, the days are continuous. It was hard certainly in the light of that steady fire not to interpret all fire. Besides, he had an affection for his belching and hairy father, and quite sincerely cried when the blacksmith finally died of the rum bottle and a stroke.

Then, more than at any time, the nostalgia of permanence and the fiend of motion fought inside the boy, right there at the moment when his life was ending and beginning.

"At least you will be a comfort to your mother, Stan," said Mrs. Parker, her nose grown thin and pink, not so much from grief as from remembering many of those incidents which had pained her in a world that is not nice.

The boy looked at her in horror, not understanding altogether what she implied, but knowing for certain he could not be what she expected.

Already the walls of their wooden house were being folded back. The pepper tree invaded his pillow, and the dust of the road was at his feet. One morning early, while the dew was still cold outside his boots, he got up and left, in search, if he had known it, of permanence. And so he went and came for several years, getting nothing much beyond his muscles, scabs on his hands, and on his face the first lines.

"Why, Stan, you are a man now," said his mother once, when he walked in across the creaking board in the doorway of their house at Willow Creek and caught her going through the things in a drawer.

It was as if she had come out of herself for the first time in years, to take surprised notice.

And he was surprised too, for his manhood did not feel exactly different.

They were both awkward for a while.

Then Stan Parker knew by his mother's shoulders and the gristle in her neck that she would die soon. There was, too, a smell of old letters in the room.

She began to talk of money in the bank. "And there's that land that was your father's, in the hills back from here, I don't just know the name, I don't think it ever had one, people always called it Parkers' when they spoke. Well, there is this land. Your father did not think much of it. The land was always uncleared. Scrubby, he said. Though the soil is good in patches. When the country opens up it will perhaps be worth a little. The railway is a wonderful invention, and, of course, assistance to the landowner. So keep this property, Stan," she said, "it's safe."

Mrs. Parker's voice had been scrubbed clean of the emotions. It was bare and very dull.

But the young man's breath thickened, his heart tolled against his ribs—was it for a liberation or imprisonment? He did not know. Only that this scrubby, anonymous land was about to become his, and that his life was taking shape for the first time.

"Yes, Mother," he said. As always when she spoke of matters of importance. And turned away to hide his certainty.

Not long after that she died, and he touched her cold hands, and buried her, and went away.

Some people said that young Stan Parker had no feelings, but it was just that he had not known her very well.

Nobody took much notice when the young man left for good, in a cart that he had bought from Alby Veitch, with a shaggy sort of a brumby horse. As the wheels of the cart moved over the melting ruts and screaming fowls made way, only a face or two, released from the beating of a mat or kneading of dough, remarked that young Stan was on the

13

move. Soon there would be no reason to remember Parkers in that place. Because the present prevails.

Stan Parker drove on, through mud and over stones, towards those hills in which his land lay. All that day they rattled and bumped, the sides of the sturdy horse grown sleeker in sweat. Under the cart a red dog lolloped loosely along. His pink tongue, enormous with distance, swept the ground.

So they reached their destination, and ate, and slept, and in the morning of frost, beside the ashes of a fire, were faced with the prospect of leading some kind of life. Of making that life purposeful. Of opposing silence and rock and tree. It does not seem possible in a world of frost.

The world was still imprisoned, just as the intentions were, coldly, sulkily. Grass that is sometimes flesh beneath the teeth would have splintered now, sharp as glass. Rocks that might have contracted physically had grown in hostility during the night. The air drank at the warm bodies of birds to swallow them in flight.

But no bird fell.

Instead, they continued to chafe the silence. And the young man, after sighing a good deal, and turning in his bags, in which the crumbs of chaff still tickled and a flea or two kept him company, flung himself into the morning. There was no other way.

But to scrape the ash, but to hew with the whole body as well as axe the gray hunks of fallen wood, but to stamp the blood to life, and the gound thawing took life too, the long ribbons of grass bending and moving as the sun released, the rocks settling into peace of recovered sun, the glug and tumble of water slowly at first, heard again somewhere, the sun climbing ever, with towards it smoke thin but certain that the man made.

A little bird with straight-up tail flickered and took the crumb that lay at the man's feet.

The man's jaws took shape upon the crusts of stale bread. His jaws that were well shaped, strong, with a bristling of sun about the chin. This was gold.

Down through him wound the long ribbon of warm tea. He felt glad.

As the day increased, Stan Parker emerged and, after going here and there, simply looking at what was his, began to tear the bush apart. His first tree fell through the white silence with a volley of leaves. This was clean enough. But

14

there was also the meaner warfare of the scrub, deadly in technique and omnipresence, that would come up from behind and leave warning on the flesh in messages of blood. For the man had stripped down to his dark and wrinkled pants. Above this indecency his golden body writhed, not in pain, but with a fury of impatience. Anæsthetized by the future, he felt neither whips nor actual wounds. He worked on, and the sun dried his blood.

Many days passed in this way, the man clearing his land. The muscular horse, shaking his untouched forelock, tautened the chain traces and made logs move. The man hewed and burned. Sometimes, possessed by his dæmon of purpose, the ribs seemed to flow beneath his skin. Sometimes his ordinarily moist and thoughtful mouth grew rigid, fixed in the white scales of thirst. But he burned and hewed. At night he lay on the heap of sacks and leaves, on the now soft and tranquil earth, and abandoned the bones of his body. The logs of sleep lay dead heavy.

There in the scarred bush, that had not yet accepted its changed face, the man soon began to build a house, or shack. He brought the slabs he had shaped for logs. Slowly. He piled his matchsticks. So the days were piled too. Seasons were closing and opening on the clearing in which the man was at work. If days fanned the fury in him, months soothed, so that time, as it passed, was both shaping and dissolving, in one.

But the house was being built amongst the stumps, that in time had ceased to bleed. It was more the symbol of a house. Its prim, slab walls fulfilled necessity. There were windows to let the light into the oblong room, there was a tin chimney, shaped like a matchbox, through which the smoke came at last. Finally he stuck on a veranda. It was too low, rather a frowning addition, but which did not forbid. Seen through the trees, it was a plain but honest house that the man had built.

If there had been neighbours, it would have been a comfort to see the smoke occur regularly in the matchbox-chimney. But there were no neighbours. Only sometimes, if you listened on the stiller days, you might hear the sound of an axe, like the throb of your own heart, in the blue distance. Only very distant. Or more distantly, a cock. Or imagination. It was too far.

Sometimes the man would drive off into that distance in his high cart. Then the clearing was full of the whinge and

15

yelping of the red dog, left chained to a veranda post. Till in time the silence grew, and his yellow eyes watched it. Or a parrot flurried the blue air. Or a mouse glistened on the dirt floor of the house. The abandoned dog was at the service of silence at last. He was no longer attached, even by his chain, to the blunt house of the man's making.

The man always brought back things in his cart. He brought a scratched table and chairs, with mahogany lumps in the proper places. He brought an iron bed, big and noisy, of which the bars had been bent a bit by kids shoving their heads between. And he brought all those necessities, like flour, and a bottle of pain killer, and pickled meat, and kerosene, and seed potatoes, and a packet of needles, and oaten chaff for the shaggy horse, and the tea and sugar that trickled from their bags, so that you crunched across them, almost always, on the hardened floor.

The dog's collar almost carved off his neck when the man came, and there was always the joy and excitement and the smell of brought things.

Then, once, when the man had been gone some time, longer than normal perhaps, he brought with him a woman, who sat beside him in the cart, holding the board and her flat hat. When she had got down, the dog, loosed from his chain, craned forward, still uncertain of his freedom, on trembling toes, in silence, and smelled the hem of her skirt.

Chapter 2

DOWN along the coast there was a township of Yuruga, to which Stan Parker had paid visits, to a cousin of his mother's called Clarence Bott. Already as a boy in large boots he had known that town, and had, in fact, worked near Yuruga for a few months, on a dairy farm. In later life, whenever he approached Yuruga, the man recalled the sleepy, morning smell of cows, the smell of warm milk-buckets waiting to be rinsed, and the feel of cows' teats, proud and rubbery at first, then dangling empty like a silly glove.

It was as a young man, rather, that Stan Parker had paid the visits to his mother's cousin Clarrie, a draper, whose stomach looked like a small melon underneath his calico apron. Altogether unlike the heaving paunch of the young man's blacksmith father. Clarrie Bott was quite unlike. He did not overflow.

Still, the draper had managed to get three rollicking girls, Alice, Clara, and Lilian, who had all three put up their hair and were taking an interest about the time Stan Parker had become interesting. These girls were continually baking fluffy sponges, and writing scenty letters to friends, and embroidering mats and table runners, and playing the piano, and thinking of practical jokes. So that it was quite natural for the kind of cousin, Stan Parker, now a young man with shoulders, to gravitate towards their house. Not that it was intended any of the Bott girls should marry the blacksmith's son, himself with hard hands and a shack somewhere in the hills. Oh dear, no. But the Bott girls themselves were not above sticking a sponge finger into a young man's mouth, to see whether he would bite, and fizzing like their own sherbet as they waited for signs of intimacy. Alice, Clara, and Lilian were taut with interest as they waited to repulse their Cousin

17

Stan, or to rend him, if there were no need to repulse. They waited. And their sherbet fizzed.

The young man did not propose to or even attempt to kiss his cousins. Why he did not, it is difficult to say. He was backward or something. Because, with their small waists and dainty fingers, and talent for folding table napkins and paper fans to put in grates, he should have been overcome. Consequently he became a bitter subject in the Bott household. Particularly when, on almost his last visit, he broke the corner off the marble washstand in the best room. At once it was confirmed that Stan Parker had been designed to do the wrong thing, and they should never in their senses have expected anything else from the blacksmith's son.

The evening Stan Parker broke the washstand was the evening of a dance in a hall to raise church funds. Such an act on such an occasion should have shaken Stan, but he kicked the marble into a corner, as if it had been tin or wood. His mind was quite steady, and the window of his room, he saw, was full of stars.

All that night the fiddle could not have been more watchful that sawed the waltzes up and down. The grave face of the young man sitting in conflicting clothes followed the logic of the lancers. He was not surprised. Their golden patterns merged and opened. The giggles flowered on the faces of girls. The young man's deep eyes protected him from any who might have struck. He was quite defenceless. But nobody dared.

Then, after a time, when it looked as though he might almost fathom the figures of the dance, after he had sighed and crossed the hot serge of his legs, the parson's wife came across, still warm from the cakes she had baked, and the programmes she had copied out, and children fed, and napkins changed, and people pushed together how many times that night, came across and was arranging, between the gasps for breath, and the ends of hair that got in her mouth, some contract of elaborate and refined importance.

Almost before he could uncross his legs Stan Parker saw that the parson's wife had gone, leaving in her place a thin girl.

The girl was turning her head, he saw, in almost every direction but his.

"Sit down," he commanded her.

While watching his own feet slide back and forwards on the glazed boards in some act of deference or defence.

The girl sat.

Her arms were very thin.

"This is the first ball I have ever been to," said the girl.

Her hands, which were less elegant than those of Alice, Clara, and Lilian Bott, picked at pieces of her blue dress. This was obviously too big, and had, in fact, been lent by Mrs. Erbey, the parson's wife, from a box in which it had been put away.

Stan Parker wished she had not come.

"Well, anyway," he said, "it is hot."

"It is cold outside," she answered, touching something that might have happened to her dress.

"But all these people," he said, "breathing in the one room."

"Do you know," she said, "Mrs. Erbey once told me about a diver, she had read it, see, in a book, who used up all the air in one of those suits."

Then they looked at each other, under the sea of music. The brown man was yellower. At any breathless moment the girl's black hair might stream.

"Don't you dance?" she asked.

"No," he said.

She was about to confess, what suddenly she would not tell. Courage had made her craftier. Instead her face embarked on a little smile.

"It is just as much fun," she said, "to watch."

She did not sense dishonesty. Already he had seen her thin dismay, and that was too much.

"What is your name?" she asked.

"Stan Parker," he said.

The whole room was filling, and filling, with music and the laughter of dancers, so that it was difficult to hear the obvious question, but she knew that this had been asked in turn.

"Mine?" laughed her thin mouth.

Then she bent her head and quickly scribbled on the piece of paper with the little pencil that Mrs. Erbey had given her that evening to note the partners she would not have.

He saw the eyelids on her lowered face grow dark, and the shadows beneath the bones of her cheeks.

"There," she laughed shortly.

"*Amy Victoria Fibbens?*" he read in a slow voice that clearly doubted.

"Oh yes," she said, "that's it. Still, you have got to have a name."

Intent on her lowered eyelids, his eyes had already abandoned that name as an unnecessary label. But her eyelids did not notice this.

Now Stan Parker had begun to remember the thin girl.

"You one of those Fibbens from Kellys' Corner?"

"Yes," she said, her face thinking. "But I'm not one of those really. My mother and father is dead. I'm an orphan, see? And I live with Uncle and Aunt, who are those Fibbens at Kellys' Corner."

Her blue dress was quite anxious, and the narrow sash that had been tied too many times.

"Go on," said Stan Parker. "Now I remember."

Which made it worse.

Because he remembered the shed at Kellys' Corner. He remembered the kids playing in the rain. There was a mob of Fibbens kids, and when they walked out they walked in a string, their bare feet kicking dust or slapping mud. He remembered this girl, the mud halfway up her bare legs. He remembered her also once in shoes, so raised up it was perhaps the first time, and the string of Fibbens kids that walked behind.

"What do you remember?" she asked, trying to see it in his face.

But she could not. All she saw was the face of a young man, and it seemed she had never been so close before.

"What do you remember?" said her hollow mouth.

"You," he said. "I dunno there was anything else."

If this man's skin is not honest, she said. For two pins she would have touched it.

"As if that's not bad enough." She laughed, rocking safely on her hands.

"I was working then for Sam Warner, out at Narrawan. Of a Saturday evening sometimes I'd come in to town."

"Uncle," said the girl, "worked for Warners for a bit."

"Go on," he said. "What was his job?"

"Oh," she sighed. "I forget."

Because Old Man Fibbens had been employed shovelling up the cow manure and putting it into bags. It was only for a bit, because, where Uncle Fibbens was concerned, it was always only for a bit. He liked to lie on a bed beneath a tree and look at his toenails from a distance.

Amy Fibbens had not got great affection for her uncle or her aunt. She had not felt affection for any human being, except in a respectful and unsatisfactory way for Mrs. Erbey, the parson's wife, whom she went to help by day when she had turned sixteen. There her life was not so different from what it was in the Fibbens shed. She wiped the noses of a string of children. She stirred the morning pan of porridge. But she also ate the remains of puddings. And she did wear shoes.

So she was fond of Mrs. Erbey. But Amy had not yet been loved, except by her mother, fretfully, for a short time before she died. The thin girl did expect something to happen eventually, because it does, but these expectations were timid and wholly theoretical.

Thought had made her silent in the middle of the music, and the young man, exhilarated by the questions and the answers, was brought a little closer, and was glad.

Stan Parker thought he had never been so close to any girl. Not even to the mouth of the unknown woman yearning on the window-pane. The thin girl became familiar to him in the ages of silence in which they sat. For the wobbly music had receded, and the voices of the dancers, assured of their beauty and their cleverness. Only the girl's face, from which the subterfuge had slipped, was not so sure. Stan Parker knew this girl. As all oblivious objects become known, and with the same nostalgia, the tin cup, for instance, standing in the unswept crumbs on the surface of your own table. Nothing is more desirable than this simplicity.

"I must go now," said Amy Fibbens, standing up in her awkward dress.

What is Stan, on whose arm somebody had spilled a custard, doing all night with the Fibbens girl? Clara asked Lilian.

"It is not as late as that," said Stan.

"Oh yes, it is," sighed the girl. "I have had enough of this."

That was true, he knew. His own face ached. He was only waiting to be told.

"But don't let me take you away," said the girl, with a measure of borrowed tact.

He followed her out of the room, his back obscuring her departure for those who watched.

Their steps, if not their voices, were mingling through the empty streets of the dead town. Iron lace hung from dark pubs, and the heavy smells of spilled beer. Dreams broke from windows. And cats lifted the lid off all politeness.

"I wonder if this town will still be here in a thousand years," yawned Amy Fibbens.

His mind fumbled lazily and failed. He did not see the point. But he did not doubt permanence.

"I shan't worry if it is not," sighed the girl.

Her shoes were hurting, and the ruts were deeper on the outskirts of the town.

"I could easy do with a thousand years," he suddenly said. "Why, you'd see things happen. Historical things. And you'd see the trees turning into coal. You'd be able to remember the fossils, how they looked when they were walking about."

He had never before said anything like this.

"Perhaps too much would happen," the girl replied. "Perhaps there'd be a fossil or two you wouldn't want to remember."

Because now they were on the outskirts of the town. They stumbled past the hulks of cows. There was a smell of sheep, and of water drying in a mud hole. And soon the yellow Fibbens' doorway, leaning outwards, and the yellow straws of light that fell from the cracks in walls into darkness.

"Well," she said, "this is where I take off the shoes."

"It looks like it," he said.

He wondered if, after all, this girl might not be a box of tricks. She was a skinny one, and sharp.

The whimpering of a waking child was not contained by walls.

"A-*myyy*?"

"Yes, Aunt," called the girl.

The shadow of Mrs. Fibbens heaved into fresh shapes on its frail bed. Her belly was fretful with her seventh.

"Anyway," said Amy Fibbens, "we have had a talk. About a lot of things."

It was quite right. They had talked about almost everything, because words occasionally will rise to the occasion and disgorge whole worlds.

Just as the darkness will disgorge a white face under a dusty tree.

"Will you be coming to this place again at all, perhaps?" asked the girl.

"On Saturday week," said the usually slow man.

And again he was surprised.

Under the sad tree, more frond than bark, beside the girl's blurred face, less shape than longing, in an amorphous landscape of cows' breath and flannelly sheeps' cud, his intention was absolute.

"Oh," she said. "In that case."

22

"A-*myyyyyy!*" called Aunt Fibbens, the shadows knotting on her dreadful bed. "Stop maggin. An come inside."

"Yes, Aunt," said the girl.

"A person could be dead," complained the shadow, "an only the flies would cotton on. Here am I, reachin, ever since I swallowed me tea."

There were people in that place who said that Mrs. Fibbens was as rough as bags.

Chapter 3

STAN PARKER did not decide to marry the Fibbens girl, if
decision implies pros and cons; he simply knew that he
would do it, and as there was no reason why the marriage
ceremony should be delayed, it was very soon performed, in
the little church at Yuruga, which looks a bit cockeyed, because built by hands less skilled than willing, on a piece of
bumpy ground.

Clarrie Bott came to the church, because, as he explained
to his reluctant lady and disgusted girls, the boy's mother was
his dead, or rather his defunct, cousin. Uncle Fibbens was
there too, in boots, with a handful of family, but not Aunt,
whose seventh was at breast. Only Mrs. Erbey benefited emo-
tionally by the ceremony. The parson's wife was happy at a
wedding, especially if she knew the girl. She gave Amy Fibbens a Bible, a blouse as good as new (it was only slightly
singed near the waist), and a little silver nutmeg grater that
someone had given her at her own wedding and with which
she had never known what to do.

Amy Parker, fingering the silver nutmeg grater, found it a
similar problem but the loveliest thing she had ever seen, and
she thanked Mrs. Erbey gratefully.

The day was fine, if cold, on the steps of the blunt church,
when Amy Parker prepared to stow herself and her goods in
her husband's cart and leave Yuruga. Her nutmeg grater in
her pocket, her singed blouse concealed beneath her jacket,
she carried in her hands the Bible and a pair of cotton
gloves.

"Good-bye, Ame," mouthed Uncle Fibbens.

The wind had made him water, and the rims of his eyes
were very red.

The cousins clawed.

"Good-bye, Uncle," said Amy calmly. "Good-bye, youse!" As she smacked a random bottom.

She was quite calm.

Meanwhile the draper, who had given several yards of calico, was telling the bridgroom to make the best of life, and the young man, because his attention had been bought, was screwing up his eyes and nodding his head in a way altogether unlike him. His face too had grown thinner since morning.

"After all, it is respect," said the draper in some torment of moustaches, "it is respect that counts."

The young man stood nodding like a boy as the draper struggled to soar on wings of wisdom.

Finally, when the kids had thrown a handful of rice, and Mrs. Erbey was standing on tiptoe to wave, and dab, and smile, and pull the ends of hair from out of her mouth, and wave again, and the cart was beginning to pull away from the stumpy church, under the needles of dark twisted trees that tore at hats, the Parkers, which was what they now were, knew that it was over, or that it had begun.

The cart drove away, over the ruts in that part of the town. The gay horse tossed his forelock. Thin clouds flew.

"Well, there we are," laughed the man's warm voice. "It's a long ride. You mustn't mind."

"Wouldn't help if I did." The girl lazily smiled at the landscape, holding her hat.

Their different bodies jolted with the cart. For they were changed, since what had been agony, for a split second of confessed agreement in the church. Now they were distinct, and one, they could look without effort into each other's eyes.

Only, as the town of Yuruga jerked past and away from them, Amy Parker's eyes were at present for the landscape. What she had just done, whether momentous or usual, did not concern other people. She did not belong to anyone in that town. Her fat aunt had not cried, nor had she expected it. She herself had never cried for any specific person. But now she began to feel a sadness as she struggled against the possessive motion of the cart. As if the cart, with its aspiring roll, and the retrospective landscape, were fighting for a declaration of her love. To force from her an admission of tenderness that, until now, she had carefully sat on.

The cart rocked. The road pulled at her heart. And Amy Parker, now in the full anguish of departure, was torn slowly

25

from the scene in which her feeling life had been lived. She saw the bones of the dead cow, of which she could even remember the maggots, of Venables' Biddy with the short tits, that had died of the milk fever. Ah, she did feel now. It came swimming at her, that valley, from which the nap had been rubbed in parts, by winter, and by rabbits. Its patchiness had never coruscated more, not beneath the dews of childhood even. But what had been, and what was still a shining scene, with painted houses under the blowing trees, with the carts full of polished cans in which the farmers put the milk, with staring children and with dabbling ducks, with blue smoke from morning fires, and enamelled magpies, and the farmers' wives, spanking into town in sulkies, wheezing inside their stays and the red foxes at their necks, all would fade forever at the bend in the road.

For this last look Amy Parker turned, holding her hat in the wind. There was a sheet of iron on the ground, that had come off Fibbens' roof in a gale once, and that they had always talked about putting back. Ah dear, then she could not hold it. She was all blubbery at the mouth.

He had begun to make the clucking noises at the horse, and stroking with the whip the hairy rump.

"You are sorry then," he said, moving his hand farther along the board, so that it touched.

"I've nothing to lose at Yuruga," she said. "Had me ears boxed, and roused on all this time."

But she blew her nose. She remembered a bull's-eye she had eaten under a bridge, and the wheels ground over the planks of the bridge, and there in the hollow afternoon swallows flew, the scythes of their wings mowing the light. She could not escape her childhood. Out of her handkerchief its slow, sad scent of peppermint.

So he stayed quiet beside her. There are the sadnesses of other people that it is not possible to share. But he knew that, in spite of her racked body, which he could feel fighting against the motion of the cart, she was not regretful. It was something, just, that must be fought out. So he was content.

It was a long ride. It was soon the sandy kind of bush road that there is no consuming. But they crunched and lurched. And the horse gave strong, leathery snorts, flicking the health defiantly out of his pink nostrils. The man would have liked to tell his wife, We are coming to This or That, or we are so many miles from So-and-so. But he could not. The distance was quite adamant.

26

Well, she could sit a lifetime if necessary, she said, once the crying was done.

The girl sat with her eyes on the road. She was not concerned, as, at odd moments, her husband was afraid she might be. Because in her complete ignorance of life, as it is lived, and the complete poverty of the life she had lived, she was not sure but that she might have to submit thus, interminably bolt upright in a cart. Life was perhaps a distance of stones and sun and wind, sand-coloured and monotonous. Dressed too much, as she was, for her wedding, and in an unfamiliar, undistinguished place, she could have believed anything.

But once they passed a tin nailed on top of a stump, and in the tin were a stone and a dead lizard.

And once their wheels thrashed through brown water, and the coolness of fresh, splashed water drank at her hot skin.

That, he said, was Furlong Creek.

She would remember, she felt, gravely, this that her husband was telling her.

The cart was livelier after that. Wind flung the sweat from the horse's shoulders back into their faces. There was a reckless smell of wet leather, and broken leaves that the wind had been dashing from the trees in that part of the bush. All and all were flung together, twig and leaf, man and woman, horse's hair and ribbony reins, in the progress that the landscape made. But it was principally a progress of wind. The wind took back what it gave.

"Does it always blow in these parts?" She laughed.

He made a motion with his mouth. It was not one of the things to answer. Besides, he recognized and accepted the omnipotence of distance.

But this was something she did not, and perhaps never would. She had begun to hate the wind, and the distance, and the road, because her importance tended to dwindle.

Just then, too, the wind took the elbow of a bough and broke it off, and tossed it, dry and black and writhing, so that its bark harrowed the girl's cheek, slapped terror for a moment into the horse, and crumbled, used and negative, in what was already their travelled road.

Achhh, cried the girl's hot breath, her hands touching the livid moment of fright that was more than wound, while the man's body was knotted against the horse's strength.

When they were settled into a recovered breathing the man looked at the cut in his wife's cheek. It was the cheek of the thin girl whose face had become familiar to him the night of

27

the ball, and whom apparently he had married. And he was thankful.

Oh dear, she gasped thankfully, feeling the hardness of his body.

Their skins were grateful. And unaccustomedly tender.

They had not kissed much.

He looked at the bones in her cheek, and in her neck, exposed willingly to him.

She looked into his mouth, of which the lips were rather full and parted, roughend by the wind, and on his white teeth the blood from the small wound in her cheek.

They looked at each other, exchanging the first moment their souls had lived appreciably together. Then, quietly, they rearranged their positions and drove on.

No other event disturbed the monotony of emotion, the continuity of road, the relentlessness of scrub that first day, until, about evening, just as their faces were beginning to grow grey, they came to the clearing the man had made to live in.

Now his modest achievement was fully exposed. The voice of a dog, half-aggressive, half-hopeless, leaped into the cool silence.

"This is the place," the man said, as if it must be got over quietly and quickly.

"Ah," she smiled, withdrawn, "this is the house you have built."

It is not much better, oh dear, than Fibbens' shed, she said, and you can cut the silence.

"Yes," he grunted, jumping down, "it's not all violets, as you can see."

As she could see, but she must also speak, she knew.

"Once I saw a house," she said, in the even dreamlike voice of inspiration, "that had a white rosebush growing beside it, and I always said that if I had a house I would plant a white rose. It was a tobacco rose, the lady said."

"Well," he said, laughing up at her, "you have the house."

"Yes," she said, getting down.

It did not help much, so she touched his hand. And there was a dog smelling at the hem of her skirt, that she looked down dubiously to see. The dog's ribs were shivering.

"What is his name?" she asked.

He said that the dog had no particular name.

"But he should have one," she said.

The moment a conviction had animated her bones she began to take the things from their cart, and to arrange their belongings in the house, as if it were the natural thing to do. Carefully she went here and there. She gave the impression she was not sticking her nose into what was already there. In fact, most of the time she was so careful to look straight ahead in her husband's house that there was a great deal she did not see at all.

But she knew it was there. And would look later on.

"There is water," he said, coming and standing a bucket inside the doorway.

The level of the water lapped quietly and settled down.

She went to and fro in what was becoming her house. She heard the sound of his axe. She thrust her shoulders through the window, outside which it was determined she should plant the white rose, and where the slope of the land was still restless from the jagged stumps of felled trees.

"Where is the flour?" she called. "And I cannot see the salt."

"I shall come," he said, rummaging after the sticks of wood.

It was that hour of evening when the sky is bled white as scattered woodchips. The clearing was wide open. The two people and their important activities could not have been more exposed. About that importance there was no doubt, for the one had become two. The one was enriched. Their paths crossed, and diverged, and met, and knotted. Their voices spoke to each other across gulfs. Their mystery of purpose had found the solution to the mystery of silence.

"I shall like it here." She smiled, over the crumbs on the table, when they had eaten the damper she had slapped together, and some rancid remnants of salt beef.

He looked at her. It had never really occurred to him, in the deep centre of conviction, that she might not like his place. It would never occur to him that what must be, might not. The rose that they would plant was already taking root outside the window of the plain house, its full flowers falling to the floor, scenting the room with its scent of crushed tobacco.

Already, as a boy, his face had been a convinced face. Some said stony. If he was not exactly closed, certainly he opened with difficulty. There were veins in him of wisdom and poetry, but deep, much of which would never be dug. He would stir in his sleep, the dream troubling his face, but he would never express what he had seen.

So instead of telling her smooth things, that were not his anyway, he took her hand over the remnants of their sorry meal. The bones of his hand were his, and could better express the poem that was locked inside him and that would never otherwise be released. His hand knew stone and iron, and was familiar with the least shudder of wood. It trembled a little, however, learning the language of flesh.

The whole night had become a poem of moonlight. The moon, just so far from full as to be itself a bit crude, cut crooked from its paper, made the crude house look ageless. Its shape was impregnable under the paper moon, the moon itself unperturbed.

So that the thin girl, when she had taken off her dress, and put her shoes together, and rolled into a ball the gloves she had held but had not used, took courage from the example of the moon. The furniture, huge in the moonlight, was worn by and accustomed to the habits of people. So she only had a moment of fright, and chafed that easily off.

Flesh is heroic by moonlight.

The man took the body of the woman and taught it fearlessness. The woman's mouth on the eyelids of the man spoke to him from her consoling depths. The man impressed upon the woman's body his sometimes frightening power and egotism. The woman devoured the man's defencelessness. She could feel the doubts shudder in his thighs, just as she had experienced his love and strength. And out of her she could not wring the love that she was capable of giving, at last, enough, complete as sleep or death.

Later, when it had begun to be cold, and the paper moon had sunk a bit tattered in the trees, the woman got beneath the blanket, against the body of the sleeping man who was her husband. She locked her hand into the iron pattern of the bedstead above her head and slept.

Chapter 4

LIFE continued in that clearing in which Parkers had begun to live. The clearing encroached more and more on
the trees, and the stumps of the felled trees had begun to dis-
appear, in ash and smoke, or rotted away like old teeth. But
there remained a log or two, big knotted hulks for which
there seemed no solution, and on these the woman sometimes
sat in the sun, shelling a dish of peas or drying her slithery
hair.

Sometimes the red dog sat and looked at the woman, but
not closely as he did at the man. If she called to him, his eyes
became shallow and unseeing. He was the man's dog. So for
this reason she had never given him the name she had promised. He remained Your Dog. Walking stiffly past the stumps
and the tussocks of grass, stiffly lifting his leg. In time he
killed a little fuchsia that she had planted in the shadow of the
house, and in her exasperation she threw a woody carrot at
him. But she did not hit the dog. He continued to ignore her,
even in his laughing moments, when his tongue lolled and increased with the laughter in his mouth. But it was not laughter for the woman. He did not see her. He licked his private
parts or looked along his nose at the air.

Never far from the dog the man would be at work. With
axe, or scythe, or hammer. Or he would be on his knees,
pressing into the earth the young plants he had raised under
wet bags. All along the morning stood the ears of young cabbages. Those that the rabbits did not nibble off. In the clear
morning of those early years the cabbages stood out for the
woman more distinctly than other things, when they were not
melting, in a tenderness of light.

The young cabbages, that were soon a prospect of veined
leaves, melted in the mornings of thawing frost. Their blue
and purple flesh ran together with the silver of water, the

31

jewels of light, in the smell of warming earth. But always tensing. Already in the hard, later light the young cabbages were resistant balls of music, until in time they were the big, placid cabbages, all heart and limp panniers, and in the middle of the day there was the glandular stench of cabbages.

If the woman came and stood by the man, when the sun had risen, after frost, when the resentful blood had settled in the veins, he would show her how he was chipping the earth in the rows between the cabbages.

"Not this way," he said, "because you cover up the weeds. But this way."

Not that she had to be shown. Or listened. Not that he did not know this, but had her by him. The earth was soft and exhausted after frost. After the awful numbing and clawing and screeching of the fingernails, it was gently perfect to be beside each other. Not particularly listening or speaking. He could feel her warmth. She wore a big old straw hat with frayed spokes where the binding had come unsewn, and the hat made her face look too small and white. But her body had thickened a little. She no longer jerked when she turned, or threatened to break at the hips. Her flesh was growing conscious and suave.

"Not this way. But this way," he said.

Teaching her not this, but the movements of her own body as she walked between the rows of cabbages. She walked narrowly, on account of the hummocks of earth that he had hilled up to serve as beds, but her movement pervaded the orbit of his vision. He did not often raise his eyes, chipping the thawed earth, but he carried against him the shape of her body.

So that he too was taught. She was imprinted on him.

Sometimes she would look up from her plate and speak, after tearing a mouthful of bread, speak with her mouth too full, the voice torn. He would hear and remember this voice again when he was alone. Her too greedy voice. Because she *was* rather greedy, for bread, and, once discovered, for his love.

Her skin devoured the food of love, and resented those conspiracies of life that took it from her before she was filled. She would look from the window into the darkness, hearing the swinge of metal and the thwack of leather, seeing the dark distortion of a cart with its mountain of cabbages against the stars.

"I have filled the water-bag," she would call.

32

As the man tore at stiff buckles, and cold leather resisted his hands. As he moved round and round the horse and cart, preparing for the journey of cabbages.

"And there's a slice of pie beneath the sandwiches," she said.

To say.

Because it was cold on her shoulders in the morning, and in the bed when he had gone, and the hoofs of the horse were striking their last notes from the stones, and the cart had creaked its final music. She could not warm back his body in the forsaken bed.

Sometimes he would be gone a whole day and night after the market, if there was business to transact or things to buy.

The the forsaken woman was again the thin girl. The important furniture of her marriage were matchsticks in the hollow house. Her thin, child's life was a pitiful affair in the clearing in the bush. As she walked here and there, tracing maps in scattered sugar or in the receded undergrowth, close to the ground, staring eye to eye with the ant.

Sometimes she mumbled the words she had been taught to say to God.

She would beg the sad, pale Christ for some sign of recognition. On the scratched mahogany table which the man had bought at auction, she had put the Bible from the parson's wife. She turned the pages respectfully. She said or read the words. And she waited for the warmth, the completeness, the safety of religion. But to achieve this there was something perhaps that she had to do, something that she had not been taught, and in its absence she would get up, in a desperation of activity, as if she might acquire the secret in performing a ritual of household acts, or merely by walking about. Suspecting she might find grace in her hands, suddenly, like a plaster dove.

But she did not receive the grace of God, of which it had been spoken under coloured glass. When she was alone, she was alone. Or else there was lightning in the sky that warned her of her transitoriness. The sad Christ was an old man with a beard, who spat death from full cheeks. But the mercy of God was the sound of wheels at the end of market day. And the love of God was a kiss full in the mouth. She was filled with the love of God, and would take it for granted, until in its absence she would remember again. She was so frail.

The woman Amy Fibbens was absorbed in the man Stan

33

Parker, whom she had married. And the man, the man consumed the woman. That was the difference.

It did not occur to Stan Parker, in the suit of stiff clothes he wore for town, that his strength had been increased by an act of cannibalism. He swallowed, and forgot his own body too, when once he had been conscious of it, in the presence of other men. Nor did his words hold back. He was still slow, but his slowness had become, and would remain, a virtue.

In the town in which men transacted their business, bought flour and sugar, got drunk, talked big, and spewed up under the balconies of pubs, Stan Parker began to be known. He did not assert himself but would give or receive opinions, whenever asked. People began to recognize his face. His hands, with scabs on the knuckles, were respected as they received the change.

Sometimes he stood in the pubs with other men, wrapped in the damp blankets of beerful reminiscence, and listened to what they had to say. This was endless. The stiff, moustachy, or the smooth and blubbery, or the blue-eyed, empty faces of confident men in pubs do not draw the line. Their cows had full udders. Such hams, bacon, and pork had not been known from other pigs. Tried in drought, flood, and fire, the heroic muscles of these men had performed prodigious feats. They had caught fish and killed snakes. They had hurled bullocks into heaps. They had bitten the ears off angry horses. They had eaten and drunk, lost and won, more than other men. Their involved voices spun out their deeds in the dark and swirly, damp and drooly atmosphere of the pubs. It was an atmosphere of reported fact. It was an atmosphere of branching smoke, that began, and wandered, and broke, and continued, and hesitated, and fizzled out. If the smoke began in fire, at some point or other it lost itself in patterns of ostentation.

Stan Parker sometimes listened to the voices of men in pubs, but he did not feel the necessity to translate his own life into brave words. His life as lived was enough. So that when the swing doors swung on him, it was sometimes wondered whether they liked his face, whether he was not perhaps a surly sort of cove. But Stan Parker walked away beneath the lace balconies, and the dog that had waited followed him.

Life at Bangalay, the market town, did not convince Stan, not even such solid evidence as the red courthouse and the yellow jail. He drove along the straight streets, where men were persuading themselves, and past the stone homes, where girls sat beneath the pepper trees, exchanging confidences and sipping raspberry vinegar. He would blow down his nose at times, as if to settle the flies. His cart crunched almost insolently through the outskirts. He sat upright, asking to be knocked off rather than acknowledge belief in that town.

And he would smile for his own secret existence, and for its most significant, most secret detail, his wife.

Once, intruding on this privacy, an old woman in a crumpled bonnet ran out into the middle of the road and asked, "Where is Delaney's, please, son? It is either Smith Street or Broad Street, I forget which, my memory is not too good. He is the big building contractor come to live here from The Glebe. His daughter is married with me sister's boy."

The young man, who knew Delaney at least by sight, frowned and said, "I'm a stranger here, mother." Pulling the shadow over his face. He had been taken by surprise. He was ashamed for some indelicacy.

"Ah," she said, her mouth doubting above the stubble, "I thought youse would know Delaney. He's a fine figure of a man."

But the young man shook his head. He was ashamed of something. Afterwards he was sorry, and anxious for the fate of the old woman, but he had kept his secret, which was also, after all, his strength.

In the comfortable silence, in a blandishment of trees, in the smell of hot leather, the young man drove homeward after market days. Distance flooded his soul. He began to open. He would remember many simple but surprising things: his mother combing the hair from a bursh, the soldiers on the battlements of Elsinore, the breath of a roan cow at daybreak, mouths biting at a prayer but not consuming. All the riches of memory were recounted on these mornings.

He had been brought up in a reverence for religion, but he had not yet needed God. He rejected, in his stiff clothes, the potentialities of prayer. He was strong still. He loved the enormous smooth tree that he had left standing outside the house. He loved. He loved his wife, who was just then coming with the bucket from behind their shack, in the big hat with spokes like a wheel, and under it her bony face. He loved, and strongly too, but it was still the strength and love of substances.

"Well," he said, hiding his love, "and what has happened? Anybody come?"

"Nothing," she said, diffident beneath her hat, and wondering whether she should offer some sign. "What do you expect," she said, "a steam engine?"

Her voice broke the cold stillness too roughly. She stood squeaking the handle of her bucket, a sound of which the air was less shy. She too was ashamed of her voice.

She was ashamed of not being able to say those things that she should. All day long she had listened to the bell on the cow, the laughing of a bird, the presence of her silent house. Her thoughts had chattered loudly enough, but took refuge now.

Anyway, the young man her husband was thudding down from his cart. His coat, uneasy on him, had got hitched up on his back.

"Your coat's too tight," she said, touching.

"Then it will have to be."

But he kissed her mouth, and at once it was clear that this had been his goal, and anything else, words, harness, the weaving of the cart between the grey stumps, even his jacket's wrinkling upward, all was part of an elaborate bird's ritual.

So she went away from this climax with his breath in her mouth. She went to find the yellow cow, that had stood this how long, her patient belly, her mouth full of her blue tongue. The old cow that the young woman called to herself Julia, because of an affection she had had for the parson's wife. And in this light her gentle cow was gentler, turning the eyes in the direction from which she came, her welcome sweet-breathed. She loved her copper cow in the orange light of evening. The world was open. Peace fell into her bucket. Her hands that had just now touched her husband's back, if casually, performed these further acts of love. All things that she touched were translated. She bowed her head against the cow and listened to the sounds of peace.

Once about this hour a stranger came, whom they remembered for many a day, because he was the first. He came up the track towards the dead tree, against which she milked her yellow cow. The man's approach mingled with the steady milk. Till the woman looked up to see. And here was a man with a long nose and a sack over his back.

He was making for Wullunya, he said, which was some

way still, where a big river ran. "Have you been to Wullunya?" the man asked.

"No," she said, "I have never been that far."

It was too far to contemplate. She was fixed now, seated with the bucket between her knees; the river flowed away from her.

"I have only been to Yuruga, and here," she said. "Oh, and to Bangalay once or twice."

"I have been to most places," said the man.

His scurfy coat had not reaped the benefit, but his face could have seen many things, his rich nose revelling in them.

"Have you seen savages?" she asked, wringing the milk into the still evening.

"Lord," he laughed, "more than enough. In many an unexpected place they'll shake their feathers at you."

So he was a sort of educated man.

"I knew a lady," she said bitterly, "who told me there's savages diving to the bottom of the sea and fetching things up in their teeth."

Her eyes had a hungry glitter for something she did not possess, or as if she had not yet walked on the bottom of the sea, and would not perhaps, seated at her cow's side, with the teats slacker in her aching hands.

"You are interested in literature?" asked the man, assuming a glitter of his own.

"What?" she asked.

"I mean, you are a young woman that reads."

"I have read four books," she said. "And I read the newspaper when I was at Yuruga."

"Look," said the man, plunging his arm into the sack. "Here's books."

He had, in fact, a whole lot of glossy Bibles in the lumpy bag.

"There's pictures," he said. "Twenty-seven art plates. Look," he said, "there's Samson pushin the temple down, and there's Job examing 'is boils. Perhaps the gentleman would buy you one of these here Bibles as a present. It's a gift as should appeal to a young lady with a taste for reading."

"We have the Bible," she said.

"But not with pictures."

"No," she said, "but there's the potatoes to peel, and the mending, and the cow, and the sticks to chop when he is not here, and I take a hoe sometimes when the weeds are extra

37

bad, after rain. When should I ever be looking at pictures, even if they are Bible ones?"

The man rubbed his nose. "You are the practical woman," he said.

She pushed back the old box on which she had sat to milk her cow. "I don't know what I am," she said. "I was never taught a great deal."

"Ever seen that?" asked the man.

He brought from his pocket a chunky bottle. *"Thompson's Genuine Magnetical Water,"* the label said, *"Guaranteed Killer of Most Pains, Safe but Sure (No Humbug)."*

"This is also a good investment in its way."

"Ah," she said, "there is my husband."

And she began to walk across the paddock with the white milk slip-slopping up the side of the pail. She was glad to leave the man, for she had begun to feel her inexperience of life.

"Who is this cove?" asked her husband.

"He's a man walking to Wullunya, with a bag full of Bibles and some funny water in a bottle."

"It's a long way to Wullunya," said the young man as the stranger was gathering his books in the dusk, wrapping them in the sheets of crumpled paper from which he had taken them.

In the clearing that had not very long ago been bush, the light drained fast. Their house looked quite frail. They were themselves strangers to their own place. Until the lamp was lit, it would not be theirs.

"Better ask him to have something. Can you do it?" asked Stan Parker.

"Oh, there'll be something, I suppose," she said.

"He can doss down outside," said her husband, "or on the veranda, on a few bags."

"Though what it will be," she said, "I don't yet know."

She was suddenly full of angry importance. Excitement chafed her anger. She was pretty now. Her important actions filled the lamp-lit room as she dealt with the business of a first guest.

And the stranger with the Bibles rubbed his hands as greed began to ease through his humility and relief, as he smelled the meat the young woman was grilling at the hearth. There were three chops and a kidney, that she cooked on a slither of wire gridiron. The chops spat fat, and the kidney swelled and shone with little drops of blood. As he waited, there was a sadness beginning to invade the stranger's eye, whether of patience or from a conviction that the angry chops might finally explode.

"Ah yes, food, it nourishes," sighed the man who carried the bottle of magnetical water, and who had not eaten that day. "There is also drink," he said. "There are those that deny the nourishin properties of alcohol, but you will'uv read, I don't doubt, you are thoughtful people, it is obvious, you will'uv read that this is also a form, a *form*, mind you, of pure food."

The stranger narrowed his eyes, as if he were squinting through a crack. It emphasized the delicacy of his argument. He was a bald man, or not quite. A few surviving strands of hair struggled across the bluish skin of his scalp. Without his hat, his burned face looked less experienced than exposed.

"I had an uncle who was nourished. Still have, for that matter," said the young woman, who was slapping down the thick white cups.

"It is only a *theory*," said the stranger gently.

But the husband was moved by some pleasure to take from the rickety dresser the bottle that he had kept for an official occasion, and why not this, they had not had a guest. Now, too, in the lamplight it was confirmed that the house was theirs. Any uneasy moments of doubt that hang about at dusk had been dispersed.

"Well," said the young man, "whether it is food or not, here is a drop of good rum."

"To warm the cockles," said the stranger, slipping it in, as you do, before turning to subjects of significance. "It reminds me of an occasion on the Gold Coast of Africa, where I had important business with the chief of a tribe of savages."

"There's your tea then," said the young woman, as if she would shut her ears.

But her husband could have heard more. His lips wondered on the fat meat they had begun to eat.

"The Gold Coast, eh?" said the young man.

As if the permanence of furniture was a myth. As if other glittering images that he sensed inside him without yet discovering, stirred, heaved almost to the surface. The seat of his pants prickled on the deal chair. His wife, who was blowing on a forkful of hot meat to cool it, could have got up and kissed the sockets from which her husband's eyes had withdrawn.

Making room for words, eventually, in his full mouth, the

stranger explained, "I was engaged on a mission at the time, you might say both private and hofficial, to investigate a possibility of purchasin mahogany from the Ashanti tribes. Very difficult natives too. Things might have turned nasty if it had not been for one chief with an attack of the backache. I prescribed quantities of rum."

"You were not in the water then?" asked the young woman.

"In the water?" said the stranger, who was tilting the bottle as if he had been invited, but at the same time with a kind of invisible air.

"Yes," she said, "the stuff that you carry in your pocket."

"Ah," he said, "that is a different line of business. Yes."

And he sucked the naked bone of a chop, till his mouth glistened, but it had also closed up.

All this time Stan Parker was torn between the images of gold and ebony and his own calm life of flesh. He did not wish to take his hat from the peg and say, Well, so long, I'm off to see foreign places. This did not bring the sweat to the backs of his knees. He had a subtler longing. It was as if the beauty of the world had risen in a sleep, in the crowded wooden room, and he could almost take it in his hands. All words that he had never expressed might suddenly be spoken. He had in him great words of love and beauty, below the surface, if they could be found.

But all he said was, again, "The Gold Coast, eh?" And reached for the bottle.

All his impotence and power flowed together in his veins.

"When I was a nipper," he said, "I read the Works of Shakespeare. I dug out bits. I don't think I ever dug out more than bits, not out of anything."

"Literature," said the stranger, "is man's greatest consolation—that is, well, there are one or two competitors perhaps."

"Here," said the young woman, scraping the gnawed bones from their plates and throwing them to the dog in the doorway.

She was oppressed by a sadness of night, and the removed souls of the men, who no longer threw her scraps. Any poetry that had got into the conversation was personal. The stranger's nose glowed for himself, whether he spoke of the Gulf or Ethiopia. Her husband's mood she had met once or twice and grudgingly respected.

"Yes," said the stranger, "if it is not the consolation of consolations, it takes a honorary mention. There's many ben-

40

efits by a good read, just as some must sing a lungful of psalm, or take the bottle down from the shelf. You will appreciate," he said, "I am bein frank."

As he killed the rum.

"You, on the other hand, are differently placed."

Hearing the man's words, feeling herself brought into focus again, the young woman leaned against her husband the other side of the table. The skin of her hand brushed the hair of his arm. She was rehabilitated.

"How's that?" she asked.

"Because the Almighty 'asn't yet shown 'Is 'and. You 'ave not been 'it over the 'ead, kicked downstairs, spat at in the eye. See?"

This old man is not only drunk, but perhaps a little bit mad, felt Stan Parker. But the warmth of his wife against his shoulder kept him distinct from any such states.

"All young married couples are a vegetable sex," said the stranger. "They don't compete. Marrows and squashes. They coil and cuddle on the bed."

"You are a nice sort of man to be peddling the Bible," the young woman said.

"There are all sorts to everything," yawned her guest from the side of his mouth. "And talkin of Bibles, I've been filled with such fire, you wouldn't believe. I was dazzled. Oh yes. Only it don't last."

His hair hung, the few sad strands. The husband and wife sat against each other. It was true, they were untouched. Their faces had the golden waxiness of closed contentment.

"And now, with your permission, I'll lay down somewhere," said the guest, easing the stuff of his pants. "Stretch out with the whirligigs. That's a pretty little thing."

Which he fingered, from a distance, on the mantelpiece.

"That," she said, "is a little silver nutmeg grater that was given me at my wedding."

"Ah, weddings! 'Ow we try to insure ourselves!"

But he was disposed of outside on one or two bags. He was asleep.

A crazy moon had risen on the deathless trees. The oblong shack lay at a distance in the moonlight. Inside, the fire had died to coals, of which the flames no longer exalted the human flesh, with the consequence that such poetry as man had dared to conceive was just silly. Habit prevailed in those who were taking off their clothes and preparing for sleep. Their backs turned on each other, they knew the next move. They knew the hands responding to each other. They recognized the sigh of the bed.

"Amy," said Stan Parker into his wife's cheek.

The silence was complicated.

"Tt-tt-tt," she said, "and that old boy outside."

But his body was flooding her with tolerance. They flowed together in the darkness. The coasts of tenderness opened to admit their craft. Sleep swam out to meet them, from under the trees.

When finally it was morning, all square and full of birds, with the red dog yelping after a rabbit in the dew, Amy Parker, again a thin young woman, her face creased by sleep, sat up and remembered that old boy outside.

"Waiting for his breakfast, Stan, perhaps, and the bacon that salt. I should have soaked it if I hadn't forgotten."

"He'll be too furry to notice a thing like bacon. He'll keep," her husband said, for whom it did not matter, only the warm smell of sleep and the shape of their bodies, with which the sheets were still full.

"Go on, Stan. *Leave* me!" She laughed.

Her slippers slapped across the floor as she elbowed her way into the dress.

"Why," she said, and she was still shaking her hair and smoothing, "why," she said to the morning, "can you beat it, he has gone."

And he had. There were the innocent bags on which he had slept, before some problem of conscience had propelled him out along the track, towards the great river for which he had been making.

Later, when the young woman was sweeping the place where he had slept, she could not sweep him out. So few people entered her life, she remembered the warts on the faces and the colour of the eyes of those who did. She would have liked to perpetuate her dreams and lift the reflections out of mirrors. So now, from desperate, retrospective sweeping of the veranda floor, she had to go back into the room to see what her possessions really were. There was nothing much of which she could be proud; there was nothing sufficiently useless, except her little silver nutmeg grater.

Then Amy Parker began to burn inside her cold skin.

"Stan," she called, ran, her skirts brushing hens, "Stan," as she ran, and the woolly clumps of horehound were crushed by her passage, "do you know," she said as clearly as her breath allowed, "what that old man has done? He has pinched the nutmeg grater!"

Her husband had earth on his hands. It was wet and black and comfortable.

He whistled. "He did?" he said. "The old bugger!"

She looked at his naked throat. All these mornings there was a glow of bluish cabbages.

"It was never much use," he said.

"Of course it wasn't."

But her words were hot and slow that trailed back towards the house. It had never, of course, been any use, except to hold, that morning they had jingled out from Yuruga across the flat, past Venables' dead cow. Or as the sparks flew, and the man with the Bibles had talked his exhilarating rot, mounting upward through the evening, this in the end had been her one contribution of treasure, her Gold Coast, only it was real, her silver nutmeg grater.

Stan Parker, who had never yet attempted to possess the truth in final form, was a lesser victim of the same deception. His Gold Coast still glittered in a haze of promise as he grubbed the weeds out of his land, as he felled trees and tautened the wire fences he had put round what was his. It was, by this time, almost enclosed. But what else was his he could not say. Would his life of longing be lived behind the wire fences? His eyes were assuming a distance from looking into distances. So he did begin then with impatience, even passion, to hew the logs that still lay, and to throw aside his axe at the end, with disgust, apparently, for something wood will not disclose. He would listen to the sounds around him too, the thick and endless murmurs, from which a theme will threaten to burst, the one theme, and continue to threaten.

In the meantime he was growing a bit older. His body was hardening into the sculptural shape of muscular bodies. And for the casual speculator there was no obvious sign that his soul too might not harden in the end into the neat, self-contained shape it is desirable souls should take.

43

Chapter 5

OTHER people came to live in those parts. From time to time they passed by, all tables and mattresses, on drays and bullock wagons, or some putting on dog in a buggy with new black paint. Sometimes somebody would come in to fill the water-bag from Parkers' tank. But most were tardy to recognize those who were already there, and Parkers returned their sideways glances with long, flat stares.

One young woman who was taken queer, and who came in to sit a while on the veranda, and to clean her face with a soaked handkerchief, said it was terrible lonely.

Amy Parker did not answer this. Loneliness was something that she had not learned about; she did not connect market days. Then the people went away, and at once the silence filled in where their rather thin presences had been. There was a ringing almost of bells of silence in the parrot-coloured morning. She was happy.

There was a rosebush now, growing against the veranda, a white rose, of which she had thought and spoken, and which he had brought to her from town. It was already a branching, irregular bush, with the big wads of shapely paper roses just smelling of tobacco. Cold perhaps. It belonged to the dank green light on that side of the house, where it stood in the long weed that is called cow-itch. Its branches would grow black and straggly later on. But the rosebush of Amy Parker was still green, sappy wood. The marble roses were solid in the moonlight. The white roses glared back at the heavy light of noon or fluttered papery down into the yellow-green of the cow-itch.

"You're a one for the flower plantun, I see," said the woman whose cart grated to a stop, though she only half-intended to.

"I have a rosebush," said Amy Parker quietly.

44

"Gingerbread never got anyone nowheres," said the woman in the cart, "but it is all right, I suppose, for them that has the taste."

Amy Parker disliked the woman, much as she had disliked her Aunt Fibbens, though this one was young.

"You've got to have something," said Amy Parker.

"Ho," snorted the young woman, and she would have flicked her tail if she had been a draught mare. "We have the pigs, two sow in farrer, and a pretty young boar, and the pullets besides, and he's for growun things as well, we're tryun the taters this spring, though it's a frost holler we're in if ever there was."

As she rolled her round words, turning her head this way and that, with its black coil of glistening hair, and the high colour in her cheeks, the broad young woman was more than ever like a draught mare.

"So you cannot say there is nothun," she said, "without roses besides."

"I shall have my rose," said Amy Parker stubbornly.

"You are not for bein wild at me, dear?" the young woman asked. "I was expressun a personal opinion. *He* says it is me life's vocation, but after all, a woman must breathe, and what is wrong if a word or two gets into me breath, like, I says."

Amy Parker had begun to warm to words.

"An it is terrible lonely here," the woman sighed. "I was born in a bog, to be sure, but you could call to other Christians on either hand."

Amy Parker leaned upon the gate. Her life, which had never been a wilderness, was becoming one perhaps, with so many hinting at it, except that for the moment it was peopled by her friend, the fubsy woman in the cart.

"We're here, for two," Amy Parker said, to help.

"Yes," said the woman, "that is so."

But she sat looking rather blank. She sat looking straight ahead. Her jaunty face was flat, and the heavy coil of glittery hair had begun to fall apart.

"Well," she said, as if she were tearing the word out of something that might get the better of her, "I am for town, with a few things. *He* will not be visible, not today, nor tomorrer. He has an affliction, I might say, except, as it is his, it is not, it is a gentleman's pastime. It is his privilege, he would have you know, to get shickered periodical, like a lord or a bastard, and fling out the marines, so that his wife will

45

break 'er ankles one fine day on the bottles floatun round the yard."

She put her hair back where it belonged and began to gather up the reins with some vehemence.

"I'm just tellun you," she said, "seeun as we've made each other's acquaintance, but for all that, he's not too bad."

She began to clack with her leather tongue, to slap with the whole bunch of reins, to jog with her bottom on the board, all of which would have started a better horse than this.

"The horse is sick?" asked Amy Parker.

"Tother one was," said her new friend. "But not this. He has got his bones dug in."

Whether or not, he was certainly all bones, and a girth gall or two, these and his eyes a liberal fly-feast.

"He is good in motion," panted the woman. "Only he stands awful fast. Hey there, now! Who's the deaf and unfeelun one?"

The cart began to groan.

"As I was sayun before, we are now acquainted, which is as it should be between neighbours. We are only a couple a mile down, where the chestnut mare is dead at the turn. If you would care perhaps for a drink of tea, and a conversation, sure, nothun could please me better. The house is easy to find, what there is, it is incomplete. You have only to look for the old dead horse that he left layun for a sign."

She called as the reluctant cart was pulling out, lurching over stones, and she leaned down, shining from her sweat of words. You could see the moles above her best blouse, and the knitted jacket, where the egg had fallen that day. She had a pretty smile, the neighbour woman. Her soaped skin was friendly to her audience.

"Oh," she called, "an I forgot to mention, but me name is Mrs. O'Dowd."

Soon after Amy Parker had told hers in return, with a boldness she used now that it was not Fibbens, the neighbour woman was gone. There were the trees again.

The young woman left the gate and went inside, thinking about her friend. Because she *was* her friend, she was sure of it, who had never had one before. That morning as she scrubbed the table, as she beat the mat, as she stirred the pot, she digested the neighbour woman's words. Some objects in the house now looked quite startling through the young woman's new eyes. The bed, for instance, of which the enormous brass knobs glowed with reflections upon the posts of humbler iron. So the young woman went about her house, and laughed at the dog that she had never liked, and he was looking at her straight, with his surprised but unforgiving eyes, just moving the tip of his liver-coloured nose.

"Stan," she said to her husband, who was not far behind his dog, "we have a neighbour who passed by. Her name is Mrs. O'Dowd, and her husband's on the bottle."

"The Irish have come," said Stan Parker, putting down his hat and filling the basin to wash for dinner.

"What of it?" she said. "It is lonely here."

"Since now."

"It is nice to have someone to talk to."

"And what about me?"

"Oh," she said, "you!" Piling the big, steamy potatoes.

He could not kill her warm pleasure.

"That is different," she said.

She brought him his dinner, looking down from under her eyelids in a way that was annoying to him.

"Keep an eye on your things," he said, filling his mouth too full with righteous potatoes.

"Why, but she was an honest woman," she said, "by the way she spoke."

"So was the bloke with the Bibles," said her husband, whom the hot potato had made sound angrier.

He sat there breaking bread in such a way that the bones of his wrists looked bigger and unreasonable.

She did not speak then. There was a speckled hen that had come in, her pet, that she allowed at times to peck about beneath the table, and now in the silence there was the pecking of the hen's beak upon the hard floor. It punctuated most firmly all that had been said.

But Amy Parker could not dismiss her friendship, nor her husband. They mingled in the drowsy noon. She was invaded by a warm melancholy that was rather pleasant to indulge, just not serious enough, and sweet as the strong tea that made her steamy-eyed, remote.

Presently her husband put down his cup and went outside. Nothing had been settled. It was the first time in their relationship that there were any loose ends, and the sad, pleasurable situation persisted through the sultry afternoon.

What of it? she said, running her needle angrily and excitedly through the sock she had taken to darn; none of it is important. There would be thunder later that day. The sweat stood out above her lip. Already leaves moved in a little

47

breeze. Clouds were swelling in the right direction. She pricked her finger in anticipation of some event, sucked it, rolled the socks into a nervous ball. All this time the big clouds, moving and swelling, pushed and shouldered each other. The little and, at first, subtle breeze became moister and more blatantly vicious. It was lifting the corners of things. The woman in the house got up and closed a door, in an attempt to secure for herself an illusion of safety, if only an illusion. Because the black clouds were bursting on her head. And the grey wool of torn clouds that the wind dragged across the sky raced quicker than her blood and began to rouse the terror in her.

The wind began to bash the small wooden box in which she had been caught.

Where is he? she asked, turning in it. Her mouth was cavernous with fright.

Just then the man her husband was down by a small shed he had been putting up. His hammering, which at first had been theatrical and impressive, was no longer heard; his was only inferior iron. But the man laughed. He felt a kind of pleasure in the mounting storm. He held his face up flat to the racing clouds. His teeth were smiling in a taut, uncertain humour at the sky, the Adam's apple was isolated but insignificant in his throat. When suddenly he was altogether insignificant. A thing of gristle. The laughter thinned out in his throat. The pants hung from his hips and blew against the thin sticks of his legs.

The whole earth was in motion, a motion of wind and streaming trees, and he was in danger of being carried with it.

When he was a little boy he had lain on a hard horsehair sofa and been carried through the books of the Old Testament on a wave of exaltation and fear. And now, brought to his knees, about to be hit over the head perhaps, a lightning flash lit his memory. God blew from the clouds, and men would scatter like leaves. It was no longer possible to tell who was on which side. Or is it ever possible to tell? Surrounded by the resentful inanimacy of rock and passionate striving of the trees, he was not sure. In this state he was possessed by an unhappiness, rather physical, that was not yet fear, but he would have liked to look up and see some expression of sympathy on the sky's face.

But the sky blew blacker. There was one steady stream of wind, and he began to be afraid.

Presently the man saw his wife running, her limbs fighting the wind and the stuff of her own dress. Seeing her tortured into these shapes he did not know, and the drained, strange face, quite suddenly he felt that this was not the girl he had married in the church at Yuruga, and loved and quarrelled with, but he forced himself to stumble on towards her. To touch.

They stood holding each other in the storm.

"What will we do?" she cried, through her mouth that was still of a strange shape.

"There is nothing much we can do," he shouted, "except hope it will be over."

They held each other. They searched each other's thin faces. When the touch of each other brought them back to their bodies. For a while again they were themselves. Their feet precariously held the earth.

"I am afraid, Stan," she said.

He should have said something reassuring, but as he was afraid too, he did not. He touched her though, and she felt better.

And the wind blew.

The yellow cow, curved to the wind as far as her full belly would allow, galloped on no set course. The dog fell against the man's legs, reduced to ribs and a pair of bulging puppy's eyes. Fowls flew, or handfuls of feathers. The wind peeled off a sheet of iron and flung it with a brittle tinkling of silver paper.

Ahhhh, cried the woman against her husband's neck, which once had been strong.

The great trees had broken off. Two or three fell. In a grey explosion. Of gunpowder, it seemed. The trees were snapped and splintered. The yellow cow leaped just clear of the branches, tossing her horns. Man and woman were flung against each other with the ease and simplicity of tossed wood. They lay and looked at each other, into each other's eyes, as the dog licked their hands with slow, rough system, as if he had discovered a new taste.

"We are still here," The man laughed whitely.

Rain filled his mouth.

"Our poor cow," she cried.

"But she is all right."

"Yes," she cried, "I know."

In the blubbery rain.

The cold wet sheet wrapped them till their bodies were naked, it felt, except for the clinging rain. The rain drove down the gully over the jagged stumps where the trees had been, then began to fall straight, as if the wind had passed. There was just the rain.

"What are we sitting here for?" He laughed in his new young nakedness.

She saw that his head was very young with the hair plastered to the skull.

"Yes," she said, "we must be a bit mad."

Looking at him with fresh wonder, and at the same time wanting to make excuses for any extravagances of action or emotion. It did not seem that she could in reason have been frightened, sitting as she was now by the blasted trees with the new young naked man. If she were to have a son, she thought, he could be like this, with the shining teeth, the streaming skin, and the clean, beautiful skull. She would have liked to kiss, only it would have been to destroy their present state of purity, after all they had gone through. So she got quickly to her feet, arranged what had been her skirt, because there was a lot to do, and no reason to suppose their lives would become different by thinking of it.

"Clean through the old shed," her husband was saying, "but they missed the new one, so we've got that."

"And the old cow by inches," she was saying in wet, helpless words.

The dog shook what remained of himself, for he was now his own skeleton.

The man and woman continued through the rain, holding each other, not because they needed support, now that the wind had passed, but because they had grown accustomed to it, and besides, they wanted to.

At least we shall have this, said Stan Parker, and he remembered again the figures that had plodded through the pages of his boyhood in the face of drought and famine and war, and the great deserts of human and divine injustice, as he lay on the horsehair sofa. And here he was, still fumbling his way through the more personal events. He could not interpret the lightning that had written on their lives.

"See if you can find a piece of dry wood, dear," his wife was saying as she stood in their intact house and wrung the water from her hair.

And he did, after a time, and there on the hearth was the reasonable little fire. And soon, outside, there were the grey patches of still cloud, and the orange fire of evening, burning and blazing in its distance with a prophetic intensity that would no more be read than the flash of lightning.

The man, who went about his evening work, did not try. He was tired. He was also at peace under the orange sky. Events had exhausted him. He had not learned to think far, and in what progress he had made had reached the conclusion he was a prisoner in his human mind, as in the mystery of the natural world. Only sometimes the touch of hands, the lifting of a silence, the sudden shape of a tree or presence of a first star, hinted at eventual release.

But not now. And he did not ask for it.

His dull feet went into the house, where he was grateful for the sound of his wife chafing her skin before the fire.

Chapter 6

Soon there was very little evidence that the lightning had struck. Three squashed pullets were fed to the dog, the boards of the demolished shed were again in use, and any jagged emotions were tidied away. Even the hulks of the shattered trees were slowly being hewn and dragged into neat heaps by the ant-man. The ant-woman watched him in the pauses from her own endeavours. She saw him stagger, but advance, over the uneven ground. There was no real doubt that he would eventually accomplish what he had set out to do; only the path was tortuous, and his once apparently boundless strength seen to be comparatively limited.

Sometimes, in the sonorous afternoons, when faith is at its feeblest and haze at its heaviest, the cock drooling in the nettles and hens brooding in the dust, the man and woman would look out from under their sun-frowns and watch the progress of other ant-activity. Down their track, of which use was slowly making a road, just within sight, beneath the stringybarks and peppermints, another family had squatted down. This was Quigleys'. There were the old people, an old, yellow, bristly man that they laid on a mattress, and there he stayed, and the old woman, whose vague surprise stared at these parts to which she had been transported for no apparent reason at her age. She sat beside her husband, wondering, her hands opening and closing, as if they were waiting to take up what they had dropped at the other place. In the meantime she sat beside her bundle of a husband, amongst the bundles of mattresses and bunches of hens, and her daughter and her sons moved about her, trying to find what had been mislaid.

The two Quigley sons, with long, sinewy, veined arms and slipping pants, were preparing to build a weatherboard house for their parents to live in. But the two ingenious boys, who could devise almost anything out of wire or tin or bag, would afterwards return to Bangalay, it was told, where they worked in a road gang. As they moved about, sorting and improvising, the mother included her long sons in the gaze of wonder that she kept for all objects, as if she had not given them birth. Life had already passed on from her and left her sitting amongst bundles.

"Your dad don't look good, Doll," said the mother to her tall daughter, who was freeing a bunch of red hens.

The tall young woman came and bent above the body of her father.

"He don't look no worse," she said, shooing flies with her long hand.

Like her brothers, she had long limbs. But her body was short. Like her brothers, she could have been carved from wood, but whereas the young men were crude gods, she was an unfinished totem, of which the significance was obscure.

Just as the fates of the boys could not have been fitted into the family circle, the unfinished Doll was born to live inside. If she was not herself the circle that enfolds. Some kind of natural dignity clung to her with her cotton dress. Many people would call her *Miss* Quigley even when her feet were bare, and her nephews and nieces, still unborn, would be brought to see her in carts, buggies, and eventually Fords, as an object of respect. It was difficult to tell what age Doll Quigley was, and she would remain that age, more or less. She was a dry, sandy girl, the sort that the sun soon plays havoc with, so that there is nothing left on which age can practise malignancies. Early on she had developed a prim, upright handwriting, that she had learned from the nuns, and her people were proud of this. They brought her things to write, and she sat at a deal table beside a lamp, and crooked her neck above the painful saltcellars of her chest, and made little elegant passes with her hand above the paper, to form the words in air first, and her family looked on in pride and wonder, waiting for her to write. She was above them, though she did not choose to be. People coming to the door with a message or request asked for Miss Quigley, preferring to give their words into her keeping. She was a reliable repository, it seemed.

Lastly, of the Quigley family, there was Bub, his child's face on a young man's body. He lay beneath the trees and chewed a twig. An implicit simplicity seemed to hold together the long blurred form of his face. He was obviously good.

53

His blue, blurry eyes were wide open. His indeterminate nose ran, but not offensively, and not much. Nobody, except occasionally a stranger, was upset by Bub Quigley, because he was inoffensive as water. And as passive. He had to be taken and poured from here to there, and contained by other people, usually the will of his sister Doll.

Quigleys settled down and began to live in the place that they had chosen, under the peppermints and stringybarks, beside the turpentines. Their house was quite like a house, because of the ingenuity of the two boys, who knew by instinct how to do so many things. They were fortunate, too, in finding a spring just there, and Bub Quigley would sit beside it on a stone amongst the tussocks, watching the water ooze out, while people went ahead, and arranged life in spite of him. Watching them as closely as he watched tadpoles, he never resented it. He was only resentful when his sister Doll left him behind. Then he would run up and down on his long, clothesprop legs, looking and crying, and his dribbly desperation was terrible in the landscape.

Sometimes Doll Quigley took her brother Bub and they hung around the back door at Parkers' to have a talk. Or if they did not exactly and continuously talk, they shared the silences of that place, and this was a nice change. Amy Parker accepted Doll and Bub because there was no choice. They were good people, and if she lapsed into a private yearning for intricate relationships and immeasurable events, she did not rightly know why.

"I used to think once I would have a little shop," said Doll Quigley, sitting on the doorstep, with her thin knees under her long chin. "I would sell doilies and towels and mats and things, you know, fancy things that I would make myself, and soap and things. Now, Bub, don't scare the chooks. Because I learned to make a lot of things from the nuns, hemstitch and transfers and all that. There was some that learned baskets, but that was not for me."

"I'd like to make a basket," Bub Quigley said, "with red and yeller lines."

"And why did nothing come of your shop, Doll?" said Amy Parker, in one of the remote questions she sometimes asked of people, and Quigleys in particular.

"It didn't work out in that way," said Miss Quigley, without further elaboration, but as if she knew.

What way things were working out for herself, Amy Parker was not sure. She had not thought till now, but was it not now, perhaps, a reason for panic? A slight gust of panic just touched her skin. Here in this house her life was suspended, a bubble ready to burst.

"What is it, Mrs. Parker?" asked Miss Quigley, getting up with a grace and kindness that she could suddenly command.

"Is she sick?" asked Bub.

"I just felt a little queer. It is nothing, Doll," said Amy Parker.

She sat on an upright chair in a beam of sunlight that was too hot. Till now she had never sensed sharply and personally the division between life and death.

"It is all right," she said.

"Look," said Bub Quigley, bringing in his hands a cat's-cradle he had made. "Can you play?"

"No," said Amy Parker. "You're real clever, Bub. But I can't play."

She was looking with sudden loathing into his innocent hands, on which the intricate and grubby string was stretched. She was looking at a working-out in string.

"Perhaps it is what they call a nausea," said Doll Quigley.

"I am all right," said Amy Parker.

But her words could not sweep Quigleys out. And the hands of Bub were drawing fresh shapes out of the string.

"See?" he said. "That is a mattress."

Amy Parker ran to the side of the house and began to be sick.

"That *is* a nausea," said Doll Quigley with grating gentleness. "They say if you wet a dock leaf and hold it to your forehead—"

"It will pass," said Amy Parker, holding her agitation.

If Quigley's would too.

And in time they did, long and slow across the yard, through the slow-stepping fowls.

When Stan Parker came up from the gully that evening he said, "What's up, Amy?"

"Ah, those Quigleys!" she said.

She dug her elbows into the table, because that way her arms would not shake.

"They're good enough people," said her husband. "No harm there."

He was slowly stirring the thick soup into which he had dropped big chunks of bread. Physical exhaustion and the presence of his wife made him content.

55

But Amy Parker was angrily tearing bread. "That Bub Quigley makes me feel sick."

"What's he to you? He's harmless," her husband said.

"Oh, go on!" she said. "Say it. But I can't stand it."

Her mouth was full of hot, doughy bread. The disturbed lamplight made his eyes shine, that looked at her out of his thick, unseeing face.

What is happening, he wondered, in this strange room in which we live?

"Stan," she said. "I was looking at that long, loopy boy, and I got the wind up. I don't know much. I don't understand the way things work out. Why, for instance, Mum Quigley? I'm going to have a kid, Stan. I'm sure now. He was showing me a cat's-cradle he'd made, and I began to feel myself slip, as if I hadn't a hold on anything in this world. I was afraid."

Then she was not afraid. Now the lamplight was bland. Her words had released her. And his seeing face. There are moments when the eyes flow into each other. Then the souls are wrapped around each other across a distance.

"There's no need," he was saying needlessly, "to be afraid. You'll get through it like anyone else."

Already it seemed unreasonable to dwell upon the instance of Mum Quigley, who had conceived Bub.

"Yes," she said peacefully.

He could have put almost any word into her mouth.

"We'll have to build another room," he was saying. "Or perhaps a house. It'll be a tight fit for three people walking around in this shack."

And the boy, because that was what it would be, stood in the centre of the floor, of a new house, holding in his hand things to show, a speckled magpie's egg, a piece of glass with a bubble in it, or a stick that was meant to be a horse. Stan Parker's positive vision gave even to the furniture a certainty of shape that his wife had never noticed before, so that she was ashamed of her lack of faith.

"It'll be nice to have kids about the place," she said quietly, bringing a plate of spotted dog, that was not a great success on account of Quigleys.

"Chop the wood, eh? And wash the dishes."

He laughed for the first time since receiving his wife's news, and if his mouth had tightened a bit she did not notice, or did not appear to, with her own thoughts inside her. If Stan Parker's vision was less positive than before, it was be-

56

cause there were so many bits of himself that he did not know how to unravel, and here was a fresh life, a whole tangled ball of mystery in his wife's womb. It gave him the gooseflesh to think. The man sitting in the small, frail box of light, himself glowing and waning within the limits of his soul, was perhaps greater, but also less adequate, than the husband who had begotten the child, and who sat offering advice and the consolation of his body's presence as he chewed the plateful of soggy pudding and generally performed the acts that are performed.

But his wife was comforted.

She went about. She went to Quigleys' once, where the house was almost finished that the boys were building, and Doll took her to see a slope at the back, which they would plough up, she said, and plant with orange trees, and she would have the fowls and the oranges.

"I am glad we have come here," said Doll Quigley. "I didn't want to. But it has begun to be our home. It's funny the way you take root. You get to like people."

Standing in the paddock, with her arms held awkwardly across her stomach, she was not unlike a tree, of which something had roughened the bark in passing.

And Bub Quigley showed Amy Parker the tadpoles he had caught, and she was not disgusted.

A great many little coloured parrots lit on the hills at that season, flirting and settling, stalking woodenly in the stubble, destroying the silence with their hard cries. It had become a season of activity. Life was simple and benevolent on many evenings. The wattles were in flower. Now their black trunks were less desolate, now that the sun shone through the tears of oozing gum. Amy Parker, walking beneath the froth of wattles, broke off pieces of transparent gum, stuck it in her mouth for its prettiness and promise, but the gum was nothing much, neither sweet nor particularly bitter, just insipid.

Still, it was a season of activity and life, that might hold almost any issue, as she walked with her pail, evenings, to the waiting cow. They had soon begun the new house, and were working day and night, to have at least one room finished before Mrs. Parker's time had come. She heard the hammer in the evening, and the voices of her husband and the Quigley boys, who were giving a hand. Then the whole landscape would seem to be built around the woman, which made her silent and important.

How still it was those evenings after the wind had died, the

57

stillness made stiller by the sound of milk. The wattles, which had been turbulent all day, stood penitent then. Their clouds of dying light guided the gathering darkness. The milking tree, of which the dead wood had been polished by the cow's neck, was white as a tree of bone.

This cow, their Julia, that had had the mastitis in one teat, and for that reason they had got her cheap, was again heavy in calf. Her laborious sides palpitated with the unborn calf. She chewed and sighed. Soon they would dry her off. But she would continue to chew, and sigh, and look, and stand beside the milking tree, waiting for attention to be paid, and to take part in the ritual of the milk.

She was an aged cow.

"Better to sell her," said Stan Parker, "while we can still get a price."

"No," said Amy. "She's my cow. She's a good cow."

Stan Parker did not argue, because he did not feel strongly enough. It was not important at that moment.

So his wife became fonder of the cow, especially now that she would have her child. She buried her forehead in the cow's soft side, and there was a continual stirring, and the gentle cow smell. The whole air those evenings was soft with the smell of cow's breath, as if the blue tongue had slapped it on. The old cow stood wisely waiting. Her ears were held twitched back, as if she were pleased. Her brown eyes looked inward, it appeared. There were little dots of passive moisture on her granite-coloured nose.

Stiller even than the dusk was this peaceful relationship between Amy Parker and the yellow cow. Their soft, increasing bodies were in full accord. I shall have a little girl, said Amy Parker, and she smiled for this luxury into the acquiescent belly of the cow. The child sat on a smooth log. She was as pink and white as painted china, and the hair, parted in the centre, smoothed in the mornings with a wet brush, sprang at the sides into little tinkling curls as yellow as the waning wattle trees. Yes, said Amy Parker, I would like a girl. Then she remembered that this was not her husband's wish, and looked downward into the milk.

When the time came for the old cow to go dry and rest before dropping her calf, the woman was at a loss. She would walk in the sharp evenings, from the shack to the skeleton of their new house, and along the edges of the paddocks, wearing an old jacket she had knitted, that had a darn in the left elbow, chafing her hands together, that were sud-

58

denly dry and papery in their inactivity, the bones frail. Then her own pregnancy stretched out before her in heavy days. The thorns of the straggly rose bush caught at the harsh blue of her jacket as she passed. An early bud was white and sickly on its stem.

"You look pale," he said, meeting her kindly in the path, his heavy boots coming to an abrupt stop at the toes of her more pointed woman's shoes.

He took her cold hands. There was a smell of sawdust about him that was reassuring, and his hands that had been working with the timber.

"Oh," she laughed into his eyes. "I feel no different. Well, of course, you do feel different. But I'm all right, all the same. It's funny though, not to go down to the cow. She's standing there, Stan, expecting me."

She looked into his eyes, expecting him to offer her some assistance, while at the same time knowing he could not.

Even her hands at times, he felt, are distant. Even the mystery of possession is a mystery that it is not possible to share. And now, as they stood in the path, verging on the discovery of half-veiled shores, the child was not theirs, and he was already embarrassed by those things he would be unable to say to the stranger-child.

"That old cow is nothing to worry about," he said out of his kind face.

She bent away and continued along the path, feeling that she was in herself, anyway at that moment, too thin and dry to encounter his goodness.

I have a good husband, she would say, not aware that she was specifically unworthy, yet unworthy she was in some yet-to-be-discovered way.

"As you say, there is nothing to worry about," she said. "Only the cow is old."

She walked slowly on, taking care of herself, and the harsh blue of her woolen jacket flickered through the evening colours of the garden, the colour of moss, almost of foreboding, and her skirt in passing stirred up an intolerable scent of rosemary and thyme, that lingered after she had gone.

Sometimes Amy Parker sat on the edge of the bed, and the sensation of love and joy for the child she would have became unaccountably one of sadness and loss.

If it would be over quickly, she said; I am ignorant of almost everything, I am ignorant of the sensations in my body, and of the meaning of almost everything; I cannot really believe in God. Then she recoiled also at the thought of the man with whom she lived in a house, whose strength was no substitute for her ignorance and weakness, and whose passion was disastrous. As she sat and listened to the spidery motion of leaves moving against the wooden wall.

"Amy," said Stan Parker at last, "your old cow's had a nice little heifer."

It was as if this at least was something he could recount to a little child.

"Ah," she said feverishly, "and what colour is it?"

This of course was what had been upsetting her peace of mind. All would now be well. She got up at once, intending to go quickly to the cow.

"A sort of piebald," he said. "And strong as they make them."

There indeed was the spotted calf, curled in the bracken, and the mother stood, her nose outstretched, surprised, it seemed, even now, although this one must be her seventh. The woman began to make noises of love. She wanted to touch this prize. The little calf got to her feet, all legs and umbilical cord. She stood glistening, and swaying, and licked, in the curled bracken.

"Coop, cooop, cooop!" called the woman. "A little love, Stan! You little darling!"

The cow snorted and tossed her head, but not with feeling, as if she were ready to stand, and allow somebody to take over. Her flanks were hollow. She was still bloody.

"Poor Julia," said Amy Parker. "We shall call her Jewel. See, Stan? Jewel! Julia's calf!"

And she laughed in the coloured morning. It was over. She was a girl again, standing on the flat at Yuruga, with her thin arms outstretched towards miraculous life.

All that morning she was running to look, to touch, to be with the calf that had been born. She was all the time murmuring, improvising some new tenderness with which to express her relief, until this relief flooded her, and she was impervious to the trees that stood, to the cow even with its awkward calf, that had released her. She was translated into a serene air. She was herself the blue morning in which the event had taken place.

Later in the day, when the shapes of things had hardened and she had been caught up in her life again, the man her husband came abruptly to fetch hot water from the kettle.

"What is it?" she asked.

He said it was the cow.

"But she was all right," she said, almost in anger, to defend her own peace of mind.

"She was," he said sulkily, filling an old iron basin. "But now she's down. She's crook. It looks like the milk fever," he said.

And the cow was indeed down in the bracken, but peacefully, unobtrusively, her mild shoulders rising from the bracken like a statue.

"How do you know?" the woman asked.

"She's got a bright eye," he said. "And she's lost interest. She won't get up. Look," he said, and he kicked her in the rump and twisted her tail, as if she had in the meantime become an object. But she would not get up.

"And the calf?" she asked.

"We've got to get the cow right. It's a mess," he said. "We should have sold her. That's what comes of keeping old cows."

"Blame me," said the woman.

"I'm not blaming you," he said, wringing the boiling water out of a rag.

"I don't know what else you're doing," she said, because she was superfluous and wretched.

She watched him hold the steaming cloth to the cow's udder, and the cow stirred and moaned with hot breath.

The woman watched the man. She did not feel he was resentful of her. He was absorbed in what he was doing. He had flowed away from her into his hands. These had forgotten they had ever touched her, it appeared. She was useless and desolate, standing there, and she began in a sick twinge to be anxious for her child.

"We've got to feed that calf, Stan," she said, or her voice, taking possession. "I'm going over to O'Dowds'. She told me they have cows. So they ought to have the milk."

"All right," he said, just as if all that were secondary, as if his whole being were flowing out of his hands into the body of the sick cow.

She looked away from his hands to which she had no right, and clung to her fresh purpose. She went away to harness the horse.

As she drove down to O'Dowds' behind the clinking little horse her self-pity fell away. She had a bitter taste in her mouth, but the cold wind tightened the flesh on her cheeks. She drove purposefully. The trees opened before her, as if there were no track and she were blazing one. And in no time there were the bones of the dead horse, just as the neighbour woman had told, and in the scrub there was a blur that might well become a house.

So Amy Parker came to O'Dowds'.

"Well, I do believe it is Mrs. Parker," said the neighbour woman, who was herself standing on a step, surveying everything and nothing, as if there was something she ought to do but she could not bear the thought of it.

O'Dowds' place had evolved out of a series of impulses, it seemed. Out of the original room sprang evidence of the complications of living, in the shape of further rooms, or protuberances, in slab, iron, and bark. Nothing harmonized, except that the whole was a barky, rusty brown, and this had settled into the landscape well enough, under and amongst the trees. Round about on a crust of mud hens picked at their own feathers. The red sow ran inquisitively to inspect the arrival, her dugs flipping her sides like leather, her farrow squealing over cabbage stalks. Cows stared from where the mud was becoming grass. There was a smell of ducks.

"I do believe it is Mrs. Parker," the neighbour woman said, and she came down, or, rather, the step on which she was standing pitched her into the yard.

"Yes," said Amy Parker.

The wind of her journey died about her, leaving her wretched again, and in that yard.

"I came to ask a favour," she said. "We are in trouble, Mrs. O'Dowd."

"What is it, dear?" asked the fubsy woman, intending already to be lavish.

On this occasion she was less festive. In several places, indeed, she was done up with safety pins, but her breasts were not less cordial in their motion, and blood was moving in her smooth cheeks.

"We have a cow calved this morning," said Amy Parker. "Of a little heifer."

"Lucky you are! The lovely little calves!"

"But the cow is down with the milk fever. It is an old cow," she said.

The neighbour woman sucked her teeth.

"A bugger of the old cows. Poor things. 'Tis always the same."

"But we must rear the heifer, Mrs. O'Dowd."

"Sure you must."

It was already her anxiety.

"Hey!" she called. "Where are yer? There's a lady visitun. Show yerself for God's sake, an they'll know I've got yer. Ah, it's terrible, the men, when all is said and done, an him officiatun, and the fowls not fed. But if it's milk you want, dear, we are swimmun in the stuff. We're milkun the two big beasts hand over fist, and the bally heifer comun in. You are welcome, Mrs. Parker dear, whatever he says, it is me that says last."

"What are yer squawkun for? Ain't I comun when I found me boots," her husband called.

And he did. He was there.

"This is him," said his wife.

She jerked her head towards the back door. Her black hair was coming down, that on this occasion she did not put up.

O'Dowd was a broad man. He had two black holes for a nose, that you could look right up. He was rather hairy, and his laugh was black and white.

"Trouble with the cows, eh? The milk fever," said O'Dowd.

"There ain't no need to recapitulate," said his wife.

So that everybody was surprised, and not least herself.

"Kerosene," said her husband. "There is nothun like kerosene for milk fever, or anythun."

His own breath was testimony.

"He's a one for the kerosene," said his wife. "He'll pour it into a sick beast, either end, no matter. I go in mortal terror meself whenever I have the wind."

"There is nothun like the kerosene," said her husband. "If you will take a bottle of beer, an empty it, an fill it just so full, to where me finger is, see, no more, no less, which is about a two-thirds, I should say, an after that the danger begins, as Paddy Connor knows who was too enthusiastic, an his little beauty of a Jersey heifer writhun in the dust, but just so full an you will not look back, if you insert the bottle, like, in the beast's mouth, an ram it gently down till the liquid's took, a course she'll protest, but it's too bad if she does, an the fever will pass, you'll find, like Sunday mornun."

"But it ain't the kerosene that she wants," his wife began to nudge. "For everybody's got his own treatments. It's the milk."

"If it ain't the kerosene," said her husband, "least she has the information an that it free."

"An so is the milk. For a little heifer just calved."

"Ah, the milk is free."

63

"Then what are yer maggin for this half-hour?"

"A man must say somethun," her husband said.

Standing in the hugger-mugger yard, Amy Parker was groggy at the knees, but love lapped at the muddy puddles with the bills of ducks. Even the bottles that were lying where they had landed had a rightness now, because it was O'Dowd himself that had thrown them out of the window, for what better purpose than to be rid of them inside.

"Have you a bocket?" he asked.

He took it and walked across the yard, with firm pleasure for his generous deed.

"Mrs. O'Dowd——" Amy Parker began.

"What is you today is us tomorrer," said her friend. "Tsst, tsst!" she sucked, withdrawing her rather greasy hand. "I will be forgettun me own name. There's the goat as kidded Thursday night, of a buck, an we hit um on the head, poor thing, but you are welcome, Mrs. Parker, to the doe, an her with a bag of milk that will make you happy. Hey," she called, "Mrs. Parker will have a loan of the doe! They do say, dear, there's many a child would 'uv wizened right away but for the blessed goats. And as for the lovely little heifer——"

Acts of kindness fall, at some times, with the force of blows. So Amy Parker hoped she could withstand.

"Do you have any kiddies of your own perhaps?" Mrs. O'Dowd asked.

All this time the sky was fading. It was now quite white.

"No," said the white young woman, whose nakedness was only for her husband. "No," she said, "I have no children."

"Ah well, not yet perhaps," Mrs. O'Dowd said.

And she hummed some tune that had stuck in her head and that vibrated strangely against her teeth.

"We also are not endowed," she said, "though 'tisn't for want of tryun."

Then her husband came with the goat.

So Amy Parker took O'Dowds' struggling goat, and began to poddy her newborn calf, that was soon mumbling at her fingers in the bucket. Its blundering gums could not suck in too much life. So that while she felt her calf grow in strength and gaiety, the woman was inclined to forget their sick cow, that had huddled in the bracken two days and nights, now truly a statue of patient bronze.

"But she is no worse," the woman said, trying to explain her passing indifference; she did have a true affection for the cow.

"And she's no better," said Stan Parker.

The man still tended the cow in the space that had got trampled by so much bringing and squatting. He had stuck quills into the teats, to drain them off, and would bring the bowls of steaming water, because he had begun, or to see whether his own will added to a hot rag might rouse the cow from her torpor. But his will was not strong enough. And once when he was alone, after staring at the gentle, staring eye of the cow, he began to kick the beast in the rump.

"Get up!" he cried, kicking her with all his strength. "For God's sake! Get up! Get up!"

He was exhausted.

Amy Parker, who had come through the trees just then, did not know her husband. The rough, uneven volume of his voice.

"Leave her for a bit," she said, touching a clod of earth with her shoe, as if here was the strange aspect of life she had just perceived. "I'll stay with her for a little. The tea is on. Lie down on the bed, Stan, and afterwards we shall have a bite to eat."

So he went away as he had been told.

She did not remember having experienced such power before.

If anything, it made her melancholy, in the damp hollow with the sick cow, to see her husband resign his power and authority in her favour. Because she who should now have been strong was not. The gathering darkness and the nets of blackberries pressed her thin soul into greater confinement, and the child inside her protested, perhaps sensing some future frustration, already in the prison of her bones.

"Poor Julia," she said, going and putting her hand on the passive neck of the cow.

Now it seemed as if there was nothing the woman could touch to life. All those moments of joy or knowledge that she had ever lived might not have been experienced. At present she was destitute.

She began to walk away from the cow. She walked through the trees of the piece of land that belonged to them. There was a blurry moon up, pale and watery, in the gently moving branches of the trees. Altogether there was a feeling of flux, of breeze and branch, of cloud and moon. There would be rain perhaps, she felt, in the dim, watery world in which she walked. In which their shack stood, with its unreasonably hopeful window of light. She looked through the window of this man-made hut, at her husband lying asleep on a bed. There were the pots standing on the stove. A scum from potatoes falling from the lip of a black pot. She looked at the strong body of the weak man. Her slippers were lying on their sides under a chair. She realized, with a kind of flat, open-mouthed, aching detachment, that she was looking at her life.

It should have been quite simple to break this dream by beating on the window. To say, *Look* at me, Stan.

But this is not possible, it seems.

So she was forced back from the poignant house, into the world of tree and cloud, that was at present her world, whether she liked it or not. Her feet drifting through the bracken. And this child that I am to have, she said. That her body was making in spite of itself. Even the sex of the unborn child had been decided by someone else. She was powerless. Her skirt drifted against the rough bark of trees. Everything she touched drifted out of her grasp almost at once, and she must grow resigned to it.

Then she saw that it had happened to the cow, while she had been gone, that which she had hoped at least it would not be her lot to discover.

The cow was lying on her side. She was stretched out black in the moonlight. Her legs stuck out straight. She was stiff as a table. The woman prodded it with her foot. Their Julia had died.

So that now the woman was alone with the moon.

She began to run, accompanied by her own animal breath. Wet leaves of flesh spattered on her marble face, or discovered whips, and cut deeper. She had to get back, to tell, to leave the dead cow, to run, if her ankles and the branches allowed. She was running through a slow and solid moonlight. Vicious shadows held her hair. She could not run fast enough through the agonizing trees, towards the houseful of light that she had in her mind's eye. Running. But the farther she left their dead cow behind, the closer she came to all that she had not experienced. So that her skin was cold as she ran through the nets spread to catch her, straining without much thought, except to escape as directly as possible from her own fear.

In this way Amy Parker, when not quite within reach of their house, fell against the shadow that was by day a heap of stones, and matters were taken out of her hands for a while.

Now there was the moon.

When the woman returned to her body, the world was in the grip of a relentless moonlight. I have been running away, and I have run too fast, the woman said through her teeth. The pains had come on. She began to cry gently, for the sadness of the cow, for the sadness of the white light, for the sadness of her own soft, dissolving body, over which she had no control. There was nothing, indeed, over which she had control, as she stumbled again weakly over the wet bracken.

When she arrived at the house the man her husband was stretching himself. He had been wakened by the smell of burning, of some potatoes that had almost boiled away, and had got up to move them from the stove. He was still mealy with sleep. His sense of responsibility was not yet at war with his kindly nature, and she could have come very close to him if she had cared. But she did not want to see him now.

"What," she said, "did you let these potatoes burn?" And would have turned it into a major issue.

But he looked at her shoulders and said, "What is it, Amy? Is it the cow?"

Through the door that she had left open stood the halls of moonlight filled with secrets.

"The cow is dead," she called through her shivering lips, that she was biting now, whenever the pains recurred.

She could not bear her husband to be there. Her body was slipping from her, and a great flood of tenderness that she could have offered if it had been allowed.

"Well," said the man, looking at the earth floor, "that's— why, that's bad. But you mustn't take on, Amy. There's the heifer. And this one was an old cow, and not particularly good; she had the trouble in her teats and all that."

Sitting on the edge of the rather lopsided bed, he was going over it thoughtfully, while she had grown older than facts, and was looking down on the crown of his head, at a little whorl that was open in the hair.

He was looking up at her then, and she saw how well she knew his face.

"It's nothing else?" he asked, hesitating, in his wooden voice.

She sat down on a remote corner of the lumpy bed, so that he could not touch her.

"I want you to go and get Mrs. O'Dowd, Stan dear." Her

67

voice shivered. "Leave me now, Stan," she said. "I don't think we shall have our child. But fetch Mrs. O'Dowd. She will know, perhaps, what there is to do."

So that the incommunicable misery was his too. He could not communicate, he could only fasten cold buckles on the horse, and trail his long shadow through the white night.

Chapter 7

SEVERAL times in those years Amy Parker attempted to have their child, but evidently this was not intended to happen.

"This is a barren stretch of the road," she said, laughing.

For nothing was coming out of Quigleys or O'Dowds, and now Parkers were adopting the evasions and pretences of a childless intimacy. They had persuaded themselves that their neat house, which Stan and the Quigley boys had built, was not the box which enclosed their lives. They were still young, of course, so that their fallibility had not yet been revealed, except by flashes, which can be dismissed as dreams. Even though circumstances had started them to think, it was in a tangled way, in which they made little progress against the knots of thought. They were praying too, more or less regularly, in accordance with the fluctuations of belief. They loved, sometimes with inspiration, also occasionally with resentment. They desired each other's presence perhaps less than before, cherishing the moments of peace, even of past sorrow. Sometimes they made excuses for each other.

"We can get along all right as we are," said Stan Parker. "If you have kids, they can blame you for it forever after."

It was like that.

More often than not, Amy Parker was a bright, industrious young woman, shaking a duster off the veranda or sitting on a log to shell peas. If the floods of life swelled inside her, they were not seen in those parts, where she was respected, and also liked. Only sometimes her face devoured the landscape, or she waited for the roof to be torn off, but only sometimes. So Parkers continued to be respected in those parts. There was no one could sink a post hole like Stan Parker, or fell a tree, or shoe a horse at a pinch, with improvised tools, in shorter time, which he had of course from his dad. If a poetry sometimes almost formed in his head, or a vision of God, nobody knew, because you did not talk about such things, or, rather, you were not aware of the practice of doing so.

Halfway to Bangalay a church had been built, for people of the surrounding district to keep their Sundays in. And some did. Prayers were read, and the lurching hymns were sung. You could not call it worship so much as an act of decent behaviour, as least for most. Amy Parker went out of respect for the gentler moments of her upbringing. And she liked to sing a sad hymn. If she ventured beyond acts, it was to consider the remoteness of her husband's shoulder. What does Stan, in his Sunday clothes, think of in church? she wondered, brushing from her face the flies and a shadow of resentment. She resented some personal experience enclosed in him, subtler than her own yearning occasioned by the sad hymns. Her voice had a slightly voluptuous curve. She kept a bottle of scent, that she shook up and sprinkled on her front for Sunday church, and that scented the hot horsehair and the dust. As she sang through her rather moist lips, she was glossy to look at, her substance was indisputable. But you could not put your finger on what there was about Stan.

The man himself could not have told. He was confused, because his wife was watching, and the words of worship expected too much. His body too, of which he was partly ashamed, made him kneel with an awkwardness that he did not connect with humility. But he was humbler. When he failed to rise to the heights of objective prayer he would examine himself, or the grain of the pew, finding such flaws in each that there was little hope of correction. At times, though, peace did descend, in a champing of horses' bits at a fence outside, in some word that suddenly lit, in birds bringing straws to build nests under the eaves, in words bearing promises, which could perhaps have been the grace of God.

At about this point in the Pakers' lives their neighbour Dad Quigley died. On a morning of frost, on the path to the lavatory, he fell amongst the docks, and lay there till they found him. He was quite dead. Expert women washed him, and he was taken in a cart, with much jolting, to his grave in a paddock of long grass, which was the micks' cemetery at Bangalay. The dead man's widow, who by this time was present only in body, stuck a bunch of marigolds in a jar, which goats robbed the same day, so that the old man was spared the final pathos of brown flowers.

The same evening the mourners returned to their districts, and all of them forgot Dad Quigley, except his widow, who was old and dotty, his daughter, who was ugly and tender, and Stan and Amy Parker, in whom the uneasiness of thought would sometimes stir. These last lay in the darkness in each other's arms, together resisting the possibility of death. They breathed into each other's mouths, and their spirits were strengthened. Their hands compelled each other's bodies into a temporary life.

Apart from these intimations of mortality, their lives stood four-square. Now they had a string of cows, and two heifers, and a young chubby bull. Parkers were going over to cows. Their mornings were lit by the yellow light of lamps. Their silver breath went before them in a cloud. They were stiff as the bucket handles that clanked beside them through the frosty yard, towards the milking.

When times were hard Stan Parker worked with the road gang at Bangalay. He came home at week-ends. He was silenter then, more dried up, harder, the dust of road metal had lodged in the lines of his face. But they put by a bit. And Amy milked the cows. She would take the milk round afterwards, to those parts north of Bangalay which were becoming more closely settled.

For one stretch of several months Stan worked for Mr. Armstrong and got good money. Mr. Armstrong was a rich butcher who had built a country house. He had made so much, it was time to become a gentleman and perpetuate his importance in red brick. So his country house was built about a mile from Parkers', in gardens and a maze of laurel hedges and ornamental trees. In some windows there was coloured glass. And there was a stone statue of a woman modestly disguising her nakedness with her hands.

Stan Parker worked for a time in the butcher's garden, and about the place generally. He chopped wood, and dressed fowls, and burned leaves, and weeded the oval beds of roses and the oblong ones of cannas, that decorated the garden with the florid impersonality of a public park. But the butcher was pleased. He had achieved magnificence. He wore leggings and was a country gentleman. He spoke in a jolly, familiar way to his servants, turning the money in his pockets, that made Stan Parker lower his eyes, and other servants take advantage of confidences, becoming either predatory or insolent. But this, the butcher felt, was something you bought with your money, the privilege of being fleeced or wounded. When he saw that Stan Parker did not react in this way, Mr. Armstrong himself was embarrassed, cleared his throat a lot, and looked here and there. But he respected Parker and would have paid him more money if he had dared exceed what was already liberal.

When Stan Parker was no longer employed by him and had returned to work on his own farm, Mr. Armstrong liked sometimes to ride down, and, sitting askew on his thickset horse, would give advice on the cutting of sorghum or the stacking of lucerne to the man who had been his man, and an old German called Fritz, who was lending a hand in those days at Parkers'. Then Mr. Armstrong was very content. His well-shaven face and his leggings shone. He shaded his eyes with a fringe of leaves to look across the land, and his attitude expressed condescension and approval for one whose modest advancement could never increase and equal his own. On these occasions he was particularly condescending and jokingly ironical to the old German, both because he was a foreigner and because his exact status at Parkers' was something the butcher could not assess.

Fritz had arrived one night with his swag and was allowed to doss down in a shed, which was the original Parker shack. He was sick at that time. His guts were rattling awful bad. So he stayed in that shed. He made a compound of bran and treacle for the sickness in his stomach—it was never clear what this was—but he reported on it from time to time. Parkers would give him a shilling or two and a lump of boiled brisket. They liked his clear eyes, that were of a German blue, and accepted at once the permanence of his attitude.

"Here is a chair, Fritz, that you can have," Amy Parker said. "It wobbles a bit, but no doubt you can do something with it."

Fritz made many things. He helped milk, and scalded the big cans, and would take a turn on the milk run. Most mornings his lamp was first across the yard. And in the evening he brought his chair to the door and sat amongst the wide-open sunflowers he had put in, and of which he would also chew the seeds, after he had dried them, and spit the black shells of the pointed seeds.

Like a bloody parrot, people used to say.

And they laughed at this ridiculous though simple act that was taking place before their eyes, and would have willed it not to, because all things that existed or took place outside the sphere of their experience had no right to.

But the old German said, "The oil of these seeds is good for the health."

He did not mind. No one could contest his faith. So the people turned away, shaking their heads, their lips grown resentful at the shells of sunflower seeds.

Not long after Fritz came the rains began. It had never rained in this way. It began normally enough, the usual surly clouds, the usual lulls in which the sheets were hung, and in which the cows, no longer rumps to the weather, glutted themselves with cold young grass.

"It will rain plenty," said Fritz.

"Yes, it's set for rain all right," said Stan Parker, shallowly, because it did not concern him yet.

He went out across the mud. But the old German shook his head for other rains. And the cows stared opaquely into his transparent eyes.

When the rain began in earnest, after the honeymoon of blown showers and blue patches, the lives of men and animals appeared both transitory and insignificant events beneath its terrible continuity, although in the early stages of deluge the rain was still rain, the flesh accepted it as water, and the spirit grumbled only over what must end.

But it was bad enough. The house was no longer a house; it had been reduced to a pointed roof on which rain fell. People in their houses at night no longer occupied themselves but sat sideways, with thin and yellow faces, doubting each other's motives, as they listened to the iron rain. It fell always. It fell in their sleep. It washed through the dreams of sleepers, lifted their fears and resentments, and set them floating on the grey waters of sleep.

"Listen, Amy," said Stan Parker, waking in the night, "there's a fresh place in the kitchen."

There was the sound of water in the bucket that they had put beneath the first leak, and now there was the fresh sound of water on wood. The rain was entering their house, at first only a little, but it was coming in.

"We've still got a basin or two," laughed Amy Parker from her unprotective bed, from against the body of her husband, that she might perhaps pit against the rain, but without great confidence. "Put that old iron dented thing, Stan, that I was going to throw out. Good thing I didn't. It will hold a bit of water. Put that."

So she heard his feet on the floor, for a step or two, and felt comforted, but not for long, for soon she heard the rain.

It was the rain that possessed their lives to exclusion of themselves. The frames of their bodies, under protecting sacks, walked across the yard to perform the necessary acts of the day. Their hands slithered customarily amongst the teats of cows, to make the milk stream, but it was a poor, white, pizzly stream beside the solid magnificence of rain.

"The river is up at Wullunya," said Stan Parker the day he got back from town, the fragile, hairless legs of the horse halted in the water, the straps swollen in the buckles. "They're cut off at China Flat."

"We are on a hill," said his wife.

She tried to sit on her hill, in warmth and confidence. She held the iron to her cheek. It was ironing day. She would not listen to the waters of Wullunya.

"Yes," said her husband, "we are on a hill. But what about the poor buggers at China Flat?"

"I don't wish any harm to anyone at China Flat," said the woman, in the warm smell of pressed sheets that came from under her determined iron. "I was just stating something. We are on a hill. I forget how many hundred feet Mr. Armstrong said. I can never remember figures."

And she flung her weight and that of her iron against the steaming sheet. Or against the rain. That is what it amounted to. All acts or facts ended abruptly in rain. This was falling still, and would. The waters parted above their heads where the roof met in a peak. The waters parted and streamed, and it was only by grace of a piece of iron that they lived beneath that canopy of water, and grudged each other their opinions.

"I'm hungry, Amy," said the man. "Got anything to eat?"

He was standing looking out of the window, into the solid rain.

"Yes, dear," she said. "There's a nice little bit of pickled pork. And a piece of apple tart. But wait till I finish this. Then I'll get it."

In the contenting smell of sheets and her warm kitchen, the woman once more possessed her husband; why, she would not have held her children with firmer hand, if they had lived. So she was pleased.

But the man was looking out of the house into the rain. He had escaped from his wife, if she had but known it. He was standing on a small promontory of land above what had

74

been the river at Wullunya, which he had not visited but knew. He knew the old woman in her apron, and the two or three younger women, and the long boy, the poddy sheep, the cows, and the yellow-eyed hens, all with the common expression of disaster, congregated on the last island. Because this is what their promontory had become. And the shiny horns of cattle swam and sank in the great yellow waters of what was no longer river. It was no longer possible to distinguish the cries of men from the lowing or bleating of animals, except that the old woman made some protest to God before gulping at the water with her gums. But the arms of men, like the horns of cattle, were almost not protesting, as they were carried sinking away in the yellow flood that had taken the lives from out of their hands.

"Why," said Amy Parker, who had brought the nice plate of pickled pork and put it on the kitchen table, "aren't you going to come and eat? The tea's stood a bit since Fritz and I had our cup, but you like it strong."

"Yes," he said.

The man sat down at his table to eat what his wife had brought.

She brushed against him, to unite her warmth with his apparent coldness, and he looked up at her and smiled with his eyes, which was what she wanted.

It's the rain that gets on your nerves, she said, we're forever having words, or almost, and over nothing.

She looked out at the rain and was temporarily pacified, because she had reduced it to the simple reason for their behaviour.

But the rain continued to fall. There was nowhere you could hide your head and say, Well, here am I.

This rain was no longer personal that streamed out at the wrists of Stan Parker as he went about his business. It was so many weeks, it had got beyond that. So that when the old German came and said the cows were not feeding, they were nosing the grass but would not touch it because of the silt that had been washed down, he would have liked not to feel that this was a problem, or that the cows were his even. The sense of responsibility had been sluiced out of him in those weeks, and if he were to take action it could only be on behalf of someone else.

Then it went round that they were asking for volunteers at Wullunya, to take supplies to those who had been cut off, to carry off the women and children, and to help with the destitute. So Stan Parker, together with O'Dowd and other men of their district, went down towards the river, to exercise their strength, to exchange anecdotes, to get sucked under perhaps, but, in any event, to be released by some process of flowing water. The men went down to the river, singing and laughing, in a dray belonging to old Mr. Peabody, with a bottle brought by O'Dowd.

But Stan Parker was silent, because he did not have anything to say. He sat holding his coat around him, inside the rain, and waited for his first sight of the great river.

Till there it was at last.

Ah, they all said in the dray, becoming silent.

The great yellow mass, pricked and dimpled by the grey rain, was there before them where the plain had been. The world was water now. It went in at the windows of houses and swirled at the roots of a steeple. The heads of dead trees were weathercocked by perching birds.

When the dray reached the township of Wullunya, where the mayor was directing operations in his oilskin and ladies in smocked raincoats were dispensing soup and bread in the School of Arts, the volunteers were brought to a flat-bottomed boat and, after an explanation of local geography, were asked to row in the direction of Red Hill, where two farms were believed to have been cut off.

The world of water was very quiet. The rowers did not speak, because of a sobriety that had caught up with them, and because their muscles were uncertain of this work. Their torn breath sounded against the hissing of rain on water, their hearts thumped with the monotony, and only the ultimate certainty of rowlocks.

"Are we getting anywheres, Mick?" asked Ossie Peabody.

"Nowhere much," said O'Dowd, whose breath poured metal on the air.

Then Les Docker broke wind, and everybody laughed.

Everybody felt better as they rowed across what had been the paddocks of Illarega, and the close branches of trees scrored their taut ribs. Conflicting currents and yellow eddies played with their small and clumsy boat. But the men pulled in their dumb fashion. It began to appear strange that they had been set afloat on the flood waters. It began to appear strange to everyone except Stan Parker, who by this time knew in himself that you can expect anything, and that it was not necessarily the hand of the mayor of Wullunya pointing the way to the flat boat. And as he rowed, accepting the

76

strangeness and inevitability of their position, which nevertheless he could not have explained—he would, in fact, have smiled sheepishly at the inquisitor—the half-submerged world became familiar as his own thoughts. He remembered things he had never told, and forgotten. He remembered the face of his mother before her burial, when the skull disclosed what the eyes had always hidden, some fear that the solidity of things around her was not assured. But in the dissolved world of flowing water, under the drifting trees, it was obvious that solidity is not. The rowers rowed. He listened to their men's-breath, but from a distance. As they rowed under the liquid trees the sound of leaves, swishing, dipping into his wet skin, was closer to him.

It was not unexpected, then, when Ossie Peabody called out there was something sort of round bobbing against the anthill on the right, and they eased in that direction, and turned up the rubber body of a man, in clothes that water had translated into uniform darkness, the smooth man's-face nibbled at by fishes.

Crikey, said the rowers, when the body lay in the bottom of the boat.

Their crisp skin did not believe in death. Their nostrils, grown white and grisly, refused it, like those of animals finding evidence in the undergrowth.

Stan Parker bent forward and covered the rubber face with a bag. Then they cleared their throats, somebody spat, somebody copied him, and they rowed on.

As they rowed, fragments of the still, safe lives that are lived in houses flowed past. There was a chair with no one in it, there was a piece of bitten cheese, and letters grown spidery, and a hassock in the blackberry canes, a hat with a drowned feather, a baby's chamber pot, a Bible open at Ezekiel. All these things came and went. It was the boat that was stationary. And the house, almost, that they touched upon.

"Hello there," O'Dowd shouted, sticking his head in at the window. "Anyone at home? It's the postie called, and the fire brigade, rolled into one."

Everybody laughed, because by this time they were doing things in unison.

In the still house the table was set for dinner. A snail dragged across the tablecloth. The chairs stood round in a glug of water, which had come in without the welcome of an open door. Water, at least, was united. Only the people had gone. So that in the circumstances, as they rowed round, clawing the outer wall of the house, O'Dowd felt that he might put in his hand, and take the bottle that stood on the shelf, and give it a swig, like, for the sake of his circulation, and even put the bottle in the boat.

Someone said that was thieving.

" 'Tis not," said O'Dowd through his moister mouth. "Anyone can see, plain as day, there is no value attached to the bottle, left, you might say, abandoned on a shelf, as good as throwed out."

No one was dry enough to reply. On the edge of a washstand, in a slimy room, a set of teeth was shut tight.

Then the boat was rowed away. The crew was all arms now, and ribs; they had left their bodies behind. Just as the people had left their houses to the water, the men were possessed by motion and breath.

In one place Stan Parker saw, stuck in the fork of a tree, the body of an old, bearded man. But he did not mention this. He rowed. All omissions were accepted by the blunt boat. And soon the old man, whose expression had not expected much, dying upside down in a tree, was obliterated by motion and rain.

At a house on what had been a rise but was now an island, a small, spry woman with a heavy coil of hair ran down to the shore.

"I thought youse were never coming," she called. "I been waitin and waitin. Dad is gone in a little gimcrack bit of a boat the kids made one summer. I said, 'You're mad, you'll never do no such thing.' But he'd seen a ram stuck in a tree."

She stood on the shore, in the scum of water and a fringe of sticks. There was a slight white scum of excitement on her open mouth.

"Did any of you men see Dad?" she asked. "An old man with a white beard?"

But nobody had.

"There now," she said. "I said they'd send from town. I got me things fixed."

She began to run.

"But what about Dad?" She stood in her tracks, on the tips of her toes.

Perhaps her dad had put in somewhere else, they said.

"Yes," she said. "Let's hope. There's the machine, you know. I got to take the machine."

"Eh?" said Les Docker.

"Yes," she said. "The sewin machine."

That she dragged from the veranda, barking her shins on the treadle.

"There's only three things I care for," said the small woman. "The two goats and the sewin machine. An the goats is gone."

"So the sewun machine, missus," said O'Dowd. "Or we're on the bottom."

"Well, I'm stayin," said the woman, whose name was Mrs. Wilson.

She began to cry rather loud, with her fingers in the iron of the sewing machine.

So that they had to put her in the boat, as if she had been her own wicker port, in which her things were stuffed, with a strap around.

"You didn't ought to," she cried. "I'll never get over this. The goats, an now the machine.

"Ah," she said quietly, touching the bump beneath the bag on the bottom of the boat. "What's this? Don't tell me it's a body!"

It was, they said, some poor young cove they picked out of the water.

"I never seen a dead person," she said thoughtfully. "Not even when Mother died. I was away at Muswellbrook, stayin with relatives. It was them that gave me the machine."

And she began to cry again, mingling with the rain.

The presence of the woman in front of him as he rowed made Stan Parker return to himself out of the great abstractions of death and water. He bit his lips, apparently on account of his exertion, but actually because he had failed to mention her dead father. He would soon, he said, but later, not now. He rowed on, in friendship for the rowers, and pity for the woman. She wore an old blouse with sprigs of little purple flowers. And Stan Parker, remembering baking day, saw the loaves risen in their tins, and his wife's hot cheek as she pricked the loaves. All that day as he rowed he had not thought of her, but now, as he did, he was glad to remember.

That evening he sent word by old Mr. Peabody, who was returning to their district, that he would hang around a day or two and see what he could do to help.

The team of volunteers that had come down from the hills spent the night at a livery stable, in a loose box, of which the new straw pricked their necks, and all night there was a pawing and stirring and velvety whinnying, through the stables, through their sleep. O'Dowd, who had taken a drop at the Oak, lay down outside in the rain. He had the intention, he said, of breathing the fresh air. But they took him by the armpits and the ankles and brought him in. Then again there was the warm stirring of sleep and horses in the velvety night. You forgot the rain in the stables.

Once in the night Stan Parker woke and remembered that he had not spoken of the small woman's dead father, even as friends took her with her wicker port when she landed from the flood. He could not communicate. There are certain things you cannot tell. So he fell asleep tranquilly, sinking deeper in the stableful of warm straw, inside the night of rain.

It continued to rain.

It was a national disaster, said Mrs. O'Dowd, the farms washed out, there was poor souls without a stick to their backs, and the governor's wife to take a collection round, and ladies making a sale of knickknacks and things of which they had plenty over, because the destitute and orphans had not the bread to put in their stomachs, even if politicians, inspecting the scene, of course, in a boat, each with a mouthful of speeches, promised the subsidies and what not, better a decent loaf of bread and a warm pair of combies.

"Because," said Mrs. O'Dowd, "air never did no good in the stomach, except to come out, an words never clothed the bottom, not of a newborn bastard baby."

Then she put up her hair that was coming down, and the rain in it too.

Amy Parker, who had lain alone in bed those three nights, on the warm side and the cold, and chafed her feet together, and listened to the drip from the kitchen ceiling into the basin and the bucket, said, "I'm just about sick of this bloody rain."

"Listen, dear," said Mrs. O'Dowd, who had begun to sound wheedly, "shall we be goin to look at the floods?"

"All that way!" said Amy Parker. "I have never been to Wullunya."

"Ah, it is a fine place," said Mrs. O'Dowd. "Four pubs an a flour mill. There was a circus once that we saw in a tent. Ah, it's not so far. We can cut a bite to take with us. It'll be a jaunt, dear. An us stuck here."

The rosebush by Parkers' veranda, the rose that they had moved from its original position in front of the old shack, had begun to look formidable. The rain sluiced its staggy limbs and parted at the black thorns. The brown sods of dead roses were rotting in the rain.

"It's not much of a life here," said Amy Parker, "mucking around, waiting for it to stop."

"The mould growun on your shoes," said Mrs. O'Dowd, "while you shred the cobbage."

"And we would see them perhaps," said Amy Parker.

"Sure," said Mrs. O'Dowd, "they'll be important men, all them that volunteered. Beer on the house, I'll bet, for fishun the poor souls out of the water."

Till the young woman was kindled for her husband, whose face was the bravest. She saw him again, sitting in Peabodys' dray, not looking; he was not for her, but all those men. So men drive off together as if they are ashamed of women.

"But it is out of the question," she said, in hope of a rescue, "unless I am back by milking time."

"An if you are not, what is wrong, may I ask, with the old Hun that you have, eatun 'is head off, and bustun 'is pants in the shed out there, if he cannot pull an extra tit an deliver the milk?"

So there was nothing more to say.

They were riding down to Wullunya in O'Dowds' spring cart, all ajingle on the yellow road, lashing the water with their wheels. The horse, tossing his thin mane, struck at the surface as if he meant it. Anyway, in these early stages, his bones had lost their resentment. Even his wind was gay.

"In that circus I was tellun you of," Mrs. O'Dowd said, "there was a lady dancin on the rumps of two white horses, from one to tother, and through a hoop, with the band playun beautiful. Oh, I like a circus, for a change, and so does he, if he is sensible, like, at the time. Well, at this circus that I was tellun you of, we had paid our thruppence to set on the grass—or straw it was, it had been trampled on—we was settun eatun our little pies, when *he* becomes as bold as brass. Mind you, it was no more than a pint, or two perhaps—you know what he is—that he'd took at the Oak, or was it the Bunch of Grapes? No matter. There he was, hitchun up his pants and all for ridun a buckjump nag, with me hangun on 'is arm. 'Hold hard,' I said, 'you obstropulous man, haven't you circus enough? An clowns?' I said. 'An ackrybats? If they happen to break their limbs, that is what they are there for. But I have not paid thruppence, O'Dowd, to see me own husband in splinters.' Oh, but I am tellun you, it was terrible, Mrs. Parker, an me by rights a sensitive woman for scenes in public. Anyways, they played the band. To distract attention. An they run up a dago girl on a rope.

81

There she was, hungun by one toe from the ceilun, and out of her teeth a cage of birds. 'There,' I said to His Nibs, 'observe,' I said, 'what we have paid to see.' But he was too far gone, Mrs. Parker, to expect much from the ceilun, when he was not adjusted to the ground. He fell down after that, an I was fannun the flies from off of his face, while I got me own money's worth. But it was a lovely circus, I shall never be forgettun, and the smell of elephants and monkeys that night."

Mrs. O'Dowd drove down towards Wullunya, in command of both the past and the present, slapping the landscape with her whip.

But Amy Parker, the commanded, was silent all that mile, hushed by the tinsel of the neighbour woman's words. How drab she was, dressed in bags against the wet. Under the wet bags she held her feverish hands. Whip cracked. Cart rocked. Drops hung from the wire of moving fences. Skies reeled above, opening for a moment on an act of blue, but groggily, from which the cage of birds must fall.

In that moment of tinsel sunlight and slashing swords the grave hillsides were tinkling and rustling with repentant drops. A whole slope gurgled with a yellow torrent. From out of the varnished leaves the sun was bringing the greeny-golden balls of oranges, to juggle with. For a moment. And exit. To make way for rain.

All along the road to Wullunya the trees hung, but expectantly, for some entrance to animal life.

"Listen," said Mrs. Parker, chafing her neck on the wet bag. "Did you hear something, Mrs. O'Dowd?"

"We have company," her friend replied.

For by now you could hear wheels, and at some rate.

"He will belt the daylights out of the horse," the neighbour woman said. "An no mistake. If he has not robbed the bank, then his lady's pains is comin on."

The two women became quite nervous waiting for the urgent wheels. They sat upright on the board. Their necks were thin.

Till the wheels were round the last bend, and it was a sulky that they saw, turning in their seats, a sulky splashing, with three flash young coves jammed together in a row.

"Good day, missus," they said, slowing down, or it was the one that held the dancing whip. "Is this the way to the floods?" he said. "At Wullunya?"

"It is all floods," said Mrs. O'Dowd, looking ahead. "And all ways is one."

"Funny, eh?" said the cove with the whip.

He was a big young cove with a gold tooth in front.

"We are two decent women out for the day," Mrs. O'Dowd said. "Enjoyun ourselves too. Or was. Till you all come along."

The young cove spat through his teeth at the rain. There was another one that laughed.

"Go on," he said.

"That is what I am doin," said Mrs. O'Dowd. "And I may add, at a decent pace."

"Huh!" said the young man, digging his mate in the ribs. "Then you haven't 'eard 'ow me grandmother is dead? Drownded fore they could row 'er orf."

"Huh!" said Mrs. O'Dowd. "Your grandmother and Bridget Duffy! All that is dead of yours is the marines you left behind."

So that Amy Parker was both trembling and exalted from the neighbour woman's audacity. She turned her brightened cheek and looked tautly at the wire fence, on which the rain was running beads.

"That is a bloody insult for a man," said the young fellow.

He was wearing an overcoat that was greeny-old and made him look bigger than he should have been, though this was big. And it squeezed his mate, the little black nuggety one, with the bloodshot eye, but bright and inquisitive, in his burned face, into the ribs of the outside passenger, who in turn was squeezed against the rail. This did not seem to matter much. He was the thin sort. He was the sort that does not speak but laughs in the right place, and out, or snickers. He was the egger-on.

"Insults?" said Mrs. O'Dowd, flicking her thin whip. "What will you be expectun? Violets perhaps, with a ribbon round?"

And Amy Parker wished that she would not go on. The delirious tightrope on which her neighbour walked was more than she could bear. So she turned her face and would not look.

"You there, the one that says nothun," said the nuggety mate of the big cove, leaning out from behind the greatcoat, so that his face was detached and pointed and particularly inquisitive. "You ain't doin justice to the occasion. Ain't I seen you somewheres before? Bangalay? Dingwall's Commercial perhaps."

"I don't go to Bangalay. Or very seldom."

She was mortified. Although her blood leaped she could not walk the wire. She was clumsy and atremble.

"My friend is a lady," said Mrs. O'Dowd, who was experienced. "She has led a sheltered existence. My friend has not kept company with all and sundry."

"If a couple a good-lookun tarts is also ladies, I'm not one to pick a quarrel," the big fellow said.

All this time the horses were ignoring each other, that walked at even pace, wet and relaxed.

"Saucy man," breathed Mrs. O'Dowd. "I never met such a bold feller."

The outside passenger in the sulky laughed.

"Listen," said the cove in the overcoat, "we got a drop of the real thing underneath the seat. What do you say to findin a dry spot an havin a talk. Boil the old billy if you like, and talk."

"Ah," said Mrs. O'Dowd, handling her reins, "it's too wet for talk."

"She's got the answers," snorted the small bloodshot man.

He had begun to have a hungry look, and shifty also. He sniffed the air with his long nose that was inflamed up one side.

"Oh dear, 'tis nothun," said the fubsy woman, " 'tis nothun to the answers you'll be gettun when me husband comes along."

"What's a husband?" shouted the small black bloodshot man, who was more inclined to take over from his mate the hungrier he got.

"I could tell yer in detail," said Mrs. O'Dowd, "if I had the time. But as I haven't, I must be brief. This is a very big sort of man, let me tell yer, with muscles on um like the pumpkins, an fire comin through his nose for the likes of you. There's nothun that me husband so dislikes as a little, creepun, lousy, crow-be-daylight, scoot-be-darkness bantam. So help us God."

And she dealt her horse a smart cut, so that his wet ears started, and he dashed his tail against the shafts and protested with his wind.

Sounds of a confused anger now arose from the sulky, in which the three coves were packed tight. Opinion was divided, it seemed, on whether to use words or blows.

"Job 'er one!" somebody said.

" 'Usbands!" said another. "Which 'usband is she flickin well talkin of?"

While the outside passenger sniggered and shifted in his seat.

"If you would wish for an interduction to me husband," said Mrs. O'Dowd, "Constable Halloran of Bangalay will oblige. It is him that is just commun over the rise. I would know his whiskers at a mile."

It was, indeed, the long young policeman with the shining whiskers, of which the wax repudiated water, jogging along on his loose bay, and a bump of distance on his own back.

The sulky became rather surly. It rumbled a lot, then crunched away, and was gone at its former pace of chariots, before you could say knife.

"Good mornun, Constable Halloran," said Mrs. O'Dowd. "We are makun a day of it to the floods. To see what we can see, like. Poor souls, an dumb animals too. An we're for pickun up our husbands perhaps, who have been givin a helpun hand these two days, or is it three."

After more pleasant conversation of this kind, in the warmer rain, with the agreeable young policeman of long legs and white teeth, the cart with the two women continued on its wet way.

Amy Parker, who had been exalted out of her dull life by circuses and personal danger, and relieved and pleased by the encounter with the constable, was settling sadly down to the last stages of a journey on an unfamiliar road. If at the end it was just trees, and again grey, wet trees, she began to wonder why she had come. She tried to think of her honest husband's face, that she would see, and of course welcome. She tried to rekindle her friendship for her neighbour, still jogging on the board at her side, still admirable, she knew, and still surprising, but interminable as herself.

"Oh dear," she said, stretching her cramped limbs under the wet bags, "when do you think we will arrive?"

"One day," yawned Mrs. O'Dowd, who was also feeling flat.

And the road continued.

Mrs. O'Dowd, sunken in her carapace of stiff bags, denied the possibility of circuses.

"It makes you wonder," she said, "what you can'uv done. I remember, it was the time he was kicked in the guts with the big black wall-eyed horse, that I never liked, and we sold, not too soon neither, with himself all but passun into the next world; I said, 'Will you have the priest?' I said. What with runnun all night with the hot plates to hold on his guts, an the hot clouts—he was that blue, but nothun to the yeller he afterwards became—I was fit to lay down meself, but I didn't, you see, I was wound up. So I said, 'Will you have the priest?' Like that. 'Have the priest?' he says—he was in the spasms. 'After all these years I would not know how to be havun the priest. Give me a good-size goat, in a weskit, with a book, an I will sooner have that. It will not'uv learned to hold out its hand, besides.' Because O'Dowd is tight, you know, as tight as the wallpaper round the room. Not that I blame um. It is a shillun here an a sixpence there with priests, an overnight a pound. So I said, 'Yes.' Knowun his weakness. 'Pour me a tot of rum,' he says. 'You cannot have priests and bottles, an if it is the priests that has to go, it is just too bad.' And him sweatun in agonies, and hardly a stick on his body. O'Dowd is a hairy man."

Now at that part of the road the trees were rather close, and the clouds met blacker than before, in conspiracy over the small cart, which crawled up over the rise, and was alone.

"Still, he did not die," said Mrs. O'Dowd, "for all that he cheeked the priests. I would not like um to die. An me not knowun where I stand. Because some people choose one way, Mrs. Parker, and some another."

"How do you mean, Mrs. O'Dowd?" Amy Parker asked. She could not, would not, help her friend. Her handkerchief had become a ball.

"I mean, we were married before God," Mrs. O'Dowd said. "I mean, there was no priests. Seein as his views. And mine—why, I never went nap on the priests meself. There is God an there is priests, I allus said. An a few shilluns saved. Though who is to know for sure, dear, who is to know?"

"Then you are not married to Mr. O'Dowd?" Mrs. Parker said.

"Silly thing!" said the neighbour. "What do you think I have been tellun yer this five minutes, in elegant speech, seein as some take offence!"

It was enough to fascinate. Amy Parker was struck dumb.

"Well," she hesitated, when something was awaited, "I don't expect that you are any different," she said, or lied.

"Oh, there is nothun I regret," Mrs. O'Dowd said. "If we have thrown things at each other and used words, it is because we are inclined to it. Only I would like to'uv been married in ivory satun, an a big hat."

It should have ended there, but did not. For Mrs. Parker it would never end.

They were passing a bit of a shack, of wood and tin, with two children outside, paddling in the water with their bare feet.

"This is perhaps the beginning of a town," said Amy Parker hopefully.

Now that her friend was different, she would have sat sideways and looked at her. Because she could not, she was burning.

"I shall be glad when we are there," she said. "I am sick of this."

Mrs. O'Dowd did not reply, but was sucking her wet lip, as if experienced in endlessness.

Continuing to look to left and to right, in search of something round which she could throw a rope, young Mrs. Parker would have liked to offer her friend words of love and assurance, but she was prevented. And they were being washed farther apart. The waters were lapping at the spokes of the wheels. The two women began to accept the distances. The wheels hissed through the water. Later I shall make amends, Amy Parker felt, who was neither cold nor cruel. Later, she said, but not now. She had been washed too far. She swam against the strong current, in which the circus dancer bobbed, and the naked body of O'Dowd.

And Mrs. O'Dowd was singing, because she was feeling sad.

Suddenly, though, the road lunged towards the present island of Wullunya. The causeway was quite firm, that their wheels ground along, through a mob of sheep that was going across.

Now, to be sure, there was hope of husbands.

"Do you think we will find them easy?" Amy Parker asked. And bending down, her hand would have dawdled in the backs of the greasy sheep.

"The place is not all that big," Mrs. O'Dowd replied.

As they went along in the comforting smell of warm wool the women were united again in their common hope. As they were carried, it seemed, on the bunched backs of sheep, they listened to the scattering of pellets and the sound of frogs, and sighed their satisfaction.

So they came on into the town, past the flour mill and the

paddock in which the circus had been pitched, past the pale tower of the church, in which the clock had stopped. And underneath, someone was being buried in the long wet grass.

"Ah dear, it is terrible," Mrs. O'Dowd said, her head caught between looking and turning away. She had the gooseflesh. Remembering some funeral of her own, this one had become personal.

But Amy Parker looked at the spindly umbrellas of the relations of the dead as if her eyes had opened for the first time on the road to Wullunya, with the advent of the floods. She could not die yet.

And they came on into the town, where the shops were full of hardware and gloves and coconut ice and withered beetroot, but the people, even the old, had gone down to the water's edge.

You would not think it, said a woman who came down a side street, carrying a Muscovy drake by the legs, you would not think it, but the place was chock-a-block, what with victims and volunteers, and the Governor had come; they were airing the sheets at the Oak and killing a whole yardful of fowls.

"We are looking for our two husbands," said Mrs. O'Dowd. "Stan Parker and Mick O'Dowd. They are here to do the rescue work. Have you seen them?" she asked.

But the woman had not.

"They are big men. Both," said Mrs. O'Dowd. "An mine has a black moustache."

But the woman had not seen. Her eyes had a blank look, as if she were gathering behind them fragments of her own life, which, when assembled, she would offer to these two visitors to her town.

"We was nearly washed out Friday," the woman began.

But the duck that she was carrying raised his nubbly head from the street and hissed, and Mrs. O'Dowd herself was not a one for others' tales.

"Which is the way to the water?" she cut short.

The woman swung her body and pointed with her whole arm. Her dank hair hung and swung. She was the supreme messenger.

"Down there!" she said, and it issued like a forked tongue from between two fangs, for the middle teeth were gone. "Not the first, not the second. See the balcony? Turn right. It's down at the common."

The great yellow animal was already grazing on the grass.

"It's halfway up the common," the woman said. "It's as far as Trelawneys'. It's in at the windows, and ruined the new suite."

Mrs. O'Dowd clacked her tongue, whether from sympathy or not, but the resigned horse moved on towards the terrible scene.

The whole world was involved in the floods at Wullunya, either watching the water or lending a hand, or led from the boats that had rowed them from one dream to another. Some had even woken and were carried out. From these the spectators generally turned away, either from good taste or because they were afraid to accept the evidence of those bare faces. Only Bub Quigley, who had come with his sister Doll, could endure the smiles of the dead.

"That old fellow is good," he said, meeting the face of an old man with his own rapt smile. "See it?" he said. "He is good. Good. You can tell."

And he touched the smile of the old man, that they had found hanging upside down in a tree.

Many people, including men who could crack whips and throw steers, turned away in disgust, saying it should not be allowed. So that Doll Quigley had to hush her brother and hold his hand.

He had found a curious round stone, that had been rolled and polished in other floods, and now that he was restrained he stood looking at his stone, surrounded by the forms of spectators. He was a tall young man, but he could look down, and it did not matter. The world was concentrated in his hands.

There was much talk going on all the time amongst those people who were watching the flood. There was the undisciplined expression of the emotions that is found in all gatherings of spectators, but there were those also who spoke with authority and public feeling, whose faces seemed to think they might solve a problem. Some people said they should cut a channel to the north; others said it was obvious that such a channel should only be cut to the south. Some, who had had experience of floods, considered the waters must soon fall, taking into account their present, apparently fixed level, the direction of the wind, the texture of the sky, and some intuition of the bones.

And the Governor, who had been brought by an official party, asked questions demonstrating his sympathy and tact. He stood with one foot advanced slightly in the direction of the waters, merely to ease his stance, because of a wound he had once got, but some people asked themselves whether this position had not a particular significance. They watched the toe of his slender English boot and waited for something peculiar to happen. But the Governor continued to radiate tact, in his overcoat of a good stuff, with velvet at the collar. He was a greyish man smoking a cigar, of which the exquisite, pearly cloud of smoke had got mixed up in all this by mistake.

"There will be funds, of course, and a distribution of garments," said the Governor to the mayor, easing his neck inside his well-fitting collar, intensifying the cloudy sympathy of his well-bred eye. "But in the meantime," he said, lowering his voice a little, out of respect for a situation, "have the people enough soup?"

The mayor said he thought that there was no lack of soup, thanks to the generosity of some landowners and butchers, and that the ladies had the matter in hand, the wife of a certain butcher, in particular, and an ironmonger had lent stoves. The mayor stood beside the Governor with his legs apart and bent at the knees. His hands hung open like bunches of bananas.

All this time the crowd stood, or moved, as their emotions or curiosity drew them here and there. Many of them were wearing bags, not from poverty, of course, but for practical reasons; they kept the water out. So the crowd held its Gothic hands to its breast, to maintain its covering of wet bags. At times, and in certain obvious attitudes, this gave an impression of prayer. Some did pray to themselves, either in fragments of mutilated prayers remembered from the churches or else in their own jagged words. But mostly it was just a holding of wet bags. There was a smell of bags. There was a slight mash of bran and pollard about the shoulders and the breasts of some.

As they walked and talked, or stood, daring to think or remember, you could open the cupboards of their souls on the objects arranged neatly or immoderately inside. Some overflowed. There was the wife of a storekeeper, for instance, who could not contain her lust for a policeman; she wore whole nights of tortured sheets, her lips were quite swollen from biting on her lust. But Doll Quigley, who did not move much from her one place of mud, except to restrain her brother, who wanted to see a Chinaman—Doll, the stationary Doll, contained a lamplight. As the water lapped to and fro she remembered her father. Her thin, drowning, but also rescued smile dwelt on the faces of nuns, from whom she had learned the copperplate of which her family were proud. Doll Quigley was sitting with several nuns that were engaged in various works of thread. The cones of their anonymous faces were teaching Doll the yellow light with which she was being filled.

But the crowd frowned and said, "Ah, those Quigleys."

Because Bub Quigley was brushing up and down, demanding a Chinaman, or, worse still, he stood looking into the faces of people with such candour that it became obvious he was mingling with their thoughts.

"She ought to control him," they said.

So that Doll Quigley was compelled away from the lapping of the past, to say, "Sh, Bub! The people don't like it. Stand here and see who the boats bring in."

"It'll be over soon," he sighed.

His washed eyes were embracing fresh simplicities.

"Look," he said, "it's stopping. It'll be over."

Although the fall of the floodwaters and an end to the rain had been discussed, it was only theory. Nobody believed that this would happen, and many, in their hearts, would not have wanted it. Some, following Bub Quigley's finger, looked at the sky, and now for the second time that day there was blue, but a considerable blue, and folding of clouds. In it flew an arrow of black birds. Even if no dove, the formation of birds suggested possibilities, and the Governor went so far as to make the joke, at which those who were protecting him from pressure laughed with almost physical violence.

The naked faces were immodest without their habitual clothing of rain.

"It seems that the boats would be landun about here," Mrs. O'Dowd said. "An perhaps we shall find our men."

The two women, who had left their cart a little way back from the crowd, chaining the wheel, and sticking on the horse's nose a nosebag, from which the chaff had trickled long before the floods, advanced towards the water on stiff legs, in ponderous wet clothes. It made Amy Parker feel rather ridiculous to have come that long and arduous way to recover her awkward body at the end. So she held the wet bag round her shoulders and looked angrier than she was.

"Have you seen Stan?" she asked Doll Quigley.

"No, Amy, I ain't. But we ain't been everywhere."

Because she was humble, Doll Quigley accepted as perfectly natural what she presumed to be Amy Parker's anger.

And gradually everything was natural. Amy Parker stood in the crowd, that concealed her awkwardness, with her friends, in the first shy sunlight, that was becoming by degrees more metallic and blatant. The trees, isolated in the glistening brown water, crackled with green light. A windmill flashed, and slashed at any remnants of grey. And a boat began to approach, that people were trying to identify, making jokes and even laying bets.

Then Amy Parker was seized with terror, that this should be the boat, and that she would not know what to say to her husband in public. The stranger-faces all around her were not stranger than her husband's skin, which for the moment was all that she could remember of him.

"It is Ernie," someone ventured from under his hand. "It is Ernie Oakes all right."

"We grass widders," said Mrs. O'Dowd, "would not be reckernizun our men, with three days on their chins, at half a mile."

"It's Ernie Oakes all right," said the confident man.

Then Amy Parker knew, with a slight scorn, that this would be the boat. She knew. Wind took a tail of her hair and mingled it with her smile, which was the smile of knowing. And with her conviction, her husband's face returned to her, in its least line and pore; it might have been her own, and she was holding it in her hands, devouring it in her mind, down to the bones, so hungrily that she looked round quickly to see if she had been seen.

But of course she hadn't.

And Mrs. O'Dowd had begun to call, "See? 'Tis our boys, whatever you like to say. It's the black devul himself, pullun fit to trip all the others into the water."

The boat was rowed on through the lively air, on which Mrs. O'Dowd had painted sails. Some said it was the Tingles and little Mary Hunt that had been taken off this time. It was Mary Hunt holding the tabby cat. It was old Mrs. Tingle—you could begin to see her goitre. And the boat was rowed on, and after much straining, and slewing, and manœuvring, and breath, and advice, was brought to the side where the people stood.

Then Stan Parker looked up as he sat, he was tired, and saw that his wife was there. She stood in her dark wet clothes, with the bag falling from her shoulders and her hair drying in the wind. He was not surprised. He did not wave and make jokes, as other men did with acquaintances and relations. But he looked into her and was content.

"Don't you have nothun to say to your husband now?" Mrs. O'Dowd asked her friend.

But Amy Parker looked away. She had looked into him, into his eyes, and had never looked deeper, she thought. There was very little to say.

"Go on," Amy said, "don't be silly." She bit the tail of hair that was flying into her mouth and frowned.

So that Stan Parker remembered coming into the room where she stood at the enamel basin, pushing the dark hair back from her face, and there was a greenish light in the white skin of her thighs. In that window, in summer light, there was the greenish gloom that the white roses made.

"Hey," said Ossie Peabody, leaning across, "your missus's come."

"Yes," said Stan Parker.

So that Ossie Peabody did not advance further into his mate's privacy.

It was decided that the mob that had come down from the hills in Peabodys' dray should go back home that night. Interest in the flood was waning. Some began to point and show how the water had fallen, only a little, but a little. It was cold in the mud on the edge of the yellow waters. People began to trail back into the streets. A lamp was lit in one window. A woman, pouring tea, held the pot high above the cup, so that the red stream appeared to be fixed.

Parkers walked against each other in the dwindling light.

"What about the cows?" asked Stan Parker, because he was expected to speak.

"The old man'll see to them."

In the presence of their friends, as they walked back to find Peabodys' dray, their conversation was almost guilty. But they were close. Their clothes touched. And in the dray, waiting for the leg of pork that had been promised to Ossie Peabody's mum, Parkers were interchangeable.

"Ta-ta!" said Mrs. O'Dowd, who was already slapping her horse.

She would make her own way, with her husband, and a bottle or two.

"See you this side of Killarney," Mrs. O'Dowd called.

She was gone then, in a jingle, into the friendly night.

All that night would remain friendly. Someone had a twist

of peppermints that they handed round in the dray. There was a fumbling of hard hands as they waited for the leg of pork. And Amy Parker, who did not care for peppermint, took, and bit, and rejected, and put the bitten sticky half in the place where she knew her husband's mouth would be. He took the strong sweet, laughing, in his teeth, and was pervaded by peppermint right to the backs of his eyes.

"Whose little boy are you?" somebody asked.

There was a child crying in the dark.

"Ah, look," said the butcher's wife, coming out with the leg of pork wrapped in the advertisements of the local paper, "he's been up an down, up an down. That kiddy's been crying all day. 'Who do you belong to?' I says. No answer. He only looks. An cries. 'Come in, then,' I says, 'an I'll give you a lovely cake.' But he just cries. Up an down. I says I'll go to the police, give him in charge, as a lost child, of course, nothing nasty. People, you know, can't stand it. 'Can't you do somethin to that child?' they say. As if it's mine. Cry, cry. As if it was the last Christian left on earth. There, Ossie, is as sweet a piece of pork as your mum will ever put tooth to."

While the child cried in the dark.

Perhaps he was washed down from somewhere, they said in the dray.

He'd be washed on farther if he squalled like that, was the honest opinion of a second body.

But without malice. There was only the tolerant kindliness of intimacy in the dark. They were returning home.

Then Amy Parker had to see the child. "Let me down. Let me see him," she said.

She had to get over the side of the dray, as if some purpose were forming in the darkness. She had to touch the child.

"What is your name?" she asked, holding him in the light that fell from the inside of the butcher's shop, that was really closed.

And the child's face was fully closed. The mouth and the eyelids would not be prised. She held in her hands the body of a caught bird.

"Don't they call you something?" she said, aware that they were waiting in the dray, shifting and coughing and gathering reins.

But the child eluded her, except for what she was holding of his bones.

Come on, they called, it would be morning.

"Get up, Amy," her husband called.

"Then we'll find you a name," she said, "when we get you home. Stan," she called, "we're taking the kid along with us."

Then the child gave her a long look, as if he doubted whether it would be possible. And Amy herself was not sure.

Her husband had begun to grumble, what would they do with a stray child.

"Well, perhaps for a day or two," he grumbled, "until we find out all about him."

"There," she said. "We shall soon be happy."

Though she herself had begun to doubt, her bright voice embracing the silence to which it was addressed. Still, she began to bundle the child over the awkward woodwork into the dray. He did not protest. Nor sitting in the crowded dray, that had begun its long homeward jog.

"I have forgotten the stars," said Amy Parker.

She was tenuously happy. There were whole quarters of still sullen sky, but that from which the cloud had been torn away glittered with a new jewellery of stars. As the dray reeled across the stones you could breathe the cold stars, that shivered, and glittered, and contracted, and lived.

"Yes, the rain is gone," said a man called Ted Fosdick, who was getting a lift home.

But Ossie Peabody slapped with the leather and said he would never believe that, not till the drought was on.

People in dreamy voices began to recall the flood, that was already history, and to enumerate those articles they had acquired. Because in a flood many objects change hands. There is no vice in this. It is not a stealing. It is merely a change of ownership. This way various pots and pans, a cheese, a length of rope, a world gazetteer, even a hip bath, had passed honestly enough to the passengers in Peabodys' dray.

"An Parkers got a bran new kid free for nothin."

They laughed in their friendly, dreamy voices, and passed to other subjects.

But Amy Parker rocked with the stars, and Stan Parker looked out into the darkness, past the skeletons of trees, into darkness. The child was sitting between them, hearing perhaps, you could not tell, the words of the detached passengers.

"Are you warm?" the woman asked him, with a kindness that sounded as if she was trying it out.

He did not answer. He sat stiffly. All three of them were stiff, the boy, the man, and the woman, apart from the other

95

passengers. Packed together, their bodies listened to one another; later perhaps, in a lull of suspicion, on a wave of sleep, they might even flow together in love.

Amy Parker rocked with the wheels. Her head glittered with the events she had lived that day, growing and contracting, eluding or consuming. She was at this moment quite feverish with life, with all those events she possessed in her head, inside her glowing skin. As she was jolted against the hard side of the dray, seated stiffly, on the floor, the road was interminable, that she could have accomplished quickly in her mind. Even her failures were taken from her by the child that she might now perhaps possess.

They were going over a wooden bridge. There was the touch of leaves on their faces, and the man called Ted Fosdick was singing a song about a drummer boy.

Stan Parker sat with his own awkward, uncommunicative childhood all along the inevitable road. He could feel the resentment of the strange boy pressed against his side. He did not want to possess this child as his wife did. But if he would not attempt, he would also not refuse. So the dray carried him equably through the flowing darkness. In his exhaustion his own life ebbed and flowed, along other roads, or he opened doors and went into the houses that he had known, in which the familiar faces were looking for him to behave in an expected way. But because he too, for all his apparent solidity, was as fluid and unpredictable as the stream of life, he left them standing with the words half out of their mouths and a surprised row of teeth. He would have liked to satisfy people, but he could not. He would have liked to subscribe to their gospel of the stationary, but he could not. He would have liked to open himself and declare, Here am I. Then they would have looked inside and recognized with smiles of approval their own desires, standing in rows like objects at the ironmonger's. Rigid. Instead, his star palpitated, and his cloud drifted, threadbare.

Here and there along the road the passengers in Peabodys' dray were climbing down with stiff limbs, out of the sleep of those that remained. Soon there was only Ossie Peabody, and Parkers, and the lost child. In its emptiness the dray was quite cold, and there were even less chances of escaping one another.

So that when Ossie Peabody said, there they were, delivered safe at their own door, the child was desperately exposed on his platform in the starlight. He stood as if waiting for his benefactors to decide what form his sentence should take.

At the moment they were having a slight argument about something the man was bringing out of the dray.

"What is that?" the woman asked suspiciously.

"That's a bath," said her husband, banging it awkwardly against the side of the dray, before he heaved it out.

"Whatever for?" she asked. Her voice thickened, as if this second problem was too much.

"To wash in," her husband replied.

"Make yerself sweet for church on Sunday," said Ossie Peabody, spitting at the darkness.

"I didn't know," said the woman, "that it was you brought the bath. How ever did you get the thing?"

"It was there," said her husband, kicking the hollow object with his toe, not by design, though it sounded like it. "It was there," he said. "Nobody seemed to want it. So I took it. It will come in useful."

"Oh," she said doubtfully.

The lost child sheltered behind their words, against the stars.

"Anyway," said the woman, her voice exhausted by the weight of possessions, "we're home."

"Give us your hand," she said to the boy in a revived but dangerously personal tone. "You can jump down, can't you? You're quite big, you know."

"Of course he can," said the man, who was shifting about, and stamping, and avoiding the bath, "he's a sollicker."

So the child jumped towards them, as he was told, and they were calling good-bye, and bundling through the darkness, past the twigs of a rosebush, into a house.

In the room of the house where they went, that was all bumps and thick airless darkness from being closed, the woman let go the child's hand. For the moment she thought only of reacquainting herself with her shell. She breathed the warm darkness and was relieved. Oh, I shall talk to him, she said, but later, and take his hand, and sit on the edge of the bed, and talk about animals. She knew already the shape of the face she would take in her hand, and for this reason perhaps was less afraid of losing it. For the moment she thought only of finding things. The matches.

Both the man and the woman were bumping about.

"Here's the matches, Stan," she said.

Then he made the light. There was a table and chairs, and a black stove, and dead ash lying in a hearth.

"This is the kitchen," said the man, jerking his elbow in a spasmodic, jovial way.

The tone of voice was not his, but he had felt it his duty to speak, to explain something to the child.

After that he went outside to make water, and to put the bath in a shed, where it remained quietly. Parkers were always uneasy about that bath.

The woman, who was moving about with authority and relief in her recovered house, placing and shifting things, began to talk to the child, not yet with the directness and tenderness that she ought, but to talk.

"We're going to make up a bed for you here," she said. "He'll fetch a stretcher that we've got. Then we'll find the sheets. But after we've had something to eat. There's some cold beef. Do you like beef?" she asked.

"Yes," he said.

"Some prefer mutton."

"I had pork once," said the boy, "with crackling on it."

"Your dad kept a pig, perhaps," said the woman, making a careful pattern with plates and forks.

"It was a pig that Mr. Thompson killed and give us a bit of."

"Ah," she said, listening. "Mr. Thompson did, did he?"

But the boy had closed again. Deliberately. It was as if he had determined to originate on that night, outside the butcher's shop at Wullunya.

Soon they all sat down to eat in separate silences. The man and woman chewed their food. They eyed their furniture with contented eyes. They too had turned their backs on events that had been too exhilarating or too shameful to bear. In this room there were many objects that had been shaped and worn by their own hands. These are the things that exist.

But the boy had none of these things. After he had gobbled down his meat and some cold potato that had been fried up quickly in beef dripping, he sat looking thin, and after a bit took a piece of glass from his pocket, that he sat holding half-hidden.

What's that? they asked, through a complacency of digested food.

"That's a piece of glass," said the boy.

Poor kid, said the woman, I shall speak to him, but later.

98

She had to ward off some recollection of sadness, for a little at least.

And the man thought about his cows. But at the back of his mind was the flowing of the brown waters, and the doors of houses choked with water, and on an island a sewing machine.

"Well," he said, "if we're not careful, it'll soon be milking time."

So they all began to go to bed, the child in the kitchen where he had been told. He did all that he was told.

"Good night, Stan," said the woman. "What a day!"

She put her mouth on his. She was his wife. Her mouth was rather moist, and familiar. But as he leaned on his elbow to blow out the candle he remembered the strange, dark figure of the girl standing above him on the shore as he sat in the boat, and the greenish-white shadows, the shadows of the white roses in the thighs of his wife once when he had come quickly into the room. He turned quickly from his thoughts. He was tired and could easily have become irritable.

"Yes," he yawned. "Those poor buggers that lost their homes. And that kid. Do you think he's all right?"

And now the sadness that she could no longer ward off was floating over the woman who had kissed the mouth of her husband good night. She smelled the sad wick of the candle flame.

"I don't know," she said.

Her position in the bed was intolerable.

"You would bring him," he condemned.

She did not feel she had ever loved the man her husband. She had forgotten the moment on the river's bank, when they had been cast up into each other's eyes. She longed to be pervaded by a permanence.

"Yes," she said, lying in the darkness. "I am to blame. I brought him. But I had to."

Which her husband did not hear, for he had fallen asleep.

Then she got up quickly and smoothly, as if it had been determined long before that evening that she should do this at that moment, and went straight through the cold into the kitchen.

"What are you doing?" she asked gently.

The kitchen still glowed. The boy lay on his side, looking through his piece of glass at the dying coals. He did not look up, though accepting her presence.

"You've still got that old thing," she said, shivering in her nightdress on the edge of the bed.

"That is from the church," he said.

"You lived near a church then?"

"No. That was afterwards. After I had left the others. It was near the willows. I thought I was dead," he said.

"Was it your family you were with?" she asked.

"I can't remember that," he said glibly, looking through the piece of glass, that she saw was colouring his cheek; as he moved the glass his skin was a drifting crimson.

"It doesn't matter. If you want it that way," she said, touching him with her hand, but without much hope.

"What are you doing here?" the child asked.

"Why," she said, "I live here. This is my house."

But her skin was cold. She was uncertain of her furniture.

The child was looking at her hand. It was lying with some lost purpose along his arm. She still had to learn the words that she might speak.

"Would you like to look through this?" he asked. "I broke it from one of the windows."

"You broke it!"

"No one else needed it," he said. "I wanted it to look through."

It was obviously his.

"At first it fell into the water. But I fished it up. You see, there was water inside the church."

She took the piece of glass and held it to her face, so that the whole room was drenched with crimson, and the coals of the fire were a disintegrating gold.

"I will tell you about the church," he said. "There were birds there too, that had come in through the holes in the window. I slept there most of the day, on the seats, with one of those things that they pray on, a sort of cushion, under my head, but it pricked. There were fish swimming in the church. I touched one with my hand. And the books were floating. The water was moving, you see. Everything was floating and moving."

"Yes," she said, "it was."

Now the purplish-crimson flood possessed her too, as she crouched on the pew with the child. There were dead things. There was almost the face that floated beneath the willows.

"Did you say your prayers?" she asked, pulling the glass away from her face.

"No," he said. "There were no prayers being said, not any more, in that church."

They looked at each other. Released from the glass, their skins were white.

"Listen," she said, her voice coming to their rescue, "you can stay here, you know. If you like. This is your home."

"No, it isn't," he said.

She put the glass on the counterpane.

"You'd better go to sleep," she told him.

She was again an awkward young woman with a confidence she had learned from others. Her voice was grating and superficial, when it should have come up warmly from a great depth. And in this voice she had to say her piece.

"In the morning we shall see. Are you warm enough? You want feeding up, you know. You're thin. But food will set you up."

It did not seem that he intended to speak to her again, lying curled on his side, with his head in the crook of his arm. She would not possess this child. So she went away, treading through the crimson light that clung to her still, through a wind of dead prayers in the drowning church. She went to her room, to wrestle with sleep.

Then she saw, suddenly, her husband was putting on his pants. The light in the lamp-chimney was smooth and very yellow.

"Whatever time is it?" she asked.

"Time to get up," he said, as hard as the thwack of his belt. "Fritz has gone across the yard."

She could, in fact, hear the familiar buckets, and the cock tearing apart the last rags of sleep.

They were going to do the things that had to be done; air and water cold on the skin, they were passing and repassing, each closed in himself, solemnly round the room, knotting or brushing hair, filling their empty clothes. It was obvious that these lives had never shattered into coloured fragments. They went out through the kitchen, quickly and quietly, past the body of a boy sleeping on a narrow bed. They barely glanced at him, as if they were anxious not to disturb, or for some other reason.

There in the stalls across the yard, in the light of lanterns, stood the rumps of cows. There was also the face of the old scrubbed German waiting to tell things and be told. The cows were munching chaff. The scent of slaver and the cows' breath mounted higher than the cold as the woman and the two men sat on their blocks with the buckets between their knees, prepared for the opening of their ritual.

"Rain stopped," said the old German, wringing his first teat.

"Yes," said Stan Parker, "it stopped all right."

Hanging on the nail the rag with which he had wiped the udder of the blue cow.

"I knew it would," said the old man.

"How, Fritz?" asked Amy Parker.

"Ah," he said, "I knew. You can tell," he said.

Then there was the music of the milk.

"How was the floods?" asked the old man.

"The floods were terrible," said Amy Parker. "Stan saw more than I did. But I saw a little. Some people lost everything."

The old man sucked his teeth above the gentle milk.

"We brought back a bath, Fritz," Stan Parker told.

"Stan found it," said his wife.

Then they sat dashing the milk from the rubbery teats of the big placid cows.

Stan Parker, with his feet firmly on the clean bricks, waited for his wife to tell the story of the lost boy, but it did not seem as if this would be told, or not yet, anyway.

They sat dashing the milk, and an anxious froth began to fill the bucket that Amy Parker held. It began to be an interminable milking that morning, and afterwards, while the men were clanking cans, and the cows were forming aimless groups, their empty udders flopping at their legs. Then she ran up from the bails and across the yard. To reach the house. But quickly. Now his eyes will be open, her breath said. She would say many things. By the light of morning it is possible to accomplish what the night refuses. She would imprison the child in her house by force of love.

But when she went into the kitchen, slowing up so as not to look silly, and shaping her breathlessness into a smile, the clothes of the narrow bed had been pushed back, they had already taken a cold, permanent shape. So that she did not bother to call. She looked at the piece of crimson glass that had shattered on the boards into other crimson pieces.

Not long after, her husband came in for a quick breakfast before taking the milk. She had put everything before him, beyond reproach. There were the frilly fired eggs, and the red tea that he liked to drink, standing waiting in a blue enamel pot.

He began to cut across the eggs, as if expecting them to be of harder substance, or out of absence of mind.

"Jewel has two months to go," said the woman, tearing the old leaves off a calendar that a store had sent. "It's time we dried her off."

"Where is the boy?"

There is nothing wretcheder-looking than a hash of eggs on someone else's plate.

"He's not here," she said. "He's gone."

"We coudn't have kept him," said her husband. "He didn't want to camp down here. You could see that. He didn't belong to us."

"Yes," she said.

Though she could not altogether see, nor explain why.

She could not explain that a moment comes when you yourself must produce some tangible evidence of the mystery of life. And now she was going round their kitchen, her daylight skin grey and drained by early rising, her hands performing blunt acts in no way related to the transcendent moments she had lived. This made her frown, and shove the furniture into correct positions, and pick up a grey potato peeling that had fallen from the bucket some time before.

"Amy," he said, trying to make his voice adequate, touching her, after he had finished and pushed back his plate. "It's all right," he said.

"Yes," she answered. "Of course it's all right."

They were close. Their lives had grown together. They would continue in that way, because it was not possible to divide their common trunk.

Now that they stood at the window, their arms touching, present and absent, she did not deny the goodness of their common life. He could feel this in his whole being, through the early-morning weariness, that was also achievement. Now the cows swaggered through the trees, their tails switching, their blue noses touching the pale grass that had begun to rise from the silt, or rubbing their necks against the black bark of the wattle trees. Do you know this? he would have said; and this? and this? That he saw with his eyes and felt with his bones. But as he did not know how to say such things, he stood pinching up the skin of her hand. And it was not necessary, perhaps, to speak, he began to feel in the skin of her hand. She had begun to see the shapes of the trees, the white columns, and the humbler, shaggy ones, stirring and inclining towards them in the morning light. The sky was moving in an extravagance of recovered blue, so that the man and woman arrested at their window seemed also to move for a moment, to sway on the stems of their bodies, as their souls stirred and recognized familiar countries. For that moment they were limitless.

Then the man returned to his stiff boots and began to remember what he must do. The woman put away the tablecloth, folding it as if she loved it. She was contented. If she thought of the lost boy, it was for a slight squint in one eye that she remembered from the firelit night. As for her own inadequacies, she was now stronger than they.

"Perhaps we should tell the police," she said, "about that boy."

He said that he might ride in to Bangalay if there was time, later, in the afternoon.

Nobody heard what became of the lost boy that Parkers found at Wullunya in the floods. There the waters subsided soon after, leaving a squalor of yellow mud and quantities of brown snakes. The inhabitants sorted out their furniture, and the bits of themselves that they had recovered, and by degrees forgot to mention the subject.

Only sometimes at Durilgai it was recalled how the noble draylord of volunteers went down to rescue the victims of the flood. It is not known how or why the district in which Parkers lived got its name, but it was about the time of the floods that the official voice began to refer to it as Durilgai. And this meant "fruitful," a friend of Mr. Armstrong's who was a professor, or something, said. But the people who lived in that district were disinclined to use their name, anyway for a long time, except in postal matters, as if something was expected of them that they could not, or did not care to, fulfil.

Amy Parker slowed up her rather slapdash hand in writing it, and spoke it to herself with full, thoughtful breath. Her expression withdrew into her face when strangers mentioned the official word, and she continued to refer to their district by the names of those people amongst whom the land was parcelled out. Sometimes she sat beside the bush of full white roses, her arms awkward in unemployment, at the place that was "Parkers'," and looked at the road.

PART II

✿❀✿

Chapter 8

ABOUT a mile from Parkers', where the road forks, a store had been built, and a post office was added in time, so that Durilgai did exist physically, these two buildings proved it. And as the inhabitants gained faith they trailed up the direct, dusty roads towards their village, and down the several, meandering, gritty tracks, the women to dawdle through their shopping, the men, with less excuse, to waste time.

Summer was a time of white dust and yellow grit. In the glare of sky and iron, in the scent of dry eucalypt and crushed ant, men rounded their shoulders and screwed up their eyes as they leaned against the veranda posts of the general store or frankly sat. Some exposed their particoloured foreheads in the shade, preferring flies to wet felt. There was a smell of relaxed exertion on the veranda of the store. Words would lose their direction, without censure from the audience, for time is so immense; while those who did not talk, the silenter, closed ones, would be writing in the dust with stick or whip, and erasing, and writing, in their own private codes, from which they would look up out of pale eyes.

At this stage of its existence the simple face of the general store at Durilgai still glowed with brown paint. It was a child's game in wood and iron. Many honest objects stood primly in the window, buckets, and lampwicks, and millet brooms, and axe handles, and darning wool. Nothing perishable in the window was the policy of the storekeeper who had arranged these goods so painfully. They looked timeless and did acquire a permanence. They could have been painted on the wooden backing by some awkward brush that had not yet learned the dishonesties of art.

This store, or *establishment*, as it was referred to, belonged

107

in the beginning to Mr. Denyer, a rather floury man, but good, who said his prayers and kept bantams for pleasure. Mr. Denyer liked to walk amongst his fowls, looking down at them from his height, and smiling at their neatness through thick spectacles. He was, in fact, the complement of his shop, simply, even awkwardly made. But he would endure. People driving from Durilgai along the road to Bangalay could look back and see Mr. Denyer in the simple attitudes he adopted, fixed at his counter, or in the doorway of his shop. This in turn was fixed in the landscape, of gentle green hills, or later in the season, scruffy ones. Beside the door stood a tamarisk Mr. Denyer himself had planted, that in the early summer waved its pale flags of dusty pink, and in the later summer hung in sad plumes of pink dust. As the trunk thickened, the feathers of this straight tamarisk became something to look for. Strangers often asked Mr. Denyer what his tree was, but this was something he did not know. He smiled. He said it was something he had bought, because he wanted a tree, he had to have something, and this was what it had become. But his thick spectacles were obviously pleased.

In all that district the names of things were not so very important. One lived. Almost no one questioned the purpose of living. One was born. One lived. The strings of runny-nosed, black Irish children, and the sandier, scabbier Scotch that spilled out of the bush onto the thin tracks that struggled up to meet the greater roads, were soon becoming elongated youths and girls, that hung around, and avoided each other, and met, and locked hands magnetically, and mingled their breath together in the hot evenings. New patterns of life, of paddock and yard and orchard, would be traced on the sides of the hills and the little gullies. But not yet. In time. In slow time too, of hot summer days.

Even the post office at Durilgai, with its faint echoes of a world and suggestions of other activity, stood still. The post office, which was across from Denyer's, beside the signpost that the white ant soon got into, was less imposing than the store. Its official importance was by no means obvious. The post office was a creaking cottage, in the side of which was fitted a kind of hatch, through which Mrs. Gage shoved the letters and her desperate face, and hung out afterwards to grapple departing backs with those last comments on the weather, that stood between her and silence. She was a woman in a flat hat, like a dried palm, and she wore brown-paper sleeves. In that office, which it was of course, you could also see the dressmaker's dummy, on which the post-mistress ran up cotton frocks for those who cared to submit. There were great drifts of snippets, and an orange velvet carrot filled with emery dust. And there was the dust of the road, that filled the inkwells and clotted with the postal ink, and lay on the official papers that grated together or flapped into new positions when there was a wind.

Mrs. Gage was always coming and going, to untie the string that bound the bundles of letters or to look for things. On Sundays she drove out, with a red fox around her neck and a blue dog beneath her gig, and she would rein in, and talk, in yellow tones of statement from behind her broad, unconscious teeth.

The postmistress had a husband who was no good. It was not clear in what way, except that he could not make money, and once had painted a picture of an old wooden fence with a couple of dead trees behind, that made you wonder. Mr. Gage's remunerative jobs were varied and mysterious. Sometimes he was there and sometimes not. He was a shadow in a singlet.

If anyone spoke he would look up before he had listened and say, "Ah, good, good, I'll run and fetch Mrs. Gage." And he would, at once, furtively, as if he were a boarder in that house, on charitable terms. It was the postmistress's house.

Once Mr. Gage had thrown himself on the ground and looked so intently at an ant that the eyes bulged in his head, and he was swallowed by fluctuating brown waves, and his arms were fixed to the ground at what appeared a permanent angle, their grey flesh quivering. When he recovered himself there was a soldierbird in the spider bush, and Mrs. Parker, who had come along the road.

"Is anything the matter?" she asked.

"No," he said. "I was looking at an ant."

"Ah," she said, in doubt, moistening her lips that were hot and dusty.

She did not question his attitude further, and he was surprised.

Perhaps she was absent for the moment, or perhaps it was the heat. Because it is not usual for a human being to resist an opportunity to destroy. And she could have crushed with her foot such ecstasy as remained in his ant-body.

So he continued to kneel and look at her, a scrawny object in his singlet, but the intensity of his eyes penetrated the woman's unconscious face almost to the darker corners, as if here too was some mystery he must solve, like the soul of the ant.

Amy Parker, who was half for pausing to satisfy some unrevealed need of the kneeling man, and half for mounting higher on her way, was at this time a young woman broadening into maturity. Her pointed face and bony cheeks had filled with almost satisfied desires. She was a honey colour in the summer day. Her thickening arms could lift great weights, when there was no man to do it, but they were better seen putting up her hair. Then her strong, honey-coloured back with the lifted arms was a full vase. She was filled with the thick, honey-coloured light of the heavy summer days.

"Is Mrs. Gage there?" Mrs. Parker asked.

"Yes, yes," replied the husband of the postmistress. "She's in the office or round at the back. She's there. She could be sorting out the mail."

He picked a blade of yellow grass.

"Aren't you going to get up?" Mrs. Parker asked. "It can't be comfortable kneeling there."

"All right," he said.

And he got to his feet, and went farther into the bush, trailing the yellow stalk of grass.

After the husband of the postmistress had removed himself Mrs. Parker continued to mount the hill. In company she might have questioned the behaviour of Mr. Gage, but, alone in the heat of the day, he was a child, or an animal, or a stone, from none of which she could have hidden herself. Dreamy bits of life that she had lived floated to the surface and mingled with the hard light. She looked up into the face of the sun her husband, and because she was blinded did not see that the bushes had observed her nakedness.

So she went on, touching the fence, on which there was a tinkling snakeskin that somebody had hung to dry. It was the post-office fence already, and the lavatory which a gale had knocked sideways, and the hatch in which was the face of the postmistress, looking out.

"Mrs. Parker," called Mrs. Gage. "I say, Mrs. Parker! Is it hot enough? No sign of a breeze. No sign of rain. And the big tank is nearly dry. Because I'm doing what I can for the termarters. I do like a nice termarter."

No one but the postmistress suffered from the weather. It was recorded on her that her days were unbearable.

"Is there anything for us, Mrs. Gage?" asked Mrs. Parker.

110

"No, dear," said the postmistress. "Anyways, I don't think. Not that I can remember. But I'll look."

Withdrawing her hat from the hatch in a chattering of dried palm leaves.

"You never know," she said, "what you mightn't overlook. In this weather. It drives a person potty."

The postmistress removed the string from the bundle with great skill. When she licked her yellow thumb it was more than an official act, a ritual rather, to soothe the humble suppliant, who would stand snuffing the scent of melted sealing-wax as it mounted in the sanctuary behind. It was improbable that any of those letters, elevated like a host to the level of the postmistress's eyes, could belong in substance to anyone. Many of them never did. But Amy Parker continued to attend this ritual, because it came at the top of the hill, and sometimes there was a catalogue, with pictures of things, and once there had been a letter from her Aunt Fibbens, dictated to a lady who could write, about some unpleasantness.

"No, dear," said Mrs. Gage, "it's as I thought. People are not writing in the heat. There was a storm, though, on the North Coast, and a young fellow struck by lightning on his horse. It ran up the stirrup irons. Had a baby, it said, only six months. He was a timber cutter. Can you understand?"

"How should I understand, Mrs. Gage?" said Mrs. Parker, who at this moment was strong.

She began decently to walk away.

But the yellow postmistress wrenched her hat through the hatch, her face desperate in its pleats for the state of lightning and her own impending loneliness.

"But it does somebody good," she called. "You've got to admit. The rain. And the tank half dry. They say there'll be a southerly buster later in the afternoon. But no rain."

Holding her hat in the wind of her own words, the desperate woman was a victim of her own roots. Ah, strike me, she would have said, into shapes of fire and radiance. But lightning was a thing of horror. So she withdrew her head, rearranging her hat, that rustled like her brown-paper arms.

Mrs. Parker walked away, as if exempt from the weather. For this reason some people did not care for Parkers. But lightning is a personal matter. She remembered their own lightning with some tenderness, how they were both untouched, and at the same time open for each other's eyes.

Now she quickened her pace. Now she wanted to get home. Now she wanted to tell her husband all kinds of simple things, even if he did not listen. Quite apart from the words of the postmistress she had reached that point in the road where she always experienced the anxiety of not belonging. Faces on the store veranda, pasted there some time past, it would appear, stared at her out of their permanent positions and dared her to approach.

There was a gig too, outside the store, that did not belong by rights to that scene. No dust lay on the splendid varnish of the bright gig. The horse, hardly in a lather, shook the flies from his dark face, and with them a shower of clinking brass, that slashed, and flashed, and dared. Altogether there was an air of great daring about the horse and gig that made Mrs. Parker shy. So that she approached determined not to look, with her awkward, wooden movements exposed, she felt, in the open wastes of dust.

It was Armstrongs' turnout, she began to realize, that young Armstrong sometimes drove. At that moment he was not present. Inside the store, perhaps, buying something unimportant, for anything of importance was brought from Sydney to the brick house. And now the horse waited, striking at the ground with his shapely hoofs, shifting the gig gratingly in which sat the two young women.

Amy Parker did not so much see this as know, in shame beside the tamarisk. That the women rocked with the gig, laughing and eating caramels and tossing the silver paper onto the road. No other pastime could have been theirs, because none would have been careless enough. They belonged to that gig, under the parasol that one of them held, and that shifted indolently and mottled their skins.

Any words let fall were not interpreted by the woman on foot as she passed in the shadow of the tamarisk; nor could she have looked at the faces, she was too displeased with her own. This was now brick-coloured, with a little down of hairs. She wore a hat that once she had thought pretty, with a bunch of shiny cherries, but now she held her head away, to hide the silliness of cherries on her cheap, crushed hat.

And all the time the harness of the gig jingled cruelly, like the words of a distant conversation that would seem to have a personal bearing, even though unintelligible. As the young ladies laughed, and twirled their parasol for occupation, and tossed the silver paper onto the road.

Several men on the store veranda were admiring and resenting the rich man's turnout, and making indecent remarks about the girls. When Mrs. Parker went up, old Mr. Peabody said something, as if he felt he had to, but what, she could not have told, in that scene of excitement and distress. With a blue ribbon winding through the parasol. And young Armstrong coming against her, whom she had known from a wristy boy, now a man with thick lips.

"Hold hard," he said, steadying her by the elbows and laughing distantly, thickly, in his throat.

He stood back looking at her, as he did now at women, at their breasts, but in a permissible way which some liked. And into her burned face. But it would not open for him. A draught coming from the shop carried her skirt between her legs, that were thick, and even ugly.

"Mrs. Parker," he said, seeing at last. "Sorry," he laughed. "That was a near thing."

But with some redness for his remembered boyhood of long wrists. Then he ran down the steps, in a splendid pair of pants, towards the gigful of girls, who had been brought from Sydney for him to choose from.

"Some people always make it an occasion," said Mr. Denyer, whose watch chain cut the gentle gloom.

"Oh yes, I suppose so," said Mrs. Parker, building with her burned hands an abrupt monument out of boxes of starch.

She began to remember what she had come for, and to name these innocent things almost brutally, as if one might compel them to assume some superior significance. But the pearls of barley were dim and artificial, that fell on the grocer's brass. And she gathered up her clean-smelling, ordinary parcels, and paid, and went out.

The gig had gone of course, but the air was still turbulent. Some men took off their hats, others put them on; some were shifting in their clothes and telling stories of horses, while most remembered the throats of the two young women and accepted thoughtfully the insolence of their white skins.

And Amy Parker began to accept, as she returned along the deserted road. Its monotony was even comforting. Now the incident of the gig was the faintest tingling in her blood. Her feet tramped calmly where wheels had disturbed the dust.

In this state of recovered calm and prickling silence she was again close to her husband, though he spoke to her with the thicker accents of the rich young man, and their mouths exchanged a lazy sensuality. So that she had to laugh, and redden, and shift her basket. Because, of course, it was not like this. Her face grew thoughtfuller, and thin. Many aching inci-

113

dents of regret and tenderness came at her from the ridge, from which she looked down and saw the willow, spread above the muddy water of the dam, and the first intimations of their wooden house. Although their district had become more closely settled the house still appeared to stand alone, and it was this isolation, this silence, towards which she now quickened, and which fitted her like a skin.

Looking this way and that, she began to feel possessive even of the tufts of shivery-grass that stood outside the fence. She was both possessive and possessed. Cooler leaves spattered on her face, and the first mouthful of a breeze was blown upon her elbows and the nape of her neck. So that the paddocks undulated with a greater joyfulness, in which the blue crane stalked, and neat peewits tumbled, and young calves managed their tails in awkward play. She herself was hastening over stones, in that disguised pace which is between walking and running. Because it would have looked silly, running home for what reason, except to embrace the cat at the gate and feel his rough tongue on her salt skin.

But she was in her own place at last, in which she would not be expected to find answers. Inside the house a tap dripped, boughs scraped the roof, sounds fitting into silences with such justice that already she was refreshed. Before she went out to where, beside the well, he stood treadling the grindstone, that he had brought from Bangalay in the beginning, in exchange for something that she had by this time forgotten.

"Well," she said, approaching the grindstone, and the smell of wet stone, "I got back. And it was white hot. You should have seen, Stan, there was a gigful of ladies at the store, that young Armstrong had brought. Society ladies. With a white parasol. It was lace, I think. Fancy, a parasol."

But he did not look up or say anything much, not did she expect.

He held the blade of the gleaming knife to the uneven surface of the stone, and the stone sang and lapped at the brown water in the little trough beneath.

Ah, she sighed, sitting on the edge of the well, and her skin drank the cool.

She watched the white knife in her husband's hands, that he pressed with his strength against the stone. She held her throat up, in the dim cool light of the tree above the well, offering it almost to the gleaming knife, that she would have received with what cry of love.

114

Then when he had finished he felt the knife with his thumb, and looked at her at last. He looked into her in the cool gloom of the old tree, biting his lip with some thoughtfulness. Outside the circle of the cool tree there were his cleared paddocks, burned to a white-grey by the heat of summer, and the house he had knocked together, and enlarged, and improved, and that had finally taken its place with some dignity in the fields, even pretending a bit beneath the tendrils of vines and a shower of roses. All was ranged round him, radiating out from him in the burning afternoon. So that Stan Parker was pleased.

And he was pleased with the strong throat of his wife.

It seemed that a firmly founded architecture had risen at Parkers'. Even in the flesh. Though Stan Parker himself had dried up a bit, though the back of his neck was wrinkled as he bent down to pick up an axe that he would grind next, though his eyes were somewhat cavernous, from surprise and acceptance; he had withstood the battering and would continue to withstand.

Let all things come, his body suggested, his shoulders rounded above the grindstone, his foot controlling the treadle as metal ate stone, and stone metal, with the harsh gurgle of their consummation. All was good, almost, that could come to this pass. The stone leaped and was restrained by the controlling wire. The strength of his hands shaped the metal. It would have been possible at such times to shape almost anything into a right shape.

But he sensed her restlessness as she sat at the well head and tossed her foot. So he said, "Perhaps he will marry the girl in the gig."

"I don't think so," she said dryly. "There were two girls."

She tossed her foot now for something that eluded her, in the stance of his body, in his impervious skull. But she looked at his hands and was glad that her husband was a poor man.

She got up. Ah, she felt, restlessly, how can I prove he is the best of men? And was suddenly very restless, and empty.

"We'll have a cup," he said, squinting at the axe's edge. "Then it'll be time to go down to the cows."

And after, as they walked with the buckets, out from the leafy borders of the house, out to where the heat began, she was again all restless to prove to herself some perfection. In the lesser heat of the evening the long shadows of the fenceposts lay, and the cows dawdled towards the yard. Some young heifers jumped and ran, but it was the slower, gentler

115

progress that prevailed, of the older, swollen cows. All was heaviness, yet apparent perfection in the yellow drawn-out evening. And anticipation. The cows were twitching their ears. The heifers looked.

"It's the wind that's coming," said the man, who was possessed by a great fondness for his evening paddocks; he would have liked to point to things.

So that he was glad of the opportunity to raise his arm with the bucket at the wrist and say, "Look, it is the wind all right."

As the crests of the trees bent over in an obeisance of silver, as dust flirted, as a young cow jumped in fear or pleasure, tossed her rump in the air and farted.

It was the postmistress's predicted southerly buster that struck the figures of the man and woman, sluiced them with cool, and would have torn the buckets from them.

Now the old German came out, smiling, and white with bran that he had been tipping to the stalled cows. And they laughed and made jokes. They made the standing joke about Tricky, who was *her* cow, they must not touch her—a man's hand on her side, and she lashed out and flung herself on the ground.

It was fun at the bails that evening in the wind. There was a soaring sound of wind, boisterous without malice, that almost drowned the hissing of the milk. This mounted in its loveliness. The cows came, and gave, and were content. It was the contentment of absolute perfection again. Till the man grew thoughtful at mouth. His substance, which had been solid enough, omnipotent even, at the grindstone an hour or two before, had begun to thin out. The draughts of glad wind, almost liquid in their cold, made him wring the milk from the last teats, anxious to be finished.

"What is it?" it was now her turn to ask, as they stood together afterwards in the shed they had built, on the wet floors they had just scoured down.

But it was nothing of course. Except a desire that had never been fulfilled, to express himself in substance or words.

When, in the night, after the cans were scalded, and the big pans of subtle milk were standing in a row, and she had laid the dishes on their sides to drain, and he had done some accounts on a scrap of paper and got the final answer, then he sat with the piece of pencil in his mouth, waiting to fill an emptiness. The wind had died by now, though the cool it had brought still eddied and lapped. On hot evenings the house

116

was compressed and mean; now it opened. The house was not excluded from the largeness of the cool night. The roof of the house was opening, so that the feverish stars were reflected in the pans of milk, and many other harmonies were proved, of skin and feather, of chair and bough, of air and needle.

For the man's wife had taken wool, and the cool needle was weaving in and out. He watched her hand, and the old sock that she held on the wooden acorn. And she drew the wool together, sitting at the centre of the night. He watched, and they were indeed the centre, but precariously, and he wanted to be certain. This made him chew the little stub of pencil, and would have undoubtedly resulted in something final, if it was to have been given to him to express himself in this life. But it was not. Except sometimes he had formed the lines of prayers.

Then the woman put down the sock, because this velvet night was not to be resisted. She went and took her husband's head and held it against her, as if now she did possess something. She rubbed her lips on his eyelids, that were set rather deep, scored his face with her lips, till she could begin to feel his skin answering. Till they were melting together in the night, and were led by the hand, mysteriously, glidingly, into darker rooms, in which the flesh of the bed was opening to receive.

In the cool of the released world, amongst the dreaming furniture, at the heart of the staggy rosebush that pressed into the room and wrestled with them without thorns, the man and woman prayed into each other's mouths that they might hold this goodness forever. But the greatness of the night was too vast. The woman fell back finally, almost crying. And the man withdrew into his own fleshly body. He lay on their bed and touched what was almost a cage of bones, that his soul was beginning already to accept.

There was then, in the end, sleep, and work, and a warm belief in some presence. And sleep.

But the woman got up. She was recovering her identity. The woman, Amy Parker, went and leaned against the window frame, which received the shape of her body. All shapes. sounds, seemed to fit together in the quiet night. It was no longer vast, but familiar, the darkness moving with the intimacy of old owls that have nested years in the same place, the air stroking her skin like her own relaxed hand. She stood there some time, holding her full body, and could have continued well into the night, obsessed by wonder and contentment. Wondering if she would conceive the child that she knew by heart. Holding the slow throb of her heart in her folded arms.

Chapter 9

WHEN Amy Parker did finally have her baby, the neighbours moved their faces into all the correct positions of congratulation and approval, but of course it was quite an ordinary act. Many fruitful women were lying down and having babies regularly, after the laundry, or the baking, or a hot morning in church, and no fuss at all. But Amy Parker exalted her own act on the quiet. She walked about on the shady borders of the house, and now indeed she was the centre of the universe. Light converged on the white cocoon she was holding in her arms; the course of birds invested it with mystical importance as they hovered above it, almost, in fussy flight; flowers and leaves inclined above the head of the woman with the child or gave blessing with long, benevolent wands when there was a breeze.

"It'll be nice for you to have," said the postmistress, pressing her yellow thumb on a dry sponge. "Company, like. Is he good?"

"Of course he is good," said Amy Parker. "Only sometimes he has the wind. And Friday he was upset. It was the heat. You know, the diarrhoea."

"Ah," said the postmistress, beneath her straight hat, in the tone of voice for other people's problems, "there is something that you give them."

"Oh," said Amy Parker, "I *know* what you *give* them. And now he is all right. Oh yes, Mrs. Gage, he's a very healthy boy."

He was the child of their bodies. She would unwrap him to look at his healthy nakedness. She called him Ray. It was a name that she had not thought of before, and had not heard used much, but it fitted itself to her mouth, and to the little, perfect boy, lying in the gold of the morning on the open bed. The sun glittered on his mouth and the first down of hair.

Now that the house was full of the warm, soft smell of the baby, the father of the child entered with greater diffidence. He performed quite a ceremony, humming to himself and stamping on the brick path to the kitchen, so that the clods of earth flew off his boots and made the fuchsias tremble. Then he went in arrogantly, or so it seemed, straight to where the baby lay, in a cot, or in his mother's arms, and looked him straight in the face. To get it over. The baby returned the father's stare but gave no glimpse of himself through his clear, shallow eyes. His glances and expressions were reserved for his mother. The cord between them had not been cut. He did not yet recognize and only tolerated his father, sensing perhaps the diffidence that shimmered between the man's hard body and his own soft but also powerful one. He looked at his father with a grave arrogance of his own that was more convincing.

"Seems to be doing all right," the father would say.

Then he would turn his back, glad of this release. Later on he would speak to him, he said, and teach him to make things. They would go off into the bush with axe or gun, and there would be many things to say. They would wipe the sweat from their faces, and drink cold water from their hands, returning at evening with the carcass of a fox that his boy had shot. Whether he would be able to convey to his son the quivering of his own soul on the brink of discovery remained to be seen. Or whether he would want to. He would perhaps suspect the flinty, inquisitive face of the sturdy boy.

"You never touch him," said the mother. "I believe you don't love him at all."

Taking her baby that she alone could love enough.

"What am I to do?" he asked, offering his empty hands. "What can you do with a baby?"

A baby is an abstraction, still an idea, to which you have not yet had time to adjust your opinions and your habits.

"What can you *do?*" she said. "Why, you can eat him!"

She could have. She could not love him enough, not even by slow, devouring kisses. Sometimes her moist eyes longed almost to have him safe inside her again.

"I'd put it down," said the father. "It can't be healthy to maul it like that."

"What do *you* know?" she said the mother. "He's safe enough with me."

120

But "safe" is an optimistic word. Her hands would withdraw from the child she had put to sleep, and already the future was growing in the house, making a tangle of the present. Already she was powerless.

The father and mother would sometimes watch the sleeping child, and in this way were united again, as they were not when he was awake. Released from this obsessive third life that they seemed to have created, the lives that they had lived and understood were plain as cardboard. Affection is less difficult than love. But the sleeping baby moved his head, and the parents were again obsessed by vague fear, the mother that she might not ride the storms of love, the father that he would remain a stranger to his son.

The clock ticked in the kitchen. It was an ugly clock, in dark marble, of which they had been proud in the beginning. As the little boy grew, firm and gilded, he would ask to be held up to the clock, to watch its progress. Then he would press his red mouth to the glass and drink the minutes, so that for a moment the ugliness was swallowed down, and the dim face of the clock was outshone by the golden cheeks of the boy. One day, about the time when he had begun to run about with confidence and become a pest, the clock stopped for good, and it was about this time also that Amy Parker had her second child.

This time it was more difficult. What if I do not succeed? she had said, again remembering those children she had lost, and recoiling from her helpless and unreliable body. There were days when she had no strength. She grew yellow and repulsive, waiting for this baby, and she could feel the pity in her husband's mouth pressed against the nape of her neck.

"There's no reason," he said, "why anything should go wrong. You had the boy."

These were words that he had used before, so that she could only twist her lips into a stiff smile. She would take into her lap some preferably monotonous piece of work, or hold the boy's cheek to her own, to burn some warmth into her skin. And she would wait for her husband to go away, because he was momentarily distasteful to her. She resented the veins in his strong arms.

With the withdrawal of his wife into her preoccupations, Stan Parker grew closer to the little boy. Quite often he dared to touch him, and once or twice looked deeply into the child's eyes, as if in search of some country he could recognize. But the child laughed out of his clear face, and felt the

121

stubble on his father's chin, and screamed and wriggled with pleasure. By degrees the father got used to the boy, even forgot the child's presence as he squatted to play with tins or stones or the black cakes of cow manure. The child grew dirtier away from his mother. If people had come to the farm, the kind of people who made such remarks, they might have said, He has a neglected look. But he was content and strong. And when he grew tired he slept. Once the father found him in a chaff bin and lifted him out like a warm and drooping cat, still sleeping, in a rain of golden chaff.

Not long after this the ugly clock in the kitchen stopped, and Amy Parker had her second child. They got a doctor from Bangalay. She was sick this time. But eventually she began to notice that everything was still in its place, and she got up, and was walking in her strange clothes with the new child, a rather fretful girl baby, wrapped in a shawl that her neighbour Doll Quigley had knitted for the little boy.

Again people came on the occasion of a birth, and drank tea, and exclaimed, and talked about themselves, and went. But Doll Quigley and her brother Bub would come and stand. They were like the furniture, or doorposts rather, their long wooden frames. Sometimes Doll nursed the baby, and the folds of the shawl hung from her long arms in long folds of carved wood, as if she were holding the child not according to her own instinct, but after some honest sculptor's plan.

Then Amy Parker would take her baby and cry, "Doll, you are so awkward!" And quickly mould the shawl along the lines of her own facile love.

"Yes, I am," said Doll Quigley. "I was awkward. Mum always said." Rubbing together her empty hands, that made a rough sound of wood.

Quigleys seemed the antithesis of that fullness of love and summer which Amy Parker now sensed, herself all roundness and warmth as she held the baby in her arms, and the head of the little boy against her skirt. She was at last continuous. She flowed. Her large, full breasts had become insolent in fulfilment. She could not raise her eyes without an effort towards the forms of Doll and Bub.

Yet Doll Quigley was full of love. She would have suffered willingly if she had been asked. But she was not.

So she took a broom and swept crumbs and dust with long strokes from round the feet of Amy Parker, who frowned because the act was humble.

"It's all right, Doll," she said. "Leave it. I'm behind with everything, I know. But we'll catch up."

She frowned and looked out through the door at a shade of pepper trees, where Bub Quigley had run with her little boy. Now the simplicity of Bub was terrible, his bluish face on which the hair had not properly come, his mouth wandering after words. Now Amy Parker did not see what she had escaped, but knew there was something, and hated it.

"Look," said Bub, "that is a leaf. See? But a skeleton leaf. You can look right through it. It's like a sheep's skeleton, or a cow, only this is a leaf. My sister says it is made of lace. Fancy, a lace leaf. From a lace tree."

The little boy held the leaf to his eyes. He was beautiful.

Bub Quigley laughed to see.

"I want it," said the little boy.

"No," said Bub. "It's my leaf. It's my favourite thing."

"Ray," called the mother, "give the leaf, and come inside."

"I want it," said the little boy, who had begun to cry and jump. "I want. I want."

His storm was violent.

"We shall find another leaf, Bub," the sister said.

She had learned that things do not matter.

"But this is the best leaf," said her brother.

It was of most curious, mysterious workmanship, which he kept in a book that had belonged to his grandfather, and which nobody read. He could not part with the leaf. Circles of mystery, beauty, and injustice expanded inside him, distorting his face. He began to whimper.

"Oh dear," cried Amy Parker.

She went and struck her child, not to punish, but out of repugnance for Quigleys, and the little boy began to bellow and dropped the leaf on the ground.

"There, Bub," said Doll.

"It's torn," he whimpered. "It's all crumpled. It's not any use now, not any more."

He began to trail away, like an umbrella that somebody had crushed.

But Doll Quigley smiled, because there was nothing else she could do.

"I'm sorry, Doll," whispered Amy Parker, though it seemed silly to whisper, and such a pandemonium, and what could she say. "He's tired and cranky. And I must feed Baby, if you don't mind."

As she bundled Quigleys out of the yard she knew that very quickly it would all be over, and she the mistress.

Soon she was alone with her children, and not even her husband could have denied her sovereignty. Giving her breast to the little girl, she had forgotten her husband, who was out and about somewhere, doing the things that had to be done. His functions were remote as the baby sucked and the boy grew drowsy on the bed. If the father had come in at just this point, which fortunately he did not, the mother would have raised her shoulder to ward him off, to shield those acts of peacefulness and intimacy which were hers alone to watch, or bird trembling on a hollyhock. Nobody, of course, ever admitted any of this. The mother would often go and laughingly put the children in the father's arms, making him accept that fatherhood of which he appeared diffident. These were gestures she could afford, because at such moments she realized she was strong. Sometimes, though, more particularly in the evening, when the children were sleeping and their empty clothes hung from lines in the kitchen, the wife rose from where the mother had sat and began turning in the room, wondering whether the father, who was also her husband, would still recognize her. Then it was his turn to laugh at diffidence. Often he ignored her nervous closeness, because he was tired or because of the sleeping children, who were his achievement, and now he was content to rest on this thought.

But the preponderance of strength was almost always hers. It flowed confidently from her breasts, and the frail body of the baby received something of this bland strength, and the little boy, calling to her from a dream, was comforted by a hand.

Once when the baby was fed, and Amy Parker was buttoning her blouse, and the little boy had taken his rest and was rubbing the sleep from his swollen eyes as he wriggled on the bed, there was the grating of somebody's cart, someone that had come, and before long it was evident that this was Mrs. O'Dowd.

"Ah well, you are with your family, I perceive," said the neighbour woman with a kind of primness, turning her head even, and speaking east when it should have been north.

"I am with them most hours of the day, and why not?" said Amy Parker, who had by this time arranged her blouse.

"No, an why not," said her friend. "If it's breedun a person is up to, it takes their time, and no mistake, as I know meself, if only from the little pigs and calves."

Amy Parker brought her friend right in, whom she had not seen for some time, though why, she did not know.

"It is from one thing and another," said Mrs. O'Dowd, herself guilty and anxious to explain. "He has been on it, for one. And then the house fell down, that we have been puttun up again these few month, with improvements, and paper on the best room. It is pretty enough for a honeymoon, but for that drunken bastard that I got. You will see. An roses on the paper. Then, you will observe, I have had the teeth taken from me. There was a travellun gentleman come round, with whom I took the opportunity to remove the stomps. All but one. I would not part with that bugger, not if me whole life depended on it. Not one more. My dear, you should'uv seen the blood, and the poor man with his boot against the wall, strainun like a bullock. Ah yes, it is terrible," said Mrs. O'Dowd. "So this is the little boy. He is growun fit to beat the corn. An the baby."

Now Mrs. O'Dowd, who had seen the boy when he was scarcely dry, was inclined to keep quiet for the girl, who had slipped past her, so to speak, for no reason that anybody could explain, though it may have been the teeth.

"She is smaller than the boy," she said. "Though a little girl would perhaps be small."

"She is doing nicely," said the mother, again exploring the baby's face.

"An not of such a good colour. But that could well be the heat. We all take on a better colour when the autumn comes."

So that Amy Parker began to resent the presence of a friend who could turn her child into a delicate one before her eyes.

"Would you care for a piece of cake, Mrs. O'Dowd, with your tea?" she asked, still polite. "It's a little stale, but this was a surprise. After all this time. You have caught me out."

"I want cake too," cried the little rosy boy.

"An so you will have a piece," said Mrs. O'Dowd. "An a kiss from your auntie."

But he began to look at her, stuffing his mouth with the cake, that she might replace with kisses. He looked at her hat, with its butterfly in sparkling stones, and at her face, that was gathered in towards the gums.

So that she began to be uneasy, and even melancholy.

"Boys," she said, "never go much on kissun. That is," she said, "they will, but up to a point. It is funny."

A great sheaf of bridal roses hung from the window frame, that she looked at when his eyes let her. They were the big papery roses of crushed country brides.

"It is the girls," she said, "that is the hungry ones, however they crook their fingers an refuse."

While the little boy munched and looked. Till the fubsy woman was impressed by her body's insubstantiality.

"If you must stare till Sunday," she said at last, "what is it that you see, sonny?"

She would not have looked over her own shoulder, not in the dark, not for the world. And remembered a funeral too, she had seen from an upper window, wiping the white suds from her arms, and a girl called Beatrice, who was in the same situation, straightened her cap and made a joke about a dead man as the expensive roses passed in slow rain.

"Eh?" she said. "What do you see?"

"What did you do with the teeth?" asked the little boy, whose face was all wonder and crumbs.

"Sure, I put them in a tin," she said and sighed. "To keep. An one day I will have them threaded on a silver wire, to wear with me best dress, on partickler occasions."

Then the little boy hid his face against his mother, because he was no longer sure how he was being used.

"Run along now," said the mother, "and play some game. You don't want to hang about here. It is better outside."

He went, but unwillingly, his eyes still thoughtful for those glimpses of life that he had just been given.

Then Amy Parker settled down to being with her friend, to drink the pot dry, to the dregs of intimacy. The neighbour made her, by turns, satisfied, anxious, contemptuous, forgiving, superior, ignorant, pure, hypocritical, giggly, bored, breathless, possessive, even cruel; yet all these phases were impersonations by her true self, that loved the lives they had shared on that road of ruts and raggedy trees. The two women sat, and a sweat of words or tea was appearing round their noses, at those pores which open first, after disguise is laid aside. As it has to be, of course, in time. Either you turn your back forever on those who have seen your youth, or else you will admit its nakedness, and even shame has some sweet melancholy. So the two women were riding again to Wullunya in the rain, and the fat woman tended the other the night she slipped her first child, the night their Julia died.

"Tt-tt," sighed Mrs. O'Dowd, sucking her thoughtful gums

when all was said. "I would never'uv thought you would take to breedun, Mrs. Parker, in the end."

"It was intended," murmured the mother.

Because she had not known what to say, her reply conveyed a flat conviction, which could have wounded, and perhaps did.

"Then, if it was intended, and by who," said Mrs. O'Dowd, "it was a long time up his sleeve, in a manner of speakun. And then two. Well, good luck, an God save um, the little children."

So, delivering her final blessing, she got to her feet, and rumbled, and the crumbs were falling off her blouse.

If Amy Parker continued to sit, it was because the rose is rooted, and impervious. The big milky roses nodded on the window frame. She was firmly rooted in the past, as old roses are. This was her salvation in the face of words, as she sat, and stirred, and drowsed, but could not move beyond her fate, even if her neighbour waited. She had grown up full and milky out of the past, even her little girl must wait for roses, while nodding and stirring her mind twined again, twining through the moonlight night on which it had half-spoken, half-dreamed the rose.

"I will not be denyun you are lucky," her friend was saying. "Only it is the little girl I would be worryun after, if she was mine, which she is not."

"There is nothing wrong with the baby," said Amy Parker, torn from her chair. "Nothing. As I have said before."

"There is nothing wrong," said Mrs. O'Dowd, "but she is pasty."

"What do you know, Mrs. O'Dowd?" Amy Parker said.

Her throat was full of knots.

"Sure, an I know nothun, o' course, but it is sometimes those that knows nothun that knows."

They were going to the door, and soon along the path that had known their friendship these many years. There was a scent of rosemary that they brushed, and of some crushed weed that stank of cat, tightening to the chest.

"You're a fine one to talk," said Amy Parker.

"I'm not sayun nothun at all."

"Like nothing, you aren't."

"And a fine little boy. But boys, they're indiapendent. You can have boys. Turn their heads away. Then go off and leave yer."

Then Amy Parker curled her lip. Her house was full of the

127

children she had made, and the fat woman her friend, whom she had loved at times, was a ridiculous, an empty figure.

"Boys," said Mrs. O'Dowd, who was opening the little gate, "boys," she said, "turn into men, an the only argument in their favour is that they are necessary."

And now she pushed the stiff gate.

"I will be paying you a visit one of these days," said Mrs. Parker, who could now afford to be kind, "in spite of all the things you say."

"Yes, dear," said her neighbour, "an we will have a talk."

She loosed the chain from the wheel of her cart.

"There is nothun I so much enjoy," she said, "as a talk on interestun subjects with a friend."

No one else found fault with the health of the Parker children, or if they did, they were too polite to speak their thoughts. The mother reared her children, first with diffidence and a cyclopædia, then with arrogant infallibility as her experience grew. Very soon no one could tell her what she did not know. Indeed, she became oracular, giving advice to others in flashes of inspiration, for which the younger and more timid were grateful, but which older women received with slow, sour-sweet smiles.

Amy Parker was not deterred, now that she had achieved her family.

If there had been delay in christening Parkers' second child, it was because the baby did show some signs of delicacy in her first months, however her mother might deny. But finally the parents grew used to their fears, and arrangements were made with Mr. Purbrick, and they drove the little pale girl to the plain brown church in a buggy the father had bought from a baker's widow in Bangalay. The family sat up against one another in the still quite presentable buggy, in their best clothes, which were too dark for the heat of the day. The mother held the baby tightly, hotly, in her best shawl, shooing the flies away with her glove. The father's large, hard hands lightly and expertly held the reins, making a glad business of it, as if on that day he were playing an enormous, playful fish, as he whistled through his lips that were cracked by the sun. And the little boy blew out his red-brown cheeks and kept on making an obscene noise with his mouth, till his mother had to tell him to stop.

"You get on my nerves," she said.

"Why?" he asked, his voice sulking towards a cry.

"Because," she answered wearily, bending to search again

128

the sleeping face of the wax baby, that did just flicker under the fly's wings.

"Look," said the father in an amicable, masculine, peace-making way. "There's Peabodys' twin heifers. We'll be there soon. I wonder if old Purbrick's dusted his voice."

"How?" asked the little boy.

"Your father's being silly," said the mother. "He means that Mr. Purbrick doesn't always speak very clearly. What's that?" she asked suddenly. "How did you cut your knee, Ray?"

"I didn't," he said.

"But there it is, as large as life. I'll trouble you not to tell me lies, please. Or play with knives."

"He gave me one."

"He? Who?" she breathed.

"Dad."

"When you're not to play with knives!"

She drew the shawl tighter on the baby, as if to protect it out of existence.

"A boy has to begin," said the father.

Today he was too lazy to defend, to resist or protest. He half-closed his eyes to the sun, and knew that he owned the horse and buggy, and even the woman and the two children beside him. As much as you can own anything. But the hours of lightning are usually far between.

"Here we are at the church," he said.

Doves were drooling on the roof to emphasize the peace-fulness of the occasion, and the mother began to feel both happy and sad. Churches took her that way.

"I hope she will be all right," she murmured tearfully.

Then she prepared smiles for the old parson, whose wrinkles were opening and closing in anticipation of the holy words, and for the godparents, who were standing in a group, wondering what would be expected of them, both then and afterwards, in life. Would they have to give advice or, worse still, money, forever and ever and ever, to someone they had not begun to know? Or would they, if careful, be quietly forgotten? The parents themselves were uncertain why just these people had been chosen. You had to have somebody, though. So here were Ossie Peabody, in a hat that he had tortured into a most extraordinary shape, and Mrs. Gage, and a Mrs. Firth, a kind sort of woman that no one had anything against.

The church had the smell of a closed wooden box, and of birds' droppings, but the words were marvellously simple that fell amongst the hassocks and glowed in the shafts of amethyst and ruby from one or two smouldering windows, that had been given by the rich, and that told with crude directness the stories they were meant to tell.

Under one such window the group stood for the child's christening. She was to be called Thelma, that the mother had first seen in a newspaper, the name of a grazier's heiress. The father had been doubtful at first, but he was won over finally by his wife's silences. Anyway, he did not think much about names. So Thelma the little girl became. The mother spoke it to herself, filling her mouth with it like a satin sweetie, except that the word had about it something richer, rarer, less attainable.

When the old man pronounced the name of Thelma Parker in a sound of cool water, the little boy, her brother, smiled for something which he recognized out of the welter of words. The name was already losing its mystery, and would in time become something short and common, to be carved on a tree.

The baby cried of course, and the mother was proud and agitated, prickling with the woollen shawl.

Stan Parker, the father, was trying to recapture the sense of ownership that he had experienced on the journey to the church, but now that his daughter was labelled with his name he was less sure. He was uncertain even of his own boots as he listened to the words of the unfamiliar service chasing one another in the moustache of the old man. So Stan Parker felt the strain of his immediate vicinity. Inwardly he edged a little farther away from the christening group. Soon he was wandering quite frankly beyond the confines of the crude church, unashamed by a sudden nakedness that had fallen upon him. Simultaneously with this pleasing nakedness, the flow of words, the flesh of relationships, were becoming secondary to a light of knowledge. He held up his face to receive he did not know what gift.

Then the water fell in a tinkling shower, not only onto the baby's face but onto the father's skin, and he was ashamed. He began to worry about the fee, when it should be paid to the parson for his services, and coughed, and was awkward; he was too big, and the dirt of manual labour was shameful in his hands.

"What?" he asked in a guilty whisper.

Because his wife was speaking.

"She behaved beautifully," she repeated with round satis-

130

faction, as if it had been she and not the baby, and arranged the fold of the shawl.

The touch of the old clergyman's hands was the touch of cool, papery, blameless skins, and his words too were blameless, as he gave advice and made attempts at jokes, not altogether successfully, for he was not by nature a jolly parson, though he felt he should have been.

"She'll soon be a big, bouncing girl, making mistakes in her catechism. Won't she now?" Mr. Purbrick said.

But he could not convince himself. He was happiest observing birds in the silence of his garden.

The little boy, who had been running up and down the aisle ever since the service was ended, and standing on hassocks under cover of his elders' conversation, and reading the prayer books upside down, now began to cry.

"Whatever is the matter, Ray?" asked the kind Mrs. Firth, giving him a hand.

But the little boy continued to bellow.

"Well, if you won't tell us, we can't help."

But the little boy cried, walking stiffly on chafing legs, as the result of an accident he had just had.

The group was soon drawing away from the church except for the old clergyman, who remained behind on the step, smiling not so much for his departing parishioners as for his own approaching solitude. At the moment of departure, foreshortened in the yellow light of summer, everyone, even the united family, was a bit solitary. The half-grown, raggedy pine trees dared the personality to assert itself. The more recent graves in the churchyard had not yet begun to furnish the landscape. They were too close to the act of death. This was still present in the wounds of yellow clay that had not healed up. But the family drew away, past the jars of dead flowers, through the yellow, clinging burs, and very soon all feelings of awfulness, exaltation, doom, or self-importance began to be translated into the comfortable and earthy crunch of the buggy.

On the journey home, and afterwards, the children predominated. Their childhood was the usual lengthy one. This lengthiness would impress itself sometimes also on the parents, as they dragged up hot hills or sat on long evenings listening to the sleep of children in another room. These were, on the whole, becalmed years, in spite of the visible evidence of growth. Any reference to the future was made, not with conviction, but in accordance with convention.

131

"I would like Ray to be something in the government, or a famous surgeon, or something like that. In dark clothes. And we would read about him in the newspaper," said the mother in a dream voice.

The father laughed, remembering how his own mother had failed to contain him. He laughed and said, "What will become of the cows?"

"We can sell the cows," said the little boy, who was already listening to most things. "I hate smelly old milk. I want to be rich, like Armstrongs, and have horses and things, and a pair of yellow boots."

Then he ran across the yard, to put an end to speculation, still without belief in the efficacy of this. He was surrounded by sunlight, and the warm, hard forms of stones, and the fluffy, melting ones of red hens in the dust. He lived for what he saw and did. He took from his pocket a little catapult that an older boy had made, and was looking about to let fly when he heard his father call, "I'll tan you, Ray, if I catch you again at those hens."

So he began scratching at a tree, to scratch his name, to impress his will with his hands on some thing. He was already quite strong. Stronger than his sister, whom he liked to persecute. She had a kind of fretful pallor that is altogether distasteful to strength.

"Go away and leave me alone," she learned to say with a round mouth. "Boys are a nuisance."

She liked to play neat games with a doll, and handkerchiefs for sheets. She smoothed the sheets of her doll with the palms of her small, moist hands, bending over the box in which it lay, so that her thin pale hair hung. This was not curled, as her mother had once wished. Its pale gold shone more sinuously in straight lines, but there was a little joy in Thelma Parkers hair. She got tired, and was a worry to her mother, and coughed at times. Later this was diagnosed as asthma.

"You mustn't worry your sister, she's delicate," the mother said.

"Why?"

He could not understand this. He roamed about a lot by himself, and flung stones into the distance, and buried his face in the creek water where it ran between rocks, and watched animals, but failed to become absorbed into his surroundings. He could not do enough.

132

Sometimes he hit his sister in retaliation for all that he did not understand. The scapegoat went bellowing.

"I'll tell Mumma," she howled.

But sometimes, more especially at evening, after exhaustion had set in and the light was gentler, they would hang together, or on their mother, in a conglomeration of love and tenderness, and tell stories that rose out of their imaginations, and finally doze. At these moments the mother was crowned with satisfaction. The closeness of her children excluded all else.

By this time Amy Parker had grown greedy for love. She had not succeeded in eating her husband, though she had often promised herself in moments of indulgence that she would achieve this at some future date. But she had not. He retreated from her once again. She knew him down to the pores of his skin, and through many acts of kindness, but it was perhaps just this kindness that defeated her. So it continued to be for some future date. As she smiled lazily in her kitchen. One day she would love her husband enough. As she gathered the rustling onion skins.

Amy Parker had broadened with age, was almost what some people would have called a little coarse. Her hands and back were broad. She was filled with a deep breathing, that conveyed itself to people of another kind as contentment, and especially to children, who liked to be near her, and hear her, and touch her. Her skin was particularly pleasant, clear, and brown, and comforting. Sometimes, though, she could be sharp, sour even, as if the thin and anxious girl were still buried in her flesh, and she could complain and sting. At such times her dark hair hung in tails, that she would not bother to put up. Then her husband would walk quietly, or round the other side of the house. His face looked long and grave on those days.

"Come here, Ray" she would say. "Do you love me?"

As if he might answer, instead of kick the ground.

"Thelma does then," she would say, dashing the water from her glistening arms and burnishing them with a rough towel.

But the little girl would continue to talk in a low voice to her doll, as if she had not heard.

The mother could not compel. Even though there were moments, those evenings, when she gathered her children into her now placid arms, and held in her arms that conglomeration of love from which not one of them was separable,

133

there were times also when she could not read their thoughts, when their faces became like little wooden boards, promising forever to remain flat and impregnable.

Then she would go and look along the road, along the dust and strands of rusty wire.

"What's up, Amy?" her husband asked, intruding cautiously on one of these occasions.

"Nothing," she said. "Oh, nothing."

Looking out through her frown into the glare of the white road.

"You look long in the face," he said and laughed tentatively. "I thought it must be bad."

Which made her tragedy at once seem thin and ridiculous.

"I said it was nothing."

Biting on her own laughter, which was still a bit sour.

"Oh dear, it's silly," she sighed. "Isn't it, Blue?"

As the bitch came sidling towards her.

"Poor thing," she said as she extended to the bitch the pity she had for herself, and stroked it in the voluptuousness of shared pity.

The bitch's teats were swollen and irregular and scratched by the claws of the litter. However devoured, she herself remained hungry for love. Her hot tongue tasted. Her jaws could have swallowed you down.

"They don't leave you alone, do they?" said the woman, sitting on the veranda and soothing the torn teats with her hand.

The bitch curved and fawned. And the woman was pacified.

"You're my dog, eh?" she said. "Good Blue. What a good thing it is sometimes not to have to expect answers."

The blue bitch had replaced the red dog, which had died a few years back.

"This is my dog," Amy Parker had said at once of the blue bitch. "And this one's going to have a name. Not like that ugly red thing that never liked me a bit."

Because they had never named the red dog, in spite of her intention. He had remained The Dog. But the blue bitch she had called, precipitately, Blue.

And the bitch had remained all attention and affection. Rather clumsy. Clawing with her paws for an audience. Knocking things over with her tail. Rolling on her back and shaking the dust from it when she rose, and the slobber from her pleased mouth. She had pups regularly, and lay on her side for them to suck, till she was exhausted and a skeleton.

134

Still she would come and hungrily look for affection in other quarters. The woman's eyes would be appeased as she soothed the coat of the dog.

"She's ugly," said Ray.

"No, she's not," said the mother, lazily dawdling with her hand. "What's ugly to some is beautiful to others. Now your father had an old red dog, an ugly thing if ever there was, didn't like me a bit either, but he meant something to your father. I remember the night I came. We lived in that shack then."

But the child had turned from his mother's thoughts. His eyes were for the present.

"Ugly old tits," he said.

The woman did not hear her child. She stroked her warm thoughts.

So she could not help loving the clumsy, fruitful dog. She liked to hold in her hands the warm, blunt puppies, to change them round from teat to teat, and see that the runt was fed. She would go there often, and kneel beside them in the gloom of the barn. Like this too, alone with the dog, she was young again. Nobody saw her, and she would not particularly have wanted them to see. It was a private sensation that she was holding warm as a puppy to her cheek. Her hair straggled at the nape of her neck.

Then once she came quickly into the kitchen at dinnertime and said, "Stan, three of Blue's puppies have gone."

Everyone was standing there. Her mouth was moving with the horror of it.

"Must have been the rats," said her husband.

"Rats leave bits," said Fritz, the old German, who had just come in with his mug and plate. "Was there no bits?"

"There was no sign," she said.

She felt cold and grey. She remembered her dog's warm pups, and for the moment she did not want to be with these people who were her family, and who were discussing what might have happened.

"Perhaps she ate some," said Ray, starting to mess the stew with his fork.

"Not at that age," said the father.

Thelma had begun to cry. She did not particularly care for puppies, but other people did, and other people cried, so it was right.

"The puppies are dead," she cried.

"Perhaps some swaggie lifted them out of the nest because he liked them," said the boy.

He had built an island of potatoes, and a frail isthmus, past which he was persuading the brown juices, that he did not want today.

"Eat your food," said his mother, who unfolded a napkin with great savagery.

"She had too many, anyway," said the boy. "She still has five. Eight is too many, isn't it Dad?"

"Eat your food, your mother said," said the father.

"I won't! I don't want to," cried the boy.

He jumped up. He hated his parents and the kitchen table. The crockery was against him, and the plate of messed brown stew.

"Old stew!" he cried.

And ran away.

The father began to mumble, because for the moment he did not know what to do. To the mother it was obvious that at present nothing could be done. Her personal misery possessed her, and the clash of wills in the kitchen, the muddled table, and the thick white plates were not a part of this. Her sadness was for herself. The fate of the puppies had become an intimate part of her own life, and she turned her head sharply, in pain, as the thought crossed her that their necks could have been wrung.

"Well, we're not getting anywhere by dwelling on it," said Stan Parker, pushing back his plate after a bit.

But he thought about his son, how little he knew him, and wondered how soon it would be before both would have to admit this. He was still a little boy, and they kissed each other and pretended to closeness, even when they failed to reach each other. The boy tried to tell him things and failed, stood looking up at him, with words that trailed away and did not express. Once he had smashed a pane of glass with an iron bar nearly as big as himself, and had stood panting and shivering in the scattered fragments.

"There's the pudding, dear," said the wife.

But Stan Parker did not think he wanted pudding today. He was convinced there was some connection between the boy and the disappearance of the pups.

His wife's eyes had known already. In the heat of the day they shared this coldness between them, so it was better that they should remain apart.

Only in the evening, darkness and walls forced them to-

136

gether. They talked about flat, measured things. Or he read pieces from the newspaper, that he held upright beside the lamp. Or they listened to the frogs, that surrounded the house with an illusion of water. But it was dry just then.

Once the boy called to his mother from his sleep, and she went in to him.

"What is it, Ray?" she asked, bending over him.

In the lamplight her brown skin was golden. She had grown to proportions that were both magnificent and kindly.

"What is it?" she asked.

"I was dreaming about those pups."

"Dream about something else," she advised.

As if she had the secret of all things and could remain above acts and subterfuges.

So that he turned over.

If I could know for certain, she said, her eyes burning into his sleeping head, what should I do? And will this remain a matter of importance, although it is important now?

The episode of the pups faded, and was probably forgotten at Parkers' by most people, if not by everyone.

Once or twice Thelma said, "We never did know, did we, what became of those poor little pups?"

"Why do you want to bring that up, Thelly?" the mother said.

She frowned. She loved her daughter less than her son, though she had tried to make it otherwise, and did take immense pains to do all that was best for the girl. Thelma remained thin. Her soul was thin.

Once when the mother was standing with her little girl by the gate, in the white glare of summertime, the trees limp with exhaustion and shabby with dust, there came a figure on a horse, that the standing figure shaded her eyes to see. The horse was advancing with the loose indolence of an animal that is kept for pleasure, turning his head from side to side, flicking the fringe of forelock from his eyes, and blowing out his rather naked-looking nostrils in such a way that it was not quite timidity, not quite insolence, but lovely to see. He was a lovely horse. Glittering with jet and sweat, he continued to advance, till his rider also began to assume features, and became a woman in a habit, no less grand than her grand horse, as she sat with her leg cocked across the horn of the saddle, and swayed with that same indolence of the beast, and swayed, and thought.

So the dark-figured woman on the black horse advanced

137

beneath the white trees. Although the dust of the road was unfurling beneath the horse's feet, it scarcely reached the woman's spur, she sat so high, and in the sea of dust in which she floated was god-like and remote.

"Isn't the lady lovely, Mum?" said the little girl with a prim, mincing mouth.

She hoped she was saying the sort of thing her mother herself would say. She attempted at times almost slavishly to do the right things.

But Amy Parker did not speak. She stood shading her eyes, and it was as if she were opening in the silence to receive and unite with the rider and the horse, as if her life craved to be set in the same slow and stately motion, free above the dust. So she held her breath. Her strong throat was quite swollen with the effort. She felt rather than saw the passage of the horse and rider. The chink of their metal was vibrant in her.

So the creamy woman rode by. She was smiling for some situation of which undoubtedly she had been the central figure, and this had pleased her, and in it certainly she had known success. But the smile just drifted on her creamy face. As she flowed by. While the rusty strands of the wire fence were paid out, and out. While the hairy trunks of trees jerked past.

The little girl wondered whether the strange and beautiful woman would speak, but the mother did not expect this. The woman's smile drifted over the head of the puny child, and on, without glancing at the mother, magnificent though she was too, in her own rooted way. But the woman was passing. She obviously did not intend to form unnecessary relationships even of the most transient kind. She was drifting by. Drawing arabesques on the air with the ivory handle of her raised crop. Her perilously brittle stem was carried past. Already the bronzy sheen of her hair was breaking in the distant light.

"Well, she's gone, Mum. What are we standing for?" complained the little girl. "I wonder what she is called."

In time they knew, for Mrs. O'Dowd had found out.

Mrs. O'Dowd said she was a girl, or woman was closer, she was not a chicken by any means, woman then, if you liked, and her name was Madeleine. Whatever else of a name she could not tell. No matter, said Mrs. O'Dowd, for neither you nor me will be any the wiser. Anyway, this Madeleine was a famous beauty like you read of, going to places, and the

138

races, and the picnic races, always in demand, it seemed, and above all at picnic races. This Madeleine had also been Home, and to various foreign countries, hawking her looks around; she should have married a lord, it wasn't for want of trying, only she was out of luck. So they said. But still courted. Now, it seemed, and this was the important part, according to that Mrs. Frisby, cook at Armstrongs', whose husband had been a sailor that never came back—now it seemed that young Armstrong was shook on this Madeleine, was moving heaven and earth to have his way, with presents and horses, and she sometimes cold, sometimes warm, but mostly cold, for she was no fool. Many a wealthy man would have taken this Madeleine, it seemed. She had only to say the word, and had perhaps, the diamonds were there to see in a black velvet case, and ivory brushes with monygrams. But that was on the side, like. She was playing a cool game. It is the ring and the establishment that counts with most, and with this Madeleine, and why not.

After this the neighbour woman, who was passing in her customary fashion, clapped her reins and went. And Amy Parker remained where she was.

All her acts after this became secret silk. She thought of Madeleine. She drew from her hands the gloves of soapsuds. Her body had grown indolent.

Till her children, asking for permission, would cry in exasperation, "Can we, Mum? Oh, *Mu-uummm?*"

Her eyes wore the glaze of self-indulgence as she answered, "Yes. Of course. Why not?"

They were surprised at her remote complaisance and went out quietly and thoughtful, no longer anxious to do whatever they had been allowed, while the mother continued to stare at her inner self in a glare of diamonds.

One day after rain she said they would walk across the paddocks. It would be a change, from what, she could not have answered. But she put on an old hat, that was brown and rather ugly. And her children came, sulking at the injustice of a walk. They followed her through the dead, wet grass. All through the paddocks where they walked there was the smell of wet grass and of turpentines. There was a breeze too, that turned the leaves of the trees back to front, till they were silver and more festive. There was a restless moodiness in this gentle weather, that was only a lull in the more positive blaze of summer. Damp breezes and the passing touch of cool leaves invited to retrospect and fantasy. Till Amy Parker floated, and her children, conscious of this levitation, became eager and melancholy.

"Mum," said the boy, "can I climb some trees?"

Because he loved to shin up and clamber from branch to branch, until he was almost the bending crest, and now this sensation was most imperative. To touch the thick wood. To struggle with and finally overcome it.

"Do you really think it'll do you any good?" the mother asked with an effort, as if she had been ascending a hill, though the slope they were on was still gentle. "Last time you tore your pants. And your knees are all scabs."

"Ah, please, yes," he sighed, clasping her hand and pressing against her like an animal. "Let me."

"I don't want to climb old trees," said the girl.

She shook her straight pale hair.

"You couldn't," he said. "You're soft. You're a girl."

"I'm not," she cried, twisting her thin mouth.

"What else are you?" he said. "A heifer perhaps?"

"If I'm a heifer you're a bull," she cried. "They keep heifers. But they kill bulls."

"Not all of them," he said. "Not the best."

"There. Run and climb," said the mother.

She walked on slowly, and sat on a log on the edge of a wattle grove, leaning her back against the black bark of wattle, and playing with the stalks of dead grass, while the little girl looked into rabbit burrows, and gathered a bunch of flowers, and threw it down, and picked up an interesting stone, and fretted, and wanted to go.

"Why do we have to stay in this old place?" she asked.

Amy Parker did not know, except that she was lulled, except that here she could indulge her fancy with a lesser sense of guilt than in her solid home.

"Can't we go?" Thelma said.

"Soon," said her mother.

She began to wonder whether she could have resisted the advances of a lord, if he had driven up, and she wearing a mauve dress such as she had never owned. What words she would have spoken she had not yet formed, but felt, but knew. As the lord, in shining boots, descended on the grass and smiled at her with the thick lips that had breathed upon her that day, as she mounted the steps of the store. She would have had children perhaps, as well as diamonds from the lord, whose features were permanently and irresistibly those of young Armstrong. She recognized with a shudder the same dark hairs at his wrist. But his eyes had a tenderness, a kindness, remote from the sensuality of the body, that was also her husband's.

So that she straightened her back against the hard tree.

"Why don't we go?" asked Thelma.

She came and stood there. She was their child.

"Yes. We'll go," said Amy Parker. "Where's Ray? Tell him it's time."

Because there was the house, and the trees that had grown round it, and the sheds it had accumulated, and the paths they had worn with their feet, all suggesting reality and permanence. And at the core of this reality, her husband, who would not even raise his eyes as she walked up one of the paths that radiated from their house, because he knew she would come. She was his wife. Or he would look up, and she could not always tell what he saw. He would not let her in behind his eyes, even at the moments of his greatest kindness and intimacy, even when she held him in her arms and he was printed on her body.

"Ray!" called Thelma, running fretfully between the trees. "We're go-ing! Ray! Wherever *are* you?"

He was above by this, grappling the branches. Any wounds to his flesh drove him on. He looked contemptuously into an old nest, that he would have robbed if it had been full, but as it was not he tore it from its fork and flung it to the ground. He climbed on, round and under and up. He looked coldly at a sleek young magpie, that he would have killed if he had had the means. Then, feeling the sweat behind his knees, he had reached the top, and was dipping and swaying, sheathed in a cold wind that brought the blood to his face. He was a beautiful little boy in his exaltation. His exposed position gave him an innocence. He looked dreamily out across the waves of trees and was momentarily content.

"Ray!" called Thelma, who had found the nest of musty grass and rather repulsive old feathers, and who had looked up, and seen. "I'll tell on you! You had no right to go up so high. Come on down. We're going."

But Ray continued to look out, hearing her voice or not. The house in which he lived was more acceptable seen as a toy. Roads were less distasteful in the abstract than as dust and stones underfoot. Here and there, slow, oblivious life dawdled, cows near the creek, and, along the lane that ran on that side of their land, a dark rider.

141

"We're waiting," called Thelma on a desperate gust of wind.

"All right," he murmured. "I'm coming."

Only because he had seen enough.

"What did you see, Ray?" the mother asked, to speak, when they had reached her.

"Everything," he said.

His voice had grown dull as an aftermath of achievement.

"Home, and paddocks, and cows," he said. "And someone riding down the lane."

"I wonder," said the mother, "who that could be. Mr. Peabody perhaps."

Her words were dead as yellow grass.

"No," said the boy. "It was a lady."

"Ah," said the mother. "Are you sure?"

"Yes. I could tell. You could see her skirt."

Then Amy Parker knew that she would diverge a little through the grove of wattles to where the lane ran along their land. So she walked her children a little quicker. Not knowing what she would say or do, except stand at the fence, enclosed in her own dowdiness, and watch the progress of the dark rider. Because it could only be. Now she knew that she had come for Madeleine.

"Perhaps it's that lady we saw," Thelma was saying.

"Pick your feet up, dear," Amy Parker said.

Thelma began to whimper, for some injustice sensed.

But just then they reached the small lane where it cut through the wattles. These stood thick on either side, and straight, and dark, so that anything coming down that stretch of the lane was at once intensified. And it was down this that Madeleine was passing on her shiny horse.

"See?" said Ray. "I told you I could see her skirt."

Beyond this he was not interested. It was a woman on a horse.

That day the horse of Madeleine was less inspired. He was more horse. Or they had ridden far perhaps, and he was even a little bit lame; there was something ugly and uncertain in his gait as he came on. He stumbled at a pothole, and his pasterns looked weak. But he was still a fine horse, insisted Amy Parker. The horse ambled closer, flinging his mane and showing the whites of his eyes. She could see the veins in his wet shoulder and the motion of his bones. She saw the horse so closely that she knew exactly how he felt to her touch.

But she must look also, not now, in a moment, at the

rider, but soon. In a stumble of hoofs she must look. Her heart was trampling on her.

Amy Parker looked up to see the rider, whom she had known intimately for some time, but from whom she could not hide her shyness, even her ridiculousness. For a close moment she looked at Madeleine. Today the rider wore no smiles. She was tired, or headachy, or involved in relationships with human beings. Her mouth was thinner in her creamy skin, as if it were biting on something. Her eyes did not see that part of the lane. Except for a moment perhaps, when she frowned and jerked at the reins. She rode on. The sturdy woman with her two children continued standing amongst the trees. There had been no mingling. There was no reason why there should have been.

"Why does she ride around like that?" Thelma asked when they had begun to trail across the paddocks of grass.

"I don't know. For something to do, I suppose," Amy Parker said.

"Can't she do other things? Can't she go shopping?"

"Hasn't she got a dog?" said Ray. "I'd have ferrets."

"She's a lady," hissed Thelma. "What'd a lady do with ferrets?"

"What's the good of being a lady?" said Ray.

He began to whip his sister's calves with a little wattle switch that he had picked up.

"Ah, stop *it!*" she cried. "Mum, make him *stop!*"

"Now you're both being silly. Ray!" said the mother. "Let's have peace. And no questions. I don't know this lady, so I can't very well answer them," she said.

And hoped that this would end it.

But she thought of Madeleine as she lay straight in her bed. Whole skeins of sleep flowed from the brims of their hats as they rode together through the wind of darkness. They were exchanging secrets. I have never had one, murmured Amy Parker, not of any importance, not with anyone. There, said Madeleine, is one. Amy Parker opened her hand. It was a piece of glass, or a rather big diamond. The confused cry of birds that came from her throat folded her words up. Madeleine laughed. They rode, and their stirrup irons held hands. There was no longer even a chinking, they were so close.

"What is it?" asked Stan Parker.

"I was dreaming," sighed his wife. "It was funny. About a horse."

He cleared his throat, and was asleep.

She lay gently, hoping if she fell slowly she would recapture that same part of her smooth dream. But the horses had ridden on. And when she woke in the morning it was indeed funny, not to say ridiculous, that dream. She stuck the pins in her hair and fixed a glossy bun. She who had been dreaming of the dark rider all those days could not have told how she longed for them to share a precipice. If they were to meet, which they would not. Their lives were disparate. She put down her brush, of which the bristles had been worn short, and went out to get the buckets.

Chapter 10

A BOUT this time Amy Parker received a message from her neighbour, Mrs. O'Dowd, by hand of a little girl called Pearl Britt, whose father worked on the road.

Mrs. O'Dowd had written on a piece of paper:

Tuesday mornin

Dear Mrs. Parker,

    I am in some trouble, and would take it kindly if I could see a friend.

Your ever truly,
(Mrs. K. O'Dowd.)

"Thank you, Pearl," said Mrs. Parker to the little girl, who continued to stand there, picking her nose and stamping her hard feet in the dust to throw the flies off her ankles. "I shall come down pretty soon."

Then Pearl ran away, pulling the head off a daisy as she went, to play a game of petals with.

When she had changed the position of one or two things, and put on her hat, Amy Parker was ready to go. She caught the mare, who was swishing her tail under a willow, and got out the second-hand buggy, which by this time had grown dilapidated, while still showing signs of its decent origin. Then she would have gone in search of her husband, but stopped herself. I will not say anything, she said, in case he is angry. Now she was really ready.

All along the road that had once been theirs exclusively people were now living, so that O'Dowds had ceased to be neighbours, except in history and by sentiment. Some people nodded to Mrs. Parker as she jogged along, but others considered she was trying to find out something about them, and frowned. In fact, she was thinking of her friend and neighbour, and the lives they had lived on that road, when it ran through the unbroken scrub. But people were not to know this. Fences had made the land theirs, and they resented the intrusion of a strange face. For Mrs. Parker was by now unknown to some. She drove on through scenes she could no longer claim.

The bush had opened up. There was a man tilling the chocolate soil in between his orange trees. Outside a grey shack an old man sat beside his hollyhock. Children spilled from the doors of bursting cottages. Washing blew. It was gay on this morning, as Amy Parker had not seen it, along the two miles to O'Dowds'. Bright birds fell from the sky, and ascended. Voices could be heard where once the sound of the axe barely cut the silence, and your heart beat quicker for its company. But man had come, if it was not the Irish. Wire wound through the scrub. Many uses were found for bags and tin. And at night they sat around, the men with their shirts open on the hair of their chests, the women with their blouses easy, and drank whatever came to hand, as a comfort. If it was sometimes the kerosene, well, that too is drinkable. And more children were got to the tune of the iron beds.

The old mare that Mrs. Parker drove jogged along this rather joyful road, but her hoofs began to drag as she eased down that last stretch into the dip before O Dowds'. The brakes were on now, so that the wheels grated on the sandstones. What is this trouble? asked Mrs. Parker, moistening her fresh lips, as she remembered it *was* a trouble had brought her that morning to O'Dowds'. And she would have prolonged her journey, that seemed to plunge down.

It was a poor lot of land before you came to O'Dowds' selection, and that too was inclined to be poor, but there they had camped down, in the beginning, and got used to it. They were possessed by the land, and the land was theirs. Now all the country round about appeared quite desolate to Mrs. Parker, driving down. All trees in this part seemed to have taken desperate shapes. Some definitely writhed. Some were stuck with black hairy knobs or dismal grey cones. There was a monotonous drumming in that part of the bush, of heat and insect life. Nobody would ever want it. They threw things into it. There was a glint of old tin, and the ribs of dead animals.

So Mrs. Parker grew lower. Although a comparatively young and robust woman, of some experience, she began to

146

feel inside her a thinness of insufficiency. She had never come close to death, and wondered whether she could deal with it. If death it was that beckoned from O'Dowds'. Though there was no reason to suppose. Instead, she began to think of her two growing children and her solid husband, and to persuade herself of her own strength. By degrees it did become plausible. Turning in through what had once been the gate, her strong young shoulders swayed with the buggy and tossed off all doubts. There were moments when she was superb, and this was one. Her strong, rather thick black eyebrows glistened in the light.

So Amy Parker drove up to O'Dowds' door, and if there was no sign of death, there was little enough of life. There were two brown ducks with pointed sterns paddling and dipping in some thin mud. A red sow lay on her side and exposed her leather teats. Under the pepper tree the meat-safe hung, and swung, round and round, slowly, on a wire. And the house was the same as it had always been, supporting itself on itself, and the hole in the side window still stuffed with a bag.

Amy Parker went looking for someone when she had chained the wheel, and eventually the face of her friend did come at her through a crack, and it seemed as if shortly everything must be explained.

"You will excuse me," said Mrs. O'Dowd, manipulating her moist gums, so the words would pass, and the stubborn door, so that her friend Mrs. Parker might squeeze inside, "you must excuse me," she said, "if I sent for you in writun, my dear, makun it seem official, like, an I did think at the time, but the kiddy is forgetful that brought it, if her legs are strong. So for that reason I put pen to paper. An now you'uv come. An I am glad."

She held a dishcloth in her hand, and that cloth was very grey, and gave out a smell of all the old dishwater it had ever been in, probably grey water too.

"Yes, I am here," said Mrs. Parker, who was feeling out of breath.

It was perhaps constricted in the kind of hugger-mugger back kitchen, or storeroom, or dairy, or larder, in which they stood, and in which it seemed most of the possessions of O'Dowds were cluttered. There were the buckets not yet washed from that morning's milking, and the bodies of several flies in that morning's milk. Several lines of old washed-out shirts and chemises—or was it rags?—hung from

147

overhead, sawing at each other, stiff and dry, catching in the hair, in the small dark space of that room, where your ankles jostled the empty bottles that O'Dowd had not yet flung away. There was a rat trap on a deal table, baited with a lump of yellow cheese, and beside it on a big white dish a piece of dry mutton. Everything that was gathered there seemed to have been put where it could be found, and that is more than can be said for tidiness.

"It is homely, like as you know, but what can you do?" said Mrs. O'Dowd with a sideways look as she flicked at a fly with the dishcloth and trimmed a splinter of meat from the mutton.

"Then you are well?" said Mrs. Parker her friend.

"An why should I be sick? It is not me health that has ever troubled me, Mrs. Parker. It is something far more complicayted."

She sucked the air between her gums, as if the teeth were still there, and looked at the little window that the cobwebs had almost closed up.

So Mrs. Parker waited, till her friend should give her a glimpse of something interesting, or horrible, or sad.

"It is him," she said finally. "It is that bastard. He is on it again."

"Is he ever off?" asked Mrs. Parker, who had begun to mark time.

"Not that you could notice. But there are occasions when he makes it a welter. An this is one of those. This is the biggest welter," Mrs. O'Dowd said.

"And what am *I* to do?" Mrs. Parker asked.

"Why, talk to him, my dear, as a woman, an a mother, an a neighbor, and an old friend. Wheedle him a bit."

"How am I to wheedle that you can't?"

Because this was something that Mrs. Parker did not care about. She was all red and spirited in the small room.

"I don't see," Mrs. Parker said.

"Ah," said Mrs. O'Dowd. "I am only his wife, an that not quite. It is different for a friend, for he will be less inclined to punch you in the face or kick you in the stomach for your pains. Just talk to him reasonable, an you so nice, he'll be cryun salt tears of remorse in a winkun, an all will be over, you will see."

"Where is he?" Mrs. Parker asked.

"He is on the back veranda, settun with his shotgun, an a bottle of eaudy Cologne, which is all we'uv got left. But the gun is only for show, Mrs. Parker, take it from me, I know his ways."

"I think it would be better," said Mrs. Parker, who did not like this a bit, "I think it would be better if we allowed the eaudy Cologne to run its course, if that's the end of the bottles, as you say. Then he will fall asleep. That is the more natural solution, it seems to me."

"Ha," laughed Mrs. O'Dowd. "No solution is natural where that bugger's concerned. He would go to town on his own breath if he was put to it. No, Mrs. Parker, it is his conscience that must be appealed to. You wouldn't forsake an old friend."

All this time the house had been quite still. You would not have thought that it contained a situation, and that a difficult one. The walls of the small room were simple slab, that they had pasted over with the newspapers, and the flies had done the rest. Amy Parker had never particularly noticed before that there was print to read, but began now to pick out, in slow words, the life of a grazier who had died after an accident with a bull.

Then the feet began to stir. There was a slurring of boots over boards. O'Dowd, she remembered, had large feet.

"Hsst!" said his wife behind her hand, on which was the broad wedding ring that she wore for convenience, "That is him. He's for condescendun. Whether it's for better or worse remains to be seen. Sometimes I think it is better if he sets."

The feet had no intention but to move. They came on. They were moving over boards, some of which protested. The house was groaning. A body, and that of a large man, was jostling those rooms through which it passed.

"I think we will be movun ourselves," Mrs. O'Dowd said. "Come, dear. This way."

And Amy Parker felt the grain of her friend's hand.

"If it is a crisis he wants," said Mrs. O'Dowd, "then it is better to have a choice of avenues, as I discovered on a former occasion, an have not forgot since."

So they were whirling through the kitchen, through the smell of cold fat and ash, and were in a kind of small passage, frail certainly, but with several openings. There was a sound of listening, as loud as the silence could make it. Mrs. O'Dowd stood with the lobe of her right ear cocked on a finger.

Then he burst through a door that was obviously cardboard, as was the whole house. It flapped. O'Dowd was terrible. His mouth was moist, and the hairs were black in his nose.

"Ah," he cried. "Two!"

"Surprised I am," said his wife, "that you are not seeun more."

"Why," O'Dowd bellowed, "as if two flickun women is not enough."

And he stood there most positively, holding an ugly sort of a gun, that Amy Parker hoped would not go off.

"Mr. O'Dowd," she said, "don't you recognize me?"

"Yes," said his wife, "it is our old friend Mrs. Parker. Come to pay us a visit for old times' sake."

"My arse," said O'Dowd. "A couple o' flickun women, an you have a funeral."

"That is a nice way to speak to a lady," protested Mrs. O'Dowd.

"I am not nice," said her husband simply.

His eyes frowned on this truth as if he could not look at it too long or too closely. It was a pretty pebble of a thing that required much examination.

Then he took his gun and shot if off.

"God help us!" shrieked his wife, holding her hair, that was coming down in bundles about her ears. "That we have come to this, in our own home. Christians notwithstandun."

"Are you hit?" asked Amy Parker, who had felt the wind.

"I can't answer for every part of me body," Mrs. O Dowd cried. "It's the fright I got. You black bugger! You devul! You'll kill us yet!"

"What else do you think I am flickun well aimun at? Damn woman!"

And he took the gun again.

"Quick," said Mrs. O'Dowd. "Mrs. Parker, we must make tracks."

And in that small space of brown passage, with the flinty smell of the gun and its hot oil, there was such a flapping of women, revolving, and beating against the walls, as they chose some opening through which to escape. In this scrimmage Amy Parker became separated from her friend and found herself in the best room, with the bit of a door to shut and hope against. Where her friend went to she did not know, only that she had removed herself in that same gyration of anxiety and skirt.

"Flick me if it ain't finished," O'Dowd had begun to bellow.

He could have been breaking his gun the other side of the door, and there was such slapping of his pockets, as if he were on fire.

"Sold out," he roared. "But I will get her," he said, "if I wring her bally neck."

After a door had crashed, and the house had shaken and settled again, they seemed to have entered a fresh phase, of peace, or inverted frenzy. In the room in which Amy Parker stood, which was the best at O'Dowds', and for that reason never used, even the soul suspected it would never rise. Roses had been pasted in wrinkles over every possible crack of escape, with the result that life had given up and was littering the window sill with wings and shells and pale spidery legs. The intruder, already petrified, was received into the presence of the greater mummies, the sofa, with hair sprouting from the shoulders, and on the mantelpiece a long cat, that O'Dowd had stuffed for his wife, who had been fond of it.

Turning with an effort from the sad cat, Amy Parker looked through the fog of the window and saw her neighbour elongate herself catwise round the corner of a shed, the ears appearing to be flattened back, and in her glassy eyes the desperate hope of self-protection. Then the observer would have told her friend that she need no longer fear the gun, but she could not tear the window open, and as the sound of knuckles on the glass was terrible in the deathly room, all attempts to attract attention were fizzling fatefully out. So Mrs. O'Dowd continued to crane and flatten, as if she were expecting death to appear from some direction she could not think of, much as she racked her brains.

As Amy Parker was struggling to break the terrible bonds of her protective room, O'Dowd came round the corner of the house, carrying the cleaver as if it were a little flag.

Then it is true, Mrs. Parker could not scream against the glass.

She saw the gristle come in Mrs. O'Dowd's throat as she flattened herself still flatter against the shed. Before she ran, round the corner of the house. And O'Dowd running, carrying his little flag.

Then Amy Parker was freed. She burst out, she ran, not because she was brave, but because the thread of her life had become attached to the same spool which was winding O'Dowds round the house. So Amy Parker ran too, down the rickety step, against the fuchsia tree, that tingled as she

151

passed. She ran, in turn, round the house, which had become the only pivot of existence; without it they were lost.

They were running and running, though sometimes also lurching, whether it was from the grog, or the slippery pineneedles on that side, or the stones and the potholes on the other, or just because somebody's corns gave a twinge that was extra bad. But running. That was the desperate thing. And bits of the house flashed past, through windows and doors, the boxes in which they had led their stale lives—why, there was the loaf lying that the woman had cut crooked that morning, and the pair of pants the man had let fall from his thighs, and let lie, in black coils. Such glimpses flittered. And the flattened cat on her varnished stand on the mantelpiece. She had been called Tib, Amy Parker remembered, from behind her breath.

Where are we going to? she asked. At the moment death seemed terrible hard to catch. The back of O'Dowd fluctuated. At times she wondered what she would do if she could run fast enough. But the back of O'Dowd lurched round the next corner. Always.

There were moments when, through the straining air, she swore that she heard the man hack off his wife's head with the chopper. She knew the thud, and had seen before, somewhere, the white pipe gasping words of forgiveness in the dust. We will have to do something with the body, she said, before the constable comes.

But in the meantime she was running, in the same cloud that several fowls had formed, as if disturbed by the prospect of chopping. The fowls' long skinny necks were stretched right out. They were extended in the general motion. And a pig too. The same red sow raced in the race, her teats hitting her ribs, grunting and farting as she galloped, with every sign of mirth, or perhaps terror, it was difficult to tell. The fowls shot off at a tangent, but the sow continued out of dedication to man.

Round and round man ran, till he had come on quite a distance into that country in which he is prepared to suffer, sometimes rolling his eyeballs, sometimes giving, in the depths of his fixed eyes, melancholy glimpses of the static world of peace that he has lost. In this way Amy Parker, when she had all but bust, saw her husband and her two children, seated at the kitchen table, drinking tea out of white cups, the crumbs of Tuesday's cake falling yellow from the corners of their mouths. And she could have cried. She did, in fact, just begin to blubber, for herself, no longer for her friend.

"Mrs. Parker," Mrs. O'Dowd was panting just then.

So that Mrs. Parker, looking round, saw that Mrs. O'Dowd, by exerting herself tremendously, had managed to catch up. The grey blur of her face was mostly mouth and eyes.

"What are we to do now?" Mrs. Parker panted in return.

For they were still running and running round the house, somewhere ahead, or else at the tail of O'Dowd.

"Pray to God," Mrs. O'Dowd hissed.

And the two women did, after a fashion, resuming an acquaintance they had not kept up, even hinting they had been neglected. They ran and prayed.

Then at the corner by the big tank it happened quite suddenly that they met O'Dowd, who had had the brilliant notion of running in the opposite direction. He was wet, and black, with the chopper in his hand.

"Ahhh!" cried his wife. "It is you at last. I am ready for whatever it is you intend to do. It is not me that ever denied you nothun. Here I am."

She stood still, in the last fragments of herself and her tormented hair. Out of her bosom, onto her blouse, had bumped the holy medals that she wore for safety.

"So help me God," she said, "I was not bad, an I was not good, so chop quick, an let us have the judgment."

Then O'Dowd, who was bigger than ever, and the drink lighting him up with intemperate fire, began to tremble, and his flag flapped, the little chopper that he carried in his hand.

"Ah," he cried, "it is the devul that got inter me. An the eaudy Cologne."

Till he was crying and protesting, and his lips, that had been thinned out by sun and running, were full again.

"It is me nature, I am like this," he cried. "I am up an down. It isn't that there is actual bad in me, if there is not actual good. I am a middlun man. It is only when the drink takes hold that I get a bit above meself, and then would do no harm, onyway, I am pretty certain not."

"Then we know now," said his wife, who had sat down where she was, in a few tufts of yellow grass and dead leaves and dust. "Then it is all cleared up quite convenient, an we are more alive than dead. That is the main thing. It is obligun of you, my dear, to explain the situation."

"Yes," he said, wiping his nose, that was getting out of

153

hand, "it is all over now. An I will take a little nap, Mrs. Parker, if you don't mind. It will be good for me. Just now I am not meself."

Mrs. O'Dowd sat shredding grass, and her friend, who was above her, had become a monument. As O'Dowd began to move his body with some care across the yard, stepping so as to avoid the dead emotions, and carrying his little implement as if it were a piece of paper, that he would roll up, now that it was no more use, and put away. Then he went into the house, after bashing his forehead on the lintel, and crying out because he did not deserve it.

Mrs. O'Dowd began to hum. She shredded grass. She was making a comb-and-paper noise. And her hair was hanging down.

"Will you leave him?" Mrs. Parker asked.

But Mrs. O'Dowd hummed.

"I would not stand for any such nonsense, not from any man, not from a husband," said Mrs. Parker, shifting her stone limbs.

"But I like him," said Mrs. O'Dowd, throwing aside the dead grass. "We are suited to each other," she said.

And she began to manipulate her legs, that were under her, and that had begun to set into a permanent shape from being poured there molten.

"Aoh," she said. "I could'uv killed him, notwithstandun, if it had been *my* hand had held the little axe, an us runnun round the house for fun."

Now Amy Parker had gone to release the wheel of the buggy, in the shafts of which the old horse stood looking, and her friend had turned and gone back into the house, putting up her hair through the long trance that life can become.

"Oh, an Mrs. Parker," she said, putting her head out through a window, "I had forgot. Would you like a nice piece of cheese, that was made by me own hand? It is mature an nice."

But Amy Parker shook her head, and the old horse pulled. They were going. Through a trance of trees and all that had not happened.

Chapter 11

STAN PARKER would sometimes fail to recognize his wife. He would see her for the first time. He would look at her and feel, This is a different one, as if she had been several. She was, of course, according to which dream rose to the surface. Sometimes she was beautiful.

Or again, they would look at each other in the course of some silence, and she would wonder, she would wonder what she had been giving away. But he respected and accepted her mysteries, as she could never respect and accept his. Then she would become sour and strident, from thinking about it, and she would wring out the dishcloth tight, and slam it on the hook, and shake the water from her hands. At these moments too he saw her for the first time, and was surprised how sour and ugly she was, a greyness in her coarse face, that shone with the exertion of some work. Yes, she is ugly and bitter, he said, and he could not have touched her unpleasant skin.

But walking in the garden in the evening, after the children were fed, and the milk vessels scalded, and the dishes in the rack, then she came into her own. He liked to come along the path, and find her by accident at these times, and linger with her or put his arm awkwardly through hers, and stroll beside her, also awkwardly at first, till warmth and her acceptance made them part of each other.

So they would stroll through the rather overgrown summer garden before night fell, and the plants of the garden lifting their heads from the dust and the cicadas in full throat.

"Ah," she would cry, "that old thing!"

And draw away from him, and stoop, to pull at a plant or weed that they called Wandering Jew. She did not believe in the efficacy of her act; it was simply a rite that had to be performed, and she would straighten up and throw away the pale stem that she had pulled, as if she had already forgotten.

So they would stroll in the dusk of the garden.

"Peabody," he said once, "is coming tomorrow to look over Nancy's heifer. I think he'll buy."

"What, that poor heifer!" she replied. "I did not want to sell Nancy's calf."

"We have too many," he said.

"Poor Moll," she said, "she'll fret."

And she picked the sharp leaf from the oleander that she was passing. She was speaking for the sake of speaking, for she knew in her heart, all things happen that are intended. She threw the sharp leaf away.

"She'll fret," she said. "Thelma was crying tonight. She got a splinter under one of her fingernails. I took it out, but she is still upset."

She thought of her pale child, now asleep in the prevailing dusk, and for whom she could do nothing beyond take out splinters.

"If she never gets anything worse than splinters," he said.

For he too was speaking for the sake of speaking. Their presences were sufficient, but some feeling of guilt made them speak in code words to hide their wealth. Her face was creamy, porous, absorbing what remained of the light. His longer, sharper one, almost a hatchet, cut the darkness. Now they were looking at each other, face on, absorbed in the mystery of the moment. But they were forced to speak. They spoke about their delicate child, Thelma, who had developed asthma, until he began to tell again about cows, how Nancy's heifer reminded him of one he had known, that threw a bull calf with two heads.

She made a noise of protest, because she did not want the drowsy peace of that moment to be disturbed, with flowers melting in the dusk, and her husband.

"It is all cows with you," she said. "Don't you ever consider your children?"

"What am I to do?" he laughed.

But his face quickly composed itself, returning to a suspicion that it was she who had moved the children out of his reach after they had created them together. Still, it was less important now, in the disappearing garden, and the children themselves lost in sleep.

She began to move closer to him, sensing some thought of which she might not approve. The darkness was moving with

156

them. Soft shapes of bushes brushed against them, the heads of flowers passed silkily against their legs and cheeks. He should, by rights, have been chained by her power of soft darkness. But tonight he was not. It might have been hard daylight in which they walked.

So she said, in a voice that blamed him for it, "I am going in, Stan. We can't walk about like lunatics all night. There are things to do."

But he did not detain her.

She went in and began to wind wool for clothes she would knit for the winter, fixing the skein on the backs of two chairs, since she did not enjoy the luxury of someone to help her by holding it on his hands. And as she wound she thought recklessly of the moment at the mulberry tree. She had been gathering mulberries, and was stained by them. Big glistening leaves waved upon their stalks as she worked. There was a continual opening and closing of the tree, an interplay of sky and leaves, of light and shade, so that she was mottled with it, as well as stained by the juice. Then her husband had come, and they stood together, inside the envelope of the shining tree, talking, and laughing at nothing, and gathering fruit. Then she had kissed him suddenly on his surprised mouth, with such vehemence, she remembered the impact of their teeth, destroying the soft ripeness of mulberries. And he laughed and looked almost shaken; he did not hold with kissing by daylight. So that she began again quietly to gather the fruit, ashamed of her ripeness and her purple hands.

The woman in the kitchen wound the wool skilfully, if not fiercely, and looked over her shoulder for her husband to come. But he did not. How flat the leaves were afterwards. Some fruit had little maggoty things, but frankly, these would cook up. Her husband had continued to gather with her for a little while. He was drying up, as the result of working hard for many years in the sun. She was conscious of his face beside her as they picked. His skin was almost the skin of a sandy man, but he was not sandy, no particular colour of hair. His muscles, which had been developed by work, were beginning to look too obvious, at times even ludicrous. So they gathered fruit together, and after a while he went.

The woman winding wool held all this enclosed in her face, which had begun to look sunken. It was late, of course, late for the kind of lives they led. Sometimes the wool caught in the cracks of the woman's coarse hands. She was without mystery now. She was moving round the winding chairs on flat feet, for she had taken off her shoes for comfort, and her breasts were rather large inside her plain blouse. Self-pity and a feeling of exhaustion made her tell herself her husband was avoiding her, whereas he was probably just waiting for a storm. This would break soon, freeing them from their bodies. But the woman did not think of this. She continued to be obsessed by the hot night, and insects that were filling the porcelain shade of the lamp, and the eyes of her husband, that were at best kind, at worst cold, but always closed to her. If she could have held his head in her hands and looked into the skull at his secret life, whatever it was, then, she felt, she might have been placated. But as the possibility was so remote, she gave such a twist to the wool that she broke the strand.

It is time I went to bed, she said.

And she did, when she had drunk a glass of tepid water, and mastered a burst of flatulence that surged up out of her discontent. She went in her stockings, leaving the wool, which was grey in colour, and only half-wound from the two chairs. There would be all the days in her life in which to wind wool.

The husband could sense all this happening in the house as he sat outside in the darkness, agreeably, softly, lost in it. He was watching for the storm. Events of immense importance would take place if only the moment of lightning could occur. But it did not yet seem that the little soft flashes playing about the mountaintops would gather themselves together to achieve supreme power. There was a sense of loitering in the warm darkness. As the man waited he lazily passed his hands over his relaxed body, of which the strength had created nothing significant. So he became restless, moving from side to side on his buttocks. His strength was powerless. He could not gather himself together. He flickered like the little bursts of lightning on the mountaintops. In his vague restlessness it would have been easy for him to go to his wife, and touch her, and fall asleep. But he did not.

Even his wife flickered mysteriously in his mind in that darkness. He remembered a morning at the mulberry tree when he had found her gathering fruit, and the goodness and familiarity of her face had pleased him so much that he had neglected what he had intended to do, to gather fruit beside her for a few minutes. Their hands glided through the leaves, sometimes touching each other, scarcely by accident, and this was good too, with the simplicity of true love. So the leaves

158

opened and enfolded. Till they were so close he looked with surprise at her kind of burnt beauty, and she was pressing her mouth into his mouth, they were hanging on each other with sudden hooks. But the desire to grapple with the unknown woman, who was also his wife, quickly dried up. Her importance had dwindled in the brilliance of the day. Their skins passed across each other like paper across paper. For she had felt it too. She went on gathering fruit. And he, after gathering a few more handfuls, to make it appear more natural, went back up the path, wondering.

But as the man Stan Parker sat in the flickering darkness waiting for the storm, the form of his wife faded into insignificance. A great fork of blue lightning gashed the flat sky. He listened to the drums of thunder, of which the first rolls shook the silence. The still, stale air had begun to move.

The man's breath came in gulps now, as if he had never been free to breathe enough. He was palpitating and shivering with the leaves of the garden, the wood of the house even, against which his face was resting. The storm came. It bent the garden. Large flat drops of rain were plastering the leaves and hard earth. Soon the land was shining whenever lightning opened its darkness. That torment of darkness, of lashing, twisted trees, became, rather, an ecstasy of fulfilment.

The man who was watching the storm, and who seemed to be sitting right at the centre of it, was at first exultant. Like his own dry paddocks, his skin drank the rain. He folded his wet arms, and this attitude added to his complacency. He was firm and strong, husband, father, and owner of cattle. He sat there touching his own muscular arms, for he had taken off his shirt during the heat and was wearing his singlet. But as the storm increased, his flesh had doubts, and he began to experience humility. The lightning, which could have struck open basalt, had, it seemed, the power to open souls. It was obvious in the yellow flash that something like this had happened, the flesh had slipped from his bones, and a light was shining in his cavernous skull.

The rain buffeted and ran off the limbs of the man seated on the edge of the veranda. In his new humility weakness and acceptance had become virtues. He retreated now, into the shelter of the veranda, humbly holding with his hand the wooden post that he had put there himself years before, and at this hour of the night he was quite grateful for the presence of the simple wood. As the rain sluiced his lands, and the fork of the lightning entered the crests of his trees. The darkness was full of wonder. Standing there somewhat meekly, the man could have loved something, someone, if he could have penetrated beyond the wood, beyond the moving darkness. But he could not, and in his confusion he prayed to God, not in specific petition, wordlessly almost, for the sake of company. Till he began to know every corner of the darkness, as if it were daylight, and he were in love with the heaving world, down to the last blade of wet grass.

Soon a new gentleness had crept into the rain, because the storm was passing. Sound became distinguishable from sound. The drops were separate on the iron roof, the last cold gusts rubbed leaf on leaf.

Stan Parker, who was still standing there, holding on to the veranda post, had been battered by the storm. His hair was plastered to his head, he was exhausted, but he was in love with the rightness of the world. Smiling at his own daring in accepting this conclusion, he began to go back into the clinging, sleepy darkness of the house, feeling his way between the furniture, of the house in which other people lived. He was quite distinct in this fuzzy world of sighs and clocks. Still smiling, he took off his clothes, and sleep swallowed him at one gulp.

The next morning they all threw the sheets off as if life were waiting for them. Summer wore a fresh glaze. It was also the morning that Ossie Peabody was to come about Nancy's heifer.

"Poor thing," Amy Parker said again, later on, after she had hung out the rags with which they dried the teats of the cows. "And Ossie Peabody, Stan, they say he's mean," she said, "so watch out."

"Ossie'll buy at our price," he said, "or we shall keep the heifer."

"That is all very well, now," said his wife. "But you are too soft. We shall see."

Stan did not answer that, because it was unimportant, and he was feeling good. He tightened the belt on his waist and went out.

Liquid breezes were licking the trees into tender shapes of green. The fowls were round the yard, burnished or mottled. The blue bitch came sidling, her mulberry nose moist in that morning of light.

"OO-er, *Ray!* I'll tell on you!" Thelma cried.

Because he had rubbed her face with red mud. She was

dirtied. That day was too much for Thelma's thin face. She shrank away from it. And Ray flung a ball of moist red mud, for good measure, that flattened on her pinafore.

Thelma screamed.

"Go on," said Stan Parker between his teeth.

He would have to stop and play the father. He cuffed the boy's head that was bristling up at him. On this morning he could have spoken to his children, but the boy, seeing this, was shy and ran away to stir up an ant's nest.

"It's all right, Thel," said the father, mumbling between contented lips. "It's going to wash off."

"I hate him," she screamed. "I'd kick him in the stomach if I could, but he always runs away."

Then she went into the wash-house, and when she had washed her face, looked at it in the glass, wetting her lips and pursing them up, till she had become quite dreamy with her own reflection.

Stan Parker went on towards the cow yards, where he would meet his friend and neighbour and transact this small bit of business. He walked a roundabout way, for the pleasure of it, across the stubble from which he and the old German had already brought in the oats. A wind was flattering the trees. They tossed and curved to it. And the man's spirit was lifted on the wind. He half-remembered a tune that he had whistled as a boy, on a horse, behind cattle, hunched forward on the pommel of the saddle. What if he was still this whistling youth? he wondered. It was a cold thought, that left him tingling in the callous wind, but possible. He went on. A crane rose from water in a lower paddock and set slow sail, back across the blue morning.

Just then Stan Parker saw his neighbour Ossie Peabody open the side gate, bending down from the matted bay gelding that he almost always rode. The neighbour was going quite casually through the rather complicated manœuvre of gate opening, while searching the landscape for things that would make him jealous. For many years Ossie Peabody had envied Stan Parker, in private, with many a slow twinge. Now he saw Stan walking across his land. Both men looked away. They had known each other so long, each took it for granted that he was recognized. Eventually they would meet and talk together, or shape words between grunts, and silences, and glances, and memories of all that had happened to each other over the years.

Ossie Peabody was a man with a long nose, of Stan's age

161

perhaps, but drier, and always showing several scabs. The good nature with which he had been born had turned rather sour since he drove the volunteers to Wullunya for the floods. He had closed up. He lived at home still with his mum and dad and a young, negative wife, who bore children, and that was about all. Ossie Peabody did not like his children. He did not like much. He respected his parents. He liked a good cow. Somewhere in his fastnesses there was a kind of affection for his neighbour Stan Parker, but complicated by much that was envious and sour. Because he would have liked to talk to Stan, mostly he avoided him. He drove his spurs into his shaggy, patient horse and took another road, feeling, to his increased sourness, that he would not be missed.

Now the two men were converging on the cow yard at Parkers', where the meeting would take place. They came on, with their heads down, pretending.

They said, "Lo, Stan." "Lo, Ossie."

Almost with surprise.

Then Ossie got down. He stood disgruntled on the ground, in his old strapped leggings, with his feet apart, realizing he was a shorter man than Stan.

"Where's this three-legged, flickin heifer you got?" Ossie Peabody asked.

Stan Parker smiled but did not reveal yet, as if he would release his dove all in good time.

"Well, how are we, Ossie?" Stan Parker asked.

But Ossie Peabody sniffed; he could have had something up his nose, and it so long, and flushed in summer.

"Nice oat crop, Stan?" he asked.

"All right," said Stan Parker.

He was feeling good. He was glad even to be with this sour man, his neighbour, whom he had watched dry up and get longer in the nose. Often he thought of things he would have liked to tell Ossie, but Ossie was not there, and so he forgot.

"Nice rain," he said.

"What there was," replied the neighbour. "Nice day, anyway."

He looked at Stan, wondering whether he was playing a game. Because Ossie Peabody was now aching to see the little heifer, whose great beauty he could only suspect. She was Stan's too. He wanted to own this. So Ossie Peabody looked at his neighbour, and wondered, and resented, and thought perhaps that Stan was clever, and that was why he was a

162

queer bugger, he was always coming round the corner, up to something. So Ossie spat.

But Stan Parker only felt good.

"Want to see the heifer, eh? All right, Ossie," Stan Parker said.

He was stretching himself, as if he had risen from sleep, and his bones cracked, in a way that was most irritating to his neighbour, who flicked at the dust with his long black ugly whip. Ossie Peabody was taut, but the day had lulled Stan Parker into a sense of security as sure and soft as cranes' wings. Once or twice he remembered the storm, in which he had confessed his weakness, and which he should have denied now, though he did not, for actually there was no need.

Suddenly he went from the yard in which they were standing, through another and smaller yard, in which hung a pepper tree, and flung open a grey gate. At this point in the ritual Ossie Peabody did not know how he felt about Stan Parker, his sure step, and his well-repaired yards. Ossie was biting his lip, in a long old green greatcoat that he was wearing for the change in the weather. His bronze skin had a tint of verdigris.

But there was the little heifer. Her shining nose suspected life, as she advanced on props of legs, rolling her soft eyes and butting the air with buds of horns. Stan Parker made all kinds of consoling noises. He walked behind with his hands spread like fans. The heifer advanced. The fronds of the tree stroked. But she was unwilling. Her beauty trembled.

"Not a bad sort of cow, Stan," said Ossie Peabody in a clear, metallic voice that was not going to give much away.

The heifer plunged into the last yard. Her feet would have been playful if they had not been distressed. They were lost on that earth. She sprayed the air with fear.

"Nicely built. I want to handle her," Ossie Peabody said.

He was throwing back the sleeves from his wrists. He was urgent. He could not wait to touch this cow flesh.

Stan Parker was coming round on soft feet. Now the whole air was slow, the bright morning trembled, it waited for a moment. Before he touched the rope her glistening neck wore.

"Quiet enough," said Ossie Peabody, who was examining cow.

He began to prod and squeeze. He touched her with a re-

163

sentful excitement, as if this were the only pleasure that would ever ripple on his still life.

And Stan Parker held the little heifer. There were magpies calling to each other, and falling in play out of the sky, in bundles of pied feathers. There was a scent of fresh dung and recent rain. He was powerless against all this, and anything that might happen: he stood smiling foolishly at whatever Ossie Peabody said.

"Yes, Ossie," he said, "she's got the milker's lines all right, the milker's rump."

He stood there smiling. He was a big man, and rather erect. Now he had in his face all that simplicity and goodness that he sensed to be paramount. Why, each frond of the pepper tree could not have hung otherwise. He looked down, a bit ashamed of his happiness, at his clods of boots.

"Could be short in one tit," Ossie Peabody was saying.

"Calf'll pull it down."

"That's all right. What if she's barren?"

"Sell her for beef."

"Ah, no, no, Stan. I don't want to waste me time."

And he began to give reasons why.

But could not compete with the upright posts of that yard, which Stan Parker had felled, and shaped, and tamped the earth round. Through the interstices of the high yard the sky showed. By now it was ablaze. Stan Parker closed his eyes, accepting the foolishness of words, and disintegrating into little spasmodic waves of knowledge and contentment. His knowledge of goodness was impervious.

Ossie Peabody looked sharply at Stan Parker and thought, You're a funny sort of bugger all right, simple, or is it clever?

"How much are you askin for this beast?" he said suddenly in a low quick voice.

"Six," said Stan.

"Gor struth, six for a little bit of a thing! Unproven, Stan. You'll have to look somewhere else. I'm a poor man. With a family. There's the kids' education. An clothes. An sickness. There's the flickin doctor's bills. The wife's crook too. She's never been right since the last kid. It's her womb's fell, Doc Pillinger says. Well, that's just my luck. They tell me I got to send her to Sydney, see a specialist or somethin. Course, I dunno. But I ain't got the cash, Stan, for cows."

Then he watched that Stan Parker twisting the bit of rope that hung from the heifer's neck.

But Stan did not speak. He wished that he had been on his own, because he could not contain the greatness of that day. So he twisted the piece of rope.

"I might be able to do three," Ossie Peabody said and watched. "If I tighten up on one or two things. But a man's human, Stan. You got to have one or two smokes, and a flutter with the books, Stan. But I could do three if you are willin'."

Then the magpies were calling those long clear cold calls, and the immense sky expanded still farther. So Stan Parker opened his hands that were holding the rope. This Ossie Peabody was a miserable sort of man.

"All right, Ossie," he said, "you can take her, if you like, for three. You've got a good cow."

"Ah, I don't doubt that, Stan. You've got the right strain. Now here you are. I have it with me. We'll count it out."

And they did. Note by note.

Stan Parker took the money, which was rather crumpled, and put it in his pocket. He doubted the importance of this transaction, and of most acts. People who did not know him might have thought he was uncertain of himself. But on this morning he was certain, if never before. So much so, he tilted the hat over his eyes to hide his knowledge. The glare was blinding also by that time of day.

Then the miserable Ossie Peabody was climbing onto his matted horse and was heading the little heifer towards the side gate, stretching out along his horse's neck and flapping his elbows, in case he might lose her even yet.

When they were gone Stan Parker returned to the house, from which his wife was shaking a duster and looking out.

"Well," she said, "did he pay?"

"Ah," he said, "I got what I wanted."

From under the brim of his hat.

"You did!" she said. "Then I am surprised at you."

She compressed her mouth into a tight shape to deny some tenderness.

"But he's a miserable sort of coot," he said, "that Ossie Peabody. He says his wife's womb has fallen."

"Ah," she said, her duster suspended. "It could have."

Then she drew back into the room, though she could have hung there a long time on the sill, looking at her husband in the sunlight.

Chapter 12

SUMMER took hold of the country, and it dried up. The leaves of the trees were sandpapery together, and when a wind blew through the yellow grass it rattled in dead yellow stems. There was a scurf of dry seed on the grey earth, and where the cattle gathered at the waterholes and creeks, nosing the green scum, the earth had set in craters. There were many dead things in the landscape—the grey skeletons of trees, an old weak cow that had stuck in the mud and did not rise again, lizards that life had left belly upwards. It seemed at times during that summer that everything would die. But people did not care, as they shaded their feeble eyes or mopped their greasy skins. They just did not care, that is, in the early, passive stages. Later on, when the fires broke out, and got out of control, and scorched along the gullies, and arrived in the fowl yards, and entered windows, so that the limp curtains were a pair of demoniac flames, then the people woke up at last and realized that they did not want to die. Screams came out of the throats of those that were caught. They remembered their childhood, and their sins, and could have reformed altogether and become saints, if there had been question of a second chance. Some did receive this, but only fled out of themselves for a short time, then returned worse than before.

However, it was before the fires that Armstrongs sent for two pairs of dressed ducks, that Amy Parker took up one evening to the house, after she had made things tidy. Armstrongs had company at this time, several ladies and gentlemen from the city, people of wealth, if nothing else, Mrs. O'Dowd said. It was on account of the girl Madeleine, she thought, that there was great doings in the house, so Mrs. Frisby said, and ducks ordered, because this Madeleine could no longer hold young Armstrong off, she was taking him at last.

Amy Parker set off that evening through the dry world with Armstrongs' dressed ducks in a shallow basket on her arm. She was neat enough in her clean blouse, with her arms still red from scrubbing off the blood of ducks. She walked with a slight breathlessness, wondering already what she would find and say, and whether she would see Madeleine. Most probably not. So that she grew slower on the hill, and red, for she was plump at this time, if not actually fat, and her limbs became awkward, with their smell of innocent, best soap.

So she came to Armstrongs' gateway, which had cost a great deal of money and showed it, in volumes of iron and brick, and on each pillar of red brick the name was printed in white flints. Armstrongs' property had been called Glastonbury, since a gentleman of education, after a few drinks, said it was not unlike the place of that name, of which nobody else had heard, in the old country. So Mr. Armstrong was pleased. He spoke it softly to himself, and looked it up in a book, and his place became Glastonbury.

At this time Mr. Armstrong was quite the man of leisure, though his skin had never lost its beefy grain. But it was so long now since he had put the apron off that people had forgotten. Only sometimes, eating his meat, the malice stirred in some, and they would look up, and feel superior above their plates and take what he had to offer, and get out. But most just ate. Or strolled on his lawns and spoke about Europe. And were obsequious to his son, who smelled of bay rum, and to his daughters, who wore the scent of gardenias. There was, in fact, an English lord dangling after one daughter, Mrs. O'Dowd said. So Mr. Armstrong was pleased. He had a crest now, and a club, and a great many parasites who did him the honour of relieving him of his cash.

Even on the drive at Glastonbury prosperity was obvious. It shone in the mirror leaves of laurels, and lurked in the glimpses of shrubberies and lawns, and in a little summer-house, in which a hand of cards had been abandoned beneath the cloying roses. Before she dived down that drive reserved for tradesmen and servants, Amy Parker noticed with some shyness the statue of the naked woman near the front door. Most people were hushed by that statue into a state of respect. They did not look at it, or only casually, and, after enjoying in a furtive flash the suggestiveness of the dimpled

167

hands, accepted it as a respectable symbol of the wealth that had put it there.

But Amy Parker became hot, and wished that the statue had not been there, as she turned along the side of the house to reach the door which would admit her. On this side they had planted a grove of gardenias, of which the formal leaves and melting flowers might have resisted her in that dusk, if she had not looked through a window of the house and felt impelled. So she loitered, and brushed through the gardenia leaves without thought of guilt, to see inside the window at which she had at first only glanced.

The room into which she looked glowed in the dusk, for they had lit a big opalescent lamp, and there was a silver branch of candles, of which the flames batted in the breeze. They had encouraged a draught in that heat, throwing the curtains open, and the door, which led back into the house, to other mysteries and other lights. Several people were gathered in the room, Amy Parker saw; the black-coated, elderly, respectful men, and the more ostentatious younger one. But all absorbed into shadow, except for their white shirt fronts, and their faces held to listen. They were the audience. It was Madeleine by whom they had been sculptured. She stood there. She robbed the lamp even of its light.

So that Amy Parker came a little closer, drenched by the scent of flowers in the heady darkness, into which the arms of jasmine reached out from the side of the house, and embraced the intruding face with little tremors. From here she could watch, anonymously as a moth, but not hear. She did not want to hear. She would have been afraid. Besides, she could hear too plainly her own deafening heart.

Now Madeleine raised her arm, and the eyes of the men looked along it, as if it had not been flesh but something more extravagant. They were commanded by it, just as they laughed when the shape of her mouth told them. The old men laughed as if they had been hit, shaking idiotically. But the young man, who had become young Armstrong, laughed for what he hoped was Madeleine's own deepest satisfaction, as if they had been there alone, and he was holding her. His laughter tried to stroke. But Madeleine did not pay any particular attention to those who were with her in the room. She was speaking for herself. Or she arranged her pearls. Or glanced along her naked shoulders. Or into the cleft of her breasts that she had hidden with a rose. Madeleine was ice. Her icy dress grew from her splendid body, and could have

168

been no other. At this moment Amy Parker quite forgot she had seen her in other circumstances or in other clothes.

Then Mr. Armstrong got up from where he had been sitting beside the window, in the cool of the evening, looking over some papers, letters evidently, before the light failed. Mr. Armstrong had been undeterred, it appeared, by the other people in the room. He had paid for their presence there, and was rich enough to ignore. So he moved through the solitude of his room, with the opened letters flapping from his hand, and poured himself a glass of wine the others had been drinking, and drank, and encouraged his own thoughts. But he had cast a gloom on the narrative of Madeleine. The men's laughter trailed away into real but slightly bitter smiles. They shifted and drained their glasses, and Madeleine looked into hers, at the wine she did not want. Till Mr. Armstrong came and took her glass and put it down, without her asking him. She would obviously have preferred to break it.

Then it seemed they were all standing or sitting to no purpose, the figures in the room. They would never melt together, for their natures were insoluble. They would remain a fragile metal that one breath of hate could twist. And Amy Parker began to feel she had stayed too long. The breeze had got behind the tapestry, an expensive thing that the butcher had brought from Europe, of lords and ladies on silver horses, and the forest rippled, and the horses shivered in the breeze. The whole room had become unstable, like the rippling tapestry. The flames of the candles flowed out, like hair, the gold foil of the wine bottle was brittle in the blowing light. Madeleine had gone and sat down in a chair which young Armstrong, the man it was said she would marry, was holding to the ground in an effort to give it stability. Unconcious of his strength and devotion, she sat upon the carved chair, controlling her boredom behind the sticks of her fan. The old men, who had been taught to laugh, and got over the initial annoyance at their host's approach and now stood there detached and grinning, waiting for the breaking point.

Amy Parker had begun to feel the weight of the dead ducks on her arm, and of much that she did not understand. So that she sighed and went from the scene she had been watching. It was over, anyway, or had entered a fresh phase. So she trod through the dark grove, in which there was a smell of something rotting, fuller now than the scent of night flowers, and went towards the maids' door.

This was opened on a gust of basted beef and mingled

169

laughter and complaints. She trod in shyly, on the clean floors, ashamed of even her best stockings, and battered by the lights.

"I have brought the ducks for tomorrow," she said in a voice that would have made her children glance up.

"At a fine time," said Mrs. Frisby, who was not unkind. But she slammed the oven.

"Damn thing," she said. "Damn oven. Them and their ovens," she said. "I'm sick and tired of everything. Next week they can find another girl. I shall retire to the seaside."

"And live on their thanks," said Winnie, who was training the ears of her cap to look even sharper.

"Oh dear, no," said Mrs. Frisby. "There is a lady would give me a home just for the pleasure of me company. And breakfast in bed for a treat, if I didn't mind the crumbs."

Everybody roared, till Mrs. Frisby hushed, and particularly a young girl called Cassie, with a raw face just out of Ireland, who was beating up some eggs.

"But we are forgetting Mrs. Parker," Mrs. Frisby then said. "Sit down, dear, and we will share a secret with you."

She took from a cupboard a bottle that tinkled with gold paper, like the one from which the butcher and his guests had drunk, and after winking, and crooking her finger, poured an elegant glassful.

"It is out of fizz," she said, "because it has been open this little while. But it should lift you up to where you want to be."

"I have never drunk wine," Amy Parker said.

So that Winnie's face looked longer and thinner, and she took a buffer from the pocket of her apron and began to attack her nails.

"In the last situation I was in," she said, "we girls did particularly well in wine. There was so much entertaining. Luncheons every other day. He was a real gentleman. Not like this one, still warm from the making."

"Tt-tt," sucked Mrs. Frisby. "He pays well. And he's not a bad poor devil." Wine and steam were softening her, and sad thoughts, drifting with the wind she belched, of her lost sailor. "Pardon me," she said, looking into a saucepan. "I am troubled with a bit of resurrection. That is the price of wine."

So that the young Irish girl hung trembling and splitting above the basin of egg, that she beat and beat.

"And you take care, my girl, or you'll rise the floussay too high."

It was by this time warm and scintillating in the kitchen. Amy Parker sipped from her glass, which she held delicately, as if it had been a flower, and looked inside, while listening for some indication of the life that was lived in the other part of the house. As the wine flowed through her veins and sparkled in her head, she could have got up and fumbled her way through the baize door, to stand before Madeleine.

"She is beautiful," she said.

"Who?" said Mrs. Frisby. "This lump of a girl from County Cork?"

And Cassie giggled, and beat the eggs, as if these two functions were all that she could manage.

"Madeleine, of course," said Amy Parker soberly. Her lip curled tenderly to pronounce the word she had never dared speak.

In the silence Winnie returned the buffer to her pocket and pulled the apron closer to her straight breast.

"It is Madeleine who is beautiful," Amy Parker said again, now that she dared.

"Ah," said Mrs. Frisby, plunging a ladle into soup, "we have not seen her in bed."

"That will be somebody else's business," laughed Winnie.

And Cassie tittered in a shower of egg.

Mrs. Frisby produced great clouds of steam, through which her prophetic face showed, and the soup cascaded into plates, with the little shapes of carrot in the liquid gold.

"Somebody else's business. If somebody can bring it off. And who is somebody?"

She poured, and her grey face had grown tragic in the steam.

"The bloody stuff is not clear enough," she said gloomily. "Well, they can lump it. For all I care. And a little bit of grease too. The plates is French, anyway."

But it was all splendid to Amy Parker.

"I would like to sit beside her," she said, "like she was, sitting in there, under that curtain thing, with the horses. And sit beside her. I would tell her about my dream, if I could remember it. I have never been able to talk about the things there are to talk about. When we were married I planted a rose, but we have not talked about it. And it is one of the most beautiful things. You see, I know quite a lot. But it is not possible to tell. Between you and me, Mrs. Frisby, it is that that is wrong with the husband of the postmistress. He knows something."

171

"Strike a light, Mrs. Parker," said Mrs. Frisby, "it is time you were going home."

"And on one glass," said Winnie coldly, who was arranging soup and balancing a tray on her hand, as if suddenly jealous of it.

"Yes," said Amy Parker.

"Here is the money for them ducks of yours," said Mrs. Frisby, flinging a few coins. "And if they are not tender, it won't be me that cares. Stomachs, I am sick of em. I had a friend once that died, and when they cut him open—would you believe it?—it was duck. He was stuffed full."

Amy Parker could have believed it.

"Duck!" screamed Mrs. Frisby. "Ha-ha-ha!"

So that it must have entered by the doorway through which Winnie slipped. Then the baize shuddered and settled.

"I will never speak to her," said Amy Parker, gathering her basket.

"You won't miss nothing," said Mrs. Frisby. "She's out of tune. It's all in the eye with Madeleine."

But Amy Parker stood with her empty basket.

Mrs. Frisby realized this.

"Here," she said and wrapped up some nice remains of cold corned beef.

She hoped that this might do some good, but, remembering her lost sailor, she doubted it.

So Amy Parker went from the kitchen, and from the house, with its conflicting noises. Night birds confused her still more, drowning the velvet voices that had dawdled over soup. For the rich people had gone into the dining room and were seated there behind the drawn curtains. In the open room in which they had drunk their wine only the tapestry remained.

So Amy Parker walked faster through the garden. It was full of the wings of night birds. Once she heard, she thought she heard, footsteps on the same gravel, that she avoided by taking to the pine needles. She strained and hoped. But if Madeleine had escaped from the dining room with a headache, she would have discovered, walking beneath the dark trees, only a stocky woman with wood in her mouth instead of words. So Amy Parker ran on, hating her own breath, and threw the parcel of corned beef into some bushes near the front gate.

When she came in her husband said, "Well, what happened?"

"Nothing," she said.

"Haven't you anything to tell?"

"No," she said. "There was a lot of silly talk. They gave me a glass of wine. And my head feels hot."

"You got drunk?" he asked.

"I don't know if it is that," she said, bathing her face. "I was never drunk before."

But she bathed her forehead, and was afraid of what she might have said in the kitchen. She was obsessed by the memory of some nakedness. But the cold water clothed her soul, and she became neat and familiar to her husband, with no suggestion of the poetry she had seen and lived, at the window in the dark garden, or in Mrs. Frisby's steaming cave.

And the summer dried her up as if she had been a blade of grass. The wind, when it blew down the hot funnels of summer, stirred the flags of dry corn. There were many insects that Amy Parker noticed for the first time, and the veins of dead leaves. During this period, while her husband went about his work, doctoring a sick cow or doing things with wire, while her little boy played with a green bottle in the dust, filling and emptying as if it were the sole importance, she was looking over their heads, waiting for something to happen. As it did eventually. In this position, and frame of mind, she saw the first smoke, in that part of the country which is called The Islands, in the direction of Wullunya, where the floods had been.

"Here is the fire now," she said, wondering whether she should be frightened.

The smoke grew skywards, small still, a sapling of smoke, but growing.

So she went and told her husband.

"Yes," he said, "it's a fire all right."

He looked up, with the pliers in his hand, from the knot he was tying in a piece of wire. He had seen the fire already, of course, but he was not telling. He half-hoped it would vanish into smoke.

All around, people were telling each other, the women full of information, the slower men less willing to accept fact. Some men swore when they were told, and one even hit his wife with a bucket, so that she fell down and the blood gushed out.

But the men began to gather together, after the first moment of hesitation and desire to turn their backs on the fire.

173

They looked for their āxes, and fetched out sacking, and filled their water-bags, and asked for a bit of tucker to see them through while they were gone. They they climbed onto their horses or into their carts, and made off in the direction of The Islands, where the fire was.

By this time it had grown angry. Passionate volumes of smoke towered above the bush, and in that smoke, dark, indistinguishable bodies, as if something were being translated forcibly into space. The men of Durilgai straggled along the bush tracks, in groups, discussing other fires, or singly, looking at the ground. The latter were surprised at the details of sand, stones, and sticks they saw. They had discovered in the earth an austere beauty that they now loved with a sad love, that comes when it is already too late. The fire causes this inevitably to happen to solitary men. They are reconciled to the lives they are leaving behind, as they ride between the black trees, and the yellow light lowers, and animals begin to run towards them instead of away. Even some of the jocular individuals, who are boasting of bigger fires, begin to sense the approach of the intolerable, try to cover it up with obscenity, and when this fails, ride, and spit, and jerk the mouths of their horses.

The volunteers from Durilgai had gone several miles when they met a man called Ted Doyle, coming towards them on a wet horse.

The Islands was as good as burned out, said Ted Doyle, waving his arm in the direction of the fire, in which he had lost his hat and his courage. It was the biggest, flickin fire, protested the messenger, as his sweating horse revolved nakedly on thin legs. And Flanagans' burned out, and Slatterys'; he had seen the walls cave in on the old man, and there was a woman took fire at Glassons', a sister of Mrs. Glasson's, had run and lain in the creek, that was dry that year, and had lain twitching on the dry mud—for all they had beat her with the palms of their hands and an old coat or something, she was dead. All that district was just on cleaned out. The messenger flung this fact with his open hand, which trembled in the yellow air. There was some hadn't a mattress that was not a stench of feathers. And they opened the yards for the fowls to fly out. They flew flaming, or opened their beaks for air, and died decent like, turning up their eyes, their wattles gone black. The messenger's eyes were hollowed out by smoke. His white eyes told more, and the Adam's apple jerking in his scrawny throat. When the wind took the fire, the

174

man said, stretching his arm from his side and moving it gravely as a curtain of fire, the heat withered up the leaves before the fire, and the hair was shrivelled from your hand. They looked at his hand, and it was, in fact, singed of all hair. The hair of his head was frosted with the burnt ends. He had a smell of burning, that they snuffed up, to persuade themselves. And the animals were burning, he said, the wild ones, and snakes, they were lashing on the hot earth, as their flesh burned they lost shape, and knotted, and shrivelled. He had seen a snake bite on itself before it died, to hold some-one responsible.

Then the men who had been listening decided to turn back and find a position from which to defend Durilgai. Old Mr. Peabody, who was now very old indeed, sitting like a prophet in a sulky with his son, suggested they should make a stand about a mile back, where there was a stony hillside and a natural break in the scrub. The others listened to his old voice issuing miraculously from between skin and bones, and decided to take his advice. They turned their horses obedi-ently and followed Peabodys' sulky. Some of them guiltily remembered their fathers, and almost all were grateful for the frail protection of the old man's authority.

So they prepared to meet the fire, if it was carried so far by the wind. It was poor country just there, of rocks and rab-bit warrens and dead, listing thistles. Along the hill they cleared the scrub, making a wider belt, across which it was hoped the fire would never leap. There were voices and the thud of saplings in that quiet place, all during the day and into the night, with the nickering of horses that turned their muzzles homeward and wondered.

The fire did not come that day, only the smell of it, and the sight of smoke. And at night the wind died, so that the men began to make jokes again. The fire would not move at night, to any great distance, without a wind. They decided to go home and return early in the morning. Some of them hoped secretly there would be no need, that they would wake on a radiant day in which the fires of their own fears had burned out.

All through the days of fire the women went about their business, almost as if the men had not gone. They had really never learned to do otherwise. Only sometimes they looked up at the dirty sky, and seemed to walk more heavily through the yellow light. But the silences, broken by the cries of chil-

175

dren, were the same. The sweat running on their skins was the same.

The women made jokes about the fire. Some said they would jump inside the watertanks with what cash they had from the vegetables or the pigs.

"I would pray," Doll Quigley said.

And probably be saved. But not everybody was in the same boat as Doll Quigley, who had learned something from the nuns. Still, they practised stiff phrases of prayer in quiet embarrassment, and looked at the sky, and waited.

And at Glastonbury they waited. As the crisis deepened, and the yellow sky, they felt more isolated. Mr. Armstrong, who had set off in the direction of the fires, returned, cut the end off a cigar, walked through the orchard, and returned. He had developed a slight twitch that had not been visible before.

"For goodness' sake, sit down, Father, or *something*," said his two daughters, who had come out onto the drive.

The daughters of the butcher stood on the gravel, their unused hands hands folded, and smelling of eau de Cologne. Miss Dora, who had put on her hat, had more or less decided that she would leave for Sydney, where her brother was conducting their father's business. But Mabel, the younger sister, who would eventually marry the lord, was always unable to decide. She was amiable and pretty, with faithful eyes that made people think she was listening to them.

"What will you do, Madeleine?" asked Dora Armstrong.

Madeleine had come out just then onto the terrace. She too was wearing a hat, but because it suited her, its large, lazy brim moved as she walked with slow, indolent steps. She wore a white, cool, and obviously expensive dress, which on that morning defied circumstance.

"Why," she said, "I shall read a book probably, and eat a peach I have just seen on the sideboard in the dining room."

Unlike most people, Madeleine remained clean after peaches. Dora hated her skill, for she was anxious in most things. Now she frowned and said, "How can you talk about peaches with those dreadful fires!"

"Somebody will put them out, I expect," Madeleine said.

Or else she would be immolated. In spite of her apparent coolness the palms of her hands felt hot. She sat on the stone balustrade and tossed her ankle for an occupation.

Bronze arms of fire suddenly shot up into the sky in the direction of The Islands, out of the clouds of dirty smoke. It appeared as if something had given way. There was now a visible savagery of destruction in the progress of the fire, which made the Armstrongs admit to themselves that it would not stop at Glastonbury. For the first time they were vulnerable. They could not pay to stop the fire.

Madeleine sensed this. She thought about her lover, now sitting at his smooth desk, at which she had visited him once, and kissed the top of his sleek head, because it was hers. It was a devoted head. This admirable virtue was what she supposed she had desired. Tossing her ankle at the balustrade. But doubted since. Her face let fall few shadows of doubt, to the average observer, anyway. They did, however, find expression beneath trees at night, when she would sometimes cry herself hollow, or in the vague shapelessness of sleep, from which she always woke before making a discovery.

But she did not really suppose she would not pocket her doubts in the end, together with Tom Armstrong's money, and live in broad outline the life she had always intended to live, of parties, and jewels, and mahagony, and candlelight. Only on that morning she was tormented by the fire that could consume, apparently, whole intentions. Anything might go up. So she waited, and exposed her complexion to the sun, in a way that, in normal circumstances, she would not have done, and broke one of her fingernails on the stone balustrade.

In the meantime Miss Armstrong had given up hope of influencing anybody and had gone round to order the horses that would take her to Bangalay to the train. She wished to get away as quickly as possible, and not to think any more about the fire. But her younger sister, although afraid, would have liked to see something happen. She was more emotional, and soft. She had once bandaged a man who had cut himself with an axe. Temporarily she was in love with that man. She was always falling in love, and wondering what to do, before time or her parents solved the probelm.

The two young women on the terrace, who did not usually care for each other, except officially, were for the moment united in their indecision and their fascinated acceptance of a situation. They came close together. They almost held hands, only that would have been silly.

"That was a good one," said Mabel Armstrong as trees fell and the fire leaped higher.

"Oh, the poor people, and the little children," cried the

butcher's wife, who was holding her jewel case at an upper window.

She was a softhearted, rather directionless woman, in the style of her younger daughter. Mrs. Armstrong was inclined to apologize for her wealth, and to give freely to charities, without realizing she was the cause of them. She was too slow. She spoke slowly, in an improved voice, through a mouth from which you waited for the egg to drop. After several years of perseverance she could recognize a few words of French, in print of course, and consequently felt pleased enough to relax. She liked to put her feet up, and would tell the surprised about a bunion, of which nobody seemed able to rid her.

This was before the fire, still at a distance, had burned through several layers of amiability and sloth, leaving her exposed. That morning she had walked through her house, filled with other people's china and glass, and realized that the servants had been laughing at her for years. She moved from here to there a priceless little goblet in Bohemian glass, which fell off. But it did not seem important. The butcher's wife was already too shattered to shiver again.

So they waited for the fire, and had been waiting many years of their lives. And nights. At night the clouds burned along the horizon. There was an intolerable ticking of clocks, and crickets, and the heart wrapped in its wet sheet.

Down below Durilgai the men who had prepared the break awaited the fire the following morning. It seemed inevitable that it should come. The twiggy framework of the bush cracked in the silence, in the intervals between the gusts of hot wind. Then, about eleven, when one or two of the watchers were snoozing in some thin shade, and several more had almost forgotten, in the drone of anecdotes, the reason for their being in that place, the air suddenly seemed to thicken into molten glass.

"It is coming," they said.

Those who were sitting and lying got to their feet. Those who were without their shirts ostentatiously moved their muscles and rubbed the hair of their chests, to get a hold on their strength. But nearly all of them expressed the secret quandary they were in by spitting on the ground, and the hot grey earth swallowed their spittle up, and there was not a sign of it.

Old Mr. Peabody, however, had been sitting all this time on a rock, wrapped up, in spite of the temperature, in a coat

178

that looked as if it had once been the inside of a horse rug. He appeared undisturbed by anything that might happen. It was his age perhaps. He was really very old. His skin stood up on the remains of his flesh in transparent scales. His hands were spread out like matches on the knobs of his knees. In the event of a disaster he would have been useless, a liability even, but now the men liked to have him there. He consoled them because he had survived.

Now he began to move his tongue between his dry lips in little lizardy motions, and to compose a prophecy.

As the men prepared for the fire, shifting on their feet, trailing their cut branches, with which they proposed to beat the flames, or fastening bags with wire to the end of strong sticks—as these preparations were going on, old Mr. Peabody spoke.

"Change is on its way," he said, probing the dry air with his tongue.

"Change!" said somebody. "We shall be changed all right, with the fire lickin at our arses. We shall be changed into jumpin monkeys. Up the hill an over. With the smoke comin out."

"Ah, no, the wind'll turn it. Change is comin," said Mr. Peabody in his weak voice, and winced, as if someone had walked across his grave, or the cold wind he promised had actually got amongst his wrinkles.

But everyone else sweated in the molten morning. And the bush began to dissolve into stray tendrils of grey smoke, wreathing and twining between the leaves and twigs, like leaves and twigs released. The watchers began to breathe the stray smoke, and to stare into the tangled distance for the first flame. Each one realized the insignificance of his stature as he prepared to grasp the fire in a final wrestling.

Then a fox ran screaming from the scrub, his fire fierier.

It was coming indeed.

Several bursts of yellow smoke were released all of a sudden, as if from a bag. There was a smoking, and smarting, and crackling, and breaking, and crashing. The fire was reaching upward from the undergrowth, and higher upward, to embrace whole trees. There was a sighing of sap. A bird fell, flaming from the beak upward, into an agony of writhing twigs. Snatches of sky showed mercilessly remote and blue in the welter of smoke and fire. Flags of flame were flying from the highest branches, and a victory appeared inevitable.

But when the fire reached the natural break in the side of the barren hill and the strip that the men had prepared for this emergency, it did happen much as old Mr. Peabody had predicted. The fighters who had run out to meet the fire with their branches and flapping bags, and who were slapping at the first few lizards of fire that were wriggling out across the bare earth, hitting at these live animals because they must do something, however ludicrous, these men began to feel a change, of little cool puffs at first, in the shoulderblades. They scarcely noticed in the beginning. It was too gentle. But as the fighters hit at the fire, and their arms and chests began to get singed, the wind was gathering strength, till its cool southerly force made itself felt even on the borders of the fire. The wind and the fire swayed together amongst the hot rocks. The men even began to feel they were achieving something. They could laugh.

"I told yers," said old Mr. Peabody, to whom nobody listened now, because what had happened was something personal.

Each man breathed the wind that blew the fire. His miracle exalted him. His strength and stature returned, for the fire was cornered, if not by his efforts, at least under his eyes, so that he could tell about it forever after.

By late afternoon the fire appeared to have exhausted itself. After veering up the stony gully, holding the wind for a time, it was forced back on itself, into the country it had burned out, and died there of its own achievement. The wind swept over the blackened, smoky country, morbidly trying in its turn to rouse the few last tatters of flames, but there was nothing for these to live on. Once the enthusiasm was gone, it was difficult to think what it had all been about, in all those smoking miles, or to decide whether greater virtue springs from ashes.

Anyway, the firefighters stood once more in the round after the considerable experience of feeling the smoke pass through them. Now they wiped the sweat from their faces, and laughed, and told each other it had been nothing. Only Stan Parker, who was putting on his shirt, kept his head inside it as long as he could without exciting comment, so as to avoid being picked on to express opinions. And Mr. Peabody had shrunk inside the remains of himself, overcome by age, and the truth of his prophecy, and the knowledge that he was no longer needed.

The men were dawdling rather, enjoying their relief and

friendship, when three or four children came running along the ridge, as if looking for them. These children had come with a purpose, it seemed, the way they headed for the men, without relenting, their hair streaming straight in the wind, running and running, till they were very close, you could see the freckles on their faces and scabs on their knees, running to a standstill.

The children's ribs were struggling inside their clothes, but they did find breath, among them, to tell in pieces the story they had brought. There were fires, they said, had broken out to the west of Glastonbury, had broken out that morning, Billy Scrivener had seen one, then there were two, there were several fires, joining and burning, people were frightened that the wind, it was in the right direction, and several farms were burned out already between Durilgai and Bangalay.

The children came to an end, and you could hear their breath as they looked at the men and expected them to do something.

They would, of course. Only for the moment the flesh had shrunk again from their faces, and they would have liked to deny the existence of fire. But on the blackened hillside, exposed to the children's eyes, which obviously were in the habit of seeing truth, each man remembered his house, whether of brick, wood, iron, or bark, which until now he had considered solid, and all those objects he had accumulated and without which he would not have been himself. So that after rubbing a palmful of tobacco, or biting off a wad for the journey, they saddled their caked horses or guided them into the shafts, and soon had started home.

All that part of the country to the west of Durilgai, through which the road rose from Bangalay, seemed to be under fire. A perverse wind that had no apparent intention of dying down for the night was helping the fire, which was duller, less passionate and spasmodic, but more determined than that which had consumed The Islands. The men began to feel their limbs ache and their eyes smart as they rode towards their homes and the new fire, so that they were irritable with their wives when they came to the gates to tell them things they already knew. As they flung down from their horses and walked on legs that felt bowed, they were heavy with a responsibility they could not throw off. Cattle, excited by the fire and so much coming and going, threw up their heels and ran to look at the men. Old dogs that had stayed at home crawled through the fences and grinned, between hoarse

barks. Children showed off. So that the expectancy and welcome which surrounded the men made them nervous. They
would have liked to crawl in somewhere and take refuge in
sleep.

After they had messed about the meat their wives had
put before them, and scalded their mouths, and belched a
few times, the men began to debate where they should go
next, for old Mr. Peabody seemed to have exhausted his inspiration, or else had got the sulks. Anyway, he had disappeared. A few got on their horses and rode into Durilgai, to
be in the centre at least, if that centre was no more than the
signpost, the post office, and the store. But the postmistress
was glad. She was yellower in that last light. She came out
into the dust, folding her brown paper sleeves over each
other, and was able to give information received from people
passing through. She was important.

So the defenders gathered and loitered, and those who
lived farther out looked desperately for a neighbour, to
whom they might attach themselves. In the dissolving evening
there was no evidence of direction. Bits of burned stuff
floated and settled on the dead grass.

Then the fire itself gave a lead. It began to be obvious that
it was heading for those slopes which climbed to Glastonbury. The wind had livened it up. Down in the valleys jaunty
tongues of flame rose from the dark mouths, and licked. Patterns of gold emerged from the dark undergrowth as the
evening deepened. There was a chalky moon up, lopsided and
apologetic, in the white branches of the trees.

Now the people who would fight or watch the fire began to
converge on Glastonbury, and children even, as if it had been
fireworks. Some women came in their slippers, for comfort,
and because it was close. But the men, who had already
looked into the depths of the fire that day, and seen goodness
knows what, were hollow-eyed and serious. Although it was
not far, most of them stuck to their horses, because that way
they sat above the earth. The evening was full of the jingling
of bits, the chink of stirrups, and breathing, and talking. Mr.
Armstrong was glad to see all these people come across the
paddocks and up the roads, and was worrying already how
he could reward them if they quenched the fire.

A few lamps had been lit in the big house, for nobody
could really believe in disaster, somebody would find some
way out. But in spite of this hopeful belief most of the in-
mates had come outside. Moths or maids' caps flickered

amongst the trees, and there were frequent giggles from a full bosom as the soul of the kitchenmaid struggled to extricate itself from her uniform and meet its fate in the dark. The kitchenmaid had nothing to lose beyond a tin box, so that she went more than halfway to meet the fire. With blunt hands she touched for the first time the trunks of trees, and particularly those that exuded gum. Soon she was lost, except for her long, nickering giggle whenever she bumped into other bodies, and once when she took a header into a pricking bush and grasped it, gasping, gulping at the leaves, and embracing it dreadfully.

Down the gully, which in days of peace was the view from Glastonbury, the men had gone to fight the fire, or had trickled rather, in thin streams, hoping they might conceive a plan before they reached the bottom. Darkness had robbed most of them of any powers of thought, or even action. They were not exalted to the level at which miracles take place. They were drawn on mercilessly to the fire, that was running up the trees and falling from the elbows, to roll amongst the dead bracken in balls of the same protean fire, to shatter into sparks, to divide and join, but whatever activity engaged in, whatever form disguised in, always burning. In the midst of such unity of purpose the fighters did not stand a chance. Their leathery faces, emptied by exhaustion and filled with awe, showed it whenever the fire flung itself closer. Some of them had begun to thrash the flames with branches they had torn off, but like men who did not hold the key to their own mechanical limbs. Their lack of faith was in conflict with their actions.

Up at the house, however, everyone was comforted that the men had gone down, and many of them big and strong. Mabel Armstrong who had destroyed her diary that evening, remembered a ship's officer she had been in love with for the voyage. She half-enjoyed, half-trembled at the anarchy of the evening, the rank bodies gathered on the lawns of the house, as she went amongst the crowd of spectators and was jolly with them. Nobody was particularly grateful; the spectacle was staged as much for them as for the owners of the house. Some women had already made themselves at home in chairs. Children had fallen asleep in heaps on the crisp lawns, or else were staring at the house, as if they could have broken a piece off and sucked it. Mabel Armstrong, whose rather shallow blue eyes had grown deeper in the darkness, began to feel ashamed of a tapestry, on which huntsmen blew

183

interminable horns and ladies in farthingales stood holding fans, pomanders, and other agreeable things of no obvious justification. Mabel Armstrong turned her back on the lit window, to which the alternative was the fire. It seemed to be roaring now, and against it the black specks of men with charred branches at the ends of their arms merely looked ridiculous. Mabel Armstrong, who was by this time quite alone in the crowd, would have liked to kiss. She would have held her lover's head and drained him to the dregs. But at this period she was not in love, though half-engaged to the English title, not then present.

How far the fire had advanced could be seen by the size of the black men, who had grown big and distinct against the flame. Their grave actions could now be followed in detail, and frequent stillnesses wondered at.

The fact was, the fighters had become not only exhausted but fascinated by the fire. They stared into it, into the golden caverns that yawned and tunnelled through the framework of the bush. Some were by now so apathetic and hollow they could have entered, to add their bones. There were very few who did not succumb to the spell of the fire. They were swayed by it, instead of it by them.

So they withdrew always, and it looked as if their arms were opening to receive it, when Stan Parker, who was on the left wing, looked along his unprotected shoulder and shouted, "Hi! It's coming up from Barrel Creek!"

The spidery figures of caught men looked down to the left, and there it was certainly, a second hand of fire. As it advanced, and it must with that wind, you could see they would be held in a little pocket below Glastonbury, and ringed round, and roasted in those shapes in which their writhing consciousness had left them.

So everybody naturally began to scramble back, until they were standing on the lawns of the garden, in the smoke that they had brought with them, and the questions asked. Nobody could answer questions, nobody really wanted them answered, but to ask them was to assert themselves. The fire rolled along. Many of the spectators were now standing sideways, and would soon begin to trail back towards their own homes, to rescue the mattresses.

Up the gravel drive a few volunteers were dragging a reel on which was wound a hose. The hose was fastened to a tap of poor pressure, from which emerged first a few ribald noises and a frog, then a slack stream of water. But it was comforting, as the fire, down the hill, went from tree to tree, and won them over, and the reinforcement of fire from Barrel Creek climbed the gully, hand over hand, of flame and smoke.

It was by this time pretty murky at the big house, round which the butcher and his wife still hovered. Mrs. Armstrong had dropped her jewel case somewhere, but had forgotten, in remembering she had left unpaid several debts to God. She parted the smoke with diamond hands and whimpered at so much shapelessness.

"Perhaps the wind will turn," said a calm young woman who was standing there, "or a storm break, madam. It is that close, and thundery."

"It will never happen that way," sighed Mrs. Armstrong. "It is not intended to. I know now."

It was obvious she did. So that the younger woman looked at her closely in the smoky darkness.

"Only I would like to bring out a comfortable chair I had for sitting in," said the butcher's wife. "Louis This and Louis That is all very well. But a comfortable chair is something you cannot buy with money. I had one there I could spend whole hours in, it could have been my own body. But where," she said suddenly, rousing herself from her nostalgia, "where is Madeleine? I don't remember seeing her all night."

"Madeleine?" said Amy Parker, who was the young woman standing there.

"Yes," said Mrs. Armstrong. "A girl who is my son's fiancée. She has been staying with us for several weeks."

As if others did not know.

"Madeleine!" called Mrs. Armstrong, tottering on swollen ankles, and asking here and there.

But nobody could tell.

"No," said Mabel Armstrong. "I cannot remember where I saw her last. She had a headache. She was going into the garden, she said, I think, for air. But I saw her standing in her room, reading some letters. That could have been before. Or was it afterwards? I couldn't say exactly," Mabel Armstrong said.

She felt guilty, although there was no reason why she should. As the fire swept closer and the thick smoke filled her nose, choking and making it swollen, there were many sensations that she could not have explained, nor impulses controlled, if she had wanted to. She had torn her dress on something, and water from the hose that men were aiming at

185

the house had soaked her breast, till she was naked. There was no real reason to regret Madeleine now, alive or dead, or even walking downstairs, which was an act of hers that people used to watch, only starting to talk again when she had reached the bottom.

But Amy Parker, who had dreamed of Madeleine, and spoken to her often in the more inspired moments of sleep, knew that she was in the house. Lying on a bed with her eyes closed, or watching the fire from a window in a state of indecision, her long hair hanging down.

"Ahhhh!" they cried. "Did you see it? Nothing will turn it from the house. Those old pines were made to burn."

The pines had been waiting, dedicated to fire. The fire reared up out of the gully, and after executing several complicated figures pressed itself against the huddled pines. Such a passionate torch was lit by this embrace that every face was illuminated in its most secret visions, and Mabel Armstrong covered her breasts with her arms.

Then Mrs. Armstrong, who was gulping and reeling in the stench of resin, began to call for a sacrifice.

"I must find the girl," she said. "Tom will never believe. He bought the ring only the other Wednesday."

Of diamonds, Amy Parker saw, ringed with fire.

"Stan," she said, touching her husband, who had come up when the pines caught, to be beside her in the chaos, "Stan," she said, "you go into the house and fetch the lady out. You know, the one that rides along our road. With reddish hair."

Just then Stan Parker was not prepared to do everything his wife asked. In the presence of such brilliance he was a dull man, he knew, and passive. He was waiting, not to give, but to receive. His feet were rooted in a wonderment. His veins almost ran resin. So that his wife had to touch him again, which she did with authority, knowing his body off by heart. But the worshipping man would not have moved even then if he had not also been touched by fire. Is it, possibly, better to burn? He shook his clods of feet, on which he had never got very far. Curtains, blowing outward, were restrained only by their rings. The gentler jewels of lamplight, with which some windows were set, flickered nostalgically against the barbaric blaze of fire. All that he had never done, all that he had never seen, appeared to be contained in this house, and it was opening to him. Till his head began to reel with fiery splendours of its own, and he was prepared to accept the invitation, and follow the passages of the house, or fire, to any possible conclusion.

"I'll have a go," he said and began to walk across the tingling grass, while Mrs. Armstrong called directions that he did not listen to.

Amy Parker felt she was losing control of her husband, and had perhaps done something foolish, for which his bravery would be the only consolation.

Everyone was already very glad that Stan Parker was committed to something positive. A weight was lifted from them. They could now enjoy the spectacle without a conscience. So they sighed and settled themselves, and even those men who were training the feeble hose on the house, as a prelude to its other baptism, let the water spray more aimlessly as they watched Stan Parker, who was going in.

There was a stillness in the house, of which the fate was withheld as the fire wrestled with the willing pines. It was an uneasy stillness, though, with some slight movement in it. A cat had dragged a ball of wool down from the lap of a tapestry chair and was playing with it in a quiet room, drawing out the long grey threads of wool to tangle in. The air was woolly too, with a grey woolliness of first smoke. Threads of it were wound about a chandelier. One long yarn, unravelling from beneath a door, attracted the steely cat, who slashed at it and passed through.

Now that he was there, Stan Parker had no doubts that he should have come. Lamplight made him bigger than he was, from the one lamp lit and left beside a book. His shadow, as he walked, became involved with the dormant chandelier, which tinkled faintly. He smiled in the gloom of this musical cave in which he had found himself, and remembered a play of Hamlet that he had read in a book of his mother's, the teacher, and forgotten, till walking through a houseful of poetry, of which he only had to touch the doors and they would open.

He went from that room, brushing a tapestry that shivered at his shoulder, and rippled, and regained eternity. All things in the house were eternal on that night, if you could forget the fire. Time was becalmed in the passages, and especially at their ends, in the depths of which brooms stood, and possessive winter coats, and scarred garments in old leather. There was a horse that rocked at a touch, with something rattling in his belly. A woman's scratchy straw hat hung from a hook, still smelling of roses and sun. So close was that protective darkness, which the smoke had not yet entered, it was not possible to be afraid. You listened for voices the other side of the wall, of people who had not died.

So that he had to tear himself from the passages and return to a desperate situation. Flinging open a door, he was in a long room of quivering mirrors and impassive chairs. His cloddish boots were quite shameful here. Not that it mattered now. If time had clotted in the stuffy cupboards of the passages, here it flowed again. Outside the window of the room a cedar stood, of which the bark was visible to its last knot and crack, as fire rolled the darkness up, and red clouds of smoke drifted in the branches, hanging and drifting, and entered the room. So the man, like the tree, was set adrift, and his botched reflections tried to remember their mission. He had come, of course, to look for someone, who was sitting somewhere in one of the rooms of the house, in silk and diamonds. If she would not expect him to speak, he would carry her quickly down, holding her sideways like a stook of oats. But he was afraid of the introduction in words that she would wait for. And touch. He was already nervous of her soft skin.

Outside, the fire had gained a fresh foothold. Something crashed, a bough, even a whole tree, and whole sheets of shattering light shot into the room, where the man, who had, in fact, only been dreaming there an instant, was again all energy and intention, and trod back against a harp that nobody had ever played. The shocking melancholy of the harp at once propelled him out of the room, in search.

Now the dark was lighter in the bosom of the house through which Stan Parker ran, in which he found the staircase, stumbled, mounted, paying the banister out through his burning hand, feeling his swift shirt sail against his ribs as he mounted on a mission of some mystery into the pure air of upper rooms. Here too the glare had entered. Huge furniture loomed, bursting its mahogany almost in that light, and the common iron bed that the butcher had chosen to do his penance on was gilded with a sharp importance.

Approaching some climax, the breath of the saviour or sacrifice, it was not clear which, came quicker; he hurtled in his heavy boots, flinging behind him the leaves of doors, kicking the furniture even. Similar haste was evident in some of these rooms, from which the occupants had run, leaving drawers dangling, cupboards gaping, secrets revealed. The prettiness had shrivelled up. It had died in the vases, and at

188

the dressing tables, which were now without reflections. Someone had left her hair on the carpet, and there it lay, duller when confessed, waiting to shriek as the fire reached into the room and licked it up.

But not yet. Stan Parker, in a wind, broke his way to the heart of the house, it seemed, and saw that she was standing there, her back towards him, because the fire was of first importance.

Madeleine was wearing some kind of loose gown that shone in the firelight with many other lights. Above this sheath and onto it her hair flowed, for she had loosened it that afternoon in the heat, so that when she turned to him, because she could not very well avoid it, he had never seen anything glowing and flowing like this woman in her shining dress. He stood there feeling the lumps of possible words he might bring out, and almost hoping for some disaster to consume them both. If the ceiling would cave in.

But Madeleine said, "I was watching the fire. It has got into the schoolroom down there. There's an old papier-mâché globe that the girls used to learn the capitals from, that seemed to go up in a puff. It was horrible."

But it might not have been. The words welled out of her in slow waves, of disgust or pleasure, rippling in her throat before they were released, or it might have been the light that made her supper. Her mouth was rather thin, that remained open after its disclosure. Madeleine did not like her mouth and wished it could have been fuller, though as it was nobody considered it a blemish. Her appearance as a whole defied detail to detract from it.

Stan Parker did not listen to what she said, because this too was unnecessary. Bursts of sparks flew up and past the window, together with tufts of purplish smoke. These were a relief, for he did not need to look any longer at Madeleine. He could say, "They sent me to bring you out. And we oughtn't to waste any time. It'll be on the stairs if we're not sharp. Follow me, please, and I'll take you down."

"Oh," she said. "They sent you."

She came towards him over some old letters that she had been reading and let fall. She came, but was not yet obedient.

"Of course it is ridiculous of me to be here. And I don't quite know why I am. You must think I'm mad."

All this was what he most dreaded. But she was not yet close. So he shuffled his feet and longed to substitute action for any need to touch.

"There are moments of madness," she said, "in anyone."

Then she was beside him, and he saw that the skin round her eyes had only just dried, which made him all the more mistrustful, to be handed an unhappiness.

"I hope I shan't be a liability after all this," Madeleine said.

She was ready to follow him but doubtful that he could save her. All the practical and faithful acts he might perform she could receive only with irony. And in spite of herself it made her sad.

It made him wonder if, out of his own, different experience, he might produce a clue, but this possibility passed like a shadow through the doorway.

"If we go along here," he said to her gently, "I think we'll find a way down through the back."

"I should be showing you," she said. "This is the first time you've come to the house." Whether this was so or not, her arrogance claimed it. "If we go through the baize door we shall come"—not to the servants' staircase, she softened it—"to the back stairs."

She was gentler too, doing him this kindness, and flinging open with her own hands the stuffy door that divided the classes.

But the fire was there too. It was snapping at the common wood of the servants' stairs. It was writhing upward to make fresh finds. The woman and her rescuer stood there looking down, their eyeballs large and gilded. They were a bit deformed by this fresh development, and drew closer to each other for strength and encouragement.

"Looks like it will have to be the other way," Stan Parker said.

Because here only the dead ends were left. They turned back past the small boxes in which the maids had been contained, to change their caps, to wash their bodies, and to dream of what the tea leaves had told. The royalty and the saints they had stuck on the walls had lost their power. Only the paper remained, drained of its mysticism, and spotted by flies.

Madeleine moved quickly. She had taken him by the hand and was showing him things.

"When I was a child, quite small, in arms, I believe, I was in a fire," she said, in what had become a loud voice, willing to share with him everything her thought conceived. "I have just begun to remember. It is the light of fire on these high

190

white walls. I can remember a birdcage, but not what happened. Not yet. I think it was too horrible. And now I am in a second fire," she laughed, tossing the dark, reddish hair back from her shoulders, as fire is flung out. "It looks as though I am condemned. But you——" She paused.

They had come to the head of the front stairs, on which smoke still disguised the intentions of the fire.

"And I know nothing about you. You haven't been able to tell. You won't now."

"There isn't anything to tell," Stan Parker said.

She had turned sallow, almost ugly, he was close enough to see, and it made him comfortable. On one side of her nose, that was very beautiful and fragile, there was a little mark, like a pockmark. And suddenly he wished he could sink his face in her flesh, to smell it, that he could part her breasts and put his face between.

She saw this. They were burning together at the head of the smoking staircase. She had now to admit, without repugnance, that the sweat of his body was drugging her, and that she would have entered his eyes, if she could have, and not returned.

Instead they had begun the last stage of a journey, groping down the soft stairs, moving in the grey and yellow smoke, confusing hands with banisters and banisters with hands. Once their eyes swam together and retreated before admission could be made. Because that between-world of smoke and shapes was more tender.

Then they came out onto the half-landing and felt the first tongue of fire. The breath left them. Now Madeleine's beauty had shrunk right away, and any desire that Stan Parker might have had was shrivelled up. He was small and alone in his body, dragging the sallow woman.

"Don't," she said. "I can't."

She would have fallen down and burned, because it would have been easier.

Till he picked her up. It was not their flesh that touched but their final bones. Then they were writhing through the fire. They were not living. They had entered a phase of pain and contained consciousness. His limbs continued to make progress, outside himself. Carrying her. When her teeth fastened in his cheek it expressed their same agony.

"Look! He is there," they were crying. "They are there. He has her."

The people who were gathered round the burning house,

watching that sight of fire, and who had reached the climax of their emotions, began to scream out affectionate and encouraging words, or just to scream, as they saw Stan Parker stumble out, carrying the young woman. They were blackened, but how burned it was not yet possible to tell.

Stan Parker came on. He was holding the body of the woman curved and rigid in his arms. He came on. The cooler air had returned him to his senses, and with them a certain sheepishness for all that had happened.

"Is she dead then?" the people asked each other in quieter voices.

But she was not. She was holding her face in the hollow of his neck, from which she could not yet bring herself to look out. Till she began to rub her face against his neck, waking almost, and coughing, and crying.

Then young Tom Armstrong, who was her lover, and who had come from Sydney on hearing of the fires, ran out to take possession of her. He looked handsome and clean, with his white cuffs, and was smelling of bay rum.

"Madeleine," he called.

But she continued to cry and cough, and when she was put down, said, "Leave me now. I'm all right. Only it was a terrible shock."

Then she fell on her knees and began a kind of dry retching, holding her head, and falling even to all fours. Most people were silent, from surprise and pity, but one or two let out loud explosions of laughter.

"Madeleine, darling," said young Tom Armstrong, overcoming his disgust, and putting out his hand, in front of everyone.

"Please," she said. "Leave me. Not now."

And got to her feet and staggered farther into the darkness. Her hair had been burned off.

Is this Madeleine? Amy Parker asked without regret. Her novelette was finished.

At this point the holocaust at Glastonbury could have consumed even the spectators, only there were fresh developments. Much had been taking place above the smoke and the emotions. Other clouds, hanging above the furnace, began to spill their first heavy drops. A child held out his hand to collect these jewels, and laughed as the big rain fell into his hand. And doubted as the lightning split the bungling fire. And finally cried in terror as thunder crashed and the grey scene of ashes, in which they were all standing, shook.

Storm's broke all right, they laughed, drinking it, and steadying themselves against the thunder.

And the water poured down, proving that even fire is impotent. People wandered in the rain, themselves rivulets. It ran between the breasts of the women and filled the pockets of the men. They were saved. They smelled the ashes and knew. It was doubtful that there would be a tongue of fire left this side of Bangalay, or on the other, as far as Wullunya.

So the people began to creep back into the world they knew, and from which they had only been forced out by smoke at the openings.

Amy Parker, who had laid hands on her husband again, could have asked him many things.

"Let us go, Stan," she said. "Are the burns bad? We must dress them. Tell me," she said, "do they feel crook?"

"No," he said. They are not bad."

Wincing as he felt the rain sting the burns on his shoulders and arms. But these were the superficial wounds of the flesh. If he was trembling, it was because he had come out of the fire weak as a little child, and had seen his first faces by flashes of lightning. But he did not return to the woman with whom he had been standing at the head of the stairs. He put this away and did not think about it.

But his wife did, as they walked through the rain.

"She was frightened, poor thing," she said, looking at him through the darkness. "Such an experience."

What this experience was she would have liked to live, and could not. It was nagging at her. What could Stan have said to Madeleine when he found her in the burning house? She longed to take possession of her husband by honest lamplight, and hold his face in her hands, and look into him.

In the meantime the rain poured as they walked, bumping against each other in the darkness, and the flashes of lightning lit her face in which the thoughts turned, but his face was closed.

So she had to be content with the bravery of his act in rescuing the woman from the fire.

Chapter 13

THAT deluge which quenched the fire at Glastonbury was, in fact, the first of the late summer rains, so that the land was not long naked. The charred hills and the black scars of gullies were blurred again with green almost before the people could get out and have a look for what remained. Some people, of course, did not have the courage to return to a framework, and chose to live in other parts of the country, where they imagined the passions of fire could never rise. But those who did go back to their burned-out farms were on the whole glad. The green blur, which was increasing all the time, first in veins and pockets, then spilling over, made them feel young and hopeful. As they hammered and sawed, and rounded their cattle into rough yards of saplings, and untied bundles of fowls bunched together at the legs, they were full of resolutions. Because they had looked into the fire, and seen what you do see, they could rearrange their lives. So they felt.

Bub Quigley did not rearrange his. Bub's life was too plain. He rose and rubbed the sleep from his eyes. He chewed big hunks of bread and dripping. He watched tadpoles in a jar. He knew that part of the country from earth level and treetop. He was both bird and ant. So his life continued to form instinctively outside his deliberate boy's mind. So he felt the green blur grow, of grass and leaves, before anyone else, and was itching in his long palms, and rubbing his face against his shoulder, and could not rest, but had to go off on those long loping walks that other people, even children, would not have thought to go.

Bub was out through The Islands before anyone else. He tore the first fronds of hickory and put them in his mouth. He stroked his nose with the brown down of bracken crooks. And laughed. Sometimes, to vary things, he would run downhill. Then his limbs almost came apart from his body, and his long feet struck the earth like boards. But he laughed. And plumped on his knees to look down a rabbit's burrow, in which the tail of a snake had dawdled. His boy's eyes were bright in his older face, looking for things.

Bub visited all those human habitations which had been burned out and abandoned, to see what he could find. But there was not much. There were iron vessels and the skeletons of beds. In one place he lay on the framework of a bed and looked through the roof at a slice of cold moon that had got there early, till the distance to that moon began to make him feel afraid, and he threw down a tin in which he had put some beetles, that staggered out across the charred floor to freedom.

It was livelier at Armstrongs', where Bub went too. He watched the workmen hitting the bricks with their trowels, and drinking black tea. For Mr. Armstrong had ordered a new house, just like the old one, of which he had been proud, and no expense spared. So it was being done by degrees, when the men were not sitting in the sun, telling of horses. One man, who made jokes, stuck his hat on the statue of the naked woman and did a lewd dance, of renunciation and possession. Bub Quigley laughed and clapped his hands. He loved to see horseplay of any kind, though he would have been shy to act that way himself. All such charades—boys squelching in mud and throwing handfuls at each other's bottoms, young men wearing their girls' coy hats, especially if feathered, the grotesque man in the embrace of the stone woman—these ventured into dreams. It made the laughter tremble on Bub Quigley's wet mouth. His eyes were full.

Other people went up to look at the new house at Glastonbury, though the Armstrongs themselves never went. It was enough to leave it to architects and builders. They were rich enough to ignore the process. But they had also, perhaps, been burned a little by the fire, and were afraid to visit the scene while it was still a ruin. They continued to live in Sydney, or to visit people in the country, provided they were of the same financial status.

Although they were not seen at Durilgai, Mr. Armstrong did write to Stan Parker, enclosing a handsome reward for his act of bravery, and adding the thanks of the young lady who was to become his son's wife. At least he was *sure*, the butcher said, that the young lady would add her thanks to his, only at that moment she was visiting in another state, for health reasons.

Stan Parker could afford to be a bit disgusted at the cheque, but his wife, who had not experienced exaltation by fire, considered the many things they might buy. In time she persuaded him to share her material pleasure, and they even kept the cheque for a while, to look at and show.

Mrs. O'Dowd, who came to see Mrs. Parker about this time, and who had been prevented from viewing the fire on account of an attack of the shingles all round the waist, as big as sixpences, and in other places too, sat holding the glossy cheque as if the paper itself had some intrinsic power from which she might benefit by touch.

"There now," she said, holding the paper in a dainty loop, the better to see the writing on it. "Healthy is healthy, and wealthy is wealthy, but I would like to know which is the more worth havun, an never shall, most likely, with him down the road. But I am real glad, Mrs. Parker, you have struck lucky, both with your man an the bank balance. But I am glad it is you. An no sour grapes. It is simply this, that I would'uv rather it was Stan an not O'Dowd to rescue ladies from the flames, an them in their nighties, or whatever it was I am told she was dressed up in for the occasion."

"What do you mean, Mrs. O'Dowd?" Mrs. Parker asked.

"I shall not say nothun," said Mrs. O'Dowd, "for I was not present, an other people's eyes never see so well. Only I am sayun, my dear, glad I am it was not O'Dowd come dawdlun through the fire, with a lady round his neck."

"There was no dawdling, I assure you," said Mrs. Parker, who was put out. "There was a fire, see? And as for O'Dowd, he would not have been rescuing anyone, but in the pantry, making up to the bottles."

"That is nasty, from a friend," said Mrs. O'Dowd. "But I do not mean to part with bad blood. For that stuck-up thing too, ridun up the road as if you was the dust upon it, and no mention of the weather even, to pass the time. But they say," she said, and this perhaps was why she had come, "they say that it is all called off. I have had a letter from a lady of authority. If you must know, it was that Mrs. Frisby, who was helpun at Armstrongs' for some time, whose husband was at sea, poor thing, she was goin to give notice, but didn't, I forget why, and may yet, for that Mrs. Armstrong is a perfect cat. Well, Mrs. Frisby says in her letter to me that young Armstrong, not a bad young feller neither, all considered, young Armstrong is ropeable since this Madeleine has gave him the slip. Nothun has been said, mind you. But it is known by all who know. Things become hazy, like. An Madeleine has gone on a prolonged visit, not on account of her hair being singed off, but because she was without feelun, Mrs. Frisby says, an what little she had, got burned right up the night of the fire. So young Tom must lump it."

Then Mrs. O'Dowd drew in her chin, and arranged her lips on her gums, and went. Amy Parker was glad. It was her intention not to see her friend again, though she did, in fact, that Thursday, on account of a side of pork they decided to share.

But Mrs. Parker did not encourage Mrs. O'Dowd to elaborate the information she had given. This information Amy Parker took, and shut up, and picked over in cold pleasure, for Madeleine, since a burned thing, retching on all fours in the ash and grass, was exorcised. She no longer saw her riding coldly on her horse. This had belonged to a time of great foolishness. Now she stood above Madeleine, against the burning house, and could have practised some cruelty. If it had not been for her husband and the fire itself. Her husband's silence propelled her perpetually into those flames, whether in sleep or at the sink, till she was herself turning and dancing in them, guarding her hair, while she looked for some sign obscured by smoke.

Stan Parker, whose burns had soon healed, leaving only a few small scars, took the cheque to Bangalay one day, to bank. Stan had never loved that town, filled with hardware and the yellow jail. But by this time it was his town. He knew the Christian names of most of those men he saw. He knew their backs, and their habits, and who was to be found in which pub, with whom.

That day Stan Parker went in search of a man called Moriarty, from whom he had borrowed a few shillings a few weeks before, and who would be found, if true to form, at the Grand Railway Hotel. So Stan went there, into the sour cavern, which on that day for some reason was filled with a momentous air, along with the slops of beer, and the smoke, and the faces. They were discussing some great news which had just reached the flash town, and which threatened temporarily to intimidate it, making its yellow paint and iron lace a degree less flash.

Snatches of this news came to Stan Parker, gradually numbing him as he pressed through the pub, until finally he saw Moriarty and asked, "What's up?"

"Why, don't you know?" said Moriarty, who was several minutes better informed, and for that reason inclined to despise the ignorant. "Why," he said, "a war's broke out, over the other side."

"Yes," said Bob Fuller, "we're all orf to fight the Hun."

"No bloody fear," said some. "It's too far."

They downed their beer, to fill up quick, and feel better.

"What'll you do, Stan?" somebody asked.

"I don't know," he said.

Which was true. He felt slow.

In spite of moments of true knowledge that came to him, animating his mind and limbs with conviction, telling him of the presence of God, lighting his wife's face when he had forgotten its features, bringing closer and closer a trembling leaf till its veins and vastness were related to all things, from burning sun to his own burned hand—in spite of this, Stan Parker had remained slow with men. It was a kind of unrealized ambition to communicate with them. But so far he had not done this.

And now he said, "I don't know."

He didn't either, though he might soon. Problems resolve themselves, as day eases out of night.

"That's one way out," said Moriarty, scratching his short, sweaty hair.

He was a fencer by occupation, a good enough cove, but one that you would not remember for anything in particular. He lived alone in a bark humpy, and hung his bits of washing on the scrub. Some years before, his wife had left with a shearing contractor and not come back.

"Cripes, yes," laughed Bob Fuller, laughing as if he was shickered, which he was.

Then the girl who was rinsing the glasses, and whose white, shiny indoor skin was smelling of soap, said, "You will, Mr. Parker. You'll look lovely in a uniform. I'm all for big men. They're better-tempered. I was going with a little runt at Cobar, coupla years ago. It was like going with a barbed-wire fence. Look, I said, at last."

But what she said was not material.

In the bar of the Grand Railway Hotel at Bangalay, though many men were talking, few were listening to anyone but themselves. They had to tell all that they knew, all that they had done, for fear that silence might discover nothing.

So they talked, and some had come to blows, to show that they were brave, and one man could not keep his misery down, it rose up, and he vomited, and passed out. It was all very impermanent and inebriating in the Grand Railway Hotel the day the news came, with a train coughing at the platform outside, and the smell of the trains, which made men feel they were going somewhere, that they had been waiting to do so all their lives, and whether it was to be terrible and final, or an exhilarating muscular interlude to the tune of brass bands, would depend on the nature of each man.

Stan Parker slipped away after a bit and drove home. As he came down the last hill, and he saw the sticks of the willows by the dam, and the paths that his feet had worn round the house, the man supposed that he would go to war. He even wondered whom he would kill, and whether he could do so with the conviction that it needs. He saw the life fading from a face, from some Ted Moriarty. Or was it his own face? Sweating at the neck, he drove on, but now his own impermanence was in conflict with the permanence of all that scene, of bees and grass, murmuring and bending, murmuring and bending.

Still, he was a bit of a hero within the limits of flesh, and he jumped down when he got there, and made short work of the harness, and felt that he would enjoy praise with the pudding, though it would not be decent to show it.

When she was told, however, his wife Amy Parker went on cutting the bread.

"When will you go, Dad?" asked Ray, who was by now a big small boy, eager for events, so that he hung wide open on receiving the news, and his dinner would not go down. "And will you bring us things," he asked, "from the war?"

He wanted a sword, and a bullet taken out of a German.

"Eat your food," his mother said to him, and to her husband, "How do we know that this isn't something that they have made up to talk about in pubs?"

But it was not, Amy Parker knew, and for this reason she threw the plates together harder than usual, and swept the crumbs with more vehemence, and called the fowls and flung the hateful crumbs, after which she looked up and saw that the landscape had survived the first ghastly tremor and resumed its natural glaze. Only she was still trembling and foolish, and had to hide herself from her children, sitting on the crocheted quilt she had made not long after Ray was born, on the bed she shared with her husband. Outside, the sounds of afternoon were no different, but made her desperate to hear.

After Stan had enlisted and it was time for him to go into camp, they all waited for a cart which was to come, for O'Dowd was going too, and a boy was driving them as far as the village where they would meet other enlisted men.

So Parkers waited on the veranda. They were so stiff, it might have been Sunday after dinner.

"Will you have blankets in the camp, Dad?" Thelma asked.

None of this touched her personally, but there were moments when she took a vague interest. She was a neat child, who liked washing her hands. She would not miss her father much, although she would cry.

Just then Ray called that he could see the cart, and there they were too, Mrs. O'Dowd as well, who had come for comfort, she was quite swollen up.

Then it was time to gather up with quick nervousness the few things. Everybody's limbs were stiff and shy, except O'Dowd's. He had taken something for the journey and was singing a song of some patriotism.

"Listen to the man," said his wife through her blubbery big face, that could not hide itself and had given up. "It is we women should be singun, but we can't. Get on, you buggers, and let us at least have a good cry, an be done, it is near on milkun time."

The cart prepared to take her advice, while Stan Parker kissed his wife. How stiff she was in that white blouse. Some people called her a stout woman. She was not fat, but she was well covered. And now she stood firmly, waiting to be extricated from this enormous event, which she would be, if she waited long enough. It was not so very different from other departures, to the fires and the floods, the backs of men disappearing in a cart. It was only more formal. So she stood and held her breath in.

They were all standing. The children without their shoes, which they wore only for church and school. Mrs. O'Dowd, who was by this time quite reduced. And old Fritz, who had grown very old, but who still pottered, and mended his shirts in front of his hut of an evening. They stood and waved even after the cart had stopped taking notice; they waved because they had not yet thought what they should do next. The gentle, soothing rise and fall of hands filled their emptiness.

Stan Parker returned home once on embarkation leave. He was different then. His hair was shorn extra short, and there was a smell of khaki on him even when he went about the place and did his jobs in his ordinary clothes. Sometimes he would sit and wind his puttees, as if he had taken a liking to this ritual, and wind and bind, till he was shrouded. Then he was more than ever closed up.

"You must like all this soldiering," said his wife bitterly. "There is no telling what a man will like, even the one you know best."

"What else should I do?" said Stan Parker. "Run my head against a wall?"

"Do they give you enough to eat, Stan?" she asked.

Food, after all, was something you could touch and talk about. If a professor came, or a rich man, you could roast him a round of beef, and feel safe.

"Are you ever hungry?" she asked. "What do they give you?"

"Stew," he said.

He looked at a piece of brass he had just polished, that glittered in the lamplight as if it had been precious.

Because it was the last night, and because the mysticism of evasion and self-destruction in which he had been immersed ever since he wore a uniform had finally made her lonely, she asked, "Don't you ever feel lonely, living in tents with a lot of other chaps?"

"How can you feel lonely," he said brutally, "when your thoughts are so close to the thoughts of the next bloke they jog each other? Even on the lavatory."

Then he got up and went outside. It was a cold night of stars. He went up onto a little rise beyond the house, on which a couple of ironbarks stood, the stars shivering in their leaves and branches. Then he too was cold and shivering, his flesh was flapping; he leaned against one of the trees, but it was no support. He would have prayed, but he was afraid at that moment it might not have been answered, nor any prayer.

So he returned to his wife, who was about all the certainty he had, and she received him with conviction. They clung together as if they were drowning in darkness and would at least sink together. As they reached the depths they no longer cared.

After Stan had gone, together with the other enlisted men, in the public conveyance to Bangalay, with tears and cheers, and a bit of a flag that Mrs. Gage had run up over the post office, it took Amy Parker some time to realize all that had

201

happened. Mercifully she did not cry. She had the cows and the children. She ran at once to do whatever had to be done next, and she continued to do this, by clockwork, for many days, till the muscles cracked in her broad back and her detached face met her in mirrors at night with some surprise.

Mrs. O'Dowd, whose arches had fallen since the men left, said that it was up to the women. She was full of kindnesses for her neighbours, at any rate in the beginning, and would come when there were potatoes to be dug, or would hold the cow to the bull. Or everybody went to Quigleys' for the oranges, and made short work. There was Doll standing amongst her wooden cases that everyone had nailed, smiling, and counting, and smiling her sandy smile. Even Bub learned to do a few simple things, but mostly he was too obsessed by the great joke of war, neighing with laughter as he made the sound of guns. Once he announced that he was dead and it wasn't half bad.

Anyway, the women and children at Durilgai got along, and in the beginning shone with those virtues they were exhorted to discover in themselves.

Ray had begun to milk. He pulled the stiff teats in the sleepy darkness, his head lolling against the full belly of a cow.

"Gee, I'm tired, Mum," Ray said at night.

So that she kissed his full mouth with passion. Even Thelma's prim face above a sock, she looked at with less disappointment and more affection, and took the sock, and picked the stitches up. Amy Parker at this time performed many such acts, from above, as it were. Because her weakness had not yet been discovered, she was still strong.

About this time, though, people began to take notice of old Fritz, who had been with them all those years, tiring, and going, but always returning, to chop wood, and dress fowls, and scald the milk cans, and pull each thread of pale weed by the roots from round the sunflowers. Now people had begun to notice Fritz for the first time. He had shrunk a good deal since the war, as if he were sick or something. He would chop, and leave off, and go inside. He no longer sat outside his door, but in his hut, neither at the window, but sideways, just sitting, the knots of his bones and the last vestiges of old flesh.

Perhaps Fritz will die, Amy Parker began to fear with a first foreboding.

But Fritz would not be allowed to die, not before he had been wrung. His downcast eyes knew this.

People coming into the yard tried to get a look at Parkers' Fritz. They would have prised his face open and picked his thoughts over, if they had been hardier. But as they were not, they looked and pretended innocence, or looked with slow candour and frowned.

Then Amy Parker, returning from the butter factory at Orwell, to which they had begun to take their cream, met Ossie Peabody on his matted horse. As it was decent to speak about the weather, Ossie stopped. He was a sharp man, with excuses. He had not enlisted because his parents, of course, were old and of uncertain health, and his wife was mostly sick since that trouble. He was ready to give such reasons, and many others, if people had asked him why he had not gone, but they did not, because they had forgotten Ossie Peabody. He was not memorable. His eyes had frosted over since those transparent days when they had all driven down to Wullunya to the flood.

"That old Hun of yours, Amy," said Ossie Peabody when he had come to the point, "surprised at you keeping him on, these days, a German. I only say, because people are wonderin, and Stan not here."

So that Amy Parker was amazed at this thought, and her eyes proclaimed such innocence that Ossie Peabody was pleased. He had violated something.

"I would not send away my father, if I had one," Amy Parker said. "I do not understand these things. But Fritz is good."

"It's nothin fer me to decide, of course," Ossie Peabody said and smiled.

"It is not for any of us," said Amy Parker, urging on her horse. "It is for Fritz."

But now she was uncertain of her life.

"Women," said Mrs. O'Dowd, who liked to propose an abstraction in her steamier moments, especially after a cup of tea, "women are the half without the men. It is the men that make the round figure, even such men as we may have, some of us, they know how much of what we know to be right, is right. It is not enough to know that something is right if you cannot add an subtract an get the final answer. Do you see what I mean, Mrs. Parker dear?"

But Mrs. Parker was not sure.

"It is that old man that ought to go, Amy, an our boys

with the bayonets in their guts, and innocent little children that have died with such dirty Germans, I would spit on them willingly, any day, Sunday too."

"No!" Amy Parker cried.

But it was decided.

It was a day of rain. The old man, his good face now quite destroyed, had gone across the yard to chop a few sticks, because doing this, if he could for a little, he would feel less numb. And in the drizzle children stood around, screaming, and pushing, and telling secrets, and killing time. The children had become brutish with boredom and rain. They would have liked to break something. But they were not brave enough to smash glass, or take the axe and start gashing the house, so instead they began to imitate their parents, and nudged, and told each other about Parkers' German, and laughed, and whispered.

Ray and Thelma hung around, apart from the other children, and kicked the mud with their toes, and felt ashamed. He was a good old man, whom they had loved, they knew, but they resented the indignity he had imposed upon them. In their hot shame they began to hate him worse than anyone.

Then boys began to shout and sing:

"Fritz the German,
Fritz the Hun,
Wait till you see him
On the run. . . ."

How they laughed then.

Somebody began to throw little pats of red mud that flattened on the old man's patched back.

"We shan't give him
Even a chance,"

sang Jackie Holloway, who was good at rhymes.

"Not even to button
Up his pants.
We'll put a cracker
Under his tail,
To blow him right
To the doors of jail."

204

How the girls in their jumpers shrieked, and the scabby-kneed, knobbly boys. Then Eileen Britt, who had got the hiccups, she had laughed that much, stooped and picked up a big, daring handful of mud, and shrieked, and flung it smack in the middle of the old man's turned back as he was gathering a few sticks of kindling at the woodshed.

Then he turned. He was quite white and papery. He did not protest. He was bled too weak. He began to walk towards his shack, in his shambling way that was now so ridiculous and hateful.

Some children had qualms, or were perhaps afraid when faced with the front of him, and were silent. But several continued to scream and chant.

It was altogether hateful, and Ray Parker, who was panting, his mouth open with excitement or disgust, wished that it had not happened, or that worse would. He was shining with sweat and exaltation as he picked up the stone that laid Fritz's lip open. They heard the stone strike his teeth. Then the blood began to run, to trickle down his clean chin. Ray was horrified, but he had freed himself. Now he could hate the old German that he had loved, and stand amongst the other children without doubts.

The old man continued to walk across the yard and into his shack, and the children melted away into silence and rain, and wondered if they should forget what had happened. They were torn between respect for the old man's face and the stirring and patriotic nature of Ray's act, in which they had all participated.

When Amy Parker went outside to see what the row was, though by then, of course, all was rain and silence, she found the old German sitting on the chaff bags that covered his bed.

"Why, Fritz," she said, "whatever is it? Are you hurt?"

"No," he said, "I am not hurt no more. But I must go from here," he said. "It is not good for us that I should stay now."

"No," she said, "you mustn't go."

She stood twisting her ring, and helpless, like a little girl in a wedding ring, touching it for an inspiration of maturity that did not come.

"Yes," he sighed. "I will go."

She wondered what she could say to comfort them, but knew that there was nothing in that wooden room.

So next day Amy Parker drove Fritz the German to Bangalay. He was wearing his black suit, which was decent if rather thin, and he had a case with a strap around it, and a pollard bag, into which was stuffed a variety of soft or awkward things. The woman drove, but the road was the active element on that journey; they would simply remain on it until it had exhausted itself, and the road did momentarily deaden pain by its sheer monotony and length.

When, however, they had reached the edge of the town, and the scattered tins, and the tethered goats, the woman began to feel desperate. Because it was plain now that everything must come to an end.

"Where do you want me to take you, Fritz?" she asked, nervously jerking her whip.

"Anywhere," said the old man. "I can get down. It is all the same."

"But there must be somewhere," she said, shepherding with care her lost voice.

The old man did not answer. He sat fingering a kind of medal on his tarnished watch chain, touching an inscription that for a long time now had been unreadable. His face too was almost beyond interpretation, and was entering a state of intense and original purity, of air.

"This will do," said the old man, his hand on the rail.

By this time they had driven fairly deep into the town and had become involved in its self-importance. They were in the vicinity of the market. Ducks were being brought by scaly, yellow women. There was a bellowing of hopeless calves. A dray lurched, with its dense heads of cabbages piled in a blunt pyramid.

"I thank you," said the old man to the woman, who did not dare speak.

Then she saw him standing on the ground with his possessions, and she reached down and seized his hand.

"Ah, Fritz," she cried, and the desperate sounds of a bird with the knife at its throat came out of her mouth.

"Good-bye, Mrs. Stan," said Fritz, taking away his hand, because there was nothing else he could do.

Then he went up some side street that she did not know, and she did not see him again.

So she hung there crying for the lost world. Now that the structure of her life was shaken, full misery smote her, as it had not when she kissed her husband good-bye, whom she loved nevertheless, in tenderness of spirit and with sensuality of body, she loved and would. But she loved the old German for that contentment of first light, with the strong clank of stubborn buckets, for the drooling hours of midday, when leaves hung and hens drowsed in the dust, for the hours of evening, of which the face was a wilting sunflower. And these were lost.

So she hung crying, lopsided and ludicrous on the seat of the buggy, with her hair coming down, and the little greenish flies almost permanent on her dark back. People passing looked at her and wondered why she was taking on. There was something almost obscene about a strong, healthy woman blubbering in the sunlight in that public place.

A boy carrying a halter, and walking on assured feet, did snigger and ask, "What's up, missus?"

But as she continued to cry he was afraid, realizing that this was not a toothache but some pain that he had not experienced. So he went on and did not look back.

And in time the woman righted herself, and put up her hair, and blew her nose, and turned the horse, because she must resume omnipotence in her house.

The stones were cruel that strewed the road to Durilgai.

At one point she met Bub Quigley and took him up. He was very pleased.

"Well, I am alone now, Bub," Amy Parker said.

"Ah," he said, looking at her in some surprise, as if he had not expected anything else.

But he could not see her face; she was keeping it away from him and was looking out over the country, or into herself.

"Fritz has gone," her hunched shoulders said.

"Who will chop the wood?" asked Bub.

"Oh, we shall all have a chop," she said.

"I don't like chopping wood," said Bub. "I'd rather my sister did. Then I am free."

This ageless man was singularly free, Amy Parker realized. That was his one blessing from God. For a moment the woman thought that she would pray, but she had lost her faith, or else had put her trust in the strength and goodness of her husband.

"Look," said Bub, pointing vaguely everywhere. "It is green again now. It has never been so green as after them fires. There are ferns in the gullies," he said. "Sometimes I lay down in them and sleep a bit, and my sister goes crook because I don't come, but I come in time, of course. You can't stay there always, you get hungry."

It was true, she realized, she was herself quite hollow.

"There's some young foxes I know," said Bub, "in a hollow log. I have a nest of mopawks."

She was wide open, on a gaping emptiness, but he was filling her with hills and valleys, and down of birds, and balm of fern.

After a bit he said, "Let me down, please. I'm going down to them foxes. Here's the place."

When she had let him down he began to run down the slope, his boards of feet slapping the ground, his wild arms steadying himself on the air.

Then Amy Parker continued on her way, through that fresh and innocent landscape of her own solitude and sadness. At the end of the road her children were waiting for her to affect that strength which they expected, and cows did not doubt, and fowls would fling themselves towards her, sensing that her hand would dispense from on high.

It seemed that her life was planned, and she was glad. She was glad of her house, even if it looked frailer in that drawn light of afternoon, standing amongst the raggedy rosebushes, and the oleanders that she did not care for, they were too stiff.

PART III

PART III

Chapter 14

W HEN the years of mud and metal were over, Stan
Parker would seldom talk about them. He would not
be coaxed into telling the interminable boys' adventure stories, as some men will after wars, for chaos was not his opportunity. At the height of violence, when even the seasons
had been destroyed, his functions appeared to have gone
from him, who had been happiest looking at the sky for signs
of nature, listening to oats fall, picking up a wet calf that had
just dropped from the womb, and showing it that its legs
worked.

Things were made to work. But the contrary process of
destruction was far more convincing, once perfected. So his
skull saw, as the green lights drifted in the night. The lovely
fireworks showed him the hand that had just fallen at his
feet, thrown there. The fingers of the lost hand were curled
in its last act. It lay there like a tendril that had been torn off
some vine, and dropped when the motive, if ever there was
one, had been forgotten. So the living skull of the green sol-
dier looked at the suppliant hand. He was waiting in the
darkness for an order. Which did not come. But would, he
hoped. He was standing there. He was the last man on earth,
to whom the hand had begun to beckon. Then the order
came through the greeny, drifting darkness, and his sweat ran
again. He kicked aside the soft hand-thing. What else could
he do?

Often afterwards, in the silence of mud and exhaustion, or
when the bombardment opened the flesh and laid out the
nerves in grey skeins, he would wonder about the hand, how
it had taken hold of things, whether it had shaken after drink
or in touching women, and to whom it had written home.
Once in a village he had seen the arthritic hand of an old
priest make the sign of blessing on the air. He looked at it

with longing, for this hand too seemed irrevocably lost. In the broken villages he would have talked to someone, if it had been possible. But it was not, he lay in a ditch, and held the hot hands of a woman he had not seen for darkness, and they offered each other their longings in the desperate convulsions of such love, and went away separately afterwards, arranging their clothes, and wiping their confessions from their mouths. As he went, the man thought with increased longing of a God that reached down, supposedly, and lifted up. But he could not pray now. His stock of prayers, even his chunks of improvisation, no longer fitted circumstance.

He wrote home, though. Stan Parker sucked his pen until his cheeks grew hollow, thinking of all those things he would not write, but knew. He wrote:

Dear Ame,
    ... I could tell you a thing or two if only I could write it, but then we have never been ones for talk, anyway. I have not, you have done the talking, you have been the tongue of both of us, and how I would like to hear that tongue telling what has happened since dinner time—even if it was disastrous, like the roof blowed off, we could always put it on again. I could always do most things with my two hands. That is the terrible part of all this. It is taken out of my hands. I am weak, Amy . . . .

My dearest Amy,
    You did not tell me if Cherry had calved yet, only that Dorcas and Ally had dropped theirs, that will be nice to have two such heifers, you say they are good. Now when Cherry is ready next I want her put to Regan's bull, the one that he got from Bega, and that you say is extra special, so that perhaps we shall have a little heifer jumping and butting by the time I open the gate, and we shall call her Peace, eh?
    I do not feel so bad since I knew that I would come through all this, that I did not tell you, I think. It was in the entrance to the dugout. It was particular bad that night. Then I could smell the grass, like it was after a storm, and the smell of wet lucerne, I could have sworn there was sunlight up above, but it is night and winter here. And I was that happy and sure, I was groggy at the knees with so much happiness. I would not be swallowed down into the mud. I would go home. Then they

said, what was I doing there. I looked as if I was drunk, and nothing to drink. I said I did feel queer, and went and laid down, and had a dream that you was reading the paper beside the quince tree, I could see the big grey quinces, with the fluff on them, not yet ripe, and you looked up.

Tell Thel I got the socks, and no knots. I thank her, and for the photograph with plaits. She looks neat. And Ray, I have the helmet and the hand grenade.

You have made the dress out of the old blue, Amy, and I am glad. I am glad you tell me all these things, because I can see you then. I can see you sitting in the rooms, and walking down the path. I can see the rosemary bushes. We must bear up, Ame, and soon it will be over. . . .

He held his head on one side, and wrote slowly, but surely, once he began, in the respectable hand that he had learned from his mother, who had been a teacher. He was a bit excited at himself, writing these letters, of which the words became transformed—they were grass, and slow cows, and the bits of paraphernalia, axes and hammers and wire and things, that lay around a place, and that he liked to remember. The words became, too, contained in their bluntness, experience of death, and exaltation, and love.

Stan Parker wrote:

My dear Ame,

I have thought it over and it is best for you to spell the Creek paddock after summer, unless it rains real hard this autumn, and divide the herd between the Sally wattle and the Square paddock. I think this is best. And get the oats in if you can, with the help of some man, perhaps that old Skinner with the gammy leg would come from Wullunya if you make it worth his while.

If Ray has blunted the good axe chopping into nails and stones, he must learn to sharpen it. If anything should happen to that axe, I don't know what I would do.

Tom Archer is gone, and Jack Sullivan. They were good men. Tom knew he had it coming for some time, and was changed. Jack Sullivan was a noisy sort of coot, but you could not help liking Jack. He could do a trick

213

with a penny, it was that quick you could not see it, and another with an egg, if he had one, that brought the house down. Well, they are gone.

I sat awhile in a church in one of the villages here last week. It was what remained of a church. It was all sky. There were the frames of the windows, but the glass had fallen. But people come there. There was a priest poking about as if the roof was on. There was a wind blowing, and rain, and dogs coming in. I could have sat there forever doing nothing. I could listen and watch and think of home. Good God, Amy, it is a long time, but there is a lot that has been longer. There was an old woman in that church, skin and bone, praying as if she had just begun to pray. She could have told a thing or two. But we cannot speak, we can only look at each other.

Some of the coves reckon it will soon be over. They heard something. Mick O'Dowd says he can only hear the guns, and will believe when he is deaf from silence. Tell his missus that Mick is good, and will write when he has got his muscle up. . . .

He did in time:

Dear Mother,
I am all right. You shod see the girls (ha! ha!) you shod see the beer here, it is like piss.
Hopun this leaves me as it finds you, your ever lovun hossbarnd

M. O'DOWD

214

Chapter 15

DURILGAI did not suffer from the war. In some houses, certainly, women ached for their husbands, and some women who were afraid of the silence or interested in variety went out and took other men, sleeping with these with varying degrees of guilt or appetite, and some women were crushed as if they had been empty eggshells when news came that their men had been killed, and some ate the potatoes they sowed, and would have gone hungry but for these and the milk they pulled out of some old horny cow. But Durilgai was not touched, by and large, because it was a long way away, and besides, in those parts the earth predominated over the human being. The grass still grew and bent in the wind. The hot wind still blew from the west, and the cold from the south, and the languid, moist breezes came in from the east, from the sea. Sometimes in stormy weather gulls came, even from that distance, and glided and dipped above the black wattles, crying with their cold, starving voices.

Once Ray Parker shot a gull, and took it quickly, and hid it, because his mother would have been annoyed. He buried it in the gully, after he ripped it open, to see. He would have liked to do something memorable and heroic, but as he could not think of anything great enough, and yet within his reach, he had shot at the gull on that afternoon. For some time after, he had the fishy smell of the bird on his hands, and was half-pleased.

"Shall I go out to work when Dad comes home?" the boy asked.

"I expect so," said the mother. "You can't hang around forever. What do you want to do?"

"I don't know," he said sullenly.

He slashed at the air with his knife. Because he did not know, he wandered in the paddocks, and cut his name into green trees, and made stones skim on water, and put his hand into the secret depths of nests and stole the jewels of eggs.

He did not want these much. He wanted the souvenirs of dead Germans that his father would bring. He wanted to wear the steel helmet, and would charge through the dusk to challenge strangers.

"Ray," called his mother, because it was time she asserted herself, and stood there wiping her hands on her apron to do so, "can't you stop mooning about and do something useful, and chop a bit of wood?"

He did so, silently.

When he brought her the armful of wood, with his face closed above it, he reminded her of her husband, whose letters she had tied with a piece of string and stuck behind the tea canister. She tried sometimes to remember her husband in such minute detail that she would make him stand before her. But she could not. Outside her love for him, which was real and permeating, he was by this time vague. Most often she remembered him lifting his leg over the side of the cart, getting in to sit beside O'Dowd, when they were leaving for the war. His back was turned to her.

"Come here," she said when the boy had let the wood fall in the box beside the stove.

"What is it?" he asked suspiciously.

"Give me a kiss," she said laughingly, as if it had been a red apple.

"Oh, why?" whined the lumpish boy.

He dragged his cold cheek away from her face, and bit his lip, and looked hot.

"What good is it?" he said.

"No," she said, "I suppose it is not much *good*."

And she began to sort some clothes she had washed, and to sprinkle them with water, and to roll them into bundles.

She too went into the paddocks. She went in the evening when the work was done. There were times when she could feel so peaceful that she awoke from her peace with a start of guilt, to urge herself on to some fresh restlessness, in this way to do homage to her absent husband. From the peace of her finally achieved self-sufficiency, of farm and children, he was absent. But in the restlessness of her footsteps over grass, in the restlessness of wind in tumbled grass, in the crying of gulls, in the uncompromising line of a black wire fence, he was always present. It was right that she should torment herself, though sometimes it was possible that even these torments were for her own pleasure. Years of sorrowing will bring a voluptuousness of sorrow.

When the children were at school she would go down to the edge of the road, about midday, and stand in the steady but not oppressive sunlight of those early autumn days, waiting to see who would pass. People would talk to the woman by the road, and tell her about their relations, their ailments, their animals, and about their dead. They would take the woman into their confidence, because her face was asking for it. Sometimes they would even tell her thoughts they had just had, that they would not have told their families, but they would never see this woman again. And the woman thought about all she had been told, which filled what would have been an emptiness. She entered into the strangers' lives, as she strolled in the garden afterwards, picking off the dead heads of flowers. She entered into their lives, forming relationships of sympathy, and even passion, which nobody would ever have surprised her into admitting. So that in this way her husband's absence became reduced to a dull unhappiness. It was there. But sometimes she did not stop to think of the cause. Her surroundings, of sunlight and dappled bark, and her relationships with the departed strangers, were too vivid, far more vivid, indeed, than the strangers themselves, or the natural landscape.

One day as she stood by the road, longing for events or faces, shading her eyes to bring them into her vision, a young Digger passed along with his hat on one side. As he came along the road he hung his head at first. He was brassy, but not enough, not in these surroundings, which were foreign to him. So he came on, and spat because he was being stared at, and turned his face, so that he was looking at the paddock opposite. For all his strength and brassiness, caught like this he was like a girl.

The woman who was watching him, and not, saw that now he would probably pass without recognizing her right to conversation. She blushed and nearly cried for her concealed weakness, because she would have hung over the fence and said, I am waiting for you to tell me things, of war, and death, and love.

But the young man was passing on. He looked at his red boots, that the road had made white. His eyes denied her presence. Then suddenly he turned to her, as if only at that moment he had thought to do so, and tossed his head with its cocky hat, and still not looking at her, or only sort of, through his transparent eyelids, said, "How are we doin? Know anyone down this way name of Horner?"

"Horner?" she repeated, starting, as if she had only that moment seen this young, strange man, with the leather strap of his hat caught on his lower lip, it appeared, now that he was full on.

"Why, no," she said, collecting herself, and putting back a strand of stray hair behind her left ear. "I have not heard of anyone of the name of Horner. Not down this road. But it is a long road, and down that end where you are going it is not all closely settled."

"Ah," he said, "doesn't sound too good."

He came to her, to the side of the road, where she was standing by her fence, where the garden became raggedy grass; it was too hard and dry there for anything else to grow.

"They're relatives of Mum's," he said, tossing a coin. "Jack's got a few acres. He's crook in the chest. Mum wanted me to come down here and see em. That's why I come. I don't go much on Horners. Jack sits around and spits. It turns you up to watch sick people like that. They put a bucket in the kitchen for him to spit inter. They say one of his lungs is gone. He was a shearer. From Bombala."

"Oh," she said.

On these occasions she did not give, in words; she received. But people seemed to take to her. They had confidence in the eyes and the brown skin of the quiet woman. So the young Digger was prepared to grow in the shadow of her quietness. There was nothing that he would not reveal of his own shadowlessness.

"I only come back a few weeks ago," he said. "They took a piece out of me leg, the bloody bastards. Look," he said, pulling up a leg of his pants. "That was near Dickiebush. They grafted on a lump of skin."

"It must have hurt," she said, looking at the wound, neither with disgust nor emotional sympathy, almost as if she were examining the limb of an unusual insect that had been crushed or torn off.

Yet she was not cold. And the Digger knew this. Her distance was part of the dream of dust and sunlight that they were sharing in the long grass at the side of the road.

"Cripes, it hurt all right," said the young Digger. "But I'll go back and have another go at the bastards. If they'll let me. Or in the next. I like a good fight," he said.

218

"My husband is over the other side," she told him, in her detached and at the same time warm, lingering voice.

"What's his mob?" asked the young man.

She told him the figures and letters, which added to the grave mystery of her conversation.

"He was wounded once. They took some shrapnel or something from him. He has it for us in a box. He won a medal," she said.

"Ah," said the Digger, looking inwards. "There are all kinds of medals."

He was more interested in his own, still unmutilated ego, and the muscles of his hard body.

"All kinds," he said.

"But I am sure this is a good kind to have," said the flushed wife of the man who had won it.

"It's funny the way things happen," said the Digger, unclasping his collar and leaning on the fence, so that she looked inevitably at the Adam's apple in his taut throat. "I got sort of engaged to a girl over there. She was a Belgium. She wasn't a bad-lookin sort of girl. They're different there, or course. Her old man had a charcootery business—that's kind of small goods, see, sausages and things."

The weight of his body drew the fence down in the lovely sunlight. He was hanging on the wire, swinging slowly to his confession, and she waited for his words with fixed eyes. She looked at his bony temples and realized she was older.

"And didn't you stay engaged to the charcootery girl?" she asked.

"No," he said.

"Why?"

"I dunno. It got taken out of me hands, like," he said simply.

He had stopped swinging. For an instant the man and the woman were intensely conscious of some same fear that they shared. Now the woman also stood exposed to the possibility that all things might be taken out of her hands.

"Getting sent back an all that," said the Digger, more to himself. "I was gonna write in the hospital. I got the paper out. I didn't write. I won't now," he said. "I can't."

The woman chafed the skin of her arms.

"I got a picture I'll show you," he said. "That's her. It's not took too good. But you can see. Of course, the French and the Belgiums are different, but you can see she's a decent sort of girl."

The woman, standing now in a chalky world of long perspectives, mercilessly exposed in the light of all human experience, examined the face of the charcootery bride. It was hopeful. With the confidence of love, it attempted to reveal any depths it had. The face had not yet received the fist.

"What was her name?" Amy Parker asked.

"Whyvonne," said the Digger readily. "I could never get the rest."

Amy Parker was very calm, though she shuddered for all crushed or mutilated birds. She continued to stare at the brownish photograph that the Digger held in his callused fingers, and at the man's thick wrist with its hairs of dominant bronze.

"One side of the shop," the Digger was saying, "they had a coupla little marble tables, where you could sit an have a drink. I used to go in. They have different drinks over there, all colours, an a kick in the pants. She was standin there. The boys had drawn on the tables, but she did not seem to notice these things. She came an sat down after a bit. She often sat with me, and it began to be taken for granted. It wasn't exactly, I wouldn't say, any fault of mine."

But his eyes were less positive than his mouth. And Amy Parker, staring at the charcootery bride or the man's wrist, could not help him. She asked for help herself. All that she had taken for granted trembled. Her miserable body waited for some touch of assurance.

"You got a nice place here," he said, putting the picture in his pocket and buttoning it up, because the present is more important.

"It is nothing much," she said, withdrawing a little into the shadow of the dahlias. "We made it. I have lived here most of my life."

She could see the clear animal eyes of the inoffensive young man try preceptibly for a moment to look inside that life that she would not open for him.

"Go on," he said, leaning more heavily on the fence and looking at the mysterious greenish flesh of her face, that the dahlias made, the big, heavy cushions of magenta dahlias rubbing and crowding her into their green gloom.

She could not breathe in the horrible stuffiness of fleshy green, so that she came out, and began to look up the road, and murmur about her children.

"You got kids?" he pondered between his lips.

When the shade was dragged away from her face he realized again that she was one of those women whom he passed in the street, or who sat opposite him in trams, with parcels, and whom he did not think about. They had reached an age of uniformity.

"I have two," she said lightly. "They are growing bigger every day. Sometimes they are quite useful."

The young man, she realized, would soon go. She was a strong figure in her white starched apron, except that, as she watched him with the detachment of a stranger releasing a stranger from further obligation of confidence, she saw the callousness of her son's eyes, and something of his full mouth that she had frequently been driven to devour.

"I gotta be goin'," said the Digger. "Find those relatives of me mother's."

"Good luck," she said in a clear voice, but it was obvious she was not used to those words.

When he had gone she went into the room in which her husband, ironic at being photographed, gave her an uneasy, proxy smile. She lay on the bed then, in her starched apron, and rubbed her arms against the crocheted quilt, and sank her neck in the pillow. Great unhappiness oppressed the wooden room, in which flies vibrated, and a big grey moth pressed itself like dead against a wall. Till she began to cry, whether it was for the charcootery bride, or her husband, or the aching afternoon. But that way she was emptied.

And when her children came in, and hovered, and began to ask what was the matter, she sat up, crumpled, and said that she had had a headache. They were convinced, and she saw then that the boy's eyes were without that callousness which she had suspected, they were the eyes of her husband, so that she was filled with renewed gentleness and hope.

In time Stan Parker did come home. Through some postal delay he was unannounced, and walked down the road carrying his pack and the helmet he had brought for the boy, and came in about that same time of day the young Digger had passed, early afternoon, and said, "Well, I got here, Amy, at last."

Because it was unexpected, and she had been engaged on one or two jobs of urgency and importance, his wife gave him quite a small kiss, which was different from what she had imagined and rehearsed, and began almost at once to tell him about a hinge that had come loose on a door, and by which she had become obsessed in her unseccessful efforts to screw it tight.

"All right," he said. "We'll see about it. But later. There's plenty of time now. For everything."

There was, it seemed, on that afternoon. The house stood open. Great carpets of golden light were spread on the floors. Bees passed through the windows and out the other side of the peaceful house, in which the man and woman had sat and begun to look at each other.

"You'll have to tell me all about it," she said shyly as he sat drinking the tea she had poured, and making noises because it was still too hot.

He pulled his mouth down in defence. "Give us a chance," he said.

But she did not intend to hold him to it.

She was not, in fact, interested. She believed only in the life they had lived together, and would now begin to live again, when she had got used to the different man, her husband, read the the new lines in his face, and generally reassured herself by touch. Only at the moment his eyes were coming between them.

"All those letters we wrote," he said, "we shall be rid of all that. It's a waste of time. But what can you do?"

"I have them," she said, picking at the cloth. "I like them."

"It doesn't do to keep old letters," he said. "It's morbid. You start reading back, and forget that you have moved on. Mother was a great one for that. She had a drawerful of old letters. They had changed colour."

Because he had given this brown-skinned, opaque woman, who was also his wife, bits of himself that were secret, laying himself open in the night, he was now uneasy. Because he had revealed himself, he found her a stranger. She put up walls round her knowledge, and sat smiling at the tablecloth, and you could not tell. Her hair had begun to fade, but her face was still bright, whether beautiful or irritating he could not at that moment decide.

Then he stirred his tea again, and from the round red eddies of tea contentment began to radiate. She sat opposite him, smelling of scones and permanence. There would be every opportunity to learn her off by heart.

"How are the kids?" he asked, to break the silence.

"They're good," she said. "They're leggy now. Thelma puts her hair up sometimes for fun. Then she looks real grown-up. But she's too sorry for herself. She's got that asthma. Oh, she'll be all right, I suppose. She'll have to go from here. And Ray. They'll both go. Ray is a strong boy. Violent sometimes.

He has a temper. Ray could do anything he wanted to. Or burn the house down in a fit of temper. He doesn't like to be messed about. He won't let you touch him. I could love Ray, Stan, if he would let me. I could make him into something, but he is ashamed of gentleness."

The father did not reveal that he no longer believed anything can be effected by human intervention. Instead, he listened with foreboding to the tale of the children he still had to meet. He burned his mouth with the tea, and looked across at his wife, animated by her love for their children, and realized she was the stronger for her knowledge of them. He would look to her to do something. She would stand between them. So he felt better.

So the afternoon was passing, towards the return of the children, and the procession of the cows. The man and woman began to look at each other with less strain and more compassion. He was glad now that he had opened the secret cupboards of himself on all their contents. The woman was no longer ashamed to touch her husband's hand, which she had wanted to do for some time. Now she took it and looked at it as it lay, and chafed it with her own burning one, and bound it to her again with the bones of her fingers. So they were reunited at last. Their mouths and their souls were open to each other. They could not press closer than they did, their closed eyes admitting no barrier of flesh to this complete mingling.

That night, after the shynesses and the standing about, they were all laughing in the lamplight of the kitchen, for no great reason but their happiness, and this laughter overflowed the house into the world of moonlight and sculpture, of white horses and solid trees, of watertanks and headless birds, that a big moon had fixed there. The children, who were getting to know their father, laughed for silly things, and for the sake of laughter. By this time they were exhausted really, but a feverishness held them upright. The sturdy boy, his head almost lost in a German helmet, wondered whether he could clown some more and get away with it. The thin girl stood shaking back her annoying plaits and twisting a celluloid armlet that she had exchanged with another girl for a brooch in the shape of a dog's head.

Stan Parker almost asked the ages of his children, before realizing he should not have forgotten. The little girl had moments of solemn maturity.

"Thel'll be taking a boy before we have come to our senses," he said, half to himself.

"Whatever will you come out with next?" the mother said. "We haven't finished school yet."

"I hate boys," said the girl, twisting her thin neck. "I shan't marry, never ever."

"Never ever," chanted the boy, who was astride a chair, so that he could rest his head on the back, and yet it would not appear evident. "I wouldn't marry. I want to do something. I want to ride in a race, or walk across Australia. Do you know there's water in the roots of some trees, and you can pull up the roots and suck the water, if you know which trees? That's what the blacks do. I could be an explorer perhaps. Or a boxer. I can fight with my hands. There's a boy called Tom Quodling that I gave a bashing to, because he wouldn't give up a marble that he said he would if I won, and I did. So I took the marble. It was a green taw."

"Now you *are* talking silly," said the mother. "It is time you went to bed."

"Oh, whhhyyy!" grumbled the boy, rubbing his sleepy head on the chair.

"I *said* why."

"Boys are all silly," said the girl.

She stood in a corner, holding an elbow behind her back, and the hour had left her pale skin greenish. She was frail, but possibly capable of great virulence. She liked secrets. She exchanged secrets with other girls. She even wrote them down in a book, which she kept locked in a trinket box, of which the key was hidden. She would have liked a piano on which to practise the pieces she had learned from the postmistress, but as there was no piano at home, the cracked and metallic themes that she brought home from the post office remained in her head, and she would hum them to herself sometimes with a thin and superior air of secrecy.

"Boys are loopy," she said, swinging her body from side to side, and speaking as if she had to repeat this opinion before her father to leave it on record forever.

"I'll kick you," said the scowling boy, placing the same emphasis on each word.

How could they hate enough? As this was not evident, they were frustrated by their hatred, except during moments of indifference or sleep.

"Now we have had enough of this," said the father, who

had to do something, they were his children, he told himself again with a qualm. "This is a day of peace, isn't it?"

They looked at him incredulously, at the strange man who was also their father, and began to slide off towards their beds, disguised by masks of love. The peacefulness of the night did, in fact, begin to insinuate itself into the house, till they were bound by this more than by the father's words. The boy yielded up his mouth to his mother, who drank his kiss with such ease that she began to wonder if what she had done was not shameful, and went out, shutting the door. The little girl looked out of the window for a time without noticing the beauty of the night, because she was obsessed by the problem of herself. She fetched a little bottle of French scent that her father had brought her and smelled it several times. Only then was she drenched with peace and beauty. The mystical flower of her face shone in the mirror as she said her prayers from behind the long, unopened bud of her hands. She prayed, arranging relationships, as she had been taught, into the categories of love. Then, when she had disposed of these, she got into bed and dreamed of herself walking down the long corridors of anxious music and sleep.

The days after war unfolded slowly but headily at Durilgai. Stan Parker went about his work again. Many people did not know yet that he had come, some did not care, some had forgotten who this man was. A few looked at him for the first time and resented his intrusion on the edges of their recently acquired property. But he was not disturbed by any of this. He went about. His head was sometimes sunk, as if peace were too heavy. He was older, of course. He began to put on weight. He was a heavy man, whose muscles would become gnarled soon. But he was still in his prime. He could toss a bag of feed onto his shoulder without much effort, and carry it against the grey stubble of his burned neck.

He was a grey man now, of strength, but also great mildness. His eyes were lost in hopefulness. He had already observed the behaviour of ants, the flight of hawks, calves moving in the belly, men calculating money and thinking about death, observed these in some detail and with the greatest accuracy, but from the dream state of the sleeper, in which he was slowly stirring and from which he would one day look out perhaps and see. So he went about, and for the moment was a bit lost. In the early mornings, when the cloth clung to his legs with dew, and the mists lay, and the spiders' webs on the taller grasses raised their little targets by the paddockful,

225

blurring things, fact and promise, dread and object, were fused in the same half-world. Even when the sun came up, a bit ragged at first, but red, then breaking through the cobweb of mist, slapping the light across the land by strong acres, standing the trees up solid in the blaring unequivocal light, it was difficult for Stan Parker to look altogether convinced. In that peacetime he was still diffident of accepting anything as solid, factual, or what is called permanent. Much had to be proved. Only he could prove it.

Doll Quigley came soon after he returned. Miss Quigley, as she was called now by all but those who had known her as a scrawny girl, without her shoes for greater ease. Doll had not changed much. She had been born old-young, or had grown young-old. Her dignity was as simple as her grey dress. It was a long, straight dress, of what material or ornamentation you did not notice, only that it covered her and was a decent garment. She wore a brooch too, of enamel perhaps, of some small design that people would never look into. But it was there under her long throat, of which the sandy skin had grown somewhat goitrous. Still, they would not notice that, except the fascinated children. It was the face of Doll that mattered.

"I brought these," she said, shading herself with her long, sandy hand.

There were some little yellow rock-cakes in a box.

"They are a change," she said, or hoped.

Grains of sugar glittered on Doll's crude cakes. She offered these with her second long hand, on which the pollard had dried, and of which one finger had gone in a chaff-cutting machine.

"Thanks, Doll. They look all right," he said, taking the awkward yellow cakes.

The man and the woman were all awkwardness as they stood in the light of exchange and inquiry. She continued to shade her eyes with her hand. Her slow, sandy words slid through the waters of time, till he was standing on the edge of the river at Wullunya, and many smooth, miraculous, quite complete events of his youth flowed by. That is what Doll Quigley put into his hands on the morning of the cakes. She put completeness.

"Well," he said after a while, "why are we standing? Won't you come in?"

"No," she said. "There is nothing to tell from here."

226

She would not ask about his wounds and his medal as other people did.

"No," she said. "The fowls is layin. I have turkeys now, you know. Fine young poults."

And smiled. She had clear pale eyes that had not yet recognized evil.

"Well," she said, "I'm glad you come back, Stan. I knew you would. I prayed for it."

What was the secret which, he sensed, he might share with this woman? Their souls almost mingled, as well as their lives.

But the cakes were jostling in his hands, in the frail box in which she had put them. So that awkwardness returned, and he thanked her for her prayers; there was not much else he could have done.

After that Amy Parker came out with some signs of amusement. She was looking very handsome that morning, so that he should have admired her. But at this moment he was disturbed. There was something he had to protect.

Soon afterwards Doll Quigley said good-bye and returned to her brother, her turkeys, and her fowls.

"What is that?" Amy Parker asked and peered.

"She brought these," he said, because he was forced to show the dedicated cakes.

"Well, I never," said his wife. "Doll's old rock-cakes. A lump of raised-up pollard, I bet."

She had seen the cakes, but she had not seen his hurt, or she might have been pleased. He was a boy on the back doorstep, awaiting further developments.

Amy Parker took the cakes, it was natural that she should, and he heard them landing in a tin, too quickly and too hard.

"Poor old Doll," his wife said. "She's a good old thing. Fancy baking those cakes. She wouldn't have dared tell me. I expect she's sweet on you, Stan, like these old maids get on some man."

He heard her rubbing her hands together to get the crude sugar off, that clung.

But Stan Parker continued to think of Doll Quigley, her still, limpid presence that ignored the stronger, muddier currents of time. It was through ignorance perhaps. Or else the purposes of God are made clear to some old women, and nuns, and idiots. At times Stan Parker was quite wooden in his thick bewilderment. Then for a moment he would be laid open, as he was by Doll Quigley's glance. He would begin then, watching his own hands as they did things, or he would remember the face of an old woman in a shattered church, or a tree that had been blasted, putting on its first, piercing leaves.

Armstrongs came once or twice to Durilgai after Stan Parker returned. They were obviously confused. They came in a motorcar, high up, and did not speak to people that they met, not out of pride, but because they preferred never to stay long in any one place. Since young Tom Armstrong was killed, who had been a lieutenant, and mentioned in dispatches, and decorated—there was all about it in the papers—the old man had a kind of stroke, so that his face was down on one side. You felt sorry for old Armstrong. Now he sat in his green car, with the brass snake that wound along the side and gave warning, he sat in his flat cap and good coat of English tweed, and looked ahead, except when his wife nudged him to recognize something or somebody. Then he would slightly raise his hand, offering in the air a greeting that anyone who cared might take. Only old Armstrong himself was indifferent. The skin of the fingers of his dead hand was gathered in cold pleats.

His wife, though, had a kind of brightness, as of flapping corn. Her hair hung from her scalp like the corn silk, and looked quite moist and vegetable by comparison with her dry but suitable gestures. She smiled as she had learned, and would have liked to talk of illnesses, short, bright ones, or minor operations, surrounded by carnations and grapes.

When the Armstrongs came to Durilgai they would drive to Glastonbury, where they never lived now, because it had not been finished. The men had been withdrawn when the news was recieved of young Tom's death, so that the staircase continued to open into the sky, and mortar hardened into rocks where it had been mixed, and people had stolen the loose bricks on dark nights. The old Armstrongs would take a turn or two in the deserted garden, holding their clothes tightly to their bodies, as if in this way they might appear disguised, and Mrs. Armstrong would still look for scars of the terrible fire, and would stand where the beds had once existed under the milk thistles and the cow-itch, to tear the roses from their bushes in guilty handfuls. Great handfuls of her own roses. She could not gather too many too quickly, almost as if she wanted them and they were not hers. Then Armstrongs would return in their motorcar, for the afternoon breeze blew dangerously on the hill at Glastonbury. Their

legs were uneasy as they sat beneath the Scotch plaid, and
the roses wilted on the old woman's lap, and sometimes she
would throw them over the side of the car, wondering why
she had picked the lolling heads of spent roses.

Stan Parker once had cause to go to Glastonbury, after
that big Muscovy duck, that flew from the pen because they
had delayed cutting its wing, though they had talked about it
often enough. The duck made straight for Glastonbury, to
stalk and hide in its wilderness, and to endure all kinds of
frights and elements in order to preserve its illusion of freedom. Stan Parker went up the hill in pursuit, parting the tall
weeds, so that the seed flew from them, and the dusk was
floating with a fine down. There was a cabbage gone wild in
one place. It had a rank smell beneath the foot. In the stalks
of Paddy's lucerne, of which the sour lashes sprang where the
gardenia grove had been, and was still, only sickly and unrecognizable, with pale leaves and buds that had clotted and rotted into wads of brown paper, he stooped and picked up a
bundle of old letters. These also were pale and mouldy. Their
secrets were more secret in the faint but firm hand of some
man, it looked, who had dipped his pen and said what he
wanted to.

How Stan Parker wanted to read the sodden letters in the
suffocating grove and discover something that he did not
know! There is always a guilty yearning for anonymous advice that makes the hands tremble. So he was prepared to
immerse himself in guilt and knowledge, if he had not
remembered Tom Armstrong, whether the letters were his or
not. He threw them down then and went inside the half-fin-
ished house, which no one had thought to shut, because there
was no reason to.

Unreason abounded in the identical twin of the house that
had been burned. Some swaggie had camped there once in
the twin of the room in which the tapestry had hung, and lit
his fire in the twin fireplace, and smeared his excrement on
the blank wall. Someone had written of his love in terms of
physical urgency. But it was the reasonable face of young
Tom Armstrong that recurred to Stan Parker as he walked in
the room in which his heel had struck the harp that other
evening of fireworks. Because it was not fire, he had realized
later. It was the fireworks before the fire. Tom Armstrong, in
his good collar and brilliantine, had everything cut and dried,
with the confidence of the rich. Unless outside the burning

229

house, with Madeleine on her knees, or when, finally, his face was blown off.

Stan Parker trod through the house, which did not, in fact, belong to Armstrongs. Vines had taken possession of the half-built staircase; it was not clear through what crevice, but unfurling and writhing where the smoke had been. The man stood at the top, as high as he could go, and from his vantage of vines looked out, and wondered about Tom Armstrong's girl. She had not been heard of, neither married, nor dancing; Madeleine had vanished, and would never have existed, if it had not been for the moment on the stairs.

Then Stan Parker leaned his head against the unfinished brickwork and thought quite distinctly how he would finish this unfaithfulness to his wife if the opportunity occurred. Now the dispassionate evening allowed him no feeling of guilt. Under the wide sky, thickening into night, at the top of the deserted, desecrated house, vines crumpled in his hands with a fleshiness, a soft muskiness of flesh. Only he could not remember enough. He could not remember the pores of her skin, the veins in her eyes, her breath on his neck, however hard he tried to. Whole rooms of his mind, in which each separate detail had been stored, seemed to have gone, like those rooms of the top and most significant story, through which he had run, matching himself against the bravura of the fire, to find her, as he had not expected in his youth and diffidence, awake.

Now the middle-aged man stood crumpling the vines at the top of the ugly house. Unpleasant lines had come in his face, almost of consummation. But nobody would see, of course, because the place was quite deserted. Except for the duck, that was stalking heavily in the undergrowth, showing its yellow eye. Why, he had come there for the duck, he realized, crumpling the hot vines, and glad of a reason.

So he swore at the bird, "I'll get that bastard," he said.

While the duck continued to stalk, the man ran down and out at the back, his large body grown riduculous as it hurtled far outside his recollections. Then he recovered himself and his breath, picked up a long branch of a tree that wind had torn off, and that he noticed lying, rushed at the now desperately regretful duck, and pressed it to the ground with the fork of the branch, pressed as if he would crush the bird through the earth, out of existence, rather than take it alive.

"Got the bastard!" he exploded.

The duck hissed, and beat with its wings, and lashed with

its long, strong neck. Its ugly wilfulness, and the knobs at the root of its bill, had become quite pathetic. But at present the man could not hate it enough.

Till suddenly he slid to the end of the bough, still holding it, stooped, and picked up the bird from the fork. After a hiss or two the duck hung neatly, if heavily, from his hand.

The man turned back and began to go down the hill. Nobody had seen any of this. He walked in the tracks he had already made, through the flattened weed. Nobody would know of any spasm of lust on that evening, which was already growing cold, it was autumn.

So Stan Parker walked home with his recaptured duck, and felt the cold begin to creep through the sweat beneath his clothes, and an uneasiness in one shoulder that had over-reached itself. The crumb of goodness is irretrievable in the light of one lapse. So he was disconsolate. He thought with longing of his wife, whom he loved, and of the soggy bread she had baked when they first lived together in that bit of a shack. He thought of Doll Quigley, and that purity of being, which he recognized but could not apparently convert into terms of his own reality. So he walked through the docks and mallows. In his heavy boots, heavier with moist, gathering earth, he thought of those clods of words he was in the habit of heaping together in some shape of prayer, on which ordinarily he could expect to climb at least in the direction of safety. In the dusk, though, of cold passion, the chances were reduced.

When he got in he went to his wife's workbox, and took a pair of scissors, and hacked through the satiny but coarse feathers of one of the duck's wings.

"That'll fix it," she said, looking up calmly through the glasses she had taken to wearing for close work.

He only grunted, and went in the dark to throw the duck into its pen.

Amy Parker continued to darn the sock with neat skill. It was the duty she had imposed upon herself that evening, seeing her husband go in the direction of Glastonbury, to catch the duck, he had told her deliberately, looking into her eyes. Remembering her own mission to Glastonbury, on a former evening of ducks, she had wondered what he would find. But Stan was different; he was not given to doubt or recklessness; he strained fences, and planed wood, and gave people the last word on things. So Amy Parker wove the neat, square patch on the man's thick sock. So Stan would

231

quickly find the duck, even in that undergrowth, which she had seen lately for herself, to satisfy curiosity for what people said of the ruin. So she wove and snipped. She was in her own way skilful and precise, her work wore well. She was a steady, amiable sort of woman now, whom people liked, to look at her pleasant skin, and to ask what she did when the jam did not jell or when the hens were getting the white diarrhoea.

Then Stan had come in, as she had promised herself he would soon, and hacked off the feathers.

She had made her comment, not because it contributed anything, but because they were married to each other, and these words of no significance wove then closer and more confidently to each other, and similar threads of daily words, weaving and uniting. Or was it patching?

Amy Parker cut the last thread she would put that night. She did not intend to do much on that occasion, or go deeply into anything. But if she could have put down the sock, and gone into the darkness of the yard with a hurricane lamp, and held it to her husband's face to see, she would have done that. She would have liked to reassure herself.

It will be different now, they had said, when Stan came home at the peace, it will be different, they said, meaning it will be the same as before. Only nothing is ever the same. She could not look too often at his face to wonder what was happening. She would invent excuses for watching, call him to change a washer or lift a weight, and she would find reasons for touching even, some convenient roughness of his skin or shadow of dirt. She would laugh a little then, in apology, and he would frown sometimes. But it gave no clue to the progress of his mind, whether it was making provision for her or whether she had dropped behind, inside the network of acts they performed necessarily together, and words spoken.

So the woman began to wonder whether their life together was too comfortable for him, or whether he had learned by heart all those thoughts and opinions she was in the habit of expressing. Of course there were others that she kept hidden, which was only natural. And some that she sensed only as an uneasiness, or even terror.

"Stan," she said once, "we must take the children one day and go for a picnic or something."

"All right," he said, "if you want to."

Because he was a good-tempered husband.

"It was an idea," she said. "It would make a change in our lives. And that's important, isn't it? I would like to look at the sea again."

"All right," he said. "Whenever you feel like it."

His full agreement almost disappointed her. She would think about it, she now said, as if the idea had been his, and in doing so her desire to see the ocean remained theoretical. Standing between pine trees, she was overawed and almost sucked under by the glassy rollers. It will be exhilarating, she said, as if all currents are a spectacle in green glass.

So the days swelled, and rose out of each other, and were folded under, and her idea of the picnic became a silly whim, then a cause for resentment, that she hadn't the will to achieve it, or achieve anything much. Resentments bred.

Not long after the war Stan Parker bought a motorcar, and they felt they had come a long way. Stan learned to drive his car with pride, if not with ease, sitting there too stiffly, with stiff neck and arms, as if he were screwed fast at certain key joints. The car was a Ford, rather a loose thing, but it hung together; no errand was too surprising for the Ford. When Parkers drove out, Amy Parker put on her hat with more than usual formality, and streaked some powder on her face, and took a handbag with lozenges and things. Some neighbours looked and smiled from their verandas; others turned away in anger and pretended that they did not see. But Parkers drove on, fascinated only by the road.

Sometimes Stan would take the car and drive out quickly, though, before his wife could ask him where he was going. He could feel that she had run out from the house, and was standing in her clean apron watching the car as it disappeared. But he did not look back and wave, or shout an explanation, because he did not know yet where he was going. He drove down sandy side roads, on which the body of the car was almost torn in pieces, and along which, except for the fact that the road did exist, there seemed no reason why human beings should go. It was too sour in that part of the bush, or too pure, to suggest prospects of gain or possibilities of destruction. Black sticks pointed on the sandy soil, in which struggled bushes of stiff, dark needles, and greater trees, of which the bark came away in leaves of blank paper. There were the anthills too, their red, brooding domes perfectly contemplative.

Stan Parker would draw up in those parts. He would roll a cigarette. He liked to be there. He would sit with his hands on the still wheel, till their dried-up skin had disintegrated in the light of sand and grey leaf, so that his body was no longer surprised at the mystery of stillness, of which he was a part. If his wife continued to stand, in his mind, beside the house in her clean apron, with the anxious and thwarted look on her face, it did not avail her for the moment; he could not have done much to answer her poignance with rational assurances, or even the deceptive gestures of the body.

So he forgot about her for the time being, knowing that he would return to her, to share their habitual life. There was no question of its being otherwise, even if his soul ventured out beyond the safe limits on reckless, blind expeditions of discovery, and doubt, and adoration.

Stretching himself finally on the creaking seat of the frail car, till his bones cracked, he would long to express himself by some formal act of recognition, give a shape to his knowledge, or express the great simplicities in simple, luminous words for people to see. But of course he could not.

There were individuals who said Stan Parker had gone a bit queer from the war, after all he had been through, and him a husband and a father. Now these people began to avoid him. He had never been a talkative man, except on direct practical matters. His advice had been good. But they preferred to take their troubles elsewhere, rather than have his eyes discover any cracks in their demeanour. Stan Parker was queer.

Once he had told his boy to get into the car, and said that they would go for a drive. Where? Well, just to those parts to which he had grown attached, he could not say it was anywhere particular. The boy was naturally embarrassed, and sat looking at the sober speedometer or gloomily out at the side of the road. He did not like to be with his father, anyway.

But Stan was full of hope. Now I must speak to this boy, he felt, and convey to him something of what I know; it will be easier if we do it like this; and already he had greater confidence, seeing the sandy bushland, in which stood only the essentials of tree and shrub, the absorbed mounds of ant-hills, and the black sticks pointing in different directions on the ground.

"This is pretty poor country," said the father. "Sour. But I sort of like it. It gets a hold over you."

"I don't know what we've come here for," said the boy, looking with gloomy distaste at the bushland.

Although he had never seen a city he longed for it. Much

of his unhappiness was due to the fact that he had not discovered the herd.

"Aren't we going to do something?" the boy asked.

"I just wanted to go for a drive," said the father, "and have a talk."

His heart had begun to fail, though.

"About what?" asked the boy, who was suspicious, thinking it might be some explanation of sex.

"Nothing in particular," said the father.

He was glad that he had the wheel to guide, and could employ himself in this way to some effect.

"We don't know each other too well, do we, Ray?"

The boy was quite unhappy. So was the man.

"We know each other all right, I suppose," said Ray in self-defence. "What is there to know, anyway?"

The father could not answer that one.

"I haven't seen you since I got back," he said.

"What can I do?" complained the boy. "Hang about all the time?"

He now definitely disliked his father. He even disliked the smell of him, which was the smell of the solider, steadier men of that age, smelling of tobacco and work, of their regular and reliable bodies. For a moment the father had excited him, at the return, with his rough khaki tunic open at the neck, but it was perhaps more the excitement of the barbarous and foreign objects he had brought with him, the little polished grenade and the sullen helmet, which had been taken, he said, from the head of a dead German.

But this was already some time ago. Ray was a bigger boy. He had grown at the wrists. And the helmet had been dented and the grenade was lost. He had, in fact, almost forgotten these talismans capable of averting the ordinary, the safe, the good, while his father remained.

There beneath that tree, under which they had pulled up, a gnarled, difficult native with harsh, staring leaves, the man and the boy were resenting each other for their separateness.

Not without sadness and a sense of his own failure, the father said, "I'm going to smoke a cigarette, if you want to poke about a bit."

There was nothing else the boy could do, except continue to sit beside his father, which would of course have been intolerable. So he got down, slamming the tinny door of their car.

There was a lizard amongst the stones that the man saw,

235

and to which his attention now clung with the hope of the hopeless. As if he might suddenly interpret for his son, by some divine dispensation, with such miraculous clarity and wisdom, the love and wonder the horny lizard had roused in him. That day could still become transparent, which remained opaque.

"Look, Ray," said the man, looking along his own pointing finger, that just did not tremble for its daring tactic.

"What?" said the boy. "Oh, that's only an old lizard. There are plenty of them."

And he almost aimed a stone at it, only desisting because it was a small fry, and what was the use.

"Yes," said the father. "But I like to watch it. I like to look at these things."

The lizard closed his eye, shutting it up in its pocket of stone. Then the man was really alone. He began to roll a cigarette, and to lick at the thin paper with his dry tongue. That part of the bush was very grey. Its symbols would not be read.

It was to the boy, wandering apathetically through the scrub, the same monotonous bushland that his youth had become. He was perpetually wandering through bush, hacking or scratching, looking for birds or something to kill. He had lost his beauty and was not yet handsome. His skin was thick and dull, full of the tortuous secrets of puberty.

Ah, if he could escape, he said, bending a sapling till it broke. And do what? He thought that he would become a policeman. He remembered the admirably virile leggings of the young police constable, Murphy, who had shot at a man and killed him, they said, that was wanted for the murder of a rabbiter out Wullunya way. The young constable had no time to speak to boys, for writing reports at the police station, and looking distantly important out of blue eyes.

Ray Parker took aim with a stick. He could have shot the fugitive as cleanly as Murphy, if with less righteousness. His eyes were not blue. They were a deep brown, which did not yet suggest what they were looking at, or perhaps it was just inward, at those images of himself in a variety of postures, in leggings or without, or naked, clothed in a brooding nakedness that was both fascinating and awful. He looked back over his shoulder and saw the hood of the car. To which he must return. To his father.

When they had driven home, with much painful changing of gears, and manœuvring past and out of ruts, they were both conscious of some guilt, common or unrelated, of which the mother was at once aware. She watched the return secretly, with bitter pleasure, and was determined that she would give no assistance whatsoever in any emergency that might arise, because this was something the boy's father had brought upon himself. For once the problem of her son was not hers to solve. So she went on sardonically drinking the strong cup of tea she always took at that time of day, just before they all went down to milk. She stood by the window, to one side, holding the saucer rather high, and the steam from the meditative tea, or else the queer pleasure she derived from sensing some hurt to her husband, whom she loved and respected, made her nostrils appear finer than they normally were in her full, by this time almost coarse face.

Then she stepped aside quickly, coughed, shoved the cup and saucer on the table, and was all busyness as the men came.

She did ask something about their having a nice drive, but she made it sound their exclusive business, as she smoothed back her hair in the glass and put on the old felt pudding-basin hat that she always wore for milking. The origins of that hat were forgotten, though it must originally have been bought for beauty.

Then when the woman had fiddled a bit more and gathered up buckets and some clean rags, and the men had taken tea in silence, to the heavy chink of the kitchen cups, they all walked down towards the bails. It was a healing autumn light of reddish gold that sluiced the trees. The play of light and wind dimpled the liquid leaves. A poplar they had planted some years ago beside the yards was plashing like glad water. So that the boy emerged from himself and began to sing, furtively, in his breaking voice, but sang, and soon he was running amongst the cows, separating and guiding them, driving them into their respective bails, through the plop-plop of falling dung, pinning their heads, roping their legs, knotting the switches of tails about their hocks. Soon that contentment of cows eating had spread to him, for the father had filled the troughs with dry feed, into which the beasts stuck their melting noses, to gather up succulent, overflowing mouthfuls, and the crumbs fell back.

"Gee, Dad, Nancy's springing all right," Ray said and paused in spontaneous pleasure.

237

Stan Parker came, and together they looked at their swelling heifer.

They met and parted. They passed along the line, and sat, and milked their cows. Once the father bumped the boy, who was passing with two buckets weighing his wiry, youth's arms. Stan Parker put his hands for a moment on the boy's hips, to steady him, and the boy laughed, he did not mind. What were you to believe then? Stan Parker was too wry-mouthed from that afternoon to consider. It was, besides, the hour of cows. The white pools of milk rose beneath the milkers' satellite hands. The moons of milk were in themselves complete. Everyone sensed this perhaps, and bowed the head.

Amy Parker would look up, though, from out of the abstraction of milk. She was the steadiest milker of all, and would milk along her line without a pause, either for yarns or to ease the ache out of her hands. She sat with the bucket between her strong legs, her buttocks overlapping the little sawn-off block she had always used as a milking stool. What saved her from appearing ludicrous was the harmoniousness of her rather massive form beside the formal cow. Still, there were many people who would have laughed to see the farmer's wife, in her rubber boots and old hat, pulling out the milk with swollen fingers. They would have laughed at the calves of her legs. Or wondered. For she would dart looks here and there.

Now she looked up. Her eyes had grown deep in that light of evening, in the shadowy cowhouse. As her son passed back and forth, and released a cow that had been milked, and scraped up its droppings, and drove in that lean heifer with the uneven teats that they would get rid of later on, she intended to say something to the boy that would make him respect her for her wisdom, or more, respect himself for discovering he could share in it. But she was unequal to the situation, and he passed by, whether a boy still, it was difficult to say, or some strange man, for a shaft of light had come in at the door, striking the uncertainty from his face, anyway momentarily, and giving strength to his throat. So the woman continued to sit huddled on the little milking block in the shadow of the cow. It was doubtful she would ever gain upon her son, whose lead had been established the moment they took him out of her body.

About this time Parkers took on a young Greek as a hand. It was difficult to know why he had left the shops and come to those parts, looking for work, for Con the Greek was still

238

shut up inside his language, but he was hungry, and anxious, you could see that. They took him on without giving it much thought. Amy Parker brought him a big plate of overdone meat, with lumps of pumpkin and a good hash of potato, with which he filled his mouth, so that he could not close it, besides, the potato was that hot. Afterwards she showed him the shack where old Fritz had lived, and into which he trod with the unhappiness of a man entering into something sad but necessary. He smiled, though, and nodded his head. The gooseflesh showed on his rather livery skin as he stood holding his hands together. But he stayed. They were paying him a small wage.

People laughed, of course, because there was Parkers taking on another foreigner. They remembered the German. Only this was worse, the speechless Greek, who could only make signs, and laugh, and run to it, in order to express his willingness. Was it possible that somebody might be made to suffer? They thought it was, though how, they were not sure. Then, when everyone at Parkers' seemed pleased with one another, they turned away, their hopes gone sour.

The Parker family, once they had recovered from the strangeness of the situation, expected great things of the Greek. Secretly they hoped he would be able to answer all kinds of questions. But he was still a cipher, or a smile. His eyes, which promised frankness on the surface, withheld secrets in their liquid depths. His greenish skin was still repulsive. But he did finally begin to emerge, woodenly at first, leaning on learned phrases, that might give way if he did not take care.

He was a small, muscular, rather hairy man in his singlet, which he wore mostly for greater freedom, and because his skin seemed to crave the sun. This skin, which at first had been green, or yellow, because he was nervous, or because he had been a bit repulsive to them, because he was foreign, began to be golden, they noticed with some interest and surprise. When he chopped the wood or bent above the tin basin to sluice his neck and shoulders, sinuous lights shone from the golden Greek. He laughed a great deal, to speak to them in this way. Then they looked at his struggling mouth and wanted it to tell them more than it could. They thought about him constantly.

"That young man, Stan," said Amy Parker, "do you think he is happy?"

"I suppose so. Why not?" said her husband. "You don't

239

have to understand words to feel happy. But he will learn to speak in time. Then you can ask him how he feels, if he doesn't tell you."

"It's none of my business," she said. "I only wondered."

But a feeling of sadness began to develop in her for the imprisoned Greek, and she began to think what kindnesses she could do him, mend his socks perhaps, see that he went out covered in the rain, like a son, because he was a young man, though not so young.

Once she had given him a red apple and watched him bite it. His teeth clove the apple with a hard, animal sound. His lips were shining with the white juice.

"That is an apple," she said in a flat voice, watching him in the peaceful yard. "Apple," she repeated, nodding her head, but diffidently.

"Epple?" he asked, or laughed, from his wet mouth.

Almost as if he were returning it to hers, this word, or fragment of apple flesh, that he had tried in his. So that she blushed for the intimacy of the whole incident.

"Oh," she said, laughing roughly, "you'll learn in time."

She did not know what to say next, so turned away with a moisture in her mouth, of apple juice.

Thelma came running. "Con," she called, "I was looking for you." She took his hand.

"Yes?" he laughed, embarrassed by so many tendrils. "Oh. You look me. Orright."

"I want to be with you," she said, chafing his hand.

"Orright. I here," he said. "I work now."

"You can work, and I shall be with you," she said with complacency and determination.

The little girl, who had begun to write in notebooks and have secrets, and who was hiding things in the hollows of trees and under stones, watched the young man raking the fowl yard for manure. He rose above that squalor. He had climbed back into his past life, and they were separated by the bars of language and his silent face, that looked down with a kind of withdrawn modesty, it did not see her.

Ah, she loved the Greek then, quite desperately. She stood twisting a bangle she had received for her birthday, which floated loosely round her spindly wrist, getting in the way of things.

"Are you married, Con?" she asked, looking round to see whether somebody had crept up.

240

But he laughed foolishly, because he did not know what this was, and raked the dung.

"Haven't you got a girl?" she said, the breath becoming tight in her chest.

"Girls?" he said, his face breaking out of its withdrawn beauty into a convulsion of sinews, and bone, and pointed teeth. "Yairs! Oh, yairs! Girls!" He continued to laugh.

They were standing in the fowl shed. She did not like him then. Besides, she had reached that point where anxiety and down stifled her. Her breath came tearingly. Possibilities of shame presented themselves to her beneath the oppressive roof of the dark shed, till she went out into the sun and walked away with her head down.

But it was the tenderness of music that best expressed her feelings for the Greek. She could play now with some bursts of emotion and an exerted pedal, advanced pieces at the postmistress's piano. She played out many scenes of love, touching the golden, slightly warped skin of music.

"Thelma," insisted the postmistress and her ruler, "it just ain't in the notes."

As if it ever was.

Once she had kissed the Greek for some festive occasion, a birthday or something, when they had given him a bottle of beer, but the episode was so brief and public, her act was swallowed up by others more boisterous, and was not even considered funny. His skin was slightly greasy and mysterious.

Then Ray found the diary and exposed whole pages of her nakedness. He read and laughed, barely digesting the words before he spat them out.

" 'I love Con,' " he read, " 'I would let him cut my veins open.' "

How he laughed. And let her bleed.

"This is good," he sighed.

She threw the mirror at him. Then when they were faced with the cold fragments of their hate he said, "I could show Mum all this, you know."

"I'll give you anything," she said.

"Mightn't want anything. It might be more fun showing."

"Go on," she said. "Anything."

Then he threw the book back where the mirror lay, knowing perhaps it was not worth much, now that she had given her soul. It was a sixpenny notebook with marbled edges that she had bought from Mr. Denyer one day, in which to write something, anything, then this had come out. Now she picked up the book by its cheap and gluey covers, but would have to think where to put it.

Thelma was silly because it was not possible for her to be otherwise. But Ray was a boy. Ray went down to the Greek, down to the shed where he lived, because he was his friend, and they talked together in hard voices about objects, nails and saws and knives. There was not such a great difference in their ages, except by reckoning. Their sex and limitations united them closely. They could even look at each other and say nothing, not even looking, but being together.

"Let's see the things in the box," Ray said.

This was the little box that Con the Greek had in his swag, with private and valuable and interesting articles, as well as some things that he had forgotten why he kept. His essence was contained here. Ray liked to look at the contents of the box, which he coveted, not for any purpose, but to own. The eruption of coral and the luminous saint, these he did not understand, they were frightening even. For the faces on old photographs he had contempt, old women and black, thin girls emerging from the twilight and the fingerprints. He dropped these back onto the buttons and sprig of dry rosemary.

"What is that old plant thing?" he often asked, with only slight interest.

"That is good," said the Greek. "Dendrolivano. Smell."

"There's no smell left," the boy said.

But the Greek did not bother to reply, knowing that this was not true.

Then the boy took the knife, which was the best thing of all in Con's box and had the smell of clean, oiled metal. The boy held it in his hand and supposed with cold fascination what would happen if he closed his hand, just that bit closer, and closed. His skin was pricking.

"The knife is too sharp," said the Greek, taking it, and shutting it in the box, and putting the box away.

He was tired of the boy now.

The boy began to be consumed both by contempt and sadness. The Greek's box was a miserable sort of box, but he could not possess it. He could not possess the Greek, who sat on the edge of the bed, and sucked his teeth, and had his own thoughts.

Then the boy was shaken by a fury of contempt and frustration. He seized the Greek by the wrist and shouted, "Anyway, I bet I'm stronger than you!"

He plaited his hand into the Greek's hand and bent it back for all he was worth. Then the Greek came to life, coldly at first, glitteringly. His attitude was not yet determined. As he held the struggling, gangling boy. Their breath fought together. They were wrestling on the narrow bed. It was a game, or not, it was not possible to tell in that Laocoön of man and boy. Then the Greek began to laugh explosively, which made his muscles more fluid. His sinuous arms were pinning the boy. Their flat, breathless chests were boarded up together, so that it was difficult in that moment to extricate the hearts one from the other. They boy listened to the thumping and breathing and shouted with rage because he could not possess the intolerable Greek. He would have liked to kill him. To dig his hands into the congested throat. But he was powerless. And presently his resistance dissolved. He wanted to escape from his embarrassing weakness, and the still more embarrassing proximity with the Greek.

"Let us go, Con," he wheedled. "Go on. Call it quits."

But the Greek refused. So that the boy who was writhing on the rack began to fear that still greater weaknesses than his lack of strength might be discovered. They were panting together, and the Greek was laughing.

"I hate you!" cried the stifled boy. "I hate bloody Greeks!"

Then the mother came in with some things she had mended for the Greek. She had not expected to find her son.

"Ray," she said, putting on an improvised voice, "it's time you went to work. We must speak to your father about it and decide."

The boy got up and went stupidly across the yard, followed by the mother, who was trying vaguely to remember what she had intended to say to the Greek if her son had not been there. In her distraction she could not.

Similarly she forgot for the moment that they must decide something about the boy. The days of autumn in which she walked were perfect in themselves. The wind dropped at that time of the year. Birds rose indolently and alighted with ease. Quinces fell and rotted after a time; she sat on a doorstep and could not pick them up. All shapes, tree or fence or the merest, tottering skeleton of a shed, were clear-cut and final in that fixed landscape of autumn. Only the human being might still erupt, and assume fresh forms, or disintegrate. She watched her husband walking through the stubble. He had

243

begun to shrivel a bit. His neck was old. What if she should find Stan fallen in the grass with his face lost in an expression she did not know? There was no reason, of course. He had never faltered for a moment. His eyes assured permanence. But she had gone cold, that she could think the thought, and worse, that it could happen.

So she stroked her own strong arms for warmth, inside the old cardigan. There was the Greek, walking with armfuls of corn stalks and withered, twitching corn leaves. He was burning the dead corn in little heaps, on the paddock from which the grain had been stripped. Grey ribbons of smoke unwound. There was a smell of burning. She thought about the Greek, and her ever-present concern for him, that had still taken no positive direction; she could not express for him her sympathy, except in dull gestures of mending and words taught. Children you hold to you, but she could not do that, except once in the darkness, before sleep, released from her conscience, she had held his head in her arms, forming it against her breast, and anticipated the coarseness of his hair. It was a dog's coarseness. That was it. She was kind to dogs. They came, lolloping and friendly, but did not attach themselves to her with passion, they never became hers. And that was right. So it was a kind and friendly relationship, hers with the young Greek, of dog and mistress. She was glad, she said, it was like that. She was glad he was walking at a distance between the heaps of smouldering corn stalks. That way they exchanged no words, nor fumbled them.

Amy Parker stirred on the step.

"We should encourage that young man to go about more," she said when her husband came up. "He's a human being," she said.

"I'm not stopping him," said Stan Parker, who was tired of thinking about the Greek, not a bad lad, but who would not be told. "He can take his days, but he won't. I can't force him."

Again she was glad, for some inner devotion that she liked to think did exist.

Still, he did go sometimes. She watched him walk up the road to the bus in his tight, best clothes, to which his body would never reconcile itself, he should not have worn clothes. And he would be gone all that day, and sometimes she failed to hear him return, she had fallen asleep from exhaustion, in the still, white morning where the cock crew, and wooden horses shifted their legs.

244

Con the Greek went to the city, where he began to have many friends, and relations came, and people from the same island, and the friends of relations. So that Amy Parker knew that it was only a matter of time, as he went silently about his work, or singing softly, but always meditating something. It will have to come, she said, and was glad that the fate of the young man, that she lacked the courage or was powerless to direct, would be taken naturally out of her hands. Still, he persisted in her life, one of the many people she had never spoken to.

From the city he brought presents, bright, childish sweets in sticky little bags, for which the children jostled each other. When he had saved up he bought the guitar. Then in the evenings the kitchen was full of a brittle music, that she could not keep out, much as she frowned. He told her bits of his songs. He told her about his island. Most of the year the men were away diving for sponges, he said; they came back to get drunk, and beat their wives, and make more children, they they went away again. Till she knew the bare island. The women of the island were the hollow-faced dark women of the photographs in Con's box, but they spoke with her voice as they looked from the islands of their houses. While his muscular hands were tightening the guitar for some further music, she wondered what kind of children she would have made with the Greek. But her courage did not dare pursue this road very far.

"A fine sort of life those women lead," she said in a loud, objective voice.

"Why not?" he said, forming his lips into a trumpet, from which the words of a fresh, impatient song were waiting to slip. "They dunno no better. It is good."

"Everybody knows better," she said.

He did not understand this, or else he did not want to hear.

"This is a love song," he said.

"A love song!" she whispered with some irony to her husband who had come in, as if she had to punish someone, or herself.

"Ah dear," she sighed, and laughed as she folded the cloth.

When the Greek had finished his song he assumed an awkward position of official announcement and said, "Mr. Parker, I must go from here very soon. I shall marry one widow. She have a business at Bondi, and this is good opportunity. It is orright for me."

245

"It is all right for us, Con, if you are pleased," said Stan Parker.

He was a bit relieved. There were certain objects, particularly an axe and the hacksaw, that he could not bear other people to touch.

"A widow," said Amy Parker. "Well, Con, that is interesting."

"She have five children," said Con. "It is many. But plenty hands good for business."

"You are certainly provided for," said Amy Parker, "in every way."

"Yes."

What, then, was so disturbing about it all? The young man, whose socks she had mended for a while, would leave the house, as was natural. But she might have told him something of herself, any day now, something that nobody else had been told, that she might have told perhaps to the child they had found in the floods, who was that blank sheet of paper which is necessary for such confessions of love, but who had gone while she still fumbled. That was it, she grasped, the young Greek picking at the guitar in the kitchen, and satisfied to smugness by the way his life was shaping, was the same oblivious, escaping child. There were moments when the young Greek's muscular cheeks relaxed into the innocence of childhood, picking at notes of music, for instance, before or after a song. That is it, or must be, she decided with some tenderness.

"I hope you will be happy, Con," she said.

But her husband was tempted to remark between coughs of tobacco and preparations for bed, "It is not a funeral, Amy."

"I will be orright," said the Greek, picking over the bones of the guitar for some last shred of music, of the love song.

"Is she nice, Con?" she asked.

"She is fat," he said, looking up. "She cook good."

He smiled luminously, with the light of innocence or complacency, it was difficult to tell which. There were certain expressions of the Greek's face, when his complacent flesh was lit by simple joys, that did invite entry into his soul. So that Amy Parker went away, saying she was tired. She bit her lips. As it was time for bed, she took down her hair and began to brush it. That night she could not brush too much, brushing out the long shadows in the mirror. Her hair was shorter than it had been, not grey, but at that stage when in her own mind she had always felt that what she had of looks was distinct. But she was not beautiful, it was obvious. She brushed back her hair and let it fall loose, apparently in some formal exercise of hair-brushing.

"Aren't you coming to bed, Amy?" her husband asked, from sense of duty, it appeared, not of loss.

"Yes," she said. "I am doing my hair."

But she could not evade the floods of time. She was by now rather a fat woman. She went across the roses of the carpet and got into bed, and in darkness tried to think of her children, of her husband, of a pan of jam, of a field of oats, of the great bounties, in fact. Until she had swum beyond them and, in spite of sinuous strokes and the bristles of her brush that she used as a reminder, was sucked under.

Then her husband touched her, and she woke up and said, "Ah, I was drowning."

She lay there thinking about it with persistent horror.

The day the Greek went was a clear day. There had been some frost early, from which the country leaped out and flaunted. In the clear, still air they could listen to the preparations for departure from the shed across the yard. Then Con came out of the shed. He had a new case with a yellow strap around it, and some things tied up in a sugar bag. He wore his tight clothes.

"Good-bye, Con," Parkers said, eyeing him curiously, almost as if he had never been anything to them.

Their everyday clothes gave them a desire to feel superior to anyone so obviously lifted out of the context of daily life as Con in his best. Ray, in fact, got into positions of some insolence and would have liked to hurt someone.

"That is a small present," said Amy Parker, handing the Greek a scarf that she had made in blue wool, and done up in a piece of tissue paper that she had fished out from somewhere, it had a network of electric lines.

She put her hand on her son's shoulder. The ceremony of presentation had made her sentimental but safe. She was a kind woman. Her motherliness overflowed, both to her son, who did not want it, and to the young man who was going out from their house, and who had been surprised into trembling by the unexpected present.

"Oh, theng you, theng you, Mrs. Parker," he said, growing moist-eyed with spontaneous emotion.

She noticed his beauty for the last time, almost casually. In the homely daylight, in her comfortable slippers with the pompoms on them, with her reliable husband beside her, and her brash son, any divergence from the obvious course of her life would have been ludicrous.

"I will bring my lady," said the Greek.

"Yes. Yes," said Mrs. Parker.

But she did not expect he would, nor did she want it.

"Where is Thelma?" asked the Greek.

"Saturday morning is her music lesson," said the mother, and because she was in the habit of repairing the omissions of her children, added, "She asked me to say good-bye."

"It is a pity," he said.

Then, as there was nothing more for him to do, he went.

He went up the road, and Ray said he would come and muck around for a bit up that way. That morning he was surly, and awkward of body. It seemed to the boy himself that he would never form but remain gangling on a road, and he resented the man his friend who was leaving and whose future was ordained. The man walked with strong, deliberate steps, carrying the heavy, common case and the little, awkward sugar bag. He wanted to talk, so he described the things they passed in stiff, rudimentary language. Till the boy could not bear it any longer.

"I'm goin down here," he said, balanced in his old pair of sand-shoes on the edge of the bush. "I'm not gonna come any further."

"Why?" said the surprised Greek. "You no come to the bus?"

"No," said the boy with contempt. "There ain't no point."

"Then we must say good-bye," said Con, putting down the bags.

He came forward, the sleeves still rucked along his arms from carrying the heavy bags. It was obvious he intended to make a ceremony of this farewell also, so the boy's courage failed him. He could not very well have hit his friend in the face to prevent his creating this formal but agonizing group at the roadside, so he drained his own face, till it had the texture and thinness of paper, and said, "Why can't people just go without making a song and dance about it?"

The Greek was arrested. He looked stocky and ridiculous. In his injured simplicity he began to wonder what he had done to this boy, to fear some power that he must possess without his knowing. But it would never be explained. The boy's face gave no clue, and the thin grey leaves hanging from still twigs excluded all possibility of elucidation.

"Orright then," he said, backing.

Ray Parker went off down into the bush. It was thin and grey there, but sympathetic in a way. He did not have to think about it. He had thinned right out, till he was exclusively of that place, as exhalation of leaf or bark, his hanging hands no longer idle, except that they did nothing, otherwise there was purpose enough in being, amongst the grey scraggy trees. So he edged along from rock to rock. He bent down to examine ants that were carrying something, or rather, he performed the act of examining, for he did not see.

He had begun again to think of the man who had gone, and whom he would have kept, he almost trembled to admit, though kept for what. Because if he did not love the Greek, and it was obvious he could not love him, then it was hate. Keep him on a chain perhaps, to kick on the quiet, like a dog. The sun was up now above the boy's head, a bland, dispassionate globe of autumn, as he walked through the bush, peeling off bark in search of some answer, and feeling the swollen misery of those cruelties he was perpetrating, and had still to perpetrate on his memories of the man. This way he would become stronger. Though he did doubt his strength. He was still pinned by the arms of the golden Greek.

After a bit he stopped. It was under a tree. It was a big old banksia, full of dead heads, the trunk and branches of the tree tortured into abominable shapes, full of dust and ugliness. All beauty and goodness were excluded from that place, and sky being obliterated for the moment. The boy was shivering that took out the knife, which was, in fact, the one from the Greek's box. He remembered the Greek's intent face telling him about the knife and those other things of beauty or interest in his box, or telling him about his family, in difficult sentences, about his mother, who was an old woman in a kind of cap. The boy held the knife. Trembling in anticipation of his act, he took out the photograph of the old black hollow woman. As he stood there, trying to impress her disinterested features on his memory, his hands that held the Greek's belongings, which he had taken because he wanted them, had become quite possessed. The hands were not his. The hands took the knife. It began to cut through the yellow snapshot, to cut in zigzags, to saw and destroy. When it was done, and he could press the blade no deeper into the heart of his friend, the boy threw away the knife and the shreds of paper, somewhere, he did not look.

He had slipped down onto the stones, with which that sour slope was littered. He ground his cheek into the sharp sand. Dry, desperate cries for some lost simplicity that he had himself dispatched racked the boy's body. It seemed that his daemon would never be exhausted, but it was in time, later that morning, and he even fell asleep for a little, and woke up with a fresh mind.

Chapter 16

STAN Parker finally decided to apprentice his son to old Jarman the saddler at Bangalay, to see, he said, though what would be seen he was not quite sure; the move was more than anything a lame answer to his own puzzlement. Stan's mother had had a cousin a saddler, a decent man. Leather was honest. So leather it would be.

"Ah, why, Dad" said the disgusted boy, this throat protesting desperately. "Who wants old saddlery? I don't."

"What do you want?" asked the father.

"Not that," said the boy, because he did not know how to make a more concerete answer.

He turned his head away, not liking to be alone with his father. He was a strong youth by now, handsome at times, with a ruddiness that gave his face a touch of carelessness. Many people would forgive Ray Parker his more detestable acts on account of his bright skin. His admirable hair, which his mother would have liked to touch, was a dark brown. His healthiness of body quite disguised any trace of disease; only the neurotic could have had any misgivings about the corners of his mouth, or found in his rather bold eyes reflections of their own hells.

"Try it anyway for a bit," said the father. "There's always room for a couple of saddlers in a town of any size."

The boy held his tongue.

Soon he was at Jarman's in a calico apron, sweeping up the snippets through the too heavy sunlight that always lay on the floor in that shop, together with a heap of cats and an old ruptured terrier. Ray was learning the trade too. At slacker times Mr. Jarman made him sit on a stool at his side, and cut the simpler shapes, and learn to sew with waxed thread. It was heavy in the shop on those afternoons, filled with the smell of wax and new leather. Ray Parker did not

251

think he could endure the full extent of monotony that he had found in that place of life, and would go often to the lavatory to escape from the spectacle of becalmed virtue. There then, encased in white-washed boards and vine leaves, that monotony was certainly intensified, but to a point where it became personal, and for that reason regenerating. As he heard time pass, the boy stroked his flat belly and looked at himself. He was confident that he would achieve anything if the opportunity offered itself. But would it?

Sometimes he thought about his father and mother, and doubted that it would.

The father came often to the shop. Nobody would have said it was to see his son, but rather to talk with other men. These men all had scaly hands. They were so slow, anyway, for the moment, the flies stood still on them. They began to tell things and became entangled in their narratives, and when they had made such knots that could not be untied they would return hopefully towards the starting point, expecting they would find what they had begun to say. But if it led nowhere, nobody was there for that. It was a communion of sunlight and local history that they celebrated.

Few of the men who were watching the saddler's hands seemed to realize that Jarman's apprentice was Parker's boy, or if they did, they did not let on. Through some shyness the father did not produce his son. It was as much as he dared to think how that straight nose had been detached from his own flesh. Once he did speak to the boy in the presence of other men, but looking ahead, as he was leaving the shop.

He said, "That Bella threw twin heifers, Ray."

But as he went out of the shop. And the boy blushed and looked angry. He made himself feel glad his father was gone.

Ray came home seldom now, only sometimes on a Sunday. He found the house a bit lopsided and, in spite of his childhood, unfamiliar. He poked here and there, feeling the air cold about his ears. The fowls in the yard moved out of his way more precipitately, it seemed. And his mother called him to do little jobs that she had invented, to have him there, to command him, to look into his eyes, to examine the pores of his skin, to break open his sealed mind through the deaf-and-dumb show of gesture that human beings carry on. At this period she treated him with a brisk friendliness, that would not admit he had escaped her but at the same time was rather desperate, trying to establish a relationship that was final, and that other people would believe in. He could feel her disappointment as he sat in the kitchen, unable to help her out as he stared at some object, a cake of yellow soap in a saucer, or a little bunch of hot flowers stuck into a jar in a hurry.

Much as he disliked Bangalay, this was worse, and he would escape soon, walking up the road in long pants, to stand at a corner with other youths, or often at the signpost, waiting for the time to pass, or something come.

They had taken a room for him at Bangalay in the house of an old Mrs. Northcott, whose husband, now dead, had been a railway official. It was a small, decent house, thickly pasted with brown paint. It had an elderbush on one side, and a smell of sink water. On that side, opening onto the blank wall of the next house, but with some light of shifting elder leaves, was Ray Parker's room. It was very private, which suited him well enough, as he was at that time shy, and would not have entered windows if they had existed. As it was, the blank wall acted as a screen on which his dream life was played, and at the same time screened his naked acts. Sometimes he would lean at the window, smoking a slack cigarette that he had rolled himself, and consider on the blank, but in a way responsive wall, whether some girl, preferably of a class superior to his own, might not have the coolness, the directness, the experience that he desired but also feared. He would stand there, absorbed in the porous surface of the wall, half-closing his eyes to the upward smoke, and breathing rather greedily and uglily through one corner of his mouth, as he had seen smoking men do.

Life at Mrs. Northcott's was predominantly brown. It was the kind of furniture, and that wall, and Mum Northcott's face, she had always been one of the brown-skinned women. But the boy did once wake from a dream of great beauty and tenderness, which he tried to remember, but could at first only sense. He had been sitting at a table, at least, he believed, a simple table of white deal. Faces were opening to him, though which faces he could not tell. And there was a clock face that he could accept, like all things, on trust. Awake, he lay and looked at the hard washstand with its set of involved china, and wondered whether he should condemn the beautiful and trustful simplicity of his dream.

Finally he got up angrily out of the sheets that were holding him back, and thrust off that vision of goodness that he had been contemplating. Putting on his clothes, he condemned his parents for those of their virtues that he had

253

glimpsed. He must eventually bruise his parents, so he was furious with them as he brushed his stiff hair, remembering his mother looking through the window for a solution to some problem, and his father wrestling with words as if they had been tangled nets. He threw down the brush. He was still too young to have seen his parents' vices. There was nothing that he could forgive.

He went out to a dark, brown, outer kitchen, or breakfast room, where Mum Northcott had his breakfast for him, a dark, brown chop with some vegetable that had been warmed up.

"Well, Mum," he said, throwing his arms and legs about coltishly, to convince himself of his independence, "Did you sleep good?"

"No, dear," she said. "I had the stones again. They was with me all night, I slept terrible. I got up and warmed some plates to hold on me side."

"What you want is a hot-water bottle," he said.

But she did not answer that; she would want to think about it for some time.

Mum Northcott had the gallstones. She sighed a great deal. She was a rather lonely, if mean, old woman. To help out the savings of her husband the official, now dead, she took in a little washing as well as a boarder. But the arthritis in her hands would not allow her to do much.

She had grown fond of this boy, which he had allowed, for sentimental attachments are easier to maintain than relationships which demand love. His mother might have devoured him, if allowed, but the gallstones and the aches of her bones must predominate in the last years of this old woman's life.

"You want to take care of yourself," he said, "and not do too much, and have a lay down after dinner."

Nobody was listening, and it did not cost anything to say. He sat picking his teeth after meat, and even began to believe in his own concern for Mum Northcott's health. His callousness softened a little. He felt creeping over him that nostalgia for what he would destroy. There were times when he did almost cry for his mental destruction of his parents. If he had been rich he would have gone out and bought them things. As he was not, he patted the old woman's back with the flat of his hand and smiled that affectionate smile which was only in the experimental stages of its evolution.

Mum Northcott sighed and grumbled. She enjoyed the

254

touch of the young man, who might have been her son, and was not.

"It is all very well laying down," she grumbled, through the startling hair of her otherwise unremarkable face, "but there's the dust, the dust is accumulating all the time, and fluff too. I don't know where the fluff comes from in a house."

He did not care to inquire into the origin of this phenomenon. He did not, in fact, care much about the problems of other people, and fortunately nobody had thrust them on him yet. Still, he was generous that morning, and wondered what he could do, and took the towel to dry the dishes as the old woman drew them from the water.

He wondered what he could do further to advertise that generosity which at times he possessed in theory. Then he remembered the banknote he had seen in a cookery book in Mum Northcott's drawer, laid between the pages and obviously forgotten. Presently, when the old woman had taken the additional problem of her constipation out to the lavatory at the back, Ray Parker had a look and found that the note was still there. It was quite cold and unlike money, like all money that has been let lie too long away from contact with the human body. So he took the note and put it in his pocket, where it recovered its purpose with warmth, and became his.

That evening Ray Parker brought home a hot-water bottle in a pink flannel cover that he had bought for Mum Northcott.

"There y'are, Mum," he said. "Slap it on the gallstones, and it will do them good. Leave the water loose, though."

Mum Northcott, who was sitting with a Mrs. Pendlebury, her friend who had come in, was touched to the extent that her brown and crinkled face began to nod foolishly.

Mrs. Pendlebury said, of course, that it was the act of a son.

Then Ray went into his room to luxuriate for a little in his simple act, which was not reprehensible really, and gave pleasure. That he had kept the change and would go to the pictures later on in his best clothes detracted only a little from the virtue of his original generosity. Virtue is, anyway, frequently in the nature of an iceberg, the other parts of it submerged.

So he went out, still virtuous, into the street in which the lights had formed, disguising with their blaze the dearth of life. He stood around for a bit, sucking a lolly, then collected with other people at the picture show. It delivered them. Horses' feet were beating on the face of boredom, and the patent-leather lips sucked them down. Ray Parker adopted several of the positions of oblivion on his cooperative chair, but when he went out the loneliness came on, and that desire to exchange his identity with something tangible.

Later that night, underneath some pepper trees, at the back of a livery stable, he touched the jumper of a girl wearing her first high-heeled shoes, who smelled like a slut, and was, who breathed and trembled a good deal, but who was willing for the darkness to accomplish most things. When it was accomplished she ran off, crying for her loss. So that he too trembled. He shrank for a moment into a boy and went away, treading through the soft dung of horses.

When he got in, changed, half-exalted, half-afraid, the old woman called to him from her broken sleep, "Is that you, Ray?"

"Yes, Mum," he said, swaggering at himself a bit in the hall, in front of a bamboo hatstand, on which a hat of the late official still hung.

"Be a good boy," she said, "and put out the billy for the milk."

Her voice trailed off into relief and sleep. Her belief in his goodness was confirmed by his presence.

But later in his room, after he had hung the billy on the hook and heard it settle, clinking in the starlight, he was displeased with his youth's face, that did not seem to proclaim his recent act with any conviction but had gone soft and vulnerable.

He sat down on the edge of the bed and began nervously to nick at the leg of the little bedside table with a knife he had, and to wonder whether he would ever shake off that part of himself which was rooted in memories, of sunlight in the cracks of boards, of quinces rotting in the long grass, of rising from the chaff bin and scattering the sleep from his eyes in golden showers with his fists. At such moments it seemed that the best had happened, and he could not retreat towards his mother's apron. He was involved in progressive guilt.

To hide some of this he quickly turned the little bedside table so that the mutilated outside leg was facing the wall. Then he got into bed. Usually he fell asleep at once; the whole house approved of him. But tonight there was a smell of fresh horse dung that persisted and persisted, the horses pawing and whinnying and raising their long shining necks, to strike.

That Sunday, Ray Parker wanted to go home and see the faces of his family. So he got the bus early. He walked down the road from the post office at Durilgai, where the whole landscape led down to Parkers', in jubilation and hopefulness, to the rather ordinary but real house.

His sister, who was combing her hair at the window, looked up, and made it obvious she no longer believed in his existence.

"This is a surprise for you," he said, so as not to appear deterred.

"I hope it is a pleasant one," she said, and threw from her the pale hair that she took from the comb, the hair drifting and soon dissolving into light.

Thelma Parker was an older girl now, who could remove her secret life into protective corners, and for this reason was more irritated than upset by her brother's visit. She wore a ring now, too small to proclaim itself as cheap, and would bathe herself frequently, and powder her skin, and press her best blouses, till such neatness and cleanliness became oppressive, even insulting. But she carried her eyes downcast, and so was unaware of any effect she might have on other people, not that she wanted to know. She was too cold, except for her own mysteries, then she warmed. Her parents had decided that Thelma should start next term at a College for Business Girls in the city. They were impressed by, rather than fond of her. They went on doing whatever they happened to be doing, but with one eye on Thel, frightened by her aloofness and immaculacy.

"Ray is here," Thelma said now, passing through the kitchen with a towel.

She did not express her disgust with more than one petal. Her camellia graces were not of the generous, blowing order, but tight and small, greenish-white, and not for picking.

The whole family was a bit aghast that something unforeseen should happen on that day. The mother, who had abandoned system on Sunday morning, was dawdling in her felt slippers. The father was reading Saturday's paper, but would go very soon to solder a can that he had saved for Sunday; he liked to see the glittering metal flow beneath the iron.

But they said, Ah, Ray is here.

Of course they loved their son, only they were off their guard. The mother was even caught at the throat by the love

257

she had for him, its quick spasm surprising her by its strength. She would show him this time, she decided.

The father cleared his throat, and rattled the newspaper, and looked desperately from column to column, hoping to find in a moment and few words the secret of life, which he was long overdue in offering to his son.

But by this time the youth was cocking his leg over the window sill, and was coming in through the congested canes of a white rose, which his parents had once planted, and which had practically taken possession of the house. He was extricating himself in a shower of papery petals. An old bird's nest fell. Then he emerged, looking red but rational.

"That's no way to come into the room, Ray," said the father.

"But it's the quickest," said the son logically.

The boy would have defended himself mathematically, if necessary, out of pigheadedness.

"Nice if we all came in that way," called the pure young girl his sister, who had flounced into the bathroom and was scrubbing her clean nails.

But the mother, picking up the bird's nest from the floor, stopped frowning and said, "Anyway, you are here."

She would make it obvious she was his mother, proclaiming her love by tolerance. It was most important that he should return that love and treat her with kindness.

Instead, he wondered what she would try to sell him.

All that day he was on the defensive, though in the morning, as he came down the road with the wind behind him, things had been clear; it was that deceptive morning light, Then the landscape had begun to change. It was not so much in himself. He had genuinely wanted to see his family and feel himself part of it. But the sadder lights of afternoon prevailed, the trees darkening, and the dead colours of grass. In the afternoon a wind got up, and handfuls of brown grass were blown aimlessly by the gusts of wind, eddying in the sour back yard amongst the clumps of ruffled hens.

For a while he roamed in the paddock. Thistles had sprung up since he was there last, and there were places in which he had to walk carefully. But even so his hand, he saw, was striking against a thistle, which, while seeing what must happen in the next second, he could not avoid. He accepted the sharp and melancholy pain as something that his flesh must in the end suffer.

Returning to the house, he saw that his sister, whose prettiness and pale hair, as she stood at the window that morning, combing and dreaming, should never have been destroyed, had now grown thin and ugly. She was seated at the same window, sorting some of her possessions, girls' things, and had pinned paper round her sleeves, as she had seen the postmistress do. This is not for me, felt the boy. The paper sleeves alone told him that. So he continued to tread clumsily round the house, and Thelma frowned and did not see him.

"Look, Ray," said his mother, coming up against him unexpectedly, which made her breathless, for she was not quite ready, "I found this little notebook the other day. It was given to me years ago by a parson's wife, I think. I never wrote in it, because I don't write easily. Did you ever keep a diary? Some people do. I thought you might like to try. Then you could send it to me at the end of the year, and I could read what you have done."

It was a silly idea, and not quite fair. She had thought of it on the spur of the moment, as a means of approach. Now she regretted it as they stood there beside some strands of inactive honeysuckle. The boy looked as if he was going to be sick.

"Pffh," he said. "I don't want to keep a diary. What am I going to put? What I had for breakfast!"

He continued round the side of the house, and she followed him patiently.

"I only thought," she said.

The more stupidly she behaved, the more desperate she was to retrieve the situation. And it did seem to her that she could only behave stupidly towards her children. She remembered how, as a young woman, she had looked inside their minds and seen their desires, or they had brought her their thoughts without disguises.

"Are you happy, Ray?" she asked when they had stumbled inside the kitchen, for it seemed there was nowhere else they could go, there was no real escaping from each other, except in the end by the boys' actual, and what she feared would be his natural, flight. "Are you happy?" she asked.

He was too young and callow to realize that this was a means of telling him she was not.

"What do you mean, *happy?*" he asked lumpishly.

He did not like this kind of catechism. It bordered on air. It was like opening a door and finding that the floor had gone.

"I would like to think," she said, "you were getting the most out of life. It's only natural, as you are my son. I have been very happy," she said.

She did tell herself with conviction.

"I only want to be left alone," he said.

The dark shapes of trees were altering all the time, combed into long tresses by wind. It would rain soon probably.

"But Ray," she said, leaning on the table.

Thelma came in, throwing back the leaf of the door with ease. She could afford to. She had been reading the ridiculous things she had written in a notebook when younger. She was tingling with her present superiority to all that was childish and laughable.

"Aren't we going to have some tea?" she asked loudly.

She looked in the mirror to watch herself speak, and was pleased with what she saw, for that moment anyway.

"Yes," said the mother, as if wondering why she had not thought of this solution. "Shall we bake a few scones?"

"We?" asked Thelma, wrinkling up her face in a way that was both pretty and amusing. "My scones are always sods."

While her mother took flour, she brought the more agreeable things, and particularly the cake, which she had iced herself in pink sugar, and decorated with a laborious and runny white flower.

"Did you hear about the College, Ray?" she asked, beginning to set the more important crockery that they used on Sundays.

"No," he said thickly. "Oh, I heard something."

He would go from here to that alternative, Mum Northcott's, from which he must go in turn. At night the streets are filled with the desperate echoes of departing footsteps.

"Next term," she was saying. "I am going to board in Randwick with the Bourkes. Mrs. Bourke is a relative of Dad's. They had a quarrel or something, but it is made up."

"It was not a quarrel," said the mother. "People often fade out, leaving you to guess the reason, and there's always many."

"Anyway," said Thelma, "I shall go to the city. I'm a bit afraid, Ray. I shall have a season ticket, and travel by tram from Randwick every day. Mrs. Gage knows people too, who will invite me. They have a small-goods business. They are quite rich. Mrs. Gage is helping with a dress. It is a beige

260

dress, with little tucks and a pleated skirt. There are little red buttons, three on each sleeve, and a row down the back."

When the wood moved in the grate Thelma glowed. She was, after all, pretty, or feverish, holding her neck high, which was too thin certainly, as she sat gathering crumbs with correct fingers.

The mother listened to all these far-off things, eating her comfortable scone, and would have liked to feel comfortable. Do the children take over perhaps?

Ray looked out of the window. He was struggling with a sense of injustice and the cake in his throat. Long whips of vicious rain began to lash the gooseberry bushes, which had never done well in that district, though they continued to try them.

"What'll you do then?" he asked, not yet decided what form his insult, or self-defense, should take. "In your beige dress?"

"Why," she said, flushing, "I shall pass the necessary exams, in typing and shorthand, and take a job, with a stockbroker or solicitor, something like that. And make something of my life," she added smoothly, taking out her handkerchief, which she had not yet used, and which had been folded in a perfect oblong, to stay in her belt.

"And marry some bloke," he said.

"I'm not thinking of anything like that."

"And play the pianner," he laughed, "while he brings the dough home."

His rich, metallic laughter, that he had discovered all of a sudden how to make, rocked him regularly, and he liked the feeling of it. He had a strong throat and rather heavy eyelids. He sat looking out of the window at skeins of grey rain that were being flung across the paddocks, and black trees restrained so far by their roots.

"What's she done to deserve this?" asked the mother.

"Nothing," he said, quietening. "Only you get fed up."

"Because you get fed up, I am to pay for it," said the girl.

Self-pity made her mince with a new gentility, that was perhaps instinctive, or else she had listened to a stranger and learned. Her skin had the soapiness of righteousness.

"Perhaps I should keep a diary, eh, Thel? And write it all down. Wonder what happened to that Greek?"

"Why the Greek?" asked the mother, remembering something she had forgotten.

"He came into my mind," said the boy. "Not a bad cove, for a dago."

Now the rain wrapped the trees and house with grey sheets, folding and falling. If you had not heard it, this rain would have appeared quite solid. But the sound of rain and wind and spitting fire dispersed the illusion of solid rain, of all solidity even.

The mother remembered that time of the floods when furniture was no longer rooted. She forgot her joy in standing on the riverbank with the muddy water swirling at her feet, and her solid husband in the little boat; she forgot for remembering the transitoriness of most things, and most of all her own life, it seemed, as the strong young Greek walked in the field and turned the withered corn stalks to smoke.

"He was a good young man," she said, looking at her broad and still sensual hands, with the yellow wedding ring. "A good fellow," she said, as if by repeating no one could accuse her of concealing.

Nobody did, because each was his own globe, or world of thought.

The boy began to be afraid of this isolation, to which it all boiled down in the end. He longed to substitute movement for his fears, so he got up and went from the kitchen, running through the rain, past the shack in which he had wrestled with the Greek, down to the feed room, where his father used to lift him sleeping from the bins, and shake the sleep from him as if it had been chaff, and there his father, the daylight, would be standing. They would have a talk then about objects of interest.

There was his father now, he saw when it was too late. The father was bending over a bucket, mixing up some kind of mash. On the walls there were bottles and jars, of liniments and ointments, that rats sometimes knocked down. The father looked up. He also saw immediately that he was caught. He had across his shoulders an old bag he had been wearing in the rain, which did not seem to have been much of a protection, except a moral one.

Now he looked up and shook the wet mash from his hands back into the bucket. "This is from the right quarter," said the father, to investigate what was uppermost in his mind, hence safer. "If we don't get three days of it, we shall get three weeks. The dam is low," he said. "It will bring the sorghum on."

To the boy, weather, like fruit and vegetables, was unimportant, even hateful, but he supposed, grudgingly, he was glad his father had chosen to talk about this now. Each of them was afraid that some explanation of the boy's sudden presence in the shed might be called for.

The wind continued to blow the bending rain in the grey paddock. In the uproar of wind and rain a black tree fell, at a distance, without being heard.

Now that things had begun to suffer for their existence, it seemed more than ever likely that explanations must be dragged out. Souls unite in the face of violence, if only on the common ground of frailty.

The boy pressed his face against a pane of the cobwebby window, that did let some light, slow and pearly, into the obscure shed.

"Perhaps there will be more of those floods that we had," he said, "that you and Mum talk about. I would like to see them," he said, his voice grown hollow on the glass, "and things floating, and houses carried away. I would like to see a tree torn out by the roots. Or struck by lightning. They say you can smell a struck tree, and it smells of gunpowder."

The father paused with a pang, for normally he could have taken refuge in the virtue of his own activity, in warm, moist bran.

"What good would that do you?" he asked.

"It would be something happening," said the boy.

Acts of terror had exhilarated Stan Parker too, before he had built his house. After that they had confused him, made him feel he had been taken in. Then when he had accepted his confusion, and lived longer, much later, not till now perhaps, in the shed with the confused and rebellious boy, who was his son, those acts of terror did begin to illuminate the opposite goodness and serenity of the many faces of God.

If he had been able to come closer to his boy and tell him this, he would have done so now, but he was a slow and awkward man with bran on his hands.

The boy looked round, suspecting his father of being too close. He did not want to be touched. The humble, familiar shapes of the shed were looming round him. He could have kicked the walls down, and with them the face of the humble man his father, whom he would have loved, if disgust had allowed.

"We'll have to get you out of that hole in Bangalay," said the father as an alternative. "I did wrong perhaps to put you there."

263

"I'm not asking for that," said the boy raucously. "I can fit in there as well as any place."

The truth of this had still to be proved.

As a lull had come in the rain, or it blew more than it ran, and above all the sounds were less disturbing, Ray Parker made his getaway from the place that had been his home. He went up the road with his head down and his hands in his pockets. The emotions that had been knotting in him actively all that afternoon had settled down, at least temporarily, into a passive coil.

The parents took it for granted that something like this must happen, and were grateful that it was not more bewildering. Until they were asked for information, first from old Mrs. Northcott, then from Mr. Jarman the saddler, on the whereabouts and intentions of their son.

It appeared that Ray had gone.

He wrote soon, a letter from Brisbane, in which he said:

Dear Mum,

I come up here on the spur of the moment, and think I have done right to make the move, whether it was the right move, but I had to make one, as Dad said, only it was me that had to make it.

I am working on a steamer on this coast. I am working in the galley. The cook is a Chinaman, but clean. He gave me a piece of pearl shell with some carving on it, that I will keep for you, it is what you will like.

Well, cheer up, Mum. Nothing is for always, though there is life enough on the coastal run. I wake up at night and see the cranes loading up, or else it is horses driven up the race. I could go to the Territory if I like with a gentlemen who made me an offer as a hand on a station, but I don't think that I will. I will look around. I could go anywhere. Last night I dreamed I was swimming to the islands, the sea was like oil and full of phosphorous, and I was swimming and swimming without a stitch, the water full of light, but I did not get there before I woke up. . . .

When the father was handed this letter to read he said, "It is natural, Amy."

He gave it back to his wife to keep, because they were not accustomed to receive mail, excepting bills and catalogues. He remembered his own youth, and how easily his clothes

264

had sat upon his body, making him forget his nakedness. Whichever steps he had taken were hardly determined by himself. But this was not what his wife would have wanted to hear.

She found him, as often at moments of crisis, disappointing.

She said, "That is all very well for you. You have not had the trouble." Her voice swelled up for the injustice of it, and because she was taken unawares.

For he had gone, slipping from her as easily and naturally as the seed from the pod, to become lost in the long grass. If she suffered a great spasm at the moment of realization, with lesser ones recurring over many days, it was more perhaps for her vanity, though she did remember the little stubbly-headed boy in short trousers, and the baby gorging itself with placid confidence on her breast. So she cried at times, mostly at dusk, standing at a window, when shapes have grown tender, and she herself was disintegrating, and sucked onward, the years streaming behind her like skirts in the wind, or hair. It was frightening then. Her face abandoned the mealiness of personal sorrow and became a brooding skull, or essential face.

I have paid too much attention to Ray and not enough to Thelma, said Amy Parker, rousing herself. After all, a girl is more reliable than a boy, a girl needs to be.

When Thelma left for Sydney and the College for Business Girls, the mother packed her daughter's case. She put in a sachet that she had made for the occasion, and some packets of chocolate in case her girl felt hungry at night; she would eat with gratitude, rustling the silver paper, and think of her mother.

The last night Amy Parker went into her girl's room, and put her mouth in the long pale hair, and held her, and said, "Who'd have thought, Thel, all by yourself in the city, but you must not worry."

"I'll be all right, Mum," said the cool girl, taken by surprise and anxious to extricate herself. "Besides, there will be Mrs. Bourke. Dad says she was a good sort, in spite of the misunderstanding there was at that time about some things."

"Oh yes, there'll be Mrs. Bourke," said Amy Parker. "But it won't be the same as home."

Through the nightdress she felt her daughter's thin, secretive body, and wondered if this had ever belonged to her. Anxiety transferred itself to the body of the girl, who

265

coughed a good deal during the night, and had to burn a little powder that she kept against such an attack. When it was dawn she got up, groping through the bitter fumes of the powder. The steely knives of morning cut deeply into the feverish girl. As she prepared to wash, baring herself for the operation, she shivered and winced. But she was glad. All unpleasantness and pain were necessary to achieve her final, perfect shape.

Thelma caught the train in Bangalay, in a grey suit and neat hat. She never showed any nervousness in public. Her parents, who had brought her to town in the Ford, stood beside the window of the compartment, and wondered about things. The father did not struggle, because the situation was being taken out of his hands. For a long time, though, the mother put up a show of authority and advice, till it was time to bow her head, under the large dark hat. Then the children do take over, she was forced to admit. She received on her mouth with gratitude, even humility, the last kiss, wondering if it signified love; she would have liked to believe this.

The girl watched the last of the handkerchief, feeling a pang for her departing childhood, that was made more poignant by the flatness of the country streaming by. Finally she settled down to her own reflection in other people's faces. It was a new and voluptuous sensation, to try to solve its mystery in such mirrors.

So Thelma Parker came to the city, and went to the College for Business Girls, and became efficient. She was as cool as the bell on the typewriter that rang at the end of the line. She would fling the roller back, just not angrily, but disdainfully, looking at nonexistent objects at the far end of the room. Her paper was always spotless. She was, indeed, very clean. Her long, slightly oval nails were pink, and she smelled of lavender water, which she kept in a drawer of her desk and sprinkled discreetly on her clean hands. On her thin white wrist she wore a small gold watch, cheap but in good taste. Her skin was very white, almost unhealthy, and always ready to react to worldliness in other people, so that when her friend Genevieve Johnstone made some joke, she was bathed in the pink of pleasure or shame, it was difficult to tell which.

Genevieve Johnstone, whom Thelma Parker first met at the same business college, lived at Bondi, whereas Thelma was with the Bourkes at Randwick. Sometimes the two girls went for rides together on a tram, because it was cheap and passed time. These rides were of great importance to Thelma, because they emphasized her freedom. The loose tram clanked and swung. People laughed electrically on those nights. The two girls sat together, friends, but not particularly fond of each other, feeling their hair grow dank in the salt air. They swung and laughed at their own motion, and the bony knees of men sitting opposite, or passing, pressed their knees. Genevieve Johnstone liked to look at men. She was a dark, smudgy girl with a bust. She was anxious to give generously to some man, whereas Thelma looked away, holding her handbag in suddenly hot hands. It was doubtful whether generosity was in Thelma's line; either she valued herself too highly, or else she was afraid.

In the end it was these differences of temperament that caused the friendship between Thelma and Genevieve to lapse. Thelma grew afraid of the company of the dark, smudgy, big-busted, laughing girl, on whom the glances of men hung, on her dank, salty hair, and the swing of her breasts in the tram. The night was too powerful in her company. So Thelma broke with her for weak reasons. She continued to go on tram rides by herself, for the air, but looking away from people, into the flashing night. This way she could still enjoy her freedom. She loved the city, she said, translating its garishness into a personal poetry. Were not its asphalt and metal a mark of her own progress? So she rode the trams at night, looking down from her compartment into the windows of people's lives, noticing them at table, having differences, easing their clothes, picking their teeth. If she had not yet made definite plans for the conduct of her own life, she was pretty confident she would succeed in whatever she chose, and would not be surprised in awkward attitudes.

This confidence was occasionally shaken if she heard laughter as she closed a door. Particularly the laughter of men. For this reason she hated the stablehands at Bourkes'.

Horrie Bourke, who had married Stan Parker's relative, with whom Thelma boarded, was a trainer of racehorses. He was an honest man and consequently had not succeeded as he might have. Even so, he had known some good wins, and had bought diamonds for his wife, and a fox fur, that had got its head squashed in a taxi door during the Easter meeting some years back. Horrie Bourke himself was never dolled up, though he approved of it in his wife, and in the rich, his patrons. He preferred his slippers. He would wear a collar but no tie. Just the brass stud that held together his slightly yellow starched collar. This way he went about his stable yard and gave directions to the lads, and to the one or two older men who were experienced and supercilious in horse matters, though obedient to Horrie, who was a decent cove.

This was what Thelma Parker saw when she looked from her window of the Bourkes' brick home, for her room was, humiliatingly, on the stables side. There were the lads in their singlets, swinging buckets of shining water, and the older men, bandy-legged, and the glistening, muscular, trembling horses.

Horrie Bourke said that Thelma must make herself at home. He gave her a box of chocolates the second day, with a big pink satin bow, and said she could pick out an occasional soft one specially for him. He was the kind of man who likes to practise an elaborate ritual of courtliness with girls. He liked to see young girls with bows in their hair and bangles on their wrists, and to make the kind of jokes they giggled at, eating chocolates in the afternoon. But nothing nasty in his relationship with these girls. His innocent vanity was appeased by giggles and the acceptance of his simple presents. He was of that school which seems to think women are a different breed, which does suit some women.

Thelma Parker soon sensed that Horrie Bourke was amiable but not of much account. She learned to accept the ritual of his courtliness and to laugh at his jokes without conveying any deception.

"Poor Dad," said Mrs. Bourke, "he is so good."

As if he were suffering from an illness.

Mrs. Bourke had been a Bott. She was Lilian, one of those three girls to whom Stan Parker did not propose, and for that reason she developed a habit of screwing up her eyes at Thelma, to look a little closer, it seemed, with ever so much quizzical tolerance. But you could not say that Lily Bourke was not a good sort. She rouged a bit, but it meant nothing. She liked to have a few friends in for the evening, and a glass of something, preferably stout, when she would sing all the old songs at an upright piano, after she had removed her rings.

How do you like Mrs. Bourke? You do not say, Thelma's mother wrote.

Mrs. Bourke is all right, she is very kind, wrote Thelma to her mother.

Mrs. Bourke approached her powder to Thelma's face and

told her she must call her Aunt Lily. But Thelma decided she would not be trapped into calling her by a Christian name. She did not think she wanted a permanent cosiness of Bourkes, already feeling she was dedicated to some higher form of discomfort.

So she did not commit herself, and went to her room to buff her nails.

When Thelma Parker graduated from the business college she very quickly got a job as junior typist with a shipping firm. It was not what she wanted, but it would do for then. Soon it became apparent that she was most efficient. Special bits of work were given her, with the result that she was hated by those who did not want to do it. But she was undeterred. She had her hair cut off about this time, and the nape of her neck was unassailable as she passed through the offices between the rows of desks, carrying a sheaf of fresh papers, or returning from the washroom with her towel and soap.

She did just think about her home sometimes, eating her anchovette sandwich, for instance, in the half-hour she took off for lunch. The discomfort of such thoughts distressed her but could not be avoided. Her mother persisted, who deserved really all affection and compassion, in spite of the ugliness of her clothes and clumsiness of most things that she did, continually knocking over buckets and pots, or cutting herself as she shredded a cabbage, her face bungling after thoughts she had forgotten, that she was afraid she would not retrieve though everything depended on it. Thelma Parker would become hot with an ashamed and irritating love for her mother. Her father was a man, therefore of less account, except economically. Her father was given to abstractions, so his face indicated, and in that wrestling was defeated, and for that reason could be despised. Besides, she did not understand what needs her father had. She despised and feared what she did not understand. Till she remembered that her father's neck was shrivelling up. So she was pulled back. The cracks of his hands were catching in her dress. So she could not escape, not so much from the humiliation of her parents as from their humility, and would in the end perhaps not be brutal enough.

She would sweep up the crumbs of her insipid sandwich, which was still adequate to her needs. She would make a little screw of paper, containing the miserable crust of the sandwich, because she did not like crusts.

Thelma did not think at all about her brother. She closed a

lid on him, and persuaded herself he was not just choosing his own time to burst out.

Several nice people had found Thelma Parker nice. There were the Goughs, those friends, or, more likely, acquaintances, of the postmistress at Durilgai, whose business was small goods, though in a better way; they were no longer in aprons behind the counter, nothing of that sort. The Goughs lived in a better suburb, though not the best, with quantities of shining furniture, including a smoker's-table-cum-drink-cabinet, that you approached on all fours to fish out a bottle of banana cocktail. After washing her hands Thelma Parker fingered their towels, which were embroidered with *Guest* in a wreath of pansies, quite artistic. The Goughs gave evening parties, nothing formal, but bridge rolls and semi-evening dress. Thelma soon knew what to do. She had the gift of looking all ways, of assuming correct attitudes, as if her limbs were wax to the moment, of conjuring phrases, as if they had sprung from her own throat and not someone else's. She was doing all this, exhilarated by so many discoveries, possibilities, and surprises.

One Sunday at Bourkes' an elderly but imporant grazier, after feeling his horse's fetlocks and discussing prospects with the trainer, complimented Thelma Parker on her looks. It was, of course, silly. But she remembered how his boots shone, and that his suit, however carelessly worn, was of expensive stuff. She remembered that his name was Letourneur, although she did not see him again.

Buffing her nails at the window at Bourkes', Thelma had many things to think about, and watch, as the horses were led up and down, or pawed at their doors in the evening, and snuffled dustily. Some of the boys hung around in the evening, to fool or play at cards or toss coins. Boys in the yard held each other's heads beneath their arms, practising forms of torture. They laughed in broken voices and smoked, they told jokes and made obscene gestures, for or in spite of the girl at the window, who was, anyway, oblivious. Nobody spoke to Horrie Bourke's stuck-up sort of relative, except when it was necessary, and then calling her Miss. Never taking liberties. Except blowing a raspberry from a distance, which could, of course, have been an expression of joie de vivre.

There was Curly, though.

Thelma had begun to be impressed by the way she was arranging her life—they had given her a rise at the office and she had bought the half-coat in dyed lapin—when Curly spoke to her. Quite insolently, in fact. He came across the strip of buffalo grass that Mr. Bourke kept mown himself. He walked quickly and straight in his sandshoes on the coarse grass, with that motion of his buttocks she had noticed, swinging his muscular, unconsciously insolent young man's arms, and stuck his chin on the window sill, and said, "Got any thoughts for us tonight, Thel?"

She looked at him with her lips open, less thin, as if they had been stung. She was at the same time shocked, stimulated, and a little frightened.

She looked at him. He was younger than herself, which made it worse. But his face was well cut, rather blond. He might commit crimes, but in a good-humoured way.

"Eh?" he coaxed.

"Not that I know of," she said, wishing she could turn away. "Not for cheeky boys like you."

Wishing to destroy him, she was at most prim, looking at his arms that were laid along the window sill.

"Ah," he said. "I'm not all horse crap. Scratch me an see. I'll allow yers to use a fork.

"I'll tell Mr. Bourke," she said.

He began to laugh then. She could see his big teeth.

"No jokin," he laughed. "I got a message for yer," he said. "How much will yer pay me for it?"

"What sort of message?" she asked.

Her head, in spite of herself, had taken on a tick-tock motion of badinage, as she struck her nails and carefully did not look at whatever else she might be aiming at. It had begun to be a game that she liked almost. The inexorable smells of liniment and hay made her reckless, and the squeals of the filly rolling in the sand behind the palings of the exercise yard.

The young man had begun to pick the hard putty in a crack of the window frame.

"What message?" she asked.

Against the hot wall he shifted his body into a fresh position of indifference, indolence, and self-possession.

"From your brother," he said.

"From my brother? How do you know my brother?"

"Ar!" he said. "I seen im Saturday at Warwick Farm."

"It can't be my brother. My brother is up North."

"He come South, see, recently."

"I can't believe you know my brother."

"Aren't you the sister of Ray Parker?"

271

"Yes," she said. "But—"

"Ray says, 'Tell Thel I'll be out one of these days to pay a social call.'"

She sat thinking. She was a thin girl in a window, disturbed by the thought that something might intrude beyond the sill into the shadowy privacy of her room.

"Well," said the boy, "I'd a thought you would a been pleased to see yer brother."

"Oh," she said, "I shall be pleased."

But she pushed back her chair, and the boy began to go, sensing that she was older than himself. He was a boy, really, at most times, big, and inclined to assume the attitudes that his body took. Now, of himself, he did not know how to continue, so he went away in his sandshoes, over the spongy buffalo grass.

Thelma Parker was disturbed. She went into the lounge, and sat on her Cousin Lily Bourke's Genoa velvet settee, and looked at a magazine, at the photographs of brides and furniture. Unattainable heights caused in her a breathlessness, and possible loss of foothold a first dry spasm. She coughed and flicked the pages of the magazine. Many bright vistas opened and closed. Waning light brought with it the sweet sadness of coconut ice and childhood. She got up, to change her position into one in which her breathing would be less constricted, sitting at Lily Bourke's piano, in which the candlewax had run that last time there had been a singsong, onto the walnut veneer. Now Thelma touched the keys. Pieces of music returned to her, with feeling and even a little talent, out of the postmistress's workroom. She should have been a musician perhaps. Distinguished music flowed from her hands when she was alone. She would have had, or would still have, a grand, with a bowl of mixed flowers and a photograph of herself in evening dress. Then some man, her husband, his face shadowy at the hour, is coming in and touching her on the shoulders with careful, dry hands to assure her of his admiration.

"You ought to go out and have a good time, Thel," said Lily Bourke. "At your age."

Mrs. Bourke, who had been lying down with an aspirin, and who looked bright under her fresh rouge, and the brandy she had just knocked back, for her health, had heard or read somewhere that specific behavior belongs to different ages, and so she prescribed accordingly. Looking at Thelma through her migraine and the gloom, she would have thought her a poor sort of thing if kindness had allowed. Lilian liked rollicking girls, engaged in the perpetual lancers of a good time. She would have taken a turn herself, if it had not been for her husband's rupture, and her moral standards, which did not encourage other men. So she invited people round and played the accompaniments in royal blue.

Lilian Bourke said, "When our dad had the shop at Yuruga, there was always such a coming and going, we three girls were never at a loss. It was a small town, but there was life in it. There were the dairy farmers. There were business associates of our dad's always passing through, and your father coming down from his place. Yes, I remember the night he broke the washstand. Yes," she said.

"But I am content," said Thelma, on the relentless bench which contained the ballads.

She did not play much more, except in a last trickle of notes, because her music had lost its privacy.

"If you are content," said Mrs. Bourke, shaking out the beads of a lampshade that had become tangled at a party, "you are content. Though, mind you, there is no knowing without you have sampled the alternatives."

Then she went out to cook the tea. It was a nice piece of steak that she had that evening, with a little frill of fat, just enough to lubricate the lovely meat. Because, it was obvious, men must eat meat.

Thelma Parker only picked that night, and for several days she was off her food. She wondered whether she should write and tell her mother that Ray was now in town. She did not write, though, for wondering what she should say, and then Ray came.

"I am Ray Parker," he said on the step.

"Well, now," said Mrs. Bourke, "you are like your father, or is it your mother? I wonder. Your sister will be pleased, she is just in, and will no doubt invite you to stay for something to eat. As you see, I am going out."

She was fitting the kid, in fact, onto her rather small hands, of which she was very proud.

"If it's not convenient," he began.

He was a broad, open-faced young man, with clear skin, that encouraged the faith people put in him. He was looking up with that expression of trust that he kept for those to whom he was not closely related.

"If it's not convenient," he said, "I can come back another
273

time. You are Cousin Lil?" he asked with a tentative smile, of a rough but somewhat practised charm.

"I am a sort of cousin," admitted Mrs. Bourke.

"Dad often speaks about you," he said.

"Oh," she laughed, believing it because she had been told. "It is good to talk about the old times."

He might have insinuated himself still further into her graces, but she was fat and ugly.

Thelma met her brother in the lounge. They sat together on the Bourkes' furniture, feeling its pressure during the silences, the swelling of horsehair and the rustling patterns of the Genoa velvet. Thelma wished he would go quickly, that all her relations would leave her to meditation of her own higher good. But Ray had still to tell about himself. He would stay in Sydney, it appeared. He had a job with a bookie, as his clerk. The money was not bad. Still, he was looking around.

Thelma explored the piping on the lounge settee.

"You have always hated me, Thel," he said, lighting a cigarette with accomplishment.

Because she had never seen him do this before she experienced anger, as if he had stolen somebody else's gesture.

She shifted sharply, drawing up her knees and putting her neat feet together, and said, "I don't hate you."

"It is that diary perhaps."

Blowing long smoke.

"Pffh," she said. "I had forgotten about that. The silly things you put in a diary when you are a kid!"

But he remembered, through the ramifications of smoke and memory, a queer thing, his own passion for the Greek.

"Some people," he said, "don't like you to know too much about them."

"What do you know about me? You know nothing, nothing. We might not be related even, except that we are."

Whether either knew anything of the other was both possible and doubtful, as they looked at each other sideways in the lounge, or waiting room, that preserved only an uneasy sort of collusion. Or whether even, inside the clothes they had adopted, they knew about themselves, which way they might strike or drift. Uncertainty began to make the young man restless. He got up and moved about, handling ornaments and looking into boxes. But the girl only clasped her hands together tighter on her knees, holding the hot ball of her handkerchief.

"You think you'll stick it out down here?" asked the brother, without much interest in an answer.

"Of course," she said.

She could still feel indignant if it was suggested she would not accomplish what she had intended to.

But the brother wanted to talk about the place in which they had lived together.

"You remember those Quigleys?" he asked.

"I hadn't thought about them," she said dryly. "But I haven't forgotten."

She did not want to be drawn back.

"She was an ugly old bitch," he said. "That goitre."

He was disgusted but melancholy.

"But clean," he said. "You could see how she'd scrubbed the table half away. I remember they had a lyre-bird's tail in a vase on the mantelpiece. I said I'd give the loopy brother six red maggy's eggs if he'd let me have the tail. And he did. But I didn't bring the eggs. He was cryin mad."

"Why did you cheat him?" asked the girl listlessly.

"I don't know," he said. "I wanted the tail. And I didn't have the eggs."

In that light, and in his rather pleasant voice, it seemed logical. So that the girl turned her head aside afresh. She did not want to see Doll Quigley's plain table, because in its presence she too became suspect. Her past dishonesties, and those she had still to commit, were turning in her.

"I don't think there's going to be enough for everyone to eat," she said, to make him go away.

But the young man, now that he had made his sister share in the crime of his childhood, craved her company. He sensed that some kind of reality had been established between them at last. So he did not want to relinquish it and said, "That's all right. I didn't come for that."

Quite forgetting that he had.

Presently, too, Horrie Bourke came in, and had to meet the young man, his relative.

"You are a fine feller," said Horrie, putting his arm in its shirt-sleeve, with the elastic-metal armband, along the shoulder of this young man. "A fine feller. And one that your dad can be proud of."

Whenever he was convinced, a little drop of saliva appeared in the corner of Horrie's mouth and began to follow a furrow down. He was an unsavoury old man in some respects, but good. He would cry if his horses strained themselves, and give directions to the stable-hands between on-rushes of saliva, and finally seize the liniment bottle, identifying himself with the injured limb and experiencing great pain as his hand trembled on ligament or joint.

Now, as a sign of appreciation, he wanted to expose the tenderest, the most vulnerable part of him, and tell Ray Parker about horses. He continued to stand with his arm along the boy's shoulders, otherwise in rather a formal position, which his rupture forced him to adopt. When he knew Ray just a little better he would also tell him about his rupture. Horrie would have liked to have had children. Now he was treating Ray as he thought he would have treated his own, to the sentimental intimacies of confession, and to un-broken narrative. Naturally it put the young man who was not his son in an awkward position. Forced into acceptance, he acted as a son should but does not act, which gave him a passing expression of malevolence, that he should have had but normally did not. The trainer, however, was too pleased to notice anything but what he wanted to.

Oh Lord, said Thelma.

For Cousin Horrie had begun to tell Ray about a race.

"When Don Antonio had gone a couple of furlongs," he said, "or perhaps it was not so fur, an Harcourt was comin up, an Cantaloup—or no, it was the Witch—Georgie Abbott did a funny thing. I did not say much at the time, but I seen it, an I made a mental note, see. I seen Georgie look round over 'is shoulder, like, and drop 'is near-side elbow. I said this is some funny business. I said to Cec Docker, Cec was standing there—poor old beggar died of a growth the year after. I said, I remember, to Cec, 'Did you see what I seen, Cec?' 'Well, Horrie,' he says, 'it depends what you seen.' Because Cec was awful careful. He was what you call a real nice bloke. Well, Harcourt was comin up and up, an Cantaloup—or no, it was the Witch—"

Then Lilian Bourke came in. She had taken off her fox, and had a quick dash at her face in the bedroom, and they would open a couple of bottles of stout, she said, as a little celebration for Stan's son, and what was Thelma thinking about, there was that round of beef and half a chicken on the bottom shelf of the ice-chest, staring at her, if she opened the door.

The Bourkes were very pleased with Ray. They looked at him devouringly; they were hungry for his youth as they tore the bones from off the cold chicken and chewed the shreds of brown skin. They pleaded for anecdotes.

Ray was embarrassed. He looked shyly into his full glass. He told them one or two. Obviously he had begun to like best to talk about horses with the old man. He asked Horrie about Eggcup's chances for the Gold Plate. The old man, whose lips had grown greasy from a lovely forkful of yellow fat, tempered with a sliver of red beef and harshened by half a pickled onion, looked at the piece of bread he was trimming for use and admitted that Eggcup's chances were fair.

When Ray went away the Bourkes longed for him to come again. Which he did. He came quite often. They were all three in the grip, it seemed, of a fresh and stimulating, almost a passionate relationship.

"Your brother is not a bit the boy we expected," Lily Bourke said to Thelma. "Your father was always a slow one. Oh, we all liked Stan. But slow. It was your mother who married him, we all said."

"It is difficult to say what Ray is like," said Thelma. "I feel I know. I cannot say. I am prejudiced by being his sister, I suppose."

"You are a funny girl, Thelma," Lilian said.

While this was happening Thelma continued in her employment at the office of the shipping firm, where she was disliked, if also respected. No girl kept her pencils sharper. If Miss Halloran was engaged on some piece of work, as she frequently was, the boss would call Miss Parker in and dictate a letter, which she would run off, tear from her typewriter, and there was the cool paper in Mr. Fulbright's tray before he had put the telephone down. But she did not encourage jokes.

Then, suddenly, Thelma Parker left the shipping office, where she was getting on, and took a position with a solicitor at a lower salary. She could not have explained with any conviction why she had done this, only that it had to be. Soothed by the smell of discretion and timelessness perhaps. Many of the women clients wore fur coats and pearls, and were ushered out by the partners with signs of discreet intimacy and social connection, and a touch of dry hands.

In the circumstances her life at Bourkes' became more and more distasteful. Ammoniac smells from the stables clashed with the lavender water with which she refreshed her long hands, and the hooded horses sidled monotonously out, led by the hairy older men, or with boys up, hunched into shapes of arrogant responsibility. None of this concerned Thelma

Parker or was concerned about her, but it was there. And the uncouth shapes of the men, who spat through the gaps in their yellow teeth. And the wrestling boys, like the boy Curly, who had spoken that day when he became, briefly, the messenger.

Ray came sometimes to see Curly. He was his friend, it seemed. At the stables Ray removed his tie for ease, he hung over Curly's shoulder and they studied form in the supplements of Sunday newspapers; they shared confidences that were sometimes serious and sometimes, from the pantomime of their participant bodies, lewd. Sometimes on a slow Sunday afternoon, of baked brick and sleeping cats, Ray would wrestle with Curly on an old stretcher covered with sacking in the saddle room, as he used to wrestle with the Greek, and the young man in his turn would imprison the boy, who would struggle and finally cry out, wanting to escape from the humiliation of his own weakness. Before this, though, the girl who had been engaged in mysterious rites at her window would have pulled down the blind. Her anger and superiority preferred to stifle in that brown-papery gloom, from which a blowfly could not get out.

Sometimes Thelma went by herself to concerts. Her music, which had not developed, both through apathy and from fear of the consequences, was a sadness to her, which she liked also to indulge. The surge of music sounded notes in her of exquisite sadness and self-pity. She was drenched by the violins.

Once in the street in the evening she met her friend Genevieve Johnstone, who was less respectable than formerly, but pleased and even grateful to find Thelma, who was at least surprised. Over brown stew and boiled pumpkin, Genevieve told Thelma she had had an abortion on account of a married man she knew at Wentworth Falls. Thelma did neat things with her fork in the gravy. Almost as if she had not heard. But Genevieve was telling.

Then Thelma tore her superiority from the debacle and said, "I am on my way to an orchestral concert, Genevieve. Why don't you come along? It will do you good."

"Classical music isn't in my line," said Genevieve in some doubt. "But it is a way of passing the evening, I suppose. If it is cheap."

So the two girls listened to the music, or Genevieve sat and Thelma soared; she could rise to great heights on the apathy of her friend. Her own evolution seemed to depend on the brilliant passage of the violins. So she followed with headachy devotion. Her interminable but rapturous pathway led somewhere. Her own life, in trams and offices, filing her nails, reading the future in cups of tea, was not less inevitable. Only little glistening pearls of notes littered the way before the dark gulf. It is Ray, she admitted, I must not think of Ray. She trod carefully along the bridge of awkward, thin slats. In that slow field, toothed with awkward stumps and brackeny growth, it was the mother and father that became insistent. How very plain and boring they were, especially the father when explaining the workings of a fence-strainer or the ailments of cows.

This is a part on which I must concentrate, said Thelma Parker, crossing her legs and leaning forward a little. She was sometimes horrified by the difficulties of music. But it was by concentration that she had made herself appreciated, and by superior men. No percussion could make her recant now. No triumph of her smudgy friend whose mouth gratefully extracted tunes where audible. Horns issued commands to willing women. She herself liked, in her reluctant way, the dictatorial manners of brass instruments, and of some men, if their hands were well kept and restrained. She brought cups of milky tea and left them anonymously for oboes to drain.

The architecture of the composition could not be destroyed, if its intention. Thelma Parker wandered beneath the dome of music in her best shoes. Get a room somewhere, she said, with her own four-square walls, and perhaps use of kitchen. The clash of her own cymbals could not destroy her privacy. So she mounted farther, on firm steps now; it was possible to follow their winding, however intricate, even doubly spiral, in which were set the little mirrors reflecting the past, of roses, and of fowl manure, even the shattered one in which her silver face was splintered, but quickly shoved behind the flat boards of woodwind. Ah, she sucked the air between her teeth, putting the hot strands behind her ears, then it is in sight. A little farther, across a formal platform, and up, just a little, tremblingly, was the bell of victory. She reached up, so high that her breasts had disappeared, and placed the wreath with her own hands.

"Is it over then?" asked Genevieve, for whom there was no other reason to clap.

"Yes," said Thelma, resuming her outward person.

When they had pushed out and were in the damp street Genevieve said, "What do you think about all the time, all

279

through that kind of music, when you're listening to it, if you are?"

"You don't exactly think," said Thelma slowly. "You live with it."

"I don't live that way. Not any way like it," said Genevieve. "Ah, you're too deep."

Thelma was pleased but also too embarrassed to answer. She had no experience of the tolerant ways of friendship, and words could turn her rigid, or a gesture. For Genevieve had taken her arm.

"There was a bloke there playing a fiddle," said Genevieve, "you may have noticed, with the hair parted in the middle, that I think I met once on a ferry. He was from Manly. Gee, it was rough that day. And he was keen, this boy, if it was the one I think it was. But what could you do? It's one thing on a rough sea. But going with a bloomin fiddle case."

Possibilities are sown at night in damp streets and purple mist.

"Is your boss nice, Thelma?" asked Genevieve. "Is he old? I never ever knew a solicitor that wasn't old. They must begin, though."

"They are all right," Thelma said. "One is old. He doesn't come when he has lumbago. The other is younger, but not young. Mr. Forsdyke. He's a bit bald. But not bad."

The trams were cutting in now.

"Go on," said Genevieve.

"Why," said Thelma, "really, Genevieve, there isn't anything to tell."

"It would give me the willies working with a bunch of solicitors. They talk funny."

Thelma had begun to laugh. "He has a way of drawing up his stomach," Thelma said, "of drawing it up as he talks. And letting it go again."

Thelma laughed.

"He has a stomach then?" laughed Genevieve.

"Well, yes," laughed Thelma, "but not much. He lifts what he's got, I mean. Oh dear."

"The stomachy solicitor," shrieked Genevieve.

The two girls rocking at the tram stop could not stand upright. They rubbed against each other in the purple light. One or two men paused, put their hands in their pockets, and watched, spat, and walked on. The two girls laughed.

Is this perhaps life? asked Thelma, under the influence of

words and friction. But at once she was annoyed, drew herself away from the heaving Genevieve, and stopped laughing.

"I'm going to look for a room somewhere," she said quite brutally, "or a flat or something. I can't go on any longer living where I am."

"I wouldn't like living in a room," said Genevieve. "You might get bashed. Or even murdered. By some man."

"If you have got to have a man," said Thelma.

"But you have got to."

"I shall be content with a room, with a door," said Thelma.

Knowing she was not always so cool, but would have lied again, because it was necessary.

"Here is my tram," she said.

And was glad.

"Better get yourself tied up with that solicitor," shrieked Genevieve. "In red tape. The one with the stomach that lifts up."

Thelma was by that time high in the tram. She could look down with white indifference on the purple face of Genevieve. The sluggish purple waves sucked her down, while Thelma rode on, without pity for her friend, and wondering why she had attempted friendship. Offering the cold pennies to the tram conductor, she might have been buying freedom. She craved for this, like most men, before anything, while remaining uncertain of its nature. She would have liked to ask someone—but whom? Not her parents. You don't ask parents. Ray had perhaps bought it, but at what price she did not know.

Once he bought her a pair of silk stockings. He opened the door and threw them across the carpet, so that they lay there contorted, inseparable from the feelings she had for Ray.

"There y'are," he said, looking through the half-open door. "A present for you."

He waited for a moment to see whether she would accept. She still showed no sign when he went away, but his face was pretty sure that she would. And she did, guiltily, pick up the stockings from the carpet and fold them over her hand. She put them in a drawer and did at last wear them, trying to forget, and finally forgetting, that they were a present from a brother.

It was not clear what Ray intended by the pair of stockings. It was certainly that debt laid up against the future, in which spirit most of his presents were offered, but whether there was also some impulse of love in giving he was not

281

sure. He would have liked to enter into a blameless kind of relationship with some human being. He would have liked to sit down and talk with someone about the flat things, as blameless as paper, about which it is necessary to talk. It is not possible with parents, any more than with corkscrews. His mother would bore right in, hoping to draw something out. Nor with the Bourkes, they were the old children of life. Nor with any mob of friends or business associates, who expected you to act in certain preconceived ways. So there was Thelma. If they could have resisted for a moment those separate currents which were carrying them on, they might have entered into that negative kind of relationship for which he felt the need.

At that time Ray was still associated with Bernie Abrahams, the book, whom nobody had met yet, because Bourkes did not go for bookies. None of Ray's mob found their way to Bourkes'. Lily drew the line. She was afraid for her jewellery too, of which she had several real pieces in amongst the paste. There was Curly, though, who they knew was Ray's pal, and who was from Bundaberg, they knew, but what else. Ray lived somewhere above a fruit shop. There was talk of some Italians, and two Italian girls, sisters, it appeared. Ray brought the Bourkes paper bags filled with big pale apples, or the purple foaming ones, or the head of a pineapple sticking out at the top.

Horrie was pleased, like a child, but Lily was less pleased, who had had time to recover a little from her love.

"That boy is too good to us," said Lily, screwing up her eyes. "Why should a boy be so good?"

"Well, what is wrong?" said Horrie, peeling an apple. "The boy is away from home, he misses his dad and mum."

Thelma had come into the room to look for some belonging, and went out again with the quietness of discretion she used in that house. She was passing through their lives.

"You are right, Horrie," Lily said. "We didn't ought to talk about the boy like that. And in front of his sister. What will Stan say?"

But Thelma made no comment.

All this was so much regrettable cardboard of other people's lives. She must find the room, with use of kitchen. Until that time she would ignore.

So the horses continued to sidle out. In the early morning as she did her hair, and on Sundays as she sat, their monastic figures clopped out across the asphalt and through the wooden gates. The men and boys were talking of some big meeting for which the horses were being prepared. It was esoteric talk, of weights and anatomy and odds and paces, to which the girl did not listen, except as fragments fell and unavoidably were picked up. That Malabar had been scratched. Eggcup was a cert, they said, for Horrie Bourke, his big chance. As she combed her hair and thought how disparate other issues were from her own desires.

Eating soft eggs at breakfast, the old trainer trembled over the importance of this race. Then for a moment the girl did see not so much the pathos of men's fragile lives as the pathos of her own in similar isolation and unimportance. The old man's skull was frail as an eggshell waiting to break under some blow, that somebody, not now, but sometimes, must deal. And her own blouse did not protect her shoulders. She scalded herself with the bitter red tea that she was pouring from high up, and bit her mouth, and asked, "When is this race then?"

"What?" he said incredulously. "The race! Why, Saturdee."

Shocked by the discovery that he might not exist, he scraped up raspberry jam and opened and closed his mouth once or twice.

"Where is your brother?" he asked this girl, about whom he began to think now, about what kind of life she must live, shut in her room, in the same house certainly. "We ain't seen him since I don't know when."

"I don't know where Ray is," she said. "He has never told me much about his business."

She also had not seen him, she realized, with satisfaction or mistrust, not even in the yard with Curly. Curly was there, but she was noticing him less. He went on softer feet. He was grave at times. He had come out in spots, and was just a boy about the place. He whistled, but more often he would stay silent. Really she would not have noticed Curly if Ray for a time had not breathed life into his limbs.

So she wondered why Ray did not come, and there it was Saturday, it was the day of that race for which Horrie Bourke lived.

On the day Thelma did not go to the races. She never went, because when the house was dead, then she lived. She would take off her dress, and improvise on the walnut piano, or write in her diary, and make cups of tea. That day she was extended on the lounge room settee in a position of luxury and abandonment, foreign to her rather precise nature,

283

but instinctive now as she practised that life of discernment and privacy which she would lead later, by choice and, she was convinced, inevitability.

When Mrs. Bourke came in.

Lily Bourke could scarcely force the latchkey in. Or find breath to wrench out. She was a victim of her corsets and whatever had happened.

"I will tell you, Thelma," she said, "but first I must lay down."

So Thelma waited, by now in her dressing gown, full of misgiving, for she avoided all passionate events, and this must be one, as Lily Bourke was puce. Her fox was staring from a chair.

"It was a cruel day," said Lilian Bourke at last, flat, in her slip and her stockings. "I will tell you, Thelma, what happened."

So Thelma listened, and later that evening, after thinking it over, wrote a letter to her mother.

Dear Mum,

I am writing to tell you what has happened here. It is in the papers, so you will have to know, and better from me than some kind friend. Mum, it is about Ray. He has been mixed up in a racing scandal. He has been, and he has not, that is, for they cannot pin it on him. But it is pretty obvious from what they say. You know how you can only feel about Ray, there is not always proof.

Anyway, you may have heard of the big race, the Gold Plate, that was run today, and which Mr. Bourke's horse Eggcup was supposed to win. Well, it did not. It appears that the horse was somehow interfered with. There has been talk of dope even, and an inquiry is being held. A strapper from the stable, a raw sort of boy, who was a friend of Ray's (I have often seen them here together, when they could, as one sees it now, have been hatching some plan), has more or less confessed to giving something to the horse, but under the influence of Ray. The boy is in a great state, but will just not say enough. It appears that the winner of the race, an outsider called Sir Murgatroyd, was backed by Ray for a lot of money. . . .

Two days later, events and a suspicion that she was the martyr inspired Thelma to write again:

284

... We have not seen Ray since all this happened, not that Mr. Bourke would allow him on the place. Mrs. Bourke has been sick, I have had her in bed, nursing her at night and working by day is no fun. She is letting her hair grow out, she is so upset. As for Mr. Bourke, it has turned him into an old man, who was always so full of kindness for Ray, he can talk of nothing else.

All this is, needless to say, very difficult for me. As his sister, I have to bear a great deal of it. I do think Dad should come and see if he can do something, or talk to Ray. Although I am sorry for these people and am related to them a little, I would not have chosen them, and feel that that relationship is purely accidental.

I shall tell you later about my plans for the future, when they will have come to a head. I am getting on all right at the office. I think another girl may be leaving, and that I am pretty sure to benefit by it, judging from something Mr. Forsdyke, one of the partners, said. ...

Thelma Parker did, at this point, want to have a cry on the pale mauve notepaper that she kept for more important correspondence, like writing to thank Mrs. Gough for an evening party. In sudden detachment she remembered cats in the sun at the back doorstep. She bent down to touch the heap of sleeping cats. The scent of crushed mint made her desperate in the brick room. Whether she was looking forwards or backwards to that freedom which she so desired she was not sure, but her suspicions were horrible. She finished her letter with an action that was less upright. There were softnesses even in the pauses, of sleeping fur.

... I shall be back, I hope, for Christmas. I would like to do nothing, and wake up in the morning and see the roses, that white rose. I have a plant in a pot that I bought, it is an ornamental chilli, though some people call it a "love apple," whichever may be right. It does not do very well, I am afraid, and should, I suppose, be put in the ground.

I hope you are well, Mum dear. Look after yourself. The asthma has not been so bad, except when the mornings are foggy, or when I am over-tired. I do work quite hard you know! I have headaches at times, and should see about glasses, I think, but a rimless kind. Still, I must not talk about me!

You said in your last the roof is leaking. It is too bad.

Almost everybody seems to have a leaking roof, or patches on the wall. . . .

She never knew how to end a letter, and was even a little embarrassed by it, but finally she wrote quickly:

Yours ever, with love,
Thelma.

And read the whole letter over, to see whether she had said too little or too much.

If she had suggested her father should come, she had not altogether bargained for his coming, for his honest look, which left her speechless. She had been thinking more of her mother as she wrote, and her mother, though not dishonest, was like herself, a woman. Her elastic code could be made to fit circumstance.

But Stan Parker came.

He could not have avoided coming. In the beginning, as a young man, when he was clearing his land, he had hewn at trees with no exact plan in his head, but got them down, even at the expense of his hands, though these in time became hard, and there were boulders to be moved, that he strained against with his horse, till the soft bellies of man and horse grew hard and stony too, and the stone of will prevailed over rock. It was in this frame of mind that Stan Parker, the father, blundered into town. He had no plan. He was bewildered by much of what he had been told. But he would, if given a chance, harness his will to the situation, and move it by strength and determination. He supposed. In the end he had hewn a shape and order out of the chaos that he had found. He was also an improvisor of honest objects in wood and iron, which, if crude in design, had survived to that day. His only guide in all of this had been his simplicity.

So he came, and waited at the door of the Bourkes' brick home, till it was opened to him; it was Thelma, he saw, was there.

"Why, hello, Dad," she said. "I knew you would come but thought you would let us know."

To this he did not make any intelligible reply, because it was a gimcrack remark, stuck on as a formal decoration. Silence had perhaps taught him more about the usages of speech than the practice of it.

"Anyway," she said, "come on in."

He was wearing a watch chain across him that she could not remember having seen, when she thought that she knew everything he had. In his awkward serge he was rougher, she saw, the man her father, seated amongst the tassels and fringes of Lilian Bourke's lounge, uneasy but respectful on leatherette. Soon he had decided somewhere to put his hat, laying it on the floor beside him. She noticed with surprise and slight disgust the hair on the backs of his hands, and grey hair in his nostrils. Ah, she said desperately, this is my father, whom I have not known, and began to talk about train journeys and meals. She even told him the history of an oil painting of a mountain, done by an aunt of Mr. Bourke's at Richmond when a girl. She wondered at herself, that she could talk so fluently to her father, but of course it was his strangeness that made it possible. She was talking to an uncouth but good man in serge, but not her father.

"What's all this about Ray?" he said.

"It's more or less as I said," said Thelma. "Mr. Bourke will tell you the details when he comes in. Because I have never taken an interest in racing, and never shall. But the inquiry has not got to the bottom of it. That boy has retracted some of what he said. Whether he said it about Ray out of spite, in the beginning, I can't tell. Anyway, they can't pin anything on Ray except a feeling that he is guilty."

"So he is not guilty," said the father.

"I have been remembering something about some puppies," she said very slowly, "about some puppies that disappeared. What was it? They were in the shed where the plough is. I just can't remember."

"I don't know," he said.

She was forcing him into a convention of dishonesty that was not his. He was glad at that moment that he did not know his daughter better. He would have liked to think clearly about his son, and to arrive at some decision, as people are reputed to. But the presence of the furniture and his daughter's eyes held him constricted in a clumsiness of body and numbness of mind.

"I would like to think better of him," she said. "Because he could be good too."

Sensing that this was what her father expected, she had begun to convert herself. She did want to believe. Because goodness is, of course, desirable.

"He used to come here sometimes," she said, "and talk about Quigleys and people at home. He brought me a present

287

once of some stockings. I don't know why. They were expensive stockings."

So that she made herself believe, and was sad, for the handsome young man her brother, who was standing there by the window in his city jacket with the light from the half-drawn blind on his golden skin.

But the father did not want any of this.

"Where is Ray?" he asked.

Then Horrie Bourke came in, with his handkerchief tucked into his collar, and when he had sat down said, "If I had not believed in that boy I would not'uv believed in me own self."

He was a fat old man with veins in his face, brimming over with the injustice that had been done him, and afraid that someday, if not soon, even tomorrow perhaps, he would have a stroke. So that mixed up with the tears that he shed for the son who was not his but might have been, a recipient of presents as well as a giver of them, was hate for the healthy young man, whose muscles were impressive in his singlet, who stood laughing by the dung heap in a sheen of horses, and threatened him callously with a seizure. Ray was walking across his puffy body as it lay in the yard.

"Whether it was dope or not, or too clever riding, those young fellers were mixed up in it. Tom Schmidt the jockey, him that was on Sir Murgatroyd, is no better than any of em. There was an incident at Toowoomba, I am told, though told only. So you came here today, Stan?" said Horrie Bourke.

"Yes," the father said.

He shifted his thighs to make some speech which should be made. But could not. Words and wallpaper were getting the better of him.

"Lily will be glad to see you," said Horrie Bourke. "I will retire from racing," said Horrie. "It is a rich man's hobby, and a fool's downfall. To think," he said, "it begins with horses. Poor hinnocent beggars, they cannot be sure of their own legs."

Stan Parker had not made water since early. Somewhere was the lost intention. To see his son, and all would be made clear.

"I want to see Ray," he said, his own voice growing, and growing, into the room, till it took possession.

"Yairs, yairs," said Horrie. "A course. Lily, this is Stan. My wife has been laying down with a headache. This business has hit her hard like everybody selse."

"Stan!" said Lily Bourke. "Why, what do you know! I often remember how you broke that washstand at Yuruga. Mother was ropeable. If it had been a piece of the set, but the slab was solid. And now this awful thing. You have changed, Stan."

Her face told him that a great deal had happened, in *his* life, that is, she would not have believed it possible in hers. Lilian would have liked to sit and read his face, with a mingling of irony and regret. But, like a person at a funeral, she remembered continually that she must show grief.

"It is terrible," she sighed. "Horrie will be exonerated, of course. There is no question of his honesty. But we have both suffered, and it will not make amends, in no way, Stan, for the inroads on our health."

Did she want money? She wanted dreams.

The powdery Lilian, all cloudy from aspirin, had been a girl with finicking ideas, but not a bad sort. Would she be able to accept the men who did not ask, she had never been able to make up her mind, and was forever brushing hands, and glancing sideways into mirrors, and asking conundrums after the roast pork. The woman of the girl was still uncertain. She had a habit of looking at her wristwatch and wondering whether it was time for a snack.

"You will stay to tea, Stan. Amy was thin," she said, "in those days. You could see the saltcellars in her, and the elbows. We always said that those Fibbens were reared on parrot and skim milk. But of course it was the kind of exaggeration that people make. We girls were always ready for a joke. Poor Clara was unlucky—did you know?—lost her husband and is in reduced circumstances. Alice died of an incurable disease. Yes," she said, "how we danced then. Till it was time for the boys to go home and milk."

Lilian was in a sense appeased by the past, its movement and its multicolour, and would have whirled still in that room, in spite of the lampshades and the Genoa velvet, if her visitor had been willing.

But he got up and said, "I came here to see Ray. Where is he?"

"Oh," they said. "Yes."

Because this shock to their own worlds set up a positive collision of globes.

Then Horrie Bourke felt for his rupture and said, "We don't know where he is, Stan."

"He has disappeared," said Thelma. She touched the seam of her skirt.

Stan Parker was left standing. There is nothing you can put your hand on, unless it is wood or ion, but not other people's motives.

He could ask, they said, but it was doubtful. Bernie Abrahams, the book who had employed Ray, was not too happy about the whole affair and was not saying much. Then there was the boy Curly—he had come back for a pair of sandshoes he had left behind but did not or would not know anything of Ray. Ray had lived above a shop in a certain street, which they had written on a piece of paper, in a drawer.

"There," said Lily, holding it up and reading. "It is Highclere Street, Surry Hills."

It was a dago shop, she said, and he had mentioned a couple of girls, one still a kid. Their names were Rose and Jean.

"Then I shall go and ask," said Stan Parker.

The people in the room all agreed that he should employ himself in this way.

"Ray has been warned off, Stan," said Horrie Bourke.

As an afterthought. Because Ray had gone. It was Horrie's health and honour that remained.

"Terrible for his mother," sighed Lilian. "How did she take it, Stan?"

He murmured, because he did not know, because at that moment, when his wife had been reading words, he had been living them.

Thelma came and let him out, after she had gone back for his hat, which he had forgotten on the carpet.

"I am sorry, Dad," she said, making the affair his. "I'd come with you if I thought it would do any good."

Then she kissed him, and did quite enjoy being an affectionate daughter for its passing novelty. She thought how his skin was unfamiliar to her.

Stan Parker took her kiss and went. He would find Ray now. He had great faith in his own legs and staying power. He took trams when they were suggested. He took streets. Some people gave him directions with minute, antlike fidelity, as if they were receiving him with confidence into their own ant-world. Others scuttled across the asphalt, scowling at him, and shook him off. He told one man that he was looking for his son, who was living above a fruiterer's in Highclere Street, but the man wondered whether the stranger was mad to expose himself thus nakedly at a crossroads.

So Stan Parker went on his way over the asphalt. Once he thought he saw Ray looking at him from a window, but was mistaken apparently. A young woman who was pinning some material to her bust pulled down the blind. In one street two cars rammed each other, crushing the occupants. He went on, sad to think that the impulse to run to their assistance had been taken from him; it would have been different on a dirt road. Now he no longer looked at people, but for the names of streets nailed to corners. He went on, over a rime of rotting vegetables, and old newspapers, and contraceptive aids.

In what seemed like the last street to which he might penetrate, then or ever, a man lay spewing in the gutter. This is Highclere St., he read. He began to look for, and found, the fruitshop, of which the door was closed.

One window of that shop was blind with green paint, the other was boarded up, so that its use might have appeared equivocal if the smell of old fruit had not come out, a sweet, thick rottenness of brown fruit. There was a padlock on the door, but presently a girl looked from an upper window, then a similar girl, though younger, both in coloured jumpers that they would have knitted themselves. The two girls looked down. They were sisters. They had the same greenish skins. Their noses were good.

"Hello there," said the riper girl, who would have been Rose. "Who are you lookin for?"

"I am looking for Ray Parker," said the man who had come.

They looked down at his stiff clothes, that had been stuck on him by circumstance. The nostrils of the green girls were afraid this was some plant of a particularly honest-looking kind.

The girl Rose gave a thick grunt. Jean looked. Her eyes were continually looking at scenes from a life which at any moment she might be called upon to enter. But not yet. It was her sister's life.

"I am his father," said the man.

Whose leathery face was looking flat up, giving itself as a pledge to the girls.

"Ah," said Rose.

Her sister Jean wriggled closer, pushing back her live hair behind her ears, and would listen all day.

"Ray ain't here," said the sullen Rose.

"But I've come to see him," said the man. "I came up from Durilgai on the early train. I could get back perhaps tonight. Not for the milking. But I could get back."

Rose listened to incredible things. But she did not speak. With her finger she was tracing a vein of the sick house.

"Tell him," breathed the man's upheld face.

"I cantellim," she sulked. "Ray's gone away."

"Where?" asked the man's breaking face.

Then the young girl who was listening also began to break up. She began to giggle. She began to snicker and laugh. She laughed, and hid her face, and burrowed deeper into the flesh of her sister's side.

Till Rose laughed too. But deep, common, bubbly laughter from over her short teeth.

"Go on," begged the man.

He began to laugh too, but slower, haltingly, as if he had not yet grasped the full extent of the joke. And the sun was in his eyes.

"Where?" he said with less strength.

"Up North," shrieked Rose, waving somewhere.

But Jean unfastened her teeth from her mouth, and hung down, and in a couple of awful, dry spasms said, "Don't you listen, mister. Ray went out West. Honest."

She could only just say. She was quite young, and convulsed, and sweating from having taken part, as she drew back into the house of rotten fruit.

Then Stan Parker stood in the street with his shortcomings and omissions. He knew now that he would not see Ray. He no longer felt very strong. His face ached from the expression of youth and indifference it had worn for the two padlocked sisters.

Some way back, after several streets, roughly in the direction from which he had come, an old woman showed him a bag of plums she had bought.

"Look," she said. "When I bought these they were big luscious plums. Anyways, on the barrer. See these little runts of things?"

Indignation made her walk by the stranger's side.

"It ain't right," she said, moving her teeth. "A person is always had."

He agreed, because that was all he could do.

The woman walked. She began to tell him about her son. He was a miner.

"Is he good?" he asked with a stupid smile.

"He is all right," she said, looking away. "Some people perhaps have different idea of what is the truth. That is all."

Then she broke away, as if she had no further need to

know the stranger, and he saw her pitch the paper bag of runty plums into the gutter.

I am lost by this, he realized. He continued to walk, fumbling through the shapeless, ineffectual state in which his life had ended. Although he had acquired the habit of saying simple prayers, and did sincerely believe in God, he was not yet sufficiently confident in himself to believe in the efficacy of the one or the extent of the other. His simplicity had not yet received that final clarity and strength which can acknowledge the immensity of belief.

So instead of praying he went into a café and ordered a plate of food.

It was a Chinese café. When the dish of chop suey was brought he sat looking at it, or more especially at the large joints in his inactive finger bones.

"You feel crook," said the young Chinese, coming and moving the cutlery into a different pattern.

"No," said Stan.

"Someone died," said the Chinese, still making a statement rather than asking a question, in a high, flash, second-generation voice.

Then he went away and began doing a sum, adding on paper over and over again, his Chinese face clear and honest, in spite of his flash, high voice.

So Stan Parker sat there and began to see he must go home. There was nothing else he could do in that city.

After a couple of days he did go. His daughter Thelma came with him to the station. It was early, and she was dressed for business in a grey costume and white blouse, her importance barely pent up as she shook her cuffs and looked at her clean nails. Her successful appearance made him rather shambly, but he was proud to be with her. He walked beside her, swinging an old Gladstone bag, that had been in his mother's house at the time of her death, but to whom it had belonged he did not know, he had never seen anybody use it. The bag was hard and awkward, in spite of the fact that he had given it a coating of saddlesoap before leaving home.

"That funny old bag," laughed Thelma, making it into something quaint, for otherwise it would have been awful. "Can you really pack your clothes in it without rolling them into a ball?"

"It serves its purpose," he said.

She began to feel that she should talk to him of tender, in-

293

timate things, but the horror of that was too much for her, so she said in a determined voice, "We seem to be hours too early."

He had taken her into a shop and, before she could laugh at him or protest, was buying her an ice-cream horn.

"Have I got to eat this?" she asked.

"Why not?" he said. "You used to like them."

I used to, her memory echoed as she licked the child's stuff perched on top of the wafer horn. She did not want to cry, but she was being compelled to. It was in her throat, cold on hot. On grey mornings she would wake and hear the lamps flower, and the unbearably white voices of the cocks predicting the future with sad conviction for the past.

"When you were a kid," he said, "you liked them."

"Are you harping on that!" she said. "Listen, Dad, about Ray, it has been terrible for you, I can see, but he is no good."

"It is too early," he said, "to say who is good."

Then she had not exorcised her brother.

"I cannot explain," she said.

She suspected simplicity, and would have liked to avoid it altogether, so she was glad when they had come to the trains, and it was time to kiss.

"Good-bye, Thel," he said and flushed a bit for the young woman he was kissing, who was his daughter and not.

His children were let loose. Steam had begun to blow through the station, like fine grey seed. The incredible had begun to seem more natural, or perhaps it was the homeward journey.

Thelma Parker watched her father go. She had resumed her life. It was cruel but necessary. She walked along the platform and down the steps. She had taken a room in the house of a doctor's widow, and would begin to live there soon, next week in fact, it had been agreed, with use of kitchen and bath, of course. Thelma Parker caught the tram. If it seemed that her life had begun to crystallize, there was still no need to tell about it. It was peculiarly hers. To be drowsed over, in the docotor's widow's bath, in waves of sandalwood and lilac, in a good suburb.

Stan Parker continued to travel home, and was guiltily eased by the appearance of familiar features of geography. He knew the contours of the landscape more intimately than he did the faces of men, particularly his children. Children are learned by the mother, he said. He would have liked it that way. But his unhappiness was less obtrusive, the train disclosed. From Bangalay he took the bus which runs over the hills to Durilgai. There he got down and walked across the paddocks. He would sometimes choose that more solitary approach, slowing through the yellow grass and black trees, looking about as if he were a stranger there, looking at the scrolls of fallen bark, which is a perpetual mystery. Then the ignorance of the man was exchanged for knowledge. His rough skin was transparent in that light.

❦

Chapter 17

AMY PARKER accepted the absence of her son; as time
passed, it was not so very different really from his
presence. If she thought about him, it was as a baby, or a little boy that could not run far, or would hide and she would
find him, in a game. Then she would blind him with kisses
and devour the angle of his neck. He could only struggle
against her love. In this way the past was made more concrete than the present.

But Ray did once send a postcard, from Albany. That
writing she had forgotten, if she had ever known. It was an
emanation of a strange man, that she looked at respectfully
through her reading glasses, as if it had been a flickering of
lightning. He was in business, he said. She was proud in the
end to have the card, though she did not love this man. She
loved the little struggling boy, to whom her own full face was
held on a summer's day. She showed the card to people, after
she had dried her hands, she showed it to people who had
come, and received their congratulations with decent pride,
and spoke of her absent son with natural affection. But she
did not love this man.

She would have liked to love. It was terrible to think she
had never loved her son as a man. Sometimes her hands
would wrestle together. They were supple, rather plump
hands, broad, and not yet dry. But wrestling like this together, they were papery and dried-up. Then she would force
herself into some deliberate activity, or speak tenderly to her
good husband, offering him things to eat and seeing to his
clothes. She loved her husband. Even after the drudgery of
love she could still love him. But sometimes she lay on her
side and said, I have not loved him enough, not yet, he has
not seen the evidence of love. It would have been simpler if

she had been able to turn and point to the man their son, but she could not.

Often, again, it was as if she had had no children, for it had not been given to her to love her daughter, except by intermittent gestures. Then she would think about the child they had picked up at Wullunya in the floods, and brought home in Peabody's cart, and who had quickly gone. This boy, if she had tamed him, would have been her son, she felt. It was possible. All those things that did not quite occur during the floodtime of their lives had the nostalgia of possibility now that she was drying up.

At our time of life, said the postmistress, who was withered in the beginning, but who did not seem to mind.

Amy Parker hated the postmistress, but because they had formed the habit of friendship she would stop to yarn a while those days when she went to the village. It was a pause, besides, on the hill.

She would say. "Are you there, Mrs. Gage? There is nothing, I suppose?"

Then Mrs. Gage would rush out.

"I have not looked yet, dear," she would say. "It is the telephone. It would drive you dilly. Not that it is not an education. I am here all day listening to the wires. We had Lithgow this morning. You would be surprised. But of course I am an official, not a person."

So that Mrs. Gage was manipulating the lives of people with her yellow hands, and for that reason was doubly distasteful, if mysterious and impressive, to Mrs. Parker.

But there was that day when Mrs. Gage failed to manipulate the wires, or one was cut. She was in a muddle. She ran out. She had china balls for eyes, and her breath was bad.

"Mrs. Parker," she called, "I was waiting for you. Oh dear. It is terrible, as I would never ever have expected. It is Mr. Gage."

Amy Parker, who had forgotten the husband of the postmistress, as most people did, was holding back. But the postmistress took her by her hot hand and led her with her dry and fibrous one.

"Took his life, dear," she announced, now piteously for her situation, "on a tree down the yard. By two belts. One was an old thing I had not seen before, that he must have picked up. He was hanging there. Oh dear, it was terrible to see. He was swinging. Very slow. But his face was quiet."

So Amy Parker, who was not prepared for doom, was led on. She looked ridiculous and hot.

"Mrs. Adams came and helped me with the body," the postmistress said. "It is quite decent. It is all right to see. These ladies have just seen it, and have sat here sympathizing with me a while."

In fact, there was Mrs. Hobson, and Mrs. Mulvaney, and a woman in a veil.

"At least you have company," said Amy Parker, who did not want to see the body just then.

Mrs. Mulvaney sucked her teeth.

"A nice way to leave a widow," Mrs. Hobson said.

"Yes," screamed Mrs. Gage. "Yes."

Everybody was surprised, because until then she had appeared comfortable and resigned.

But Mrs. Gage was choked by the enormity of her life. Suddenly she had to tell. She was the daughter of an inspector of schools, domiciled in some coastal town. They had lived in a neat cottage almost buried beneath hydrangeas, of which her father had been proud, but which had made of them a pale family, from living beneath plants, looking out through the big leaves and breathing the moist green air. She had met her husband while he was fishing from a breakwater with a rod. She saw the fish glisten as he landed it, masterfully, though his arms were thin. It was a lovely fish. Then they had looked at it together. She had been afraid to spoil his pleasure by any remark, for he was engrossed in the fish, or to accept, when he was forced against his inclination, by some dreadful impulse, to offer it. At home they had eaten the fish, boiled, with a white sauce, inviting the young man to share it, but he had declined, saying he was not interested in fish after they had been cooked. Not long after that he had married the recipient of the fish, for no reason beyond an awful inevitability. Then they began to know each other. They went from place to place. Mr. Gage was a weak man, as everybody knew; he had no chin, he had weak, if refined, eyes, that would not look quite at you. They went from place to place, living in hot brown towns, in cottages that smelled of dry rot, in tents, or even under bark. While the husband took up work, and put it down. He was a fettler till his hands gave out. He had a talent for carpentry, but the sawdust affected his breathing. Sometimes he would sit for days without saying a word, to insult a woman. He would sit looking at an empty plate as if it were an object of importance, or on the old iron bedstead under the pepper tree, in his singlet, as everyone had known him, just sitting. It was many years, of course, since the woman had taken to postal work, from bravery, through necessity. She had been many years at Durilgai, and before that in another small town. She would have liked to tell of many more details of her life with the dead man, even physical details, and might still.

"Just to show you," she said, "what a woman can endure."

Her hair had begun to look abandoned.

But Amy Parker remembered the husband of the postmistress on his knees beside the spider bush, and hoped he would not be so mercilessly exposed.

"He is dead now, Mrs. Gage," she said.

"And what am I?" shrieked the postmistress. "I am alive. Or just about."

She was making dry noises, like a palm.

"I was never ever hit about, or split open, but I was led to understand I did not understand myself," she said, "nor anything."

Mrs. Mulvaney sucked her teeth.

"Look," said the postmistress, unmatting her desperate hair above the forehead where it had grown wet, "I shall show you ladies something that will explain what I mean. Come this way, please," she said, shifting the waistband of her dark skirt. "It will illustrate," she laughed.

Everybody was afraid, but all followed, Mrs. Mulvaney, Mrs. Hobson, Mrs. Parker, and the woman in the veil.

In face of the possibility that there might be a human soul somewhere in a box or pinned to paper, it was forgotten there was a dead man lying in the house. There was a breathing of women as the postmistress opened the door of a room. There were pieces of furniture in the room of a kind that everybody knew, and a dull clock swinging its measure of time. There was also perhaps the smell of a man brooding there. It had persisted after the man had gone out, after he had died even.

"Look," said the postmistress, in a voice that was more detached, almost official. "These! I never let on to anyone, of course, that anything like this was going on. But now that he has passed on," she said, quite respectfully, because after all death must be respected, whatever the individual worm, "and seeing as we are friends, I am making it public for the first and, I should hope, last time."

"What are they?" Mrs. Hobson asked.

"Those things are oil paintings," said the postmistress in the same even official voice.

She was pointing with her toe at the objects that stood against the furniture, stacked in layers or exposed singly. Then she ran at them like a young girl, very lightly, and began furiously to arrange the paintings in lines of shame. She would reveal the depths of her life to the women she had brought in. She was morbidly excited by the prospect of complete revelation.

"There," she said, on her knees, looking back at her friends, giving them her yellow face, to be stoned or exonerated, by this time she was indifferent to which, either would have fulfilled her longing. "This is the story of our life."

Mrs. Mulvaney sucked her teeth.

"He was mad then?" said Mrs. Hobson, who did not know what was going on.

"I do not know," said the postmistress in an awful voice, which seemed to open right out, and which was addressed to herself more than to her audience.

The woman in the veil had come forward to look with greater ease. After moistening her lips with the tip of her tongue and encountering the veil, she lifted this, which was either a bit old-fashioned, or else it had gone on and become fashionable again.

She said, "Very interesting. But, of course, works of art really prove nothing. They must be judged for themselves."

Mrs. Hobson and Mrs. Mulvaney looked with hate at the stranger, at what they did not understand. It was a dark face that had spoken, and what was worse, perhaps foreign.

"It is all very well for you, Mrs. Schreiber," said the postmistress, getting up from her uncomfortable knees. "You are in a position to judge what you have not suffered. I have sweated blood for every stroke of these," she cried, "these things!"

And she kicked a picture.

Mrs. Mulvaney and Mrs. Hobson gasped and recoiled for the audacity of her act. Because she had struck the blasphemous Christ that her late husband had painted, apparently on the side of a tea chest, which by this time had warped somewhat. And it had been in the beginning a poor sort of a scrawny fettler-Christ, a plucked fowl of a man that had not suffered to the last dregs of indignity, but would endure more, down to gashing with a broken bottle, the meanest of

all weapons, till left to suppurate under the brown flies, beside the railway lines.

"Ahhh," sighed Mrs. Mulvaney and Mrs. Hobson. "It is
terrible."

They were shocked and afraid. They wanted to turn their
backs, and run out of that room of madness, and not think
about it again.

But Amy Parker, who had been quiet all this time, because
she was opening to an experience of great tenderness and
beauty, had not suspected such jewels of blood as the husband of the postmistress had put on the Christ's hands. Then
the flesh began to move her, its wincing verdigris and
sweating tallow. She knew this, as if her sleep had told her of
it. Great truths are only half-grasped this side of sleep.

So she looked at the picture of Christ, and knew about it.
Without moving much, she looked about at the other pictures
that the husband of the postmistress had left. He seemed to
have painted a great many trees, in various positions, their
limbs folded in sleep or contemplation, or moving in torture.
And the dead trees. The white forms of these did not look a
bit dry and sceptical, as bones do in a paddock. So also a
bottle can express love. She had never before seen a bottle of
adequate beauty. This one tempted her to love her neighbour.

Then the women who were looking were beginning to
laugh.

"What about this?" laughed Mrs. Mulvaney.

"Oh, I say! Eh?" laughed Mrs. Hobson behind her wedding
ring.

The women began to shriek, and to labour inside their
stout stays, and to darken at the armpits.

"Yes," said the postmistress, eagerly enduring it, "that one
is the vilest."

She would have welcomed a blow on the back. She was
herself teetering on the brink of cruelest laughter, for the laborious woman, almost carved out of paint, that Amy Parker
saw.

This figure was just waking. There was a small kernel of
knowledge in the almond of the eye, that was growing, and
would soon put on leaves. Otherwise the figure of the waking
woman was naked, except for the tendrils of hair that
preserved those parts of the body in an innocent poetry. Her
simplicity was that of silence and of stone. Her breasts were
as final as two stones, and she was reaching up with her ponderous but touching hands towards that sun which would it-

self have been a stone, if it had not glowed with such a savage incandescence.

All this time Mrs. Mulvaney and Mrs. Hobson were rocking and mocking. "What next?" they shouted as the tears gushed out of their leather faces.

The smell of their mirth had become oppressive.

Then Amy Parker, who had been standing inside the uproar, noticed in the corner, at the feet of the woman, what appeared to be the skeleton of an ant that the husband of the postmistress had scratched in the paint with some sharp instrument, and out of the cage of the ant's body a flame flickered, of luminous paint, rivalling in intensity that sun which the woman was struggling after.

Ah, said Amy Parker, remembering, and blushed.

"Now you will understand," said the postmistress, turning on them all. "I have nothing left to hide. I just had to show somebody," she said. "And yet we were happy at times. I cooked him the things he liked. He was very fond of a kidney. We would sit outside together of an evening. He knew the names of the stars."

Then she swept the window sill with her hand, and the bodies of several dead flies fell down, and a little dust.

By this time nobody was listening particularly. They had either seen so much they could not see more, or else they were anxious to climb back into the room of their own thoughts. So they began to sidle out.

"It was kind of you, Mrs. Schreiber," said Mrs. Gage, in the snivelly sort of voice that is often put on for a person of wealth and some power.

Because Mrs. Schreiber, who was foreign, was also rich. She had bought a property in those parts, and would sometimes make the butter, to feel it on her hands.

"It was very interesting," said Mrs. Schreiber in her thick dark voice, drawing down her black veil. "I should forget about it for a little, Mrs. Gage. Then it will appear differently."

"But it will not leave me," cried the postmistress, as the veiled woman went away in thought.

Others were moving.

"Mrs. Parker dear," called the postmistress and came after her in a sound of rushing skirt. "I would not say anything about it," she appealed, "not to anybody else."

Amy Parker lowered her head and said that she would not.

When she got in her husband said, "Where have you been, Amy, all this time?"

"With the postmistress," she said. "Mr. Gage has taken his life. He hung himself on a tree in the yard."

Stan Parker, like everyone else, had not known the husband of the postmistress, but marvelled that death could have caught up with anyone he knew by name.

"Go on," he said.

And asked why, before he realized.

Amy Parker brought cups and plates.

"Mrs. Gage showed us some pictures he had done," she said finally.

"What sort of pictures?" her husband asked.

"A kind of oil paintings," she said. "But we are not to say anything."

She began to set the crockery. She began to tremble for the strangeness of her own house. Her own hands were strange birds blundering and flumping amongst cups.

And Stan Parker wondered why it had never occured to him to want to take his own life. Where is the point at which this necessity arises? He cut bread. He wondered. The thin air of the morning drifted about the house, rubbing at the paper walls and moving them. At what point does solidity dissolve? But this was not decided yet.

After the body had been buried in the scrub beside the cemetery, Stan Parker forgot, but his wife remained preoccupied, less with the act of dying than with what could have been her relationship with the dead man. She would remember his grey face as he knelt that day upon the stones. It had looked at her, but possibly with some expression that she had missed. Or supposing there was something she could not remember? She searched herself feverishly, but it eluded her, until she did, in fact, resemble the turgid woman reaching for the incandescent sun. Her body was what she had.

So she grew restless. She would harness a horse and drive out, with the reins lying in her hands. The sky, of that blue, was moving with little whorls of impatience. A whole field of corn would pursue her blatantly with secrets to be guessed at. Then she would become angry and frighten her placid horse. On such an occasion she said, slapping with the leather: I will visit O'Dowds, this is what I know. And she drove down, with her hands grown firm, pleased now that this solid objective had materialized. A confusion of spirit would not enter into the presence of O'Dowds. So she drove on, in a jingle, in

303

a smart little trap that she owned at that time, with a good solid taffy pony. Trees fled. I shall not think, she said, of what I do not understand.

When Amy Parker drove up the track towards O'Dowds', again in full possession of assurance and her broad back, there was no sign of inhabitants. There was the house, and pigs, and a little yellow runty pig that had been sick, of worms or something, and was nosing after a cabbage stalk in a halfhearted sort of way. It was many a day since Amy Parker had seen her friend and neighbour Mrs. O'Dowd, through no actual quarrel, but rather because there had been no special favour for either of them to ask. So now she looked around, looking at a strange house, which she had known then, and forgotten. It was standing there, supporting itself, as it were, by some special grace of gravity. Pieces of it hung. Pieces had been pulled off, for comfort, on a wet day, to make a little fire with, and save a soul a trouble with an axe in the shed.

Now, in fact, there was a fire in the middle of the yard, or a sulky black heap of ash with smoke upon it, just rising and coiling, dirtily. There was the fire, and there was a stink. This reached out, and down the nostrils—there was no mistaking they were two pipes in the skull, exposed to unreasonable torture.

Amy Parker groped through this stink and tied her little snorting horse.

After the neighbour woman had looked out, and put in her teeth that she kept on a shelf in the kitchen, and come out on the step, and pulled her blouse about a bit, Amy Parker said, as if it were yesterday she had seen her friend, and what else could she, it was so long, "What is it you are burning, Mrs. O'Dowd?"

"Ah," said the neighbour woman, shielding her mouth, "it is a little fire."

"It is a little fire. It is a big stink," her friend Mrs. Parker said.

"Ah," said Mrs. O'Dowd behind her hand, "it is the old rubber we are burnun."

"But what rubber?"

"It is the old tires that he bought cheap."

"Then you have your own car?" Mrs. Parker asked.

"He would not drive anythun that goes on spirit," said Mrs. O'Dowd from behind her hand. "He would drink it up sooner," she said. "No, this is old tires that he bought as a speculation, like, an then got sick of, so we are burnun them."

"That is one way," Mrs. Parker said.

"Dirty things," said Mrs. O'Dowd, giving the fire a kick.

So that her teeth shot out from behind her hand and were caught mercifully in the V of her blouse.

"These are new," she said with her gums. "It is a plate that I got by letter, an it is the bugger for poppun out."

It was like a shining shoebuckle that she stuck back.

"It is the devul," she said from behind her hand. "If they should fall an split it would be money wasted. That is why I am forever holdun me hand in front of me face, as you may have wondered at."

"I would take them out," said her friend.

"Why," said Mrs. O'Dowd, "that is an idea. It is not that I am wearun um for social reasons, only they are bought, you see."

Then she put them in her pocket, and they had a laugh. They were glad to see each other when they did. Each was reminded by the other of her own substantiality. She discovered that she had endured.

So they laughed agreeably together, and forgetful, till the smoke got them.

"Old black-in-the-guts," coughed Mrs. O'Dowd. "It is not us that is to blame, it is the constable."

"What is the constable to do?" coughed Mrs. Parker back, she could have choked with black smoke.

"I will tell you as a friend of years," said Mrs. O'Dowd, taking her by the hand. "An show. But Mrs. Parker, you will never, never tell?"

Amy Parker promised, for she burned to hear, and they went back into the shaky house.

"It is because they will not let decent an freedom-lovun people alone, the police an all," said Mrs. O'Dowd, "who are stickun their noses in. 'Well,' says he to me, 'let um stick, an we shall give um somethun to be smellun at.' So we built this fire of most convenient tires."

By this time they had come into a kind of little larder, which may or may not have been there before, through a curtain of bags that had been stretched there for some reason. All was obscure, and smells too had become more complex. Amy Parker in her groping kicked a drum of mutton fat that was standing there, for greasing of boots and such like, and which the rats had been scratching at.

" 'This fire will fox um,' he says," the neighbour woman said. " 'It will make a royal smell, though not so royal as tother.' "

This other smell had indeed begun to predominate as they blundered on towards the kitchen of the house, over boards that threatened, and some that frankly let you down.

"Ah," said Mrs. O'Dowd, "draw your foot out, dear. It is the white ants. They are terrible things. We shall be fixun it one day when he finds the time."

So they came on, and into the kitchen, where the royal smell smote them in the nose, and Mrs. O'Dowd smiled.

"It is ale then?" asked Amy Parker, who was gasping from the impact of fumes.

"We never mention it by name," said Mrs. O'Dowd with a lovely smile.

She stirred the pan, from which a lazy steam laved her face, giving it a warm colour that it did not normally have; she was more the colour of bark and leather and old dried-up brown things, for the sun had been at her quite a while.

"We was driven to it," she explained, "since he was warned off the hard stuff, and the expense too is somethun to consider. So we sit in the evenun and take our innocent glass. Afternoons too, it is no harm to knock a couple back, but quicker like."

"Then you are on it too?" Amy Parker asked.

"What do you mean, on it?" paused Mrs. O'Dowd. "If a poor soul is so afflicted, the least a person can do is to bear him company, insofar as she can. I do not drink, Mrs. Parker. I alleviate the sufferun of me husband only, by sympathizun a little."

Then there was such a belching, such a rocking of the house and a bell-pulling, that she dropped the spoon.

"That is the bugger now," she said. "He is after his midnoon ration."

As the bell belted brass. As the lungs lifted up.

"Old woman, old woman!" called the voice of O'Dowd, and it was black and leathery.

"That is his joke," she explained, uncorking a bottle from a former brew and pouring the conciliatory liquid into some receptacle that happened to be at hand. "An he has fixed up a sort of bell arrangement, as you have heard, and will see, it is quite clever."

If Amy Parker did not want to see, she was compelled by that force of circumstance which swept her friend and neigh-

306

bour down a passage with the tin tray, and on, and out. They were soon fanned out on that side of the house on which O'Dowd sat, on a veranda, beside some fuchsia bushes.

"Stop yer bellerun," said his wife. "Here is a lady that has come to pay us a visit."

"What lady?" he asked, and did stop, though the bell, which was controlled by a string from his toe, continued a while longer to jerk and clap.

"I was never shook on the female visitors," said O'Dowd. "But if it happens, it happens. Mrs. Parker," he said, "take a glass with us. I will answer for all consequences. If it don't rot your guts, it will lift you op."

"Thank you. I'm not in need of it," Amy Parker said.

She had by this time repented of her impulse to visit O'Dowds. Her sobriety had made her prim.

"She is above it," said Mrs. O'Dowd, whose own nose was not unwilling to nuzzle in a glass.

"I am not. And you know it," Mrs. Parker said.

"She is a great lady in a hat," Mrs. O'Dowd pursued, removing a fly or two from her glass.

"I am nothing that you say, but sober, and with every intention of staying that way."

"That is terrible in onybody's life," shuddered O'Dowd. "To stay stone cold. I could not look me own reflection in the face, if it was not kept warmed op."

But Amy Parker was looking at the fuchsia bushes. She wondered why she had come.

"All tastes is not one," Mrs. O'Dowd supposed. "Still, it is nice to have a conversation with a friend, an her droppun in."

She had taken to swilling her glass round and round, and rocking her ankle easily, and cocking her head to one side, as ladies do.

She said, "That boy of yours, Mrs. Parker, young Ray, is he keeping well, I hope? We have not heard of him this long while."

She was looking, Amy Parker saw.

"Ray," said the mother in a clear, easy voice, "is out West. He has written. He is in business," she said.

"In business? That is nice. An what kind of business? Groceries perhaps, or hardware?"

"He did not say," said the mother in the same clear, assured voice. "It is not always easy to explain a business, an important business, in a few words."

"That is true," Mrs. O'Dowd said.

But she was looking. Her eyes were rather small. She was looking for a crevice, through which to turn a knife idly on an afternoon.

"Ah, business," said O'Dowd gloomily, "I should'uv been in business, ef I had not'uv been done in by a feller that I knew from Forbes, for an invention that I thought of some years ago, for pluckun a cockerel by mechanical means. It was at a contraption like this," he said, spreading his fingers into Vs and half getting up, to demonstrate the intricacies of machinery.

"You kind of catch the chickun by the neck, like. An give it a sort of twist. See? An roffle his feathers till there is no hope but they must fall out. You onderstand? It was the simplest device, Mrs. Parker, that this feller pinched, an has never looked back, they tell me, since that day."

"That old machine!" said Mrs. O'Dowd. "An your Thelma, Mrs. Parker, we have heard that she is doin well."

The mother cleared her throat. "Yes," she said directly. "Thelma is engaged."

"Well now," said Mrs. O'Dowd. "You don't say so. Thelma is engaged."

"To a solicitor," said the mother, "a Mr. Forsdyke, whose confidential secretary she was. Is still, for that matter."

"I could'uv wrung that feller's neck," said O'Dowd, "as if he was a cockerel himself. I forget what he was called."

"Fancy, little Thelma," Mrs. O'Dowd said. "An such a pasty child I would not'uv been surprised if she had died."

"But she did not," the mother said.

As they rocked in the perilous boat of friendship.

Amy Parker did wonder why she had come. Or she had known and forgotten. Or habit is the motive force of most acts. Anyway, they were sitting there, all three somewhat at the mercy of one another's balance, in the bland light of afternoon, through which little birds came and went, to and from the fuchsia bushes.

"With kiddies and a business, we would'uv sat pretty," said O'Dowd, spitting between the teeth which were his own.

"It is what you are blessed with," said his wife, draining the brown dregs. "An it is you that would be sittun on the same rump, come Thursday, blessuns or no blessuns, so help me."

And she put her glass down.

"You are a cow," he said, "that likes to use the truth as if it was a weapon. To bash the first poor bugger across the head that answers to its description. You are a bloody cow of a woman," he said.

And he sat farther down in his seat, after spitting a second jet between his teeth, which were still very white, Amy Parker saw, and remembered that O'Dowd could spit walnuts with those teeth and land the shells quite a distance off.

Now he was dejected, though.

And his wife began to hum, putting her arms up, still monumental in their way, to fasten a comb of imitation tortoiseshell that she wore. She hummed that same tune which had pursued her remorselessly from girlhood.

So they sat leaden. They were not quite statuary. O'Dowd was sunken. He sat with his chin upon his chest, looking at Amy Parker, as if she were almost connected with his thoughts. He was a hairy man, she saw, and shuddered.

Ah, she said, I must get away from here. What had been a fair day had turned to lead. She longed to be raised up out of that heaviness from which it is difficult to stir.

"Do you happen to know the time, Mrs. O'Dowd?" she asked.

"It is an acquaintance I have given up these many years," said her smooth friend, who was determined to destroy somebody, and perhaps herself, that afternoon. "But you will not be goin yet, Mrs. Parker, it is too soon. An if he is in the dumps, he will lift op again. An sometimes is most entertainun if he is in the mood."

So she poured him another to put him in it, and another for herself, in sympathy.

"Here's luck," Mrs. O'Dowd said. "Me husband will perhaps tell us a story or two."

"I have forgot um," said O'Dowd.

"Ah, I did hear," said his wife, "that the husband of the postmistress was doin oil paintun all this while, before he hanged himself, an that nothun curiouser than these pictures was ever seen. Did you hear tell perhaps?" Mrs. O'Dowd asked.

And her breath listened.

"I have heard," said Amy Parker, "what people say."

"What sort of paintuns, for heavun's sake?" asked O'Dowd, yawning till his uvula stood up.

"Dead trees and Jesus Christ," said his wife. "And naked women. Mad things, it seems."

"Hold hard," said her husband. "Is it mad then to paint a

naked woman? What would Mrs. Parker say? What sort of a mad, naked-woman paintun was it that you saw?"

"I did not say I saw," Mr. Parker said and blushed.

"You are drunk, you," said Mrs. O'Dowd to her husband, looking at Mrs. Parker all the time.

"I would paint a naked woman," he said, rolling his red eyes, so that they almost turned their inward visions out.

"But you cannot paint," said his wife. "An you are drunk."

"If I could paint I know what I would paint," roared O'Dowd. "I would paint the guts of a sheep, because it is a pretty thing, an I would paint a naked woman," he said, narrowing his vision and looking at Amy Parker, who was afraid she had been caught in some situation, terrible, but also half-expected, "a naked woman in a wicker chair, with a bonch of fuchsias in her lap."

"Dear, listen," laughed his wife, putting up her hair nervously. "An it all began as conversation. But you are drunk, you bugger, if I know. It is too much good stuff. You a painter, then what am I?"

She began to laugh, and looked curiously at Amy Parker, who had got up to go.

"Wait, dear," said Mrs. O'Dowd, looking at her. "There is somethun I want to ask yer. When I come back. Oh dear, pardon me."

And she went off, and out to the back, looking carefully at the step of the veranda, which threatened to throw her, but just failed.

In this way Amy Parker was left with O'Dowd. She did not look at him, but waited. Their figures were huge on the veranda at this moment, and gave every indication that they would grow even larger.

"She will not let a person speak," said O'Dowd, who had got up too, and was looking at his toe-caps, and steadying himself, and looking most carefully at the dry leather. "She will kill a man, if he does not kill her first. But I cannot succeed in this. She is a good woman, Mrs. Parker, and that is what makes it so much the worse. Whether it is paintuns that is in me, an that is perhaps a manner of speakun, or ideas, the ideas I have are well worth lookun at, if they are not stillborn, if they are not *killed*, or pinched like the cockerel-pluckun machine, I am a man that has been mucked up."

"If you will sit down, Mr. O'Dowd, perhaps you will feel better," Amy Parker said.

Because their over-life-size group had become oppressive

to her. She was tempted to ward off any further encroachment by raising her arm.

"But I am tryun to tell yer somethun," said O'Dowd, striving for that something with the bones of his fingers. "An I feel good."

"Oh dear," sighed Amy Parker, looking in the direction from which her friend did not return.

While those little flowers with which the fuchsia bush was hung trembled feverishly; their scarlet notes had never been so shrill.

"You see," said O'Dowd, leaning over, "I have never told onyone about meself. Not all of it. To onyone."

As he leaned right over and looked inside Mrs. Parker's blouse. Then he came up and stood quite straight.

Then Amy Parker knew that all her life she had been expecting O'Dowd to do something of this nature, or not O'Dowd particularly. So she did not instantly resume her correct body. Big sticky lilies are too heavy to hold their heads up after rain, or with the dew even, but bask in their fresh flesh.

So she was moister at that instant, recovering some luxuriance. Until she was disgusted. Then the sound of disgust came in her throat.

"We was speakun of somethun," said O'Dowd, confused now that he had wandered off the map.

"There was somethun I was after rememberun to ask you, Mrs. Parker," said his wife, returning just then.

Mrs. O'Dowd had stuck her head in a bucket, it appeared. She was all smoothed down, even piteous, with the drips upon her face.

"I was a little flushed," she said. "An I still do not remember that bloody thing."

"Then, if you cannot remember," said Amy Parker finally, "I think I will be going."

"All right," said her friend. "You will not be sayun things about us?"

"What should I say?" Amy Parker asked.

"How should I know rightly?" said Mrs. O'Dowd, looking into Mrs. Parker as far as she could. "You are a funny girl, Amy, an always has been."

Mrs. Parker went down the step.

"I cannot answer that," laughed the rejuvenated woman, of smooth face and firm arms.

So that Mrs. O'Dowd was stuck with doubts, watching her

friend glance back, the blood in her face, or light of fuchsias. Amy Parker was still warm. Light broke in her at times, and coruscated, under the brim of her large hat.

She drove away then, leaving O'Dowd, who had sunk back into a shapelessness, of lost opportunities and mistier desires, beside his wife, who had found the grievance she was looking for perhaps. O'Dowds omitted to wave. They were too preoccupied.

And Amy Parker drove on. The sleek horse belted the road, because it was the road back, and the trap rocked, bringing to the soul of the woman that drove an easy indifference to matter. She flowed, easily and smoothly as light and the streaming trees. All those anxieties which had possessed her on the way down were now cleared away. By instinct she could have grasped an abstruse problem if it had been put to her.

But of course it was not, and might not be. So that the power in her hands which held the reins did eventually begin to fret her. She looked recklessly through the smooth trunks of flashing trees. And she remembered again, with disgust, the shambling, hairy body of O'Dowd. In the end, all that proud freedom of motion and recovered youth was overlaid by the feeling of disgust, that became also fear. She had never tipped herself out of any vehicle, but it might happen, she realized, by ramming the hub against a gatepost, or from one wheel mounting even a small log.

When she drove into the back yard Amy Parker was perspiring and throbbing, and her husband, who was gathering together the buckets, looked out of a window and frowned.

"It is late," he said. "I am ready to start."

Coming outside with the shining buckets.

"I shall not be a minute," she said, climbing down from the trap rather quickly for a woman of her age, rather ungainly in her precipitation.

She must have guessed this, for she blushed and looked down.

"I was with O'Dowds," she said. "I have wasted a fine lot of time. They were drunk, dirty brutes, shickered in the middle of the afternoon."

She went into her house, throwing back at her husband fragments of her experience, which seemed incredible as she crossed her orderly kitchen and into the bedroom to pull off the dress she had worn for that outing.

But her husband laughed in all kindliness and went on,

appeased, towards the bails. He liked sometimes to listen to the reported sins of other people, and to think about them, and laugh. As he was in no way vicious, tolerance was perhaps his vice.

Amy Parker, who was in her flat feet, got into that old woolen dress she wore for milking. How shapeless she was sometimes, she saw now, and blotched by haste or excitement. A coarse woman. And she began again to think about O'Dowds, and of that word which she had used in connection with them.

Shickered, she said again, heavily, to herself.

It was not her word, but she had used it, and now was fascinated by the sound. Its brutal and contagious ugliness. She smoothed herself inside her old dress, still standing in her stockings. She was disturbing to herself.

It is milking time, she said, holding her hands flat to her face, so that it was framed in her hands and the mirror.

Then great sadness invaded the house, or it was just the silence that she was listening to, as she walked on flat feet over the carpet towards her shoes. If something were to happen—what, she did not dare to think—would she conduct herself with delicacy, or that brutality which sometimes threatened her? She looked out of the house. Or a letter would arrive—her trial could take this more merciful form—to say that Ray was coming, and she would make everything nice, and keep the excitement from bursting out of her veins, and run out, and take his head as he was standing there, it was hers to gather.

But she was pulling the shoes onto her heels.

Stan is waiting for me, said the heavy woman. He will be annoyed.

She went out then without any further thought or silliness, though looking about, in case somebody might come, asking for directions, or to tell some news.

Chapter 18

WHEN Stan Parker had reached this age of life he did sometimes wonder what was expected of him. He was respected. He was inseparable from the district, he had become a place name. His herd was small, but of good quality for the herd of a man in a small way, neither rich nor ambitious, but reliable, the cans would always reach the butter factory to the minute, without fail. He went to church too, singing the straight psalms and rounder hymns, in praise of that God which obviously did exist. Stan Parker had been told for so long that he believed, of course he did believe. He sang that praise doggedly, in a voice you would have expected of him, approaching the music honestly, without embellishing it. Standing in the pew, singing, the back of his neck was by this time quite wrinkled, and the sinews were too obvious in the flesh. But he was a broad and upright man.

What then was wrong? There was nothing, of course, that you could explain by methods of logic; only a leaf falling at dusk will disturb the reason without reason. Stan Parker went about the place on which he had led his life, by which he was consumed really. This is my life, he would have said if he had expressed himself other than by acts of the body. But there were seasons of stubble and dead grass, when doubts did press up. There were certain corners of his property that he could not bring himself to visit, almost as if he might have discovered something he did not wish to see. It is all right there, he said, and persuaded himself that nothing does alter that is established in the mind.

Once he had been looking at a crop of remarkably fine sorghum that was almost ready to bring in, when he remembered that same stretch of land after he had cleared it as a young man, and on it the white chips lying that his axe had carved out of the trees, and some trees and young saplings still standing and glistening there, waiting for the axe. So that he forgot his present crop and went away disturbed, and thinking.

At times he indulged in great physical exertion, excessive, in fact, for a man of his age, to atone perhaps for those weaknesses with which he was assailed. He prayed too, in prayers that he had learned, avoiding improvisation now, for he no longer trusted himself at this, and he tried to fit those stern and rather wooden prayers to his own troubled and elusive soul. He prayed hopefully, desperately at times, always woodenly, and wondered if his wife knew.

I should tell her something of this perhaps, he said, but how to mention, and what to mention, so he could not. He realized that it was some time since they had spoken together. Except to ask for things and recount incidents, they had not really entered into each other. She was closed, he saw. He was perpetually looking at her eyelids, as she walked or sat with these drawn down, in a dream.

If their life and love had not been so firmly founded on habit, he would have been troubled by this too. As it was, he was not. He accepted his wife's face as further evidence of that uneasy dream-time to which they had come at last, and through which they floated restlessly towards whatever was in store.

One evening the woman, in looking for something, had begun to turn out a cupboardful of junk, pieces of old ornaments that she had put away, knowing that almost certainly those pieces would never be joined together again, a knot of insertion turning brown, old catalogues from big stores, the teeth of children in a bottle, many valueless and transient things which some tenacity or avarice in herself had tried secretly to elevate to permanence and value. Down on her knees, turning over her possessions with some irony and helplessness, she also came across a little notebook.

As she was turning the pages, looking at them, or merely turning, the man her husband who had been watching her, waiting for some act or exposure that might illuminate the present and many other situations, sat forward and asked hopefully, "What is that that you have got, Amy?"

"Ah," she sniffed, or grunted, that evening she was in her slippers and her hair was loose, "that is a little notebook that was given me by Mrs. Erbey, I remember, the parson's wife at Yuruga. I wanted to give it to Ray, to keep a diary in. I thought it would be nice. But he wasn't taken with the idea."

Then she added, "It was a silly one perhaps. To expect boys to write down what they do. I don't think boys look back. They go on doing."

"Give it to me," said her husband, coming forward. "I can use it for something, to make notes or keep lists."

She was glad to give him the silly book, putting it into his hand without rising from her absorption.

The man returned to his chair on the edge of the room, and looked at the blank book, and tried to think what he would write in it. The blank pages were in themselves simple and complete. But there must be some simple words, within his reach, with which to throw further light. He would have liked to write some poem or prayer in the empty book, and did for some time consider that idea, remembering the plays of Shakespeare that he had read lying on his stomach as a boy, but any words that came to him were the stiff words of a half-forgotten literature that had no relationship with himself.

So the book remained empty. He went about, ploughing, chopping, milking, reaping, emptying buckets and filling them. All these acts were good in themselves, but none of them explained his dream life, as some word might, like lightning, out of his brain. Sometimes, though, he was appalled by his foolishness, and would look at his wife to see whether she suspected.

She did not.

"Stan," she said, "do you think it will rain yet? There is a little cloud down there in the South."

She moistened her lips and rose guiltily to the surface of her mind, because she realized he was looking at her.

These were years of drought, and they often made such remarks, going out from under the heat of the roof to the vaster heat of the sky. To look. They would moisten the dry skin of their lips and make prognostications, sometimes hopeful, to encourage each other. They stood, and were watched by their own lean cows, as if these expected a revelation from men similar to that which men expected from the sky.

Then everyone grew accustomed, more or less, to the yellow drought. They watched it and each other less. They even discovered moments of detached beauty.

Stan Parker found a dragonfly, as long as his finger, which he brought to show his wife, it was trembling on a yellow mulberry leaf.

"Why, that is beautiful, Stan," she said.

316

She was pleased but detached, humouring him as if he were a little boy. She was kneading dough at the time.

"Put it on the sill," she said, "and perhaps it will fly."

After delivering it from his hands, from which the skin had been knocked in one or two places, there were scabs on them, he went out, and afterwards remembered the incident as one that had been insufficient.

If they had been dependent on those frail wings to rise together, the woman would not have been able at that moment to infuse them with strength. Eventually I will speak to him, she felt. It was as if she could not bring herself to take the final vow of love and submission. She was incapable just then, because she was not yet ready. In the meantime she kneaded, she could only knead dough, or tear the pages from the calendar, or look out of windows at the spectacle of yellow leaves on dying twigs.

That autumn was no yellower than summer in which she walked, saving one or two shrubs with a drop of water that she had kept from the sink. Dust blew down the road from Durilgai, in hungry tongues or in eddies, playful until they acquired the force of madness. In the first stages of the drought, while resistance to it was still related to self-respect, the windows of the house had been kept shut, but as the months drew out, and it became obvious that there was no real barrier to what was happening, that dust would settle, and the brittle leaves and wisps of white grass appear subtly on the carpet, the windows began to stand open. Sometimes the arms of curtains waved hopelessly in the enveloping wind. Dust had entered the drawers, and was beginning to fill a little china shoe that the woman kept on the mantelpiece, which she used to fill with violets, or capricious bunches of any small flowers, but which now of course was empty.

Is this really my house? the woman thought, pausing with her empty can, looking through the dusty oleanders at the curtains waving from the shell of the house.

Sometimes the man her husband, who had his own preoccupations, would promise himself to tell her she was letting the house go, and that she must do something about it, but he postponed this, because it is something you do postpone, out of delicacy, even pity.

Now he was away, at a sale of farm machinery that was taking place on a property at Wullunya. The woman remembered his kiss as she stood there in the arid garden. His affection, which was kind and habitual, made her feel fretful in retrospect. Then she began to whimper quietly, for no good reason, except at the touch of her own dry and drying skin, slightly gritty from the dust, which she had touched, and continued touching, stroking her own arms. The can, which she had knocked over, fell with a clatter of emptiness on the hard ground.

Finally she said dryly, This is ridiculous.

And began to brace herself, and to walk upright through the bushes of the garden. Nobody had seen her.

Later, when she had drunk some tea and felt stronger, she came out again and sat on the veranda. The afternoon was full of the clear light of autumn, but dry of course, with a hard, bright twittering of birds. The wind had turned cold, which made her shiver. It came ballooning down from out of the direction of Durilgai, making things rattle in it, twigs and loose tin.

There was a car coming down from Durilgai, a small blue car, rather new, she noticed, but without interest, perhaps from the city, but trailing the dust of these parts. She sat on her veranda, looking, because you do look. In the days of horses and her youth she would have gone down to the gate, but that was not now.

So the car continued, and drew near, as she was looking, and the man got out and came up the path, after having some trouble with the catch of the gate. All through this she had sat and watched, in lethargy or with irony, when she could and should have explained the peculiarities of the catch, and with the same irony she let him come up the path with the two heavy cases, that had given him a congested look and pulled his collar down, exposing his neck below the weather line.

The man was a commercial traveller, it appeared. He asked whether he could interest her in a few lines of dress materials he was carrying. He had stockings too, and lingerie, and fancy buttons.

But the woman smiled faintly, incredulously, shaking her head. She was white as well as silent, for she had rubbed some power on her face while she had been in the house, absently and inexpertly, and this increased her expression of remoteness, giving her, in fact, the expression of some statuary in public places, almost fatally withdrawn and impersonal. She was big too, sitting sideways on a hard chair.

The man, who was on the verge of closing his mouth on a half-spoken word, dropped to his knee then.

"Give us a chance," he said. "You can at least give it a lookover. That is free for nothing."

Although discouraged, he could not shed the brass with which he had been armoured.

The big white woman laughed softly at the brazen man as she sat looking down, and at his hands. He began to draw out lengths of material from one case.

"This is just to show you," he said. "I got more back there in the car. French. This is a nice line," he said. "It's sort of quiet. That appeals sometimes to ladies of quiet tastes. But mind you, distinguished. This is a nice one. Something to stand out. Bright but not flash. Or this. It'll wear for years. But because it don't hit you in the eye, you won't hold that against it. Care for green? Some ladies are superstitious. I can show you a belt that would go with that. Very reasonable and tasteful. Something different. And a set of buttons. Hand-painted. Or pink? Lots of young girls go for this one. Of course that don't mean it's not available. If it's pink you're feeling like, then pink it is. But take your time, lady. Have a look. A *comfortable* look, I always say. We've got all day."

Then when he had heaped them in a turmoil at her feet, these and other soft snakes, in and out of the cases, on the veranda, he turned and began to look at three hens which had come round the side of the house, and were chipping at the paths without regard for him, and stalking round the stiff rosemary with fixed eyes. The man was forced to light a cigarette, from a rather tinny inscribed case that had been given him years ago, on an occasion, by a mob of blokes. The man looked at a row of pumpkins standing on the roof of a shed. He drew hard on the cigarette. All that was in the garden, and what could be seen of the sourrounding paddocks, submerged in their dead grass, was at that moment incredible to him. As he did not know the names of plants, he did not even have the comfort of thinking these over. He could only smoke his thin and bitter cigarette.

But the woman, who had been surrounded by such tribute of colour, and who had been fingering it in search of inspiration, finally said, "I am sorry. I have everything. There is nothing I want."

"Some people are lucky," said the man, not angrily, but almost.

He began to fold and smoothe, till he was ready to snap the catches of the cases. All was hidden. All the time she had been watching his hands, which were stained on certain fingers. He was one of the reddish men, of skin and hair. He was repulsive to her, she thought. Turning to fat. Without brilliantine he would have bristled. But she continued to watch those acts of conjuring that he was performing. She was fascinated by the smooth cigarette that blew smoke.

Then the man pushed back the cases, as if, surprisingly, he despised the elaborate mechanics of his slick life.

"Gee," he said, "it's dry here."

The hat pushed back, his head had begun to look naked and pitiable.

"We've had just about everything in the years we have lived here," she said, looking around. "Floods, fire, drought. But we have never starved."

"How do you account for that?" he asked, without interest.

When he put his hands on his hips, and stood that way, thickset and rather pursy, she might not have trusted him. Remembering her husband—in fact, she could never escape from him for long—she said, "My husband has a belief in God. At least I think he has. We have never spoken about it."

"Oh," said the man.

This woman was standing above him on the raised-up veranda, looking down. Because she was concentrating on her own thoughts, he suspected her of looking into his. Which he did not care about. So he moved the muscles in his jaws. She was a woman getting on, probably at that time of life, complicated but harmless.

"Are you religious?" he asked.

"I don't know," she said. "I don't know what I believe. Not yet."

"I never thought about it much," he said.

He spat into the bushes, but wondered at once whether he should have done so. She gave no glimpse of her feelings, though. She was a still woman. There was no indication of censure, only a sound of insects congregated round a lump of dark comb underneath the eaves.

The woman heard it too. It was a throbbing.

"You don't happen to have a glass of water," said the man at last, when his eardrums were bursting. "I'm dry as a snake."

"Yes," she said, just raising her eyes from under the weight of some deliberation that was taking place, and smiling with straight lips.

A bit dotty, he said, but a good-looking woman, or has been.

He began to follow her through the house, through which she was leading him, through an intimacy of clocks and silence. His flash shoes trod heavily on the linoleum, on which the dust had gathered. There was a slight grit beneath his rubber feet. And everywhere the dimness of the inhabited house was opening to him, offering him the faint smells of life and furniture. He had never penetrated deeper into any house, he began to feel, least of all into his own shallow box, which he entered rarely, anyway, and then turned on the radio.

The woman could feel the stranger in his sumptuous suit behind her as she brought him on. He was rather a big man in the dimness of the passage, moving in masses of squelching rubber, coughing in a thick voice, and murmuring those commonplaces that people who talk are compelled to utter. It was exciting and disturbing for her to reveal the intimacies of her house, but all the time she was remembering that he was repellent to her, with his reddish skin and red hair. The obscenity of his fingers too, with those brown stains.

Then they were in the kitchen, which did have an amplitude, of a comparatively big old kitchen. The common but living furniture was pleasant to the hands. So the man rested his knuckles as a matter of course on the surface of the big worn table, waiting for the woman to fetch him the glass of water, which she did soon, from a canvas bag.

"Ah," said the man, jerking back his head and wriggling his neck, because he was preparing to be funny. "That's the stuff to shake the navy."

It disguised the trembling of the water.

Because it was strange there. We are advancing towards something, he knew, looking at the woman's transparent eyes. Her smooth flesh trembled and receded like pale water.

He drank down the rest of the glassful, and it was very cool. A great innocence of object and purpose prevailed in the kitchen.

"I'd like to have a spring, like the people down the road," said Amy Parker, stepping out of the state of entrancement in which she had been shut, it seemed for many years, and the words ran out of her quickly and glitteringly, like water. "You can see it coming out of the ground. You can hold it up, and it is quite clear, no weed in it or anything. You

321

should always look for a spring before you build a house. Tank water isn't the same."

She came forward breathlessly after that, to take the glass. Her courage had grown with words, and overcome an awkwardness of movement.

"Yes," said the man unsteadily. "There's nothing like cold spring water."

She was almost but not quite his height, he saw.

She noticed the pores in his red skin, which would remain her torment.

Then they were grappling with each other. Teeth were striking on teeth. Their arms were knotting.

Ahhh, cried the breath of the woman Amy Parker as she remembered a name that she could not tear up. She could have righted herself perhaps, but only momentarily, before swirling farther to destruction.

"What's come over us?" panted the pursy man, but did not wish to be answered.

Buried in the flesh of the woman, he had returned to boyhood, from which poetry had escaped, and would again ultimately.

Presently Amy Parker took the man by the hand. Their fingers were surprising to each other's fingers. Now that their wills had withdrawn, they were trembling together in cold rooms. But after they had taken the clothes from their nakedness, fire leaped out of them, and in that blaze they would have to burn out, to whatever end.

They had gone in to that straight bed on which Amy Parker had slept out the sum of her life. She saw intermittently those possessions that she had given up to the holocaust. She closed her eyes. The man drew from out of her lovely ribbons of appeased flesh. But when she took his skull, and tried to enter it, she could not, but bruised her mouth against the sockets. It was her husband's head. Then she put her tongue, crying, against the mouth. It was as if she had spat into the face of her husband, or still further, into the mystery of her husband's God, that she saw by glimpses but could not reach deeper to. So that she was fighting her disgust, and crying for her own destruction before she had destroyed, as she must destroy. Long waves of exquisite pleasure were carrying her condemned body towards that point.

"Steady on now," breathed the man's hot breath into her burning ear.

On putting aside surprise and fear, he had quickly risen to

the moderate heights of which he was capable, of rather trite and panting sensuality, of stale words and physical cosiness. Now he tried to calm this woman, whose passion overflowed the bounds that he knew.

"Take a hold of yourself," he laughed, touching her with heavy, superior hands. "I'm not gonna run off and leave yer."

If he was her inferior in passion, he was her superior in quickly appeased lust. So he could afford to laugh, and light another cigarette, and watch the soul writhe mysteriously in her body.

Finally she was still. She was innocent in that stillness. He touched her dreamy thighs, and remembered standing on the white banks of a large but almost dry river, catching eels, when a little boy. That innocence of light which came beneath the blind lit his fleshy face, and the struggle of eels lifted from the mud, he was himself lithe and golden. That morning, it seemed, was the one solid morning of his life. The banks of the river were sculptured. All else, all experience, slithered through his hands in confusion.

"What is it?" said the woman, opening her eyes.

"Nothing," said the thick man. "I was just thinking."

He began to think about his wife, who was thin. She had a smoker's cough. She knitted jumpers, one after the other; it was a kind of vice with her, to preserve a continuity of wool, and especially when night came.

But he broke off there.

He had remembered something. He bent forward, examining the woman's skin, through smoke.

"They call me Leo," he said.

"Leo," she said dully.

She neither accepted nor rejected. In that drowsiness even her own name was not stuck on.

She rubbed her cheek against the sheet, which smelled of recent washing, and was uncorrupted by smoke. Lust leaves no immediate trace. Instead many little pictures of contentment and tenderness flickered in her. Some of these were barely stated, but she could interpret them, like the expression on the face of the postmistress's husband, or those paintings he had left as an apology for his life. She was given access also to other souls, to that of her neighbour O'Dowd, with whom she sat again on a veranda, bandying hairy words, bridging the gap between them by obscenity and drunkenness, till she could have loved that one too, embracing her own guilt. Sometimes the dreams her children had dreamed on other beds in the house, and which had never really dispersed, mingled with her own vision, and she thought that in time she might have understood even her children.

Opening her eyes again, she saw that the man called Leo was occupying the room as he put on his clothes with great masterliness. How his braces hung down, she saw through the slits of her eyes.

"Open the window, Leo," she said. "It is stuffy in here."

He was only too willing to do this, hurriedly, to oblige; he had a long way to go, and even longer to catch up with himself after the detour he had made.

"Aren't you going to get up?" he commanded rather than asked, but because his strength was not great enough, he pulled the knot of his tie so tight the colour came deeper in his face, she saw, like a congestion, and the veins in his eyes.

"In a little while," she just said.

"Well," he said, "I've got to be on my way."

It was not the moment for two people who had looked so intimately into each other to kiss. So they touched each other somehow, and she heard him going too quickly through the house, and did not think about him much more for that moment, as if he had ceased to be of importance to her. She lay there smiling and dreaming. If she was destroyed, she had not yet woken to her ghost.

Then, as the wind was lifting the curtain up and letting it fall, the cat got in, a pied tom that she had grown fond of as a kitten, and kept, and sometimes regretted after his cheeks had swelled out. This cat now eased himself through the slit of the window, jumped down on felt feet, and was all for rubbing himself against her.

"Down, Tom," she murmured, without other attempt at remonstrance.

Feeling fur, as the condoning cat rubbed and cherished her. As she lay powerless. The big cat grovelling, and bathing his cool fur in her warm flesh. Then the tail trailed, she felt, between her breasts. It was giving her the gooseflesh. It was revolting her.

"Ahhh," she cried. "You brute!"

As she recoiled, flinging the cat, which struck the dressing table. How it squawked, and rebounded, so that she was left with the silence and her own face.

This had crumbled further since morning, it seemed. It was all loathing for the glass, and the hair had slipped out of control, was hanging in switches, and masses, and grey tails. She was sagging. Now she did really begin to shiver.

"It is cold," she shivered, covering her shoulders and her breasts with her arms, as if she might stop her shivering in that way.

She began to feel her way through her clothes.

"It is late," she shivered. "It is milking time. And I am on my own."

She walked through the house in a wind of resumed activity, flinging doors behind her as she passed, gathering things, buckets, and the clean rags with which to dry the teats of the cows. Temporarily this honest and steadfast activity swallowed her up, so that she was not able to reconnoitre her position, except when she was approaching the sheds and found them square and ominous, as she had not suspected, in their white bleached wood. Slow cows stood watching her, and afterwards, in the bails, turned their heads at some difference in her hands, or uneasiness, or haste, ruminating above their blue tongues.

When Stan Parker got home he saw that his wife had probably had a headache. She had parted her hair very carefully, and the bones of her face were distinct. Sometimes after headaches, or some secret activity of thought, the flesh or her face had a grey tinge, which it had now. It looked flatter. Immediately he turned his eyes away from this, and began to tell her about the sale at Wullunya and people he had seen, about illnesses, and deaths, and marriages. She bent her head and received all this information with gratitude, even humility.

She wanted to do something for him.

"Here's a nice piece, Stan," she said, "with the fat on that you like."

She sliced, or rather hacked, for she was not very good at carving, at the solid roast of beef, and brought off a ruddy sliver with an edge of yellow fat. Although he was already full, and on the verge of pushing back his plate, he was forced to accept this, because he thought it might give her pleasure.

"You are not eating," he said.

"No," she said, turning down her mouth, as if he had mentioned something nauseating to her. "It has blown all day. I have no appetite," she said.

And began to go about.

"It has blown all right," he said. "It will dry the last drop."

So that she saw the yellow grass lying down, in that brassy light of afternoon, in which travellers appear out of a distance.

"There was a man here this afternoon," she said, in a louder voice than was hers. "With things to sell."

"What sort of things?" he asked, because their lives were made of question and answer.

"Dress materials, and oh, fancy things."

"What did you buy?" he asked.

"What should *I* buy?"

"I don't know," he said. "Why, some *frill!*"

He laughed for that word which he had not pulled out of his mouth till then.

"At my time of life!" She laughed.

Holding up her throat for the laughter to escape with passion, it seemed.

He was content, though. He took yesterday's paper, more as an occupation than to cast fresh light on that little which he already knew, because he no longer expected to learn more, except by the blinding force of some illumination. So he read solidly through the deeds of statesmen, soldiers, scientists, while keeping himself in reserve for something of greater importance that would occur. And his wife sat and sewed.

Presently he said, "I met a man called Organ at Wullunya. He was nephew of a woman we rescued in the floods. I can remember her. She was a small woman, with a sewing machine that she had to leave behind. This boy's grandfather was drowned in the floods. They found him caught in a tree."

"Well, what of it?" said his wife rather irritably. "Everyone in the district was in the floods. Some of their folks were drowned. Did this man tell you something of interest perhaps?"

"Nothing in particular," said Stan Parker.

His wife squinted at the eye of a needle. She could have been terribly irritated at that moment in the loud, pervasive electric light.

"What of him?" she murmured thickly.

"I saw his grandfather, Amy," said Stan Parker. "He was an old man with a beard, hanging upside down in a tree. And we rowed past. Nobody else saw. He was almost certainly dead. I would'uv liked to think it was a ram. I persuaded myself perhaps, while there was still time to tell. But we rowed. And soon it was too late."

326

"But if he was a corpse," said Amy Parker.

If it was, to the young man still rowing in the same boat.

"And perhaps the others did see," his wife pursued subtly, now that she had speared the needle's eye, "and were not letting on either, because it is unpleasant to stop a boat, and pull in the body of an old man."

But his guilt remained, and because of this he was humble.

"It is all too silly," said his wife.

She had her own corpse, that she could not share. She stood in great isolation on the banks of the swollen river, and strong young men rowed splendidly over the brown and flashing waters, towards her, and there was her husband whom she recognized finally, but with whom she could not communicate.

Amy Parker put away her sewing because her hands were trembling. She did not feel now that she had ever had definite control of her actions. At any point in her life the wind could have blown her with fantastic force in directions that immediately would not have seemed improbable.

Just then the wind was glowing by infernal gusts, to beat the iron that was nailed to the wooden house. The sticks of dead shrubs were scratching the walls. If the roof should lift off, she breathed.

But in the meantime she went to bed, holding her hair. She took the pins out, and let it fall, and was looking at herself, when her husband, who was pulling off his boots, said, "Was it a green car that that fellow had, who came here selling things?"

She was holding a hairpin.

"I don't remember," she said. "It could have been green. No. It was blue, I think. Why?"

Looking at her own face stranded in the glass.

Stan Parker, who was pulling off his second boot, said rather jerkily, "There was a green car down the road, before you get to O'Dowds'. The bloke seemed to be selling a woman some kind of kitchen things."

"I told you," she said angrily, "this was not kitchen things."

And did experience some twinge of pleasure for what she had lived that day. Her grey flesh glowed again. She was glowing and blowing in the gusty wooden box, in which there seemed room for both good and evil. In this mood she arranged the sheet beneath her chin, and would not look at the face of her husband, fearing that a preponderance of good might upset this satisfactory balance. Of course she loved her

327

husband. She fell asleep with this conviction. But other immeasurable impulses moved with the flapping of the blind. It was tapping on her skin with stained fingers, that reckoned up her age ten years from then, she could not, she said, laughed, it was not arithmetic or cats' tails.

Stan Parker, who had fallen asleep tired, in a draught, dreamed that he could not lift the lid of that box to show her what he had inside. It does not matter, she said, holding the dishcloth between, to hide. But he could not lift. It does not matter, she said, Stan, I do not want to see. I shall show, he said, pulling till the sweat came. But still not. No, she said, Stan, Stan, it has gone bad in there, it has been in there all these years. Pulling, he could not explain it was his act that had died, and grown wool, like a ram, and lived again. I am going, she said. The dishcloth blew through the doorway. Running through the kitchen. Grey water was flowing between them.

He woke then, stretched stiff in the bed, his feet nailing the sheet to the rail, and his neck bare, on which the sweat was cold. But she was breathing. She had not gone. Then he understood. He understood the husband of the postmistress hanging from the tree in the yard, the reason for whose action had always appeared obscure to him. I could take my life, he said behind stiff lips. But she had not gone. She was breathing. So he lay sideways against her, drawing up his knees for comfort, and her warmth flowed through his veins again, and gradually he fell asleep, and was sleeping, and sleeping because she was there.

Even so they woke a bit stiff, and were going stiffly about their jobs, and were talking to each other in thin grey voices.

We must expect this at our age, he said, and the cold weather coming on.

But when the sun rose finally, and while it remained an innocent and recognizable ball balanced on the crests of the trees, it was a magnificent and clear autumn that Amy Parker saw. The leaves had not yet all been torn off those trees which would eventually lose them. There were still golden tatters, and the dark, almost black thickets of the evergreens. Light lay in masses on the paddocks, which smoked and glistened.

Later in the day the woman would begin to divest herself of the old scarves and cardigans and hat she had put on as a precaution in the early hours, while she was still grey and grumbling and tentative, and which made her into an unsightly bundle of fraying wool and stained felt. She would shake back her hair. Sometimes when she had time, some afternoons, she would walk through the bush along the bed of the creek, where strange objects were to be found, stones, and the skins of snakes, seed pods, and skeleton leaves. She would look for things, and she would gather sprays of leaves, to have something in her hand, to acquire some reason for her being there. Then too, with the stronger light beginning to weigh her glance down, she would think more boldly of what had happened. It was the brazen light touching things. She would think about the man Leo, avoiding those aspects of him which were repulsive to her, reducing him to meet those needs of her own for destruction or renewal. So she moved thoughtfully along the dry bed of the creek, turning a stone over, picking at a leaf, trying the polished limbs of a dead tree. Silence and reckless thoughts exalted her incongruity into rightness. But finally, at the bend in the creek, when she was faced with turning, and must go back in company with her body, into that life which remained, she began to walk in a panic across grass and sticks, her nostrils grown thin. She could not walk fast enough, whether to escape or to arrive. There had been no indication that the man would come again, and when she reached the road, she was glad that she could look along it disinterestedly, following its ribbon with her eyes, right along past the little tuft of trees, and farther, to where it touched the sky.

Once when she got back to the cluster of sheds which were gathered round the house, walking with her eyes cast down, and holding her side on account of the speed at which she had come, there was her husband, with a piece of wire that he had cut off and twisted into the shape of a circle, apparently for the purpose of making something.

"Hello, Amy," he said, pausing deliberately. "Where have you been?"

"Oh, down the paddock," she said. "To get a bit of air," she said. "And up along the road. You get stale in the house."

He paused, and then asked, with the obvious intention of being kind to her, "And did you see anyone?"

"Only an old man," she replied.

Her instantaneous conception of this even turned her blood cold, but once conceived she continued to watch placidly enough as it grew.

"He was on his way to Wullunya," she said, "where he has

329

a block of land. He has pigs, and some poultry, and a citrus orchard. Poor old man, he is walking because his horse went in the feet, back near Badgerys', where he left it. He had been to Bangalay to see his daughter, who is suffering from the quinsy."

Stan Parker shook his head incredulously.

She turned away, guarding a pulse in her throat, and a coldness for that wave of falsehood which had overtaken her.

And as she walked away he realized that he no longer saw her eyes, or very rarely, as just now, and then they were filled with great distances. So he turned back to that piece of wire which he had cut, the original purpose of which he had momentarily forgotten.

They began to be kind to each other, as if each sensed the other was in need of the protection of kindness in that world of strange truths in which they now found themselves. So they performed simple acts to please each other, which had only a sadness for the recipient. One night she began to pin on him, for size, the pieces of a cardigan she was knitting for winter. She went round him, touching his body, patting, and arranging.

"Ah, it is too small," she said, standing back. "I did not allow for the stomach that has come."

Then they both laughed, as, of course, it really did not matter, all this.

"The wood will stretch," he said, drawing his mouth down and easing his weight onto one leg, as he stood with his hands on his hips waiting for the operation to be finished.

She went round him thoughtfully, touching the body of her husband. His wrists were rather gnarled now.

All round him he could sense the play of her hair. Sometimes her hands, which were rough, caught in the soft wool. As she was stooping and looking, he remained considerably taller than she, and closed his eyes while submitting. He was locked up now in some impersonal state of warm grey wool, neither good nor bad, but tolerable.

Then he opened his eyes, and they were looking at each other, for she had straightened up.

"It will be all right in the end," she said quickly and guiltily, to atone for her glance at his sleeping face. "I know what I can do, I think, to make it fit better."

He smiled, and did not intend irony, but he was tired that night.

She sat down and began to pull out part of her work, and

330

to knit desperately, paying out the thread of wool, gripping her needles nervously.

"I am worried about Ray, Stan," she said.

She really was too, as she sat on the edge of her chair.

"Do you think it was in him, anyway, all this badness? Or was it his upbringing? Or is it something that he has got from us? Together, I mean. It is like the cattle. Two goods can make a bad. We may not mix well," she said, and waited.

He sat with his chin on his chest. He would have liked to throw aside the weight of what she was putting on him.

"I have never known what to do," he said, wincing. "I am to blame. I try to find the answers, but I have not succeeded yet. I do not understand myself or other people. That is all."

He wondered whether she would leave him alone after that. He felt weak tonight, with a bitter taste in his mouth.

She continued to knit. She was propitiated. At that moment she could feel grieved and frustrated for the weak husband that she had got. All her own potentiality for evil streamed away from her in soft, elusive wool. And since she had bought her innocence, her memory crept back into the languorous attitudes of afternoon, tremulously amazed at her own desirability and youthfulness.

It was natural enough then, one afternoon when Stan had gone somewhere on some business or other, and she could see the deliberate blue car again in fact, that she should go straight out of the house, flinging back the wire gauze of the outer door so that it hit the wall of the house and quivered. The dead balls of brown roses were hanging on the old staggy bush, that brushed her as she went down, feeling in the calves of her legs a tautness that could have been confidence or anxiety. She was at the gate soon, a minute or two before the slow but fateful car, and there held herself masterfully erect in waiting sunlight.

"How are we doin?" asked the man Leo, who was driving casually enough, and had pushed his hat back, so that she could see that hair which would still have been repellent to her if she had been able to consider.

Instead she said back, in even but rather colourless tones, "Thanks. I am all right. Where have you been all this time?"

So that he was forced slowly to stop, and began to tell her how he had taken his holiday just then, and how they had made a trip to the North or perhaps the South Coast, she did not hear which, and that they had visited relatives and had a bonzer time. His voice was slower than she had remembered.

Wherever *they* had been, sitting in the sunlight in their night things, eating fresh fish and lazily sharing other lives, she realized that he was not dependent on her.

She looked down and frowned even. You are a lazy man, she said, as well as ugly.

"An you," he said, "what've you been up to?"

"Oh, I!" She laughed. "The same."

Looking down.

But she was conscious of his behaving very slowly, leaning on the wheel and spitting slowly.

Then I shall not catch fire? her dry mouth asked. All around, the garden, or what remained, the sticks, could have gone up with one match.

"The same, eh?" He spat between his teeth.

He was, in fact, remembering this full-blown woman whom he had forgotten, because of certain aspects, of which he had been afraid. He had deliberately forgotten. There she was now, blowsy was the word, and still. It is stillness that perplexes more even than the mystery of passion opening. To a thin man. For this man was thin inside his flesh.

"It is all right, I suppose, to them that likes it," the man said. "All this," he said, looking around. "The cows down there. Gettin up with cold hands. Good Christ!"

"It is my life," she said, again evenly, which gave no echo of the drumming.

For her ears were bursting.

Then she threw back her head. "And you are a flash type of man," she said. "That is all right too, I suppose. Stringing people along with all that talk. And holding out the material for women to see."

"You don't like me," he laughed.

He slammed the door, but he had come out.

"I did not say so," she said.

She was all gentleness again. He liked that inflection, which appealed to his virility. So he came on, easing one leg, which had grown stiff from his sitting in the car. And she continued to stand there, still gently feeling the situation, which was as subtle as air, and which, because it was first and foremost her situation, must be handled tenderly. That was what nerved her to look him full in the eyes, which were rather puffy, and which would teach her to say things that he expected. She could have followed the wildest intricacies of that situation because the necessity was hers.

They went into the house then.

He put his hand in the small of her back, ushering her into her own house, and she closed her eyes in its familiar gloom with complete passivity; otherwise she could not have endured its strangeness.

But today it was different. As if the revelation of passion is not revealed twice.

This time they laughed, and she saw his gold tooth. Their flesh had been made to run together sensuously. He looked at her.

"What is your wife's name?" she asked.

"Myra," he said.

Then when she had thought about it enough, she put her mouth in his mouth, as if she could have bitten out the word. And they struggled together, not heroically, but to bruise each other's bodies, and she swallowed down any suspicion of repulsion that rose in her throat to oppose her lust.

Then when they had exhausted themselves he said to her, "What's become of your old man?"

She told him that Stan had gone wherever he had.

The man beside her, who was yawning, laughed a low, slow laugh, full of collusion.

Then she sat up.

"But I love my husband," she said.

And she did. The goodness and sudden perfection of their life together were trembling before her, because lost, in the face of such obscenity, foisted on her by a strange dictatorship of the body.

"I haven't said anything against him," said the man. "I ain't made his acquaintance, and shan't neither. Probably."

He was grumbling now, as she stepped heavily about the room, gathering stockings and things. Her gooseflesh filled him with contempt for his own impulses.

They were getting up, wondering.

Get out of this mess double quick, he said, and could not find his collar stud immediately.

Her hands were fixing the disguise of her hair. Soon, she saw, nobody would be able to accuse her. She was unrecognizable, except to her own desires. These were never dead long.

"I would like to go to the city once or twice," she said.

"Yeah? What would you do there?" he asked, without interest.

"I'd walk in the streets and look at the people," she said.

He laughed down his nose. "That's one thing I ain't done yet."

"I'd sit by the sea," she said, "and watch it. And I'd listen to music."

" 'Ere," he said, "where do I come in?"

Now that he was in a position to make a quick getaway, and was altogether possessed of himself, he put his hands on her shoulders, so that the ring he wore, which was set with a very small ruby star, smouldered. In the counterfeit of this fresh situation she did just flash back, commonly enough, putting her breasts against him.

"Are there no other women?" She laughed. "Don't tell me!"

They went out, exchanging more jokes with a brutality that the time seemed to demand.

She was surprised that she could be one of the flash women.

"So long, Leo," she said brazenly, looking at the veins in his neck, into which the collar cut too tight.

His smooth car was ready. She watched him prepare a deft departure. These are easy to some.

"If I had yer picture," he said, "I'd keep it underneath the mattress."

"Good thing you haven't," she laughed.

Then she held her hand straight above her eyes to shield them from the metallic light and watch this man drive with such ease along the dust. She saw with some indifference, almost as if her life had not been broken into, except by watching, by her eyes following the smooth passage of a blue car, mingling for a moment perhaps with a man's eyes. Remembering his eyes, though, through dust, these were too close, and livery, with little red veins.

It was in this position, with her straight hand held above her eyes, that Stan Parker, driving down the road, saw his wife. He still drove with some thought, one of those old cars they always had. He saw Amy standing there. There was the plume of that dust. It was floating and disintegrating but still attached.

As Stan drove in at the gate, on which the kerosene tin was nailed for the bread delivery, he waved at his wife, because this was his habit. She was still standing there, stiff. She had not taken down that straight hand. As he got down from the car he too began to move with wooden limbs.

He cleared his throat and said, "I saw Merle. She's willing to come on Thursday and give you a hand with the curtains."

"Ah, yes," she said.

334

She had forgotten.

What would they say next? she wondered horribly.

But the machinery of their lives had soon sucked them in.

Except that they were talking in stiff voices, with words like dry sticks that would have broken under slight pressure, nothing changed much. If they did not look at each other, it could have been that, through long experience, they knew what they would see. But Stan Parker listened to his wife a lot, those sounds that she made about the house, or calling hens, or speaking to cows, or her breathing even, and most of all her silences. All these sounds with which he had been familiar too, most of his life, like the beating of his own heart, were suddenly swollen, and his own heart was intolerable in his ribs.

"Last night," she said at one stage, coming to him in horror, "the rats killed another hen. One of the good ones."

She had come to him so that he should do something.

"We must bury it," he said, moving his dry limbs.

"But what can we *do?*" she said, standing there. "They ate the head off and tore out the inside. It is a horrible thing, Stan. And if they keep on, now that they have begun, tearing our good fowls to bits—" She could not say more, but waited for him.

He did not know what to do.

"We can put down poison," he said, "outside the sheds."

"Not poison, Stan," she said. "We might poison some dog or cat."

Then neither of them knew what to do.

Amy Parker became quite obsessed over the importance of this issue, she had to, and while in the grip of her obsession three or four more hens were killed and devoured by rats.

"Now that they have begun they will not stop," she protested.

He heard her above the tapping of his spoon upon an egg, that he would eat for his breakfast, but that first he must examine most carefully. If he was unable to accept the importance of her problem, he was also unable to solve his own. But from hearing her talk he did look at her eventually, and saw that her hair was untidy, and knew that he loved her.

"Perhaps we should try the poison," she hesitated.

She had seen him look at her, which was what she wanted, and was reassured.

But he was less certain than before. He went outside and began to feel his pockets for his tobacco pouch, which was

335

not there, he realized with sudden anger, and rummaged in his pockets over and over for what was mislaid, or even lost. His hands were catching in the folds and confines of his clothes, his bony hands. Sweat was in his eyes now, and behind his knees. For it was inconceivable that habit should be thus destroyed. His pouch. And he began to walk about slowly, almost totteringly, feeling his way through the situation, like some blind man, and through his thoughts, trying to arrive at where he might have put the pouch, which was a little rubber bag with a twist at the top, an old thing that had turned black.

In the shed he used as a workshop, and in which he was searching now, he began to despair of finding the pouch, and he flung down an iron last that he used when repairing boots. There was immediately a clatter and chaos of falling tools, and a sweet smell of shavings and sawdust shot up. The lost goodness was unbearable in the narrow shed. So he stood there panting and sweating, and remembered his wife when she was thin and rather shy. He remembered her, of all times, with a mouthful of clothes pegs, fixing washing on the line.

In that rainy light, between clouds, in the light of blue, blowing sheets, she appeared so simple and touching, it was not possible for such things to happen. If I put them out of my head, he said, they cannot. But the event continued to occur. It drove back into his mind attached to a plume of dust. He heard the slamming of a car door. He imagined, or tried to, and could not imagine the words spoken. Other people, even the innocent, or strangers, speak mysterious and perhaps explanatory words, which die within earshot.

So that in the end there was nothing he could seize on. He stood there fingering the hieroglyphics of the workbench, that had been chiselled into the wood, and as he stood he remembered miserably that he had lost something, which finally his mouth told him was that old rubber tobacco pouch, which he would not have lost for anything, although perished, he was used to the shape of it.

When he did find the pouch, by kicking it with his toe as it lay on a path, he began at once to rub trembling tobacco between his palms, and to stuff his pipe with a good wad. He should have been comforted, but he was not.

There was much that comforted the woman, on the other hand, who was able still to see things in their persistent shapes, whether it was a cloud swelling, or some weed she bent to look at, and which, in the absence of true flowers, was a flower, a common blue thing, but pleasing. There was a certain amount that she allowed herself to remember, and a certain amount that she compelled herself to forget. This arrangement is admirable, if possible. And she would think too of the many ways in which she might show her affection for her husband. A great warmth enveloped her at that time, of safety and contrition. Her contrition did indeed signify her safety, it began to seem.

So the woman walked in what remained of her garden, her face fresh and absorbed in autumn air. Sometimes a dog came, a big yellow rangy thing, that had attached himself, some kind of a kangaroo dog, they said. She strolled, and the dog followed, hare-footed, or she stopped, and he lowered his neck. She did not like that dog. He would appear. He would stand there, just moving his tail, of which the joints were visible. Looking at her. That dog, she said to her husband, gave her the creeps. But he was docile. He loved her in a tentative sort of a way, moving his neck. But she disliked him so, frowning at him. Then the dog would lift his lip, smiling and conciliatory, his yellow teeth gnashing for approval. For his part he would approve any behavior he might witness, translating through the eyes of love all that is depraved and bestial. If she had lived alone she could have been cruel to the dog. As it was, she walked away, quickly, round the corner of the house. And the thin yellow dog followed. His light eyes saw her wherever she went.

The cat, at least, did not watch, and she did, after a fashion, return the advances of the cat, under cover of exasperation. The cat was furry and insinuating, as he described those slow arcs about her legs, or direct, as he backed his quivering tail against the lavender bushes.

"Dirty thing," she laughed, by now acceptant.

And the big cat yowled up at her.

One evening, when the horizon was a thin red line of cold fire, she caught up the cat, and was kissing him, holding his vibrant body to her breasts. Then she knew that she was lost, or would be, given another opportunity for total destruction. But would this occur? It was so doubtful that the cat began to struggle against the desperation that was in her arms, and scratched his way free, and scrambled down. Leaving her.

The woman Amy Parker began to turn out the house during those days, to fold quantities of brown paper, to make little hanks out of lengths of string, to glance through old letters and come across yellow photographs. In one photograph she wore a hat of flowers, and was eloquent in shyness as she seldom was in words. This photograph she stood upon a chest in the bedroom, propped against a vase, and would go there guiltily to look at it. Before resuming the business of her house. Arranging and furbishing.

"Here are some handkerchiefs that I put by, Stan, and that you have not used," she said once to her husband, with the clear overtones of voice used by one whose secret life is cloudier.

She brought the pile out to show that it was true, that there should be at least this between them. She was a good wife, putting a handkerchief in his pocket before he went on a journey, and brushing the fallen hair from his collar with her hand. He accepted all this, of course. And today, which was the day he had agreed to advise a young man, a Peabody, about the purchase of some land at Hungerford, which is the other side of Bangalay.

When she had done her duty she watched him go. He was staring up at the sky, as if to read its intentions, then starting the car, which he always did rather badly, looking closely at the panel. And as she watched this erect and honourable man she realized with blinding clarity that she had never been worth of him. This illumination of her soul left her weary, but indifferent. After all, she had done her material duty in many ways. Putting a clean handkerchief in his breast pocket, for instance. She was standing there, as she had stood many times in church, with people around her who had apparently realized their spiritual aspirations, whereas she could not rise, could not discover to what she should aspire. In time the knowledge that some mystery was withheld from her ceased to make her angry, or miserable for her own void. She accepted her squat body, looking out from it, through the words of canticles, in dry acceptance of her isolation.

So now, she was looking at her husband as he started on that journey.

Then she went back into the house, from which she had swept most of the dust blown there by the droughty winds, and which was now clean but fragile. Her circulation was not very good that morning, her bones were brittle, and she walked about nervously amongst the bright furniture. She longed for some event of immense importance to fill the house's emptiness, but it was most improbable that it would. Glittering, dusty light spilled from the mirrors. That was all.

After looking round, which was foolish, because she was alone in the house, she went to the mirror in the front room, and on this mirror she wrote the word *Leo*. She could just see it, written in the smudge of her finger. As a spoken word she disliked it, for some coarseness that she could feel in her mouth. But she had never written it before. Even here, in silence, it was shameful, if desirable. So she looked at it. In this way invocations are made. But when the breath was tight in her chest she rubbed out the name savagely.

After she had taken a bucket of scraps to throw to the fowls, and derived some benefit from having these round her in their blamelessness, she came back and found him sitting on the veranda, eating from a little paper bag.

"How did you get here?" said her mouth.

"Same way," he said, between stuffing in what were apparently peppermint lollies, she could smell them now, in his vicinity.

"That is a fine sort of welcome to give a man," he said, full of peppermint.

"I did not mean it that way," she said, putting down the bucket, bowing her head to whatever might happen, and wiping her hands, which he looked at glancingly, to see that they were broad, and cracked by cold mornings.

"I have been on the grog two nights running," he said, wincing. "Don't ask me how. These things happen. And smoke—Christ, I have curdled me stomach. I have given them away, the smokes."

He tossed the little bag, in a ball, that fell upon the hard ground and lay there. Then he belched once and said, "Pardon me."

Amy Parker looked at the little ball of paper, which was a point of burning white, and most necessary.

"I have never been really drunk," she said.

But it was not necessary to explore the shallows when she had reached the depths.

"You gotta do something," he said.

And suddenly, although it was the back veranda, he had drawn her with him into the same waiting room, very square, with blank walls. They were sitting there waiting, though presently disgust began to come over his face for some past nausea. She was so still by this time she could hear the shape of objects.

What will he tell me? she wondered.

In expectation, considerable litheness had crept into those

339

pepper trees round which fowls were scratching. There was a nervosity of fronds just twitching in a little breeze. The woman remembered how, as a girl, she had run up the side of a hill, gathering her breath and laughing, and had lain on the top. She remembered the cool touch of the fronds of pepper trees, and now this same smoothness and litheness had returned to her, if she could tell him.

But the man looked, and saw the sallow woman sitting by the scrap bucket, and her stockings, old stockings certainly, which she wore about the place, were dragged round, and wrinkled.

"Well," he said, "I was out this way. Thought I'd look in and have a word, like. Friendship don't cost nothing and is a lovely thing."

He sat with his hands resting on his pursy thighs, very deliberate. Everything he said or did would be deliberate now.

Christ, it would have to be.

"We have been busy these few weeks," she said. "We have had several calvings. There was one in the middle of the night, poor thing. Stan had to fetch the vet. But it was all right in the end. A little heifer."

She shifted on her upright chair, which grated.

Ah, she could have expressed to this man, or not necessarily man, to some human being, visions of great and permanent beauty. But shifting light destroyed that side of the house on which they sat, leaving their minds in shadow.

"I feel crook," said the man Leo, holding his stomach and thinking about himself. "It don't do to racket around. I got ulcers, or somethin."

He stood up.

When Amy Parker saw his back, which was broad and still young, inside the flash suit that had worn shiny over those country roads, she said loudly. "You should see a doctor, Leo."

"They'd skin yer," he said, "for a bottle of poison. Some of that white stuff. I know."

She passed so close to him that her hand brushed the cloth of his coat, but it did not answer.

He began to tell her of a cousin of his father's who had died of a cancer.

So that she was not to come closer to this man, she saw, or perhaps to anyone. Each one was wrapped in his mystery that he could not solve. This man and woman already

340

remembered with surprise the excesses of their bodies, and forgot what else had been attempted.

"So they buried Cousin Herb," said the man Leo. "His funeral was wrote up in the *Advocate*. And what he had done. Though not all of it. He was a bit slippery, but a decent bugger."

The man Leo's sweat had begun to cool, knowing that they had eased past the dangers into that placid state from which you can pretend that things have not happened. He might soon tell a joke, if he could think of one.

"Of course they are inventing cures," Amy Parker said, "for all those diseases, all the time."

"Oh," he said. "Yairs."

Remembering.

"It is wonderful," she said, "to read of science."

And presented to the knife the grey muscles of her throat. Grey of floorboards, she saw, and of earth, that had been tamped down by people coming and going through a drought. She pushed back a lock of hair, which was grey too. She had reached that time of grey. It would be calm, though.

"Gotta be twisting the old Ford," the man Leo was saying.

So they walked out between those stiff rosemary bushes that catch at the clothes, and he got in, and drove off, and would not come again.

In the afternoon Amy Parker began to absolve herself of all that had not happened. She felt old indeed, now that the race was run, but this state did also enjoy a kind of superiority. She began to remember disagreeable details of the man who had ceased to be the shadow of her desire, the way the hair grew on the nape of his neck, in red whorls, a habit of talking about himself, the smell of peppermint. And as her flesh slowly ceased to tick, she thought that she would love the silence.

Things that she had known began to return. The old rosebush, thorny and horny, which they had planted in the beginning. A sewing machine with an intricate treadle. A white jug with a brown crack. She looked at these with conviction.

But she would not think about her husband yet.

When, in the afternoon, a young man came and said, "Where is Stan, Mrs. Stan?" she did look up in genuine surprise.

It was that young Peabody, the nephew of Ossie, all dressed up in blue serge, that was to have met Stan Parker to inspect the land at Hungerford.

"Why, Joe, Stan went to meet you," Amy Parker said, looking at the clock. "He left here, I couldn't say when, but some time."

She could not judge time since several years of her life had passed in instants.

The young man laughed, and hesitated, and wondered what he should do. He was awkward before the wives of men that he knew well.

"I don't know what to advise you," said Amy Parker.

Young men moved on a different plane. Their eyes did not see older women. The sons even had shallow eyes for the mothers. This one, who could have been her son, stood sideways at the door, so that he should not see her. His blue, blazing tie of festive satin was arched on his chest, for himself, or a formal occasion.

Presently he drifted away, and she had not gathered what he intended to do, or what anyone would do.

Later in the afternoon, and more particularly at night, when the work was done, and everything washed and arranged in cupboards or on racks, dutifully, Amy Parker was compelled to think about her husband; he came forward, who had stood not so far back in her mind. She had been listening for him, she knew, some time now. Faint sounds of wind and animals drifted in the darkness. Darkness, stars, and cloud were streaming away from her as time passed. The frail chairs in the rooms were apathetic.

Whatever is to happen now will happen in spite of me, she realized. She was standing against a window frame, and shivering, because it was cold really. Solitary stars trembled. Then she put her head against the frame and gave way to her own solitariness, which she feared, though did expect.

When Stan Parker returned, shortly after leaving, to pick up the hundred-foot measure he had intended to take on the expedition with young Peabody, but forgotten, when he did see the blue car shining in the ruts and dust, he knew this was something he had both expected and feared. Then he felt how very frail was the little wheel on which his hands lay. Visions of violence rose up in him like blood, and boiled over. His lips were blubbery as he took an axe perhaps, or a hammer, or his own hands gave a quick answer.

But in the hollow before the house, were the cypresses were just moving, heavily, suffocatingly, under sheets of dust, his own breath began to suffocate him in his throat, and he turned the car round, with those jerky, unconvincing movements made by the steering of old cars, and drove back along the road. He settled down then to what would very likely be eternity. Or he would make some decision.

Stan Parker drove in his high, ridiculous car along those roads. Most of the flesh had left his face. He drove past Halloran's Corner, and the turn off to Moberley. People who did not know what had happened were continuing to live their lives. An old woman in a big hat was cutting dahlias, convinced that this momentarily was the activity of mankind. She looked up, shading her eyes to see, but her sun had yellow petals. And Stan Parker drove on. Two children near Bangalay were looking at something in a tin, from which soon they would begin to tear the wings. Under the cold gaze the universe had shrunk to the size and shape of a doomed beetle.

The man drove on. He entered and left suburbs of distinct similarity. People walking in the streets turn their heads sharply to look at anything that does not convince. Was there perhaps something in that car, something to fear, or hate, or just to stare at curiously, a soul exposed?

The car drove on too quickly over one crossing, then across several. At one corner a woman tilting a pram did almost scream. But asphalt was apathetic in that glare. The old but deliberate car drove on. In it a man in middle age, rather upright, in best clothes. Neither a drunk nor a madman, by any evidence; it appeared rather that some vision of actuality had got the better of him, and he was stuck in it, rigid, forever.

So the car ran on, into the city, to which Stan Parker had not come since that visit on his son's account, and which began now to swallow the loose and dusty car by previous channels. Time trickled down the man in sweat, and particularly behind the knees. It was a long time, he felt. Some walls of grey concrete had sweating pores, the cement pointing of others, in brick, had crumbled and fallen in places, the hugger-mugger shopfronts on the other hand were too intricate and brittle, and stood back beneath awnings. So he drove on, sweating with cold ooze of concrete almost, and remembering the grey face of his mother as she lay on the bed, an old woman with her eyes closed. The dead were moistening their lips as he drove that old rattle-box along, choosing a moment.

If I drive it, if I drive it now, he said, swerve in, into any wall, now. But he continued. One wheel was wobbly. He was continuing. Bitter, agonizing sweeps of grass with the frost on it, with the sun on it, trees turning up silver in a wind, or just the dead trees, to which he had always been mysteriously attracted, consoled as he rode amongst their silences, through a silence of grass, drifted this side of glass and concrete. So his life was continuing. His wife was walking in grass. Amy came up the dead grass, the long, leafy switches trailing from her hands, that she threw down afterwards, after telling him those lies which were apparently necessary at the moment.

Everything is necessary, though it is important to discover why.

He stopped the car then. It drew up neatly and soberly at a curb, after failing to rise to the heights of tragedy and passion. I could not kill myself, like that bloke Gage, Stan Parker knew, I do not know why, but I could not. All round him were the terribly deliberate faces of the inhabitants of the city, going on the errands of their peculiar lives. The man in the car, whose hands were empty now that they had given up the wheel, did not know much, except possibly his wife's form and those glimpses he had had of her soul, and those experiences in which he and she had been interchangeable. For a moment he saw Amy's face, that had died in some dream, and in the streets of sleep he was calling to her, his tie flying, and the streets were empty.

Then he got out quickly, out of the old car, bumping his head, because he was tall, and invariably forgot about opening up too soon. He got out, and went into the pub that was on that corner, and ordered a glass of pale beer with thin froth on the top, and drank it down. It tasted sour. He drank several of the wretched beers, with pauses of recognition for his act. Then he was drinking. And continued for some time.

Several men talked to him in that swill pot, which was lined with white tiles for the greater resonance of memory. Men who held their faces close to his were convinced by the jerky pageantry of all they had done. This conviction shone from their faces, sometimes spilling over in tears for motives or gestures of the past, that they had not recognized till now, in recitation. They had grown. They were heroic. All these men, rocking on their heels or inclining gravely, were anxious for Stan Parker to assume their size, to tell them something from his own heroic life. So they inclined, and waited. There was one thing to tell. But he could not.

344

"Go on," he said, shaking the hands from off the sleeve of his coat. "Leave me. There's nothing to tell."

Several surprised gentlemen mumbled through respectable lips of purple grapeskins, "What's got into yer, mate?"

"Tell what?"

"The flickin truth is not told, so nobody asked for it, or nothin. See?"

Stan Parker looked round at the place, seeing that it was now pretty full, and writhing, yet he was alone with his thoughts, could look at a wall, if he chose, between the heads of eels. So that the water, which was flowing where the grass had been, rowed past, and he could have caught at the old ram by the horn. But it was now too late. This is the key to me, Amy, he said, I cannot see things in time.

Ah, she was laughing and gurgling, it was all water in there, and slapping her tiles with strange hands that were wearing veins and rings. He could not look closer because of the extreme bestiality of what he already saw. This was the worst yet, because until now his thoughts had not put on flesh.

After this he began to go outside, many coats and yellow, thin overcoats opening willingly for him to pass, until he was out, or his legs had carried him there. He was tittuping. He was opening and closing. He got round the corner to some side street, of which he could not read the name, while trying; it seemed so necessary to locate a degradation. And old banana skins. There was a paper sky, quite flat, and white, and Godless. He spat at the absent God then, mumbling till it ran down his chin. He spat and farted, because he was full to bursting; he pissed in the street until he was empty, quite empty. Then the paper sky was tearing, he saw. He was tearing the last sacredness, before he fell down amongst some empty crates, mercifully reduced to his body for a time.

When he returned to himself a man with a wart and some mission for night-watching was looking above crates and saying, "Hi, mate, you fell down."

The purple lights of night were drifting in the side street.

"Get up," said the man, whose form could have been large, but it was nightbound.

"You have soiled yer good suit," the man said.

Stan Parker got up. There was nothing to do now but go away, which he did, on older legs, away from his soothing saviour, whom he would never know better on account of the circumstances.

The city was adrift with lights, purple and red. He drifted with them. He found the old car. Events had passed over it and left it standing. Until he made it flow. Purple and red, blossoming, fell. The white lights, though, burned from the brain. The tunnels of trams burrowed clumsily into other tunnels, of darkness, going somewhere.

So the man Stan Parker went in a direction that was chosen for him, driving round the night, on a curve, it seemed. Sometimes tramlines guided him into a groove, giving his conscience a jerk, but for the most part he just drove. Now he was less drunk than blurred. He was benign now, if unhappy. Sea air began to eat into the landscape, as into metal. He touched the sticky damp on metal, and mist on the windscreen. A violet efflorescence hung along the coast, on which soft waves sensuously destroyed effort. Here too, he remembered, some people came to kill themselves, leaving their lives on the sand together with a little heap of clothes, and swimming out to sea till the water entered into their mouths.

But this man had grown too soft in the night to endure such tensions. Nor is it necessary to kill to destroy.

He got out somewhere on the esplanade, which followed the beach round. He was looking for something. His legs were wambling for the time being, but at that age he was still a good figure of a man, without a hat, which he had lost somewhere. Walking along concrete, he looked into windows, sometimes pressing his face against them, to focus the blur in those caves into something precise and consolatory. He liked to see people sitting at tables, when they had left off doing anything and were merely sitting in each other's presence. Then he knew them so closely he could have taken part in their lives as it is not possible ordinarily.

So he was looking into the windows, and in one a face was forming in more than fact, in memory, was speaking to him out of thick lips. It was a milk bar evidently, in which the thick man stood pouring glasses of green and pink for youths to drink. Youths showed their behinds, and sipped sweet draughts, and belched because they had learned how. While the man poured, his black eyelids entranced above the silver cups.

Why, bugger me, said Stan Parker, if it isn't Con the Greek.

Ah, he was glad to find the Greek on those shores. Night

346

and the sea breezes flowed in with the stranger through the sucking door, as he went forward quickly to touch something that he knew.

"It is Mr. Parker," cried the Greek, emerging from behind his eyelids. "Go on! Waddayerknow! It is Mr. Parker, Rirí, Sosó, Kostáki, that I spoke about, the boss, remember, when I first come ere, an was workin. Go on, Mr. Parker, it is you then. An how is Mrs. Parker? Good? How do you like it here? This is my place, that my wife brought. This is my wife."

Other people quickly came to investigate what had happened. They were talking in their bird calls, mature, frizzy girls and rippling younger ones, the livery, damp boys with early moustaches and night eyes.

"Please to meetcher, mister," said Mrs. Con.

Her breasts were glad beneath an apron, and her prosperous teeth smiled.

"You stay," said Con the Greek, dashing his friend against his chest, "an we shall eat."

"No. Not stay," said Stan Parker, who had not yet rediscovered what is possible. He said, "Only for a little. I can't stay."

His bones were feeble. He sat abruptly on an iron chair.

"Yes, yes," they cried.

"I make nice spessel dinner," smiled Mrs. Con.

"Soodzookákia," spattered a long girl.

"Kephtérdes," shrieked a plumpy one.

Then they were all screaming, and pushing, and settling it.

"You wait," smiled the wife.

Her buttocks were quite confident that went out through a bead curtain. Soon the oil hissed.

"These are all the children of my wife," said Con the Greek, for whom the time had arrived to give the shape and content of his life. "All ready-made. Like this business. I come here to get rich, and I done well."

The Greek, who had grown a stomach, was stirring his pocket, which was full of money and keys. He began to give details of his business, the mathematics of success, which in that chant became like the words of the songs he had sung, mystical.

Then Stan Parker, who had lost his substance, and who was holding his knuckles to stop the cavern of his mouth, asked, "Do you still sing, Con, those Greek songs, from the islands?"

"Sing?" laughed the Greek, shaking his stomach, which was still rather small. "Nao! What do I wanter sing for? Young men sing. They walk around and stand at corners. I leave it to the kids. They gotta use their breath up somehow. They're too hot."

Then the Greek slapped his friend on the shoulder with his now fat hand, and went outside to give some direction, or make water. He was the owner there. He could please himself. He was hard and invulnerable, if also soft and fat.

Stan Parker, who was no longer certain what he owned, if anything at all, found this wonderful.

"You must like music then?" said a girl, coming to the circle of marble at which the stranger sat.

"Music? Yes," he said. "I suppose so. I never thought about it much."

He had not. His eyelids felt old and dry. Things had a habit of occurring to him for the first time.

"I like music," said the girl, who was thirteen, fourteen, fifteen, it was difficult to tell, but blossoming in an old blue jumper that someone had knitted for her, or even for someone else. "I am studying music," she said, "and poetry, and domestic science. I have also won a state prize for an essay on Soil Erosion."

"You are leaving nothing to chance," said the dry man. "What do they call you?"

"Pam," she said.

"That isn't her name," shouted a couple of lean boys who were passing just then.

"Pam!" they taunted, showing their gums.

Brothers will wrestle the truth from a sister.

"It is," she burned back. "I am going to be Pam."

"She is Panayóta," laughed the boys, pointing their fingers at her.

So that the girl was forced to sit humbly beneath her eyelids, sitting with the tips of her fingers placed together on the rim of the table.

"Panayóta? That could be worse," said Stan Parker, when the boys had passed on.

"But I don't want to *be* Panayóta," burned the girl. "I want to choose for myself. I am not Panayóta. I don't know what I am. But it is not Panayóta. I do not know what I shall be. So I study everthing. I want to do everything."

She was feverish.

In the kitchen the oil was hissing.

"Don't listen to Panayóta," laughed the moist teeth of the mother, who had stuck her head for a moment through the strands of her bead curtain. "She is crazy," she said approvingly.

The girl, whose hair had been washed that day and was fresh and brittle, got up from the table, so that her dark hair brushed past the face of the stranger, who was fixed there for the time being.

"I shan't speak any more," she said gravely. "I shall play you something. That will be better."

The man, who had smelled her hair, remembered the white roses that smell of tobacco when you crush them, but very faintly, translated into rose. So he drew back from the brink of his unhappiness, and cleared his throat, which was the dry throat of a man of a certain age.

"This is lovely," said the girl, taking a record and sticking it on an old gramophone that stood there on the counter, beside a nickel container that held the straws. "It makes you feel sad," she said, winding the box with a groggy handle. "But it is beautiful."

"Listen," she said.

Then the disc began to slur. It was going perpetually over a bump, but something did come out. The deathless voice was singing wordlessly. A faint silveriness of sea air and waves sluiced the counter. All acts, past and present, stood transfixed in that light.

The girl, who had come and got into her seat again, sliding past the man into the circle of his companionship, said intimately, "I wrote a poem once."

"Was it any good?" he asked in a loud voice.

"At first," she said. "Then it began to look terrible."

She was talking against the deathless song. She would have liked to listen, but she could not. Her own poetry was warmer, more actual, more compelling.

"I want to get hold of enough money to go to Athens," she said. "To visit some relatives. And see the Parthenon."

"Oh?" said Stan Parker.

"You know the Parthenon?"

"No," he said.

"It is a temple," she said. "It is all marble. It is, oh, I don't know, the Parthenon," she cried desperately, flinging out her arms to embrace something that was too big.

And that cold moonlight of the song was falling out of the box on the counter.

Stan Parker, sitting at the small, cold table, had by this time achieved permanence of a kind which the song could not dissolve, ebbing and flowing though it was at the iron roots of the table. But this permanence was not worth having, he knew. All things of importance, in the liquid light of the silver song, are withheld or past. All figures that he recognized were turned to marble. So he lay with his wife upon the iron bed, which still grew from the rose carpet, but their limbs were marble. They were frozen together in each other's eyes. Their vision was fixed historically on that point.

"You don't say much," said the girl, who was tired of listening to the song.

She had listened many times. She had heard most things, she done most things that it was possible for her, within the limits of her years, to do and hear, so that she longed for the expansive mysteries of other people's lives.

"I say enough," said the man.

His mouth was growing resentful. He could have taken a hammer and smashed the marble world. And this girl, of what age, in her stretchy jumper, who had appeared touching at first, was now repellent to him, because of his thoughts.

She had rested her breasts on the rim of the table, and they were the breasts of a woman.

"Did you get drunk?" she asked.

She had a gap in her teeth, at the side.

"Mind your own business," he said. "You're only a kid."

So that immediately she was a little girl, with fingers pointing at her.

Just then the song finished, and Panayóta had to jump up and release the needle from the final groove. The man continued to sit. They were both exposed now to the loud silence of that room, of which the walls were pink and yellow. The girl, who was a little girl when she forgot, biting her nails and scratching herself in those places which needed it, went to the mirror to see what the man had seen. She had begun to hate the oldish man. Who was watching her. In the mirror she assumed the positions of women, sticking out her breasts in the sagging jumper, and following the line of her lips with her tongue.

"How old are you?" asked the man, leaning forward across the table.

His own voice sounded lewd, but he was not surprised, sensing he had not reached the depths.

"How old?" asked the girl relentlessly.

So that the gap in her teeth showed.

There were saints on the ceiling, with pointed, painful faces, and heaps of fruit.

"You are the only one to ask questions," laughed the little girl, pulling her hair down in a fresh game, and sucking in her cheeks till they looked hollow.

"Hi, Pam," said some boys, coming in.

Who sat on stools, their shoulderblades showing through their singlets, and their thighs through mauve pants.

"Mint Crush'n Banana Sundae," said the boys.

"Ach," Panayóta replied.

But she went with some grace, handling the snakes of spoons, and the little cups that mould the ice cream.

Then girls came, two sisters of friends, who blushed and giggled at the same things, and who wore the same caps with tassels hanging. These girls ordered a purple juice that stained their mouths. They rubbed their bottoms on the stools and giggled. All was lewdness now as the girls and youths spoke in secret languages or made signs. And Panayóta moved above, behind the counter, of all worlds. Those eyes, remembering the poem perhaps, of moonlight, looked at the man at his island table, and beyond.

Then Stan Parker, who was surrounded by space and lewdness, was growing desperate. The brown hands of saints, descending through the leaves, offered suggestive fruit. The girls and boys were singing some song that they alone knew. But he could learn perhaps. He would follow the eyes of Panayóta, who had already told much that night, but who was withheld now. As all things of importance are withheld or past.

So the man was getting up in the end, stiff from sitting there all that time, or it was his bones, against the iron branches of the table.

"I must go now," said Stan Parker.

Everybody looked.

But Panayóta had to rouse herself out of her rapt chalkiness.

Then she screamed, "What about the soodzookákia that Mumma has cooked?"

He saw the horror in her eyes. She was sucking a lolly too, and her mouth was wet.

"I am sorry," said Stan Parker politely. "I must go now. I must."

"It is not nice," said Panayóta.

351

The girls in tassels giggled because there was no other contribution they could make, but to the boys it was unimportant, all this.

At once Stan Parker left the milk bar of Con the Greek, which his thoughts had made intolerable. But these also followed him in the moist night, as if they would destroy such parts of him as were left. In this state, in which the sea also was taking part, folding over and over, and the remote, and now tragically irretrievable song that the girl had played on the old gramophone, he walked down to where the concrete was becoming sand, and found a woman lighting a cigarette from a stub.

"Gawd," she said, "I would burn me flickin fingers off to save the last draw."

Her lips did, indeed, look greedy, sucking fire from the little point of red ash.

"I was sitting here," said the woman, "because I felt sick. I'd been mixing them at the home of a friend, whose husband had gone to a lodge. I am not always like this. I don't say I am not above a glass. Or two. Or don't keep a bottle in the ice-chest. Of nice beer. Do you like cats?" the woman asked. "I have cats. I have six, or seven, no six, Hairy died. There is Nona, and Phyllis, and Little Un. But you are not interested. And I don't blame yer. I am sick of cats, bloody cats everywhere, in the bath. Only when you wake up, before you pull the blinds up, and there is that brown light, and doves, it is morning you know, then you have got the cats, they are all around, snuggled into your arms, and some cats like to get under the bedclothes."

Stan Parker, who had listened to this woman until he had grown tired, had got down beside her on the warm sand. Here her breath came over him in a metallic blast, but the smell of the woman was less fetid than his own condition. Disgust had died in him.

So he put his head in the woman's lap.

"You feel like I do," she said, following the shape of his face with her hand.

"You are hungry," she said.

He began to caress old matted fur.

"What is it you want, dear?" she asked, swelling with hope out of that shrivelled state in which nature had dumped her.

"Shut up," he said diabolically.

He could have killed the old tart, making his necessity hers, and did put his hands on her throat, and press, a little,

352

where there was a string of beads, and a medallion, or something.

Ahhhhhh, made the woman's mouth.

"All right," he said into her face. "I was still wondering if I could kill myself. But I couldn't. Not even now."

The woman continued to scream.

He got up and ran along the beach, stumbling across many furtive lusts, and strange driftwood, and soft sand.

When he had gone some way, and the screaming woman had run down, and a whistle had pierced the darkness, and lights were gathering round the scene he had left, he began to feel sorry for the cat-woman, whose confidence he had broken, and throat bruised.

Ah, he said, holding his head till it was not his, but a melon hanging in his hands, I am finished, I must go home.

The sea did not contradict.

By the time Stan Parker was driving over the bumps on the road from Durilgai towards his place, and particularly past those few panels of fence that he had put off straining because of an apathy in him, that cinematographic strip of life which had been flickering in front of him until now, was already most unreal. But only because he had lived it. Once he had been to the pictures, or twice, to be correct, and there his blood had collaborated to the last flicks of celluloid.

Now, though, the shabby grass and scraggy trees censured things past. Only the present is real, returning to familiar places. Stan Parker, driving the rickety car, looked once more at the skin on his hands. Till that hollow in which the cypresses rose from the dust, and dust rose to choke, from under and in spite of the dew.

He was again choking, but drove on quickly beyond reach of one thought, and negotiated the gateway with smoothness, almost polish, and eased up finally in the back yard.

That big dog got up and came forward, lowering his neck and showing his yellow teeth for guilty gladness.

Why has this dog always been guilty? he wondered.

Amy Parker, who had looked out of the window and seen her husband, got the pan, because her responses had long been regulated, and threw in a dollop of fat, and broke open three eggs, which quickly curdled on the pan.

"Have you finished down there?" he asked. "With the cows?"

"Yes," she said, "I finished."

She brought him food and things to eat with.

She brought a cup of milky tea, which she stood there drinking, and chewing at a crust of dry bread in rather ugly but usual fashion. This was her habit, while talking to him.

"Last night I nearly forgot Bella's calf," Amy said. "Bella was wild. She was running round the yard hollering. She was quite desperate, poor thing, when I let it out. It is a pretty little calf, Stan. It is growing stronger. It will be a fine calf. And from Bella."

So she spoke to him.

When he looked at her, or without looking, he saw they had entered a fresh phase of life, that something was spent. Amy moved about the kitchen. Her hair was flat and quiet, that she had smoothed down. In the stove she put wood, for a moment allowing the fire to shoot out. But she quickly damped it down.

"The wood is nearly done, Stan," she said.

Yes, later he would chop some more.

Then, do we know, he said, that this did happen? But he could not answer for any of his life. Let alone the lives of other people, in particular his wife's.

In this same spirit Amy Parker went about, taking things up and putting them down, waiting to be enlightened. What she did expect, in fact, was that some enlightenment would come from without. But it did not, and she continued to feel used up, and to remember with shame and wonder the way she had torn off her stockings, and they had lain on the floor in grey pockets.

How thin her face was now if she touched it, but she did not look at it.

In time the man and woman came to accept each other's mystery, that the roof could not contain. Sometimes at night they would wake singly and listen to each other's breathing, and wonder. Then they would fall asleep again, because they were tired, and would not dream. Habit comforted them, like warm drinks and slippers, and even went disguised as love.

Chapter 19

SOME TIME after the wedding, not at once, but after they had settled into the house, the Forsdykes went down to see her parents.

"You will be bored, of course, but it is time you faced up to it," Thelma said, making her husband responsible for any delay there had been.

The husband cleared his throat but otherwise did not contradict. He drove. He selected a gap between two cars and drove through with some dash, though not ordinarily possessing it. He was a prudent man. His car, which was of an English make, neither old nor new, neither elongated nor low, of a good, negative colour, did not reveal his economic status. It had been chosen for this reason.

"You are in a draught," said Mr. Forsdyke at last, and because, as a husband recently created, it was time that he thought of some tenderly considerate but practical thing.

"Oh no," said his wife, who for some weeks had been taking time off from her health.

But he reached across her, absently or knowing better, and wound up the glass of her window.

Then she smiled, and breathed languidly, and touched the window with her glove. She was ever so content, in love, she would have said, if she did not suspect that such an admission would have been contrary to that good taste she had begun to learn about. But she was in love. She thought in amazement of her house, of which the paint shone between laurels in the afternoon, or she stood in the darkness, secretly, to look, and the house was a fixed framework of light, round which tossed an unruly suggestion of trees that other people had planted.

The parents had been to the house on one occasion since the wedding. If they had not been to the wedding, it was because, obviously, it might have been embarrassing. But on an afternoon visit, alone, they were appreciative and hushed. They brought eggs and a few enormous oranges. Witnessing the decency of her parents, the daughter was for a moment sad that she had had to abandon them, but quickly put her hands in the pockets of her cardigan, and from behind its texture recovered a sense of reality.

"They are sweet things, of course," she said now, inside her fur collar.

"What? asked Mr. Forsdyke, whose other name was Dudley.

When he drove he did not care to have his attention diverted from the road. He was a painstaking man. This capacity for taking pains was, in fact, his greatest vanity, and although an innocent one, might become unbearable.

"My mother and father," said Thelma Forsdyke.

As if his attention were necessary to those of her thoughts which she was stating.

She was fascinated by a cairngorm, surrounded by little pebbles, that her mother had worn on their visit. She had seen this as a little girl, but forgotten.

"Mother is overemotional, I should say. That is half the trouble. But Father, you will have to admit, is a sterling character."

Mr. Forsdyke drove on, frowning at the road, which should ordinarily have soothed.

"What trouble is there?" he asked.

"No exact *trouble*," said his wife, examining her gloves and fitting them more tightly, perfectly, to her hands. "Just the business of two people discovering each other by degrees, and not discovering enough, as they live together."

In the short time that they had been married, Mr. Forsdyke had grown surprised at his wife, and would also have been proud of intimations of intellect, if he had not suspected the slipperiness of human nature.

Thelma Forsdyke sighed. She read a great deal when she was on her own. Sometimes her nostrils grew quite pinched scenting all that she had to accomplish. But she did have many afternoons.

"They seem perfectly straightforward people to me," said the solicitor, to whom simplicity was a refuge.

"You do not like them," said his wife, but lightly, so that it would exonerate the husband she had chosen, and with whom she was still pleased.

356

"That is pure nonsense," laughed the husband with clear good nature. "But I did not marry them."

Their high laughter mingled in agreement. Their heads turned on their upright necks, and they looked into each other's faces. At this moment Thelma Forsdyke could have committed any disloyalty towards her parents.

Why did I marry Thelma? wondered Dudley Forsdyke.

Everybody had wondered at first how Dudley Forsdyke came to get caught by that girl at the office. Efficient, of course, but a pale girl, skinny even, with noticeable elbows, and the upper vetebrae visible beneath her oblivious skin. The care of her shining hair was obviously a duty to which she adhered with passion. Its pale, disseminated gold was kept beautifully washed. It strayed just enough to suggest nature, while avoiding untidiness. So too her mouth was just touched by hand. People were surprised that she should favour such careful artifice in an age of deliberate art. Because she was almost imperceptibly careful. But she would finally insinuate herself, like air. She had an instinct for floating. There was her voice, for instance, on which she had worked, and spent quite a proportion of her salary for a time. People remembered her voice afterwards. It was really, on second thought, a remarkably agreeable one. Cultured, without strain. Well modulated, without discarding firmness. People in the darkness of the telephone would guess at its owner's nature, or in her presence at those channels her life took on emerging in the evening from the office lift.

Thelma Parker's evolved voice had hung between Dudley Forsdyke and endless irritations, even unpleasantness. It was expert in sympathy for minor ailments, the deaths of elderly, superfluous relations, and all the personal aspects of the weather. It ignored the passionate and angry, for passion and anger do regrettably occur, and would reduce by incredulity those clients who knew better than the law. So that not everyone was pleased when that Miss Parker passed through the room again, aloof but present, carrying in her cool hands some awful deed or contract. Or placing on her employer's desk a letter that she dared him not to sign.

Some were sorry for Forsdyke, who had risked so much on confidence. But he himself began to like it. Sometimes she leaned upon his desk, but correctly, at arm's length, to explain a point with a pencil. And he could smell her hair. He was fascinated by her wristwatch. As she went out, very quietly, the baize door just breathing, the solicitor undid a button of his waistcoat and lifted up his stomach in that way which Thelma Parker had described formerly, and flicked over a paper, and flicked over another.

Where is Miss Parker? he asked.

Miss Parker, they said, has got the flu.

Then he knew the panic of uncertainty. His desk was covered with heaps of unrelated things. Charming women in fur coats and pearls made irreverent suggestions on wording. So that he knew Thelma Parker was indispensable to him. So he married her.

If his motives for doing it were sensed rather than reasoned, which was extraordinary in one so rational, it was natural that he should forget sometimes, and wonder why he had committed that act. As now. In the detached world of the car, on the road from which suburbs were falling away, in the wet landscape of a rude spring, he was trying to remember what it was that pricked his sense of satisfaction. But he could not. He was conscious of barbed-wire fences defining the road along which he drove, and his wife's coat, of some dark, expensive fur, what was it? but he had put it on her, and that little runnel of water where rain dashed itself against the glass, coming in however frequently he screwed the window up, coming in to spatter on his face. The dry rest of his body was insignificant beside that wet patch. This communed with depths of unplumbed, colder water and unpredictable events. He grimaced rather as he drove. The rain was good for the land, though, he said.

The two people drove on. They looked very delicate, also rather silly, from outside the car. They had a purpose, no doubt, but this was not apparent, without taking into account other forces, other mechanisms. Like those little, delicate, trembling springs in the guts of a watch. The people trembled and functioned inside the glass car, and were sometimes on the verge of becoming upset, but recovered themselves for invisible technical reasons.

Presently Thelma Forsdyke opened her crocodile handbag, which she had bought after noticing quietly that such a handbag was carried by those women who frightened her, she opened her bag and said, "Would you like a sweet, Dudley?"

"No, thank you," he replied and frowned.

He quite definitely would not.

But she did produce a little paper bag, and would suck a sweet. It was a habit that she had acquired. For comfort's sake. She did it still.

It was barley sugar now, it seemed. But her husband, frowning, remembered those little sweets, or cachous, scented with something like violet, a synthetic smell, that had drifted on the more irritating afternoons above the smells of sealing wax and ink.

Thelma herself heard the bell at the end of the line, though the bland flavour of the barley sugar did absolve her to a certain extent of past guilt. She remembered those little violet cachous and the way he had turned his head, some afternoons. Then many points of etiquette she had not yet mastered, but towards which she was feeling her way, holding on to expensive objects, stirred unhappily inside her. The eyes of certain women looked beyond her clothes. She blushed.

"Why do some people always have to suck things?" asked her husband.

Thelma Forsdyke shrugged, and looked away, and was obviously intending not to answer.

Rain was beating at the windows out of a large grey sky.

She wrenched the glass down and threw out the miserable little bag of hot white paper. If fell innocently.

"You should not have taken it like that," laughed her magnanimous husband, looking at her, taking a pleasure in his own power.

If his dry hands had been free he would have patted her on the back where the pearls cut across the vertebrae.

"I was not taking it in any particular way," said Thelma, who could learn a lesson very quickly. "The barley sugar was growing sticky in my bag."

She continued to look about her at the countryside, which had become uninteresting, insignificant, since she had achieved position. It was existing vaguely in spite of her, she saw, but it was not evident to what purpose. Purpose floated in that sea of leaves plastered against leaves. The paddocks were fat again. But the houses of poverty still stood in them, tumbling down or held up by iron and wire. At times a smell of wet fowl manure penetrated the discreet car and strayed amongst its fittings.

Now Thelma Forsdyke wished they had not come. She looked at her little diamond watch, not so much to read the time as to assure herself by significant movements that events did follow a sequence. For this same reason she had started to take lessons in French, and was already sitting, though cautiously, always looking, always listening, on the committees of several charitable organizations.

"This is their road now," she said, deliberately dissociating herself from the geography of that place.

The husband's features, through concentrating on the situation that must be faced, had grown thin.

"This must be their car now, Stan," said the mother, looking out from behind the curtains she had washed that Monday.

She had put powder on her face, and it looked like it, because her face was now normally rather white, drained either by her age or repentance. So the powder lay and did not collaborate. Nor did that dress, naturally her best, of a dark blue, of a rough though quite good material. It had somehow got twisted round, or it was the way it had been cut by Merle Finlayson, it did not fit at the armpits, and had split in one place, though conveniently visible only to others. Still, the mother was presentable. She had put on a white collar, stitched it onto the thick dress. She would launder such white things very carefully and beautifully, starching them just a little, and making them look quite primitive in their essential whiteness. She was decent then.

And the father, who was determined to look cheerful and creditable, foresaw himself, without great dismay, lost in the silences of odd corners with the solicitor his son-in-law. In the room of their house in which they waited, and which no longer seemed theirs since the approach of strangers stressed its ordinariness, he moved about, and listened to his boots squeak.

"Have you cleaned your boots?" Amy Parker asked.

"I have," he said, putting out his feet for her to see.

There was nothing now of sufficient importance to be withheld from her.

"Stan," she said, dusting him with her hand, "do you like this man, the solicitor?"

"I have nothing against him," said the father-in-law.

She began to laugh, like a girl, in her woman's body, which would have sounded obscene, but the husband was used to obscenity.

"Nobody will ever sue *you*," she laughed.

But her husband continued gravely, "He seems a good sort of man."

"That is all very well," she said; she had stopped laughing, and might never have begun. "It is not enough to be good."

She stopped there. His eyes, of which the sockets were hollower than they used to be, were not hurt. She had tried repeatedly to prise out some of that goodness. She had failed, but would try again, as if she did not believe in what she could not touch.

"Anyway, his car is good enough," said Stan Parker, who was determined to be agreeable.

All his movements were cheerful. At most times his eyes had a shallow confidence. Lack of expectation, he had found, is easier to bear. So too he had discovered an affection for his wife, which is less terrible than love.

Amy Parker had looked out again on hearing the mud fly up. The car was there.

"Oh, Stan," she said, "we had better go out, I suppose. Hadn't we?"

Because she was shivering, it was such a raw day, she had pressed against him, to restore warmth, and incidentally familiarity, by touch. Then they were going out together, and what had to be, was. All four people met beside the old rose-bush, which was flinging little drops of water into their faces, and pricking their flesh, and tearing at their awkward clothes. There was a kissing and a shaking of hands. All four people were looking at one another, hoping for something they could recognize.

"Well, dear, you did not have a very nice drive," said Amy Parker to her daughter. "And Dudley. Nothing is at its best, of course, on a day like this."

Even so, Amy Parker was ambitious to become on that day some character that she had never yet been.

"I told him not to expect too much," said Thelma, who realized that in spite of resolutions her powers of endurance were not great.

She arranged her good, negative clothes, and received her father's kiss. This was rougher than she had remembered. She looked at his boots. She began to smile wonderingly at all she saw, as if this might prove to be some new experience, both amusing and touching, and particularly she looked at her father, he was a dear, he had given her this hope. Men are less positive to most women, and so more acceptable.

"Dudley knows absolutely nothing about life in the country. But he is willing to learn," said Thelma, poised halfway between the natural irony of the situation and that kindness of which her father had reminded her.

"Thelma has a weakness for making the confessions of other people," laughed the solicitor.

He was lifting up his stomach a good deal just then, under-

361

neath his waistcoat, and letting it fall again. With one dry freckled hand he was persuading the corrugations of his bald head.

"He can see all right, whatever there is to see, but there isn't much to show," said Stan Parker without any effort.

The mother and daughter were surprised, and even a bit annoyed, that he should speak with apparent ease to the dry man his son-in-law. They suspected something. Still more, as he was making first moves to lead the solicitor away among the wet trees.

"But it is raining, Stan," said Amy Parker to regain control. "I thought we should have a cup of tea first."

Those thick, white, bottomless cups, remembered Thelma.

"It may clear up later," suggested the mother, though she did not much care, provided the day preserved more or less the shape she had decided on.

"It has cleared. Look," smiled Stan, holding up his hand in a goblet.

Very few drops fell. A charitable sky of cold blue prevailed. So that he laughed at his own powers. It would have mattered once, but did not now. Hence this ease which had overtaken him on his own doorstep. The difficulties of his youth lay thick behind him, even if he could not see a way through the comparatively open future.

"It couldn't have been better laid on," he said, beginning to lead his relations.

"Miraculous," laughed the solicitor, looking at the sky, at the path, here and there between bushes, to look at something.

Stan Parker was sorry for the lost man, and thought that he might like him, if given the chance, although it was improbable that this opportunity would occur.

"But so muddy," grumbled the mother, lowering her head and frowning at branches that she knew well.

They went down deviously to the cow yards. There were rounds of dung lying in their path. They trailed across the brick floor at the empty bails, and along the bank of the creek, where sticks cracked beneath the feet and cows looked at them from above blue tongues, and along the ploughed land from which corn would spring. The mother and daughter were talking about a tablecloth, a wedding present, that had got stained at a laundry, with iron mould, and the mother knew how to take it off.

"It is all very interesting," said the solicitor, touching a furrow with his toe. "The soil. It is a grand life. And productive."

Because it was his life, Stan Parker had never thought of it as this. It had taken possession of him. But nothing had ever taken possession of Dudley Forsdyke, except perhaps his wife. Suddenly he would have liked to be possessed by something, some passion, or vice even. The wind was blowing from a southerly quarter and twitching his mackintosh.

"Why don't we chuck everything and go on the land, dear?" he called back to his wife.

"Why?" she considered, drawing her fur collar slowly across her cheek. "Because you would hate it."

His legs were ridiculous in a wind.

Dudley Forsdyke was so used to examining reports of living that he had been made drunk suddenly by a smell of life. This came up at him out of the ploughed field and down the wet hill. The sky was overflowing with obstreperous clouds. The wind hit him in the chest. Then the vision of ridiculous man returned to him with his wife's words. He did not resent them, the possibility that they were meant to hurt, because he deserved such censure for his momentary imprudence. So he made noises in his throat, of agreement, or masochism, and continued to stray across the landscape, across all those other landscapes in which he had not yet lived, and in which he would not live wholly until he was beneath them.

Poor beggar, said Stan Parker, but does it matter? It did not. It no longer mattered. It was easier to walk this way lightly through the wind, which no longer opposed him, there was no opposition of any kind. The opposition of God, which was withdrawn from him, left him altogther light and carefree. Once he had been bowed down by belief. Each leaf or scroll of bark was heavy with its implications. The man had been weighted who now walked between the openings in the wind, his frank eyes watering a little from the sting. The rims of his eyes had sagged slightly with time, giving an impression of open wounds, which his wife did not like but did not know how to mention.

"He knows that he does not like to get his hands dirty," said Thelma, pursuing her husband Dudley Forsdyke's back, "any more than I do. I like to read about the country, though."

"Do you read much, dear?" asked the mother vaguely, for this was an occupation in which she could not quite believe.

363

"I shall never catch up," said Thelma honestly, "now I have begun."

"It passes away the time, I suppose," said Amy Parker, "though I never ever understood half of what it seems you can read about. It is different from what things are."

"It need not be," sighed Thelma, but it was a waste of time.

"Oh yes. It must," said Amy Parker. "It is all different. People are different in books. They would have to be. It would not be bearable."

She would have choked herself with her own hair in the mirror.

"This is the fowl yard, Mr. Forsdyke—Dudley," she found it necessary to say. "We don't go in for them properly. A few layers. And these are the young pullets."

She had not intended any of this, but they had come that way.

The solicitor was staring through the wire, smiling at or for the fowls.

"Are you interested in fowls then?" asked Amy Parker.

"No," he said. "I don't know. I hadn't thought about them before."

The smell of wet fowl manure rose up out of the mud.

"Well, they are smelly things," said the mother-in-law.

I shall scream, thought Thelma Forsdyke, inside her incredible coat, that could not have belonged to her.

"How about that cup of tea, Mother?" said Stan Parker.

It was a sensible thing. So they all went inside.

The front room had been prepared for the rites of tea with a few little bunches of early roses, some of which were opening into frail flowers, but others had been picked too tight in bud and would never break, they looked sick. The room had the dark smell of a room that has not been lived in. All the furniture was dark and awful to Thelma Forsdyke, who moved amongst it thoughtfully. She was surprised that she had been able to escape from anything so positive. Or from herself. Suspicions of what she had been lurked amongst mahogany. So that she was forced to turn quickly to present matters. At a clean sweep, it appeared, she took the gloves off her long hands, on which the rings glittered without apology.

Amy Parker, whose breath preceded everything she did, brought a big teapot ornamented with lustre, and a yellow cake, and some large scones on a glass stand.

364

She said, "Have you seen the Bourkes, Thel?"

At times she did deal blows that were not intended for a particular recipient, for those, rather, on whom they happened to land. At these times she would have said, I did not mean anything by it, it was no more than something to say.

"No," replied Thelma Forsdyke, looking gravely at her cup. "I have not seen them."

"The Bourkes?" asked her husband, who was smiling at everything he did not recognize or understand, whether the Bourkes or that erection in nubbly glass on which the scones stood.

"Some relations," said Thelma, biting off a very small piece of scone. "I lived with them at one time."

Her face was quite smooth of expression. She could have admitted the Bourkes perhaps, but not herself, in half-coat of dyed lapin. It was the age of nougat and magazines. She had suffered from spots for a few months, but treated them by correspondence.

"They were very kind," she said, rejecting a crumb.

Now from the pallor of her own tasteful room, to which the Bourkes would not come anyway, even if they read the address in some newspaper, she could afford to be charitable. She had reached that height from which charity is possible. If she did not write an actual cheque, and she *was* generous, it was said by many, she could pay off by indifference. She seldom committed herself to emotion, which was bad for her health, or to statement of opinion, for this would have meant having one. Even her restful room was noncommittal, in which she arranged big bowls of flowers and would spend whole mornings trying to control a stalk, with anxiety for the general effect.

How much Thel has learned amused Amy Parker above her tea, and wearing gloves, and reading books.

"Poor old Horrie Bourke is sick," said Stan Parker.

"He could die," said his wife, whom tea in strong doses made melancholy.

Then we are not to escape the Bourkes, decided Thelma Forsdyke. She looked appropriately sad.

She did genuinely become sad in the dark room, though it was for herself, that she was burying. The scents of little girls' flowers on sparrows' graves brought the tears to her eyes. Or nightlights beneath which she was suffocating, before a mother, with those simple, primary features that faces wear in the beginning, gave her breath back. Thelma Forsdyke sat crumbling cake, the big yellow one that had been made too hastily, it had holes. There were many bits of herself that she would have broken off and discarded, if it had been possible that these would not still add up.

"Do you play cards, Dudley?" asked Amy Parker.

"No," he said with a smile.

This decoration had got upon his face out of turn. Actually he was startled that anyone should suspect him of a taste that suited him so badly. What could this woman his mother-in-law know about him? Or his wife? Or he himself even, in that strange room, from any corner of which an unsuspected habit might arise. The glass stand was winking under a cloud of scones.

"No," he said in a crumbly sort of voice, his mouth was full. "I have never played cards."

"We don't here," said Amy Parker. "Some people like a hand in the evening, though."

I must remember to ask her about herself, said Thelma, before we go, but remember, it is enough to ask, people do not or are not able to tell what is flickering in them. Asking is a kindness, though.

Then the solicitor drew himself up inside his suit of good English material, a flecked tweed, that will stand instead of virility at a pinch, and said, "And how is the other one, Mrs. Parker, your boy, the one I have never met?"

This is what we have been waiting for, Thelma Forsdyke knew.

Because he had got himself into a bit of a mess, the solicitor was not sure but he suspected it, he was going to poke around, as cautious men do, with a stick.

The father sat forward now, rubbing tobacco between his hands, till the scent of tobacco filled the room, and his hands were over-flowing with it.

"Oh, Ray," said the mother.

She cut several pieces of cake, though everyone had finished. She left them there.

"Ray is well," she said, but cautiously. "He will be coming one of these days."

Then she looked out of the window, from which the weather was at last withheld, and they were all looking out, past the canes and leaves, into that greenish light and stillness.

"Ray was a lovely boy," she said. "You will see. Brown skin, red lips. Strong. But he did not seem to think we understood. He was dodging off down the gully. I could not follow him. Once there were some seabirds come over, and he shot one and buried it. Then he was quiet. He thought I did not know, but I could smell it on his hands. Once, that was when he was quite young, there were some little puppies that he took and threw into a pit out at the back. How he cried at night! I couldn't comfort him for nothing. He did these things because he had to. There was a Greek, I remember, working here some years ago. Ray and the Greek became mates. Because he loved him, Ray could not hurt him enough. No," she said, "I do not *understand*. But I *know*."

Then Thelma Forsdyke began to feel her chest tighten with disgust. She began to cough, and no means with her of stopping it.

The solicitor saw his hat on a chair where he had put it on coming in. He would be glad to return to where all his possessions were arranged. He had cigars in a cabinet, and a collection of stuffed hummingbirds.

"You should not bring up all these old things, Mother," said Stan Parker, who had rolled a cigarette of a most uneasy shape.

"Why?" she said. "They are not old."

They were not.

She was looking at him. Then the hands of the woman he had half-throttled were tightening on his own throat, and girls in silky jumpers singing sea songs. There was the man too, the traveller, who was big and probably freckled, would come in, sit with his legs apart, and tell of country towns, as his kind will, chewing the words on thick lips. And veins in his eyes.

All were looking at one another, knowing rather than understanding. The mother and the father were at last together in the house, in the presence of witnesses, as they had never dared to be on their own.

"Would you like a glass of water, dear?" Amy Parker asked Thelma, who was coughing, she could not stop.

No, no, she said with her head, and drawing on her dark gloves of fine suede.

"It is not an attack?" asked the mother hopefully.

"No," coughed Thelma, "it is not an attack."

"It will pass," said Dudley Forsdyke very quietly.

As if it might, indeed, before he had reached his hat, then that excuse would be removed.

The mother was making clucking noises against her teeth.

Stan Parker, who was more or less resigned to that state

of godlessness he had chosen when he vomited God out of his system and choked off any regurgitative craving for forgiveness, did experience a freedom. He looked at the time. It would be time soon to go down to the cows, and on this evening, when she would be persuaded to stay behind and see to the washing up, he would be quite free in the large, cold shed, the animals in their bails, and his knees beneath his chin, milking. Then the large, raw sky is emptiest, and free. He knew this, and was shivering for it inside his unaccustomed waistcoat.

In the meantime Thel was going, or Mrs. Forsdyke, with her husband.

Kisses had begun. Regrets hung on the air, and reluctant drops on rosebushes.

"Button up your collar, dear," said the mother.

"It has not got a button," laughed Thelma. "That would be hideous."

She had overcome her coughing, with assistance of the brutal air, or sight of her own car.

She was ready. Then, on looking back, she did remember that she had forgotten to ask her mother to tell about herself, what sort of person she was, and what was happening to her. Well, it could not be helped.

Then they were ready, and drove off. She had forgotten to kiss her father, because you took Dad for granted, he would still be standing there, his hard and surprising trunk, rooted.

Mr. Forsdyke sighed and drove.

"Those Bourkes," he said, "I had never heard of them."

"She is a purple woman," Thelma laughed. "Almost always dressed in blue. But blue."

And as if that were not brutal enough she added, "He is a horse trainer."

They drove on.

"There is no reason," said Dudley Forsdyke, "why you should not be nice to them."

The germ of good deeds emplanted in others begets a sense of nobility.

"And your brother," he said, "Ray, whom I have not met. Why have I never met Ray?"

"There is no reason," it was now Thelma Forsdyke's turn to say. "He has been away. That's all. He'll turn up, I expect."

Would he? twitched Dudley Forsdyke, wondering what kind of man his brother-in-law really was.

The Forsdykes drove on, each wondering who had the hold.

When the car had driven far enough to be eliminated, the parents who had been left behind, standing at the gate, sorting their hopes and disappointments, turned to each other and Amy Parker said, "Do you think they were pleased, Stan?"

"They did not eat, but then people don't."

"But were they pleased with *us*, Stan?"

"We are only for an afternoon."

"They are pleased with each other."

"He is a bit of an old woman."

"Well, Thelma always liked things nice."

"It is a fine shiny car."

"But has she *got* him, Stan?"

Looking at her husband's face.

"Has she *got* him!"

He averted his face, bristling at something, his hair did bristle sometimes, and on the nape of his neck.

"Who has got what?" he said.

He was glad to go and get the buckets, following those paths of behaviour, back and forth and down to the shed, which habit had made geometric.

Then Amy Parker went quickly and got the chicken she had roasted that day, and of which the smell was still hanging in the house. She took the long loaf, a bit floury, and made the basket ready. She was very quick and sure, as she was invariably in secret matters. And she thought of the letter still secret in the drawer.

Amy Parker was going out in that secret light. Deep smells of evening rose up out of long, fat grass. Shrilly birds were settling, or first spring feathers twittered on the black twigs. The undergrowth was moving. Skeins of evening hung about the creek, unwound. Some people were coaxing fire out of damp leaves, but all they made was smoke. All things are wreathing and dissolving at that hour, before stars.

But the woman on the road, in her dark dress, was solid and stubborn. Her loud feet brought the silence down. She went on. She was glad to be having secrets at dusk, and especially with her son. *Don't tell Dad*, wrote Ray, *he will go crook on me.* Of course not, she said, she lived on secrets, the handkerchief sachet hides electric letters. *And if you can bring us twenty-five as a loan, Mum—quid, I mean*, wrote Ray, *bring them in fivers, they're easy to carry, to Glaston-*

369

bury; it is quiet there about evening I will meet you in the kitchen, I will not be long about it, Mum, I have a journey to make but I will see you, your ever loving son.

So she walked on. She had taken a lamp against darkness, and this clanked.

"Why, Amy," said Doll Quigley, who was there at the cypresses in the hollow, less matter than voice, "it is you, ain't it? What do you know?"

"Not much, Doll," said Amy Parker, who was not at all pleased.

"I will accompany you for a little," Doll said, and did begin to take shape, her long body in a long dress.

Ah, this would, Amy Parker said.

"I am walking to get me thoughts straight," said Miss Quigley. "It is my brother."

"Why, what is wrong with Bub?" asked her friend.

"It is the fits," said Doll, "that he has been having, oh, for years now. But they are getting worse."

"And what do you do, Doll?"

"I stick in a cork, and if he bites it I put a second. That is all. I watch him. He must not hit the stove. But Bub is very strong, poor boy, when these fits are on him."

"You would do better to have him put away in some place," said Amy Parker desperately.

Then the voice of Doll Quigley said, "He is what I have got."

And I have got Doll, said Amy Parker, I should not be disgusted, but I am.

Then Doll Quigley told about her life with Bub, how they sat beside a lamp and looked at curious stones and the skeletons of leaves, and this life was sometimes past, but always present, its steady yellow light.

"So you see," she said, "I could not do away with Bub, he is too young in spirit."

Bub was an old and dribbly man in flesh, Amy Parker knew. She was exasperated now.

"Ah, dear," she said, her skirt lashing the darkness, "I should have brought the trap. I shall be late."

"You have an appointment," said the tranquil Doll.

"I am taking a few things," Amy Parker hissed.

And did almost add, to Mrs. Gage, who had left the district not long after her husband killed himself on that tree.

"I am taking a few things," said Amy Parker, who was just saved, "to a friend who is having a hard time."

"Poor souls," said Doll Quigley for all mankind.

She hung fire now, and Amy Parker, touching her, loving her, said, "We must think of something for Bub, Doll, of what will be best, and kindest."

But Doll Quigley was full of doubt, knowing that any solution must come from herself, but how she could not tell.

Soon after this Amy Parker lost Doll Quigley in the dusk and hurried on towards the gates to Glastonbury. These still stood, almost immoveable in rust. To open the gates was to struggle with accumulated time, but if you won, as Amy Parker did, she was a strong woman still, your heart beat harder to be inside that strange place, in which anything might be found, half-buried, objects of beauty or just a little rusted can that could be cleaned up and used again. People sometimes emerged from under the trees, from eating, or making love, or merely exorcising unwelcome spirits of their own. So the air, if it had a mystery, was also public. The dark, coarse branches of neglected shrubs, and tendrils of rank vines, had been submitted to a treatment of hands and made more ragged. Bits had been dragged or snapped off and abandoned. Once or twice goats had got in and cleaned up the lot. For a season. It was always growing, the wilderness, and forming liaisons with small animals that watched, and moving, its leaves and air, particularly at evening, when velvet scents unite with a stink of rotting.

Amy Parker pushed on up the hill, caught at by the more rigid things, torn in one place, but also destroying many of the fleshier, more supine weeds beneath her firm heels. As it grew darker she became more expectant. What did he look like now? Would she be embarrassed in the presence of a stranger? Had she perhaps grown a little deaf, so that she would misinterpret, or smile in wrong places life deaf people do, to insinuate their understanding? She was not deaf, of course. She was not deaf.

The leaves trumpeted with silence. Quigleys intruded at times, going with her, Doll's face exasperating for its beautiful perfection. I am not perfect, thank goodness, said Amy Parker, and she is an ugly thing, that bag of skin hanging from her neck. And he, Bub, pffuh! The leaves were rotting in that part. It was a slow smell, that she hurried to escape. But Quigleys would not be put off. He is what I have got, Doll said, the way she hung on. Then he is what I have got, Amy Parker said, it is not Thelma, it is not anyone else, then it is he.

So she burst out hopefully onto what had been the drive,

crunching dandelions and gravel, and looking for a sign. The constant Quigleys, if they had existed, were dissolved by will or darkness. Only the house stood, or half house, that Mr. Armstrong had begun, and left off when there seemed no further purpose for it, except as a kind of monument to the dead. Amy Parker began to be afraid now, remembering dead people she had known, or people who were not, but they might have been, they had gone away. Birds flying through the night barely touched it with their soft feathers. The hand of a statue had broken off.

When the woman of flesh and blood had gone round the back towards the kitchen quarters, and there was the door of what must be the second kitchen, she did feel comforted, remembering a basket of young ducks she had brought there in her youth. She had lit her lamp, and now went in. The room was large and shadowy and blank. Only leaves were moving, or a mouse.

Presently Ray came, though.

"Is that you, darling?" she said.

She held the lamp up, trembling for her tenderness, and the unfamiliar word with which she had expressed it. Supposing she had used it on a stranger? Or would this perhaps be preferable to her son? So she trembled.

Looking straight at the lamp, because that blaze was all that he could see, the man was frowning and wincing. This, or something, was making him edge round the room. He was big, though not as big as his shadow.

"Cut it out," he said. "You'd blind a man."

"Well," she said, putting the lamp on a sill, "I had to bring a light. If we must meet here. What made you choose this place? A wilderness. And a house that's nobody's house."

"Ah," he said, "I've always remembered this place."

"Is that all you remember?" she asked.

Now that they were normal, standing on their feet, and of their own height and substance, she came forward to look at him.

"What's up?" he laughed. "You trying to identify me?"

"You have changed," she said.

"What did you expect?"

She did not know. A reflection of herself perhaps, to recognize from mirrors. Or some body that she could kiss, and advise about his underclothes. Now she was aghast at the mystery of a man. So some people light fires, then wring their hands when the fires have got away from them. He was good to look at, though.

"You have grown up," she said, looking, half-ashamed.

She would have liked to look at him by daylight.

Then he came forward, and touched her elbow, and said, "You brought what I asked, Mum?"

"Yes," she said. "You have not shaved, Ray."

"I got a lift on a lorry," he said. "From Melbourne. I worked my way on a freighter to there from the West."

"From Albany."

"Yes. Albany. Broome. I was at Coolgardie at one time."

"You have been everywhere."

"There's always one more place."

"But we thought you were in Albany. In some business, you said."

"What's this?" he asked, looking into the basket, which was the only equivocal object in that room.

"That is a bit of tucker, dear," said the mother, who had forgotten what pleasure she would have in watching him eat.

He did so, very quickly, tearing the legs off the chicken and wrenching open the bread, of which the crumbs were scattered, or hung from his mouth. He was uglier eating. His face was fleshier, shining with such of the yellow grease as had escaped his mouth, thinking already of a patch of crackling skin still farther on the bone, he was particularly greedy for the crisp skin.

"You were that hungry?" said the woman, who was watching a traveller she was feeding, incidentally her son.

"I been on the road since yesterday."

He threw the bones into a corner, and the carcass with its little shrivelled heart.

Then he sighed, and was easier in his clothes.

"I should have brought some apples," she said, seeing his teeth tear the flesh of apples.

He was rather a muscular man, not yet set. He moved about the room, sometimes gold when the light struck him.

"I done well," he said, wiping and blinking.

She liked to watch him.

"Now you can tell me about yourself, won't you?" she asked. "What you have done and seen."

She was standing with her hands crossed low against her dark skirt. Her thoughts had abandoned her in an attitude of great awkwardness.

"You haven't lost that habit, Mum," he said, giving a kind

373

of twitch that came to him apparently at moments of defence, "that habit of cross-questioning a man. You would kill a person dead to see what was inside."

"After all this time," she said, beginning to kindle, "I am entitled to some kind of explanations."

"Ah yes," he said, looking at his toes, "but explanations don't explain."

"Then what can we expect of you?" she said, harder than before. "Haven't you anything to show?"

"No."

When she had got him defenceless she began to cry for him. She had been waiting a long time for this.

"Oh, Ray," she cried, putting her hands on his shoulders, to be comforted.

The two people filled the empty room intolerably. It was not possible to escape from each other, as it is amongst furniture. Here they had to submit. Besides, the young man had not yet got the money, and she was his mother, and she had not wrung herself enough.

After he had felt her crying against him for some time he was in fact almost hypnotized.

"I am to blame," he said.

"No," she replied. "We are all of us to blame."

She had put a soggy handkerchief against her nose, which had swollen up. She said, "At least I hope you are honest, Ray."

"What is honest?" he asked.

"Well," she said, "that you have never committed any crime."

"Why?" he asked. "Have you?"

All around the abandoned house night pressed, and trees. There were pine trees, seedlings of those which had been lit the night of the fire. These pricked the walls of the house and scratched at the windows. There was a great uneasiness.

The minutes began to force the woman into a belief that she was innocent. It could not be otherwise. She had not killed anyone, anyway, or stolen.

When the young man saw the advantageous position he was in he was quick to make the most of it.

"Listen, Mum, I got a long way to go. Let us have the money. I gotta meet a bloke at Cairns, who has a carrying concern up there. I'm gonna be in on that if I get there in time."

374

"Is that true?" she asked, bringing the money out of her dress.

He laughed, looking at the notes.

"You don't believe me. For some reason," he laughed, receiving money.

"I believe you," she sighed. "I am getting too old to argue."

He was quick at counting money.

"But stay here for a bit, Ray," she said. "Stay and talk to us. You can help your father with the cows. I'll make an apple pie. Do you remember those kidney puddings that you used to like?"

But Ray Parker was as good as gone. In trains he put his feet up on the seat opposite and felt the flash of telegraph poles. He whistled between his teeth. He played at cards with commercials in trains, with commercials in grey dustcoats, and could look after himself all right. Sometimes he cut across country on foot, leaving the road if it suited, other people's property did not deter him. He broke off cobs of corn to chew. He tore off branches of plums and spat out the sour stones. At night he slept in the backs of lorries that had taken him up, sleeping on a heap of bags that smelled of bag and whatever had been in them. In spite of the hurtling and the rough, hairy bags he slept good enough, and got down, and had yarns with people in the starlight, after making water. In country towns girls looked down at him from windows. He liked best the girls with big breasts. The iron beds creaked under the stress of girls, some of them greasy, some of them powdery. When he had had enough he went on.

"You ought to settle down, Ray," his mother was saying in the empty room. "Find some good, steady girl."

"Nah," he laughed, buttoning up the money. "I was going with a tart in Albany for a while."

"And what happened to this girl?"

"I went away."

"You know best, I suppose," said the mother with some satisfaction, and although time was slipping from her own grasp.

He was golden by lamplight, and had been also as a little boy, looking at the marble clock.

Am I turning into the kind of mug she expects? asked the young man.

"I must go now, Mum," he said.

"Let me look at you."

Then they were turning in the gigantic room, which was stuck there in the darkness for no other purpose. She was kissing him. Where is Dad now, he wondered, that I have not asked about, did she notice?—the old bugger is reading the paper somewhere, holding on to it as if it was boards. The young man averted his eyes, as he did always when kissing, but submitted. He closed his eyes, for the shock of his childhood was too great, its empty saucepans and its kisses breathing on him with the warmth of summer. She had only taken his toys away as a game, it seemed.

"Ray," she said, looking into his face, "I can't believe that you will go."

Looking into his eyes.

"You won't go."

Looking into the pupils of his eyes, though she was unable to see herself in that light.

"What it is you're looking for I don't know," she said.

Some days of summer she herself did believe that permanence had arrived in all its stillness.

So she kissed him again as she had not kissed yet, and trembled for an answer on the lips of this young man, who was only incidentally her son.

"Look here," he said, laughing now for the joke, "I gotta be going, I said."

Began to shake her off with his shoulders, as if she were some clumsy boy or dog. She made him that way. Dogs, when patted, curve round in pleased embarrassment and knock things over.

"Yes," she said in that grey voice.

She was putting her hat right. She was older. It was the hat. It was the kind that women in buses wear, sitting in line on a long seat. It was piled with some kind of ornamentation that you do not notice without going into, and then not always.

"Well, so long, Mum," he said.

Ray Parker gave people a hard slap on the elbow when saying good-bye.

"Good-bye, Ray," she said.

Her voice was flatter. It needed a lozenge, to help it over an obstruction.

"I'll let you know how it all makes out," he said, laughing, as the night blew in at the door.

Now the room which had been put there for a purpose had clearly served it. Leaves were coming in.

376

"I'll always be interested," she said, "to hear. Even if it's only a postcard."

He was laughing insanely for some joke as he went out, and looked back once.

Jesus, he said, for his hot, wet neck.

There was a house of similar proportions into which he had once got simply by breaking a window, In that house, which had been temporarily his, he had made animal noises at the portraits and stuffed his mouth with glacé fruits, till the sight of so many innocent and haphazard objects had given him a respect, almost an affection for their owners, and he went away, taking with him only a paperweight and a little filigree box.

So Ray Parker, looking back at his mother in her oblivious hat, in the room, amongst the crumbs, began to trail quietly through the darkness with sadness for something he would never achieve. He was heavier and older in his good but feckless body. He was older, but not old enough.

Then Amy Parker, who had been rolling her handkerchief into a ball, before realizing it was not something to throw away, took the basket up. There was a cloth too, with which she had hidden a chicken from sight, and which she would wash on Monday. She looked at the crumbs on the floor, wondering whether she should resume her life to the extent of sweeping them up. But a mouse came, or was blown through the flurried leaves, and at once made the boards his province. She watched this intensive activity from a great height, in the silence of the house, through which the damp pressed, through cracks, and upwards through whole masses of cold brick, and outwards from the woodwork in a slow growth of fungus.

Of course her son had gone away by this time, so Amy Parker went quickly out. Then what have I got? she asked, as the void hit her, and her lamp went jolting down the hill. Her throat was dry. She began to be afraid in the darkness, full of live, wet leaves. The night was rocking. Clouds were heaped up, and a few small stars were glittering with virulence. People had seen Bub Quigley wander from the grounds of Glastonbury at night, but that would have been when younger, before the fits got too bad. Now he would stroll in the sun on still mornings, a little way only when he was sick, one long hand locked in his sister's, almost as if they had been lovers, anyway lost in each other.

Now that Amy Parker was lost in the helter-skelter

darkness she longed for some knowledge of which others were apparently possessors. I have nothing, I know nothing, she suspected. Her breath panted to learn, as her ankles turned on stones, but there was no indication where or how to begin. If you could ask, she said. People, however, put on that face of surprise and disgust when cornered by requests in any way peculiar. She knew, because she had adopted it herself.

After straying some distance she returned to her own kitchenful of light, and there was her husband sitting in it.

"I am going to put on the kettle," she said, "and make us a cup of tea, Stan."

He looked up from the paper he was reading. Because she was exuding night air and her cheeks had a desperate glow he should have been inquisitive, but he had decided not to be.

He said, "Thanks, Amy. I don't think I'll bother. Thanks all the same."

"But it will warm you."

He laughed. He knew better.

"I am warm enough," he said.

Stan knows a good deal probably, she sensed, but he will never tell.

"Then I shall have a cup," she said. "By myself."

And was moving her black kettle.

Stan returned to reading the newspaper, in which all incidents are electrically lit. It was not ordained just then that he should take strange paths. Two people do not lose themselves at the identical moment, or else they might find each other, and be saved. It is not as simple as that.

Chapter 20

THE GARDEN at Parkers' had almost taken possession of the house. It was a haphazard sort of garden. Mrs. Parker would plant a shrub with passion, something she had seen and desired intensely, would plant it, and forget about it. Then suddenly it had grown and was sawing at its neighbours. All flowers, all leaves, were interlocked in that garden. The shrubs were blooming in each other. Sometimes Mrs. Parker would come out from the house, and push the branches aside impatiently, and look out. Her brown skin had wrinkled at the eyes from days beneath the sun. Her skin was rough. Branches of trees, twigs of shrubs, would catch at her hair and draw it out. It got in a mess sometimes, but what can you do? and she was all the time snatching at it, pulling it back, with her brown hand, with its dull ring. Her hand was rather hard but pleasing. You would look at it.

And at her, as she peered through the branches of the oleanders, that were always dusty, every summer, or as she parted the tufts of the tea tree, looking for the grub that sews them up. Sometimes Mrs. Parker would look at the people passing on the road, but she would not speak to them now, not so much. She would go back into her house, climbing the steps with precision, some old cardigan most likely caught around her broad figure, she had certainly broadened at the hips. Then she would go inside her house, rather a secret woman, into the brown house, inseparable from the garden, from the landscape in which it was.

That house had never had a name. At first it had not needed one. It had become known as Parkers' and had stayed that way. There was no one at Durilgai, no one in the surrounding districts, who could remember when Parkers' had not stood. Everybody took it for granted and no longer looked at it. Many people thought it was ugly. It was old and brown anyway, and less planned than purposeful.

Mr. Parker kept it in pretty good order, though. He kept the gutters cleared and the woodwork painted, and replaced any boards that the white ant was getting at. He was a conscientious sort of man. Slow. He was a big man, coming up the slope from his cows, or ploughing a furrow for corn. When he remembered, he was wearing glasses now, the little metal-rimmed kind, on account of some headaches he had been having. The glasses were a damn nuisance and got broke; he had mended them in one place with waxed string. But they began to suit his face. He came up the slope with buckets, and would jerk his head at people, even at strangers, to pass the time of day. People liked him. His skin was honest.

One winter, when activity about the place had slackened off, Stan Parker was going over to give Joe Peabody a hand with some fencing. Young Peabody had bought that block at Hungerford but was not yet settled, there was always something. One year he broke his leg, another he was gored by a bull. Then his mother-in-law got sick, it was her ticker, and they had to pay the specialist. Joe Peabody had married a kind of cousin, because there were not any other girls around at that time. But she was a good girl, healthy, and they were breeding the other side of the bag curtain which divided them from the mother-in-law. The kids also set Joe Peabody back, temporarily anyway, but he was very cheerful, so cheerful, in fact, that no one ever thought to pity him.

Stan Parker would go over sometimes, though, because young Peabody had been in the habit of asking favours of him, and advice. For this reason the older man liked the younger very much. He was flattered, but refreshed too, by unexpected friendship.

When Stan Parker was getting ready to assist with that fencing job, as he had promised, fetching and scraping his own crowbar, because he did not care to use other people's tools, his wife came to him and said, "You are going over to Joe Peabody's."

It was a statement, not a question, as she stood with her hands in the pockets of her cardigan, watching her husband scrape the tools. And Stan Parker made no answer, it was a noise rather, of confirmation, that she had learned by this time to interpret.

A year or two ago Amy Parker had resented this relationship. That young man cannot speak straight to a person but stands sideways, she complained. It was true. Young Peabody was shy of his friend's wife. So Amy Parker began to dislike the shape of his nose, and to say things about his young wife. Well, she is a breeder anyway, she said.

"You don't like him. Why?" asked Stan Parker. "He is inoffensive."

"I don't *dislike* him," said his wife, surprised. "But I can't take to him. If you know what I mean."

The husband did not, altogether.

Then Amy Parker remembered the blue tie that Joe Peabody had been wearing on that day, and for which she had not forgiven him. It was a bright, accusing blue that men should not wear. Or she had not been ready for it at that moment. She was accused.

"I have nothing against him," she said stoutly.

Anyway, her husband continued to frequent Joe Peabody, and in time Amy Parker accepted this situation, as most situations are eventually accepted.

"I am not putting up any lunch," she said, watching her husband prepare his tools.

"That is right," he answered. "They would not like that."

She watched his head. Ah, she said, I am fond of him. It was pleasanter than love.

When he had straightened up, and it was evident he was going, a great warmth of affection pervaded her, for all his actions, and she rubbed her sleeve against him and said, "Won't you kiss me then?"

He laughed, and kissed her, but awkwardly, with dry lips. Because hers were moister she considered she was fonder. She loved him even. Of course she loved him. Going from the yard with the heavy tools.

Then Amy Parker watched her husband start the car, which was one in a succession of old cars, and drive out, upright. In the house in which she was glad now to be alone, in spite of, or perhaps because of, her affection, peace did seem attainable. So she polished wood with long methodical sweeps until it lit the winter with a glow of old red wood, and she looked out of the window at the sparkling grass and some first wattles on the shoulder of the hill. For the moment, at least, she demanded only what she knew.

Everyone sat easy in that peaceful morning, which is possible sometimes in the still winter days. Stan Parker, who had chugged along the stony road to Peabodys', was glad also to be in it. He passed many places that he knew, and children who did not recognize him, and cows staring, and a brilliant cock that sprang upon a roof and stood there for splendour.

Eventually the car arrived at Peabodys', where the young farmer himself ran out from the shed-house in which the family was living, came straight through the children, dogs, the screaming and the barking, and after wasting very little time the two men went down with clean strides through the dew to the place where part of the fence was already standing.

Soon they were at work, the men turning up the red soil for post holes, the dogs nosing in the tussocks for rabbits. Because he was receiving free assistance from a neighbour young Peabody felt bound to work twice as hard. He would have done all.

"Give us the shovel, Stan," he said when he had flung the crowbar down.

But Stan Parker did not like this. He took the shovel and flung up earth in turn.

So they worked like this in maniacal deference to each other.

And as it grew hot and panting, and a hawk sailed slow and black across the empty sky, young Peabody tore off his shirt, and spat on his hands, and was working all the harder.

Stan Parker, who remained clothed in his shirt, watched the body of the young man, which had all the obliviousness and confidence of young naked bodies. So Stan Parker himself had moved the trees and boulders back in the dream time. So his mouth, as he watched, had to become a bit ironical. He could remember the time when it was just a matter of fencing in his land, and then it would be his. Such a belief was obvious in the clear eyes of the muscular young man, who was opening and closing like a knife in his fury of confidence.

At last they came to something which did shake the ribs of Joe Peabody. He stood there palpitating. He could have been oiled all over.

"That's sunk us for this one," he said, temporarily dubious. "Might blast it, I suppose."

It was an apparently endless boulder that the two men had been picking round.

"That?" said Stan Parker, smiling at the hole in a rather tight way. "There has been worse than that. I wouldn't let that beat us, a little bit of a stone."

So he took the crowbar.

Joe Peabody stood with his hands on his heaving hips, secretly hoping that the older man would assume control.

Stan Parker worked. The iron trembled as it struck the ground, whether with contempt or hope. The man worked. Was it hatred flowing out of his arms? But he laughed once or twice. Once or twice sparks flew out of the rock, and grey wounds appeared. The dry, fragile body of the man was fighting with the dull stone. At the bottom of the gully, he remembered, there was that stream of brown water, cool days flowed out of the molten, and the little sarsaparilla vines twined purple through the grey thorns. Suddenly he bent over the crowbar, pressing his belly into it, weighing it down with his body, with the whole of his strength.

The stone did move in the hole.

He withdrew the bar and stabbed again and again into the corners of the earth, having observed a weakness. The rock heaved, its shape was evident now.

"Good-oh," shouted young Peabody, who liked to admire his friend. "What do you know about that!"

Stan Parker smiled.

He was rather grey. He dropped the iron bar, which fell tingling. But there was a suspicion that the man himself, though still upright, had been similarly rejected. Grey mists floated in the bright morning. He felt sick. His breath was short. His back or something.

"What's up, Stan?" asked the young man, coming and touching the older one. "Go easy on it. Are you feeling crook?"

He was full of concern.

Stan Parker wiped his eyes, putting the whole of his confused face behind his hands. The whole of his body was shaking. But when he had emerged from behind his hands, as he had to, he smiled again and said, "I'm okay, Joe. I'm not what I was, that's all."

The young man looked at the old man. "You gotta take it easy," he said.

He was pleased now to take control, and when the boulder was fully prised from the ground ordered Stan Parker to sit upon it, which he did.

Stan Parker sat there in the lovely morning feeling his neck, which was gristly, and his sides, of which the ribs were weak. If he could have put his hand on his own soul and judged its shape, age, toughness, and durability, he would

383

have done so. As he could not, he was inwardly very shaken, he felt nonexistent, although he continued to smile through the haze of exhaustion, watching the young man work at a normal rate now that there was no competition, and listening to him give advice on fencing, which, to the recipient, had begun to seem inevitable rather than presumptuous.

Soon a little boy came running over the broken ground, too fast for himself, but he was propelled by the morning. His bare feet thumping, his scabby legs flashing, he came on. He was carrying a crust of bread that he had left off chewing, and of which a moist crumb was clinging to his red cheeks.

He arrived and gabbled something.

"What's he say?" asked Stan Parker, who was an old man, and out of it now.

"He says the missus has the dinner ready," said the father, bringing out a few more shovelfuls of earth, on principle.

The child stood looking at Stan Parker, thoughtful on his crust.

"What is wrong with Mr. Parker, Dad?" asked the boy. "Why isn't he working?"

"That is none of your business," said Joe Peabody. "Mr. Parker is havin a rest."

The young father clothed his nakedness. He had a fine line of dark hair dividing his body from the breasts to the navel. He did not pay much attention to this child which had sprung from him in the dark shed. He took him for granted rather, putting his hand on his friend's back and saying, "Come on, Stan. We'll get something inside of us."

So Stan Parker was led, he was glad to be, and the little boy, hopping in front with his chewed crust, hopping and turning round, skipping backwards to get a better look, cried, "Is Mr. Parker sick then?"

Once his father struck out at him, and the boy screamed, he pretended to cry, it was a great game, and the father also liked it.

In the teeming shed-house, in which the young wife had just fed her latest baby, they sat down to a stew with a few carrots floating in it. There were big heaps of grey potatoes on the men's plates.

"Bet you men are hungry," said young Mrs. Peabody, who had a brown skin, and who was a shining, joyful young woman, because of everything. "You tuck in, Mr. Parker. Mum an I 'ave had ours."

384

"I had no appetite, not today," said the grandmother, who was a Mrs. Peabody too. "Nor has Mr. Parker, I expect. It is the young ones that are always guzzlin. It's a good thing there's the pertaters."

"I am never off my tucker," said Stan Parker, though at that moment he could not look at it.

"It will come to yer that yer will be," said old Mrs. Peabody in disgust. "You are not a young man, I would not say, by any calculation."

The visitor was defenceless. Some of the children had ceased to respect him.

" 'Ere, cut it out, Mum," said the host through a full mouth. "Leave a man alone."

"You won't get no lolly," said her daughter, winking at their guest.

"If you must all bully me," complained the old woman, whose hair stood out from her parrot skin in grey tufts. "I have reared seven daughters, Mr. Parker," she said, "and got pitched from one to the other of em. Like a parcel."

"You were lucky," said young Mrs. Peabody, "to 'ave 'ad so many. Otherwise, you would not'uv got pitched so long. The parcel would certainly'uv got dropped."

She gave her mother a slap in the back with such good humour and gentleness that the old woman began to cry for all the mercy she had received, and went off through the bag curtain, beyond which she lived.

Stan Parker pushed away his plate after a bit.

Young Mrs. Peabody looked at those potatoes in the sea of stew.

"Eh," she said, but did not continue.

She had an idea that her husband's friend was a subject for protection, so she curved her arm round him to reach the plate, and as she swept by he felt her protective warmth.

"I'll give yez a cup of tea," she said. "You want to drink it, though," she said, turning on this old man.

Stan Parker was full of humility, not that he had ever been a proud man. But he looked humbly at the knees of his pants, and at Peabodys' earth floor, from which the face of a child was staring back at him. From the end of life he was drawn towards the limpid child. He would have liked to say something to it, but it was too far.

"There you are," said the mother, placing the cup of sloping tea. "There's sugar. You can sugar yourself. Don't you hurry him, Joe. Let the poor man enjoy a nice cup of tea."

Stan Parker was no longer hurried. His slow lips drank the tea. He sat making distant conversation, and did go down with Joe Peabody to the fence, but it was advancing without him. Stan wandered off during the afternoon, and Joe Peabody was secretly pleased, thinking, The old cove has become a liability, and for the little he has done, but a good old cove.

When Stan Parker got home his wife said to him without looking up, "You are back earlier than I expected."

"Yes," he said. "I cracked up."

"How?" she asked. "Cracked up?"

She started back from him, although he had not hit her.

"We were getting a stone out of a post hole. I went as weak as a little child. It was only a sort of dizzy spell. But it lasted. I was no good today, Amy."

But by evening he was again a man of strength and prospects. And they made one or two hilarious jokes about age, underneath the hard electric light in which the room stood square. He was so far recovered that she dealt him a blow at one point.

"We'd better sell up those damn cows," she said. "What has our life been? But plodding up and down that path to pull the milk out of a mob of blessed cows."

She watched even, to see if she had wounded him. He did not flinch, though.

When she had hung up the damp tea towel to dry she came towards him. The smell of the cold garden flowed in at them through the window, a smell of woodbine and of early violets. She had smoothed her hair down that day, so that he saw, or remembered, her beauty. They kissed, quite fiercely, and were comforted by the illusion of their returned bodies. The man was fortunate enough to fall asleep in this illusion, but the woman lay longer in the bed in which they had slept their sleeping lives, and was moved by gratitude or curiosity to touch his head. She touched his skull, for all the flesh seemed to have gone from it in sleep. He did not object, but lay there breathing from a distance. Not long after, she did fall asleep in the uneasy framework of the house. This time it was she who strained to move the rock, which lay beside her heavy in the bed.

By daylight, of course, it is easy to resume confidence in flesh. On placid days of winter Amy Parker sat, in that lull of afternoons, on the front veranda, to watch from behind vines, and the canes of an old rose, that must go, it was too possessive and too old. Here she sat, though, in the mean-time, watching for something to happen, though mostly it did not.

Except one day, it was June, there was a cold wind bending the grass down, there was sunlight of that thin kind which is dispelled before it reaches its objective, but that day a car passed, a neat enough small car, it had been polished with some pride and care. Mrs. Parker bent a cane down to watch. She could not see that far in any detail. It was aggravating. She could not. Except there was a woman squinting out, looking about, looking for confirmation of some kind. She was dressed in black fur.

"Is that, can you tell me," called the woman, who had stopped her small car, "does Mrs. Parker live here?"

"I beg yours," replied Mrs. Parker with caution.

She came out in anonymity, to see.

"There used to be a Mrs. Parker," said the stationary woman, her voice loud and lonely in that cold country place in which she had pulled up.

She is an elderly woman to be driving herself around, considered Amy Parker.

"Why, yes, there is," she said, but considering, but clearing her throat.

This woman had a yellow face, like soap. Her voice went into Amy Parker, ferreting after something.

"But aren't you," said the woman, "you are surely Mrs. Parker?"

Mrs. Parker blushed.

"Yes," she said. "Mrs. Gage, is it?"

"I would not have known you," said Mrs. Gage. "You have put on quite a lot of weight."

"You have got quite stout yourself," said Mrs. Parker, looking at the landscape.

But she was pleased, it seemed, for something she had seen.

Then both women laughed, a high laughter, as if thin wooden bats had been slapped together in midair.

"Well, I never," said the ex-postmistress when they had exhausted themselves.

Amy Parker watched the face, which was yellow and strangely mobile, it could have been filled with liquid soap. She saw that Mrs. Gage was comfortably situated, and hoped that the postmistress would tell her story, which soon she did, fingering the nickel knobs of her little car, and looking misty for the past.

"When I put in for a transfer from Durilgai," she said, "after Mr. Gage had taken his life, as you will remember, I was sent to Winbin."

At this cruel township in the South, ice crackled on the puddles. You could hear it. You could see the long, yellow rain come down the valley and strike the yellow grass. There was the street with the blacksmith and the pub. There had been a murder once, but many years ago, and then never another. At the office, which was brown, on piles, above a lot of empty kerosene drums and broken chairs, the wind had loosened some of the woodwork. In the brown office, in which Mrs. Gage stood, there was a smell of stoves and dry ink. Ink, other than the dregs of ink, frequently froze, so that you were not encouraged to put it. That frozen ink just made you feel bad. So Mrs. Gage, chafing her chilblains and listening to the sound of her brown-paper sleeves, offered the public a pencil instead.

"I got quite thin at Winbin," said the postmistress. "It was on account of Mr. Gage really, passing over in that way. I developed a nervous condition. I began to have difficulty with some of the forms. Would you believe it, I could not account for several sheets of stamps? And most distressing of all, I would fall down sometimes while checking a telegram, I was conscious, mind you, which made it worse. I could hear my pencil bouncing on the boards. I could see the ceiling, quite a distance up. Well, many people did not like this. Because they do not know what to do when a person falls down. So I resigned."

Mrs. Gage dabbed at her lips with a handkerchief. Her life in the telling always began to seem real.

"It was high time, Mr. Goldberg said," she said. "Otherwise much valuable information would have been lost forever."

"Mr. Goldberg?" asked Amy Parker, who had folded her arms over each other, she was marmoreal now.

"I will tell you when the time comes," the postmistress said. "When I left Winbin, retiring from the service, I went to Mrs. Small, a second cousin, at Barangoola. She nearly killed me with kindness, soups in winter and jellied fish in summer. She suffers from a stammer, poor thing, from being scalded as a girl. Barangoola is a summer resort, you know, and in heavy seasons Mrs. Small would take a visitor or two.

In this way we got Mr. Goldberg, a gentlemen of some education, who read books and had even written some poetry—anyway, he showed me some, and it was quite nice."

Summer evenings on the breakwater, which was a rocky mole, too sharp to be anything but discreet, Mr. Goldberg gave sympathetic attention to the unfortunate story of Mrs. Gage. He listened to the swish of sea lettuce and watched the mouths of anemones, sometimes offering them a crab. Sometimes Mr. Goldberg would raise his head like a horse and appear to whinny at the madness of Mrs. Gage's husband.

"Because of course," she said, "I had to tell him about all that. But I did not at first show him the paintings, which I had brought from Durilgai to Winbin, and from Winbin to Barangoola, tied with a cord, as I hardly knew what to do with them.

"Well," she said, spitting a little, "if I did eventually show the paintings, it all happened in this way. We was in the street one morning, en route for a lending library that Mr. Goldberg patronized, when a person came up, who was known to him, it appeared, they had many acquaintances in common with unusual sorts of names. This person stayed chatting for quite a while, but looking at me, and smiling, and looking, though in a ladylike way. Of course, I looked at a shop, because I know my own business. Then this lady come to me, she was tastefully dressed too, she took me by the hands, she was that excited. 'Mrs. Gage,' she said, 'it is you,' she said, 'that I have wondered, and the paintings your husband did, I have been positively haunted all these years.' You would never guess, it was none other but that Mrs. Schreiber, who was there the day that Mr. Gage passed on, and saw the paintings with yourself and other ladies, no doubt you will remember, her face was different, but you cannot say it was not refined. So now the paintings was out. There was nothing for it but to show Goldberg. He pressed me. I refused at first. Then finally I did.

"Well," said the widow, shiny now, "it appears as Mr. Gage was a genius, would you believe it?—though all that were acquainted with my husband, poor soul, knew as he was on the unusual side. You did not know my husband."

"No," said Amy Parker, though she did.

"I was soon an object of interest," the postmistress continued, removing something unwanted from her fur, "on account of the enthusiasm of Mr. Goldberg and several other gentlemen for my husband's oil paintings. Poor Mr. Gage himself would have been surprised as one thing, if he had been there. I was only sorry he had gone, as I could see we might have worked up quite a little business. Anyway, to cut the story short, I sold the paintings. I must tell you I did well. I sold all but one, which I would not part with, for sentimental reasons, and because it is a work of art, Mr. Goldberg says, unequalled. I have it above the fireplace in the lounge. The frame alone is worth fifteen pounds. It is the one of the woman, but you will not remember. She is standing there—well, she is naked, to be frank. But why not? I am broadminded now, since I know it is worth the while."

"I remember that picture," said Amy Parker.

"You do?" said Mrs. Gage, provoked. "And do you like it?"

"I don't know," said the heavy woman. "I do not understand it."

She did not understand herself, standing heavy in the road, at that moment, or at any. She did not understand the eyes of people. And the dead man, had he seen her as she could not conceive of it? Should she have loved him then, walking between trees at night, his arms no longer skinny? I have not loved someone, she felt. She was agitated. She was a bit afraid.

"Anyway," said the ex-postmistress, "I had soon got my own home. It is all modern. I have just finished paying off the fridge. And how are you, dear?" she asked, looking around her in surprise. "It is like old times. And Mrs. O'Dowd?"

"I can't say if Mrs. O'Dowd is well or not," said Mrs. Parker formally.

"Ah," said Mrs. Gage.

"Oh, we never ever had a actual row," Mrs. Parker hastened. "But friends blow cold."

Then it was the children that the postmistress had to ask for, in that voice that she put on for the children.

"Thelma is good," said Mrs. Parker with precision. "She is married with a solicitor. She did well."

"And Ray, was it?" asked Mrs. Gage.

Because you had to.

"Ray," sighed Mrs. Parker, smoothing out her apron with long, silky sweeps, "Ray grew up too. He is selling motorcars, I think. He is to be married soon, to a good girl."

"Who?"

"To Elsie Tarbutt," Mrs. Parker said. "She is from Sydney."

"Fancy that," said Mrs. Gage.

It is more than strange that other people's lives are lived. Mrs. Gage's own life had filled the foreground. She could not have believed in much else. Now she began to press and pull the silver knobs that studded the panel of her little car.

She said, "If you are ever down Drummoyne way, you must look in, and I shall be pleased to see anyone for old times' sake."

Because she was pretty certain that Mrs. Parker would not look in, it added something to the ex-postmistress's pure bounty of mind. And Mrs. Parker, who would not look in, definitely not, it was ridiculous to think, she too was pleased. She stood murmuring contentedly amongst the stones.

Just then a cold light of evening was illuminating the sky and Mrs. Gage's face, which was purged besides, by narrative.

"It does you good to talk," she said. And added daringly, "I am happy at last."

Then she pressed something and glided from that place in her enchanted car.

Amy Parker got back ponderously onto the veranda. Whole afternoons she waited for other witnesses of the past, but saw young people who had not yet lived and strangers who were blank or kind. Because she knew better than these, she was inclined to have trouble with her wind, or breathe hard down her nose, holding herself in and upright, not listening, which made her look fierce. Some people said, That Mrs. Parker is a bad-tempered old thing.

She was and she was not. She had expected something to happen, some act of miraculous revelation, and because this had not occurred, or anyway had gone unrecognized, she was becoming aggravated. She would scratch her leg in a most exasperated manner. She would crane out to look at some distant, desirable scene, which her eyesight of course did not permit her to see. So she got cranky at times, and ugly. Or appeased herself with the past. Growing serene and even wise with these snapshots that she could produce at will from out of her sleeve. The past is a miracle of minor saints.

When Thelma Forsdyke came down, which she did more frequently than would have been expected, she was amazed to find her mother sitting there, an active woman too.

"Are you all right, Mother?" she would ask.

Passive herself, she resented passivity in other people. Since she had discovered literature she would disguise her indolence by holding a book. Though she did read too, a lot. She was obsessed by ethics. She was studying anthropology. But to sit unashamedly was suspect or a sign of illness. She was terrified that her mother might develop a cancer in her old age and need intimate attentions. For which the daughter would pay, of course, she was rich. But to come down to the furtive, insinuating smells of illness in a modest room. So Thelma Forsdyke searched her mother's face for signs of such withering.

"I am not sick," said Amy Parker. "I have sat down for a bit because I like it."

She smiled incredulously at her daughter, at the cloth of her coat, and a string of pearls. They touched cheeks. It was mildly pleasing to the mother. She no longer experienced any desire to possess her daughter, because she had failed to do so. But she did take part in the legend of Thelma Forsdyke, she had indirectly created it, and would at times demand her rights in censure or advice on purely natural matters.

"You should have a baby, Thel," she had said once.

Then the woman who was her daughter turned her head aside and said, "I am not ready. It is not just a matter of having a baby." She drew her shoulders up tightly. She was angry.

"I don't know about that," said the mother, pursing up her lips.

She looked at her daughter's hands. The mother was superior, of course. She was incredulous of the hands, lying in the lap, folded like paper fans. But she did not say any more on that subject.

Sometimes she inquired after her son-in-law.

"How is Mr. Forsdyke?" she would ask.

Mr. Forsdyke would be preparing for a fishing holiday with other businessmen, or having sinus trouble, once he developed a duodenal ulcer. Almost always he sent his regards to his mother-in-law, because he was by nature a polite man. Passion had not made him rude.

"I am terribly grateful to Dudley," Thelma Forsdyke would say, her eyes moistening even.

Such humility was surprising, but she refreshed herself in it. She had grasped so much, materially, that she had exhausted most avenues for further gain, and so she turned her attention to spiritual aggrandizement. She would have liked to be a martyr to someone, particularly her husband, who failed to give her opportunity, except in a certain manner he had of clearing his throat, and in his cult of draughts. She was unlikely to have any children, for vaguely delicate reasons, and this at times was a sadness for her, some afternoons or evenings, when she was left alone with her hands, until she realized that she would not have known what to do with young children, knocking things over in her house, or the older ones, discovering about sex. She had her health, of course, or lack of it, she had her asthma, about which people remembered to inquire, and particularly those who were grateful.

Sometimes the rector called. Thelma Forsdyke gave to the church without encouraging the parson, who would not have fitted into her social scheme. She had become generous, deliberately so; she gave rare objects or presents of money far in excess of the occasion, her eyes reddening for her own acts. Afraid, or unable to give herself, the voluptuousness of generosity became necessary to her. It was a secret vice, her wardrobe gin or hypodermic. So far no one had discovered. Unless her mother.

She liked best to bring presents to her parents, exquisitely remorseful, thoughtfully expensive things. In a car of her own, that she had learned to drive, frowning, she slipped past the villas and the abbattoirs into the surprising country, in which she played no part. Down that road, of loose barbed wire and dusty trees, which was only distinguished by her parents living in it, she drove at anxious speed, remembering an old man who had exposed himself once in some bushes. To live in a sealed room, she feared, would not exclude all the incidents that must be excluded.

Then she would arrive. These visits were absurd, she realized wryly, if touching, as she brushed the dust from her coat. The air was full of the sound of magpies.

Once she brought her mother a pineapple, and a fresh fish, and a set of table mats painted with a hunting scene, that she had bought at a charity bazaar. She opened them for her mother, she spread out, because this was part of the game, to indulge herself in one voluptuous surge of kindness, she was so good.

"Look," she said, laying the silvery fish on her bare hands. "Isn't he a beauty?"

The fish was. He glittered. His being could not end in death.

The mother, whose eyes were playing about amongst her presents, said, "Ah, Thel, what am I to do with these?"

393

"The mats? Aren't they pretty? There will be some occasion perhaps. Keep them and see."

"You are very kind to me, Thel," said the mother, looking at her daughter, right into her.

And the daughter, who had grown into rather a thin woman of taste, took the fish and went out to put it in a cool place, in the house that she knew by heart but no longer belonged to. Her mother was inclined to be selfish, she decided, to take for granted. Whether this was so or not, the old woman continued to look ironically, not at the mats but at her daughter, although gone inside. She continued to look at the little girl pressing her mouth to the mirror until her mouth met her mouth.

However, when Mrs. Forsdyke returned, testing her cleaned hands on a transparent handkerchief, the old woman was all gratitude and kindliness.

She said, "That is a beautiful fish, Thelly. I shall bake it in the oven. Dad likes it that way."

It was an amiable game that they played, of mother and daughter. Mrs. Forsdyke enjoyed its sequence, and overlooked the fact that she had been called "Thelly," which reminded her of stones in the small of her back after school.

Sometimes Thelma Forsdyke walked round her drawing room and, remembering the abyss of her origin, closed the windows tight. That is something which it is not possible to escape. It is with you always. So that her face was not convincing to her, even at its best. Her voice would falter discussing music. There is such nastiness in the evolution of a synthetic soul. She remembered the Bourkes, she remembered the feel of Genoa velvet, the taste of nougat as she sat buffing her nails.

Once the maid came in, an elderly woman with soft ways, who had been trained by somebody else.

"There is a gentleman to see you, madam. He says it is on urgent private business. He would not give a name," said the elderly maid in a discreet cap.

How safe, how established, even the elderly maids are.

The gentleman was Ray Parker, Mrs. Forsdyke's brother.

"I bet you were surprised, Thel," laughed Ray, coming into the drawing room and pitching his hat that he had brought with him, an aggressive new brown hat, pitching it from him, somewhere. "I like to give people surprises," he laughed. "It takes them out of their rut. You're in a pretty good rut, though," he said, looking round.

"We chose this house for the view," she said, coming forward to receive a guest. "It has water on three sides. You can see right up the harbour, and on this side, out to the Heads."

Then she looked at her brother, to discover what he might want. Her face had become all bones. She would be a stringy woman later on. She was tough too, in spite of an air of delicate health, that rattly cough with which she could frighten people. She would have had to be tough to get what she wanted, almost. What she did want, that is, the ultimate in desire, eluded her, so that she was more speculative, only superficially unpleasant, when she asked, "What is it you want, Ray?"

The man who had sat down heavily on her colourless brocade, he was by this time a heavy man, meant to play her for a bit. He composed his cheeks, which had a city tan, and in which two dimples came. Some people found these interesting.

He said, "I came to take a dekker at you, Thel. Here we are, related. But anyone would think we didn't exist, anyone who didn't know about the other."

She laughed.

"What good would it do these hypothetical people to know that we do exist?"

"If it is a matter of good," he said, shrugging his noticeable suit, and hoping that she would offer him a drink.

He was a sensual man, she saw, and sensuality made her nervous, though he would not have noticed. He was probably also stupid in many, if not in all the ways. What she feared most was that he should be, as she suspected, an honest brother, as well as what she knew, a dishonest man.

"Anyway," she said, giving a concise smile and sitting down, "you are here."

"That is more like it," he said in his thick, easy voice. "And this solicitor bloke that I never even met, when does he come in?"

"That depends," she said. "Professional men don't run by clockwork."

"I can wait, though," said Ray Parker.

If this pale room will not kill him. What do people, lacking the resources of flies, do in still rooms?

"Because I have always wanted to meet him."

"I can think of no two things you would have in common," laughed Thelma Forsdyke, without weighing the possibilities.

"You never can tell," said Ray Parker. "I have got to know coves in railway carriages, and on the backs of trucks at night. You would be surprised."

"Dudley," said Thelma, "is not likely to go for any such dangerous rides."

"Is he breakable?"

She did not answer.

"I could get to know you, Thel, sitting in this room."

She did not answer.

"You're thin. Too bloody thin."

When the perspiration had begun to come at her delicate temples, under the hair which had been set the day before yesterday, he continued, "I can't stand thinness. I should have done something big, but as I never found out how, I had to content myself with doctoring a horse and busting open a safe. Oh, you need not get worried, Thel. I'm going straight enough now. That is, I am in business. I am selling cars. I have stood drinks to some of the best people. But it all costs. And I am out of dough. What I have come here for, to be honest, you will appreciate the word, is to touch you for twenty quid. I am being married on Tuesday to a girl called Elsie Tarbutt."

"Is she conscious of what she is doing?" asked Mrs. Forsdyke, going to a little bureau for which she had paid a lot of money under the impression that the adorable furniture was genuine antique.

"Yes," said Ray Parker. "She is going to reform me. She is a Methodist."

"Ah," said the sister.

She wrote off a cheque, putting that graceful signature which it was no longer necessary to practise.

"I wonder whether I would be interested to see her," she said, and smiled, as she paid her brother off.

Again she thought, Ray has failed to accomplish the grand manner. It is a miserable sum.

"To meet Elsie?" he said, looking to see what figure she had written. "No. It would not be the right thing. One crook in the family is enough."

So they stood there hating, without being able to put a finger on the reason.

Then in the silent room, in which they had exchanged souls, they began also to be moved by each other. There are moments when this thick and repulsive man starts to tremble, the woman noticed; would he be still if I kissed him, in spite

396

of the smell of smoke and drink, his teeth are brown, but kissed him deeply, as I have been afraid to kiss someone, or would he add this secret to others that he has got by heart? So the woman continued to twist her rings. And the man pitied her, remembering how he had shivered on a goods train rattling north in the night, knowing there is nothing.

"I'll be going now," said Ray Parker, picking up his flash hat. "It'll ease the situation."

"Good-bye, Ray," she said.

She let him find his own way, after giving it a second's thought, and deciding it was simple enough, and there was nothing he might pick up.

When he was gone she sat in a chair.

Her body was still, but inwardly she rushed at herself, as if she had been a chest of drawers, to turn her virtues out, and find some thing that was good. Many grateful, good, humble people had told her she was good, so she must be. Such eyes see more clearly than one's own, or one's brother's, or one's own. It was something that jumped into his head, she said, and he spoke it, to be clever. But a metallic taste had come in her mouth. She could have spat out her tongue, of thin and bitter metal. So she got a headache. She felt quite feverish. She took an aspirin then. She took a book or two.

"I have brought the tea, madam," said the elderly maid, who had put the tray on a little table.

The habits which Thelma Forsdyke had carefully selected were not of great assistance. There is some crime I have forgotten, she felt, searching between the lines, for she often glanced at a book with her tea, brushing from the pages the crumbs of expertly thin bread and butter. It is absurd to be upset, she said, by the ignorant and vulgar. She read, here a word or two. But she was busted open. And what is there inside? she asked. Her long fingers trembled. Gusts of doubt were shaking her as she read some poem, that she had picked up in a shop, pleased by her own discernment:

> There, like the wind through woods in riot,
> Through him the gale of life blew high; . . .

It was a cold poem. These words had begun to blow through her soft dress, and to sweep her mind, leaving a numbness, if also a curious clarity. She read with a kind of grey fascination:

397

The tree of man was never quiet:
Then 'twas the Roman, now 'tis I.

Perhaps, she felt, it will be knowledge, not aspirin or
ephedrene, that will bring relief. So she read on, through her
teeth:

The gale, it plies the saplings double,
    It blows so hard, 'twill soon be gone:
To-day the Roman and his trouble
    Are ashes under Uricon.

When it was finished she sat on. There was nothing she
could ring and ask for. Half-sensing the meaning of the
poem, she blamed her parents bitterly for the situation to
which she had been exposed. She also blamed God for de-
ceiving her.

Eventually her husband came in with the evening paper
and said, "You are very pale this evening, Thelma."

Correcting the position of an etching on the wall.

"Are you out of sorts?" he asked.

Touching his etching. The Forsdykes had etchings because
they would not have dared choose a painting.

"It is the northeasterly," said Thelma.

There was, in fact, a nasty wind. Little leaden waves ornamented the waters of the bay. Grit was scratching at the win-
dowpanes.

"And Ray has been here," she said. "Ray, my brother."

"What did he want?" asked the solicitor, raising his stomach nervously.

"Nothing," she said.

It is too late to practise honesty, she decided, one would
not know how.

"We had a talk," she said. "He is getting married."

"What did you talk about?" asked Dudley Forsdyke, who
had forgotten the evening paper.

"Oh, family matters," she said.

"Then why are you upset, dear?"

"Ray is always upsetting. He has some effect. He is the
wrong colour for me. It is something like that," said Thelma
Forsdyke.

The solicitor put down the evening paper still hot from his
hand. He walked about chafing his hands. He had an inordi-
nate desire to meet his brother-in-law. Whoever has not vio-

lated, or been violated, it is much the same thing, does at times entertain a curiosity. Dudley Forsdyke was a dry man, but a true man. So he shivered for the shreds of truth, to tear just once, or be torn.

"I am sorry I missed him," he said.

Ray Parker will have a vein in his forehead.

"He is a brute really," said Thelma.

"Still, we are brothers-in-law."

What intimate experience would the brothers-in-law exchange on a flight of stone steps going downward? The solicitor had gathered from some remark of his wife's that Ray Parker was a fleshy man. He felt a hand in the small of his back.

"Anyway, I am glad you did not meet," said the wife.

She felt too weak.

"I am going to bed now," she said. "I shall not bother about dinner."

He kissed her, as they did at recognized intervals, and went in to eat some fish. In the silence of the elderly maid, whose name was Dorothy, he became less obsessed by self-destruction. Discretion returned, rose towards that of the starched woman who bent and breathed above him, till their twin discretions met and mingled in a mutual admiration. In this way the solicitor was restored to the surface on which it was his custom to float.

Soon after that Mrs. Forsdyke felt the necessity for visiting her mother again. Although there were times when she would blame her mother for her birth, she did also experience a desire to return to the womb. So she drove down, and soon they were speaking together on the veranda, which was their habitual meeting place.

"I am sorry you were not at the wedding," said the mother, beginning to enjoy a good talk, with its weft of relationships, in which even flaws would be of interest.

"I was not asked," said the daughter, and wondered whether she was slightly hurt.

"I would have thought that for a wedding all differences are made up," said the old woman. "Still, everyone has their own ideas. Ray has turned over a new leaf."

The mother had decided this. She did not yet know herself well enough to doubt. Or she lowered her eyelids on doubt, over her own life, so that she had a slatted look. As she peered out she was determined to see all hopeful things.

"It was a nice wedding," she said. "Mr. Tarbutt is a grocer, at Leichardt. There were beautiful presents. Someone gave a whole canteen of silver. Ray was in his element, of course. People like him. He sang too. Did you know that Ray could sing? He is prosperous now, it seems."

Thelma Forsdyke, who had sat down on the edge of the veranda, she was sufficiently assured to do ungraceful things, wore that incredulousness which warm sunlight brings on winter afternoons. Sunlight, she realized with gratitude, is one treasure that is not debased by time.

"There was a whole big ham," said the mother, "laid open in slices for people to help themselves."

"And what about Elsie?" Thelma asked.

"Elsie is not pretty," said Mrs. Parker. "But she is what Ray wants. She will make an excellent wife."

"She is a Methodist," said Thelma.

"Did you know then?"

"And you do not like her."

"That you do not know, because it is not true," said Amy Parker, moving in her chair, which squeaked, and examining the cane for clues. "Or if it was true I would soon make it not. Elsie is an excellent girl."

Other people in the end prevail. Amy Parker sat at weddings, at her son's, and of other young ones. She watched the dancers. She ate pink cake and heard it rumble. Some such cake had sand. She went to weddings but did not like them much, in spite of their loveliness. These occasions, the elaborate movements of the dancers and of the conversations diverged too far from her own still mosaic. That she had put together. She did not believe in what she had not made, whether cake or habits.

So she watched Elsie. Under the orange blossom, at the temples, in her thick, creamy skin, the pores were rather large. Elsie had a flat face, but kind. She was expecting something as she came up to speak. She laughed at jokes, because it was the thing. Then closed up, because it was finished. She had a closed face waiting to be opened. All the time her creamy, porous skin was craving for affection.

So Amy Parker realized that Elsie was unprotected. She looked right into Elsie's glasses, through the thick lenses she was compelled to wear, and saw the girl had nothing to hide. This was disconcerting to the older woman. She could not believe it.

Thelma Forsdyke was sitting on the edge of the veranda. She was wearing long crocodile shoes that had been made especially for her, by Tennysons. Shielding her face because of the sun, she too was obsessed by Elsie, and the whole ceremony of common people. How she would have whirled, herself, with gestures of slow ice, protecting herself from the groom! That silver is probably plated, she considered, with embossed handles, and will tarnish quickly.

But why did he marry Elsie? Thelma wondered.

Ray Parker married Elsie Tarbutt like this. He was crossing a park one night in the suburb in which Elsie lived. It was a white night except for black trees, with their equally solid, gummy shadows. Some old horse that mows an oval was cropping at the stillness with a heavy, tired innocence that pursued and troubled the walking man. There were hairs, he saw, hanging from the armpits of the trees, long, still snares. It began to be intolerable. He was turning the money in his pockets. This time tomorrow I shall be free, he said foolishly. He walked across the wide park, along the asphalt, his long, flat footsteps falling about his ears.

Then there was another walking. He could hear. His were mingling with other steps. It became a desperate struggle to find or lose, in the empty white park.

When he came up, as he was trying to, the woman or girl was turning her head away from something that was frightening her. She wore a big black hat that she was holding down although there was no wind, and her figure that stumped along was thick and black, though perhaps not black, it was the still purity of moonlight which drove out all colour by its strength.

"I want to come with you," said Ray Parker, walking alongside the girl.

She bit her breath. She was flickering with terror.

"To talk to you," he said.

Why is it never possible to say this?

"Go away," said the girl. "Leave me."

Hurrying along.

If he fell behind, her calves were of a sturdy shape in moon-darkened stockings. He saw her face, once, with its blurry, moon-geography.

As the girl hurried, and they were reaching the edge of the park, he felt that he would never succeed in laying his guilt on anyone. When it was imperative. For this girl to listen.

Then she slipped into a square house on the edge of the park, behind some plane trees, beside a shop. She was going to, she did look back. Her flat white face would have listened. But the door consumed it.

Ray Parker returned to that place and hung around the house and the shop, which was a grocery store. Once from a lane at the back he watched the girl washing dishes. She was a plain girl, but she had become necessary to him. When she was drying her hands, and he saw that there was no longer any reason why she should stay at the window, he wondered where he should go next.

In time, through familiarity, and because the people themselves had not sufficient belief in evil to refuse the man admittance, he was let into the house, and would spend the evenings listening to the grocer-father, who liked to talk. When he proposed to the daughter, even confessing to her some of his minor crimes, she gave the matter her earnest consideration, she prayed over it in her room, amongst the religious literature and souvenirs of high school. The weight of the issue oppressed her earnest face, but she decided to accept, even if she were crushed by it. Elsie Tarbutt was that kind of girl. She would have liked to undertake something too big for her, and this was possibly it. To have become a missionary would have been less humiliating, so she chose Ray Parker.

"I shall marry you, Ray," she said, holding up her creamy face as if in sleep.

He had not expected it to be like this, and almost recoiled, but did eventually kiss her.

They lived in the grocer's house, or residence, it was called by many, because he was a man of substance, though unpretentious. The young couple, as they were referred to in innocence, had their own rooms, in which the husband tried to live. The wife sewed in the evening, or read. She read to him from the Gospels. Soon I shall tell her all about myself, he said, and ask for that forgiveness which is given. He would walk with efforts at quietness across the brown carpets, or sit forward in his chair, his hands locked between his open knees, veins prominent in his forehead. Listening, the simple facts of faith were the impossible knots they are. He himself was well knotted.

But Elsie Parker was happy, she believed. Even at that age she was convinced that sorrow is a happiness to be borne. So her thick body was submissive, if not yielding, that was not in the nature of it. She was quickly pregnant, of course, and had a delicate boy, that they called after the father.

Then the rooms in which the parents were living smelled of fresh innocence and became more intolerable to the man. What was he to this child beyond its origin? The horrible joke of responsibility had settled on him. On summer evenings, under the mottled trees, people passed along the street, laughing through silent mouths. Or looked up, and beyond, as if he did not exist, looking at him with blind eyes. Once he ran down, he hurried through the streets, to see a man called Kennedy with whom he had once made a deal, and went on a long ride in a cab that was Kennedy's, to transact some business that was also Kennedy's at a distant house. Ray Parker, the friend who had strung along, was sitting impotently in the car, in the smell of hot felt, waiting for the other man to return. He did not belong there. He could not escape out of his own life. Nobody would take him into theirs.

Least of all Elsie. She prayed for him, though, after she had brushed her hair.

"I would like us to pray together, Ray," she had said once, standing in her long chenille dressing gown.

"No," he said.

He who was not delicate became so.

"You won't let me help you," she said, taking him by the hands.

He blew down his nose. He was angry now that he was unable to help himself.

"You people like to think that the rest of us are wallowing in sin for your own salvation," he said.

But she would not let her faith be hurt. She went away then.

Once, after the child was born, after she had begun to go about again, she had persuaded him to go with her to a meeting. This was held in a hall, of a period of recent ugliness, with much blistered woodwork, and cement pointing loose between the bricks. When they had gone inside the young Parkers sat down on brown benches, or it would be more correct to say that Ray did, for Elsie soon got up, to share her radiance with the students, and young girls, and elderly women, who had come there as witnesses. She was relieved, the husband thought he saw, to speak her secret language with others who had learned, or, more likely, had been born with it. Then the husband became sullen, looking at his toes, shifting his feet audibly against the gritty boards, as if grinding to extinction the stubborn butt of a cigarette. What do these people know, he asked angrily, slouched on the bench, what faith can they have, who have not yet lived? Or the elderly women. He saw through these to their blameless shifts, into their breasts that had never been called upon. He blew down his nose, and sucked at a tooth, that should have been filled, only he had put it off.

All this time the gathering had continued to talk and laugh, until those who were to conduct the mission assembled on the little stage. Elsie, who was among them, smiled at her husband, but remotely, as if she must draw her lashes on such things. And they sang of sin and water. There were prayers too, but they were awkward in that place. Then Ray Parker began to grow truculent. He exalted his lusts. He ferreted out odd acts of violence that he had committed and forgotten about. The whole conception of transferring guilt, which once had seemed desirable, became repulsive when offered as salvation.

Perhaps Elsie Parker had begun to sense this even before she stood up, which she did when her turn came, to sing. She had a sincere, an agreeable, if not outstanding contralto voice, which moved some people. Her husband stood there beating another time with the toe of his shoe, so that his trouser leg quivered. Drained by his detachment, he noticed sickeningly the long green woollen dress that she put on for occasions, and the heavy but plain gold bracelet that she had inherited from a grandmother, an Englishwoman. Her wrists were tense as she sang. What is this Jerusalem? he asked, so solid, it is not possible. But everyone was convinced, everyone but Ray Parker, and now perhaps Elsie. The pinnacles of gold had begun to lean. He could not stop looking at her in amazement, his wife.

It was over in time, after an address by a minister at a little table on which some woman had arranged a glass of full roses.

Ray went out to smoke a cigarette and ease his legs at the crotch. He was blowing smoke at the stars. He smoked several cigarettes, till he could smell the nicotine on his fingers. On his forefinger there was a callus too, which he bit, spitting out the hard, bitter skin. Where he was he did not know, except in some kind of a back yard. Across from him, in the window of a cottage, an old man was taking elaborate precautions to wrap up a roll of notes and hide it at the bottom of a tobacco jar. That old bugger's head, breathed the watcher smokily, would split open like a cob of corn. Then

404

he shivered a bit, for some uneasiness of soul, some suspicion that he too could be easy money.

After he had gone inside and found his wife, who had put an overcoat over her green dress, and was sitting waiting in the almost empty hall, they walked home, where the mother-in-law had dozed off, and the child was crying.

Elsie Parker began to change napkins, to plod up and down, doing the necessary things for their child. She did not often question her husband, but on this occasion said, weakly, he had made her weak by looking at her, "Then you did not like the meeting?"

He was sitting on the edge of the bed, smoking a last cigarette.

"It was not something you could *like* or *dislike*," he said, shifting his bare feet. "I had a bellyful of it, though."

His pajama jacket was open on his chest, which by this time of life had grown hairy.

I shall not look at him, she said. There were several duties to perform. She sat and gave her breast to her child.

She would have liked to be exalted. But I have not received sufficient grace, she said, it is perhaps intended that I should be defeated early by this man. She finished feeding her child and began to fold things away. Her skin was creamy in that light, but it would be said of her later that she had a pasty look.

Elsie Parker frequently took her child to Durilgai, to his grandparents, making herself like this duty. She walked deliberately down that road, down which the buses did not run, holding her baby in a scalloped shawl that she kept very clean. Or later, when he had reached the staggering stage, she would herself stagger, with the lolling child astride her hip, and pause, brushing back the hair from his clear eyes, to look at him, while she got her breath. And later still she would meander, looking sightlessly at the paddocks, while the child who was by then a little boy ran at her side, or wandered, or stopped, and came clattering back to her, to ask the names of insects and plants.

"These are not things that I know. Perhaps Granpa will," she would say, speaking to him and not, and at the same time wondering what it was she did know.

But the boy was not cheated by her ignorance. He was not intensely interested in answers, the things themselves were enough. So he ran on, holding the leaf by its twig, or feather by its quill, and whereas his mother thought mostly of arriving, discovery kept him in a state of endless being.

When they got there the grandmother almost always had just taken a batch of currant cakes from the oven, and would come out with the smell of cake about her, and say, "You got here then."

The mother would begin to tell some details of their journey, precise but colourless, which nobody listened to, but which she threw in because she felt that something was expected of her. And the grandmother was smiling and looking out at the paddocks. And the boy was smiling and panting for breath as he pulled up his socks. On no account would the grandmother have addressed the boy on arrival, or looked directly at him, and she would certainly not have kissed him, because both were reserving themselves for subtler intimacies.

Amy Parker had not attempted to possess this remote child, with the consequence that he had come closer than her own. She was placid with him. She was an old woman, of course. It was easier. Even in her moments of irony, or foreboding that this little boy would eventually do or say some cruel thing, or invest himself with some mystery that would not be for her to solve, her well-being was not disturbed. She walked in the garden, stroking her woollen sleeves.

Sometimes, taking the boy into the house, she would show him things. There is a mysticism of objects, of which some people are initiates, as this old woman and boy.

"Come here," she said, "and I will show you something."

She did not call him by his name, which was his father's. Only strangers called him that.

"What is it?" he asked.

Breathing, she undid a box.

"What is it?" he asked, touching with his finger, his lashes resting on his cheeks.

He is a pale boy, she saw.

Inside the box there were some old brittle flowers, they were camomile flowers, in fact, that she had picked once to make a tea for a stomach ache. There were some pieces of glass too, red, broken glass.

"What is this glass?" he asked.

"That belonged to a boy we picked up in the floods," she said. "One night at Wullunya. We were all there to see the water, and your grandfather was rescuing. I thought we might keep the boy. You know, adopt. But your grandfather

406

was against it. Anyway, the boy went. He was gone in the morning. He did not like it here. And he left that glass."

"What was he doing with the glass?" asked the grandson, who had picked it up and was looking through it, the crimson streaming on his face, except at the edges which were greenish, it was the pallor which the crimson glass could not wholly succeed in drinking up.

"He was looking through it, just like that," said the grandmother.

"You are pale," she said, touching the roots of his hair at the forehead, which were damp.

"I am not," he cried, jerking away the glass. "Or if I am, some people are made pale."

"Of course," she said, with an irony which was especially for the child, and which did not hurt.

"Can I keep the glass?" he said, looking at it.

"What will you do with it?" she asked.

"I shall keep it," he said, shifting awkwardly on his legs, "as a sort of secret thing."

"But I shall know about it," she said.

"That won't matter so much. You are old, anyway."

"We shall have a secret together," she said, with a pleasure that she need not hide, because nobody else was there.

Thinking back, she could not remember having shared a secret with a living soul. Hers were walled up inside her, like lumps of lead.

She took him into the pantry, which opened off the kitchen, and which was one of those rooms that have just grown, more of a passage with shelves, it was all shelves. At one end was a window which let the summer in, after it had been filtered drowsily through slats, or in the winter a thin, a cautious light.

Here the grandmother showed her son, he was her son really, showed the jars, and the tub in which she pickled meat, and a glass contraption with which to catch flies. There were many jars. Kumquats or jewels glittered there. He held his eyes against the glass, staring into the kumquats till he had turned dizzy.

"They are whole," he said, for himself.

"Yes," sighed the old woman, who had grown sick of showing things and would have liked to go and sit down. "You prick them with a darning needle. That lets the sweetness in. Otherwise they would stay bitter. Your mouth would shrivel up. Will you try one?"

"No," he said. "Thank you."

He looked at other things.

Would he be peculiar in any way? she asked. Boys should eat kumquats, the syrup running from the corners of their mouths. Ray the father's lips were red. They shone with eating, sweets, and fat things, he had liked the fat on bacon. But this was a thin, pale boy.

"Can I see inside that tin up there?" he asked.

It was a tin with a pattern on it of little flowers. A present from a grocer, a Christmas box perhaps, she had forgotten. She took it down. In it were some seeds, that could have been the seeds of poppies, that she crunched with her teeth, a few of them, to try, and spat out.

"That is some old rubbish," she said, "that I have forgotten all about."

There were other things that she had forgotten, jars of rancid stuff that the boy had fossicked amongst, alone on other occasions, and said nothing about. He loved his grandmother, beyond question, if quietly. So he had listened to her belch one afternoon, and concealed this knowledge even from himself.

"Can I keep this tin?" he asked.

"If you like," she said, or yawned, because she was sleepy, and often closed her eyes at that hour, not exactly sleeping, because she was not yet really old, she would rest in a chair though, with her eyes closed. "What will you do with a tin like that?" she asked.

"I shall keep my pencils in it. I have fifteen pencils, not including the coloured ones."

"What will you do with so many pencils?" she asked, who had a stump in a drawer, and would use that when necessary.

"Write things," he said.

"What sort of things?" she asked.

But he was picking at the woodwork.

"I will give you a book to write in," she said. "I got it for your father, who did not use it. Then Stan took it, why, I never knew. Oh, to make some lists, he said. Then I found it in a drawer. It was still not written in."

He thanked her. But he was tired of talking.

She too was tired. So they went from the larder with its jars of still fruit. He is a quiet boy, she said, what if he should die, and pale. If she had been on speaking terms with Mrs. O'Dowd she would have feared something the neighbour woman eventually would say. Though it had been all right with Thelma.

The grandmother and the boy were walking through the house. At that age it was still a large house in the child's eyes. Soon the grandmother would sleep, in a chair that fitted itself to her body for that purpose, and he would crawl through the undergrowth, into rooms of vaster importance, and beyond the palpitating green of roof, and rafters that the sap foamed along, was the dome that he could split into a mosaic of tingling blue merely by staring at it.

So Amy Parker sat in the plaited cane chair, and thought, or snoozed. She was speaking to her boy. It is funny we are able to speak together, she said, often it is not possible with people. Under the pepper tree. These beads are bullets, he said. Don't shoot at me, Ray. I am not Ray, he laughed. You are Ray. They are not bullets, they are words. Words are bullets, she said, if you mean them to be, I shot him, over and over again, and he stood up for more. I am shooting you, he laughed with his teeth. Terrible words began to confront her, and in necklaces. Raaaaaay. Shot for shot, laughed the boy, whoever you shot. It is not Stan, she was sweating, Ray love, it is not. And what is your grandfather to you but an old man in the workshop who will go on nailing things rather than come in for his tea? Come on then like a good boy. Bending with her lips, they were foolish.

Amy Parker touched the cane chair. She had woken from a miserable sleep, only of a minute or two, but clammy. She would have liked to see someone that she loved.

But the afternoon was empty.

That boy had gone crawling off. In time, she supposed, I shall not understand him. Some tall man coming up the path would treat her as a joke. Educated men bleach the meaning out of words, there is no colour left.

So she mumbled and wetted her lips.

"What is it, Mother?" asked the daughter-in-law, who had been drying some glasses and putting them away, and relining a shelf of which the paper had got dirty, and doing a few other unnoticeable jobs.

"The boy has gone off somewhere," said Amy Parker. "Is he all right?"

Am I all right? it signified. Afternoon dreams, when they happen, are crueler than those at night. They are intensified by the life that is going on all around, that persecutes the sleeper brutally, because he has been forced to give up.

409

"He is all right, I expect," said Elsie, whose faith did not allow her to anticipate a blow, in spite of the one she had received. "He is a sensible boy really."

The young woman would have liked to add to the physical comfort of her mother-in-law, speculating that in this way they might meet on common ground. She looked at the old woman, to see whether she could arrange her in some way, but realized that this would not be possible.

Because Amy Parker did not like Elsie.

She sat and watched Elsie doing crochet work. She stared at her thick, creamy skin. Elsie would not look up, dedicated as she always was to whatever she was doing, and because there was nothing to guard against, but in innocence. Her glossy eyebrows were never raised to question, but in innocence.

Once her face broke up. She laughed and blushed. Statement, not narration, was her forte, though now, it seemed, there was something that she had to tell.

"I used to know a girl who was always doing crochet work. She would drop stitches and begin to count, but she would forget her count. So she never got anywhere. But she was always starting, all sorts of things, a quilt once, and babies' bonnets, she was making things for her nieces. Oh, once I think she did finish a piece of work. It was a doily, and then her mother helped her. Her name was Ethel Bonnington."

It was boring.

Ah dear, said Amy Parker, I cannot follow this.

Grey grass stood in the paddocks at that time of year, or lay down. Most days there was a wind. Birds floated in the air with long, slow calls, almost totally arrested, as the two women sat in the prison of each other's company.

Ah dear, Amy Parker said, once I would have burst.

But Elsie persisted, on visits of whole days, or week-ends, or she would come for long weeks. With the boy, of course. She would work too. She would wring out sheets. Once she teased a kapok mattress, it transpired she knew how. And she loved her mother-in-law, she had begun and would not end.

Then Amy Parker rose up, she was compelled, to see whether she could leave her mark on the board of Elsie's face.

They were on the veranda, as many times before. Elsie was doing crochet work.

"That girl Ethel, that you were telling me of," Amy Parker said, "was she a relative?"

"Oh, Ethel," Elsie laughed and blushed. "No."

"She seems to have been a stupid sort of girl."

"Poor Ethel," said Elsie, who had nothing against her. "She was clever at school. She passed exams and things. She had a head for facts. But life, of course, is not facts. So Ethel got confused. She took to crochet work. But she was good to her mother."

"Fancy, crochet. If it had been knitting."

"I like crochet. It is soothing." Elsie blushed.

"It is a jiggery sort of work," Amy Parker said.

Elsie breathed.

"I don't know that I particularly want to be soothed," said Amy Parker. "Where is Ray now, Elsie?"

"He has his job," Elsie said.

"Has Ray left you?" asked Amy Parker.

"I don't know," said Elsie, for whom the pattern had become complicated, of little double roses, in shiny beige silk, that she had chosen. "He has been back."

Then Amy Parker began to pity Elsie. Her skin was terribly pitiable, thick and wholesome, with that way of flushing upward from the neck. In pity, the older woman's own failure began to seem less a failure, almost a success. She began to like Elsie.

"You will not hang on to Ray," said Amy Parker.

Who had gone up to Glastonbury on some such night, of inkiness and brass, to put him in that same box in which she would have kept, for safety's sake, all human love.

"But I did not intend to *hang on* to Ray," Elsie said. "Nor on to anyone."

Whatever she did not know, she knew this.

But the older woman looked at her.

The sky which had formed above the two women in clots of cloud and veins of brass hung lower, it was on their heads. To the old woman it was unpleasant, filled with personal threats. But the young one was unmoved, or too impersonally moved to fear. In her impersonality she could have been split right open. Wind blew at her hair, revealing the secret places of her temples. For a moment her face was less flat.

Looking at, or into, Elsie, if only for the second of lightning, Amy Parker knew she had begun to love her. God save us, she said, Elsie is perhaps strong.

Then the storm was breaking on the two women. Their chairs were grating. They laughed, and recovered themselves, and chased the ball of silk that threatened to escape them,

411

and were bent by the wind into unusual, supple shapes. Their eyes were shining with the moisture of the storm and green lightning.

Till suddenly the grandmother remembered and cried, "Where is the boy? Not out in this!"

But the mother was still protected by her mood.

"He will have got in somewhere," she said, soothing, smoothing her hair.

"And Stan."

The old woman began to remember her husband, whom she had forgotten. She forgot him now for whole days.

The two women walked mechanically through the shaking house, to find whatever was intended for them to find.

"We just made it," said Stan Parker, who was standing at the screen door at the back, the gauze was still quivering, as he wiped the water from his leather face.

The boy had pressed his on the window till his nose was white, and he looked out through water.

"Look," he called excitedly, turning back into the room. "Life under water would look like this. To a fish. Come and do it. You will see."

But no one would share his moment of belief, perhaps had not even heard his words. So revelations are never conveyed with brilliance as revealed. The boy knew, however.

"I am not wet," he protested, throwing off his grandmother, who began to feel her husband with less anxiety, but to establish some authority.

"You are both soaked," she said. "To my hands, anyway." And was angry. It was her right.

"It is one of those showers," said Stan Parker. "A little bit of wet never did no one any harm."

And began to fray out tobacco, with which to roll a cigarette.

"Who will pay the price?" the angry woman asked.

She was impotent, but above all she resented his leatheriness.

"You will," laughed Stan Parker, licking the thin paper.

The boy, who was content now, in the dry, tobacco-scented room, came and stood beside his grandfather. He liked to watch minute operations. He liked the smell of the little rubber bag in which the old man carried tobacco.

"Let me light it?" he asked when the thin and tinkling thing was rolled.

"It is all very well," said Amy Parker, whose eyes were feverish with what she had suffered, with what she still had to suffer for Stan.

Once she had thought of taking a knife, not against her husband, which would have been less painful, but against herself, and there where the breasts parted, plunging it in. What would it have met, she wondered, at slow, sick leisure, and what words would he have found as they watched the drops drop, big remorseful drops, onto the floor?

"Go on, Granpa," said Elsie, to whom none of this was fatal, "go and take your clothes off."

The boy was watching the paper catch alight. It flared at first. Then settled down.

Presently the old man went to change.

Other clothes changed Stan Parker less than they do most people. Different mysteries emanated from his wife Amy with different clothes. But the husband was more honest, which also made him irritating. At this age, anyway, he could see an object as it was, and interpret a gesture as it was meant. His life was no less wonderful for this baldness. If his wife were to die, he said, he would live in a room with bed and chair, he could keep his possessions in a couple of packing cases and hanging from hooks on the walls. But his wife was not dead, and there seemed no likelihood that she would die, he was glad enough to admit. He did love his wife, though she would make him nearly crack his jaws from clenching them.

They had been together a lifetime, in which certain simple habits had formed. They preferred boiled meat because it was easier on the stomach. She expected to wake in the night and hear him groping through the darkness, he would get up round about one, and go to make water, then they would drift, and fall deeper into their last sleep.

The night of the storm or shower, when we had got wet, Stan Parker had never seen more clearly. After he had carved the beef he looked at his wife where her hair had thinned at the parting; she would not look up yet, nor speak, since her scene. He looked at his grandson, who was gathering crumbs on the moistened tips of his fingers and licking them off with cat's tongue. His mother was there ready to protect somebody.

Then the old man dropped the carving knife. It stunned.

"Ach," complained his wife, holding her heart.

Things were terribly distinct under the electric light.

413

Elsie had begun to tell one of those stories about somebody she knew.

But the brilliance of the old man's light defied all else. All began to float presently in his world of light. He recollected some bookshelves he was making, he had developed a passion for carpentry in recent years, and could now see with peculiar distinctness the grain of the particular wood on which he was working, and the little nick near a dovetail which had been worrying him because of the blemish it would leave. Otherwise the simplicity and rightness of his work was greatly satisfying.

After he had sat contemplating this object for some time, and smiling out of his rather leathery, sympathetic cheeks, he said surprisingly, "I think I will turn in now, have an early night."

"There," said Amy Parker when he had gone. "He has got a chill."

She had known it, had been herself feverish all along. Of whatever tragedy that might follow she would be the centre.

She listened to her husband in the night, and touched him once or twice. Whether he was asleep or spiting her she could not tell.

So she slept. She was sleeping when her husband woke and lay rigid in the bed, looking at the darkness. In his fever he could not have been cleaner swept. All that he had lived, all that he had seen, had the extreme simplicity of goodness. Any acts that he relived in that ample darkness of the room were performed with the genuine honesty of freshly planed wood. Yet his rigid face was not convinced. It was turning and grating on the pillow. His dry mouth would have asked questions, not of his wife, of course, because she would not have known, but of some secret source of knowledge that he had failed to discover yet. So the clear, feverish light in which he lay, and thought, and saw things, began to blur. He would have liked to read something printed in large letters. But in the absence of signs he was rubbing his cheek on the pillow and touching his joints. He was tired by now, and at times even in pain. Short pains. At times he spoke to express his pain and distress. Oh God, oh God, he was saying from time to time, but very quietly and dustily, like sawdust.

Once the man saw beneath the skin of his eyelids that they were standing in the workshop again, amongst the shavings, which curled round their ankles. It was the boy who was with him, of course, because at this time of his life it was his grandson who filled his thoughts, though he would never have admitted. Their relationship was a marvellous one, almost entirely confined to the workshop. Outside the workshop they did not exist for each other, it appeared, anyway they scarcely spoke. But in the workshop each conversation that they had was in the nature of a confession.

"See," said the old man, laying open the surface of the wood with a sweep of his daring plane, "it is like a map. There are the mountains. That is a mountain peak. The round one. That is the highest."

"Yes," said the boy. "And the rivers, and the bays."

"When I was a boy," said the grandfather, "I would sometimes draw maps and shade in the bays with a blue pencil. The Gulf of Mexico, that was a good big one."

"I can't draw much," said the boy.

"What do you reckon you'll do?"

"I shall write a poem," said the boy.

"What do you know about poems? Have you read any?"

"No," said the boy, chewing the inside of his cheek. "I know, though."

The boy was stretching his arms in the sleepy afternoon till they were embracing air. His eyes were opening.

"Don't you ever know, Granpa, about things, because you just know?"

Now that the old man was locked in the prison of the bed he could not answer. His throat was that dry. In his feverishness, his childishness, there was something that he still had to do, know. So he thrust his head back into the pillow, tilting the darkness, in hopes that revelation would reward conviction.

It was the light that shone, though.

It is time, Stan, his wife's thick eyelids said.

"I feel terrible crook, Amy," said the old man. "You will have to get Jack Finlayson to give a hand with the cows."

After that Stan Parker was sick for some time. He had a pleurisy. They nursed him through, though. Jack Finlayson came, who was agreeable to help, he was a decent sort, who had made a mess of his own affairs, and his wife Merle came and did odd jobs, and was yarning in the doorway over cups of milky tea. Stan Parker sensed all this, all that people were doing. He let them. He was in no hurry, but got up when

415

they told him, with assistance at the armpits, and was soon walking again in his large clothes.

He had gone one step farther into himself, however. During his convalescence he would look out at people from the verge of his face, and they mostly preferred to switch over and talk to his wife. He was not yet quite right, of course. He had a habit of looking at people as if there were something standing behind them, and they did not like that, because they could not very well turn round to make sure.

But Stan Parker was just surprised at the newness of what he saw.

Chapter 21

URING the last few years a number of other homes had
been built down the road at Durilgai in which Parkers
had always lived. There were the original few weatherboard
homes, of which the landscape had taken possession, and
which had been squeezed back from the road, it seemed, by
other developments. The wooden homes stood, each in its
smother of trees, like oases in a desert of progress. They
were in process of being forgotten, of falling down, and
would eventually be swept up with the bones of those who
had lingered in them, and who were of no importance anyway, either no-hopers or old. If the souls of these old cottages disturbed, any uneasiness can almost be excluded from
the brick villas simply by closing windows and doors and turning on the radio. The brick homes were in possession all
right. Deep purple, clinker blue, ox blood, and public lavatory. Here the rites of domesticity were practised, it had been
forgotten why, but with passionate, regular orthodoxy, and
once a sacrifice was offered up, by electrocution, by vacuum
cleaner, on a hot morning when the lantana hedges were
smelling of cat.

There were the old inconsiderable wooden houses, there
were the waterproof brick ones. There was also another kind,
which caused resentment, and against which it was hoped the
Council would revise its policy. There were the homes in
fibro-cement. These were to be found in outcrops, of a different stratum. It was in their favour, of course, that they could
last only a little while. But for how long? In the meantime
human beings went through the motions of living in them.
Young couples locked their doors and left their homes as if
they were not open. A child had kicked a hole in one, for fun.
And at night the fibro homes reverberated, changed their

shape under the stress of love or strife, changed and returned, standing brittle in the moonlight, soluble in dreams.

All of this which was going on all round them affected and did not affect Parkers. It did not affect them in that they had reached an age where all that was happening visibly was hardly credible. Past events in recollection will splinter brick and distribute the fragments. What is still to happen must flow with a parallel, not with the same stream. Where it did affect these old people more credibly was that their property had been subdivided and most of it sold up.

This began to happen not long after Mr. Parker had his illness. Implacable cows stood in the mellow evenings, or in the mornings, stood rubbing their necks against the grey posts. The man, who continued to go down as usual, but tauter than before, sometimes with a tingling in his skin that made him smile unexpectedly, and his wife, who was troubled by her leg, besides having grown rather big behind, and old, and resentful, clung to the cows as a motive of existence, and dared not substitute another. Like many old people who have been wound up, they could not regulate themselves, they were afraid of breaking down. So they continued to plod. It was hand milking too. Mr. Parker would not have the machines because, he said, he knew they were no good on the teats. Younger men sniggered at old Parker, who had, in any case, only a handful of cows in what had become practically a suburb. It was so unimportant to most people that they did not bother to think about it. But it was obvious that something would have to be done.

Then Mrs. Forsdyke, the daughter, drove down in her own car, they had two. Most people did not know Mrs. Forsdyke, or had known and forgotten that this was Thelly Parker. Those who might have remembered, she did not encourage, narrowing her eyes until the skin almost obscured her conscience. Those who had never known, she was above, so slid past in her smooth black car, which quickly left behind all that was in any way mediocre or in bad taste.

The father was waiting for his daughter to come. His eyelids and his wrists had gone a bit scaly, but his teeth were still strong and good. He smiled at her.

"What is it all about then, Thel?"

Because Mrs. Forsdyke had suggested in a note that there was something she *wished* to talk about. She favoured that verb, which was discreet but firm.

"Oh," she laughed, looking at him, enjoying this distant

418

relationship with a simple old man, at the same time, secretly, her father, "it is a little plan. Which I hope will appeal to you. Not because it is mine, or that I want to force anything, but it is so reasonable. Dudley agrees."

Mrs. Forsdyke was one of those women who enlist their husbands when they expect to meet resistance.

"You are looking a little tired, dear," she said, getting from her car and approaching her father.

She kissed him too. Cultivating exhaustion herself, she frequently wished it onto other people. But her father's skin was alive, she noticed, and she flushed, as much as her blood was capable of. She was a frail woman, but gristly, carrying a crocodile bag.

"I am not more tired than I ever was," said the old man.

"No, Dad," said the daughter, picking snails off a bush and crushing them with her shoe, "if you are not tired, then you are not."

She winced for the snails, but did glance back in curiosity.

"You love those cows too much ever to be tired," Mrs. Forsdyke said.

"There is no question of loving the cows," said the old man. "The cows are all right. But I am not married to them, as they say."

"I had always thought," said his daughter, "that a man was indisolubly married to his cows."

The old man made a noise.

"But if he is not," said Thelma Forsdyke, "then it is easy."

"How, easy?"

"To send them off in one of those things. What is it? A float. And stay in bed later the next morning, to see whether you like it, and then when you do, stay in bed late the following morning. Until you are used to doing nothing. Oh, when I say *nothing*, I mean you can have a hobby. There is this carpentry you have taken up. It must be great fun. Fresh wood does smell so pleasant. And you have never been anywhere. Well, you can go. With poor Mother. You can come to us sometimes on a Sunday. Normally we are very quiet. On Sundays everybody is at home. With their families. Wouldn't you like that."

Stan Parker did not say whether he would like. He would, certainly, have liked to sit a long time and watch the passage of a snail which had survived the foot. He would sit, and in his own time retrace his own path, thin and silver, through the mists. But he did not speak.

419

Old people are easily hurt, considered Thelma Forsdyke with impatience. If it had been a little child, of course she did not have one, she could have planted in it her own mind, and watched it grow, like the mango tree from sand. Forgetful of her own childhood since she had ceased to live, she had not failed to evolve theories. This old child might be difficult, though.

In fact, he was not. He would think, he was already thinking, about what his daughter had said. He could give up, if not for those reasons, to those ends. Thelma is silly, he said, I am not that imbecile, but she has got something. He could give up as she suggested, more even, land even, even his life, simply because it was not his to keep. It had become blindingly obvious.

He was looking pale, for him.

"You will see," said Thelma, patting his hand, "how much better you will feel for the rest."

Because he did not resist, then or later, on that passive morning, she went away filled with pity and complacency, pity because the poor old fellow was growing senile, and complacency as the mentor of simple people's lives. She drove off joyfully, mistaking instrumentality for power.

After she had gone Stan Parker walked about his property, slowly, and with all the appearance of aimlessness, which is the impression that spiritual activity frequently gives, while all the time this communion of soul and scene was taking place, the landscape moving in on him with increased passion and intensity, trees surrounding him, clouds flocking above him with tenderness such as he had never experienced. He could have touched the clouds. Now, when he should have been detached, he was nervous, whipping his trouser leg with a little stick. For this scene which was his, and which was not, was too poignant. So he stooped to watch some ants dragging a butterfly's wing through a desert of stones. A convinced activity of tingling ants. Then suddenly he twitched the wing away. He tossed it into the sunlight, where it fluttered and shimmered, rightly restored to air, but while it was still floating and falling he went away, shaken by the ruthlessness of divine logic.

And they began soon after this to sell off Parkers' property by lots. It was easily accomplished, because it was desirable land, in a district that was being opened up. The old man did not take a direct hand in the business transactions, because his son-in-law was there, and, more actively, his daughter. He let other people work the necessary but insignificant machinery of this phase. It pleased those concerned, his respect and docility emphasizing their superior gifts, and soon they had developed a sentimental attitude towards what might otherwise have been his mediocrity. The poor old man, they smiled, has no business sense. So they went out of their way to see that he was not taken down by anyone, not even by themselves.

When the land was sold Parkers did have three or four acres left. They had the gully at the back and one paddock at the side. They had a house cow with asymmetrical horns, and Mr. Parker grew a few cabbages in winter, between the rows of which his wife strolled, in an old cardigan, on warm days, and stooped to pull a blade of grass that had come up out of place.

One day as Amy Parker was walking between the cabbages, as was her custom now, she was trying to remember something. Some restlessness had begun to possess her, of association. Then it was her youth that began to come back in the world of cabbages. She heard the dray come up with the mound of blue cabbages, and the snap of straps in the frost, as putting her shoulders through the window she spoke to her husband. She was remembering all mornings. And the little ears of cabbage seedlings that he stuck into the earth, into the holes that he had made with a shovel handle. She remembered the arms of her husband as they worked in the sunlight, the little hairs on the forearms and the veins at the wrists. It seemed to her suddenly as if she would not see him again.

So she hurried along the rows of cabbages, they were big, green, bursting ones, unlike those evanescent plants that shimmer in the field of memory, she hurried to be with her husband, who was never far from her, they could not have escaped from each other had they wished.

"Why don't we sell some of these cabbages?" she asked irritably when she had come to where he was digging a few potatoes for their tea. "There are more than we can use. We shall be sick of blessed cabbage."

"It will not be worth the trouble," said Stan Parker. "For a few bob. And the business of carting them to market."

"Then what are we to do with them?" she asked, kicking one of these bright and rubbery vegetables.

She was standing lost amongst the cabbages, and intended perhaps that he should become lost too.

"We shall eat some," he said, looking down, because she had at least deterred him. "And give some. The cow could eat a fair few. We shall think of other ways," he said.

Then they were standing there, and what had been bright jewels in the field of past and present were ludicrous lumps of cynical rubber.

"You get worked up over nothing," he said tautly.

To explain it that way.

"I like to know the reason for things," she said, looking at and unravelling a frayed bit of the old cardigan that she wore.

But he could not explain their continued existence in that same plot of cabbages, and magpies came over, and jolly peewits, and little anonymous birds, descending and picking in the moist earth, as if the man and woman had not been there.

Other people, Thelma, for instance, say that when you are at a loss you must do things, you must take up carpentry, or knit a jumper, or go on a trip somewhere. Amy Parker, who was ignorant, did not in herself believe that there is any exit from confusion, except by living it out, though she did once try the other, making a joke of it, laughing at themselves, while hoping, she said, "Why don't we go somewhere for once? Go to the city at least, I mean on a proper visit, before we die. Do something, I mean. Even if we are disappointed we shall know."

Her husband wondered what it would cost, probably a good deal. Though he was not mean. He was cautious. And the wife laughed, ashamed that she had suggested such foolishness, and was glad that they would not go. Many horrors were visualized. Even a day's journey made her constipated. They were upset by meat that was not boiled. They ate junket from the milk of their own cow. So they would not go.

Then quite suddenly they were going to the city. It was decided one evening. It was intended that they should spend a week, in a reasonable hotel, and that Jack Finlayson should come in to milk the cow and throw a bit of pollard to the fowls. Stan Parker's hands were shaking with this decision. His wife was red. She had grown rather full-blooded, and now the fine perspiration was at her temples and above her mouth.

"I will go to the sea," she said, laughing greedily. "And sit beneath those pine trees and watch the water coming in."

"What good will that do you?" asked the husband, spilling the tobacco he was manipulating.

"You would not know," she said, as if she did.

Because she had never succeeded in loving him in full measure, there were times when she must hurt. Only he was no longer hurt.

Anyway, the two old people did go. They spent a week in a modest hotel; they could have afforded better but were afraid that people might look at their clothes. So they chose one in which the linoleum was a bit worn. They apologized to the young lady in depositing their key. It was not their words exactly, it was their attitudes.

But they were pleased.

They were pleased they had survived, and were surviving. The decent couple walking in the streets did not go down before those anonymous waves. They discovered that they were strong. Their solitary lives had perhaps built them buttresses.

Once the couple walking in the street at night listened to a radio, of which the red-gold voice was singing of sunsets and renunciation.

"What is she singing about, Stan?" Amy Parker asked.

"I don't know," he said. "It is all Chinese to me."

Then they laughed. They were superior. A mystery is no mystery that the mind refuses, it is better than unravelled. So they went on.

The city was never stationary for long, nor they, it was like dreams, only less personal. The glass caves into which the old people looked, and especially in the purple night, were opening for others. It was the dream of someone else's dream that they were dreaming. When shall we be put down again? their faces asked. Their own dreams in monochrome, although at times suffocating by hate or strangling with love, did exact less.

One night Stan said they would go to a play.

"It is the play of *Hamlet*," he said. "It is by Shakespeare."

"Oh," said his wife, to whom such audacity was dubious.

It also seemed to cast some light upon her hidden husband. It is this sort of thing in Stan that I do not like, she said, I do not like secrets. Because although he would take her to his play she could not feel that she would share it.

Anyway, they went. Pausing for breath, they climbed high up, to where they would be less noticeable, and from their they looked down, through knobs and angels, into the golden bowl that was already steaming with anticipation. All scents and dust, all laughter and hot air, rose from the depths of the bowl to bemuse the old woman at its rim. She could not see well, which made it more aggravating, or else mystical. She could see a naked woman, was it? with a bunch of violets in her breasts. Grey mists rose from the woman's flesh, before reverting to the material. They were moored. As time passed and music began to come out of the little slot in which the musicians sat, there was a great deal that had grown too solid to soar. The seats were hard too. There was a smell of hot carmels and disinfectant.

"Do the women dress like that and feel clothed?" Amy Parker asked.

"If they do not feel clothed, that was more than likely their intention," her husband said. "But it is going to begin now."

The curtain was on fire, and when it had burned up, there was his boyhood, only the words had taken on a form, and were walking and running, in silk stockings. His mother was there, with a ring upon her arthritis, pointing an explanation. But the play eluded explanations, then and now. It went on its own way, like life, or dreams. He could smell the smell of damp in that old book with the brown patches, from some deluge that she had told him about but he had forgotten. He remembered Horatio, a friend. A friend of similar understanding and manliness, older than himself, was what he had wished for, but he had gone through childhood almost friendless, walking through long grass and lying along the branches of trees, waiting to grow older.

He did, and was also faced with ghostliness at some stages, though no one had ever caught him out. They had not seen him moving his lips exactly. Speaking to the green Very light. For one instance. Which passed across the sky as slowly and as fatefully as the more corporeal ghost for Horatio and his friends. And quietly. That was what made men shout, if they were the shouting kind, the Horatios, good men he had known later and who were killed in battle, shouting at their own clamminess.

"Fancy, a ghost. That is a bit farfetched," Amy Parker said.

She laughed, but liked it.

The only ghost she had seen was her conscience in mirrors. It had a grey face, and was quickly got rid of, by not looking at it. But this green ghost, in a crown. Fancy being actors. It is not men's work, it is all talking and talking. And life is not talking, it is living. Then this old woman, who was gripping the brass rail across which she hung, wondered what she had lived. She sat upon a chair on the veranda and listened to the fuchsia canes. She would have liked to see, to think of, there and then, some solid instance of living. That man. Leo. But fading. It was the theatre rising up around her, and to which she was unaccustomed. It was the words that meant nothing.

"I have never heard so much talk," she said irritably, almost abusively.

He hushed her, and she turned her head away.

Was this Hamlet, he asked, coming and going throughout the play, a white, a rather thin man in black? That we have been waiting for. Is this our Hamlet? With poor knees. The words that he had read, and was remembering, tried to convince the old man. Once he had known an old horse called Hamlet, a bay, no, an old brown gelding, a light draught, that belonged to an old cove, Furneval was it, or Furness? who would drive into the village for groceries, flicking at the flies on Hamlet with the whip. That was one Hamlet. Or standing in the feed shed, in that trench coat that he had hung on to after the war, for years, till it became green, the buttons had dropped off, and it was separated from its origin, but that morning, or in fact many mornings, as he mixed the good bran and chaff, the real Hamlet floated towards an explanation, or was it fresh bewilderment? These grey mornings the air is all cobwebs, the sun rising through the greater nets of clouds, the white seeds of weeds falling and clinging. Hamlet is confused, after the bombardment, to witness acts of thistledown.

As the old man in the gallery continued to be bombarded by words he almost lost consciousness, but this was also refreshing. Nothing, after all, is so complicated as this play, he said. He raised his head from where it was leaning on the brass. He would hold fast to this talisman of simplicity. But we too are simple people, he said in horror, Amy is simple, I am simple, and do not know myself. So that he was swallowed again by the surf of words, and was wandering about the stage, looking into the eyes of the actors.

Because that was what they were. Hamlet was an actor. Women read about him in the papers and thought about him in their beds. They shivered when the draught swirled out from beneath the curtain and settled on their naked shoulders. Some had stuck flowers in the clefts of their bosoms. But it was Stan Parker talking to the gentle girl in riddles, which were no different from what is spoken. If he could remember what he had said as they stood at the top of the stairs, but he could not remember one word. The poetry of the burning house was not of words. He could remember, rather, how her red hair burned, how their singed hair had curled together, each head grappling the other with hooks. But never speaking. People do not speak in an exchange of souls.

"Who is mad then?" asked Amy Parker.

But he hushed her.

It is not me, she said. *Buzz, buzz!* It is a lot of nonsense. Though it makes sense at times.

Oh dear, she said. She began to look along the road, along which she had been looking all her life, and there in the distance a woman rode, violets in her breast. Poetry is not words. It is the jingling of the spurs, or of chains, the curb, it could be, that she wore, which some say is cruel. This woman will not look down. She has found the distance. So other cruel poetry rode out of the past into the violet sky. I was too humble then, said the old woman, I did not know a thing, I could have been loved in any disguise.

Then Amy Parker, who was looking down from the circle, holding the rail of memory, began to be certain it was Madeleine. It was the violets that Madeleine had never worn, but should have, in the nest of leaves. So the old woman was peering through the darkness, to where the shoulders shone, and Madeleine put up her hand, to smooth a hair, or brush the wing of boredom from out of her head, at a play.

When the lights went up for the interval, there was the woman made of soap.

"I could swear that that woman with the violets is Madeleine," said Amy Parker, leaning down.

"What Madeleine?" asked her husband.

"That was to marry Tom Armstrong. That you rescued from the burning house."

The old woman could have bent down and gathered the violets, so fresh was her memory, and dewy.

Then her husband looked at her slowly and said with the brutality of husbands, "But Madeleine is by this time an old woman. She would be older than you, Amy. And you are old."

And stupid, he saw. He could see this without unkindness. It is possible to love stupid old women, and hateful ones.

"That may be," she said. "Yes. I did not think."

Old women who have been subtle, at times terribly subtle, are stupider when they begin to be, as if their subtlety has worn them out.

Amy Parker was, in fact, tired. Slowly she ate a chocolate, and let that sweet comfort drift over her in the absence of others. Madeleine would probably be dead. It was unimportant anyway.

But she began to feel sad, or chocolatey. Chocolate has its own melancholy, at a height, in darkness. Because it was dark again by now. The perverse gallery of memory in which the old woman had been shoved to enjoy herself rustled with breathing and paper, as other people let their own puppets dance. Those in the gold frame of the stage were less convincing, because they were repeating the words of the book. And books are unpardonable. You cannot go by what is written.

So Amy Parker, who had developed a little nodding motion as she watched from high darkness, overflowed from those words or precepts. Just as she was overflowing from her bosom. She walked all satiny then, and would have been caught at by rosemary, or any other sharp plant in the garden, while talking with Hamlet. Hers was red, though. It was strange to think of this white-faced Hamlet the son of that queen, a big woman, stout even, the satin was conveying. Even queens are saddled and bewildered. Does Hamlet hate his mother? Ah Ray, Ray, she said, give me your mouth once, so that I can tell by kissing. But that room, the old kitchen, was as empty as a stage, as she remembered, as empty of true answers as Hamlet, he had gone off into the night, which was filled with lightning and the leaves of trees.

"Huh," she said, she had a piece of hard filling, caramel or something, stuck to her teeth. "These are funny-looking people now. What are they dressed up like that for?"

"They are the players," said Stan Parker, who was again reading the play, and who had always been puzzled himself by this bit. "They are going to act a play of the queen's unfaithfulness to Hamlet's father. The queen that married this present king, there."

"Ttttt," Amy Parker sucked her teeth.

The players were soon acting with stiff precision.

Stan Parker remembered how that little play, in which he himself had been poisoned, had hurt. Yet he was not hurt now. Seeing the actor sneak out and drive off in his blue car. Seeing the big arse of that commercial traveller push past the

427

door into the car. Any pain will wear out. The old man began to rub the skin of his old hands in the darkness. His emptiness surprised him. Somewhere he had read: an empty vessel. That night when he had lain vomiting in the street, when he had stood in the street and spat out at God, everything, he had emptied. For many years his light and agreeable but empty life would have pleased, if it had not been that some pea of memory was rattling about inside. It began to irritate him now. Where is this play getting to? he asked, rubbing his old hands, which would remain carapaceous although he had given up work.

"That is certainly a funny way to go on," said Amy Parker.

"What, to commit adultery?"

"No," she mumbled. She added after a bit, "To pour poison in the man's ear."

She could not bear glycerine, or hot oil, that they put sometimes for earache from a roaring spoon. She shuddered. The thoughts flowing through the passages of her skull.

It was the afternoons that had poisoned her. She could have knocked her head against the wall, waiting. That man, that bugger. And acting as if you did not want it. And acting.

She stirred for the closeness of her husband in the dark.

Well, you got over it. You did not want it. There is a time when you do not want anything. She thought. Or in a panic, it was coming over her in a draught of light and noise from the lit stage, a time when you want everything and do not know what this is. I want Stan, I want Ray, said the queen, and I am not sure that I have had anything, that I know enough to have.

There was a great rumpus on the stage as the queen and her shadows fled into darkness, away from the little stiff play. She was defeated, it appeared, by fear.

The old woman in the gallery sat on, very unhappy. She was trying to recapture her little boy. She was sitting on the iron bed, her knee touching that of her young husband.

But the play went on, the big play of *Hamlet*, madness and all.

Felia was less touching, because less personal. She does not frighten me like Bub did once, because I am used to things. While still learning. I shall learn about Stan perhaps in time. But all this madness. This play is a lot of nonsense. Loonies speak their own language, like educated people.

Still, death and burial, you have got to face it, are plain

and sane enough. They are burying her. The earth is falling down.

The great accents of doom were filling the theatre, so that people were forgetting their cramp, and the creases in their clothes, and the intolerable pressure of poetry. The end was near. All were holding daggers to their hearts, or to their violets, whichever was the case.

The lithe actors were soon slashing and pricking at each other with swords and words. Hamlet himself, who had played the Second Ghost, the ghost of memory, until now, leaped radiantly into the presence of death, which is also the present, all else has been past and future, stories and anticipation, by comparison. At one moment the actors are silent, except for puffing or clashing, when words of respect fail them. There is a lamp shining in the wet shirt of the arisen Hamlet.

Many of those people who were watching from the darkness were sweating too, because the end of Hamlet is too complicated to follow, unless lived. Stan Parker, though, the old man in the gallery, was quite cold and stony as the dead piled up. After wandering about the stage over many acres of spilled words, exchanging breaths with the actors, and experiencing similar visions all the evening, he had withdrawn to a distance at the end of the play. There he sat. A grey light prevailed, by chance or intention, similar to that which is seen in bedrooms at morning. This is the light in which a man becomes aware that he will die.

Then I am going to die, he said. It did not seem possible.

After the dead bodies had got up from the ground, and bowed as though they had been responsible for their own levitation, and the red curtain had come down, Stan Parker continued to sit and consider himself.

"Where is your coat, dear? You have not lost it?" asked his wife, who felt compelled to make some contribution to life.

"It is under the seat, I suppose. Where I put it," said the old man.

"Ah," she said, "it is all dust. Look! And creases. Your good coat!"

Then I am to die, he said. But because this was still too immense to grasp he got up, like an actor off the stage, and asked, "Did you like it?"

"I would like a good cup of tea, but don't expect we shall get that," Amy Parker said. "And your coat a ruin."

She was forever brushing and patting. To restore something. But he let her.

And she was glad he did not ask her again as they wound down by a staircase to the ground, because there were things that she had seen and heard which disturbed her. What they had said about the queen. Why, her own flesh was naked. There were the things also that she did not understand but was sensing darkly in a remembered wood of words.

So the play was over, and they went back not long afterwards to their own place.

Their return was such a return to habit that Stan Parker was soon able to reject his presentiment of death. Not deliberately. Rather, the incident slipped from him. Habit supersedes thought, or extracts the sting from it. He went about smiling more often than not on those jobs which were necessary, or which he made in order to do, and although that smile was somewhat abstracted, everybody read it as a sign of contentment and amiability. He had acquired a reputation for being a good-natured old cove, and who is a neighbour to inquire beyond the mechanics of the face into the states of soul?

The old man was evidently very tranquil, though. He had taken up netting, and was making some nets to assist a pair of ferrets he had bought. Soon he was going about, down the gully at the back of the house, and round such country as was not yet built over, carrying his ferrets in a little box in the centre of his back, carrying also an old and rather heavy gun, and followed by a dusty black dog that had the canker in one ear.

That evening which Stan Parker would continue to remember for the incident that occurred was one of the still evenings of winter, when wind had dropped, yet a cold stream of air is flowing, like water almost, it is palpable, down the creek's dry course. Twigs are snapping, and a cough is blatant under the sky of two metals, of lead and copper, beneath which the old man is walking with the old dog. It is possible to believe that one is alone in this world. The stiff, needly leaves of the bushes exude no sap of kindness. But one does not ask for kindness. Rocks and silence are sufficient in themselves.

Then the old man who was walking along stubbornly on slippery feet slipped suddenly. He was an old scarecrow with wooden arms and a gun waving at the end of one of them, and the ridiculous little box of ferrets with its airholes bumping and bouncing on his shoulderblades. As the sky tilted he pulled the trigger of the gun. It all happened so quickly that it was searingly slow on his mind. The comet was still soaring slowly past him, hot and cold, material and fearful, as he lay on the ground, and realized he had just failed to shoot himself. The black dog was sniffing round and making sneezing noises.

Then the old man got up and walked on, with the safety-catch fixed. He was tough, of course. He had worked hard and could stand a bit of knocking about. But he walked brittly now, although erect. His eyes were smarting. Under them were red rims, like those which can be seen under the eyes of some old dogs.

The black dog which was running and limping ahead of his master began to whine at the mouth of a burrow.

"Very well then," sighed the old man in agreement.

He began to walk round, looking on the ground, ostensibly to find other entrances to the same burrow over which to peg the nets. But he was searching rather too aimlessly. After a bit the old man sat on a lump of anthill. He just sat. While the black dog was swinging his tail and whining. The ferrets too were turning and rattling in the suspended darkness of their habitual box.

Soon enough, thought the old man.

He was sitting in the meantime. And ants came out across the ground.

"Oh God, oh God," said Stan Parker.

He was suspended.

Then his agreeable life, which had been empty for many years, began to fill. It is not natural that emptiness shall prevail, it will fill eventually, whether with water, or children, or dust, or spirit. So the old man sat gulping in. His mouth was dry and caked, that had also vomited out his life that night, he remembered, in the street. He was thinking about it intolerably.

What is intended of me and for me? he wondered. I am ignorant.

He was not answered, though.

After a while the old man called to the old dog, that had continued to sit in front of the burrow, pointing his grey muzzle, and shaking his cankered ear, and the two went away. The man walked carefully, comforted by his continued existence beneath the evening sky.

That evening when he got in his daughter was there. She

431

was standing in the kitchen, quizzically watching her mother prod a piece of beef in a saucepan of boiling soup, as if she had never seen such a wonderful thing happen before. All Thelma Forsdyke's visits to her parents were touched with a humorous wonder, that had come with her own success, to replace a former sense of shame. Her visits were fairly frequent, though almost always in the early afternoon, so that she could get home and rest before dressing for dinner. She liked a bath too, and afterwards could endure most things. After putting on her rings she was immaculate. This time, though, Mrs. Forsdyke was honouring her parents for the week-end, which was altogether unusual. Did she owe or expect something perhaps? It was not clear. But she had come ensured against any possible discomfort, with a ham, and a jar of bath salts, and an exquisite little pillow filled with down, in a pink slip, on which to nurse her insomnia, on top of the coarser pillows of the house.

She had brought, too, more than the usual ration of quizzical good humour towards these comical old people, who were really rather sweet and quaint.

When her father came into the kitchen she went towards him and offered her face, and after he had kissed her she said, "Why, Father, how deliciously cold your skin is. Where have you been?"

"Poking around in the gully," said Stan Parker.

The daughter, however, did not listen to his reply, which she had not expected to be of any importance. She was thinking how she preferred and even liked kissing with her father now that he was a cold old man.

"He has two blessed ferrets," said the mother.

Which once she would have resented.

I shall not tell them that I nearly killed myself, said Stan Parker.

It was too personal an incident to explain convincingly. It was already part of his submerged half. So he sat cutting his meat, at a great distance, and listening vaguely to his wife tell their daughter the story of other lives.

"I never told you, Thelma," Amy Parker said, "but Ray has left Elsie. Some time ago. Or did you perhaps know?

"How should I?" said Thelma, looking down.

The beef was horrid.

"Well, anyway, he has," said the mother, "and has been living in Darlinghurst for some time, with some other

432

woman, it seems. Not by any means a desirable woman at all."

"The undesirable woman is the loser," Thelma said.

She was examining with curiosity the grain of the meat and a strap of grey gristle.

"That is a way to speak," the mother said. "And poor Elsie."

"Ah yes, poor Elsie," Mrs. Forsdyke sighed. "Poor Elsie is delivered, I should have said."

"Thelma, you are not kind," said Amy Parker.

She was forgetful of herself.

"I am not," said Thelma. "It is my great sin. I have prayed against it, but unsuccessfully."

She had, too, and could well look moist, as now. Knowing oneself is the saddest luxury. And she had achieved this through experience and study, along with the French tongue and the fur coats.

"But Ray is not all to blame," said the mother now.

"Nobody is all to blame. How simple if some were. They could be got rid of."

"I don't know about that," Amy Parker said. "I am to blame."

"Oh, Mother," said Thelma.

She wished she had not come.

"But I loved him," said the mother.

Then Thelma Forsdyke did recoil. From the terms of love. Reading lust for love, she had preferred habitually to paddle in the tepid waters of affection. The red-faced, pursy men, the bilious-eyed, of which her brother Ray was one, looked at her from most corners.

"It is a pity," she said now, "that a second butcher has never set up at Durilgai. Competition would make all the difference."

"This is a fair bit of meat," the father said.

Because it was time he did say.

He had been thinking of his grandson, and had got some comfort from it, and was guilty.

"This is as fair a bit of meat as you would find," he said with some hostility, tapping the meat.

"In meat, as in anything, it depends on what standards you adopt, and, having adopted, accept," Thelma said with pleasure.

"He has left his job too," said the old woman, "and is working at goodness knows what. He is under the thumb of

433

this woman, who had been consorting with men, it appears, in her youth, she is not young, and is up to no good."

"Mother, I shall scream," said Mrs. Forsdyke, holding her ears.

But she could not close her eyes.

"Are we not having any pudding, Mother?" Stan Parker asked.

Then Amy Parker went and produced a spotted dog, at which she fancied herself. And Thelma ate it in a silence.

Later in the evening, when some kindness had been restored, and stomachs had rumbled, and there was a smell of tobacco, Stan Parker said, "I am thinking of going to the service in the morning."

"That will be good," his wife answered. "And Thelma can go too. While I get the dinner for you and have it nice and hot."

"It is the early service, the Communion service, that I want to go to," said the old man.

"Oh, that," said Amy Parker. "It is a long time since you went to Communion. I did not know that you meant. I don't ever like the Communion service. There are no hymns."

"Nobody need come to what they don't like," said the old man. "And liking is a matter for their conscience."

"I shall come with you, Father dear," said Thelma, bowing her head with a grave sweet smile.

He would have preferred not.

"I shall drive you," she said.

"No," said the old man.

He did not want that car.

"There is nothing wrong with the old car," he said. "It is good enough."

They would go, erect, in it.

But Amy Parker was silent.

I cannot understand this either, she said. Suspicion of people who maintained a relationship with God sometimes entered her. Of course, she had said her prayers, and would continue to do so, but conscious not so much of the words as of the hands behind which she was breathing, and of many familiar objects that she saw in that darkness. Only when she suspected that her husband had received the grace of God, and that even he, a simple enough man, was wrapping it in mystery, then she began to fret.

"Those early services are cold," she sighed now. "It is that disagreeable sitting without your feet. I wonder they don't

434

give up till the warmer weather comes. Nobody would come to worse harm, I am sure. Sin will keep like most things."

The next morning, though, when Stan had gone to milk the cow with ugly horns, she was throwing water at her face. She was shivering in the room. What else could she have done but turn in bed? So shivered, buttoning and pulling. And afterwards, gathering to go, Thelma in gloves and her most expensive humility, and Stan, with mild lines from nose to mouth, everybody was quieter for the cold, still Sunday. Amy Parker could hear her own shivering, though. Will I be any better? she would ask expectantly before church. She would have been ashamed to admit she was looking for miracles, like some young girls.

"You are coming then, Amy?" Stan asked.

"Oh yes," she said, angry for the obvious, her hat was on her head. "What would I do here after you have gone? You have not heard that car roaring out of the yard, you are always in it."

She was quite red with anger for the stupidity of Stan. But nobody noticed. And they went out counting their money.

That morning frost lay on the black earth.

Shall I be exalted or destroyed? asked Mrs. Forsdyke as she sat in her father's old car, her eyes watering.

The old man drove them very soberly between the silver trees, towards the one bell that lolled in the steeple. The church at Durilgai was the same straight church, in which souls had drowsed, and birds had died, and sin had escaped from the children, in sharp cries at the touch of water, always. The church stood amongst docks and milk thistles. Some of the stones to the dead had crumbled. But it was the new strong ones, in black granite and washstand marble, that exalted their terrible incapacity. As the car of Mr. Parker arrived, other people were going in, old women and cold girls, in black or grey, and decent men in stiff collars faintly yellow where they met the neck. There was a yellow dog too, that had been temporarily disowned, that stood showing its ribs and pointing its wet nose in the surrounding cold.

Thelma Forsdyke, who was no longer a Parker except in theory, clenched her teeth for what she was about to endure. She enjoyed the rich purples of religion. Then her soul responded in like purple. Or in discussions of personal faith with respectful clergymen. She sometimes rose to great heights, but failed to remain there, because there was nobody to hold her up, except God, and she quailed before a sustained intimacy on that scale.

"That is Mrs. Westlake," said Amy Parker. "She has had a tumour taken out."

People were looking at Parkers' daughter, at her clothes. Old ones remembered her when her nose was running, but they hid their knowledge. Young girls were moon-eyed with disbelief.

Floating on such distraction, they were going in. The box, which was reverberating still with the peals of the jerking bell, did not fill up. Too few were brave enough. Those that were had not yet risen from their bodies. They opened books and read the words for other occasions, as if they might find clues to the present. Everybody was very wooden, it seemed, in the little church, which smelled of cold wood. Tentative faces were hoping for grace to descend. In the meantime chilblains wept.

When the parson came in, shutting the vestry door with a bang, because he was a positive man, in strong boots, who might not respect her wealth sufficiently, suspected Mrs. Forsdyke, and regretted, everybody stood up in a supreme gesture of awkwardness, quite forgetting the object of their coming. The parson did not help matters. He had scrubbed the face of religion till any nostalgia that might have answered the personal ones had fled out of it. He was rather a strong man, it would seem. His own muscles would not allow him to have doubts, anyway for a few years yet, as he wrestled with the evidence of indifference. The pores of this Laocoön were permanently exuding sweat, sometimes radiant, sometimes just sweat.

Mrs. Forsdyke shuddered.

The bleakness of faith had settled upon her. Then I do not believe, she said. She would have surrendered her furs, with shameful speed, and fled. Her mother, who was holding her book in an unnatural way, and turning the pages with the method of the old, did not notice her. Nobody noticed Mrs. Forsdyke. That was the strange, the awful, even the tragic part. So that in the absence of a disposition to pray, which she did truly have at times, surging towards God, clutching her petitions as if they might break, she was forced to stray amongst the tablets and plaques to dead people, and sadden herself, adding to her own sterility their prevailing ugliness.

The service that was unfolding in the cold did warm in time. The marble phrases climbing upward, one upon the other, were chafed by some fervour, or breath of the congregation, as they knelt there, or rested their buttocks in compromise on the edges of the pews. The blood began to flow. The flesh of words grew out of marble. So that Amy Parker was brought closer to devotion. She felt the words. How they hiss at times, she heard. And drowsed, listening to them. Or kissing. Words do kiss. Yawns broke her up just then, and a thought of such obscenity that she looked to see whether people recognized in the old woman that they knew, some other. But they did not.

Each person was absorbed in his own mysteries. They bowed their heads beneath a hood of prayer, which had temporarily extinguished their personalities. Even the faces of the children had been drained, their necks were fragile and unrecognizable, as they knelt there, scratching and picking at themselves.

Amy Parker, the old woman in the dark dress, or not so old woman indeed, her skin would sometimes revive, listened to the words that the strong clergyman was delivering with such force. These words were for other people naturally, and for that reason she could bear to hear the worst of them. They fell upon her bowed head without penetrating the dark shield of her hat, so that she was able to get up eventually out of the awkward position, her leg was paining her too, and declare her belief with love and fervour, it came tumbling out of her on the strings of memory, through moist lips, and she was chafing her hands in front of her, and her wrists, and through her coat her appreciative arms, bringing them back to life.

I did not think that I could have enjoyed this service, ever, Amy Parker said. But it ran sinuously ahead of her, with its man's voice, and she listening to it, glowed, even in its darker mysteries, she could have healed pain by putting her warm hands.

Am I wrong then? she asked, looking sideways at her husband, who was not knowing her for the time being, and who looked rather thin and miserable, with his bent and scraggy neck.

The old woman would have liked to enjoy the crimson light falling from the glass hem of Christ onto the floor, lying on the floor in little checkers, in the dust, but crimsonly. Jewels glittered in her own eyes as she followed the male words of the service with the slight motion of her head that had become habit. She would have embraced a religion of her own needs, and mounted quite high. But her husband would not let her. What is God to Stan? she wondered, at his shoulder, I do not know God, Stan will not let me. She liked to blame other people for herself, and was almost persuaded. Now she went grumbling, mumbling, through the words. He has made me like this, she said, relaxing on the cushions of her own triviality. She began to think about a pudding that she would make that day, for the first time, with bottled quinces and a suet crust.

Stan Parker, though, had not thought about his wife that morning after entering the car. Standing there, he was in fact empty of all thought, which can be a state of failure, or else of dedication. I cannot pray, he said, not trying, as he knew the hopelessness of it. So he stood, or knelt, a prisoner in his own ribs.

The parson had begun to force faith into the souls of his people. He would hammer it down, if need be. *Hear what comfortable words*, said his humble yet brazen, young man's voice. *Hear also what St. Paul saith. . . . Hear also what St. John saith. . . . If any man sin. . . .*

Ah, if this were true, Thelma Forsdyke said, it is not intended as blasphemy, but I cannot believe that it is true. As she shivered into her furs. There was a draught, because they had not shut the door, and she alone would contract a chill. She attempted, shivering, to believe that this would not matter. To believe. The enviable word. It was not that she was without faith, only that there were different altitudes of inspiration. Wondering then, she looked round to see which face of these would be saved by implicit faith, the old woman who had had the tumour, the man with the hair gummed down in strips, who had learned the gymnastics of ritual, several ugly people who had risen on an impulse from their beds, or on a spring, was it, you must perhaps have the necessary mechanism wound for devotion, to shoot up to heaven.

Yet I do believe, I do, I do, begged Thelma Forsdyke.

And the priest of God, who was taking bread with the tips of his fingers and tasting wine with his fumbling mouth, was also trying desperately to transcend bread and wine. But the act in its sublimity was too difficult. His wretched cheeks continued to munch. A piece of dough had stuck to his gum.

People had begun to go up, to kneel at the Communion rail. Their bodies were terrible. The soles of their shoes, exposed to the nave of the church, did a double penance.

This is the awful part, said Thelma Forsdyke, I am afraid.

Relinquishing her expensive handkerchief, which she had rolled into a soft ball, moist, and rather scented, she also went up, solicitous of her parents, whom for the time being she had turned into invalids.

They were all going up. They were kneeling. Somebody's bones were creaking.

The anticipation was, indeed, dreadful. Some people, who in private life would have been referred to as elderly, had passed beyond old and come to death. Their masks were beyond joy and suffering. They were quite pure as they waited in suspense. Others were hungry, their stomachs rumbling not merely for that morning but for all their lives, so that when their turn came to eat they did so greedily, furtively, and licking up the crumbs afterwards, even when none were there, from the palms of their hands, on which their lives were spread. That did make some shiver. The audacity of their hands.

In spite of the weight of his strong boots, which tried to fix him on the carpet, the young clergyman was mounting at last. But in the struggle had become elongated. He had increased in stature but was held. As he moved along the line a purple light of transcendent glass flowed through his marble robes. His head, at the extremity of his body, filled with the sonorities of his voice, was touching at last in achievement. The substantial squares of bread were true by the very fact of their substance.

So the people were fed by degrees. Some felt their sins go out of them blessedly. Others, though, were stuck with them forever, except that they had received the favour of knowing those sins better.

To be forgiven, it is necessary to be very simple, very good, like my parents, said Thelma Forsdyke as she received and ate the sacrament, with the merest gesture, making it appear to observers as if the act had not taken place. Of course, she had learned discretion in all things. But my father and my mother, she said. She was comforted by their presence, kneeling beside her, more than she was by the sacrament. Their lives were transparent and lovely in that early light. Thelma Forsdyke knelt, worshipping a state of first innocence, which was the only redemption from sin, and because she could not recover this, any more than resume the body of Thelly Parker, sin would have to stay.

At this point she was preparing to wipe the corner of her mouth with her handkerchief, but because she wondered whether this would have been seemly, and because in any case her handkerchief was abandoned in the pew, she coughed. It was a rattly cough. Perhaps she would have an attack.

Stan Parker, who was temporarily as innocent as his daughter had wished, took bread, and ate. His hands were hard. He would have prayed, if he had known how. But his throat was dry. He was in every way correct, but dry.

Why have I come here ... Lord? he asked.

That word which he had slipped in last did not come naturally to him, though he could feel it. He knew it. He closed his eyes now, either to hide an emptiness, or to resist a light that was too strong. In either case the eyelids gave him no protection. He had an exposed look, kneeling there.

The light shone on the dust of the carpet, of which the pattern had worn away. Weariness was almost bliss. The flowers of the vases were so taut, so tight, that only a law of nature was preventing them from flying apart by strength of their own stillness.

The words were falling like precious blood as the priest brought the cup to each man. There was nothing between them now except his large wrists. The cup and the words dissolved most mercifully, so that with some, who were particularly grateful and ashamed of themselves, the wine gurgled hotly at the backs of their mouths.

Amy Parker, at whom the moment of forgiveness had arrived, took the cup, holding it rather high, tilting it only just, so that she should feel on her lips the infinitesimal drop, more she dared not, and as it was the blood began to flow electrically down from her neck, with poison of old thoughts. So the queen had held the other cup, the wooden one, or that was how it sounded, before she fell dead upon the stage. They poisoned the queen, who had had her conscience as well, working in her for some time. The wine worked. I have hated, said the old woman. Do I love or hate? She was confused under her best hat, a velours. It was the wine. It is Stan, she said, again with love or hatred, ah, look at me, Stan, but he cannot of course, now. Then she realized it was finally between herself and God, and that it was quite possible she would never succeed in opening her husband and looking inside, that he was being kept shut for other purposes.

Then the priest took the cup from the old woman, who seemed to be hanging on to it for some reason.

If I should drop this cup like the poisoned queen did, Amy Parker said, and shuddered, they would hear it like thunder.

The crimson wine sounded and looked intolerable as it was flowing through her.

But the parson took the cup and gave it to her upright husband, as if she had not existed.

As he received it the old man extended his lips tentatively to drink, advancing his chin, down which the vomit had run, it was still there, and bile mingling in his mouth with hot wine. He swallowed it, though. Then he hoped for God.

It was very peaceful kneeling there on the carpet, once you had got down to it, leaning on the varnished rail, which heat had cracked in its seasons. Peace is desirable in itself, he said, and so in the absence of evidence that he would receive more, he accepted this with humility and gratitude.

Why, then, was he waiting, as indeed several were, after the priest had turned his back on them, after it was all over? A fly crawling on the rail traveled across the old man's hand, that was not conscious of it. He was waiting, listening, looking at some fixed point, quite feverishly. It is not possible, he considered, that I shall not eventually receive a glimpse. Which made him smile luminously. Or else it was the warmth beginning to pervade him on a cold morning, or else the benevolence that some old men achieve for their fellows towards the end of their lives.

This has gone far enough, said his daughter, however, who always liked to tidy up a situation.

She put a hand beneath her father's elbow, to indicate a state of convalescence, or return to childhood, and drove her parents down into the body of the church, as if they had been wearing little reins attached to their upper arms, and she was guiding them.

Still, it is touching, said Thelma Forsdyke, that old people should be convinced, and enviable their lack of effort. As she walked behind them. For a moment her own soul attempted to ascend in a spasm of love and charity, but it was too weak and quickly fell back. Afterwards, kneeling in the pew, blowing her nose, almost listening to those last prayers, which did not concern her, for she had already done duty enough, she was convinced that she had caught the cold she had expected and feared, and which would be appreciated neither by her mother, in that dark hat which nobody else could have discovered, nor her father, who was smelling of old men.

When they went out it was Stan Parker who led the way.

He had recovered some of his authority, while remaining at a distance in the arrangement of objects and sequence of events. He went amongst his acquaintances at the steps, smiling from out of that queer distance and plane, as he talked to them of cattle and of vegetables. Some of them noticed his hollow voice without inquiring into it, for all were floating on their empty stomachs, in the now peerless morning, of magpies and wet grass.

They began to slip away with hesitant expressions of good will on their awakening faces. And Parkers were going. The two women were telling the old fellow what to do, for he seemed to be rather vague. He was considering, and fingering, he was contemplating his inadequacy, which also can be, in a sense, a prize.

Chapter 22

L OST at times in the jungle of her past failures, Amy
Parker had her plants, not so much those shrubs which
had grown and oppressed the house in overbearing clumps
and thickets, themselves a jungle, which enticed with obsessive smells of rot and scents of cold flowers into the lemon-
coloured light of secrets and of large leaves, not so much
these, but those plants which she kept around the verandas of
the house, the more tender, waxy ones in pots, that she
would prod and sigh over, looking into them till she saw the
insects there, and pores and knobs of dark leaves. These
plants that she loved, and for which she made moist nests of
bark and fibre, were almost all dark and fleshy. And anonymous of course. She could not name things.

She was going about amongst her plants most days,
touching them, and expecting signs of still life. Or looking
out at life led outside, in the distance, at young people knotted together at the hands, at the flat faces of strangers, from
which everything had been extracted, right down to the
thoughts and teeth. She would look out at her husband too,
going about, and try to draw him in, out of his pristine ways,
calling, "You should come in here a while, and take it easy,
Stan. It is good here in the sun, amongst the plants."

Then the dark-skinned woman would sit and listen in ex-
plosive silence.

"But it is good here too," her husband said. "I can't be sitting. I've got to fossick about while the light lasts."

He did too, squinting and smiling.

The old fleshy woman, who also knew best, sat and
breathed amongst the plants. She sat in an old cane chair,
which creaked beneath her. The chair had been unravelling
for many years, but it was comfortable. The red sun lay in
her lap, and there were moments when, identifying herself

with those plants which she had around her and which she loved best, she was content.

Two visits were paid to Mrs. Parker about this time. One was upsetting and one exhilarating, but she would examine both incidents for years, for some aspect she had forgotten. Then she would see them in a brilliant light, the features distinct and illuminated, the hard or funny words printed plainly, as if on grey cardboard, she did actually see them as she sat amongst her still plants.

The first of those visitors was a man, who came along the path in a brown hat with the bloom still on it. His head was down, so that she did not see yet, but heard the sounds of a man, of money, and leather, and a cleared throat. She heard words too in the man's voice, for he came talking with a little boy, who was all radiance, a fat, rosy little boy, jumping, and running backwards, and pulling buds off as he passed. The little boy was not necessarily on the same visit as the man. He happened to be there, as children will, and was continuing to see, and do, to live his life. But the man was preoccupied. He was too conscious of his own presence there, though he pushed back the sharp oleanders casually enough with his hands, and was making that blurry conversation with the boy.

The still woman continued to sit amongst her plants, waiting to see what would happen, and whether she would know what to do. Her heart was knocking already for the man. For whoever it was. Strangers at close quarters would assume monstrous proportions. So that she waited fearfully for him to raise his head.

He did, shaking the fuchsias. The man, then, was Ray.

Before he saw, she looked at this flash man that she had loved. Her lips were open. He was flash all right, like some commercial.

"Why, hello, Mum," said Ray. "Didn't see yer there."

His voice exploding. His foot grated back, as if he had trodden on something, some bird or cat.

Amy Parker looked amongst her plants.

"I sit here sometimes," she said, "in the afternoon. To get the sun."

The little boy had come forward to look at a person with whom he did not expect to exchange words any more than he would have with plant or stone.

"That's the idea," said Ray, who, in humouring this old

444

woman, would perhaps turn into a big, soft child. "Winter sunshine, eh?"

"I didn't expect to see you," said the mother, from inside her clothes. "What have you come here for?"

"Ah, come off it, Mum," said Ray, who was still attempting to be friendly in the manner of big fleshy men, laughing, and sure of himself. Then he remembered. "Why do I always have to be after something with you people? Can't I just arrive and hang around? I wanted to come out here and look at the place again. I been thinking about it. That's all."

But she was putty-coloured, looking along the dark leaves of plants.

He would talk, though.

"I wouldn't't'uv recognized the place," he said, conscious of his suit. "You've let yourself get overgrown. It'll push you out, Mum. What then, eh? Remember the swallows' nests? I got the eggs one year and blew them with a glass tube, and kept them in a cardboard box on cotton wool. Till they broke. They broke," he said. "Remember?"

"No," she said.

Whether she did or not. She raised her head slightly.

Then the man spat into the undergrowth of fuchsias.

He was collapsed and bilious-looking. Memories in some circumstances are a crime.

Like a commercial, she said, resenting it. She would not let herself think about it, except perhaps later, in private. I will not think about Ray, or anyone else, she said. So she sat there.

"I thought I would be able to talk to you," he said, as if the boy had not been present. "But I can't."

"Oh, we have talked," she said. "Often."

More often than in fact. She wiped her lips.

"I didn't bring you anything," he said.

Though he almost had. A big box of chocolates with a pink satin bow. Handing things, you can make better excuses for yourself.

Now he was standing without presents, at a loss.

Bugger it, he said, I have never murdered anyone. Then what are we coming to, what are we coming to? All around, the place was snoozing in a fragile light of winter, the doves, those clay birds, rocking on their feet. It was escaping him. The light was too brittle here.

The old woman had been looking for some time at the little boy, who was peering through the windows of the house to see what there was inside.

"That's the boy," said Ray now.

"What boy?" asked the mother.

"Lola's kid."

"Who is Lola?" she asked, though she knew.

Ray was telling her.

The grandmother was looking at the little boy, or at the back of his head, which was burning.

"Come 'ere, sonny," said Ray. "Come an show yourself to your grandmother."

The boy came forward. He was looking up at the old woman. He was very beautiful now. But he was watching something that made him afraid.

"This one is not mine," said the old woman. "The other boy is mine. The real one."

"This is a fine healthy boy," said the man.

"Healthy or not," said the old woman getting up.

She went inside.

"You had better go, Ray," she said. "I don't want to see you. Or the boy. I have to get your father's tea."

Closing the brown door.

"This is my son," shouted Ray Parker. "He's the dead spit of me!"

For that reason she would have kissed him, but had run from it, and was trembling the other side of the door. She must love the other one, and did truly, though rather pale, the one to whom she had given the heirloom of glass. So she was trembling.

After he had listened to his mother's breathing for some time, and cursed her, the man left the door.

"Come on then," he said to the boy.

In their best clothes they went slowly down to the dam, which was on the edge of what remained of Parkers' property. These people who had come looked foolish there, but they loitered while the man thought. The boy, who had listened a great deal, was thoughtful too on that afternoon.

"Who is the other boy?" he asked.

"Look,' said his father. "See if you can beat me at making the stones skip."

The man picked up a flat stone.

"How?" asked the boy.

"On the water," said Ray Parker.

And the stone he threw slashed the brown surface of the

dam, and skimmed, and slashed. His performance had professional grace but left him panting. His breath was stale too.

The boy, who had been frowning at the water, lit up, took handfuls of stones, greedily, and when he had made a pile began to imitate his father. Except that his stones plopped. But he continued to throw, even seeing success when it was not. Laughing as a stone sank. Saying, "That was nearly better than you, Dad."

"You go on," said the father. "You'll get real good if you keep at it."

Poor devil, he felt.

Then the flash, pursy man, who was still breathless, as well as thoughtful, sat down for a bit, while Lola's kid continued to throw the stones.

Here the shapes of tree and fence were so unequivocal that Ray Parker felt blurred. He had reached the stage at which you realize that you have nothing. The man in the strange landscape was frightened by its aloofness. The pale and lovely sky eluded him. The coppery tufts of winter grass, that he had mooned amongst as a boy, stood still. There is nothing here, he said, pulling at a blade of grass with his brown teeth.

Then his mind began to rootle round, out of that cold place, into the world that he had made do, as being of some sense and substance. Lola would be getting up about this time after the headache. They would eat a steak or couple of chops, he liked the fat, he liked the smell of meat when it rose above the gas, and reached out farther, even to the top of the stairs. He liked the smell of the evening paper, all evening smells, as this lit up, round the bend and down the tramlines, spluttering with violet sparks, and unwinding in long, in endless strips of hot rubber. Only sometimes, at late evening, when the bones return to the face, and the senses are stunned, she had a desperate smell of small rooms and hot sheets. The grey face of evening looms up then. The ash has fallen. It is this bloody headache coming on again, she says, but I will be all right with a couple of aspros. How the bed groans under a grey thigh. The oysters have stood the hell of a long while.

"Dad," said the little boy, beginning to grizzle and pull, "why don't we go home? I'm hungry. Da-ad?"

"You're right," said the father. "Howdyer like a nice piece of fish?"

He began to get himself out of an unnatural position, in

which he had grown stiff. He spat, and dented his hat with the edge of his hand, preparing himself for some fresh phase, or the old one warmed up.

"Fish?" said the boy. "Where's fish? There ain't no fish out here."

"Well, we'll find some on the way," said Ray Parker. "Somewhere."

They had begun to walk along the road that led back to Durilgai, walking in their polished yellow shoes.

"I'm ti-erred," dragged the little boy.

"You better come or you won't get no fish," said the father to his own shoes.

"Fish! I don't want fish. I'm ti-erred," grizzled Lola's kid.

Amy Parker watched this progress from a golden window, but the room was dark inside, and filled by a clock. Shall I go out? she said, they are slow. The dust was slow, the slow clock ticking in her blood. But as the man and boy mounted higher in her throat, she still stood. And that boy with Ray's mouth, kissing the face of the marble clock, or sleeping. She still stood. Then Ray had really gone, or darkness come, and something was burning on the stove.

When she thought over this incident, amongst her tended plants, on still winter afternoons, wondering whether she had done right, she would arrive at different conclusions, invariably, on different afternoons.

The second visit that Amy Parker received that winter was of a different nature altogether. It did not rend, though it disturbed. It was unexpected, and Amy Parker no longer liked that, unless she played the unexpected turn herself. Even to be caught out by her own face unexpectedly in mirrors she did not care for. Am I like that? she asked, and would then try to remember how she had been, but this was always indistinct.

Anyway, Thelma came down, drove down in the afternoon, and this was usual.

Thelma came in and said, "How are you, Mum dear?"

As if she were expecting her mother to be sick.

"I am all right, thank you," said the old woman, and began to sharpen.

Thelma was dressed well. Thelma's dress was never noticed, it was rich but too discreet. Now it was her mother looking, though, who saw that Thelma was dressed extra well.

"I have brought a friend," said Thelma Forsdyke, "who is most anxious to meet you."

This is a most dishonest friend, the old woman felt.

"What friend?" she asked incredulously.

"It is a lady," said Mrs. Forsdyke. "It is my friend Mrs. Fisher."

A dishonest lady, this was worse. And the old woman began to get up, out of the deep chair in which, unwisely, she had been sitting. To get up would have been terrible, if it had not been imperative. And so she heaved.

"There, you need not worry," the daughter said, and would have had her mother in a strait jacket, she liked people under control, then to be authoritative and kind.

"I have brought a box of little cakes. There need be no fuss," she said.

"In my house," said Amy Parker, "I will have to make a batch of scones. Do you think the pumpkin ones, or does she like them plain?"

"I am sure I do not know," said Thelma Forsdyke. "It is unnecessary."

"But she is your friend."

"Friendship is not fed on scones, Mother. We have interests in common."

It was puzzling. It was evident also that Mrs. Fisher was approaching, at leisure, though with confidence.

"Am I to come in?" she asked.

She did.

Mrs. Fisher was quite old then, or not so old perhaps, it was not possible to tell. She was not young, though.

"Mrs. Parker, we have disturbed you," she said with a deliberate smile. "You hate the unexpected, I can see. I do too. In small matters anyway. But if there is to be a genuine eruption, with clouds of smoke and sheets of flame, let it erupt unexpectedly. That can be exhilarating."

Her mouth was red.

Thelma Forsdyke was unhappy over this scene. Doubts that she had had came back to her. To know that these had been justified gave her not the feeblest pleasure. She could have sacrificed her mother, but not her friend.

"Will you sit down then," Amy Parker asked, "while I get us some tea?"

"Thank you," said Mrs. Fisher. "Lots of lovely tea. One of the things I dare to admit. When I am on my own, which happens sometimes at my age, I always drink the pot dry."

Letting a nasty little piece of fur fall upon the floor beside her chair. The little piece of fur was, in fact, sable, but Mrs. Fisher forgot this on policy.

Not so Thelma, who ran to retrieve and brush the fur. Now she trembled for her friend's daring, and her own lack of it. Mrs. Fisher, of course, had been at the game a long time, and was richer than the rich, she could afford forgetfulness.

"I will make some scones," said Amy Parker, who looked out no longer on her own room, but onto some stage, upon which electric actresses, speaking the foreign language of a play, were taking positions.

Mrs. Fisher coruscated.

"Scones? Dare we?" she asked of Mrs. Forsdyke.

But Thelma had forgotten the reply. She was two people in this room, in which she had played at ludo. She was confused.

"Why?" asked Mrs. Parker. "Are you not allowed to eat scones?"

"Oh," said Mrs. Fisher, "it is one's figure. It is always with one."

Her skin was dry. On one cheek, which tired at moments into a tic, there appeared to be a little patch of roughness, it was not sawdust, that was not possible, more likely a union of powder and down at some point of irritation. Mrs. Fisher was taking no chances, though. She was withholding her blemish even from Mrs. Forsdyke's mother, by offering her good side, so that she was seen in brittle profile, like the parrot that she wore, an old, exquisite gold brooch, with flashes of enamel in the parrot tail, and a ruby for an eye, and a little chain of gold fettering an ankle to a golden perch.

Now Mrs. Parker, who had seen the brooch, came forward, as many children had, and said, "Oh dear, that is a lovely brooch. It is lovely."

Mrs. Fisher lifted up her eyes. They were still limpid. Under the influence of admiration her skin would come alive. Her mouth had moistened. The machinery of charm was working. She smiled for Mrs. Parker.

"The brooch? Yes," she said. "But to return to scones. I would truly love to eat, well, many, *many* of *your* scones."

Because she had learned that, in flirtation, the sex is immaterial

Amy Parker was afraid that such a fever might be contagious.

"They are just scones, you know," she said, twisting her broad ring.

Mrs. Forsdyke laughed bitterly. "You will be Mother's friend for life."

This chalky woman resented grace. She became thin, narrow at the shoulders, with long hands and impeccable feet. Any evidence of admiration earned by others was a barb. So she sat. Following her lips with her tongue. Her hair, which was putting out tendrils under her hat, that she had made unfashionable by wearing it, had grown powdery with age. Her skin had become milky, not unhealthy but nervous. She was not displeased with any of this.

"Run along," she said runningly, "and make the scones. And I shall find the cups."

"I do not need any help," said Amy Parker. "Not with anything."

She had become angry about something, though she was not sure what.

"Funny old thing," said Mrs. Forsdyke when her mother had gone.

"Rather sweet," sighed Mrs. Fisher, who had relaxed.

She was looking around in someone else's house.

"And this house. It is a real room. It is fascinating to see that people do live. Darling, I am so grateful that you should have brought me."

Thelma Forsdyke winced. She was not at all glad.

"It is a simple room," she said.

"There is no such thing as simplicity," said Mrs. Fisher.

"I hated it at one time."

"Of course. What one is close to, one hates," said Mrs. Fisher.

She held her head on one side. She had her friend beneath a pin.

"But ugly furniture can be most interesting," she went on, she smiled. "It has reality."

"Are you interested in *everything?*" asked Thelma irritably.

"Oh yes," said Mrs. Fisher. "One must be interested, otherwise one would be bored."

Mrs. Forsdyke, who was made breathless by uninterrupted contact with her admirable friend, said that in spite of orders she would slip into the kitchen to investigate the situation. Her own nonentity pursued her down the passage. She was most unhappy since she had confessed her mother.

Who was at the table with that mixing bowl, the stripey one. She was rather floury.

Amy Parker did not speak.

She mixed the scones.

Breathing.

All that short time she had been alone in her own kitchen she had been gathering the brilliant fragments of her visitor, because these fell in showers, of words, and enamels, but in her doughiness she could not cope, she bumped against wood, which at its most noticeable had the dull polish of years. Once she knocked the sifter off, and it went clattering. She picked it up. Her skirt had got hitched somehow at the hem onto some garment on the inside. Yet, at times, preferably of an evening, on that side of the house where the old camellia bushes stood, her mind would flow quite subtly, backwards and forwards, revisiting obscure caves, or in the present, solving some problem for her husband if he should call out. She would stand there biting the young petals of camellias, and would have recognized poetry if she had heard it.

"I do not know what she will expect," she said to her daughter, whom she had noticed.

"I told you we expect no trouble to be taken," said the unhappy Thelma.

"Still," said her mother, "it is human to expect. Have you known this lady long?"

"Yes. That is to say, for a few months. That is quite long. People come and go."

"Here we know people for a lifetime," Amy Parker said.

"In my life," said Thelma, "it is different."

But Amy Parker considered her visitor. At this moment, what would she be looking at, in that room? Sitting, and sitting. The blinds were half down. It was greenish in there. Some people are perfectly still when left alone. They close their eyelids. But this one would take on a fresh shape. And what would her shape finally be, if not a light and a tinkling?

The old woman, who was putting her hand in the oven to feel, had forgotten her daughter was standing there. She did forget people now, unless necessary to thought or pictures.

"I do not know," she said, "what people are up to in a lot of jewellery. They cannot see it. I would like to have some in a box, and look at it, and put it away. It would be my jewellery then. It would be gorgeous. But such a brooch stuck on the front."

"You would be admired for it. Mrs. Fisher is admired for

her jewellery," said Thelma helplessly, who dared not wear jewellery herself, in case it should be lost or stolen.

But Amy Parker was angry. "Pffh," she said.

She was angry for her admiration and her longing. She had not known many things. She would not know a chandelier, and had escaped drunkenness.

Mrs. Fisher, on the other hand, who sat but did not wait, it was enough to sit in that room, which seemed to create for her the pocket into which she had desired to get, had known many things. She had started by knowing men. She had liked the horsy men, the strong-looking ones that smell of cigars and brilliantine, until she had begun to suspect the body is weak. After some consideration and rejections, she had married a rich draper, who also collected furniture, and little rare objects, and paintings of vegetables. He was rather wistful, she regretted, but nothing could be done, it was his way. Mrs. Fisher continued to know men. She had slept with a scientist or two. She could listen to theories. She had known a musician and would discuss Bach with care. Conversation is imperative if gaps are to be filled, and old age, it is the last gap but one. So Mrs. Fisher had learned. Now she would converse quite brilliantly, in diamonds, on the terrace of her house, at night, binding her guests to her with words, and frowning as she brushed aside the moths and the tendrils of jasmine that strayed into her elaborate face. Some men, foreign ones, still kissed her hand. But she would return to words. Or to the young men with Byronic heads. She was at her best in *amusing* relationships with artistic young men whose demands were decorative. As they hung about her in an esoteric group, and she fed them with their own wit, the young men would threaten to break at the hips. The old thing. They simply adored her.

Sometimes, though, the mathematics, the mechanics, of admiration became too much for Mrs. Fisher. Once in an arcade, to which they had gone to choose some little cakes, of a kind that had not yet been discovered by anybody else, she had escaped from her friend Mrs. Forsdyke while she was turned in contemplation of the cakes, and quickly Mrs. Fisher had run on brittle legs, inside the glass catepillar of the long arcade, through pale yellow light, as if she had had something to protect. For some time the two friends had made a joke of the occasion on which Mrs. Fisher had wandered and got lost, shopping.

Now abandoned in the roomful of furniture, she remembered this incident, and whole reels of other scenes in which her legs were working. I wish I could remember clearly, she said, but am I honest enough? She sat, and closed her eyes, and frowned, which gave her a black look above the nose. Trying to remember herself as a girl, but all she could see was a satin dress, with beads, were they? yes, she was always well trimmed. Trying to remember her first glimpse of life, because there is a first glimpse, to which experience cannot add, except confusion. So now confusion blurred her vision. Nor could she hear her voice. Although at some period she had said innocent, blundering things, which had even explained.

When the scones were brought in, and some cups with pansies on them, and a plated teapot that had got a dent on one side, Mrs. Fisher opened her eyes quickly, so that they flashed out into the room, and she began to turn on her pivot, and to radiate generally, like some imperious searchlight.

"Mrs. Parker," she flashed, "I have sat in your room, which is perfect, by the way, and learned you off by heart. I know you *intimately*."

"Then you know more than me," said Mrs. Parker, who was glad she had the plates to do things with, and did.

"Persuade your mother, Christine, that I am sincere by nature," commanded the glinting Mrs. Fisher.

"Christine?"

Amy Parker looked up. All of a sudden, what was this?

But Thelma blushed, It had been a secret from her mother natually, as little girls will keep secrets, it is their pastime. Letters, and pressed flowers, and names. This name was in no way shameful, except when revealed mercilessly to those it had been hidden from. She kept it for those friends, or acquaintances rather, who had inherited the senior title too suddenly, and of whom she lived in terror, lest they should break the relationship for some reason or other. So she offered them "Christine" as an earnest of closer intimacies. Besides, she loathed "Thelma" more than anything else that had been inflicted on her. The naked self can be most loathsome.

"It is a name," said the thin Mrs. Forsdyke, coughing it off, "a name that some of my friends know me by."

"Oh?" said the mother, dipping her voice.

But Thelma was Thelma.

Poor Thelly. The old woman sat there, herself reddening, smiling for strange occurrences, the butter running between her fingers from good scones. Silly girl, she said. Then she licked her fingers, and enjoyed doing so.

Between bites, for which they bared their teeth artistically, the two visitors had begun to discuss Mabel, who was married to some sort of lord. Mabel, the old woman had begun to gather, was poor in spite of motorcars.

"Because he treats her to per-fect hell," Mrs. Fisher said.

"But it is a lovely place," suggested Mrs. Forsdyke cautiously.

Not knowing Mabel, her shots were timid, even perilous, but she loved to play the anxious game.

"Oh, the *place*," said Mrs. Fisher. "We drove down to see them last time we were over. Poor Mabel would have been hurt. The place is—well, what you would expect. All oak and staircases. If you like oak."

Mrs. Forsdyke, who had thought she did, made a suitably dismal noise.

"But now they are at Antibes," she said.

In fact, she had read.

"At Antibes," Mrs. Fisher intoned. "At the Pigeon Bleu. Oh yes, poor Mabel has written, one of her famous letters. They read like a bus timetable. They are sweet. Anyway, there the poor things are. At the Pigeon Bleu," she screamed. "It is madness. In winter the Pigeon Bleu is divine. So primitive. But in summer, as we all know, it *stinks*."

Mrs. Forsdyke had contracted. She could never emulate her friend. She would never *know*.

In her misery she began to think about her husband. Why the Forsdykes had never been to Europe was something for which no satisfactory reason could be given. But they had not. So that Thelma Forsdyke had been put in many a false position, or conversational ambush, through which she came shakily.

"Of course," she said now. "In summer the South of France does smell. Give me some bracing beach of clean sand. It is my English blood, I suppose."

But Mrs. Fisher had closed. She was too angry for more. Besides, her mouth was temporarily gone. When she had put it back, and touched her hair, which had begun life as red and was finishing it redder, she said carefully and kindly, "None of this is very interesting for poor Mrs. Parker."

The old woman could not decently protest that this was not so, and consequently became restless, looking from one to the other of the sterile women with whom she was sitting.

The one was her daughter, and could be dismissed as known, according to accepted standards, if not in fact. The second woman, though, was aggravating to Mrs. Parker, as dreams do aggravate, that will not come right up and surface on the morning after. Here was this bright dream then, that tantalized with smiles, and tales, and sudden kindnesses, but would not stay still to be examined for the secret meaning of it.

Mrs. Parker shifted in her hot chair and said, "I am glad that you and Thelma should have so much in common, friends and all that, to talk about."

"Though you also most probably know the person we have been discussing," said Mrs. Fisher considerately. "Mabel Armstrong that was. They lived in this district. Their property was Glastonbury."

Mrs. Fisher had tired with this disclosure. She was looking for her gloves, and was now glad of her fur to rub against. She was impermanent in the ugly room.

"Of course I knew Armstrongs," said Mrs. Parker with superiority, because the immediate district and the past were her preserves. "Mr. Armstrong was the one I knew best. But I would see the girls about, and talk with them."

"It was a handsome house," said Mrs. Fisher, whose voice had cracked.

She was examining her skinny legs on which the stockings were a pretence.

"It has pretty nearly tumbled down," said Amy Parker brutally.

She could feel her lips peeled back, plum-coloured, in her full and still rather sensual face.

"Through neglect. You should see it," she said, because this woman had put herself in her power. "There are vines there that are taking it by the handful. The roots of the trees are opening the floors."

And, in passing, she herself was giving it a shake.

"It is sad," said Thelma, getting up, and realizing again she had not enjoyed herself, she never did, except in controllable anticipation. "And such a rich property. Mrs. Fisher used to stay there as a girl. Didn't you, Madeleine?"

Madeleine was rising from the ashes.

Amy Parker drew her breath in very quickly through her teeth.

"Ahhh," she said. "It was you then. Madeleine!"

Mrs. Fisher, who had got to her feet without assistance,

adopted one of those positions for which she was famous and said, "Why? Did we meet?"

"No," said Amy Parker. "Not exactly. You were riding a horse along the roads. A black horse. You had a habit, it was a dark green, I think, anyway dark."

"I did have a habit of bottle green," said Mrs. Fisher with feverish amusement. "It was very smart. I rode a great deal everywhere. I was often invited to stay at country properties. But I cannot say I remember your roads in particular. One cannot remember everything, Mrs. Parker, in life."

"I can," said Amy Parker, whose eyes were shining. "I think I can."

"What a terrible affliction," protested Mrs. Fisher.

As Amy Parker stood up, she had been slowed by memory, and this also gave her stature.

"Do you remember the fires then?" she asked triumphantly. "The brush fires? And the burning house?"

The two women were tingling with a fire music that had been invoked.

"Yes," Mrs. Fisher said.

Amy Parker would have continued to flame, she had not been that warm since youth, but the other women preferred not, afraid that she would be burned right up.

"It was exhilarating in its way," she said, shaking it off. "You know I was nearly lost forever in the fire. Only someone brought me out."

"I think I can just remember the fire at Glastonbury. I was quite small," said Thelma Forsdyke.

"You should be kinder than to reveal the fact," laughed Mrs. Fisher as they went out on compulsion.

Amy Parker, who followed them in slippers, she had not had time to substitute her shoes, remembered the ugly girl whose hair had been singed off.

Altogether she could not dissolve too completely the lovely effigy of Madeleine that had been hers. So poetry that has been used up must go out of the system. It must be got rid of, as bile, if necessary.

"It was over there somewhere," said Mrs. Fisher on the step, hesitating on the brink of the cold garden. "Can we see it from here?"

Her back was older than her front.

"Not now," said Thelma. "The trees have grown up."

It appeared as if Mrs. Fisher was going to make the effort to stand on tiptoe, as if her muscles were still good, but Mrs.

Forsdyke put a hand beneath her elbow, and she thought better of it.

Thelma Forsdyke had grown quite bland. She could love those who depended on her, inheriting strength from weakness.

Under that sky, which was of a lilac where it had not drained away, the women were drifting along the path of old bricks, that moss had grown on in little cushions of dark velvet. Except for a few liquid birds, the garden was silent as the women. On the one hand, these were people who were leaving, who had not realized themselves fully, but would perhaps, if time would stand. On the other hand, there was the person who remained, who could not give up even the uneasiness of company, she had formed a habit in that short time.

Presently an old man came from another part of the garden, stooping beneath boughs, and parting the twigs of bushes. He wore blue trousers that were wrinkled at the ankles, altogether his clothes were slack and comfortable, his face wrinkled, orange in that light. The leathery old man came on across the damp soil. From the earth on which he trod a damp smell arose, but good.

Amy Parker craned her neck. Her eyebrows glistened. These were still curiously full and dark.

"This is my husband," she said.

Thelma kissed the old man when he came, for she always made the most of his being her father, and Mrs. Fisher gave him her glove. They were all standing in a faint glow of golden light. Stan Parker would not look at the strange woman, it seemed, blaming it on the glare from the setting sun.

"Where were you?" asked his wife, angrily smiling.

"Down there," he said, blinking sightlessly at the sun.

Obviously it was his intention to avoid details.

"I was burning off a few bits of rubbish."

There was, in fact, a slight smoke rising, and smell of it, and a few pale tongues flickering from behind twigs.

"My husband is a great one for lighting fires," said Amy Parker. "It is a habit of most men, I think, to stand around a fire and look into it, once they have got it going."

She would have liked to find fault with this, but, remembering her husband in his strength, she did not. So they stood together in the presence of the stranger. They were together. This man is as much as I am ever likely to know, she said.

"It is a lovely smell," said Mrs. Fisher genuinely. "A smell of winter. Here it is lovely, everywhere. There is no end to it."

"Do you keep bees?" she asked, turning quickly to the old man.

The drowning ball of the sun and the little leaping tongues of flame played upon them a tender gold.

"No," said Stan Parker. "I never even thought about it, to tell you the truth."

He did look at the woman once, because it was strange, her asking him. He looked into her crumbling face, of which the eyes were still practised.

"I would like to have kept bees," said Mrs. Fisher. "It is incongruous, I know. But I would have liked to go out, and open the hives, and look inside at the bees clinging there. I know that they would not have harmed me, even if they had swarmed on my wrists. I have no fear of them. Such a lovely, dark, living gold. But now it is too late."

What is all this going on? asked Amy Parker. Too great a play of gold fire tormented her. There was no reason to suppose, however, that Stan had seen the woman for the glare, or heard her voice for the murmuring of bees.

He was smiling, though.

"They are a great deal of work," he said, "and get diseases, and die."

"Then you are one of *those* men," said Mrs. Fisher.

Though what she was thinking of him it was difficult to tell.

Thelma Forsdyke had begun to put her collar up. She said, "We shall all catch our deaths, standing here in this damp air."

In the voice she kept for people who had departed from her. It had an accusing sweetness.

After that she took her friend away, afraid that in the end their visit might have been a success and she had not shared in it. Mrs. Fisher sat smiling through the window of the car, and should have called out something, something memorable for leaving, as was her custom, but she could not. Her dry face was fixed there under her hat. It was remarkable that the bees should have come into her head with such passion, as they quite definitely had, they were not an affectation as they should have been. Now the terrible nostalgia of lost possibilities was gnawing at her as she looked in amazement at the square wooden house in which the parents of her friend lived. All solutions had eluded her. Once in the deal dressing table of an empty room, of a maid she had dismissed, she had come across a book of dreams, and had looked through it quickly, hungrily, her pearls dangling on the yellow paper. She was looking for a meaning. Then she had laughed and torn up the shoddy thing, glad that she had not been seen by those who hated or respected her.

So now, for precise meanings, she looked at the faces of the old couple, more particularly of the old man, both because he was a man and because his orange skin had a glow of quiet fire. But he is not looking at me, she said, shifting her position, resting her glove on the sash of the car, as if in one further movement she might have leaned forward and turned back the lids of his eyes. Then they would have been faced with each other.

But instead she was driven away through the smoke of the dying fire, of that rubbish which he had been burning off. Lives, she realized, can only touch, they do not join. Even on the fiery staircase, they lie along each other fitfully, the eyes do not see farther than the veins in the eyeballs.

Amy Parker touched her husband.

"It is cold," she said. "Let us go in, Stan. This won't do your back any good. Or my leg."

She liked to associate herself even with his aches.

"I am glad they have gone," she said, yawning, and easing her gums. "Aren't you? But you did not come. But she was a pleasant woman. She said some funny things."

Moving along the path in the pleasant comfort of old woollen garments when people have gone. Touching some bark with which she had been familiar for a long time. Till it began to peeve her that her husband did not speak.

"She came here as a girl," she said carefully. "That is what she said. Stayed somewhere in this locality, Stan."

But her husband had developed this terrible habit of not answering, of giving no sign. So that very soon the blood was bursting out of Amy Parker.

"How she has dried up, though," she began to laugh. "With the butter on her mouth after scones. She soon fixed herself, of course. But after a person had seen."

"In this locality. It would have been the Armstrongs' where she stayed," said Stan Parker. "Did you see her hair? It was red."

"It was red out of a packet," said Amy Parker with cold knowledge. "That is what some women do."

460

And you are so simple, or are you? she asked. But as there was no answer she went into the house.

And he was following her. It was where they lived. He was grateful for all things at dusk, and did not question the impossible. The fires of evening had died to one red line. He could not have believed, anyway, in that burning house, of tremulous harps, and hair.

Chapter 23

THOSE people who do not like to associate with death were soon keeping clear of Parkers. Who were going about as if nothing had happened. It was funny. Had not heard about it perhaps. So the death-shy began to flicker their eyelids up at the bereaved. They even came out and did good turns to those who absolved them from the embarrassment of sympathizing. They brought presents and ran errands. It made them feel morbid, though.

Then old Mr. Parker read in the paper, after the inquiry had got under way, read that his son was dead. There the old man was, standing in the frost, with his head bare, he had just gone out for the morning paper, and glanced, and was reading at once about the man Ray Parker, shot in the stomach, it said, in some club. He was dead.

It was Ray. Ray was dead, in the white frost, on that same strip of road. Ray, he said, dragging the paper at his side like a wing, flapping it. He looked along the road. It was quite empty. And began again to read the newspaper, about this thing that had happened. Or looking around. And trembling. Asking for someone to come. To see whether they also had really read this.

Everybody but Parkers had read the case, of course, but kept away as soon as there was any indication that the cat was out of the bag.

Ray Parker had gone down below street level on that night, the cloth rather tight across his buttocks, for he was a big man at the time of his death, but soft, with droopy corners to his thick mouth. He walked loosely enough in those places where he was at home, and on the spongy, ash-coloured stairs. Down below, some women were doing their faces, or combing their hair, throwing balls of hair beneath the grey tables. It was at that hour when night has gone slack. A yawning mouth will not close, but opens further, till you see right back, and there is the little shining uvula. Who would have thought that it was there, at any other hour? Or music, it is more evident, bumping round the groove, it is personal as gimlets.

Ray went straight up to Lola, who was living with him, who was in a blouse that she had had back from the cleaners that day, it was smelling of it, but still had the sauce spots that would not come off. Jack Cassidy was there, who kept a book amongst other things, and a cove he had brought whom nobody knew, nobody would ever know. There were several other girls or women, with handbags and Christian names. They had been sitting there some time in front of a saucerful of ash and some beers. Lola was nervous.

But everybody got to talking and laughing, and asking Jack Cassidy about a cert that somebody was put onto by a friend. Ray Parker was leaning across the table. He was talking to Lola, he was wondering what he would think of this woman if he came into the room and saw her for the first time, bloody horrible probably, but she had become necessary to him. And Lola was speaking to Ray in a different direction from where he was, because she did not like to speak to him in front of people. Afterwards she could not remember what they had said.

That was where Alfie came in. He went up to Ray, who had turned round, and shot him with a pistol that nobody could believe in. Death is not a bit real. Ray was shot in the groin first. He was a big man, and ridiculous. Then Alfie shot him again, and it was in the stomach, Ray said afterwards, when he had got past the stage of being afraid. When he was lying on the floor looking at Alfie, whose flesh had shrunk into yellow skin, as if he too could not believe in his intention. If he had shot Ray for tipping off the police, or for some other reason that he was looking for.

Anyway, Ray Parker was shot. He was looking into that blouse of Lola's, of a white or oyster satin, that was her colour, it was her colour in the morning. She was a flabby woman. And not very long after, Ray Parker died, in the presence of this woman, and a policeman, and a nun. They were moistening his lips when he could not lower his face to suck the brown waters of the dam, he could not make the stones skip, or tell even in those simple words with which it had been customary for him to speak. He was dead.

Some of this story old man Parker read in the silver grass

beside the road. He read the names and the ages. The man Ray Parker was well known as a receiver. He had served short jail sentences in other states for housebreaking and theft. He had a reputation on the turf. This was Parkers' son. Evidence was given by the dead man's *de facto* wife, Mary Brill, otherwise known as Lola Brown or Joanne Valera. This woman was an entertainer, it said.

"What are you doing there, Stan?" Amy Parker asked.

She was injured by his hatlessness.

"At your age," she said.

"Yes," he said, smiling.

"Well, come in," she said. "The eggs are ready."

He came in and dropped the paper down behind a dresser of heavy cedar, that she did not move, except in spring, when she would ask him to help her with it. So there the paper was, lying with the dust.

Soon after this Stan Parker said to his wife, "I am going up to Sydney, Amy, on some business."

"Oh," she said.

She was content. She did not ask. Whole days Amy Parker would spend about her house, looking into drawers, at objects she had forgotten, or at plants which were leaning out towards the sun, until she turned them round, to start them off again. These acts, performed in private, were soothing to her.

So she listened without complaining to the razor on her husband's cheek, and after she had kissed his fresh skin, and fastened the front gate with a little chain, she went back into her own thoughts and was soon bathing there.

Stan Parker, who had been shocked out of grief, would have liked to talk to someone. He would have liked to talk to his daughter-in-law, but Elsie and her boy were travelling in another state, with her father, a retired grocer, a solid man. And Thelma had gone to New Zealand with her husband, on what is called a semi-business trip. Ray is dead, said Stan Parker. He began to think about the little boy, which was what little he knew of his son. Some secret had begun to close the child's face. In the train the old man cried a bit at last, turning so that he was crying at the glass, and at the sightless houses. His mouth was all watery.

When they reached the city he was pushed about a good deal at Central Station, and realized he had very little idea what he was going to do. He would not, perhaps, do anything at all. What could he do? He was in a swirl of people going somewhere. Everyone was going somewhere. The old man's hat, which was a new one, was losing its dent, but it did not occur to him to put it back.

All the while, though, in spite of his drifting and indecision, he was making his way, it seemed, asking here and there, till he was getting close to the street in which the dead man had lived. One dry, small fellow in a canvas apron had even known Ray Parker, and looked curiously at the old man.

When Stan Parker came to the street, on one of those blue mornings from which the cold has been sucked out into the splendid sea, and the clay-coloured back streets are dream-wide, even the bugs are still, he was quickly brought to the house by some children who had learned all the details of the murder, it was the first they had been connected with.

They took him up the stairs, but on the landing they left him. The children ran down through the well, in a wind, the banisters burning beneath their hands.

Presently a woman came to the door on the landing. She stood there, waiting to be accused of something. The old man thought, What else but Ray's death could have brought me to this woman?

"This is where Ray Parker lived?" he asked.

"Yes," she said quickly, or hiccupped, from all the tears she had shed.

"I am his father," said the old man.

She was not glad. She was dulled.

"I don't know what I've got to give you," she said furtively.

Her hair was terrible that morning. It was dead stuff. But she took him in past a kind of box with a frill around it, and began from habit to do things with her hair, pushing at the tufts or twisting them, moulding her scalp, and her nails showed through the hair.

"I don't want you to talk about death," she said when they were sitting at a table with their hands in front of them. "I had enough of that. I would give you a drink if there was any. You don't know how many friends you got until there is a death and they drink you dry. After Ray was murdered we was sold out."

The old man wished he could say something to this woman, and felt foolish because he could not.

"I would have liked to help you," he said, wondering upon what crazy promise he might embark.

"You cannot help people," she said, exonerating him. "They must do it themselves. In that way, at least, you are independent."

"What is that plant?" asked the old man, of something struggling in a pot.

"That?" she said. "I am buggered if I know. I got it. Then I got attached to it."

She blew her nose.

"Will you stay here?" he asked.

The woodwork on which the flies had sat had a sick smell of rot. But there was a shining radio.

"I have not got the faintest," said the wife of the dead man, who had brought a packet of cigarettes, and had shoved one into her mouth as if it had been food, and had blown smoke from her nose in a long trumpet.

"Did *you* ever know," she asked, "what you was going to do?"

"Yes," he said with an assumed certainty.

He felt, in fact, that his own intentions had always developed like smoke. They were carried.

"I could never answer for anything that happened," said the woman, swallowing a big mouthful and belching it out with thoughtful indigestion. "At home," she said, mentioning some railway siding in the Northwest, "I would say as I would do this or that. I would be a singer, I said. Because I had a lovely voice. *Then.* I could sing 'One Fine Day' and all that, and hit the notes all right. I was artistic. I had a pink dress, pink net, with roses that me auntie had sewn on around the hem, and satin shoes. But of course there was not much life up there. Only the roly-polies moving in the wind. You could hear the watertanks make noises in the summertime, with heat. And there was the night train. I would go in and help with the urn, and serve the people with rock-cakes, the rock-cakes was well known. At night it was lovely with the lamps lit, and all the strange faces. I looked at the passengers. Nobody knew what was hid in me, and it was wonderful. I didn't know neither, as it happened. But it is different when you are young, with strangers, by lamplight. In the daytime, of course, there was only the sheep trains. Shuntin up and down. The bloody sheep packed tight. Daddy, he was the stationmaster, he would go out and swear sometimes, in the heat. There was mud on your face in no time those summer days. But the nights were starry up there. Anything could happen. It did. I got on the night train with the guard, for no

466

other reason than me foot was on the step. It was that simple. There was his face. And all that night I was thinking that a train is eternity. Well, I have made worse mistakes, but the first is always the worst. That man, whose name I forget— was it Ron, I think—he had a watch chain with some lumps of greenstone on it, was afraid by morning of his wife. That is men, they turn nasty when you get to like them, unless you are the first, and who was ever first? Well, I could not go back, and did not want to. I have never expected great things of the past. So I hung around. I got jobs with several shows. But I did not become a singer as I had intended, and had been convinced I would. It was not from not still wanting. It was as if I had been shunted off. I would wake at night, and listen to the trams pass, and know that I was fixed there. I cried sometimes, but I did not care really. I was free, anyways, to take the tram to Watsons Bay, and jump over, or buy meself a good red steak, or get some man. That that was all I did not yet know. Because I was young. I could sleep whole days, and my flesh was fresh."

Then the old man, who had been wandering in the mazes of the story, realized that his grief had become personal again. He thought of Ray's legs with the bran falling from them in blond crumbs. Then I have not come here to help, he realized, but to be helped. And he looked with some horror at the frowsy woman.

"What I was, really, was a slave," said the woman, breathing heavily. "Though I did not wake up to it for some time. Then when I did I started looking for someone to free me. I was looking and looking."

The old man, who was again anxious to talk about his son, or at least the one he knew, and to hear some good spoken of him, that is to say, of himself, asked, "How long, then, did you know Ray?"

The eyeballs of the woman called Lola were fixed by looking.

"All my life," she said with certainty. "I knew Ray in one body or another. Sometimes I would look into his eyes and try to see what else there was, but I never ever succeeded. And when he died, I was holding that body, holding it up, which was not so very different, after all, only heavier than a man who has taken all he wants, they sleep then."

"Do you pray to God?"

"I will not be any other kind of slave," screamed Lola. "And what do you, anyways, know about God?"

467

"Not much," said the old man. "But I hope that in the end I shall know something. What else is there that would be any use to learn?"

"Ah dear, I haven't the patience," said Lola, scrambling her dead hair. "Somethimes I think I will go back home after all. I want to sit. I was freer there, I think, before. Or have I forgotten? Or did I dream this since? There was a few dead trees in that plain. I want to sit there, beside the chicken wire. There was nothing else," she said, "but space. That is better than prayer."

"Freedom. But prayer is freedom, or should be. If a man has got faith."

"No," she cried. "No, no, no!"

Quickly purpling.

"You are trying to catch me," she said. "But I won't be caught."

"How can I catch you," he asked, "when I am caught myself? I am tied up."

"Old men," she grumbled, "were always the worst. They think that if they talk they will show you they are strong. I don't want any kind, not strong, or old, or any."

Her eyes shone with some situation she had created, of immense space. Her breath came out like a baby's.

"Mu-um," called the little boy, coming in. "Mu-ummm."

"What is it?" she asked, catching her freed breath.

"I want a piece of cheese."

"There is no cheese," she said.

"Just a bit."

"Little boys don't go around eating cheese."

"I do," he said.

"Well, that is too bad."

When the silence had rubbed against her for a bit she went into the kitchenette, took down a tin canister with some flowers on it, and pared a slice of soapy cheese.

"There," she said. "There is no more."

He did not thank her, because it was his due. He had to eat.

The old man sat looking. It could have been his son. He felt like saying to the mother, I shall tell you what is in store for you, but of course she would not have believed. So instead he asked the boy, "Do you know who I am?"

Foolishly, aware at once that he must suffer.

For the boy looked and said, "No."

It was obvious, with his mouth full of cheese, that he did not want to know.

"Ray never ever mentioned you," said the woman dreamily, and without callousness.

She was smoothing the boy's live hair, that she could smell faintly, and was smiling.

"This is your grandfather," she said, "come to see us."

The old man wished that she had not.

"Why?" asked the boy.

Nobody could answer that.

The boy flicked his head, to free it.

"I don't want any grandfather," he said, suspecting all that was not food or pleasure, and particularly the unknown, which disturbed his confidence.

"That is bold," said the mother in an unreproving voice.

The old man accepted what he had deserved.

"Come and let me brush your hair," said the mother to the boy, she was in love with that hair.

"No," he said. "Not now."

"Just a little bit," she begged, fetching a small brush with a handle. "Ah yes, come on, Ray."

So this one was Ray too.

"No," said the boy. "That is a girl's brush anyway."

"I cannot do anything with him," said the mother with desperate joy.

After a bit the old man saw that he must leave her to her slavery. She was drunk with love and the smell of her child's hair. So he prepared to go.

As he went along the passage, which was dimmed further by old linoleum of a brown colour, the woman called Lola came running after him and said, "I cannot thank you."

"For what?"

"You have made me see things."

His eyes that looked at her were blinded by his own confusion.

"This necessary slavery," she said, "if that is what you were trying to say."

As he went away, surprised that he could light anyone with his own darkness.

But this is one of the extraordinary things.

When Stan Parker got home, after undoing the little chain which they had put on the gate as a protection from cattle that strayed from the country lower down, he saw that Amy was sitting on the veranda, as she often did, but that she was disrupted. Would he be able to face it? he wondered as his feet went forward.

"What is it?" he asked.

Though he knew.

As he went forward he saw that there was still a thin girl encased in this comfortable old woman, and was himself cut open by the poignance of it.

"I thought I would keep it from you for a bit," he said. "That is all."

As going forward he put out his hands. He would never reach her.

"It is all right," she said, daring him to touch her, because she was finished with crying. "I have been through all this before, many times, only a little different. But you don't expect it when it comes."

When it came, Amy Parker had been sitting on the veranda in the clear day. A plant that she had watched for years had put on its flower for the first time. It was a jewel.

Then she heard the chain. It was a fumbling of someone who was a stranger to it, who came in at last, bundling past those shrubs of oleanders, and straggly roses that catch at clothes, and will even tear strangers, making them annoyed.

The stranger came on, who was no stranger, it appeared, finally, but Mrs. O'Dowd, who was Mrs. Parker's friend of years.

"Well," said Mrs. O'Dowd, "you are a nice sort of friend, if that is what you can be called, I am not at all sure."

"Well," said Mrs. Parker, "you leave things, and then the time is gone."

She doubted whether she was pleased.

"Are you good?" asked Mrs. O'Dowd.

"I am good," said Mrs. Parker, who did not get up, it could have been her leg, nor offer anything whatsoever.

Mrs. O'Dowd had a melted look, it was now seen. Her fubsy flesh was to some extent gone, leaving the loose bags of skin. She was loose and yellow all right, but mobile. She would always be an active woman. Life possessed her untidily. It was fortunate for Mrs. O'Dowd that life itself is hugger-mugger. And transient. Breaking into small pieces, of which her eyes were forever taking stock, and never seeing enough, most likely, they were restless, and black.

"How is Mr. O'Dowd then?" Amy Parker asked, because she had to. "I have not heard these years."

"He is bad," Mrs. O'Dowd said, and, as facts are unalterable, was not distressed. "He is like that dog," she said.

It was an old black dog, that was Stan's dog, with a bad ear and white eyes.

"Poor bugger," said Mrs. O'Dowd. "He has the double cattyract on both eyes. He is gettun around like a dog, you ought to see him, stickun his nose inter things, it would make you cry."

Though she did not, she was used to it.

Amy Parker did not want to witness pain beneath that tranquil sky of winter. She shifted in her chair.

"I knew someone," she said, "had a cataract on one eye. She had it lifted off."

"He will not undergo it," said Mrs. O'Dowd. "Not at his age. Says he has the feel of things, an will not be seeun nothun fresh, so he says, this side of the cemetery."

She herself, of course, knew better, looking here and there.

"That is a new little covered-in end of the veranda, Mrs. Parker," Mrs. O'Dowd then said.

"Yes," said Mrs. Parker, "that is new. There is a lot that will be new. To you."

She held up her chin to Mrs. O'Dowd, and would not show her too much. But her new-old friend, turning this way and that, in the black coat, with hair upon the collar where hair does fall, and the little brown hat that she could not have found but must have sprouted from the head, was ready to show, so it seemed, she was quite open, on the surface anyway.

She laughed frankly, showing her gums, for she had put away her teeth years ago in a box. She said, "Why, that is the benefut of neglect, my dear. Leave a friend a year or two, and you will see what is new. You will see the old too, as it is. Ah dear," she laughed.

And wiped a spot of spit off her chin.

"You will see the changes down our way too. You will see the fuchsias all cut down. You can see the house. Fuchsias I always hated, to be frank, that will not hold their heads up, silly things. So I took the tommyhawk one wet day an I chopped them all down. 'Well,' he says, 'I can *feel* the light is comun in, an do you think we can stand it after all, an what will Mrs. Parker say,' he says, 'who was all for fuchsias.' "

"I do not remember," Amy Parker said, "particularly liking fuchsias, though of course they are nice."

471

And tremble under birds that stick their beaks in, their long black beaks.

"He is white now," said Mrs. O'Dowd. "An sometimes wambly. He is a carcass of a man. He does his little jobs, though. He will split a little pile of kindlun, beautifully, by touch."

She held her head up and licked her lips.

So they were sitting again in the steam of summer, in the shade of fuchsias, Amy Parker saw. He was a black man with hair in his nostrils. She had not intended being with him ever alone, and had not, except once, and then had gone from him quickly, her skirt dragging through the fuchsias. He had not touched her, except on that one occasion, and then only with his eyes. So what was she frightened of? She was frightened rather of some disguise that would be worn later. He did come up the path, and he was wearing red. She was waiting for him there, and had intended to, she knew. He was burning. Leo, he said his name was. But he was the black one too, from whom she had run while still afraid, she could only face her guilt in a different colour.

So Mrs. O'Dowd was right, who said now, "Where is Mr. Parker?"

Nothing would come out in this place to greet an old friend.

"He is gone to the city. On business," Mrs. Parker said.

"Ahhh," Mrs. O'Dowd sighed. "The men can occupy themselves in that way. But he will be cut up, I can imagine, as men are, and will not show it."

For now she had come breathlessly to point. Her words blew like gentle feathers in a little wind. She was frightened too.

"I have been commiseratun with him," Mrs. O'Dowd said. "An with you too naturally, my dear. I say that, an it will sound foolish. An us friends."

So she traced a slow seam in that black which she had put out of respect and decency. The mothballs now were striking Amy Parker as terribly cold. The mothballs, indeed, were shaking in the pockets of her friend and issuing in blasts.

"What do you mean, Mrs. O'Dowd?" Amy Parker asked.

Then for a moment her friend did regret that she had been too daring.

"I do not understand," Amy Parker said.

"Ah," Mrs. O'Dowd gulped.

I am letting out the cat with all claws sprung, she said, so be it. but am I strong?

"I would not'uv spoke otherwise, only I thought that you would most certainly'uv heard."

"I have not heard." Amy Parker listened to her own loud, cold voice.

"Then, dear me," said Mrs. O'Dowd, looking in that bag which would not shut, and which she carried on occasions of importance, to pay the rates, to funerals, and to such like, and in which she found finally the piece of paper she had kept, for no reason, she had read and learned the sentences, except that she was not brave, she was not enough, to say, and so she gave the piece of paper.

"There," she said.

And Amy Parker, who had known in an instant of split sky, read also that her son was dead.

She was sitting there alone.

Ray, she said, I told you, I told you. Though what she had told she did not well know.

Then her love came out in a great burst, she was kissing him, and cried.

Till the neighbour woman, who was watching what she had achieved, through no personal malice but a little grudge, began herself to feel sad, the sadness of life was on her in her brown hat.

So she frowned, and had begun to sweat, before the real moisture came. Her pores were glistening as she said, "It is us women that will allus pay. Remember that, Mrs. Parker, when you take on, we are all of us in the same boat. Ah dear, it is terrible," she said.

And cried. She could gush with anyone once she had begun.

But Amy Parker was alone.

A great hollow of cold was about her, of the dark garden, of cold scents, which were violets at that time of year, with water in them. The blurry violets were all around. She would pick them sometimes, and tie them with a thread, and put them in a little china shoe that he would take when empty, he liked to take it in his bed, to sleep with it. Sleep should compensate but does not. All the sleepers she had watched were gone the instant of waking.

The pale sky was stretched tight.

I should do something, said Amy Parker, but what? There was nothing, of course, to do.

"Have you a drop, perhaps, in the house, of something?" Mrs. O'Dowd asked.

Mrs. Parker had not.

"Ah dear, the poor souls," Mrs. O'Dowd cried.

And as they mourned they did to some extent melt together. The two girls were again warm and close. Their pockets were interchangeable, for handkerchiefs and kindnesses. Their thoughts and hair strayed together. Only when they were exhausted did the two sleek girls shrink back into old and floury women, and remember where they were.

They blew their noses then. The neighbour woman was noisier, because she had been crying for her friend, just as Amy Parker was quiet, because the grief was hers.

"Now you will count on me, Mrs. Parker," Mrs. O'Dowd said. "For anythun. I would throw a little bit of grain to the hens, if you was willun."

"The hens," said Amy Parker. "It does not matter. There is Mr. O'Dowd, besides, who will be wondering."

"Oh, him," said Mrs. O'Dowd. "He has learned that impatience will not alter things. He has been made reasonable, poor bugger, who never was."

Then when she had gathered herself and was for going off, it did seem by that light of sad friendship and in the gloom of plants that her act had been virtuous. She touched her friend and said, "You will come to see me, Mrs. Parker, when you are feelun better, like, an we will talk about old times. An have a laugh, I daresay. I have some little duckluns as will do you good to see."

She would have begun again to cry for her own kindness, as well as for her friend's eyes, but went away in haste and respect.

And Amy Parker said, "Yes. I will come. Some day. And have a cup."

When she had lived in its entirety the event that was still occuring. But that would be a matter of time.

So she was still sitting, an old and heavy woman with her legs apart, when Stan came in, and from her distance she saw that he had suffered, and that she would not be able to help.

"What else are we intended to do if we have failed in this?" asked the old man, who had been creased by his journey.

His skull was hollow-looking.

"It is so late," he said.

Then she stirred, and shivered, choosing stupidity.

"There will be a frost," she said deliberately. "And I have not attended to the fire."

"At our age," he pursued. "With nothing to show."

"I do not understand," said his wife, pulling down her sleeves, of coarse stuff of ropes. "It is all above me. I do not understand a thing."

"But we must try to, Amy."

"What good will it do? Provided that we live our lives."

"But it is not intended to be easy. Even now."

"I don't understand you, Stan," she said, quickly putting her hands to her mouth.

"I am little enough to understand," said the old man.

"When we have ourselves," said his wife, forcing back her unhappiness into her mouth. "The mysteries are not for us, Stan. Stan? Stan?"

She could not bear him to escape her in a general greyness of speculation, so she began to draw him towards her, using some warmth of her own, almost as if she had been a younger woman, and when they had searched each other they began to see in the depths of their eyes that even their failures were necessary.

So the old people recovered in time, except for a stiffness of their bones, these never did recover from the beating that they got. And the paddocks remained blurred. The winter cabbages that Stan Parker put would run together in a purple blur, till at his feet, then they would open up in true splendour, the metal leaves breaking open, offering their jewels of water on blue platters. She would come to him often amongst the cabbages. They were happy then, warming themselves on flat words and their nearness to each other.

In this tranquil frame of mind Amy Parker did intend to pay a visit to her friend and neighbour, as had been spoken of, and promised. But did not go. She is all right, she said, wrinkling her face. And would, but did not, go. Her daughter Thelma had got her a little trap and pony, and she would drive about the countryside. It was a change. With an old green rug across her knees. The little horse went plop-plop, his hoofs and dung. So it would have been easy, too easy, to pay the visit to O'Dowds. But she did not. Though she was warm towards them. She could not put them quite out of her mind, they were of the moments of her life and would recur.

Then it was Mrs. O'Dowd who recurred in person, the other side of a year, it must have been, the frost was already on the ground, where there was Mrs. O'Dowd again, walking

475

against the fence as if she had been looking for sticks, and swinging a string bag.

"Mrs. Parker," said the neighbour woman in a low voice, that she made an immediate effort to raise. "We have forgotten each other, it seems. An it is a pity. Not to end as we begun."

"I am to blame," said Amy Parker humbly.

On this motionless day she could take any blame. She was looking about from under her hand. All shapes were kind.

"Truly," she said. "You know what it is. I have been meaning. And will still."

"Yes," said Mrs. O'Dowd, clearing her throat.

She was swinging her little dillybag, in which was a packet of something from the shop.

It did not seem likely that they would speak further just then. They were both of them looking on the ground at the stems of yellow grass.

When Mrs. O'Dowd, who was herself the colour of winter grass, wetted her lips and said, "I have been sick, you know."

Amy Parker sympathized. The sun was too benign to deny formal sympathy.

"In bed?" she asked.

"Ah," said Mrs. O'Dowd, swinging her bag, "what would I be doin in bed? I never did take to me bed, except nights, an sometimes of an afternoon, if that was his wish. So not now, thank you. Me feet will see me out, God willun, an if not."

"Then you are bad?" Mrs. Parker asked.

They had come together on the grey fence.

"I am bad," said Mrs. O'Dowd.

The little packet in her swinging bag poised and swung out. It fell. They watched it.

"It is the cancer," said Mrs. O'Dowd.

They were watching that packet in the grass.

"No," said Mrs. Parker.

Because her throat was full. It was the life protesting in her.

"It is not possible," she said, "Mrs. O'Dowd."

"It is," said Mrs. O'Dowd, "it seems."

She was herself looking at things in doubt. And at the little packet, which was there, and which must now be picked up.

"There will be some drug," said Mrs. Parker as she stooped, "something that they have discovered."

They were both stooping. They were exchanging hands,

476

that had the yellow wedding rings. They were bumping heads even, foolishly.

When they were again erect, and Mrs. O'Dowd had straightened her hat, and the packet was restored, she said, "They will not discover nothun for me. I am rotten with it. Now I know it is intended that way."

But Amy Parker continued to protest. "It is not," she said. "It cannot be."

Holding her own hands that had begun to tremble, for however much love and pity she did truly feel towards her friend, the experience of pain was also hers. She was aghast at her own unreliable relationship to life.

"I will not die easy even so," Mrs. O'Dowd now said. "I will give it a tussle. As it has allus been."

As she had wrung the necks of ducks, and thrown a calf, and cut the pig's throat once, at a pinch, riding its back until enough of life had gushed from it. She had let it out, who now must be let.

The two women stood awkwardly gulping at the callous air, unwilling to part, though they could not unite.

"I will harness the pony to the trap and run you home," Amy Parker said.

To oppose some small act to great facts. It is, besides, less difficult to die than to watch the dying.

"I would not put you to the trouble," Mrs. O'Dowd said. "I came up here on foot for a little stroll and diversion. I will continue that way. There will be ladies all along that will be yarnun to me at their fences. The distance is easy passed now. Remember how we had to speak our own thoughts to get an answer once?"

So the two brown women walked a little way together, over the ringing earth, under the penny sun, and eventually parted. They were the colour of dead leaves.

When Amy Parker went inside she said, "I am that upset, Stan, Mrs. O'Dowd has the cancer."

The old man replied, "Go on!"

And put his head inside a newspaper, from which his ears obtruded. He began to think about his youth, how the mornings had predominated, the morning, in fact, was almost the whole day. Anything that must happen must happen in the morning.

"When did she tell you that?" he asked, on becoming reconciled to the shocking brevity of his own life.

"Just now," said his wife. "She is looking terrible."

Her own skin would still glow at times, and to see whether this miracle might take place, she walked alongside the mirror, slowly, prolonging reflection, but barely noticing her face because her rudimentary eyes were looking inward.

The room in which they sat was puzzling to them that evening. Each hoped that the other understood their position.

Late that night it began to rain, and persisted for several days, wrapping the small house in grey rain. Then, when it had stopped, and the yellow water was no longer running at the sides of the road, and the country was emerging tentatively, colourlessly, the old woman began to sneeze. It was obvious that she had caught a cold. It was obvious also that she could not visit her neighbour in this state. But must cosset herself, putting on a thick black comforter, that she had knitted once and forgotten. Taking onion gruel. And feeling sorry for herself.

This way she was more or less released from her promise to visit Mrs. O'Dowd. Though she would, of course, later on, with something nice, some soup, or a basin of veal knuckle. In the meantime she substituted pity, for mankind, and more particularly for women. But the evenings were sad, when the black, the almost blueblack shadows lay around the well head, and the fine claws of possums could be heard in chimneys. Then the knowledge of her own powerlessness, that had become active treachery, drove Amy Parker about her house. She became nervous, suffered from indigestion, and would sometimes hiccup out loud, though as she was usually alone it did not matter. Once even she thought about her friend in the position of death. She visualized it in some detail. Then if she is dead, she said, we shall not have to talk of things that are too terrible and wonderful to mention, we shall not mention our past lives, or speak in any way of suffering. She will be dead. But the survivor was not pacified.

And was relieved one day at the turn of the season, when she was called to the door by a little girl standing there. She was wanted, said the child, she was wanted at O'Dowds'. It was little Marly Kennedy, Mrs. Parker saw, whose mother Pearlie Britt had once called her to O'Dowds' on other business.

"Is she bad then?" Mrs. Parker asked as she held the struggling door.

But the little girl took fright at words and ran. She ran showing her bare heels and the bottom of her drawers, and her hair was blown back.

Mrs. Parker did not wait long, but harnessed the pony to the trap.

She drove down through that wind which was coming from the west and filling her up. Great gusts of wind rocked her in the little trap. Her cheeks were soon plumped out. Down the funnel of her throat poured the wind, till she was big with her mission. She was a busty woman still. As they ran smoothly or lurched across a stone she got courage. It was possible that all her faults, of which there were many, would be ignored. She drove on, and it became evident that she had in no way neglected her friend, except to wait for a moment on this scale. So she was driving down towards O'Dowds', and the heroic wind bent the mighty trees, and the old woman in the trap was truly moved by anticipation, and anxiety, and love.

When she got there, O'Dowds' place had just entered on a further stage of its collapse. The wind was torturing the roof. It took a leaf of iron and tore it off. The iron, tingling and tinkling with rust, flung across the yard and slapped a pig's arse fairly hard. This act committed, the iron sank into a pond, or spill of brown water, from which a white spray of ducks shot. There was such a quarking and groaning of animals, it was near murder, but unnoticed. The house, round which several loosely made cars and secured sulkies were gathered, children playing, and blue dogs lifting their legs, contained its own diversions.

When she had hitched her horse Mrs. Parker went inside the house, which already smelled of death and a great many live bodies. They had tried to do something about it by scattering eau de Cologne from a bottle brought from Bangalay, and by burning something that had left a cloud in which the company was lost. But after Mrs. Parker had pushed sufficient way in, doubting again in that room, she did eventually find her friend, or what remained of her, on the high pillows of a bed.

For Mrs. O'Dowd had sunk in, and was all for dying, now that her body was a strait space. She had suffered that day—was it the worst?—she did not yet know. Although weak, her gums could still bite on pain and draw the blood out of it. Her cheeks were quite gone. But her eyes, to which the spirit had withdrawn, were big cloudy things. They were not her own, or rather they were that part of man which is not recognizable in life.

Some of those present treated her accordingly, as a

479

stranger, or as one who had already gone, anyway from the body, which is all that they dared to count.

"Let us hoist her up a little. She has slipped down," said one woman. "Take her, Mrs. Kennedy. There. By the armpits. Poor thing. Tt-tt-tt. She is a weight even so."

"Ah," said Mrs. O'Dowd. "When will he come?" she said.

"Who is it now?" they asked, tying her down with a crocheted quilt across her chin.

"He said that he would come if it was necessary. It is most necessary," she said. "I will not be back by Tuesday if I cannot cut the rope. That young man will do it easy, though. Just one little touch, an it is lovely. I never walked but flew."

"It is the doctor," they said knowingly.

"Dr. Smith," said Mrs. O'Dowd.

"Dr. Brown," they said, and would have laughed.

"Dr. Smith was the *old* doctor," said a small woman with a mole, bending close to the sick woman, so that she saw the mole as if it had been a gooseberry. "This new young one is a Dr. Brown."

"What is in a name?" said Mrs. O'Dowd. "Those little bristles would singe right off a pig's back."

"Whatever will she say next?" whispered the small sniggering woman as she withdrew her oblivious mole.

"Dr. Brown has been sent for, Mrs. O'Dowd. Mr. Doggett went down. The doctor is over by Fingleton delivering a baby for a young lady," said a woman, or another lady, as she had become by deed of nomenclature.

"I do not believe you," said Mrs. O'Dowd. "Ladies do not have babies. They know a thing or two."

It makes you laugh, though, they said. Poor thing.

"I had no baby," said Mrs. O'Dowd, who closed her eyes to open them. "An am no lady. Not by a bloody long chalk. But I did not know enough. I was allus terrible iggerant," she sighed. "I was iggerant of life, and of death, for that matter. I did not believe in it till it had come. How could you? With the washun in the tub, an the bread risun in the tins, an all those little pigs suckun at the mother's tits."

"It was that way also with me father. He was a most disbelievun sort of man," said an individual who was sitting there in a bit yellow collar of the stiff variety.

This was a fellow called Cusack, a relative of some kind, from Deniliquin, it was believed, who had not seen Mr. O'Dowd since passing from the landing jetty to the interior many years ago, but who happened to be in these parts, and had scented death, and come to be there, what more natural. All already knew the man from Deniliquin, and had given him a bottle of ale to keep him quiet, but this did not work. He liked best to talk about animals and money, for which he had a curiosity and respect, both for the domesticated animals and the wild ones, particularly alligators, that he had looked into the eyes of, and for money, which had eluded him, but which he had elevated by an unenvious worship and mysticism, even the colour of it.

"To return to me father, though," said the man from Deniliquin, "or to start with um, because I do believe it is the first time I have mentioned the old gentlemun. Who died of an angina in doubtful circumstances. Mind you, he had been warned, but would not take heed, no more than that shilluns do not grow on bushes. He loved flowers too, and would walk amongst the roses, touchun them, just, he said, to feel their flesh, which is most beautiful. Even when some unpleasant individuals told him he was mad he would not believe, but went through life smilun at people he did not know, which they say is a sure sign. And me mother, drivun her near demented. She could not onderstand this love he had for people, and particularly for dark girls, with dark hair upon the upper lip. She, you see, was forever darnun. She would sit with a sock upon an acorn, frowning at it, because it was ever such fine work as me mother did it, no cobblun together and snippun off. She was the darner. But me father liked to make people happy, by touch, and by less tangible means, of illuminatun things that they had not noticed before. So with his genius for life, which even me mother had to admit, an her hatin him for love, he could not believe in 'is own death, which was waitun for um all unbeknownst on the second floor of a house in Corrigan Street. I was then a bit of a boy, that they sent for as bein the next to kin, an could not naturally tell me mother, she havun a headache besides. Me father was dead, they said, an the ladies were creatun like old Harry, especially Mrs. La Touche. 'What ladies?' I asked, I was a shy sort of boy then. 'Ah,' they laughed, some of them was good enough to blush for me, 'it is the whores,' they said, 'your father was already stretched out, an now will you please come an fetch um, afore the ladies get hysterical. Naturally I went, because there are some occasions when you cannot run, I was held by the seat of the pants, by circumstance, and pushed. Well, I got there, and some was cryun, because they got a fright, an some was

481

laughun, because it was a rare occasion for a man to be carried stiff out of a bawdy house. Only Mrs. La Touche, whose establishment it was, was goin crook over the good name of her house. Well, there was much discussun of the situation, an some pinched me, an some kissed me, because I was a pretty sort of boy. Yes," he said. "An what with this an gyratin generally, we had carried me poor father to the top of the house, an never a thought of down. Even Mrs. La Touche, who enjoyed a conversation, was surprised. So again we got to work, an was pushun, and was pullun, an was carryun the body of me late poor father, an sweatun, it was the summer, you must bear in mind, an one girl told of new milk in the pail, she would never be forgettun the cows' breath, she was a big yawny sort of girl, a country girl, with muscles on. Well, we got me late poor father down. As the day was breakun, his feet were through the door. 'Well,' I says, 'what am I to do?' 'That is your business, Tim,' they laughs. 'We cannot suckle babies as well, it is not at all in our line. Call a cab perhaps,' they says. An shut the bloomun door. Me poor father that was with me was sweet-faced and agreeable even in death. An disbelievun of the worst. He took all for granted. That the day would break, as it was then doin, an that some solution would present itself, as it allus does. Well then, up comes a water cart at last, rainun on the street in that shivery light. Me sweat was cold by then, and I musta been a long-faced boy that was wonderun there. 'What is it that you have picked up, sonny?' asks the water man. 'It is me father,' I says, 'an he is dead.' Then the water man says, 'Well, if he can hop up, I can take um on the next stage.' So we made me father hop up, after a fashion, though it near killed us, an soon he was ridun through the streets stretched upon a fall of water. It was lovely there. I will never forget it. The sound of soft water goin through the grey streets. 'This is not a bad perfession,' the water man says. 'This is how the streets will look after the Judgment.' 'Have we been judged perhaps?' I says, like a cocky boy. But the water man did not hear. And I did not bother, it is not many things that will bear a second askun. So we drove on, shimmerun and yarnun pleasant enough, till it was the trumpets that became obtrusive, and I was avoidun these big brass instruments with me elbows, that would have swished us off, an the cheerun, of whores mostly, that was leanun out of most windows, in which long tables had been laid. Then one young lady opened her lips that wide I knewed I was a goner, an was straddlun the cart, an dodgun,

482

an hangun on to me late father at the same time. When he sits up an says, 'If you are to fall, son, then open your arms and legs wide, and imitate the sawdust, in that way no bones will be broke.' In that way me father took a header off the cart, and it was two streets from our own that I discovered the body, an me with a bump on me head from follerin him over the side. 'That is a terrible corpse you have got,' says the water man, lookun down. The sun was up by then. People come out to look, men in their singlets and ladies in their papers, people that we knew too. 'Why,' they says, 'it is Tim Cusack and 'is dad, who is dead drunk again, the old bastard.' That is the judgment we got. An because I knew better, I was above letting on, while it was possible not to."

"Tt-tt-tt," said the woman with the hairy mole. "What a story to tell."

"It passes the time," said the man from Deniliquin, who could feel the gas rising in him sadly from a great depth.

Then Mrs. O'Dowd, who had been asleep, or withdrawn by some other tongs of mercy, opened her eyes with the wideness of pain and said, "Now that there is too many ladies there is no more mulberry jam."

"That is so, Mrs. Parker," she said to her friend, who was sitting there at the bedside, on a chair, in a hat. "You was always a one for mulberry jam. And brawn. I can remember that brawn as if it was me own face. And never a sign of those little bristles that gets into brawn. Do you remember?"

"I remember," said Mrs. Parker, nodding her straight black hat.

They were recognizing each other, though one was a fat old woman in her disguise of time, and the other almost eaten away.

"I have not made a brawn for some years," said Amy Parker, as if startled by the presumption of those acts which she no longer performed. "You stop something, then you have lost the habit."

All her words were strange, because she was hypnotized by the approach of death. She was looking into mirrors.

"I can remember a man who had developed the habit of eatun a pint of treacle mixed with a pound of bran," said Mr. Cusack. "Every mornun."

But they stopped him.

Amy Parker looked at her friend's face, which was closing again. She is dying, she said, and I cannot grasp it, not really.

I have no understanding, she said, of anything. So began to nod her head. She could not stop.

"It will be a mercy," said young Mrs. Kennedy. "It will be over by tea."

"I would not gamble on anything in life," said Mrs. O'Dowd. "Ahhhh," she screamed, falling back. "They will have me all right, but when they are ready."

Amy Parker, who would have liked to bear some of this since she had been forced by her presence to have the courage, leaned forward and took her friend's hand, in which the life was trickling still. And in this way their two streams did flow together again, for a little.

After the neighbour woman had lain there sweating and grey, she was the exact colour of her own hair, which had been loosened and hung in two wings, she began murmuring of what she was seeing, or had seen, it was difficult to tell which, for both wore the same grey glaze. Everyone in that room, which had dwindled with the growth of pillows, and the enormous pile of eiderdown, and the heavy chains of crochetwork, everyone began to feel the tug of those same grey waters which the voice of Mrs. O'Dowd was pouring out into the room, and to bob and flow, sometimes upon the stream of their own now melancholy dreams, sometimes eddying round the objects that Mrs. O'Dowd pointed out. But it was Amy Parker, who held the drowning hand, who was carried most frighteningly upon the stream of life, as their two souls navigated its jokes and perils.

"Because there were seven of us," Mrs. O'Dowd was saying, "if I am not forgettun the eighth, the little girl that fell face downward in a bog an was drownded, or suffocated, I should say, with being sucked under in the mud, a Mary too, we was all Marys besides, named for Our Lady's sake. We would all of us children, or as many of us as was active together, row down some days in a little boat, it was a good stream, the weed in places, which would make it brown, would row down and touch the bridges at Wullunya. They are all marble there, and cold to the touch. I can feel it now. Even with the sunlight on the bridge. An moving. It was the water, but you would have said the marble. Over this bridge the lady came drivun to market in a smart gig, that give me this plant, which you can see, Mrs. Parker. Don't tell me you can not."

"Which plant, Mrs. O'Dowd dear?" Amy Parker asked.

She was confused to re-enter the close room.

484

"The red one," said Mrs. O'Dowd. "It is that pretty in the evenun. On the sill."

"Ah," said Mrs. Parker. "The geranium, you mean."

"Sure," said Mrs. O'Dowd. "That is it. That is a present from a lady at Killarney. I would not recernize her now, for she is dead too, I expect. But it was on that bridge that we stood, Mrs. Parker, you will remember, to watch the sheep go by, and were pushed and pulled till our buttons were rubbed off, sleepy animals though they be. Will you remember how our hands were full of dreamy wool, and the smell of wool? 'We are not come for an outin,' you says, 'but for a purpose.' 'If we do not choose our purposes,' I says, 'there will be no outins, an what better than a flood.' Oh dear, you were nosun after your husband through the crowd. I love a crowd. I love to look right up the nostrils of strange people. I cannot see too much of um. I could run my hands through the skins of strangers. Do you know?"

Some of those who were there, and who were being tormented by discovering lives of their own, now came out from the spasms they were enduring, to laugh.

What next? snorted some of the women, but quietly, down their noses, into their chins.

But Amy Parker knew. There are times when you know nothing, and times when you know all. So her eyes glowed.

So she leaned down from the bridge, to pick the faces floating there. Some lips were open to be kissed, some were closed tight. All bobbing in the grey flood. And the old letters, and the yellow photographs.

"You will do better to stay quiet for a bit," she said to Mrs. O'Dowd, "and keep your strength."

She was herself exhausted by too much motion.

"It is that airless in here," said the woman with a hairy mole, opening a window. "It makes you sleepy."

The man from Deniliquin, Mr. Cusack, whose eyes were smarting from the smoke and who was belching back the beer that was a rather bitter brew, would have liked to tell a story, something tremendously truthful, that would make people look round at him, and remember him afterwards, but such a story, on close thought, eluded him, and he sat back, a cavernous man with blue chin, and what had he come here for, except to receive a corpse into the world? By this time almost everyone was deceived. Only the geranium blazed, now that it was evening, upon the sill.

Then the husband came in, who had been sent out to get a

breath of air, and to divert himself generally. He was a nuisance at the bed. Sometimes his love for his wife became unsavoury, and he would start licking her hand, like a blind dog, and whining, showing his teeth, which at least were still white and sharp.

Nobody bothered about O'Dowd. He was the remains of a man. What could become of him afterwards? Would somebody be expected to feed him and mend his clothes? Sympathy can become attenuated. It will be best if, like a dog, he will lie down under a blackberry bush and die. He will do this, but not yet.

The husband was feeling his way across the room, bumping into objects that had changed their place, and into the bodies of unexpected people, a big, shambly man in clothes that had been put on in darkness, and looked like it. O'Dowd was all awkward clothes. His white eyes were running, either tears or matter. If he had lost control of his face, it was still a private grief, to him at least, since most things had become disguised by a privacy of darkness.

So he advanced across the room. Some people shifted their faces out of reach of his nubbly hands with obvious alarm. Others slipped aside with more discretion and became shadowy with their simulated unconcern.

"Where is Mrs. O'Dowd?" the man then asked helplessly, lost in the crowd. "Is she any better, can you tell me?"

"Mrs. O'Dowd is as well as can be expected," Mrs. Kennedy spoke up, whose cousin was a probationer nurse, a fact from which she borrowed no little importance. "Sit down there. But be quiet. You must not be any nuisance."

She guided the man across his own room, towards the bed in which he had been paramount these many years, and in which he had caught at much elusive poetry as it slipped by.

"What are you after now?" grumbled Mrs. O'Dowd from behind her eyelids.

She could do no more for her husband. Her hair had grown heavy.

"I will sit here for a while," he said.

Feeling the quilt, of which the pattern was a raised-up honeycomb.

For some reason she did not intend him to have her hand, perhaps because she had passed beyond him and was nothing to him now. But to Amy Parker's hand she clung. Some people will desire a new friend to tell their greatest secrets to. And Amy Parker, who was old, had become new by length of absence. So the two women held hands. There was still much to tell and show.

"I never did tell you, Mrs. Parker," said Mrs. O'Dowd with the skin of her lips.

And smiled.

"What, dear?" Mrs. Parker asked.

And bent to see. Because it was doubtful she would hear.

"The fuchsia bushes," said Mrs. O'Dowd, "are all cut down."

So that Amy Parker heard the trembling of the red trumpets. She felt the hot blast of morning. She looked deeply into the eyes of Mrs. O'Dowd, which had become a heavy golden, occupied with matters of minute importance.

"Just now," she said, "I seen your face, Amy, for the first time."

Because nobody in all her life had said anything so personal to her, Amy Parker blushed.

Then O'Dowd, who could not interpret the several languages that were being spoken round his own bed, began to hit the air with his arms, and grow nasty, and shout, "Why don't you all get out, and let us die in private?"

But they put him in his place, those organizers who consider that death is a public occasion.

And the woman with the hairy mole came and lowered it to Mrs. O'Dowd's face and said, "Are you sure you will not have the priest, dear?"

"What would I be doin with a priest?" Mrs. O'Dowd asked.

"You could try anyways," the helpful neighbour said.

Then O'Dowd, who had felt a terrible draught, and was crumpling up the quilt, cried out from the depths of his lungs, from the centre of the black room, so that everything was shaking. "Ah, Kathy, Kathy, you are not leavun me? What will I do when I am on me own?"

Mrs. O'Dowd was quite tranquil.

"I shall not be havun any priest. I am not afraid. I can talk for meself. Thank God."

Then there was such a noise, of praise, and disapproval, and teeth sucked, and the poor man crying, some people could only listen to that, because it is not often you get the opportunity of listening to a man crying, and him a big man, that they did not notice the entry of the doctor, who had performed the act of delivery over at Fingleton, and come on.

The doctor was a surprised and diffident young man, who

had so little patter that no one ever believed in him, though they went along and would even pay. At times, when he was dead-beat, he wished that he had been a conjurer.

"How are we?" he asked now, of someone and of everyone.

Or if he had become a juggler. To hold his audience with a stream of coloured balls.

She had been suffering terrible, though cheerful enough, said Mrs. Kennedy with importance. She had been asking for the needle, just a little one, a while ago, Mrs. Kennedy said.

The young doctor was only too pleased to be able to produce something from his bag, into which two children were already looking.

But Amy Parker, who sat holding her friend's hand, knew that it was dead. She must tell this now, she said. Her throat had swelled though, with great words.

"Mrs. O'Dowd," she said at last, "is dead."

And went away holding her handkerchief to her mouth, to stop it up.

She had never cried much, and would not now, in front of other people.

With the result that all those who rushed to see, to do, to compare, to lay out the body with inherited skill, and to drink tea afterwards in warm communal compassion, said that Mrs. Parker had always been a cold woman, and stuck up, for no good reason, and not well liked thereabouts, not when you came to think.

The old woman, when she went from the room, past the geranium which was still glowing, and the crying hulk of a man to whom she did not know how to offer sympathy, walked across the yard to her pony, across whose rump she had placed a bag, to protect it from possible cold. It was cold too, on that spring evening, the trees stirring with a dying wind, as the old woman drove home. Driving over sticks and leaves. In her frail trap.

When she got in the old man her husband was on his knees, raking together some embers.

"How is Mrs. O'Dowd?" he asked, looking up.

"She is gone," she said, letting the door flap back outwards.

The old people did not say any more about the death, but soon sat down to a tea of chops and chirps. As they wiped the fat from their lips, and drank cups of sweet tea, and said warming through insignificant things, they were destitute even of each other.

Later on they did begin to feel calmer, by some dispensation, and as they lay beneath the eiderdown dared to think of the dead woman as she would mingle with the sandy soil down at the cemetery. It was fantastic. Mrs. O'Dowd, if they dared, in a narrow trench. Whose words had danced, and would still dance, anyway in memory, itself a dying thing.

Till finally the old couple were dead asleep.

Chapter 24

QUIGLEYS were still there, in their house along the road.
They are the kind that grow from the landscape with
the trees, the thin, dusty, unnoticeable native ones. Some people round about, in brick cottages with waterproof tiles and
privet hedges, who were there by assault of nature, and for
that reason loved to proclaim their morality, said it was a
disgrace the way the stink of poultry manure rose on damp
evenings from Quigleys' old ramshackle place, in what was
now a residential area, the Council must be told. But it was
not. They did not in the end tell on Miss Quigley, for she
would look at them, and her face was quite open. Then those
people would retire into the brick tombs which they had built
to contain their dead lives, and tune into the morning radio
sessions, and as they stood on the floral carpet, in a blaze of
veneer, would wonder what simple harmonies had eluded
them. They would become as angry and as desperate as their
millet brooms.

Doll Quigley had not altered much, except that her skin
was more positively rough and speckled, and her knuckles
were enlarged, and that goitre which she had always had. She
was slower too, from minding turkeys all those years as they
stalked grey and pernickety round the horehound clumps, or
down the hill to where the tussocks were, always stalking
greyly. Doll had an old apron that she wore, she had made it
out of clean bag, and would put on for turkey-minding almost always. This operation was not exactly necessary, but
she liked it, and so would go stalking, a brown-grey, behind
the turkey school.

There is something convalescent about the grey slope of
turkeys' wings. Their chirp is sick, or invalid at best. This
would explain why Doll Quigley loved the birds. There were
not the buyers for compassion. Could she not go out into the

490

rain, and take the bag from her head, and lay it over some-one's shoulders? There were not enough accidents for Doll. People will accept compassion, casually, as if a component of abstract goodness, they will not take it and wear it for what it is, someone else's emotional skin. That would be embarassing. Why, even Bub Quigley was irritated at times by his sister's hands.

Anyway, everybody respected Doll, and took from her many material things, and made use of her a lot. Take her family, for instance. They would come out Sundays in their sedans, the long, muscular brothers, who had become gnarled and dry, and their long, muscular, similar sons, they would lie around, or look for something they might fancy, some tool, or piece of iron, or fat cockerel. Doll won't mind. Or the flat-ulent wives, and the wives of sons. They love to sit, and pass on the wet nappies, and tell about their operations and house-hold appliances. Sometimes they pause, and look at Doll, and look quickly back into their own lives, which are necessarily more absorbing. The bellies of the wives of the sons are per-manently filled with babies. And the children, these run around at Doll's place, and call for the lavatory, and smash things. They get into cars at evening, and do not look back, because they will return. It is the unalterable in children's lives that is the most admirable, and cruel. If Doll was not wounded, it was because she had given too much of herself, there was little left. It was logical, though. Goodness is given to give.

She was reduced by this time to the essence of goodness, which is what made people ashamed or afraid, because it is too rare. Sometimes her brother Bub, out of his simplicity, would recognize the nature of this predicament, or exaltation, better than others did. He would run along the passage and start looking at her, like some animal, like some rat that has been let live in a house unharmed, and that, while taking the situation for granted with its limited animal intelligence, will look out suddenly from its limitations and close with the hu-man consciousness on the verge of all manner of mystical un-derstanding. So Bub, now an elderly man, with his sometimes slobbery rat's teeth and his blue, shadowy face, would stand beside, though a little behind, his sister on the brick floor of the larder, which smelled cool all the year round, and within the world of candlelight would eye milk or bread, of which the shapes themselves are good and touching, beginning and end, in fact, perfection. Then Bub Quigley would sigh like

491

some animals, looking more closely at his sister for some communication of recognition.

But she, of course, moving the bowls of swaying milk, or feeling the new loaves of bubbly bread, had passed several stages further than her animal brother. Infinite love and peace will spill from candles and dissolve the flesh into silence. Then I will die readily, said Doll Quigley.

Though it was wrong, of course.

And Bub there.

Then she would step back quickly, and draw in her breath, and say, "What is wrong, Bub, treading on my heels in this small room, that is only space for one, and breathing on the milk? You should blow your nose too. You can blow your own nose."

That was angry for Doll Quigley, and she would go away knowing it in her narrow shoulders. I should love Bub more, she said, but how? And Bub was snivelling there. His handkerchiefs got twisted up to string. Though he could manage himself well enough when told.

Sometimes she would go out and sit on the front steps, the side the rail had not yet fallen off, and put her arms round her knees in the position she had adopted as a girl, and attempt deliberately to approach that state of perfection which would sometimes drop voluntarily over her head like a simple bag, but she could not always then, she was intimidated by the greatness and diversity of the universe, which dwarfed her own limited powers. And there was her brother, seated behind her, drowsing and drooping over his pointed knees. Then she had a choking feeling in the lump of her neck. She had led a happy life, but it became suddenly oppressive and sad.

"Why don't you go in, Bub?" she would say, sideways, to the darkness. "You are droppin asleep. It is bedtime now. Run along."

But even when he went, he almost always did what he was told, and the shadows of his body were jerking on the blind, and then the darkness fell, Doll Quigley herself was not released from the fiendish difficulties of constellations, they would not be solved, she sat there late, knotting her hands.

No one realized any of this, of course, because some things are too great to tell. Until that day she went down to Parkers'.

It was the summertime, Amy Parker would remember, it was a time of juicy weeds and heavy air. Doll was decent.

Her legs were very thin inside a cotton dress of some little checkered pattern, with a little purple eye. It was her best dress, Mrs. Parker noticed by degrees. There was some awkward powder smudged along Doll's jaws, she did not put it ordinarily, but now. And she wore a cameo brooch. It was a good piece. It was forgotten how Quigleys had come by it. It was too good to excite much attention, though a lady that once stopped for eggs had offered to buy it, but Doll would never sell.

"Well, Amy," she said in her long, slack, Quigley voice when the screen door had flipped back and she had sat down.

"What can I do for you, Doll?" asked Mrs. Parker, who was moistening a bundle of clothes to iron, and who was really a bit annoyed.

"I have come to tell you something," said Miss Quigley, looking at her long, gentle hands, "that I don't know who to tell."

"Well, what is it?" asked Mrs. Parker, who was not interested on such a close day.

"My brother is dead," Miss Quigley then said.

"Your brother, your brother Bub? You don't say!"

"Yes," said Doll Quigley. "I put him away. I will not say kill. Because I loved Bub. And now when I must go, I will not feel that bad, Amy, if you understand. Sometimes I do see clear, if sometimes I am confused. This I do know, though, is for the best. His face tells me so."

Then the two women were looking at each other, and Doll Quigley's face was so open that Amy Parker saw right into her soul, and began to take her friend's hands, and to lay them here and there, and to rub them, because she herself could never hope to reach such heights of simple sacrifice. And rubbed the side of her own face. And felt the closeness of the kitchen. Altogether confused, or blinded. As already there crept over her a fear and distaste for the blinding logic of Doll's act.

"Oh dear, then we must do something, and Stan is not here," said Amy Parker, who was the confused woman of ant-proportions, even smelling of ants.

"If you will ring the constable, Amy, and tell him what has happened," Doll Quigley now said.

"Oh yes," said Mrs. Parker.

She did.

It shook the collar stud that was lolling loose on Constable Tuckwell's throat.

"We had better wait at our place," Miss Quigley then said.

"If that is what you wish, Doll," said Mrs. Parker.

"Oh, he won't frighten a person. He is covered with a sheet. He is peaceful. Poor Bub."

So the two old women walked down, against many people that did not notice them from their polished cars. They were elderly, rather simple women, poor even. So the two old women walked down from the beginnings of their lives, linked together for some comfort that their flesh still craved. Everything was strange around them that they had seen before, and desperately necessary. Amy Parker went smiling at things, a tree, or a tin, or a patch of scrub, though she, of course, was less involved.

There was a goat too, an old doe called Nan, that had been the property of the dead man, and that had followed his sister up to Parkers', and now pattered back after the two women, bleating and tossing her head, because her udder was tight. Or she would forget her predicament, and crane after tender leaves, and tear them gluttonously from their twigs. But remember, and bleat, pattering, and scattering her black pellets. Hopefully following the two women.

Presently they came to Quigleys' place, and Amy Parker, who was a weak woman, who had failed in everything in life, prayed for strength, but Doll Quigley was more convinced.

They took Doll and put her in the nut house at Bangalay, which is a lovely place. Her friend Mrs. Parker visited her that winter when she herself had recovered from the shock, taking a few choice oranges and some jujubes. Doll was different. She sat on a straight chair in a bright room to speak with her visitor, whom she was obviously glad to see.

"Are you in good health then, Doll?" Amy Parker asked, wetting her lips.

"Yes, I am good," Doll said languidly.

Her face had filled out and was different from what one knew.

"Anyways, you have put on weight," Amy Parker said.

"It is the suet puddin," said Doll Quigley with a grey glint.

"Is there anything that you want to tell to people?" Amy Parker asked. "Any messages for the people round about?"

"That is what my brother is continually asking me," said Doll, sitting forward like a frank man. "And I cannot remember, Amy. When it was me that knew always, and had to say for both. I have lost my way," she said, looking about as if she could hardly divulge this frantic secret. "Any my sister is pestering me."

"But Doll, you were all boys," Amy Parker said, and could have gone through the list, because in the circumstances it was difficult to converse.

"My sister was a girl," said Doll. "She knew the names of things. She knew the saints. She would tell us about the Everlasting Mercy, sometimes at night after we had lit the lamp, just the two of us, and it was nice then. Because I never knew nothin much of me own self. I knew the ways of animals. The tracks and nests. I had a boxful of coloured stones and four skeleton leaves. So that the sister would have had to show me most things, you see, and did. She was always kind. Until that day she cut herself off. She pressed with the big meat knife that she had been slappin all Thursday with the steel. She said, 'Bub, God will receive you.' But I was not received yet, Amy. Now was this kind?"

She leaned forward to enter with the situation into her friend's eyes, and Amy Parker saw that Doll Quigley was in hell.

"We suffer for some purpose," said Amy Parker, taking her friend's hands, "but I am one of the stupid ones. I could not answer Mrs. O'Dowd either, when the time came."

"Mrs. O'Dowd? Where is she?" Doll Quigley asked, fixing her hair.

"You know. She is dead," said Amy Parker.

Doll began to rootle in the paper bag, and to chew a jujube, of a lovely orange colour.

"These are nice too," she said. "I always liked sweet things. When I was a little girl the nuns used to say that this would be my great sin."

She smiled.

Sin then, Doll, Amy Parker would have said, and left her friend to enter heaven by that way.

So Amy Parker rode home in the smooth bus, everyone together, breathing and sweating, making jokes and having headaches. She dropped her money long before the conductor came, but it did not matter. She sat quiet. She was thinking all this time of the twin knives turning in Doll Quigley and Mrs. O'Dowd. Then what tortures are in store? she asked, and was afraid, even though she was going home to her husband, a quiet man who would stand up at the last moment perhaps, and say something. Stan will know, she said.

So she was comforted. So the green sky of winter flowed

by, and all the bodies in the bus ran together. Because she was a superficial and a sensual woman, when the last confessions are made, Amy Parker was soon even thinking about that other man who had been her lover, his freckled calves, and how the suspenders had eaten in. How she had disliked him. How she would have liked to take other men and to have rocked with them on deep seas of passion, and to have forgotten their names, and to remember their features and their eyes, prismatically, some winter, in old age, after the face has fallen back into place.

The green sky streamed past the homeward bus.

"Oh," said the old woman meekly, when they were all looking at her, "I dropped the shilling some way back, and the bus was too full to go stooping around. Perhaps it is at someone's feet."

Everyone began shuffling and looking and making simple jokes for the old woman who had lost her money.

It was found at last.

"There, missus," said a hearty man. "That'ull save a walk home."

Everybody laughed.

The old woman smiled, but lowered her eyes on those people whose company she was shaming. Sometimes her simplicity would blaze electrically. And the sky was streaming by. It was late. The collar of her coat was ornamented with a piece of rabbit fur, which she now pulled across her throat, against whatever knife might be prepared to enter in. And in that way she did feel protected for a little. And then they arrived.

Chapter 25

T HELMA FORSDYKE rang her husband from a dress salon, where she had been made to suffer ridiculously over a simple detail of an important dress. The telephone box was heavily upholstered in a smoky grey, and smelled of faint smoke and the scents of other women. Thelma did not use scent, because of something it did to her sinuses, and she was frowning now, and beating on the little T-piece of the telephone, which was conspiring with other things against her.

"Oh, Dudley," she said after she had been having some difficulty, "I have had an exhausting afternoon at the hairdresser's, and with Germaine, the dress, you know, which should have been ready and which is not."

"Yes. Yes. Yes," said Dudley Forsdyke, or some reverberation in the machine into which she was talking.

"And so I have decided," she said, "to have a mouthful of something at the club and go on to a concert that I see is advertised."

She spoke terribly distinctly and with a confidence that came from long practice. You do not know a thing until you have forgotten how that thing was learned. Well, Thelma Forsdyke had forgotten at last.

"Very well, dear," said Dudley Forsdyke. "If that is what you think."

And would consume his own dinner with much the same indifference as in her presence, a little quicker perhaps, in order to escape from the restrained breathing of the elderly maid.

"I feel it will be good for me," said Thelma, smiling into the telephone for her own sensibility. "It is a lovely concert."

And I cannot go home yet, she tapped on the bakelite, I cannot, or rather, will not, not yet. It was as if she were terrified of some responsibility life might suddenly offer her.

497

"Well then, good-bye," said her husband the solicitor, who did not expect anything further, then or ever. "Have a good time," he said, out of respect for theory.

Thelma Forsdyke rang off without saying any more. Inviting husbands to play at fathers is always humiliating. So she took her persecuted gloves and left the smart shop. But looking straight ahead. Annoyance had made her suspect elegance of bad taste. She would still pay for her dress, of course, but she would wear it with the saving grace of her own especial dowdiness.

She was a thin woman of a certain age, in -black. Her stockings were exquisitely expensive, but did not help her. As she walked, and particularly down steps, she extended her legs and planted her feet in a distinctive way, as if convinced that, with less care, she might suffer a fall.

Since her friend Madeleine Fisher had been found dead, Thelma had known an increase in loneliness and discovered that her circulation was bad. Not that friendship had made her blood flow; it frequently stopped it in her veins by increasing her ignorance of those mechanics of behaviour which are considered necessary. Though no one by this time would have noticed this. Not even her friend Mrs. Fisher, whose glances latterly had been directed inward.

Then Mrs. Fisher had died. How, Mrs. Forsdyke had not been able to clear up to her personal satisfaction, owing to the fact that she had never been received sympathetically either by Mr. Fisher or any of the Fisher entourage, and on occasions, in fact, had been forced to observe the furniture. So she would never know for certain whether her friend had died, quite simply, of time.

Mrs. Forsdyke walked along the evening street with her crocodile bag.

At the club, in the presence of several gentlewomen, she ate some languid, crumbed fish.

"We shall meet tomorrow night," said Mrs. Owens-Johnson.

"Yes, indeed," said and smiled Mrs. Forsdyke, with knowledge.

And wondered whether Madeleine Fisher would have destroyed her glory with some thrust. For this would be the first occasion on which the Forsdykes had dined at Government House, with other burghers of their kind, equally rich and equally destitute. So they were all day thinking about their clothes.

But in the meantime Mrs. Forsdyke was sitting solitary at her concert. As the strings were turning up a golden rain streamed from off her shoulders. She had never been perfect, till now, her ankles crossed, the veins blue in her white skin, of which no use had been made for years. She was waiting on discreet and tasteful pleasures. Her stomach was not too full of food. Her nerves were still.

I have never felt better, she said, except the dress, she frowned, which *must* be ready, it is too tiresome of Germaine.

There were several pieces of programme music that Mrs. Forsdyke had learned never to listen to, and would treat even with disgust. Then a grave Jew with black eyelids and a violin was welcomed out to play a great concerto. Mrs. Forsdyke rolled her programme into the thinnest cylinder, and would have made herself thinner, if possible, clasping her elbows still tighter, reducing her attentive thighs. Thus compressed, she might have soared upward on the note of release. But she could do nothing about her soul. The soul remains anchored. It is a balloon tied to a branch of bones. Still, it will tug nobly.

The Jew began to play, touching tenderly at first the flesh of music. It was still within his grasp, and everyone's. Thelma Forsdyke bowed her head, which was really quite grey by this time, and submitted to such blandishment. What tenderness would she have been capable of, she wondered, if the occasion had ever offered itself? Nothing sensual, but ethereal, swayed in divine winds of music. Music was her love, of course. Even with all her hypocrisies deducted, and these were many, there were still simple strong phrases that she could lie with and understand to the last silence of their simplicity. If by opening her mouth music would enter in, and down the funnel of her throat. She sat drooping now, in a most awkward position, on her standard chair. To listen to music. This was the lovemaking stage of music, when the tendrils creep around the breasts in formal patterns.

The Jew played. Greater difficulties were reserved. Though he had played them a hundred times with virtuosity, even genius, there were passages which always frightened him on approach, the sweat poured down his shoulderblades and down the backs of his knees at the very moment when he knew they were overcome. In anticipation he had begun to wrestle with the music, though the blood had not yet started to gush out of his yellow eyes.

499

The music had really taken over the men who had been brave enough to play it, and in some cases those who were listening. Thelma Forsdyke lowered her eyelids in the face of this assault, shocked and frightened by her approaching nobility. Almost anyone can be raised at some point in his life to heights he dare not own. So this woman looked and retreated. Her understanding of the situation, which she would be allowed to forget almost immediately, was so clear and intense that the tears were coming into her eyes. Her hands had been cut, not by her own nails, but by these formidable pinnacles.

Just at that moment the music took and almost threw the Jew at the conductor's feet. Some people sniggered at such extravagance of manner. However, Thelma Forsdyke, who was by this time destroyed and frightened, merely dropped her curled programme on the floor, for which her neighbours frowned at her. She was a miserable woman in good black, with very small, too small diamond drops in the bluish lobes of her ears.

Afterwards she listened, or was played to, sadly. She was brushed in sad gusts by the branches of the music. All the faces had ripened and were ready to fall from those branches. She was walking across the paddocks. Her stomach was thin and sloping. It was a personal sadness, or sickness, that had infected the music, and that she could not bear. Her omissions were turning over and showing their true side.

She began to sidle in her uncomfortable chair, and wish that she could get out somehow, but this obviously would have been impossible.

And the violets. She was standing on the broken concrete path at the side of the house, on which the shrubby gnarled honeysuckle has grown too big, and reached over, and is scratching the side of the house. And all that side is blue with violets. Father is standing there, she saw, he has not shaved this morning, or is it?—is it?—oh Daddy, she began with horror, for she had never said this before, never.

Nobody noticed any agony, because it is not visible in discreet people, even when whole ganglions of nerves are cut.

I must get out, said Thelma Forsdyke.

She did eventually. When the brilliant interpretation of the work was at an end, she slipped past people's knees, faintly sucking a little cachou that she had had in her bag.

Mrs. Forsdyke came home by degrees to the strange house in which she lived. With its glittering white woodwork and large structure, tossing as it were in a dark-blue sea of leaves and moonlight, for there was a wind on that cold night, it was like a ship, and she looked at it as long as she could before taking the little gangway which connected it with firm land. Her feet made white notes on the dry boards, and almost at once a shadow opened a glass door, and came out along the veranda towards her, lit by the red eye of a cigar.

"Is that you, Dudley?" she asked.

"Yes," he said.

They were awkward. It could, of course, just have been their relationship.

"I tried to get you at the club," he said, "but you had gone."

"I told you I was going to the concert," said the woman, her voice rising.

All this was happening in the moonlight, which had rinsed their faces of age, and their bodies of environment.

"They rang up from home," said Dudley Forsdyke, who was being kind in that way which he had inherited from other decent males.

"Yes," she said quickly through her small mouth. "It is Father." She did not ask.

"I am afraid so," said Dudley Forsdyke. "The old man died this afternoon."

What am I to do now? asked Thelma. The moment of nobility, to which she had been lifted recently by music, would not recur in her lifetime.

"Oh dear, oh dear, oh dear," she had learned to say, walking on thin legs, her footsteps following her whitely all the length of the woodwork.

"And the funeral?" she asked.

"I gather it will be tomorrow afternoon," Dudley Forsdyke said.

"I shall go down," she said. "Tomorrow. Early. I shall drive. I would rather go by myself, Dudley. You will understand. Flowers on the way."

Arranging smoothly and with taste.

"But there is the dinner." She froze suddenly. "At Government House."

"Yes," said Dudley Forsdyke.

Tactfully, or brutally, he would not help her.

Perhaps funerals in the country, little funerals of simple insignificant people that trail through the yellow grass in hired cars and a variety of dreadful clothes, are over quickly, said the limp Thelma.

She had had too much for that day. She went into the dining room and drank off a goblet of soda water.

And in the morning had recovered herself sufficiently to mourn for her father along with herself. Poor Dad. She remembered with fascination his hands, which were those of a working man. She remembered his silences, which she had failed to penetrate, not that she had tried really, but which she suspected at times contained something of worth. Awfulness obscured further speculation as she drove down through the suburban landscape. The moments of illumination would not have been for her anyway.

As she approached the house of death, terror possessed her, though the naked canes of roses were trembling with birds and the wet earth was steaming after frost. She went up the path without identifying herself with the house in which she had been born.

A woman in an apron came to the door. It was Ray's widow, whom Thelma scarcely knew. She thought her name was Elsie. She had a flat, rather heavy, creamy face, from which the hair had been pinned back in some timeless fashion of its own. She was a plain woman. It was a clear brow, though, distinguished by the expanse of its serenity.

"How is Mother?" Thelma asked.

Though realizing fearfully, now that she had achieved it, she could lay claim to nothing in this house.

"She is in the kitchen, baking a cake," Elsie said.

Ray's wife was not surprised by anything.

"Will you go in to her?" she asked.

"Yes," said Thelma. "Oh, there are some flowers that I brought."

Which Elsie at once fetched from the car, holding them in her square hands, to bring some sense of importance to the thin woman. They were standing on the step then, breathing the rather unpleasant scent of crushed chrysanthemums. But the heads were big expensive ones.

"How lovely they are," Elsie said, for Thelma.

And would indeed love, for, strangely, this was her vocation.

Thelma Forsdyke, on the other hand, remained uncertain of the direction that life was taking, and at the most would allow herself ungraciously to be led. As she followed Elsie into this house, which, in spite of the immense event that had taken place, was open to birds and leaves on all sides, and to the picking and fossicking of gathering sunlight, Thelma's nonentity was complete.

The day Stan Parker died he had been poking about in the back garden a bit, or sitting, mostly sitting, in a coat that she had made him wear, of old discoloured tweed, because that clear, candid sunlight would withdraw swiftly and treacherously from the immediate vicinity, uncovering bottomless wells of cold and the blue pools of evening. So the old man sat there in his coat and a cap. He had a black stick, which somebody had produced from the disuse in which it had been lying, and which he walked with now, or propped against his chair, ever since the stroke he had suffered several months ago.

Amy Parker did not speak about that. You do not speak about strokes, especially those which fell members of the family. She would hand the black stick, if it was ever out of reach, hand it back as if it were not visible. How simply Stan, a big man, had fallen down with the connivance of God, and had lain there, blasted. Finlaysons were with them at the time. Jack and Merle had come over about something, and to yarn. It was round about eleven o'clock. She had poured tea. They were all looking back at Stan for long minutes, and asking what to do, not for then, it is easy enough to pick a man up, but for always. They had to have some direction, it seemed, for the future. Only the present will not wait. It is itself potential future. And so, as no communications were forthcoming, Jack Finlayson stepped forward and picked Stan up. It was all as simple as that. The old woman did not cry or anything. She was watching it all happen.

But afterwards it was obvious she had had a fright. She did not want to see people, in case she might have to explain something that was not yet clear to her.

It got round, of course, what had happened to Mr. Parker, because Finlaysons were there. They had to tell what they had seen, for nothing of a transcendental nature had happened in their lives ever before. But there were others round about who began to shy away from Parkers after this. Most people do not want to be the bystanders at death, particularly the living death of some old person. It is a different matter if it drops on you out of the sky, on the road for instance, some stranger, that can be stimulating.

The old woman was glad people let them alone, or confined their attentions to formal kindnesses. So that she was able to watch her husband in peace, and, in such time as remained, devote herself to discovering whether he had really loved her, whether he had ever been conscious that she had inflicted on him the great wounds he had suffered, and whether it was still possible at this last moment to love a person in that measure in which he should be loved.

As for the old man, he was quite content to sit in the rather cold sunlight, but well wrapped up. He was soon hobbling about proppily on the stick. He would even go down to the tool shed sometimes, and move the tools from one position to another. Followed by that black dog.

It would be Stan Parker's last dog, and was itself a great age, distracted by canker and the itch.

"All dogs like Stan," said his wife, pinching up her eyebrows tragically. "They follow him around. There was that red one when we first came here, that I could never stand, lolloping thing, would not let me touch him. Some young dog he had picked up as a boy. Look at this one now. All his teeth gone, or stumps. Yellow. His breath is terrible, I tell you. Stan will not have him put away, though. He understands him, I suppose, whatever there is to understand."

And did the dog, looking up through those milky eyes, grinning through that mauve mouth from which the frill had fallen away, perhaps understand Stan? She would have given him a push sometimes, if he had not been so mangy. But she did also stand bowls of milk for him in the grass, and go away quickly before she could notice the details of his misery.

The dog lay beside Stan Parker, gnawing at a raw place between the toes of one of his paws. He was a quiet dog. The back of his neck was innocent and unprotected. A blow could have fallen easily.

That afternoon the old man's chair had been put on the grass at the back, which was quite dead-looking from the touch of winter. Out there at the back, the grass, you could hardly call it a lawn, had formed a circle in the shrubs and trees which the old woman had not so much planted as stuck in during her lifetime. There was little of design in the garden originally, though one had formed out of the wilderness. It was perfectly obvious that the man was seated at the heart of it, and from this heart the trees radiated, with grave movements of life, and beyond them the sweep of a vegetable garden, which had gone to weed during the months of the man's illness, presented the austere skeletons of cabbages and the wands of onion seed. All was circumference to the centre,

504

and beyond that the worlds of other circles, whether crescent of purple villas or the bare patches of earth, on which rabbits sat and observed some abstract spectacle for minutes on end, in a paddock not yet built upon. The last circle but one was the cold and golden bowl of winter, enclosing all that was visible and material, and at which the man would blink from time to time, out of his watery eyes, unequal to the effort of realizing he was the centre of it.

The large, triumphal scheme of which he was becoming mysteriously aware made him shift in his seat, and resent the entrance of the young man, who had jumped the fence and was coming down towards him, stepping over beds rather than following paths, he was so convinced of achieving his mission by direct means and approaches.

Stan Parker was shrinking all this time. He did not like to speak to people now. His skin was papery, you could see through it almost in certain light. His eyes had been reduced to a rudimentary shape, through which was observed, you felt, a version of objects that was possibly true.

When the young man had reached the old one, who purposely did not look up, but at the shoe which had approached, and which was crushing the brown nets of clover, he burst at once into a speech, addressing the button of the old man's cap.

He said, "I just wanted to have a little talk, sir. I was passing, and saw you sitting here on this beautiful day."

Sir, he said, very respectful. Some kind of a student perhaps. But the old man drew in his neck, which was as wrinkled as a tortoise's.

"I wanted, when I saw you, sir, to bring to you the story of the Gospels," said the young man, "and of Our Lord. I wanted to tell you of my own experience, and how it is possible for the most unlikely to be saved."

The old man was most unhappy.

"I was a fettler. I don't know whether you know anything of conditions in the fettlers' camps," said the young man, whose experience was filling his eyes, even to the exclusion of his present mission, the old man.

The young evangelist began to present himself in the most complete nakedness.

"Drinking and whoring most week-ends," he said. "We would go down into the nearest settlement and carry back the drink. It was wine mostly. We would knock the necks off, we were craving for it that bad. The women would come up

505

along the line, knowing where the camp was. There were black women too."

The old man was intensely unhappy.

When the young one had finished his orgasm, he presented the open palms of his hands and told how he had knelt upon his knees, and grace descended on him.

"This can happen to you too," he said, kneeling on one knee, and sweating at every pore.

The old man cleared his throat. "I'm not sure whether I am intended to be saved," he said.

The evangelist smiled with youthful incredulity. No subtleties would escape the steam roller of faith. "You don't understand," he said smilingly.

If you can understand, at your age, what I have been struggling with all my life, then it is a miracle, thought the old man.

He spat on the ground in front of him. He had been sitting for some time in one position, and had on his chest a heaviness of phlegm.

"I am too old," he said colourlessly.

He was tired really. He wanted to be left alone.

"But the glories of salvation," persisted the evangelist, whose hair went up in even waves, "these great glories are everybody's for the asking, just by a putting out of the hand."

The old man fidgeted. He was not saying anything. Great glories were glittering in the afternoon. He had already been a little dazzled.

"You are not stubborn, friend?"

"I would not be here if I was not stubborn," said the old man.

"Don't you believe in God, perhaps?" asked the evangelist, who had begun to look around him and to feel the necessity for some further stimulus of confession. "I can show you books," he yawned.

Then the old man, who had been cornered long enough, saw, through perversity perhaps, but with his own eyes. He was illuminated.

He pointed with his stick at the gob of spittle.

"That is God," he said.

As it lay glittering intensely and personally on the ground.

The young man frowned rather. You met all kinds.

"Look," he said. "Here's some books that I will leave with you. Take your time. Have a read. Some of them's light enough."

506

His vice was gnawing at him. He had to get to the end of the road.

After he had gone and the tracts were flapping and plapping in the undergrowth, and the black dog had smelled one with the tip of his dry nose, the old man continued to stare at the jewel of spittle. A great tenderness of understanding rose in his chest. Even the most obscure, the most sickening incidents of his life were clear. In that light. How long will they leave me like this, he wondered, in peace and understanding?

But his wife had to come presently.

"Stan," she said, approaching, he knew it was she, crunching over the grass with her bad leg, "you will not believe when I tell you," she said, "I was scratching round the shack, in the weed, where the rosebush was that we moved to the house, the old white rose, and what did I find, Stan, but the little silver nutmeg grater that Mrs. Erbey gave me on our wedding day. Look."

"Ah," he said.

What was this irrelevant thing? He had forgotten.

Branches of shadow were drifting across his face, interfering with his sight. The scent of violets was a cold blur.

"When we always accused that fellow who was selling the magnetical water," Amy Parker said.

Her face was quite pleased. She was herself bad enough to expect the worst in others. Yet sometimes, if seldom, man is exonerated.

"Of course," she said, "it is all discoloured, and quite useless. Though we never did use it," she said.

She was going away, but came back, and took his hands as if they had been inanimate objects, and looked into his face, and said, "Is there anything you want, Stan?"

"No," he said.

What could she have given him?

She herself began to suspect this. She went away, wandering through the garden in search of an occupation.

Exquisitely cold blue shadows began to fall through the shiny leaves of the trees. Some boulders that had been let lie in the garden all those years, either because they were too heavy to move or, more likely, because nobody had thought about them, assumed enormous proportions in the heavy bronze light. There was, on the one hand, a loosing and dissolving of shapes, on the other, a looming of mineral splendours.

Stan Parker began to go then. To walk. Though his hip was stiff.

I believe in this leaf, he laughed, stabbing at it with his stick.

The winter dog's dusty plume of tail dragged after the old man, who walked slowly, looking at the incredible objects of the earth, or at the intangible blaze of sunlight. It was in his eyes now.

When he had reached the side of the house on which the shrubby, gnarled honeysuckle had grown too big, and had reached over, and was scratching the side of the house, his wife was standing on the step.

"What is it, Stan?" she asked.

Her face was afraid.

I believe, he said, in the cracks in the path. On which ants were massing, struggling up over an escarpment. But struggling. Like the painful sun in the sky. Whirling and whirling. But struggling. But joyful. So much so, he was trembling. The sky was blurred now. As he stood waiting for the flesh to be loosened on him, he prayed for greater clarity, and it became obvious as a hand. It was clear that One, and no other figure, is the answer to all sums.

"Stan," cried his wife, running, because she really was afraid that she had been left behind.

They clung together for a minute on the broken concrete path, their two souls wrestling together. She would have dragged him back if she could, to share her further sentence, which she could not comtemplate for that moment, except in terms of solitary confinement. So she was holding him with all the strength of her body and her will. But he was escaping from her.

"Ahhhhhh," she cried when he was lying on the path.

Looking at him.

He could not tell her she would not find it in his face. She was already too far.

"It is all right," he said.

She was holding his head and looking into it some minutes after there was anything left to see.

Amy Parker did not cry much, because she had often visualized this event. She got up unsteadily, she was a heavy old woman, and went through the garden with tenderness, in a torn stocking, to call those people who would come and give her material assistance. She promised herself great comfort from this, And from the grandson, Elsie's boy, in whose eyes her own obscure, mysterious life would grow transparent at last.

So she rounded the corner of the empty house. Whimpering a little for those remnants of love and habit that were clinging to her. Stan is dead. My husband. In the boundless garden.

Chapter 26

IN THE end there are the trees. These still stand in the gully behind the house, on a piece of poor land that nobody wants to use. There is the ugly mass of scrub, full of whips and open secrets. But there are the trees, quite a number of them that have survived the axe, smooth ones, a sculpture of trees. On still mornings after frost these stand streaming with light and moisture, the white, and the ashen, and some of the colour of flesh.

There is nothing else in the bush, except the little sarsaparilla vine, of which the purple theme emerges from the darker undertones. There is silence, and a stone lizard. And a dog that has died recently, that the maggots have not yet had time to invade. The dusty dog lying with his muzzle turned sideways on his paws in perfect simplicity of death.

The rather leggy, pale boy comes down later into the bush. He is mooning there, and rubbing his forehead against the bark of trees. He is breaking twigs, and making little heaps of sticks in various patterns. He is writing in the sand, and expecting precious stones in the surfaces of rocks.

The scraggy boy, who has grown too long for his pants and for the arms of his coat, has come down from the house of death because he cannot stand it any longer. Well, his grandfather is dead. An old man, whom he loved, but at a distance, amongst wood shavings. Death gave the boy a fright, but he had soon recovered, and absorbed all its strange and interesting details. Then he had begun to suffocate. What can I do? he said.

So he had come away into the bush. He had in his pocket a piece of glass his grandmother had once given him. He lay on his back, on the sandy earth, on the root fibres and decomposing leaves, and looked through the glass at the crimson mystery of the world.

What would he do?

He would write a poem, he said, dragging his head from side to side in the sand, but not yet, and what? He was tortured by impotence, and at the same time the possibility of his unborn poem. The crimson sky drifting on his face, and the purple snakes of trees. He would write a poem of death. Long words wired for the occasion, marble words of dictionaries, paper words in rat traps would decorate his poem. He was a bit frightened of it. But of course he did not believe in it, not really. He could not believe in death. Or only in passing through a dark hall, in which it is an old overcoat that puts its empty arms around him. Then death is faintly credible because it is still smelling of life.

So he would write a poem of life, of all life, of what he did not know, but knew. Of all people, even the closed ones, who do open on asphalt and in trains. He would make the trains run on silver lines, the people still dreaming on their shelves, who will wake up soon enough and feel for their money and their teeth. Little bits of coloured thought, that he had suddenly, and would look at for a long time, would go into his poem, and urgent telegrams, and the pieces of torn letters that fall out of metal baskets. He would put the windows that he had looked inside. Sleep, of course, that blue eiderdown that divides life from life. His poem was growing. It would have the smell of bread, and the rather grey wisdom of youth, and his grandmother's kumquats, and girls with yellow plaits exchanging love-talk behind their hands, and the blood thumping like a drum, and red apples, and a little wisp of white cloud that will swell into a horse and trample the whole sky once it gets the wind inside it.

As his poem mounted in him he could not bear it, or rather, what was still his impotence. And after a bit, not knowing what else to do but scribble on the already scribbled trees, he went back to the house in which his grandfather had died, taking with him his greatness, which was still a secret.

So that in the end there were the trees. The boy walking through them with his head drooping as he increased in stature. Putting out shoots of green thought. So that, in the end, there was no end.

THE BIG BESTSELLERS
ARE AVON BOOKS!